DUNE

THE BUTLERIAN JIHAD

Brian Herbert

and

Kevin J. Anderson

TOR®

A TOM DOHERTY ASSOCIATES BOOK
NEW YORK

DUNE: THE BUTLERIAN JIHAD

Copyright © 2002 by Herbert Properties, LLC

All rights reserved.

Edited by Patrick LoBrutto

A Tor Book
Published by Tom Doherty Associates
120 Broadway
New York, NY 10271

www.tor-forge.com

Tor® is a registered trademark of Macmillan Publishing Group, LLC.

ISBN 978-1-250-20854-5

Our books may be purchased in bulk for promotional, educational, or business use. Please contact your local bookseller or the Macmillan Corporate and Premium Sales Department at 1-800-221-7945, extension 5442, or by e-mail at MacmillanSpecialMarkets@macmillan.com.

First Edition: September 2002
Second U.S. Mass Market Edition: June 2019

Printed in the United States of America

10 9 8 7

To our agents,
ROBERT GOTTLIEB and MATT BIALER
of Trident Media Group,

who saw the potential in this project from the very beginning
and whose enthusiasm helped us to make it a success

ACKNOWLEDGMENTS

Penny Merritt, for helping to manage the literary legacy of her father, Frank Herbert.

Our editors, Pat LoBrutto and Carolyn Caughey, offered detailed and invaluable suggestions through many drafts to fine-tune this story into its final version. Tom Doherty, Linda Quinton, Jennifer Marcus, and Paul Stevens at Tor Books gave this project remarkable support and enthusiasm.

As always, Catherine Sidor, at WordFire, Inc., worked tirelessly to transcribe dozens of microcassettes and type many hundreds of pages to keep up with our manic work pace. Her assistance in all steps of this project has helped to keep us sane, and she even fools other people into thinking we're organized.

Diane E. Jones and Erwin Bush served as test readers and guinea pigs, giving us their honest reactions, and suggested additional scenes that helped make this a stronger book. Rebecca Moesta contributed her imagination, time, and support in all phases of this book, from start to finish.

The Herbert Limited Partnership, including Jan Herbert, Ron Merritt, David Merritt, Byron Merritt, Julie Herbert, Robert Merritt, Kimberly Herbert, Margaux Herbert, and Theresa Shackelford, gave us their enthusiastic support, entrusting us with the care of Frank Herbert's magnificent vision.

Beverly Herbert, for almost four decades of support and devotion to her husband, Frank Herbert.

And most of all, thanks to Frank Herbert, whose genius created such a wondrous universe for us to explore.

Princess Irulan writes:

Any true student must realize that History has no beginning. Regardless of where a story starts, there are always earlier heroes and earlier tragedies.

Before one can understand Muad'Dib or the current jihad that followed the overthrow of my father, Emperor Shaddam IV, one must understand what we fight against. Therefore, look more than ten thousand years into our past, ten millennia before the birth of Paul Atreides.

It is there that we see the founding of the Imperium, how an emperor rose from the ashes of the Battle of Corrin to unify the bruised remnants of humanity. We will delve into the most ancient records, into the very myths of Dune, into the time of the Great Revolt, more commonly known as the Butlerian Jihad.

The terrible war against thinking machines was the genesis of our political-commercial universe. Hear now, as I tell the story of free humans rebelling against the domination of robots, computers, and cymeks. Observe the basis of the great betrayal that made mortal enemies of House Atreides and House Harkonnen, a violent feud that continues to this day. Learn the roots of the Bene Gesserit Sisterhood, the Spacing Guild and their Navigators, the Swordmasters of Ginaz, the Suk Medical School, the Mentats. Witness the lives of oppressed Zensunni Wanderers who fled to the desert world of Arrakis, where they became our greatest soldiers, the Fremen.

Such events led to the birth and life of Muad'Dib.

⤙⤚

LONG BEFORE MUAD'DIB, in the last days of the Old Empire, humanity lost its drive. Terran civilization had spread across the stars, but grew stagnant. With few ambitions, most people allowed efficient machines to perform everyday tasks for them. Gradually, humans ceased to think, or dream . . . or truly live.

Then came a man from the distant Thalim system, a visionary who took the name of Tlaloc after an ancient god of rain. He spoke to languid crowds, attempting to revive their human spirit, to no apparent effect. But a few misfits heard Tlaloc's message.

These new thinkers met in secret and discussed how they would change the Empire, if only they could overthrow the foolish rulers. Discarding their birth names, they assumed appellations associated with great gods and heroes. Foremost among them were General Agamemnon and his lover Juno, a tactical genius. These two recruited the programming expert Barbarossa, who devised a scheme to convert the Empire's ubiquitous servile machines into fearless aggressors by giving their AI brains certain human characteristics, including the ambition to conquer. Then several more humans joined the ambitious rebels. In all, twenty masterminds formed the core of a revolutionary movement that took over the Old Empire.

Victorious, they called themselves Titans, after the most ancient of Greek gods. Led by the visionary Tlaloc, the twenty allocated the administration of planets and peoples among themselves, enforcing their edicts through Barbarossa's aggressive thinking machines. They conquered most of the known galaxy.

Some resistance groups rallied their defenses on the fringes of the Old Empire. Forming their own confederation—the League of Nobles—they fought the Twenty Titans and, after many bloody battles, retained their freedom. They stopped the tide of the Titans and drove them back.

Tlaloc vowed to dominate these outsiders one day, but after less than a decade in power, the visionary leader was killed in a tragic accident. General Agamemnon took Tlaloc's place as leader, but the death of his friend and mentor was a grim reminder of the Titans' own mortality.

Wishing to rule for centuries, Agamemnon and his lover Juno undertook a risky course of action. They had their brains surgically removed and implanted in preservation canisters that could be installed into a variety of mechanical bodies. One by one—as the remaining Titans felt the specter of age and vulnerability—all of the others also converted themselves into "cymeks," machines with human minds.

The Time of Titans lasted for a century. The cymek usurpers ruled their various planets, using increasingly sophisticated computers and robots to maintain order. But one fateful day the hedonistic Titan Xerxes, anxious to have more time for his pleasures, surrendered too much access to his pervasive AI network.

The sentient computer network seized control of an entire planet, followed quickly by others. The breakdown spread like a virulent infestation from world to world, and the computer "evermind" grew in power and scope. Naming itself Omnius, the intelligent and adaptible network conquered all the Titan-controlled planets before the cymeks had time to warn each other of the danger.

Omnius then set out to establish and maintain order in its own highly structured fashion, keeping the humiliated cymeks under its thumb. Once masters of an empire, Agamemnon and his companions became reluctant servants to the widespread evermind.

At the time of the Butlerian Jihad, Omnius and his thinking

machines had held all of the "Synchronized Worlds" in an iron grip for a thousand years.

Even so, clusters of free humans remained on the outskirts, bound together for mutual protection, thorns in the sides of the thinking machines. Whenever attacks came, the League of Nobles defended themselves effectively.

But new machine plans were always being developed.

When humans created a computer with the ability to collect information and learn from it, they signed the death warrant of mankind.

—SISTER BECCA THE FINITE

Salusa Secundus hung like a jeweled pendant in the desert of space, an oasis of resources and fertile fields, peaceful and pleasing to the optic sensors. Unfortunately, it was infested with feral humans.

The robotic fleet approached the capital world of the League of Nobles. Armored warships bristled with weapons, weirdly beautiful with their reflective alloy coatings, their adornments of antennae and sensors. Aft engines blazed pure fire, pushing the vessels to accelerations that would have crushed mere biological passengers. Thinking machines required no life-support or physical comfort. Currently, they were focused on destroying the remnants of age-old human resistance on the wild outer fringes of the Synchronized Worlds.

Inside his pyramid-shaped vessel, the cymek general Agamemnon led the attack. Logical thinking machines did not care about glory or revenge. But Agamemnon certainly did. Fully alert inside his preservation canister, his human brain watched the plans unfold.

Ahead of him, the main fleet of robot warships swept into the human-infested system, overwhelming the crews of surprised sentry vessels like an avalanche out of space. Human picket ships opened fire, defenders swept in to meet the oncoming machine force. Five League sentry vessels fired off heavy salvos, but most of their projectiles were too slow to hit the streaking inbound fleet. A handful of robotic vessels were damaged or destroyed by lucky shots, and just as many human ships exploded in flashes of incandescent vapor—not because they posed a particular threat, but because they were in the way.

Only a few distant scouts managed to transmit a warning toward vulnerable Salusa Secundus. Robot battleships vaporized the diffuse inner perimeter of human defenses, without even slowing on their way to their real goal. Shuddering under extreme deceleration, the thinking-machine fleet would arrive not long after the warning signal reached the capital world.

The humans would never have time enough to prepare.

The robot fleet was ten times the size and power of any force Omnius had ever before sent against the League of Nobles. The humans had grown complacent, having faced no concentrated robotic aggression during the last century of uneasy cold war. But machines could wait a long time, and now Agamemnon and his surviving Titans would finally have their chance.

Revealed by a flurry of tiny machine spy probes, the League had recently installed supposedly invincible defenses against gelcircuitry-based thinking machines. The massive robot fleet would wait at a safe distance while Agamemnon and his small vanguard of cymeks pressed forward on a mission, perhaps a suicidal one, to open the door.

Agamemnon reveled in the anticipation. Already the hapless biologicals would be sounding alarms, preparing defenses . . . cowering in fear. Through flowing electrafluid that kept his disembodied brain alive, he transmitted an order to his cymek shock troops. "Let us destroy the heart of the human resistance. *Forward!*"

For a thousand hellish years, Agamemnon and his Titans

had been forced to serve the computer evermind, Omnius. Chafing under their bondage, the ambitious but defeated cymeks now turned their frustration against the League of Nobles. One day the once-defeated general hoped to turn against Omnius himself, but thus far had seen no opportunity.

The League had erected new scrambler shields around Salusa Secundus. Such fields would destroy the sophisticated gel-circuitry of all AI computers—but human minds could survive the passage. And though they had mechanical systems and interchangeable robotic bodies, cymeks still had human brains.

Thus, they could pass through the defensive shields unscathed.

Like a target behind crosshairs, Salusa Secundus filled Agamemnon's field of view. With great attention to detail the general had studied tactical projections, applying the military skills he'd developed over the centuries, along with an intuitive understanding of the art of conquest. His abilities had once allowed a mere twenty rebels to take over an empire . . . until they'd lost it all to Omnius.

Prior to launching this important attack, the computer evermind had insisted on running simulation after simulation, trying to develop plans for every contingency. Agamemnon, though, knew it was futile to plan too precisely when it came to unruly humans.

Now, while the immense robot war fleet engaged the expected League orbital defenses and perimeter ships, Agamemnon's mind probed outward from his sensor-connected container, and he felt his guideship as an extension of his long-lost human body. The integral weapons were part of himself. He saw with a thousand eyes, and the powerful engines made him feel as if he had muscular legs again and could run like the wind.

"Prepare for ground assault. Once our dropcarriages penetrate the Salusan defenses, we must strike fast and hard." Recalling that watcheyes would record every moment of the battle for the evermind's later scrutiny once the fleet returned, he added, "We will sterilize this filthy planet for the glory of Omnius." Agamemnon slowed his descent, and the others followed suit. "Xerxes, take the lead. Send in your neo-cymeks to draw their fire and flush them out."

Hesitant as usual, Xerxes complained. "Will I have your full support as I go in? This is the most dangerous part of—"

Agamemnon silenced him. "Be grateful for this opportunity to prove yourself. Now go! Every second you delay gives more time to the *hrethgir*." This was the derogatory term that intelligent machines and their cymek lackeys used for human vermin.

Another voice crackled across the comlink: the robot operator of the machine fleet battling the human protective force orbiting Salusa. "We await your signal, General Agamemnon. Human resistance is intensifying."

"We're on our way," Agamemnon said. "Xerxes, do as I instructed!"

Xerxes, who always fell short of complete defiance, stifled further comment and summoned three neo-cymeks, later-generation machines with human minds. The quartet of pyramidal ships shut down their subsidiary systems, and their armored dropcarriages fell unguided into the atmosphere. For a few dangerous moments they would be easy targets, and the League's missile-and-aerial defenses might hit a few of the cluster. But the dropcarriages' dense material shielding would protect them against the brunt of the bombardment, keeping them intact even through a wild crash-landing on the outskirts of the prime city of Zimia, where the main shield-generating towers were located.

Thus far the League of Nobles had preserved unruly humanity against the organized efficiency of Omnius, but the feral biologicals governed themselves ineffectively and often disagreed over major decisions. As soon as Salusa Secundus was crushed, the unstable alliance would disintegrate in a panic; resistance would crumble.

But first Agamemnon's cymeks had to shut down the scrambler shields. Then Salusa would be defenseless and quivering, ready for the main robot fleet to deal the lethal blow, like a huge mechanical boot squashing an insect.

The cymek leader jockeyed his dropcarriage into position, ready to lead the second wave with the rest of the extermination fleet. Agamemnon switched off all computerized systems and followed Xerxes down. His brain floated in limbo inside its preservation canister. Blind and deaf, the general did not feel the heat or violent vibrations as his armored craft roared toward the unsuspecting target.

The intelligent machine is an evil genie, escaped from its bottle.
—BARBAROSSA,
Anatomy of a Rebellion

When Salusa's sensor network detected the arrival of the robotic war fleet, Xavier Harkonnen took action immediately. Once again, the thinking machines meant to test the defenses of free humanity.

Though he bore the rank of tercero in the Salusan Militia—the local, autonomous branch of the overall League Armada—Xavier had not yet been born during the last real skirmishes against League worlds. The most recent major battle had been nearly a hundred years ago. After all these years, the aggressive machines might be counting on soft human defenses, but Xavier swore they would fail.

"Primero Meach, we've received an urgent warning and a vidstream clip from one of our peripheral scouts," he said to his commander. "But the transmission cut off."

"Look at them all!" squawked Quinto Wilby as he scanned images from the outlying sensor network. The low-ranking officer stood with other soldiers at banks of instrument panels inside a domed building. "Omnius never sent anything like this before."

Vannibal Meach, the short but loud-voiced primero of the Salusan Militia, stood in the control center of the planet's defenses, coolly absorbing the flow of information. "Our last report from the perimeter is hours old due to signal lag. By now they've engaged our pickets, and they'll try to get closer. They'll fail, of course." Though this was his first warning of the impending invasion, he reacted as if he had expected the machines to arrive any day.

In the control room's illumination, Xavier's dark brown hair glinted with reddish cinnamon highlights. He was a serious young man, prone to honesty and with a tendency to see things in black and white. As a member of the third military ranking tier, Tercero Harkonnen was Meach's backup commander of the local defense outposts. Much admired by his superiors, Xavier had been promoted quickly; equally respected by his soldiers, he was the sort of trusted man they would follow into battle.

Despite the sheer size and firepower of the robotic force, he willed himself to calmness, then signaled for reports from the nearest picket ships and put the spaceguard defense fleet on highest alert in close orbit. The warship commanders had already called their crews to battle-ready status as soon as they'd heard the urgent transmission from the now-destroyed scout ships.

Around Xavier, automated systems hummed with activity. Listening to the oscillating sirens, the chatter of orders and status reports in the control room, he drew a slow breath, prioritizing tasks. "We can stop them," he said. "We *will* stop them." His voice carried a tone of firm command, as if he were much older than his years and accustomed to battling Omnius every day. In reality, this would be his first engagement with the thinking machines.

Years ago, his parents and older brother had been killed in a marrauding cymek attack while en route from an inspection of family holdings on Hagal. The soulless machine forces had always been a threat to the League Worlds, but the humans and Omnius had maintained an uneasy peace for decades.

On a wall grid, a map of the Gamma Waiping system showed the orbital locations of Salusa Secundus and six other planets, along with the deployment of sixteen patrol battle groups and the vigilant picket ships that were scattered at random. Cuarto Steff Young hurried to update the tactical projection, plotting her best guess of the location of the approaching robot battle group.

"Contact Segundo Lauderdale, and call in all perimeter warships. Tell them to engage and destroy any enemy they encounter," said Primero Meach, then he sighed. "It'll take half a day at maximum acceleration to retrieve our heavy battle groups from the fringe, but the machines might still be trying to get through by then. Could be a field day for our guys." Cuarto Young followed the order with easy efficiency, dispatching a message that would take hours to reach the outskirts of the system.

Meach nodded to himself, going through the much-drilled sequence. Always living under the specter of the machines, the Salusan Militia trained regularly for every scenario, as did Armada detachments for every major League system. "Activate the Holtzman scrambler shields around the planet and issue warnings to all commercial air and space traffic. I want the city's shield transmitter output up to full within ten minutes."

"That should be enough to brain-fry any thinking machine gelcircuitry," Xavier said with forced confidence. "We've all seen the tests." *This, however, is not just a test.*

Once the enemy encountered the defenses the Salusans had installed, he hoped they would calculate their losses to be too heavy, and retreat. Thinking machines didn't like to take risks.

He stared at a panel. *But there are so many of them.*

Then he straightened from his summary screens, full of bad news. "Primero Meach, if our velocity data for the machine fleet is correct, even at deceleration speed, they are traveling almost as fast as the warning signal we received from our scouts."

"Then they could already be here!" said Quinto Wilby.

Now Meach reacted with sharp alarm, triggering a full emergency alert. "Sound evacuation orders! Open the underground shelters."

"Evacuation under way, sir," reported Cuarto Young moments later, her fingers working the update panels as she spoke. The intent young woman touched a communication wire at her temple. "We're sending Viceroy Butler all the information we have."

Serena is with him at the Hall of Parliament, Xavier realized, thinking of the Viceroy's nineteen-year-old daughter. His heart clenched with concern for her, yet he did not dare reveal his fear to his compatriots. Everything in its time and place.

In his mind he could see the many threads he needed to weave, doing his part while Primero Meach directed the overall defense. "Cuarto Chiry, take a squadron and escort Viceroy Butler, his daughter, and all of the League representatives deep into the subterranean shelters."

"They should be heading there already, sir," the officer said.

Xavier gave him a stiff smile. "Do *you* trust politicians to do the smart thing first?" The cuarto ran to do as he was told.

~~~

Most histories are written by the winners of conflicts, but those written by the losers—if they survive—are often more interesting.

—IBLIS GINJO,
The Landscape of Humanity

Salusa Secundus was a green world of temperate climate, home to hundreds of millions of free humans in the League of Nobles. Abundant water flowed through open aqueducts. Around the cultural and governmental center of Zimia, rolling hills were embroidered with vineyards and olive groves.

Moments before the machine attack, Serena Butler stepped onto the oratory stage in the great Hall of Parliament. Thanks to her dedicated public service, as well as special arrangements made by her father, she had been granted this opportunity to address the representatives.

Viceroy Manion Butler had privately counseled her to be subtle, to keep her points simple. "One step at a time, dear one. Our League is held together only by the threat of a common enemy, not by a set of shared values or beliefs. Never attack the lifestyles of the nobles."

This was only the third speech of her brief political career. In her earlier addresses, she had been overly strident—not yet understanding the ballet of politics—and her ideas had been met with a mixture of yawns and good-natured chuckles at her naïveté. She wanted to end the practice of human slavery that had been adopted sporadically by some League worlds; she wanted to make every human equal, to ensure that all were fed and protected.

"Perhaps the truth hurts. I was trying to make them feel guilty."

"You only made them deaf to your words."

Serena had refined her speech to incorporate his advice, while still sticking to her principles. *One step at a time.* And she, too, would learn with each step. On the advice of her father, she had also spoken to like-minded representatives in private, rallying some support and gaining a few allies ahead of time.

Lifting her chin, adjusting her expression to look authoritative rather than eager, Serena positioned herself inside the recording shell that surrounded the podium like a geodesic dome. Her heart swelled with all the good she might be able to do. She felt warm light as the projection mechanism transmitted oversized images of her outside the dome enclosure.

A small screen atop the podium allowed her to see herself as they did: a soft face of classical beauty, with hypnotic lavender eyes and amber-brown hair highlighted by natural golden strands. On her left lapel she wore a white rose floweret from her own meticulously tended gardens. The projector made Serena look even more youthful, as the mechanism had been adjusted by nobles to mask the effect of years on their own features.

From his gilded box at the front of the audience, round-faced Viceroy Butler, in his finest robes of gold and black, smiled proudly at his daughter. The sigil of the League of Nobles adorned his lapel, an open human hand in gold outline, representing freedom.

He understood Serena's optimism, remembering similar ambitions in himself. He had always been patient with her crusades, helping the young woman to rally disaster relief for refugees of machine attacks, letting her journey to other plan-

ets to tend to the injured, or dig through rubble and help rebuild burned buildings. Serena had never been afraid to get
her hands dirty.

"The narrow mind erects stubborn barriers," her mother had
once told her. "But against those barriers, words are formi-
dable weapons."

On the floor of the great hall, dignitaries chatted in low
tones. Several sipped drinks or munched on snacks that had
been delivered to their seats. Just another day in Parliament.
Comfortable in their villas and mansions, they would not welcome change. But the possibility of bruised egos did not prevent Serena from saying what needed to be said.

She activated the oratory projection system. "Many of you
think I have foolish notions because I am young, but perhaps
the young have sharper eyesight, while the old grow slowly
blind. Am I foolish and naïve—or have some of you, in pampered complacency, distanced yourselves from humanity?
Where do you fall on the spectrum of what is right and
wrong?"

Out in the assemblage she saw a flurry of indignation mixed
with expressions of rude dismissal. Viceroy Butler shot her a
sharp glance of disapproval but transmitted a quick reminder
throughout the hall, asking for respectful attention, as would
be accorded any speaker.

She pretended not to notice. Couldn't they all see the larger
picture? "We must each look beyond ourselves if we are to
survive as a species. Now is not the time for personal selfish-
ness. For centuries we have confined our defenses to a handful
of key planets. Though Omnius has launched no full-scale
attack in decades, we live in the constant shadow of the machine threat."

Touching pressure pads on the podium, Serena displayed a
projection of the stellar neighborhood, like a cluster of gems
on the high ceiling. With a wand of light, she pointed out the
free League Worlds and the Synchronized Worlds ruled by
thinking machines. Then she brought her pointer to more extensive regions of the Galaxy where neither organized humans
nor machines held sway.

"Look at these poor Unallied Planets: scattered worlds like Harmonthep, Tlulax, Arrakis, IV Anbus, and Caladan. Because their sparse, insular human settlements are not members of our League, they do not warrant our full military protection should they ever be threatened—by machines or by other humans." Serena paused, letting the audience absorb her words. "Many of our own people wrongly prey on those planets, raiding them for slaves to be supplied to some League Worlds."

She caught the eye of the Poritrin representative, who scowled, knowing she was talking about him. He responded loudly, interrupting her. "Slavery is an accepted practice in the League. Lacking complex machines, we have no other choice to augment our workforce." He looked smug. "Besides, Salusa Secundus itself kept a population of Zensunni slaves for almost two centuries."

"We put a stop to that practice," Serena replied with considerable heat. "It took some imagination and a willingness to change, but—"

Trying to head off a shouting match, the Viceroy stood. "Each League planet makes its own determination of local customs, technology, and laws. We have a fearsome enough enemy in the thinking machines without starting a civil war among our own planets." His voice sounded paternal, just slightly chiding her to get back to her main point.

Sighing but not surrendering, Serena adjusted the pointer so that the Unallied Planets glowed on the ceiling. "Still, we can't ignore all these worlds—ripe resource-filled targets, planets just waiting to be conquered by Omnius."

The Sergeant at Arms, on a tall chair off to one side, rapped his staff on the floor. "Time." Easily bored, he rarely listened to speeches.

Serena continued in a rush, trying to finish her point without sounding strident. "We know the thinking machines want to control the Galaxy, even though they have been essentially quiescent for almost a hundred years. They have systematically taken over every world in the Synchronized star systems. Do not be lulled by their seeming lack of interest in us. We know they will strike again—but how, and where? Should we not move before Omnius does?"

"What is it you *want*, Madame Butler?" one of the dignitaries inquired impatiently, raising his voice, but not standing, as was customary. "Are you advocating some sort of preemptive strike against the thinking machines?"

"We must seek to incorporate the Unallied Planets into the League, and stop harvesting them for slaves." She jabbed her illuminated wand at the overhead projection. "Bring them under our wing to increase our own strength, and theirs. We would all benefit! I propose that we dispatch ambassadors and cultural attachés with the express intent of forming new military and political alliances. As many as we can."

"And who will pay for all that diplomacy?"

"Time," the Sergeant at Arms repeated.

"She is allotted three extra minutes for rebuttal, since the representative from Hagal has posed a question," Viceroy Butler said in an authoritative tone.

Serena grew angry. How could that representative worry about petty price tags, when the ultimate cost was so much higher? "We will all pay—in blood—if we do not do this. We must strengthen the League and the human species."

Some of the nobles began to clap—the allies she had courted before her speech. Suddenly, screeching alarms echoed through the building and in the streets. Droning sirens wavered in a chillingly familiar tone—usually heard only during planned drills—summoning all reserve members of the Salusan Militia.

"Thinking machines have entered the Salusan system," a voice said through built-in speakers. Similar announcements would be ringing all across Zimia. "We have an alert from perimeter scouts and the sentry battle group."

Standing next to her father, Serena read details as the Viceroy was handed a brief and urgent summary. "We've never seen a robot war fleet that size!" he said. "How long ago did the first scouts sound the warning? How much time do we have?"

"We are under attack!" a man shouted. The delegates were on their feet, scattering like stirred ants.

"Prepare to evacuate the Hall of Parliament." The Sergeant at Arms became a flurry of movement. "All armored shelters are open. Representatives, report to your designated areas."

Viceroy Butler shouted into the chaos, trying to sound confident. "The Holtzman shields will protect us!" Serena could read her father's anxiety, though he covered it well.

Amid shouts and cries of panic, the League representatives scrambled for the exits. The merciless enemies of humanity had arrived.

Any man who asks for greater authority does not deserve to have it.

—TERCERO XAVIER HARKONNEN,
address to Salusan Militia

"The robot fleet has just engaged our spaceguard," Xavier Harkonnen called from his station. "Heavy fire exchanged."

"Primero Meach!" Cuarto Steff Young shouted from the orbital grid screens. Xavier could smell the salty metallic tang of Young's nervous sweat. "Sir, a small detachment of machine ships has broken from the main robotic fleet in orbit. Configuration unknown, but they're preparing for an atmospheric descent." She pointed to the images, picking out brilliant lights that signified a cluster of inert projectiles.

Xavier glanced at the perimeter scanners, real-time intelligence transmitted from the defensive satellites high above Tio Holtzman's gelcircuitry-scrambling fields. On the highest resolution he saw an assault squadron of pyramidal ships roaring headlong into the atmosphere, straight toward the sizzling shields.

"They're in for an unpleasant surprise," Young said with a grim smile. "No thinking machine can survive that ride."

"Our biggest worry will be dodging the debris from their crashing ships," Primero Meach quipped. "Maintain surveillance."

But the dropcarriages slipped past the scrambler shields—and kept coming. They showed no electronic signatures at all as they penetrated the boundary.

"How are they getting through?" Quinto Wilby mopped his brow, brushing dishwater-brown hair out of his eyes.

"No computers could." In a flash, Xavier understood what was happening. "They're blind dropcarriages, sir!"

Young looked up from her screens, breathing hard. "Impact in less than a minute, Primero. Second wave is coming in behind them. I count twenty-eight projectiles." She shook her head. "No computer signatures on any of them."

Xavier called out, thinking ahead, "Rico, Powder, work with med-response teams and fire-suppression squads. Everything up to speed and *ready*. Come on people, we've drilled for this a hundred times! I want all vehicles and rescue equipment mobile and in the air, prepared to move before the first ship hits."

"Divert defenses to pound the invaders as soon as they crash." Primero Meach lowered his voice, swept his flinty gaze across his comrades. "Tercero Harkonnen, take a portable comstation and get out there—be my eyes on the scene. My guess is those dropcarriages will hatch into something unpleasant."

⨪

OUTSIDE, THE CITY streets were chaotic under a cloud-dappled sky. Rushing into the confusion, Xavier heard the hot metallic scream of agonized atmosphere as the inert armored projectiles shot downward like bullets from space.

An asteroid-rain of pyramidal dropcarriages slammed into the ground, one after another. With deafening thunder, the first four blind vessels punched into buildings, leveling city blocks with the explosive dispersion of kinetic energy. But sophisticated shock-displacement systems protected the deadly cargo inside.

Xavier ran down the street, his uniform rumpled, his sweaty hair clinging to his head. He stopped in front of the giant edifice of the Hall of Parliament. Although second in command of Salusa's defenses, here he was in an unsecured position, ready to issue orders at ground zero. Not exactly the way he had been taught in his Armada Academy courses. But Primero Meach was relying on his assessment, recommendations, and ability to act independently.

He touched the comline on his chin. "I'm in position, sir."

Five more unguided projectiles thumped into the outskirts of the city, leaving smoldering craters. Explosions. Smoke. Fireballs.

From the impact points, the inert crashdown pods cracked open to reveal a huge object stirring in each one. Reactivated mechanical units peeled off charred ablation shielding. With dread, Xavier knew what he was about to see, understood how the enemy machines had managed to pass through the scrambler shields. They were not computer minds at all. . . .

Cymeks.

Fearsome mechanical monstrosities emerged from the broken pyramids, driven by surgically detached human brains. Mobility systems restarted; articulated legs and augmented weapons clicked into place.

The cymek bodies lurched out of the smoking craters, crab-like gladiators half as tall as the damaged buildings. Their alloy legs were as thick as support girders, bristling with flamer cannons, artillery launchers, poison gas jets.

Xavier shouted into his comline. "Cymek warrior-forms, Primero Meach! They figured out how to get through our orbital defenses!"

All across Salusa, from the outskirts of Zimia to the farthest continent, the local planetary militia was dispatched. Low-atmospheric defense craft—kindjals—had already launched in defensive overflights, their weaponry magazines loaded with armor-piercing projectile shells.

People in the streets fled in terror; others stood frozen, staring. Xavier shouted descriptions of what he was seeing. He heard Vannibal Meach add, "Cuarto Young, issue orders for all stations to break out the breathing apparatus. See that filter masks are distributed to the populace. Every person not inside an approved shelter must wear a breather."

Face masks wouldn't protect against cymek flamers or high-energy detonations, but the people could be safe from the thick poison clouds. As he fit his own breather into place, Xavier felt a growing fear that all of the Militia's best-planned precautions would be woefully inadequate.

Leaving the discarded shells of their dropcarriages behind, cymek warriors thrummed forward on monstrous feet. They launched explosive shells and incinerated buildings and screaming people. Gouts of flame poured from nozzles in their foremost limbs, setting the city of Zimia on fire.

Dropcarriages continued to tumble from above, ready to split open as soon as they crashed. Twenty-eight of them in all.

With a howling roar loud enough to burn his ears, the young tercero saw a column of fire and smoke spinning, tumbling, so fast and bright that it left his retinas smoldering. The drop-carriage smashed into the military compound half a kilometer behind him, vaporizing the control center and the planetary Militia HQ building. The shockwave knocked Xavier to his knees, shattered windows for dozens of blocks.

"Primero!" Xavier screamed into the comline. "Primero Meach! Command center! Anybody!"

But he could see from the ruins that he would get no response from the Militia commander or any of his comrades in the complex.

Stalking through the streets, the cymeks spewed greenish black smoke, an oily mist that settled into a toxic film covering the ground and structures. Then the first squadron of kindjal bombers came in low. Their initial sweep scattered explosives around the machine warriors, striking both cymeks and buildings.

Wearing his clearplaz breathing mask, Xavier panted, unable to believe what he had just seen. He called again for the commander, but received no response. Finally, tactical substations around the city checked in, demanding to know what had happened, asking him to identify himself.

"This is Tercero Xavier Harkonnen," he said. Then full understanding hit him. With a supreme effort, he summoned his courage and steadied his voice. "I am . . . I am currently in command of the Salusan Militia."

He ran toward the conflagration, into the billowing greasy smoke. All around him civilians fell to their knees retching in the poisonous mist. He glared up at the aerial strikes, wishing he could be in more direct control. "The cymeks can be destroyed," he transmitted to the kindjal pilots. Then he coughed. The mask was not working properly. His chest and throat burned as if he had inhaled acid, but he kept shouting orders.

As the attack proceeded, Salusan emergency response aircraft swooped over the battle zone, dumping canisters of fire-suppression powders and foams. At ground level, masked medical squadrons moved in without hesitation.

Oblivious to the insignificant human defense efforts, the cymeks marched forward, moving as individuals, not an army—mechanical mad dogs spreading mayhem. A warrior-form bent back on powerful crablike legs and blasted two rescue ships out of the sky—then it moved ahead again, eerily graceful.

The front line of Salusan bombers dropped explosive shells directly onto one of the first cymeks. Two projectiles struck the armored body, and a third hit a nearby building, causing the structure to collapse, girders and debris tumbling down to bury the invader's mechanical body.

But after the flames and smoke cleared, the battered cymek remained functional. The murderous machine shook itself free of the rubble, then launched a counterattack at the kindjals overhead.

From his distant vantage, Xavier studied their movements, using a portable tactical grid. He needed to figure out the overarching plan of the thinking machines. The cymeks seemed to have a target in mind.

He could not hesitate or waste time bemoaning the fall of his comrades. He could not ask what Primero Meach would have done. Instead, he had to stay clear-headed and make some immediate decisions. If he could only understand the enemies' objective . . .

In orbit, the robotic fleet continued to fire upon the Salusan spaceguard, though the AI enemy could not pass through Holtzman fields. They might defeat the spaceguard ships and blockade the League capital world . . . but Primero Meach had already recalled the heavy perimeter battle groups, and soon all that League Armada firepower would pose a serious challenge to the robot warships.

On the screen he saw the robot fleet maintaining position . . . as if waiting for some signal from the cymek shock troops. His mind whirled. What were they doing?

A trio of gladiator machines launched explosives against the west wing of the Hall of Parliament. The beautifully carved facade sloughed to the street like a late-spring avalanche. Slabs of rubble crumbled, exposing open chambers in the evacuated governmental offices.

Coughing in the smoke, trying to see through his smeared faceplate, Xavier looked into the eyes of a white-smocked medic who grabbed him and fitted a new mask over his face. Xavier's lungs burned more now, as if they had been soaked in av-fuel and lit on fire.

"You'll be fine," the medic promised in an uncertain tone as he applied a snap-injection pack to Xavier's neck.

"I'd better be." The tercero coughed again and saw black spots in front of his eyes. "I don't have time to be a casualty right now."

Xavier thought beyond himself and felt a deep worry for Serena. Less than an hour ago, she had been scheduled to speak to the League representatives. He prayed that she had reached safety.

Struggling to his feet, he waved the medic away as the injection took effect. He tuned his portable tactical grid and requested a sky-high view, imaged from the fast defense kindjals. He studied the blackened paths of the graceful, titanic cymeks on his screen. *Where are they going?*

Mentally, he scanned from the smoldering impact craters

and the ruins of the Militia HQ, envisioning the paths made by the mechanical monsters as they pressed forward.

Then he understood what he should have seen from the start, and cursed under his breath.

Omnius knew the Holtzman scrambler shields would obliterate thinking machine gelcircuitry; thus the main robotic fleet remained just beyond Salusan orbit. If the cymeks took out the shield generators, though, the planet would be wide open to a full-scale invasion.

Xavier faced a critical decision, but his choice was predetermined. Whether he liked it or not, he was in command now. By wiping out Primero Meach and the Militia command structure, the cymeks had put him temporarily in charge. And he knew what he had to do.

He ordered the Salusan Militia to fall back and direct their utmost efforts to defend the single most vital target, leaving the rest of Zimia exposed as the cymeks blasted and burned everywhere. Even if he had to sacrifice part of this important city, he must stop the machine forces from reaching their target.

At all costs.

Is the subject or the observer the greater influence?

—ERASMUS,
uncollated laboratory files

O n Corrin, one of the primary Synchronized Worlds, the robot Erasmus walked across the flagstone plaza that fronted his lavish villa. He moved with a well-practiced fluidity that he had learned to imitate after centuries of observing human grace. His flowmetal face was a burnished blank oval, like a mirror entirely devoid of expression until he decided to form the metallic polymer film into a range of mimicked emotions, like ancient theater masks.

Through optic threads implanted in his facial membrane, he admired the iridescent fountains around him, which so nicely complemented the villa's stonework, gemstone statuary, intricate tapestries, and laser-etched alabaster columns. All plush and opulent, by his own design. After much study and analysis, he had learned to appreciate standards of classical beauty, and was proud of his evident taste.

His pet human slaves bustled about performing household chores—polishing trophies and art objects, dusting furniture, planting flowers, trimming topiary shrubs under the crimson afternoon light of the red-giant sun. Each tremulous slave bowed in respect as Erasmus passed. He recognized but did not bother to identify individuals, though he mentally filed every detail. One never knew when the tiniest scrap of data might help in overall understanding.

Erasmus had a skin of organic-plastic composites laced with neurelectronics. He pretended that the sophisticated sensor network allowed him to genuinely feel physical sensations. Under the glowing ember of Corrin's huge sun, he detected light and warmth on his skin, presumably like real flesh. He wore a thick gold robe trimmed in carmine, part of a stylish personal wardrobe that separated him from Omnius's lesser robots. Vanity was another thing Erasmus had learned from studying humans, and he rather enjoyed it.

Most robots were not as independent as Erasmus. They were little more than mobile thinking boxes, drone subsets of the evermind. Erasmus obeyed Omnius's commands as well, but he had more freedom to interpret. Over the centuries, he had developed his own identity and semblance of an ego. Omnius considered him something of a curiosity.

As the robot continued to walk with perfect grace, he detected a buzzing sound. His optic threads picked up a small flying orb, one of Omnius's many mobile watcheyes. Whenever Erasmus ventured away from the ubiquitous screens found throughout all buildings, the avid watcheyes followed him, recording his every move. The evermind's actions spoke of either a deep-seated curiosity . . . or an oddly humanlike paranoia.

Long ago, while tinkering with the original AI computers of the Old Empire, the rebel Barbarossa had added approximations of certain personality traits and goals. Subsequently the machines had self-evolved into a single grand electronic mind that retained a few of the imposed human ambitions and characteristics.

As far as Omnius was concerned, biologicals, even bastardized cymeks with human brains and machine parts, could not see the epoch-spanning vistas that the gelcircuitry of a machine mind could encompass. When Omnius scanned the universe of possibilities it was like a vast screen. There were so many ways to win, and he was constantly on the alert for them.

Omnius's core programming had been duplicated on all the machine-conquered planets and synchronized through the use of regular updates. Faceless, able to watch and communicate throughout the interstellar network, near-identical copies of Omnius were everywhere, vicariously present in innumerable watcheyes, appliances, and contact screens.

Now, apparently, the distributed computer mind had nothing better to do than snoop. "Where are you going, Erasmus?" Omnius demanded from a tiny speaker beneath the watcheye. "Why are you walking so fast?"

"You could walk, too, if you chose to do so. Why not give yourself legs for a while and wear an artificial body, just to see what it is like?" Erasmus's metallic polymer mask re-shaped itself into a smile. "We could go for a stroll together."

The watcheye buzzed along beside Erasmus. Corrin had long seasons, because its orbit was so far around the giant sun. Winters and summers each lasted for thousands of days. The rugged landscape had no indigenous forests or wildernesses, only a handful of ancient orchards and agricultural fields that had gone to seed since the machine takeover, left to propogate untended.

Many human slaves went blind from exposure to the pounding solar flux. As a consequence, Erasmus fitted his outdoor workers with custom eye protection. He was a benevolent master, concerned for the well-being of his resources.

As he reached the entry gate of his villa, the robot adjusted the new sensory-enhancement module grafted by neurelectronic ports onto his body core and hidden beneath his robe. A unit of his own design, the module allowed Erasmus to simulate the senses of humanity, but with certain unavoidable limitations. He wanted to know more than the module could provide, wanted to *feel* more. In this respect, the cymeks might have an advantage over Erasmus, but he would never know for certain.

Cymeks—especially the original Titans—were a narrow-minded, brutal bunch, with no appreciation for the more refined senses and sensibilities that Erasmus worked so hard to attain. Brutality had its place, of course, but the sophisticated robot considered it only one of many behaviorial aspects worthy of study, both positive and negative. Still, violence was interesting and often pleasurable to employ. . . .

He was intensely curious about what made cognizant biologicals *human*. He was intelligent and self-aware, but he also wanted to understand emotions, human sensibilities, and motivations—the essential details that machines never managed to reproduce very well.

During his centuries-long quest, Erasmus had absorbed human artwork, music, philosophy, and literature. Ultimately, he wanted to discover the sum and substance of humanity, the magic spark that made these creatures, these *creators*, different. What gave them . . . souls?

He marched into his banquet hall, and the flying eye buzzed away toward the ceiling, where it could observe everything. On the walls, six Omnius screens glowed milky gray.

His villa was modeled after the opulent Greco-Roman estates in which the Twenty Titans had lived before forsaking their human bodies. Erasmus owned similar villas on five planets, including Corrin and Earth. He maintained additional facilities—holding pens, customized vivisection rooms, medical laboratories, as well as greenhouses, art galleries, sculptures, and fountains. All of which enabled him to study human behavior and physiology.

Erasmus sat his robed body at the head of a long table lined with silver goblets and candleholders, but with only one place setting. For him. The antique wooden chair had once belonged to a human nobleman, Nivny O'Mura, a founder of the League of Nobles. Erasmus had studied how the rebellious humans had organized themselves and established strongholds against the early cymek and machine assaults. The resourceful *hrethgir* had ways of adapting and improvising, of confounding their enemies in unexpected ways. *Fascinating*.

Abruptly, the evermind's voice echoed from all around, sounding bored. "When will your experiment be concluded,

Erasmus? You come in here day after day, doing the same thing. I expect to see results."

"I am intrigued by questions. Why do wealthy humans eat with such ceremony? Why do they consider certain foods and beverages superior to others, when the nutritional value is the same?" The robot's voice became more erudite. "The answer, Omnius, has to do with their brutally short lives. They compensate with efficient sensory mechanisms capable of imparting intense feelings. Humans have five basic senses, with countless gradations. The taste of Yondair beer versus Ularda wine, for example. Or the feel of Ecaz burlap compared with parasilk, or the music of Brahms versus—"

"I suppose that is all very interesting in some esoteric way."

"Of course, Omnius. You continue to study me while I study humans." Erasmus signaled the slaves who peered nervously through a porthole in the door to the villa's kitchen. A probe snaked out of a module at Erasmus's hip and emerged from underneath his robe, waving delicate neurelectronic sensor threads like expectant cobras.

"By tolerating your investigations, Erasmus, I expect that you will develop a detailed model that can reliably predict human behavior. I must know how to make these creatures *usable*."

White-clad slaves brought trays of food from the kitchen—Corrin game hen, Walgis beef almondine, even rare Platinum River salmon harvested from Parmentier. Erasmus dipped the weblike ends of his probe into each dish and "tasted" it, sometimes using a cutter to penetrate the meat and sample the internal juices. Erasmus documented each flavor for his growing repertoire.

All the while, he carried on a dialogue with Omnius. The evermind seemed to be doling out bits of data and watching how Erasmus reacted. "I have been building up my military forces. After many years, it is time to move again."

"Indeed? Or are the Titans pressuring you into a more aggressive stance? For centuries, Agamemnon has been impatient with what he perceives as your lack of ambition." Erasmus was more interested in the bitter berry tart in front of him. Analyzing the ingredients, he was puzzled to detect a strong trace of human saliva and wondered if that had been part of the original recipe. Or had one of the slaves simply expectorated into it?

"I make my own decisions," the evermind said. "It seemed appropriate to launch a new offensive at this time."

The head chef rolled a cart to the table and used a carving knife to cut a slab of Filet Salusa. The chef, a toady little man who stuttered, placed the dripping slice on a clean plate, added a dollop of savory brown sauce, and extended it toward Erasmus. Clumsily, the chef bumped the knife off the serving tray and it clattered against one of Erasmus's smooth feet, leaving a nick and a stain.

Terrified, the man bent to retrieve the knife, but Erasmus flashed a mechanical hand down and grabbed the handle. Sitting straight, the elegant robot continued to talk to Omnius. "A new offensive? And is it a mere coincidence that the Titan Barbarossa requested exactly that as a reward when he defeated your fighting machine in the gladiator arena?"

"Irrelevant."

Staring at the blade, the chef stammered, "I will p-personally p-polish it and m-m-make it good as n-n-new, Lord Erasmus."

"Humans are such fools, Erasmus," Omnius said from speakers on the wall.

"Some of them are," Erasmus agreed, waving the carving knife with graceful movements. The little chef mouthed a silent prayer, unable to move. "I wonder what should I do?" Erasmus wiped the knife clean on the trembling man's smock, then stared at the fellow's distorted reflection in the metal blade.

"Human death is different from machine death," Omnius said dispassionately. "A machine can be duplicated, backed-up. When humans die, they are gone permanently."

Erasmus simulated a boisterous laugh. "Omnius, though you always talk about the superiority of machines, you fail to recognize what humans do better than we."

"Do not give me another of your lists," the evermind said.

"I recall our last debate on this subject with perfect accuracy."

"Superiority is in the eye of the beholder and invariably involves filtering out details that do not conform to a particular preconceived notion." With his sensory detectors waving like cilia in the air, Erasmus smelled the odor of foul sweat from the chef.

"Are you going to kill this one?" Omnius asked.

Erasmus placed the knife on the table and heard the toady man emit a sigh. "Individually, humans are easy to kill. But as a species, the challenge is far greater. When threatened, they draw together and become more powerful, more dangerous. Sometimes it is best to surprise them."

Without warning, he grabbed the knife and plunged it into the chef's chest with enough force to drive it through the sternum and into the heart. "Like so." Blood spurted down the white uniform, onto the table and the robot's plate.

The hapless human slid off the blade, gurgling. As Erasmus held the bloody knife he considered attempting to duplicate his victim's look of disbelief and betrayal with his own pliable mask, but decided not to bother. His robot face remained a flat, mirrored oval. Erasmus would never be required to display such an expression anyway.

Curious, he tossed the blade aside with a clatter, then dipped sensitive probe threads into the blood on his plate. The taste was quite interesting and complex. He wondered if the blood of various victims would taste any different.

Robot guards dragged the chef's body away, while other terrified slaves huddled by the doorway, knowing they should clean up the mess. Erasmus studied their fear.

Omnius said, "Now I wish to tell you something important that I have decided to do. My attack plans are already set in motion."

Erasmus feigned interest, as he often did. He activated a cleaning mechanism that sterilized the tip of his probe, which then snaked back into its hiding place beneath the robe. "I defer to your judgment, Omnius. I have no expertise in military matters."

"That is exactly why you should heed my words. You always say you want to learn. When Barbarossa defeated my gladiator robot in exhibition combat, he requested the chance to strike against the League Worlds, as a boon from me. The remaining Titans are convinced that without these *hrethgir*, the universe would be infinitely more efficient and tidy."

"How medieval," Erasmus said. "The great Omnius would follow the military suggestions of a cymek?"

"Barbarossa amused me, and there is always the chance that some of the Titans might be killed. That is not necessarily a bad thing."

"Of course," Erasmus said, "since programming restrictions prevent you from harming your creators outright."

"Accidents happen. Regardless, our offensive will either subsume the League Worlds or exterminate the fragments of humanity there. I do not care which. Very few humans are worth keeping around . . . perhaps none at all."

Erasmus did not like the sound of that.

The mind commands the body and immediately it obeys. The mind orders itself, and meets resistance.

—ST. AUGUSTINE,
ancient Earth philosopher

Though the cymeks had only begun their assault on Zimia, Xavier Harkonnen knew that free humanity must make its stand, here and now. And make it count.

The weapon-studded warrior-forms strode forward in lockstep. Raising silver arms, they launched explosive projectiles, spewed gouts of flame, spread poison gas. With each smashed wall, the cymeks drew closer to the main shield-generator station, a soaring tower of parabolic curves and intricate latticework.

At the fringes of Salusa's atmosphere, an orbital array of redundant satellites wove a crackling fence with amplifiers at each node. Across the continents, transmission towers beamed up the substance of the Holtzman scrambler field, crisscrossing it into an intricate mesh high above the planet, an impenetrable tapestry of energy.

But if the cymeks took out the primary towers on the surface, vulnerable gaps would open in the shield. The whole protective fabric could unravel.

Coughing blood from his searing throat and lungs, Xavier shouted into his comline, "This is Tercero Harkonnen, assuming command of local forces. Primero Meach and the control center have been wiped out." The channel remained silent for several long seconds, as if the entire Militia had been stunned.

Swallowing hard, Xavier tasted rusty blood in his mouth, then he issued his terrible order: "All local forces, form a cordon around the shield-transmitting towers. We do not have the resources to defend the rest of the city. Repeat, *pull back*. This includes all combat vehicles and attack aircraft."

The expected complaints poured in. "Sir, you can't be serious! The city is burning!"

"Zimia will be undefended! This must be a mistake!"

"Sir, please reconsider! Have you seen the damage those cymek bastards are already causing? Think of our people!"

"I don't recognize the authority of a *tercero* to issue orders of such—"

Xavier countermanded all of them. "The cymek objective is obvious: they intend to bring down our scrambler fields so the robot fleet can destroy us. We must defend the towers at all costs. *At all costs.*"

Blatantly ignoring his order, a dozen pilots flew kindjals overhead, continuing to dump explosives upon the cymek walkers.

Xavier growled in an uncompromising voice, "Anybody who wants to argue about it can do so afterward—at your court-martial." *Or mine*, he thought.

Droplets of scarlet splashed the inside of his plaz mask, and he wondered how much damage the poisonous fumes had already done. Each breath became difficult, but he put such concerns out of his mind. He could not sound weak, not now. "All assets, pull back and protect the towers! That is an order. We need to regroup and change our strategy."

Finally, Salusan ground units retreated from their pitched defenses, drawing back toward the shield-transmitter complex. The rest of the city lay as vulnerable as a lamb prepared for slaughter. And the cymeks took advantage with gleeful mayhem.

Four warrior-forms crashed through a statue park and destroyed fabulous works. The mechanical monsters annihilated buildings, blasting and burning museums, dwelling complexes, hazard shelters. Any target suited them.

"Stand firm," Xavier commanded on all channels, overruling howls of outrage from the troops. "The cymeks are trying to lure us away."

The warrior-forms set fire to a resonant bell tower erected by Chusuk to commemorate a successful defense against the thinking machines, four centuries ago. The ornate bells clanged and gonged as the tower collapsed onto the paving stones of an open gathering square.

By now most of Zimia's populace had rushed to armored shelters. Fleets of medical and fire-suppression craft dodged enemy blasts to fight the increasing disaster. Many rescue attempts became suicide missions.

In the midst of the Militia crowded around the transmitting towers, Xavier felt a flash of doubt, wondering if he had made the right decision but not daring to change his mind now. His eyes stung from smoke, and his shredded lungs sent shocks of agony through his body each time he drew a breath. He knew he was right. He was fighting for the lives of everyone on the planet. Including Serena Butler's.

"Now what, Tercero?" said Cuarto Jaymes Powder, coming up behind him. Though the subcommander's angular face was partially covered in a mask, his eyes still revealed his outrage. "Do we just sit back and watch these bastards level Zimia? What good is it to protect the shield transmitters if there's nothing left of the city?"

"We can't save the city if we lose our shields and open up the whole planet to machine attack," Xavier rasped.

The Salusan troops mounted a defense around the parabolic latticework of transmitting towers. Ground forces and armored equipment were arrayed on the surrounding ramparts and streets. Kindjals circled the skies and fired their weapons, keeping the cymeks away.

Gripping their weapons, the nearest Militia members seethed. The frustrated men wanted to rush forward and engage the attackers . . . or perhaps tear Xavier limb from limb. With each explosion or leveled building, the angry troops edged one step closer to outright mutiny.

"Until reinforcements arrive, we'll need to concentrate our forces," Xavier said, coughing.

Powder stared at the tercero's plaz faceplate, noticed blood on the inside. "Sir, are you all right?"

"It's nothing." But Xavier heard the liquid wheezing of his mangled lungs with every breath he took.

Feeling unsteady as the poison continued to burn his soft tissues, he gripped a plascrete bulwark for support. He studied the last stand he had assembled on short notice and hoped it would hold. Finally, Xavier said, "Now that these towers are held and protected, we can go out and hunt down some of our attackers. Are you ready, Cuarto Powder?"

Powder brightened, and soldiers cheered. Several men fired their weapons into the air, ready to charge pell-mell into the destruction. Like a rider at the reins of a willful horse, Xavier held them back.

"Wait! Pay close attention. There is no clever trick we can use, no inherent weakness that will allow us to outsmart the cymeks. But we have the will to succeed and the need to succeed . . . or we will lose everything." Ignoring the blood in his mask, he didn't know how he was able to summon unwavering confidence in his voice. "*This* is how we will beat them."

During the initial frantic skirmishes, Xavier had seen at least one of the gargantuan invaders destroyed by multiple, concentrated explosions. Its articulated body was now nothing more than a smoking hulk. However, the scattered bombers and armored ground units had spread their attacks across too many targets, diluting their efforts.

"This will be a coordinated strike. We will select a single target and crush it, one cymek at a time. We'll hit it and hit it again until there's nothing left. Then we'll go on to the next one."

Though he could barely breathe, Xavier chose to lead the squadrons himself. As a tercero, he was accustomed to being in the thick of the action during training exercises and simulations.

"Sir?" Powder said, surprised. "Shouldn't you be in a secure area? As the acting commander, standard procedure requires—"

"You're absolutely right, Jaymes," he said quietly. "Nevertheless, I'm going up there. We're in an all-or-nothing situation. You stay here and protect those towers at all costs."

Subterranean elevators brought more kindjals to the surface, ready for launch. He climbed into one of the mottled gray craft and sealed himself into the cockpit. Troopers raced to their assault ships, shouting promises of revenge to their comrades who were forced to remain behind. As he transferred the kindjal's comchannel to his command frequency, Xavier issued new instructions.

Tercero Harkonnen adjusted the cockpit seat and launched his kindjal. The rush of acceleration pushed him backward and made his breathing even more difficult. Hot blood trickled from one corner of his mouth.

Soaring away from the central transmitting towers, aircraft followed him, while a small number of armored ground vehicles moved away from the generating facility, heading for their designated intercept positions. Weapons primed and bombs ready to drop, the kindjals descended toward the first cymek target, one of the smaller machines. Xavier's voice crackled in the cockpit of every aircraft. "On my mark, strike—*now*."

The defenders pounded the crablike body from all directions until the warrior-form lay crushed, its articulated legs blackened and twisted, the brain canister destroyed. Cheers and catcalls resonated across the comchannels. Before the cymeks could react to the new coordinated tactic, Xavier chose a second target. "Follow me. Next one."

The Militia squadron came in like a hammer, converging on a single mechanical body. Mobile armored ground units opened fire from the surface, while kindjals dropped powerful bombs from above.

The second cymek target saw the attack coming and raised

its spiked metal legs to open fire with white-hot sprays of flame. Two of Xavier's flanking kindjals went down, crashing into already-ruined buildings. Stray bombs leveled a square block of the city.

But the remainder of the concentrated assault struck true. The multiple explosions were more than the robotic body could withstand, and another cymek was battered into wreckage. One of its metal arms twitched, then fell out of its socket into the rubble.

"Three down," Xavier said. "Twenty-five more."

"Unless they retreat first," said another pilot.

The cymeks were individuals, unlike most of Omnius's thinking machines. Some of them were survivors of the original Titans; others—the neo-cymeks—came from traitorous human collaborators on the Synchronized Worlds. All had sacrificed their physical bodies so they could be closer to the supposed perfection of thinking machines.

Among the troops surrounding the field-transmission towers, Cuarto Powder used everything in his combined arsenals to drive back four cymeks that had gotten close enough to threaten the vital structures. He destroyed one warrior-form and forced the other three to limp away and regroup. Meanwhile, Xavier's forces in the air crushed two more cymeks.

The tide was turning.

Xavier's bomb-laden kindjals came around again, closing on a new wave of invaders. Followed by armored ground vehicles and artillery guns, the Salusan Militia launched volley after volley at the foremost cymek. The bombardment damaged the machine's legs, obliterated its weapons. Kindjals circled around to deliver the final blow.

Surprisingly, the central turret containing the cymek's human brain detached itself. With a bright flash of ignition, locking bolts blasted clear of the set of articulated legs. The armored spherical container rocketed skyward, beyond the reach of Salusan weapons.

"An escape pod to protect the traitor's brain." Xavier's words caused him to wheeze and cough more blood. "Open fire on it!" His kindjals launched their weapons as the cymek pod soared into the smoky sky with enough thrust to reach escape velocity.

"Damn!" The pilots shot at the fading exhaust trail, but the cymek's escape pod rapidly dwindled from sight.

"Don't waste your weapons," Xavier said over the comline. "That one's no longer a threat." He felt dizzy, either fading into unconsciousness . . . or dying.

"Yes, sir." The kindjals turned back toward the ground, concentrating on the next cymek.

However, when his assault squadron converged on another enemy, that cymek also launched its escape pod, shooting the brain-case like a cannonball into the sky. "Hey," a pilot complained, "he retreated before we could give him a black eye!"

"Maybe we activated their 'turn-tail-and-run' programs," another pilot said with a snort.

"As long as they're retreating," Xavier said, barely able to hold on to consciousness. He hoped he didn't spiral down and crash. "Follow me to the next target."

As if in response to a signal, all the remaining cymeks abandoned their warrior-forms. Escape containers blasted upward like fireworks, vaulting blindly through the scrambler net and out into space, where the robotic fleet could retrieve them.

When the cymeks abandoned their assault, the surviving Salusan defenders set up a ragged cheer from the wreckage on the ground.

❧

OVER THE NEXT several hours, Salusan survivors emerged from shelters, blinking into the smoke-filled skies with a mixture of shock and triumph.

After the cymeks had retreated, the frustrated robot fleet had launched a swarm of missiles at the ground, but their gelcircuitry guidance computers also failed. Standard Salusan missile-defense systems obliterated all of the machine weapons before they could reach their targets.

Finally, when the recalled battle groups began to converge on the robot fleet, charging in from the perimeter of the

Gamma Waiping system, the thinking machines recalculated their chances for success, didn't like the odds, and decided to retreat, leaving much wreckage in orbit.

On the surface, Zimia continued to burn, and tens of thousands of bodies lay in the rubble.

Xavier had held himself together for the battle, but in its aftermath was barely able to stand. His lungs were full of blood; his mouth tasted of acid. He had insisted that the medics and battlefield surgeons concentrate on the more seriously wounded out in the streets.

From a balcony on the top level of the damaged Hall of Parliament, he gazed out at the horrendous damage. The world turned a sickly red around him, and he wavered on his feet, then reeled backward. He heard aides behind him, summoning a doctor.

I cannot consider this a victory, he thought, then retreated into black unconsciousness.

In the desert, the line between life and death is sharp and quick.
—Zensunni Fire Poetry from Arrakis

Far from thinking machines and the League of Nobles, the desert never changed. The Zensunni descendants who had fled to Arrakis lived in isolated cave communities, barely subsisting in a harsh environment. They experienced little enjoyment, yet fought fiercely to remain alive for just another day.

Sunlight poured across the ocean of sand, warming dunes that rippled like waves breaking upon an imagined shore. A few black rocks poked out of the dustlike islands, but offered no shelter from the heat or the demon worms.

This desolate landscape was the last thing he would ever see. The people had accused the young man and would mete out their punishment. His innocence was not relevant.

"Begone, Selim!" came a shout from the caves above. "Go far from here!" He recognized the voice of his young friend—*former* friend—Ebrahim. Perhaps the other boy was relieved, since by rights it should have been him facing exile and death, not Selim. But no one would mourn the loss of an orphan, and so Selim had been cast out in the Zensunni version of justice.

A raspy voice said, "May the worms spit out your scrawny hide." That was old Glyffa, who had once been like a mother to him. "Thief! Water stealer!"

From the caves, the tribe began to throw stones. One sharp rock struck the cloth he had wrapped around his dark hair for protection against the sun. Selim ducked, but did not give them the satisfaction of seeing him cringe. They had stripped almost everything from him, but as long as he drew breath they would never take his pride.

Naib Dhartha, the sietch leader, leaned out. "The tribe has spoken."

Protestations of his innocence would do no good, nor would excuses or explanations. Keeping his balance on the steep path, the young man stooped to grab a sharp-edged stone. He held it in his palm and glared up at the people.

Selim had always been skilled at throwing rocks. He could pick off ravens, small kangaroo mice, or lizards for the community cookpot. If he aimed carefully, he could have put out one of the Naib's eyes. Selim had seen Dhartha whispering quietly with Ebrahim's father, watched them form their plan to cast the blame on him instead of the guilty boy. They had decided Selim's punishment using measures other than the truth.

Naib Dhartha had dark eyebrows and jet-black hair bound into a ponytail by a dull metal ring. A purplish geometric tattoo of dark angles and straight lines marked his left cheek. His wife had drawn it on his face using a steel needle and the juice of a scraggly inkvine the Zensunni cultivated in their terrarium gardens. The Naib glared down as if daring Selim to throw the stone, because the Zensunni would respond with a pummeling barrage of large rocks.

But such a punishment would kill him far too quickly. Instead, the tribe would drive Selim away from their tight-knit community. And on Arrakis, one did not survive without help. Existence in the desert required cooperation, each person doing his part. The Zensunni looked upon stealing—especially the theft of water—as the worst crime imaginable.

Selim pocketed the stone. Ignoring the jeers and insults, he continued his tedious descent toward the open desert.

Dhartha intoned in a voice that sounded like a bass howl of stormwinds, "Selim, who has no father or mother—Selim, who was welcomed as a member of our tribe—you have been found guilty of stealing tribal water. Therefore, you must walk across the sands." Dhartha raised his voice, shouting before the condemned man could pass out of earshot. "May Shaitan choke on your bones."

All his life, Selim had done more work than most others. Because he was of unknown parentage, the tribe demanded it of him. No one helped him when he was sick, except maybe old Glyffa; no one carried an extra load for him. He had watched some of his companions gorge themselves on inflated family shares of water, even Ebrahim. And still, the other boy, seeing half a literjon of brackish water untended, had drunk it, foolishly hoping no one would notice. How easy it had been for Ebrahim to blame it on his supposed friend when the theft was discovered. . . .

Upon driving Selim from the caves, Dhartha had refused to give him even a tiny water pouch for his journey, because that was considered a waste of tribal resources. None of them expected Selim to survive more than a day anyway, even if he somehow managed to avoid the fearsome monsters of the desert.

He muttered under his breath, knowing they couldn't hear him, "May your mouth fill with dust, Naib Dhartha." Selim bounded down the path away from the cliffs, while his people continued to utter curses from above. A hurled pebble bounced past him.

When he reached the base of the rock wall that stood as a shield against the desert and the sandworm demons, he set off in a straight line, wanting to get as far away as he could. Dry heat pounded on his head. Those watching him would surely be surprised to see him voluntarily hike out onto the dunes instead of huddling in a cave in the rocks.

What do I have to lose?

Selim made up his mind that he would never go back and plead for help. Instead, chin high, he strode across the dunes as far as he could. He would rather die than beg forgiveness from the likes of them. Ebrahim had lied to protect his own life, but Naib Dhartha had committed a far worse crime in Selim's eyes, knowingly condemning an innocent orphan boy to death because it simplified tribal politics.

Selim had excellent desert skills, but Arrakis was a severe environment. In the several generations since the Zensunni had settled here, no one had ever returned from exile. The deep desert swallowed them up, leaving no trace. He trudged out into the wasteland with only a rope slung over his shoulder, a stubby dagger at his belt, and a sharpened metal walking stick, a piece he had salvaged from the spaceport junkyard in Arrakis City.

Maybe Selim could go there and find a job with offworld traders, moving cargo from each vessel that landed, or stowing aboard one of the spaceships that plied their way from planet to planet, often taking years for each passage. But such ships only rarely visited Arrakis, since it was far from the regular shipping lanes. And joining the strange offworlders might make Selim give up too much of himself. It would be better to live alone in the desert—if he could survive. . . .

He pocketed another sharp rock, one that had been thrown from above. As the mountain buttress shrank into the distance, he found a third shard that seemed like a good throwing stone. Eventually, he would need to capture food. He could suck a lizard's moist flesh and live for just a little while longer.

As he made his way into the restless wasteland, Selim gazed toward a long peninsula of rock, far from the Zensunni caves. He'd be apart from the tribe there, but could still laugh at them every day he survived his exile. He could thumb his nose and call out jokes that Naib Dhartha would never hear.

Selim poked his walking stick into the soft dunes, as if stabbing an imaginary enemy. He sketched a deprecating Buddislamic symbol in the sand, with an arrow on it that pointed back toward the cliff dwellings. He took a special satisfaction from his defiance, even though the wind would erase the insult within a day. With a lighter step, he climbed a high dune and skidded down into the trough.

He began to sing a traditional song, maintaining an upbeat composure, and increased his speed. The distant peninsula of rock shimmered in the afternoon, and he tried to convince himself that it looked inviting. His bravado increased as he drew farther from his tormentors.

But when he was within a kilometer of the sheltering black rock, Selim felt the loose sand tremble under his feet. He looked up, suddenly realizing his danger, and saw ripples that marked the passage of a large creature deep beneath the dunes.

Selim ran. He slipped and scrambled across the soft ridge, desperate not to fall. He kept moving, racing along the crest, knowing that even this high dune would prove no obstacle for the oncoming sandworm. The rock peninsula remained impossibly far away, and the demon came ever closer.

Selim forced himself to skid to a halt, though his panicked heart urged him to keep running. Worms followed any vibration, and he had run like a terrified child instead of freezing in place like the wily desert hare. This behemoth had certainly targeted him by now. How many others before him had stood terrified, falling to their knees in final prayer before being devoured? No person had ever survived an encounter with one of the great desert monsters.

Unless he could fool it . . . distract it.

Selim willed his feet and legs to turn to stone. He took the first of the fist-sized stones he carried and hurled it as far as he could into the gully between dunes. It landed with a *thump*—and the ominous track of the approaching worm diverted just a little.

He tossed another rock, and a third, in a drumbeat pattern intended to lure the worm away from him. Selim threw the rest of his stones, and the beast turned only slightly, rising up in the dunes close to him.

Empty handed, he now had no other way to divert the creature.

Its maw open wide, the worm gulped sand and stones, searching for a morsel of meat. The sand beneath Selim's boots shifted and crumbled at the edge of the worm's path, and he knew the monster would swallow him. He smelled an ominous cinnamon stench on the worm's breath, saw glimpses of fire in its gullet.

Naib Dhartha would no doubt laugh at the young thief's fate. Selim shouted a loud curse. And rather than surrender, he decided to attack.

Closer to the cavernous mouth, the odor of spice intensified. The young man gripped his metal walking stick and whispered a prayer. As the worm lifted itself from beneath the dune, Selim leaped onto its curved and crusty back. He raised the metal staff like a spear and plunged the sharpened tip into what he thought would be tough, armored wormskin. Instead, the point slipped between segments, into soft pink flesh.

The beast reacted as if it had been shot with a maula cannon. It reared up, thrashed, and writhed.

Surprised, Selim drove the spear deeper and held on with all his strength. He squeezed his eyes shut, clenching his teeth and pulling back to keep himself steady. He would have no chance if he let go.

Despite the worm's violent reaction, the little spear couldn't have wounded it; this was merely a human gesture of defiance, a biting fly thirsty for a sweet droplet of blood. Any moment now the worm would dive back beneath the sand and drag Selim down with it.

Surprisingly, though, the creature raced forward, keeping itself high out of the dunes where the exposed tissue would not be abraded by sand.

Terrified, Selim clung to the implanted staff—then laughed as he realized he was actually *riding* Shaitan himself! Had anyone ever done such a thing? If so, no man had ever lived to tell about it.

Selim made a pact with himself and with Buddallah that he would not be defeated, not by Naib Dhartha and not by this desert demon. He pulled back on his spear and pried the fleshy segment even wider, making the worm climb out of the sand, as if it could outrun the annoying parasite on its back. . . .

The young exile never made it to the strip of rock where he had hoped to establish a private camp. Instead, the worm careened into the deep desert . . . carrying Selim far from his former life.

We learned a negative thing from computers, that the setting of guidelines belongs to humans, not to machines.

—RELL ARKOV,
charter meeting of the League of Nobles

Afterbeing rebuffed on Salusa Secundus, the thinking-machine fleet headed back to their distant base on Corrin. There, the computer evermind would not be pleased to hear the report of failure.

Like lapdog servants to Omnius, the remaining neo-cymeks followed the defeated robot fleet. However, the six survivors of the original Titans—Agamemnon and his elite cadre—prepared a diversion. It was an opportunity to advance their own schemes against the oppressive evermind. . . .

While the dispersed battleships made their way through space carrying the vigilant watcheyes, Agamemnon discreetly flew his own ship on a different course. After escaping the Salusan Militia, the cymek general had transferred his brain canister from a soot-scarred mobile warrior-form to this sleek armored vessel. Despite the defeat, he felt exuberant and alive. There would always be other battles to fight, whether against feral humans or against Omnius.

The ancient cymeks maintained com-silence, worried that a

stray electromagnetic ripple might be detected by an outlying ship in the retreating machine fleet. They plotted a faster, more dangerous route that took them closer to celestial obstacles avoided by the risk-averse robot vessels. The shortcut would buy the secretly rebellious cymeks enough time to meet in private.

As their course intercepted a simmering red dwarf star, the Titans approached a misshapen, pockmarked rock that orbited close to the dim sun. There, a sleet of stellar wind and ionized particles, coupled with strong magnetic fields, would hide them from any robotic scans. After a thousand years of serving Omnius, Agamemnon had learned ways to outwit and sidestep the accursed evermind.

The six cymeks vectored in toward the planetoid using their human skills instead of computerized navigation systems. Agamemnon chose a site within a yawning crater, and the other Titans dropped beside his vessel, finding stable terrain on a rippled plain.

Inside his ship, Agamemnon guided mechanical arms that lifted his enclosed brain canister from its control socket and installed it into another mobile terrestrial body with a set of six sturdy legs and a low-slung body core. After connecting the thoughtrodes that linked his mind through electrafluid, he tested his gleaming legs, lifting the metal pads and adjusting the hydraulics.

He walked his graceful mechanical body down the ramp onto the soft rock. The other Titans joined him, each wearing a walker body with visible internal workings and life-support systems impervious to the blazing heat and radiation. The bloodshot dwarf star loomed overhead in the black, airless sky.

The first of the surviving Titans came forward to touch sensor pads against the general's mechanical body, delicate probings in a romantic caress. Juno was a strategic genius who had been Agamemnon's lover back when they had worn human bodies. Now, a millennium later, they continued their partnership, needing little more than the aphrodisiac of power.

"Will we move forward soon, my love?" Juno asked. "Or must we wait another century or two?"

"Not so long, Juno. Not nearly so long."

Next came Barbarossa, the closest thing to a masculine friend Agamemnon had known for the past thousand years. "Every moment is already an eternity," he said. During the Titans' initial takeover, Barbarossa had discovered how to subvert the Old Empire's ubiquitous thinking machines. Luckily, the modest genius had also had the foresight to implant deep programming restrictions that prevented thinking machines from doing any outright harm to the Titans—restrictions that had kept Agamemnon and his cymek companions alive after the evermind's treacherous takeover.

"I can't decide if I'd rather smash computers or humans," Ajax said. The most powerful enforcer of the old cymeks, the brutal bully clomped forward in a particularly massive walker-form, as if still flexing the muscles of his long-ago organic body.

"We must cover our tracks twice for every plan we make." Dante, a skilled bureaucrat and accountant, had an easy grasp of complex details. Among the Titans, he had never been dramatic or glamorous, but the overthrow of the Old Empire could not have been achieved without his clever manipulations of clerical and administrative matters. With none of the bravado of the other conquerors, Dante had calmly worked out an equitable division of leadership that had permitted the Titans to rule smoothly for a century.

Until the computers had wrested it all from them.

The disgraced Xerxes was the last cymek to clamber into the sheltered crater. The lowliest Titan had long ago committed the unforgivable mistake that allowed the ambitious newborn computer mind to hamstring them all. Although the Titans still needed him as part of their ever-dwindling group, Agamemnon had never forgiven him for the blunder. For centuries, miserable Xerxes had had no other desire than to make up for his error. He foolishly believed that Agamemnon might embrace him again if he could find a way to redeem himself, and the cymek general made use of such enthusiasm.

Agamemnon led his five co-conspirators across the terrain to the crater shadows. There, the machines with human minds faced each other among broken rocks and half-melted boulders to speak their treason and plot revenge.

Xerxes, despite his flaws, would never betray them. A thousand years ago, after their victory, the original Titans had agreed to surgical conversion rather than accept their mortality, so that their disembodied brains could live forever and consolidate their rule. It had been a dramatic pact.

Now, Omnius occasionally rewarded loyal human followers by converting them to neo-cymeks, as well. Across the Synchronized Worlds, thousands of newer brains with machine bodies served as indentured servants to the evermind. Agamemnon could not rely upon anyone who willingly served the evermind, however.

The cymek general transmitted his words on a tight waveband that tapped directly into the Titans' thought-processing centers. "We are not expected back on Corrin for weeks. I have seized this opportunity so that we may plan a strike against Omnius."

"It's about time," Ajax said, his voice a deep grumble.

"Do you believe the evermind has grown complacent, my love—like the humans of the Old Empire?" Juno asked.

"I have noted no particular sign of weakness," Dante interjected, "and I keep careful track of such things."

"There are always weaknesses," Ajax said, twitching one of his heavy armored legs and gouging a hole in the ground, "*if* you're willing to use enough muscle to exploit them."

Barbarossa clacked one of his metal forelegs on the hard rock. "Do not be fooled by artificial intelligence. Computers do not think like humans. Even after a thousand years, Omnius will not let his attention wander. He has enough processing power and more watcheyes than we can count."

"Does he suspect us? Does Omnius doubt our loyalty?" Xerxes already sounded worried, and the meeting had just begun. "If he thinks we are plotting against him, why won't he just eliminate us?"

"Sometimes I think you have a leak in your brain canister," Agamemnon said. "Omnius has programming restrictions that prevent him from killing us."

"You don't have to be insulting. It's just that Omnius is so powerful, you'd think he could override whatever Barbarossa loaded into his system."

"He hasn't yet, and never will. I knew what I was doing on that job, believe me," Barbarossa said. "Remember, Omnius yearns to be efficient. He will take no unnecessary actions, will not waste resources. *We are resources to him.*"

Dante said, "If Omnius is so intent on ruling efficiently, then why does he keep human slaves around at all? Even simple robots and minimal-AI machines could perform their tasks with less bother."

Agamemnon paced out of the thick shadows into harsh light, and then back again. Around him, the conspirators waited like huge insects made of scrap metal. "For years, I have been suggesting that we exterminate the human captives on the Synchronized Worlds, but Omnius refuses."

"Maybe he's reluctant because humans created thinking machines in the first place," Xerxes suggested. "Omnius might see humans as a manifestation of God."

Agamemnon chided him. "Are you suggesting that the computer evermind is devoutly religious?" The disgraced cymek quickly fell silent.

Barbarossa said, like a patient teacher, "No, no—Omnius simply doesn't wish to expend the energy or cause the turmoil that such an extermination would bring about. He sees humans as resources, not to be wasted."

"We've been trying to convince him otherwise for centuries," Ajax said.

Aware that their safe window of time was rapidly dwindling, Agamemnon pushed the discussion forward. "We must find some way to spark a radical change. If we shut the computers down, then we Titans rule once more, along with any neo-cymeks we can recruit." He swiveled his sensor-turret. "We've taken charge before and must do it again."

Previously, when the human Titans had consolidated the stagnant Old Empire, combat robots had done the bulk of the fighting for them. Tlaloc, Agamemnon, and the other rebels had simply picked up the pieces. This time the Titans would have to fight for themselves.

"Maybe we should try to find Hecate," Xerxes said. "She's the only one of us who has never been under Omnius's control. Our wild card."

Hecate, the former mate of Ajax, was the sole Titan who had relinquished her rule. Before the thinking machine takeover, she had departed into deep space, never to be heard from again. But Agamemnon could never trust her—even if she could be located—any more than he trusted Xerxes. Hecate had abandoned them long ago; she was not the ally they needed.

"We should look elsewhere for assistance, take any help we can find," Agamemnon said. "My son Vorian is one of the few humans allowed access to the central complex of the Earth-Omnius, and he delivers regular updates to the ever-minds on other Synchronized Worlds. Perhaps we can use him."

Juno simulated a laugh. "You want to trust a human, my love? One of the weak vermin you despise? Moments ago you wanted to exterminate every member of the race."

"Vorian is my genetic son, and the best of my offspring so far. I have been watching him, training him. He has read my memoirs a dozen times already. I have high hopes that one day he will be a worthy successor."

Juno understood Agamemnon better than the other Titans did. "You've said similar things about your twelve previous sons, if I recall. Even so, you found excuses to kill all of them."

"I preserved plenty of my sperm before converting myself into a cymek, and I have the time to do it right," Agamemnon said. "But Vorian . . . ah, Vorian, I think he might be the one. One day I'll let him become a cymek."

Ajax interrupted, his voice pitched low, "We cannot fight two major enemies at once. Since Omnius has finally allowed us to attack the *hrethgir,* thanks to Barbarossa's victory in the gladiator ring, I say we prosecute that war to the best of our abilities. Afterward, we deal with Omnius."

Immersed in the crater shadows, the cymeks muttered, half-agreeing. The League humans had escaped Titan rule centuries ago, and the old cymeks had always harbored a hatred toward them. Dante's optic threads tracked back and forth, calculating. "Yes, the humans should be easier to defeat."

"Meanwhile, we continue to seek a means to eliminate Omnius," Barbarossa added. "Everything in its time."

"Perhaps you are correct," Agamemnon admitted. The cymek general did not want to extend this clandestine gathering much longer.

He led the march back to their individual ships. "We destroy the League humans first. Using that as a springboard, we then turn our attention to the more difficult foe."

༄

Logic is blind and often knows only its own past.
> —archives from *Genetics to Philosophy,*
> compiled by the Sorceresses of Rossak

Thinking machines cared little for aesthetics, but the Omnius update ship was—by accident of design—a beautifully sleek silver-and-black vessel, dwarfed by the immensity of the cosmos as it journeyed from one Synchronized World to another. Finished with its current round of updates, the *Dream Voyager* was on its way back to Earth.

Vorian Atreides considered himself fortunate to be entrusted with such a vital assignment. Born from a female slave impregnated with Agamemnon's preserved sperm, dark-haired Vorian could trace his lineage back past the Time of Titans, thousands of years to the House of Atreus in ancient Greece and another famous Agamemnon. Because of his father's status, twenty-year-old Vor had been raised and indoctrinated on Earth under the thinking machines. He was one of the privileged "trustee" humans permitted to move about freely, serving Omnius.

He had read all the stories of his illustrious bloodline in the extensive memoirs his father had written to document his triumphs. Vor considered the Titan general's great work to be more than a literary masterpiece, closer to a holy historical document.

Just forward of Vor's work station, the *Dream Voyager*'s captain, an autonomous robot, checked instruments unerringly. Seurat's coppery-metal skinfilm flowed over a man-shaped body of polymer struts, alloy supports, gelcircuitry processors, and wound elastic-weave musculature.

While Seurat studied the instruments, he intermittently tapped into the ship's long-range scanners or looked out the windowport with focused optic threads. Multiprocessing as he conversed, the robot captain continued the interplay with his subservient human copilot. Seurat had a strange and unfortunate penchant for telling odd jokes.

"Vorian, what do you get when you breed a pig with a human?"

"What?"

"A creature that still eats a great deal, still stinks, and still does no work!"

Vorian favored the captain with a polite chuckle. Most of the time, Seurat's jokes only demonstrated that the robot did not truly understand humor. But if Vor didn't laugh, Seurat would simply tell another one, and another, until he obtained the desired reaction. "Aren't you afraid you'll make an error by telling jokes while monitoring our navigation systems?"

"I don't make mistakes," Seurat said, in his staccato mechanical voice.

Vor brightened with the challenge. "Ah, but what if I sabotaged one of the ship's vital functions? We're the only ones aboard, and I *am* a deceitful human after all, your mortal enemy. It would serve you right for all those terrible jokes."

"I might expect that of a lowly slave or even an artisan worker, but *you* would never do that, Vorian. You have too much to lose." With an eerily smooth movement, Seurat turned his rippled coppery head, paying even less attention to the *Dream Voyager*'s controls. "And even if you did, I would figure it out."

"Don't underestimate me, old Metalmind. My father teaches

DUNE: THE BUTLERIAN JIHAD 59

me that, despite our many weaknesses, we humans have a trump card with our very unpredictability." Smiling, Vorian went to the robot captain's side and studied the metric screens. "Why do you think Omnius asks me to throw a wrench into his careful simulations every time he plans an encounter with the *hrethgir*?"

"Your outrageous and reckless chaos is the only reason you are able to beat me in any strategy game," Seurat said. "It certainly has nothing to do with your innate skills."

"A winner has more skills than a loser," Vor said, "no matter how you define the competition."

The update ship traveled on a regular, continuous route throughout the Synchronized Worlds. One of fifteen such vessels, the *Dream Voyager* carried copies of the current version of Omnius to synchronize the separate computer everminds on widely separated planets.

Circuitry limitations and electronic transmission speeds constrained the physical size of any individual machine; thus, the same computer evermind could not viably extend beyond a single planet. Nonetheless, duplicate copies of Omnius existed everywhere, like mental clones. With regular updates continually exchanged by ships like the *Dream Voyager*, all the separate Omnius incarnations remained virtually identical across the machine-dominated autarchy.

After many voyages, Vor knew how to operate the ship and could access all onboard data banks using Seurat's codes. Over the years, he and the robot captain had become fast friends in a way that others were not likely to understand. Because of the extended time they shared in deep space, talking about many things, playing games of skill, telling stories—they bridged much of the gap between machine and man.

Sometimes, for amusement, Vor and Seurat traded places, and Vor pretended to be the captain of the ship, while Seurat became his robotic underling, as in the days of the Old Empire. During one role-playing session, Vorian had impulsively christened the ship *Dream Voyager*, a bit of poetic nonsense that Seurat not only tolerated, but maintained.

As a sentient machine, Seurat routinely received new instructions and memory transfers from the overall Omnius brain, but because he spent so much time disconnected while journeying between the stars, he had developed his own personality and independence. In Vor's opinion, Seurat was the best of the machine minds, although the robot could be irritating at times. Especially with that peculiar sense of humor.

Vor clasped his hands and cracked his knuckles. He sighed with pleasure. "Sure feels good to loosen up. Too bad it's something you can't do."

"I do not require loosening up."

Vorian didn't admit that he, too, found his own organic body to be inferior in many ways, fragile and prone to aches, sicknesses, and injuries that any machine could have easily fixed. He hoped that his physical form would remain functional long enough for him to be made into one of the enduring neo-cymeks, all of whom had once been valued trustee humans, like himself. One day Agamemnon would receive permission from Omnius for that, if Vor worked very hard to serve the evermind.

The *Dream Voyager* had been in space on a long update run, and the young trustee was glad to be going home. He would see his eminent father soon.

As the *Dream Voyager* soared between stars, undisturbed, Seurat suggested a friendly competition. The two sat at a table and engaged in one of their customary diversions, an amusing private game they had developed through frequent practice. The strategy involved an imaginary space battle between two alien races—the "Vorians" and the "Seurats"—each of which had a space fleet with precise capabilities and limitations. Though the robot captain had a perfect machine memory, Vor still fared well, as he invariably came up with creative tactics that surprised his opponent.

Now, as they took turns placing warships in the various sectors of their fanciful space battlefield, Seurat reeled off an endless succession of human jokes and riddles he had found in his old databases. Annoyed, Vor finally said, "You're making an overt attempt to distract me. Where did you learn to do that?"

"Why, from you, of course." The robot proceeded to mention the many times in which Vor had teased him, threatening to sabotage the ship without ever really intending to do so, concocting extraordinarily unpredictable emergencies. "Do you consider it cheating? On your part, or on mine?"

This revelation astonished Vor. "It saddens me to think that, even in jest, I have taught you deception. It makes me ashamed to be human." No doubt, Agamemnon would be disappointed in him.

After two more rounds, Vor lost the tactical game. His heart was no longer in it.

Every endeavor is a game, is it not?

—IBLIS GINJO,
Options for Total Liberation

On a garden terrace overlooking the scarred ruins of
Zimia, Xavier Harkonnen stood somberly by himself,
dreading the upcoming "victory" parade. Afternoon sunlight
warmed his face. Birdsong had replaced the screams and explosions; breezes had scoured away the worst of the poisonous
smoke.

Still, the League would be a long time recovering. Nothing
would ever be the same.

Even days after the attack, he still saw smears of smoke
wafting from the rubble and trailing into a cloudless sky. He
could not smell the soot, though. The cymeks' poison gas had
so damaged his tissues that he would never smell or taste much
of anything again. Even breathing had become no more that
a mechanical act, not an enjoyable inhalation of sweet fresh
air.

But he could not wallow in misery when so many others
had lost much more. In the aftermath of the cymek attack, he
had been kept alive by the heroic efforts of a Salusan medical

team. Serena Butler had come to him at the hospital, but he remembered her only through a fog of pain, drugs, and life-support systems. In an extraordinary procedure, Xavier had received a double lung transplant, healthy organs provided by the mysterious Tlulaxa. He knew Serena had worked vigorously with the brilliant battlefield surgeons and a Tlulaxa flesh merchant named Tuk Keedair to get him the treatment he needed.

Now he could breathe again, despite intermittent bursts of pain. Xavier would live to fight the machines another time. Thanks to pharmaceuticals and advanced healing techniques, he had been able to leave the hospital soon after the medical procedure.

At the time of the attack, the flesh merchant Keedair had been in Zimia on a routine sales call and barely escaped with his life. On the Unallied Planet of Tlulax in the distant Thalim solar system, his people ran organ farms, growing human hearts, lungs, kidneys, and other body parts from viable cells. After the cymeks were driven away, the secretive Tlulaxa had offered his biological wares to the battlefield surgeons at Zimia's main field hospital. His ship's cryogenic lockers were filled with sample body parts. A stroke of luck, Keedair had admitted with a smile, that he could be there to help the grievously injured Salusan citizens during their time of great need.

Following the successful surgery, Keedair had come to see Xavier in the medical center. The Tlulaxa was a man of middle height but slight of build, with dark eyes and an angular face. A long, dark braid hung at the left side of his head, plaited tightly.

Breathing in, carefully modulating his raspy voice, Xavier said, "It was fortunate you were here with new organs already stored aboard your ship."

Keedair rubbed his long-fingered hands together. "If I had known the cymeks would strike so ferociously, I would have brought a larger supply of material from our organ farms. Your Salusan survivors could use many more replacement parts, but additional ships cannot arrive from the Thalim system for months."

Before the flesh merchant left Xavier's room, he turned back and said, "Consider yourself one of the lucky ones, Tercero Harkonnen."

⊱

IN BATTLE-SCARRED ZIMIA, grief-stricken survivors searched for their dead, and buried them. As rubble was cleared, the death toll mounted. Bodies were recovered, names of the missing were compiled. In spite of such pain and sorrow, because of the attack free humanity grew stronger.

Viceroy Manion Butler had insisted that the people show only determination in the aftermath. On the streets below Xavier's terrace, final preparations were under way for a celebration of thanksgiving. Banners with the open-hand sigil of human freedom fluttered in the wind. Rough-looking men in dirty coats struggled to control magnificent white Salusan stallions that had become agitated by the commotion. The horses' manes were braided with tassles and bells, and their tails swept behind them like waterfalls of fine hair. Festooned with ribbons and flowers, the animals pranced, eager to march down the broad central boulevard that had been washed clean of debris, soot, and bloodstains.

Xavier glanced uncertainly at the sky. How could he ever look at the clouds again without dreading that he might see more pyramidal dropcarriages plunging through the scrambler shields? Missiles were already being installed, increased batteries to protect against an attack from space. More patrols would be launched, circling the system on the highest state of alert.

Instead of attending a parade, he should be preparing the Salusan Militia for another attack, increasing the number of picket ships and scouts at the edge of the system, working out a more efficient rescue and response plan. It was only a matter of time before the thinking machines returned.

The next meeting of the League Parliament would devote itself to emergency measures and reparations. The representatives would sketch out a reconstruction plan for Zimia. The cymek warrior-forms left behind must be dismantled and analyzed for weaknesses.

Xavier hoped the League would immediately dispatch a summons to Poritrin, calling the brilliant Tio Holtzman to inspect his recently installed scrambler shields. Only the great inventor himself could devise a stopgap measure against the technical flaw the cymeks had discovered.

When Xavier mentioned his concerns to Viceroy Butler, the florid-faced leader had nodded, but stopped further discussion. "First, we must have a day of affirmation, to celebrate the fact that we are alive." Xavier saw deep sadness behind the Viceroy's mask of confidence. "We are not machines, Xavier. There must be more to our lives than war and revenge."

Hearing footsteps on the terrace, Xavier turned to see Serena Butler smiling at him, her eyes flashing with a secret depth that she shared with him now that no one could see the two of them. "There is my heroic tercero."

"A man responsible for letting half a city be destroyed isn't usually called a hero, Serena."

"No, but the term does apply to a man who saved the rest of the planet. As you are fully aware, if you hadn't made your hard choice, all of Zimia, all of Salusa, would have been crushed." She put a hand on his shoulder and stood very close to him. "I won't have you wallowing in guilt during the victory parade. One day won't make much difference."

"One day could very well make a *huge* difference," Xavier insisted. "We barely drove off the attackers this time because we were too confident in the new scrambler shields, and because we foolishly thought Omnius had decided to leave us alone after so many decades. This would be the perfect time for them to hit us again. What if they've launched a second wave?"

"Omnius is still licking his wounds. I doubt his force has even returned to the Synchronized Worlds yet."

"Machines don't lick wounds," he said.

"You're such a serious young man," she said. "Please, just for the parade? Our people need to have their spirits uplifted."

"Your father already gave me the same lecture."

66   *Brian Herbert and Kevin J. Anderson*

"You know, of course, that if two Butlers say a thing, it's bound to be true."

He gave Serena a firm hug, then followed her from the terrace toward the parade reviewing stand, where he would sit in a place of honor beside the Viceroy.

Since they'd been children, Xavier had always found himself attracted to Serena; as they matured, they had grown confident of their deepening feelings toward each other. Both he and Serena considered it a foregone conclusion that they would wed, a rare perfect match of politics, acceptable bloodlines, and romance.

Now, though, with the sudden increase in hostilities, he reminded himself of his greater priorities. Thanks to the disaster that had killed Primero Meach, Xavier Harkonnen was interim commander of the Salusan Militia, which forced him to face larger issues. He wanted to do so much, but he was only one man.

An hour later, the assemblage sat on a grandstand in the central plaza. Scaffolding and temporary girders shored up the broken facades of government buildings. The ornamental fountains no longer functioned, but the citizens of Zimia knew there could be no other place for such a presentation.

Even burned and damaged, the tall edifices looked magnificent: constructed in Salusan Gothic style with multilevel roof lines, spires, and carved columns. Salusa Secundus was the seat of the League government, but it also hosted the leading cultural and anthropological museums. In surrounding neighborhoods, the crowded dwellings were of simpler construction but pleasing to the eye, whitewashed with lime taken from chalk cliffs. Salusans prided themselves on having the best craftsmen and artisans in the League. They did most of their production by hand instead of with automated machinery.

Along the parade route, the citizens dressed in colorful raiment of magenta, blue, and yellow. People chattered and pointed as the remarkable stallions passed them, followed by marching musicians and folk dancers on hover-floats. One monstrous Salusan bull, drugged into a near stupor to control it, plodded down the street.

Though Xavier made the best of it all, he found himself constantly glancing at the sky, and at the scars of the wounded city. . . .

At the conclusion of the parade, Manion Butler delivered a speech celebrating the successful defense but acknowledging the high cost of the battle, tens of thousands killed or wounded. "We have much healing and recovery to do, but we also have an unbroken spirit, no matter what the thinking machines may attempt."

Addressing the crowd, the Viceroy summoned Xavier to the central platform. "I present for you our greatest hero, a man who stood firm against the cymeks and made the *necessary* decisions to save us all. Few others would have been strong enough to do the same."

Feeling out of place, Xavier stepped forward to receive a military medal on a striped blue, red, and gold ribbon from the Viceroy. In the midst of cheers, Serena kissed him on the cheek. He hoped no one in the crowd could see him blush.

"With this commendation comes a promotion to the rank of Tercero, First Grade. Xavier Harkonnen, I charge you with studying defensive tactics and installations for the entire League Armada. Your duties will encompass the local Salusan Militia, along with responsibility for improving the military security of the entire League of Nobles."

The young officer felt awkward from the attention, but he graciously accepted the accolades. "I look forward to beginning the hard work of our survival . . . and advancement." He favored Serena with an indulgent smile. "Following today's festivities, of course."

Dune is the planet-child of the worm.
　　　—from "The Legend of Selim Wormrider," Zensunni Fire Poetry

For an entire day and deep into the night, the monstrous sandworm raced across the desert, forced beyond its normal territorial range.

As the two moons rose and shone their curious light down upon Selim, he clung to his metal staff, completely exhausted. Though he had escaped being devoured by the wild and confused creature, he might soon perish from the interminable ride. Buddallah had saved him, but now seemed only to be toying with him.

While thrusting the corroded spear, the youth had wedged himself into a gap between worm segments, hoping he wouldn't be buried alive if the demon plunged beneath the dunes. He huddled against rank flesh that smelled of rotten meat impregnated with pungent cinnamon. He didn't know what to do, but prayed and contemplated, searching for an explanation.

Perhaps it is a test of some kind.

The sandworm continued to flee across the desert, its un-

dersized brain seemingly resigned to never again finding peace
or safety. The beast wanted to wallow into the dunes and hide
from this malicious imp, but Selim pried the spear as if it were
a lever, irritating the wound anew.

The worm could only surge onward. Hour after hour.

Selim's throat was parched, his eyes caked with grit. He
must have crossed half the desert already, and recognized no
landforms on the monotonous open bled. He had never been
so far from the cave community—no one had, as far as he
knew. Even if he somehow escaped this giant monster, he
would be doomed in the unforgiving Arrakis wasteland because of his unjust sentence.

He was certain his faithless friend Ebrahim would be exposed one day, and the truth would come out; the traitor would
violate other tribal rules, and would eventually be recognized
for the thief and liar that he was. If Selim ever saw him again,
he would challenge Ebrahim to a fight to the death, and honor
would win out.

Perhaps the tribe would applaud him, since no one in even
the grandest fire poems had ever braved a giant sandworm and
lived. Maybe the saucy, dark-eyed young Zensunni women
would look at Selim with bright smiles. Dust-covered but with
his head held high, he would stand before stern Naib Dhartha
and demand readmittance to the community. To have ridden
a desert demon and *lived!*

But, though Selim had already managed to survive longer
than he had ever hoped, the outcome was by no means assured. What was he to do now?

Beneath him, the worm made peculiar, agitated noises, an
invertebrate sound beyond the loud whisper of hot sand. The
weary beast shuddered, and a tremor ran down its sinuous
body. Selim could smell flint and an overpowering aroma of
spice. Friction-induced furnaces burned inside the worm's gullet, like the depths of Sheol itself.

As lemony dawn tinged the sky, the worm became more
unruly and desperate. It thrashed about, trying to dig itself into
the sand, but Selim wouldn't permit that. The monster
slammed its blunt head into a dune, smashing a dust spray into

the air. The youth had to throw all of his body weight against the spear, digging into the raw, exposed worm segment.

"You are as sore and exhausted as I am, aren't you, Shaitan?" he said in a voice as thin and dry as paper. *Almost exhausted unto death.*

Selim didn't dare let go. The moment he dropped off onto the barren dunes, the sandworm would turn about and devour him. He had no choice but to keep driving the creature. The ordeal seemed endless.

As daylight grew brighter, he noticed a faint haze on the far horizon, a distant storm with winds bearing flakes of sand and dust. But the disturbance was far away, and Selim had other concerns.

At last, the demon worm ground itself to a halt not far from a ridge of rocks, and refused to move. With a final convulsion, it slumped its serpentine head onto a dune crest and lay like a slain dragon, quivering . . . then went utterly still.

Selim trembled with absolute weariness, fearing this was some kind of final trick. The monster might be waiting for him to drop his guard so it could swallow him up. Could a sandworm be devious? Was it truly Shaitan? *Or did I ride it to death?*

Gathering his energy, Selim straightened. His cramped muscles trembled. He could barely move. Joints were numb; nerves prickled as they awakened with the creeping fire of restored circulation. At last, risking all, he yanked the metal spear from the pink flesh between the callused segments.

The worm didn't even twitch.

Selim slid down the rounded bulk and hit the sand running. His boots pumped up little dust clouds as he raced across the undulating landscape. The far-off rocks were black mounds of safety protruding from golden dunes.

He refused to look behind him and ran on, gasping. Each breath was like dry fire in his throat. His ears tingled, anticipating the hiss of sand, the rippling approach of the vengeful creature. But the sandworm remained still.

Filled with desperate energy, Selim sprinted for half a kilometer. Reaching the rock barricade, he scrambled up and finally allowed himself to collapse. Drawing his knees against his chest, he sat gazing out into the wash of daylight, watching the worm.

It never moved. *Is Shaitan playing a trick? Is Buddallah testing me?*

By now Selim was very, very hungry. He shouted at the sky, "If you have saved me for some purpose, then why not offer a bit of food?" In the extremity of his exhaustion, he began to chuckle.

One does not make demands of God.

Then he realized that there was food, of a sort. In his flight to the rock sanctuary, Selim had crossed a thick ochre patch of spice, veins of melange like those the Zensunni sometimes found when they ventured onto the sands. They gathered the substance, using it as a food additive and stimulant. Naib Dhartha kept a small stockpile within the cave warrens, occasionally brewing from it a potent spice beer, which the tribe members consumed on special occasions and traded at the Arrakis City spaceport.

He sat in the uncertain shade for nearly an hour, looking for any sign of movement from the monster. Nothing. The day became hotter, and the desert lapsed into a sluggish silence. The distant storm seemed to move no closer. Selim felt as if the world itself was holding its breath.

Then, growing brash again—after all, he had ridden Shaitan!—Selim crawled down from the rocks and scurried out to the patch of melange. There, he raised a wary gaze in the direction of the ominous hulk.

Standing in the rust-hued sand, he scrabbled with his hands, scooping up the dry red powder. He gobbled it, spat out a few grains of sand, and immediately felt the stimulant of raw spice, a large quantity to take all at once. It made him dizzy, gave him an explosion of energy.

Finally sated, he stood at a distance from the flaccid worm, hands on his hips, glaring. Then he waved his arms, shouting into the utter silence, "I defeated you, Shaitan! You meant to eat me, old crawler, but I conquered you instead!" He waved his hands again. "Can you hear me?"

But he detected not even a flicker. Euphoric from the melange and foolishly brave, he marched back toward the long sinuous body that lay on the dune crest. Only a few footsteps away, he stared up into the face. Its cavernous mouth was studded with glittering internal thorns. The long fangs looked like the tiniest of hairs in relation to the creature's immense size.

Now the dust storm approached, accompanied by skirling hot breezes. The wind seized grains of sand and fragments of rock, whipping them against his face like tiny darts. Gusts stole around the curved carcass of the worm with a whispery, hooting sound. It seemed as if the ghost of the beast was *daring him*, prodding him forward. The spice thrummed in Selim's bloodstream.

Boldly, he strode to the worm's maw and peered into the black infinity of its mouth. The hellish friction-fires inside were cold; not even an ember remained.

He shouted again, "I killed you, old crawler. I am Worm Slayer."

The sandworm did not respond even to this provocation.

He looked up at the daggerlike fangs, curved shards that lined the wide, smelly mouth. Buddallah seemed to be urging him on, or maybe it was simply his own desire. Moving before common sense could catch up with him, Selim climbed over the lower lip of the worm and reached the nearest sharp tooth.

The young outcast grabbed it with both hands, feeling how hard it was, a material even stronger than metal. He twisted and wrenched. The worm's body was soft, as if the tissues of its throat were losing integrity. With a suppressed grunt, Selim uprooted the fang. It was as long as his forearm, curved and pure and glistening with milky whiteness. It would make an excellent knife.

He staggered back out, holding his prize, utterly terrified at the realization of what he had done. An unprecedented act, as far as he knew. Who else would have risked not only riding Shaitain, but stepping into its maw? His body trembled to its core. He couldn't believe what he had dared—and accomplished! No other person on all of Arrakis possessed a treasure such as this tooth-knife!

Although the remaining crystalline fangs hung down like stalactites, hundreds of them that he could sell in the Arrakis City spaceport (if he could ever find the place again), he felt suddenly weak. The rush of the melange he'd consumed was beginning to fade.

He scrambled backward onto the soft sand. The storm was almost on top of him now, reminding him of his Zensunni desert survival training. He must make his way back to the rocks and find some sort of shelter, or he too would soon lie dead upon the dunes, a victim of the elements.

But he no longer thought that would happen. *I have a destiny now, a mission from Buddallah . . . if only I can understand it.*

He backed away, then turned and ran toward the line of rocks, cradling the fang in his hands. The wind nudged him onward as if anxious to get him away from the carcass.

*Humans tried to develop intelligent machines as secondary re-
flex systems, turning over primary decisions to mechanical servants. Gradually, though, the creators did not leave enough to
do for themselves; they began to feel alienated, dehumanized,
and even manipulated. Eventually humans became little more
than decisionless robots themselves, left without an understanding of their natural existence.*

—TLALOC,
Weaknesses of the Empire

Agamemnon was not eager to face Omnius. Having already lived more than a thousand years, the cymek general had learned to be patient.

As patient as a machine.

Following their secret rendezvous near the red dwarf star,
he and his fellow Titans reached Corrin after an interstellar
voyage of nearly two months. The robotic fleet had arrived
days before, delivering the battle images captured by the
watcheyes. The evermind already knew about the defeat. All
that remained was for Omnius to issue rebukes and repri-
mands, especially to Agamemnon, who had been in command.

As he landed his ship under the blazing giant sun of Corrin,
the cymek general reached out with his sensor network, accepting data through his thoughtrodes. Omnius would be waiting, as always, after a mission.

Perhaps by now the evermind would have accepted the failure.

A false hope, Agamemnon knew. The all-pervasive computer did not react in the manner of a human.

Before emerging from his ship, the Titan general chose an efficient mobile body, little more than a streamlined cart that carried his brain canister and life-support systems connected to the framework. The cymek moved out onto the paved boulevards under the enormous baleful eye of the red giant. Harsh crimson light washed the flagstoned streets and white facades.

Millennia ago, the bloated star had expanded, growing so large that its outer layers swallowed the inner planets of the system. Corrin itself had once been a frozen outlying world, but the increased heat from the swollen giant now made the planet habitable.

After the atmosphere thawed and the icy seas boiled away, Corrin's landscape became a blank slate on which the Old Empire established a colony during its younger, ambitious days. Most of the ecosystem had been transplanted from elsewhere, but even after thousands of years Corrin still seemed an *unfinished* world, missing many of the ecological details necessary for a thriving planet. Omnius and his independent robot Erasmus liked the place because it seemed new and unburdened by the baggage of history.

Agamemnon trundled along the streets, followed by hovering watcheyes that monitored him like electronic guard dogs. With surveillance monitors and speakers throughout the city, the evermind could have conferred with him anywhere on Corrin. Omnius, however, insisted on receiving the cymek general in a lavish central pavilion built by human slave labor. This pilgrimage of contrition was part of Agamemnon's penance for the Salusa failure. The powerful computer understood the concept of dominance.

The electrafluid surrounding his brain churned blue as Agamemnon prepared to defend himself against a rigorous interrogation. His mobile body passed under tall arches supported by scrolled white-metal columns. Eccentric and earnest, the robot Erasmus had copied ostentatious trappings from historical records of human empires. The awesome gateway was designed to make visitors tremble, though the Titan doubted Omnius cared about such things.

The cymek general halted at the center of a courtyard where fountains trickled from gaps in the walls. Tame sparrows flitted about the eaves and nested atop the pillars. Inside terra cotta urns, scarlet lilies bloomed in violent explosions of petals.

"I have arrived, Lord Omnius," Agamemnon announced through his voice synthesizer—a mere formality, because he had been closely observed since emerging from his ship. He waited.

In the echoing pavilion, the mirror-faced Erasmus was nowhere to be seen. Omnius wanted to upbraid his general without the curious scrutiny of the independent and annoying robot. Though Erasmus fancied that he understood human emotions, Agamemnon doubted the eccentric machine would show even a glimmer of compassion.

The voice boomed from a dozen speakers in the walls, like an angry deity. No doubt the effect was intentional. "You and your cymeks have failed, General."

Agamemnon already knew how the discussion would play out—as did Omnius. Surely the evermind himself had run simulations. Yet, this was a dance that must be continued.

"We fought hard, but could not achieve victory, Lord Omnius. The *hrethgir* put up an unexpectedly fierce defense and were surprisingly willing to sacrifice their city rather than let the shield generators fall. As I have said many times, feral humans are dangerously unpredictable."

Omnius responded without hesitation. "You have repeatedly insisted that cymeks are far superior to the human vermin, combining the best advantages of machine and man. How, then, could you be rebuffed by such untrained, uncivilized creatures?"

"In this instance, I was in error. The humans realized our true objective faster than we had anticipated."

"Your forces did not fight hard enough," Omnius said.

"Six neo-cymeks were destroyed. The gladiator body of the Titan Xerxes was demolished, and he barely escaped in a launch pod."

"Yes, but the remainder of your cymeks survived. A mere twenty-one percent loss does not equate with 'fighting to your fullest.'" Around the courtyard, chirping sparrows flitted about, oblivious to the tension between Omnius and his top military officer. "You should have been willing to sacrifice all your cymeks to bring down the scrambler shields."

Agamemnon was glad he no longer displayed human expressions, which the computer mind might be able to interpret. "Lord Omnius, cymeks are irreplaceable *individuals*, unlike your robotic thinking machines. In my estimation, risking the loss of your most vital Titans was not a reasonable exchange for one insignificant planet infested with feral humans."

"Insignificant? Before the mission you emphasized the extreme importance of Salusa Secundus to the League of Nobles. You claimed that its fall would precipitate a complete collapse of free humanity. *You* were in command."

"But is the League itself worth the obliteration of your remaining Titans? We created you, established the foundation for your Synchronized Worlds. The Titans should be used for more than cannon fodder." Agamemnon was curious as to how the evermind would respond to this line of reasoning. Perhaps by setting up the Titans to fall in battle against feral humans, Omnius planned to bypass the choke-hold of Barbarossa's protective programming.

"Let me ponder that," Omnius said. Screens on the pavilion walls projected watcheye images from the battle on Zimia. "The *hrethgir* are smarter than you presumed. They saw your target. You made an error in judgment thinking your cymeks would be able to push forward easily."

"I miscalculated," Agamemnon admitted. "The humans have a clever military commander. His unexpected decisions allowed them to mount a successful resistance. Now, at least, we have tested their scrambler fields."

Agamemnon's explanations rapidly degenerated into a succession of rationalizations and excuses. Omnius analyzed and dismissed them, leaving the Titan feeling bare and humiliated.

In the serene courtyard, bright flowers bloomed and birds sang. Trickling fountains added their musical sounds . . . and

Agamemnon contained his outrage within himself. Even his sensitive mechanical body showed no sign of agitation. A thousand years ago, he and his fellow Titans had controlled these damnable thinking machines. *We created you, Omnius. One day, we will also destroy you.*

While it had taken the visionary Tlaloc and his group of rebels only a few years to conquer the sleepy Old Empire, Omnius and his thinking machines proved to be a far superior adversary, never sleeping, always watching. But even machines made mistakes. Agamemnon just needed to exploit them.

"Is there anything else, Lord Omnius?" he interrupted. Further arguments and excuses would serve no purpose. Above all else, machines craved efficiency.

"Only my next set of instructions, Agamemnon." The Omnius voice moved from speaker to speaker, giving the impression that he was everywhere at once. "I am dispatching you and your Titans back to Earth. You will accompany Erasmus, who intends to continue his studies of captive humans there."

"As you command, Lord Omnius." Though surprised, Agamemnon showed no reaction. *Earth . . .* a very long journey. "We will determine other ways to destroy this blight of humanity. The Titans exist only to serve you."

It was one of the few advantages of Agamemnon's human side: Even though the evermind was filled with a vast quantity of data, Omnius did not know how to recognize a simple lie.

From a certain perspective, defense and offense encompass nearly identical tactics.

> —XAVIER HARKONNEN,
> address to Salusan Militia

New duties, new responsibilities . . . and more good-byes.
As a mostly recovered Xavier Harkonnen stood with Serena Butler inside the Zimia Spaceport, the departure facility seemed a sterile environment with echoing plaztile floors. Even the warmth of Serena's expression did not compensate for the utilitarian structure. Window walls looked out onto the fused pavement where shuttles took off and landed every few minutes, going to and from the larger long-distance ships that waited in orbit.

In one wing of the spaceport, work crews shored up sections of a hangar damaged during the cymek attack. Large cranes lifted temporary walls and braces into place. Out on the landing field, huge blast craters had been filled in.

Dressed in a crisp gold-and-black Armada uniform reflecting his new grade, Xavier gazed deeply into Serena's unusual lavender eyes. He knew how she saw him. His facial features were not particularly striking—ruddy complexion, pointed nose, generous lips—but overall she found him attractive, especially the soft brown eyes and his infectious, though rarely used, smile.

"I wish we could spend more time together, Xavier." She fingered a white rose floweret on her lapel. The spaceport drone of other people, noisy repair crews and heavy machinery surrounded them.

Xavier noticed Serena's younger sister Octa watching them. A seventeen-year-old with long strawberry-blond hair, she'd always had a crush on Xavier. Willowy Octa was a nice enough girl, but recently he wished she would give him and Serena a little more privacy, especially now that they would be apart for so long.

"So do I. Let's make these minutes count." Surrendering to the urge he knew they both shared, he leaned forward to kiss her, as if his lips were drawn by a magnetic force. The kiss lingered, then grew intense. At last Xavier pulled back. Serena looked disappointed, more with the situation than with him. They both had important duties, demands on their time and energy.

Newly installed in his position, Xavier was about to embark with a group of military specialists on an inspection tour of League planetary defenses. After the nearly successful cymek strike against Salusa two months ago, he would make certain there were no weaknesses on other League Worlds. The thinking machines would exploit the tiniest flaw, and free humans could not afford to lose any of their remaining strongholds.

Serena Butler, meanwhile, would focus on expanding the League domain. After the battlefield surgeons had been so successful with the fresh tank-grown organs provided by Tuk Keedair, Serena had spoken passionately about the services and resources the Unallied Planets such as Tlulaxa could provide. She wanted them to formally join the union of free humans.

Already, more flesh merchants had arrived on Salusa with their biological wares; previously, many nobles and League citizens had been uneasy about the mysterious outsiders, but now that the war-wounded faced terrible losses of limbs and organs, they were willing to accept cloned replacement parts.

The Tlulaxa never explained where they had developed or obtained such sophisticated biological technology, but Serena praised their generosity and resources.

At any other time, her speech in the Hall of Parliament might have been forgotten, but the cymek attack had underscored her point about the vulnerability of the Unallied Planets. What if the machines next chose to wipe out the Thalim system and thereby eliminate the Tlulaxan ability to give sight to blind veterans, new limbs to amputees?

She had studied hundreds of survey documents and ambassadorial reports, trying to determine which of the nonsignatory planets were the best candidates for induction into the League brotherhood. Unifying the remnants of humanity had become her passion, to make the free people strong enough to put down any machine aggression.

Despite her youth, she had already led two successful aid missions, the first when she was only seventeen. In one she had taken food and medical supplies to refugees from an abandoned Synchronized World, and in the other she had provided relief for a biological blight that almost destroyed the pristine farms on Poritrin.

Neither she nor Xavier had time for themselves.

"When you return, I promise I will make it up to you," she said, her eyes dancing. "I'll give you a banquet of kisses."

He allowed himself a rare laugh. "Then I plan to arrive very hungry indeed!" Xavier took her hand and kissed it gallantly. "When we dine again, I shall come calling with flowers." He knew their next rendezvous could be months away.

She gave him a warm smile. "I have a particular fondness for flowers."

He was about to pull Serena close, but they were interrupted by a familiar brown-skinned child coming from another direction—Xavier's eight-year-old brother, Vergyl Tantor. The boy had been permitted to leave school to see him off. Breaking free of an elderly instructor escort, Vergyl ran to hug his idol, nuzzling his face into the crisp uniform shirt.

"Take care of our estate while I am gone, little brother," Xavier said, playfully rubbing his knuckles on the boy's wiry hair. "You are in charge of tending my wolfhounds—you understand?"

The boy's brown eyes widened, and he nodded gravely. "Yes."

"And obey your parents, otherwise you can't hope to grow up to become a good officer in the Armada."

"I will!"

An announcement summoned the inspection team to board the shuttle. Hearing it, Xavier promised to bring something back for Vergyl, Octa, and Serena. While Octa watched from a distance, smiling hopefully, he hugged his little brother again, squeezed Serena's hand, and strode off with the officers and engineers.

Staring at the window wall where they could watch the waiting military shuttle, Serena glanced down at the boy and thought of Xavier Harkonnen. Xavier had been only six years old when thinking machines had killed his natural parents and his older brother.

Because of interfamily agreements and the written wills of Ulf and Katarina Harkonnen, young Xavier had been raised as the foster son of powerful and then-childless Emil and Lucille Tantor. The noble couple had already made arrangements for their holdings to be administered by Tantor relatives, distant cousins and nephews who would not normally have inherited anything. But when Emil Tantor began to raise Xavier, he was quite taken with the orphan and legally adopted him, though Xavier retained his Harkonnen name and all associated noble rights.

After the adoption, Lucille Tantor unexpectedly conceived a son, Vergyl, who was twelve years younger than Xavier. The Harkonnen heir, not worried about dynastic politics, concentrated on a course of military studies, intending to join the League Armada. At the age of eighteen Xavier received the legal entitlement to the original Harkonnen holdings, and a year later he became an officer in the Salusan Militia. With his impeccable performance and rapid promotions, everyone could see Xavier was a rising star in the military ranks.

Now three people who cared about him watched the shuttle

lift into the sky on a plume of orange exhaust. Vergyl held Serena's hand, bravely trying to comfort her. "Xavier will be all right. You can count on him."

She felt a pang for her departing love, but smiled warmly at the wide-eyed boy. "Of course we can."

She would have it no other way. Love was one of the things that separated humans from machines.

The answer is a mirror of the question.

—COGITOR KWYNA,
City of Introspection archives

The temporary meeting chamber for the League delegates had originally been the home of the first Viceroy, Bovko Manresa. Before the Titans had taken over the weak Old Empire, Manresa had built the mansion on then-isolated Salusa Secundus as a way of celebrating wealth garnered from his planetary land dealings. Later, when refugee humans began arriving, driven out by the cruel rule of the Twenty Titans, the big house had become a meeting hall, with chairs and a lectern set up in the grand ballroom, as they were today.

Months ago, within hours of the cymek attack, Viceroy Butler had stood on a pile of rubble beneath the broken central dome of the Hall of Parliament. While the poisonous dust settled in the streets and fires still blazed in damaged buildings, he had vowed to repair the venerable old facility that had served the League for centuries.

The governmental edifice was more than just a building: It was hallowed ground on which legendary leaders had debated great ideas and formulated plans against the machines. The damage to the roof and upper floors was severe, but the basic structure remained sound. Just like the human spirit it represented.

It was a frosty morning outside, with fog on the windows. Leaves on the hills had begun to turn lovely autumn shades of yellow, orange, and brown. Serena and the representatives came inside the temporary meeting hall, still clinging to their coats.

She gazed at the walls of the crowded old ballroom, at paintings of long-dead leaders and depictions of past victories. She wondered what the future would bring, and what her place might be in it. She wanted so badly to *do* something, to help in the great crusade of humankind.

Most of her life she had been an activist, always willing to get her hands dirty, to assist in aiding the victims of other tragedies such as natural disasters or machine attacks. Even during pleasant times, she had joined the work crews of harvesters to pick grapes from the Butler estate vineyards or olives from the gnarled groves.

She took a seat in the first row, then watched as her soft-featured father made his way across the wood parquet floor to the antique lectern. Viceroy Butler was followed by a monk in a red-velvet tunic carrying a large plexiplaz container that held a living human brain in viscous electrafluid. The monk lovingly placed the container on an ornate table beside the lectern, then stood beside it.

From her front-row seat, Serena saw the pinkish gray tissue undulate slightly within the pale-blue life-support liquid. Separated from the senses and distractions of the physical world for more than a millennium, stimulated by constant intense contemplation, the female Cogitor's once-human brain had grown larger than its original size.

"The Cogitor Kwyna does not often leave the City of Introspection," Viceroy Butler said, sounding both formal and excited. "But in these times we require the best thoughts and advice. If any mind can understand the thinking machines, it will be Kwyna's."

These esoteric disembodied philosophers were seen so infrequently that many League representatives did not understand how they managed to communicate. Compounding the mystery that surrounded them, Cogitors rarely said much, choosing instead to marshall their energies and contribute only the most important thoughts.

"The Cogitor's Secondary will speak for Kwyna," the Viceroy said, "if she has any insights to offer."

Beside the brain canister, the red-robed monk removed the sealed lid, exposing the agitated viscous fluid. Blinking his round eyes rapidly, he stared into the tank. Slowly, the monk slid one naked hand into the soup, immersing his fingers. He closed his eyes, drawing deep breaths, as he tentatively touched the convoluted brain. His brows furrowed with concentration and acceptance as the electrafluid soaked into his pores, linking the Cogitor with the Secondary's neural system, using him as an extension in much the same way cymeks used artificial mechanical bodies.

"I understand nothing," said the monk in a strange, distant voice. Serena knew that was the first principle the Cogitors adopted, and the contemplative brains spent centuries in deep study, adding to that sense of nothingness.

Centuries before the original Titans, a group of spiritual humans had enjoyed studying philosophy and discussing esoteric issues, but too many frailties and temptations of the flesh inhibited their ability to concentrate. In the ennui of the Old Empire, these metaphysical scholars had been the first to have their brains installed in life-support systems. Freed of biological constraints, they spent all their time learning and thinking. Each Cogitor wanted to study the entirety of human philosophy, bringing together the ingredients to understand the universe. They lived in ivory towers and contemplated, rarely bothering to note the superficial relationships and events of the mundane world.

Kwyna, the two-thousand-year-old Cogitor who resided in Salusa's City of Introspection, claimed to be politically neutral. "I am ready to interact," she announced through the monk, who stared with glazed eyes at the assembly. "You may begin."

With intense blue eyes, Viceroy Butler gazed around the packed ballroom, pausing to look at a number of faces, including Serena's. "My friends, we have always lived under the threat of annihilation, and now I must ask every one of you to devote your time, energies, and money to our cause."

He gave tribute to the tens of thousands of Salusans who had died in the cymek onslaught, along with fifty-one visiting dignitaries. "The Salusan Militia remains on full alert here, and messenger ships have been dispatched to all League Worlds, warning them of the danger. We can only hope that no other planets were attacked."

The Viceroy then called upon Tio Holtzman, recently arrived after nearly a month in transit from his laboratories on Poritrin. "Savant Holtzman, we are anxious to hear your assessment of the new defenses."

Holtzman had been eager to inspect his orbital scrambler fields, to see how they might be modified and improved. On Poritrin, the flamboyant nobleman Niko Bludd funded the Savant's research. Given his past accomplishments, League members always held out the hope that Holtzman would pull some other miracle out of his pocket.

Slight of body, Holtzman moved with grace and an enormous stage presence, wearing clean and stylish robes. The iron gray hair that hung to his shoulders was square-cut, framing a narrow face. A man of immense confidence and ego, he loved to speak to important dignitaries in the Parliament, but now he appeared uncharacteristically troubled. In truth, the inventor could not bring himself to admit a mistake. Unquestionably, his scrambler network had failed. The cymeks had broken through! What would he say to these people who had relied on him?

Reaching the speaking platform, the great man cleared his throat and looked around, glancing oddly at the imposing presence of the Cogitor and the looming attendant monk. This was a most delicate matter. How could he shift the blame from himself?

The scientist used his best voice. "In warfare, whenever one side makes a technological breakthrough, the other attempts to top it. We recently witnessed this with my atmospheric scrambler fields. Had they not been installed here, the full thinking machine fleet would have laid waste to Salusa. Unfortunately, I did not factor in the unique abilities of the cymeks. They found a chink in the armor and penetrated it."

No one had accused him of lax work or poor planning, but this was the closest Holtzman would come to admitting that he had overlooked a major flaw. "Now it is our turn to surpass the machines with a new concept. I hope to be inspired by this tragedy, pushing my creativity to its limits." He then stalled and looked embarrassed, even endearing. "I'll be working on that, as soon as I get back to Poritrin. I hope to have a surprise for you very soon."

A tall, statuesque woman glided toward the lectern, drawing attention to herself. "Perhaps I have a suggestion." She had pale eyebrows, white hair, and luminous skin that made her seem ethereal, but charged with power.

"Let us hear from the women of Rossak. I gladly yield to Zufa Cenva." Looking relieved, Holtzman hurried back to his seat and slumped into it.

The pale woman carried an air of mystery about her; she wore glowing jewelry on a black, diaphanous gown that revealed much of her perfect body. Pausing at the Cogitor's life-support case, Zufa Cenva peered inside at the enlarged brain. Her brow furrowed as she concentrated, and as she did so, the brain itself seemed to vibrate; the electrafluid swirled, bubbles formed. Alarmed, the devout attendant monk withdrew his hand from the liquid.

The tall woman relaxed, satisfied, and stepped to the podium. "Because of oddities in our environment, many of the females born on Rossak exhibit enhanced telepathic abilities." Indeed, the powerful Sorceresses of the dense, barely habitable jungles had parlayed their mental quirks into political influence. Rossak men exhibited no such telepathic enhancements.

"The League of Nobles was formed a thousand years ago for our mutual defense, first against the Titans and then against Omnius. Since then, we have barricaded ourselves, trying to protect our worlds from the enemy." Her eyes flashed like highly polished stones. "We need to rethink this strategy. Perhaps it is time for *us* to take the offensive against the Synchronized Worlds. Otherwise, Omnius and his minions will never leave us alone."

The League representatives muttered at this, looking fearful, especially after the devastation Zimia had just endured. The Viceroy was first to respond. "That is a bit premature, Madame Cenva. I'm not sure we have the capability."

"We barely survived the last attack!" a man shouted. "And we had only a handful of cymeks to contend with."

Manion Butler looked deeply concerned. "Confronting Omnius would be a suicide mission. What weapons would we use?"

In response, the imposing woman squared her shoulders and spread her hands, while closing her eyes and concentrating. Although Zufa was known to have extrasensory powers, she had never before displayed them in Parliament. Her milky pale skin seemed to heat up with an inner light. The air in the enclosed chamber stirred, and static electricity crackled around the assemblage, making hair stand on end.

Lightning flickered at her fingertips, as if she were holding a barely contained thunderstorm inside herself. Her own white hair coiled and writhed like snakes. When Zufa's eyes opened again, a dazzling energy seemed ready to shoot out of them, as if the universe lived behind her pupils.

Gasps echoed through the delegates. Serena's skin crawled and her scalp tingled, as if a thousand poisonous spiders skittered over her mind. In her preservation tank, the Cogitor Kwyna churned.

Then Zufa relaxed, throttling back the chain reaction of mental energy. Letting out a long, cold breath, the Sorceress smiled grimly at the startled onlookers. "*We* have a weapon."

The eyes of common perception do not see far. Too often we make the most important decisions based only on superficial information.

—NORMA CENVA,
unpublished laboratory notebooks

After delivering her announcement to the League assembly, Zufa Cenva returned to Rossak. She had been in transit for weeks, and her shuttle now landed on a dense section of the jungle canopy that had been paved over with a polymer to seal and fuse the branches and leaves into a solid mass. To enable the trees to receive adequate moisture and gas exchange, the polymer was porous, synthesized from jungle chemicals and organics.

Toxic oceans made the native Rossak planktons, fish, kelp, and sea creatures poisonous to humans. Rugged, sterile lava plains covered much of the planet's land area, dotted with geysers and brimstone lakes. Since the botanical chemistry did not rely on chlorophyll, the general cast of all plants was silvery purple; nothing here was fresh and green.

In a tectonically stable zone girdling the equator, large rifts in the continental plate created broad sanctuary valleys where the water was filtered and the air breathable. In these protected rift ecosystems, hardy human settlers had constructed sophisticated cave-cities like hives tunneled into the black cliffs. The declivitous external walls were overgrown with silvery-purple vines, drooping ferns, and fleshy moss. Comfortable chambers looked out upon a thick jungle canopy that pressed against the settlement cliffs. People could venture directly onto the upper rubbery branches and descend to the dense underbrush, where they harvested edibles.

As if to make up for the dearth of life elsewhere on Rossak, the rift valleys teemed with aggressive living things—mushrooms, lichens, berries, flowers, orchidlike parasites, and insects. The Rossak men, lacking the telepathic enhancement of their women, had turned their talents to developing and extracting drugs, pharmaceuticals, and occasional poisons from nature's larder. The entire place was like a Pandora's box that had been opened only a crack. . . .

Now the tall, luminous Sorceress watched as her much younger paramour, Aurelius Venport, crossed a suspended bridge from the open cliffs to the foamy purple treetops. His patrician features were handsome, his dark hair curly, his face long and lean. Tagging along behind him on stubby legs came Zufa's disappointing fifteen-year-old daughter by a prior relationship.

Two misfits. No wonder they get along so well.

Prior to seducing Aurelius Venport, the chief Sorceress had arranged conjugal relationships with four other men during her peak breeding times, selecting them for their proven bloodlines. After generations of research, miserable miscarriages, and defective offspring, the women of Rossak had compiled detailed genetic indices of various families. Because of heavy environmental toxins and teratogens, the odds were against any child being born strong and healthy. But for every stillborn monster or talentless male, a miraculous pale-skinned Sorceress might occur. Each time a woman conceived a child, it was like playing a game of roulette. Genetics was never an exact science.

But Zufa had been so careful, checking and doublechecking the bloodlines. Only one of those conjugal encounters had resulted in a living child—Norma, a dwarf barely four feet tall, with blocky features, mousy brown hair, and a tedious, bookish personality.

Many offspring on Rossak had defective bodies, and even the apparently healthy ones rarely exhibited the strong mental powers of the elite Sorceresses. Nevertheless, Zufa felt deep disappointment, even embarrassment, that *her* daughter had no telepathic skills. The greatest living Sorceress should have been able to pass along her superior mental abilities, and she desperately wanted her daughter to carry on the fight against the machines. But Norma showed no potential whatsoever. And despite Aurelius Venport's impeccable genetic credentials, Zufa had never been able to carry one of his babies to term.

How many more times must I keep trying before I replace him with another breeder? Once more, she decided—she would attempt to get pregnant again, within the next few months. It would be Venport's last chance.

Zufa was also disappointed in Norma's independence and defiance. Too often the teenager spun off on obscure mathematical tangents that no one could comprehend. Norma seemed lost in her own world.

My daughter, you should have been so much more!

No one had a heavier burden of responsibility than the small clan of Sorceresses on the planet, and Zufa's burden was the greatest of all. If only she could count on everyone else, especially in light of this latest danger from the cymeks.

Since stunted Norma could never take part in the mental battle, Zufa had to concentrate on her daughters in spirit, those few young women who had won the "genetic lottery" and acquired superior mental abilities. Zufa would train and encourage them, showing them how to eradicate the enemy.

From her cliffside perch, she watched her lover Aurelius and young Norma reach the other side of the suspension bridge and begin to negotiate a circular network of ladders that led to the deeply shadowed jungle floor. Like two happy-go-lucky outcasts, Norma and Aurelius had grown close emotionally, using one another as crutches.

Engrossed in their own petty concerns that had nothing to

do with victory, neither of them had even noticed Zufa's return on the shuttle. No doubt the two misfits would spend hours poking through the foliage in search of new drug resources, which Aurelius would incorporate into his business ventures.

The Sorceress shook her head, not understanding his priorities. Those drugs the men developed were of little more use than Norma's arcane mathematics. Admittedly, Aurelius was a highly intelligent and skilled businessman, but what good were enormous profits if free humanity was doomed to enslavement?

Disappointed in both of them, knowing that she and her Sorceresses would have to do the real fighting, Zufa set out to find the most powerful young women she had recruited to learn the devastating new technique she planned to unleash against the cymeks.

⤬

AS NORMA FOLLOWED him through the fleshy underbrush, Aurelius consumed capsules of a focused stimulant that his expert chemists had synthesized from the pungent pheromones of a boulder-sized burrowing beetle. Venport felt stronger, his perceptions sharpened, his reflexes enhanced. Not quite like the telepathic powers of icy Zufa, but better than his natural abilities.

Someday he would make a breakthrough, allowing him to meet the powerful Sorceress on his own terms. Maybe he and Norma would do it together.

Aurelius maintained a benign fondness for the girl's stern mother. He tolerated Zufa's moods and scornful attitude with good grace; Rossak women rarely allowed themselves the luxury of romantic love.

Though Aurelius knew full well that Zufa had selected him for his breeding potential, he saw through the woman's stoic, demanding exterior. Attempting to conceal her weaknesses, the powerful Sorceress showed her doubts on occasion, afraid that she could not fulfill the responsibilities she had placed on herself. Once, when Aurelius commented that he knew how strong she was trying to be, Zufa had grown embarrassed and angry. "Somebody has to be strong" was all she had said.

Since he lacked telepathic ability, Zufa had little interest in engaging him in conversation. Perhaps she recognized his skills as a businessman, investor, and politician, but she valued none of those abilities as much as her own narrow goals. The Sorceress frequently tried to make him feel like a failure, but her derision only served to ignite his ambition, especially his desire to find a drug that would give him telepathic powers equivalent to her own.

There were other ways to fight a war.

The silvery-purple jungles offered a treasure-trove to cure diseases, expand the mind, and improve human abilities. The choices were overwhelming, but Aurelius sought to investigate everything. From proper development and marketing, the products of Rossak had already put him on the path to great wealth. He was even grudgingly respected by a number of the Sorceresses—except by his own mate.

As a visionary entrepreneur, he was accustomed to exploring alternatives. Like paths through a dense jungle, many routes could lead to the same place. Sometimes, one just had to hack through with a machete.

So far, though, the right drug eluded him.

In another venture, he had proudly distributed Norma's exotic mathematical work among scholarly scientific circles. Though he didn't understand her theorems, he had a gut feeling that she might come up with something important. Maybe she had already done so, and it took expert eyes to recognize it. Venport liked the intense girl, acting as a big brother to her. As far as he was concerned, Norma was a mathematical prodigy, so who cared about her height or her appearance? He was willing to give her a chance, even if her mother never would.

Beside him, Norma studied the design of a broad purple leaf, using a light-beam caliper to measure its various dimensions and the relationships among angles in the sap-filled veins. The depth of her concentration added a wistful cast to her plain features.

Glancing back at him, Norma said in a surprisingly mature voice, "This leaf has been designed and constructed by the Earth mother Gaia, or the Master Creator God, or Buddallah, or whatever you want to call it." With blunt fingers, she held up the fleshy leaf and passed a beam of light through it, so that the intricate cellular designs showed clearly. "Patterns within patterns, all tied together in complex relationships."

In his drug-enhanced, euphoric state, Aurelius found the design hypnotic. "God is in everything," he said. The stimulant he had taken seemed to supercharge his synapses. He squinted through the illuminated fabric of the leaf as she pointed to the internal shapes.

"God is the mathematician of the universe. There is an ancient correlation known as the Golden Mean, a pleasing ratio of form and structure that is found in this leaf, in seashells, and in the living creatures of many planets. It is the tiniest part of the key, known since the time of the Greeks and Egyptians of Earth. They used it in their architecture and pyramids, in their Pythagorean pentagram and Fibonacci sequence." She discarded the leaf. "But there is so much more."

Nodding, Venport touched a moistened fingertip to a pouch of fine black powder at his belt; he rubbed the powder under the sensitive tissue of his tongue and felt another drug penetrating his senses, merging with the remnants of the last one. Norma kept talking; though he did not follow her logical development, he was certain the revelations must be fabulous.

"Give me a practical example," he slurred. "Something with a function that I can understand."

He had grown accustomed to Norma spouting off obscure formulations. Her basis might have been in classical geometry, but she applied her knowledge in much more complex ways. "I can envision calculations all the way to infinity," she said, as if in a trance. "I don't have to write them down."

And she doesn't even need mind-enhancement drugs to accomplish it, Aurelius marveled.

"At this very moment I envision a huge and efficient structure that could be built at a reasonable cost, tens of kilometers long—and based upon the ratio of the Golden Mean."

"But who would ever need something so immense?"

"I cannot peer into the future, Aurelius." Norma teased him. Then they trudged deeper into the weird jungle, still curious and intent on what they might discover. Norma's face was radiant with energy. "But there might be something . . . something I haven't thought of yet."

Careful preparations and defenses can never guarantee victory. However, ignoring these precautions is an almost certain recipe for defeat.

—*League Armada Strategy Manual*

For four months, Tercero Xavier Harkonnen and his six Armada survey vessels traveled along a predetermined route, stopping to inspect and assess the military facilities and defensive preparations of the League Worlds. After many years of no more than a few skirmishes, no one knew where Omnius might strike next.

Xavier had never wavered from the difficult decision he'd made during the cymek attack on Zimia. The Viceroy had praised him for his nerve and determination; even so, Manion Butler had wisely sent the young officer away during the major rebuilding activities, giving Salusans time to heal their wounds without looking for a scapegoat.

Xavier listened to no excuses from tightwad nobles unwilling to commit the necessary resources. No expense must be spared. Any free world that fell to machine aggression would be a loss for the entire human race.

The survey ships traveled from the mines of Hagal to the broad river plains of Poritrin, then made their way to Seneca where the weather was poor and the rain so corrosive that even thinking machines would break down soon after a conquest.

The League planets of Relicon followed, then Kirana III, then Richese, with its burgeoning high-tech industries that made so many other League noblemen uneasy. In theory, the sophisticated manufacturing devices contained no computerization or artificial intelligence, but there were always questions, always doubts.

Finally Xavier's team arrived at their final inspection stop, Giedi Prime. At last, his tour was about to end. He could return home, see Serena again, and they could make good on their promises to each other. . . .

All other League Worlds had installed scrambler field towers. The shields' known weakness against cymeks did not completely devalue Holtzman's ingenious work, and the costly barriers still provided substantial protection against all-out thinking machine offensives. In addition, every human world had long ago built up enormous stockpiles of atomics as part of a doomsday defense. With so many nuclear warheads, an iron-willed planetary governor could turn his world into slag rather than allowing it to fall to Omnius.

Although the thinking machines also had access to atomics, Omnius had concluded that atomics were an inefficient and nonselective way to impose control, and radioactive cleanup afterward was difficult. Besides, with unlimited resources and a deep reservoir of patience, the relentless evermind had no need of such weapons.

Now, as Xavier disembarked from the lead survey ship at the Giedi City spaceport, he blinked under bright sunlight. The well-maintained metropolis sprawled in front of him, with its habitation complexes and productive industrial buildings amid manicured parks and canals. The colors were bright and fresh, and flowers bloomed in ornate beds, although with his new Tlulaxa lungs and tissues he could smell only a hint of the most potent scents, even when he breathed deeply.

"This would be a fine place to bring Serena one day," he said wistfully as he stood in the heat-shimmer of spaceship exhaust. If he married her, perhaps this would be a suitable world for their honeymoon. During the current inspection tour, he had kept his eyes open, trying to find a likely spot.

After four months in space, Xavier missed Serena terribly. He knew the two of them were destined for each other. His life operated on a smooth, clearly defined path. When he returned to Salusa, he promised himself that he would formalize their betrothal. He saw no point in waiting any longer.

Viceroy Butler already treated him like a son, and the young officer had received the blessing of his adoptive father Emil Tantor. As far as Xavier could determine, everyone in the League agreed it would be a fine joining of noble houses.

He smiled, thinking of Serena's face, of her intriguing lavender eyes . . . and then looked across the landing field to see Magnus Sumi approaching the survey ships. The elected leader was accompanied by a dozen members of the Giedi Prime Home Guard.

The Magnus was a thin man in late middle age with pale skin and gray-blond hair that hung to his shoulders. Sumi raised a hand. "Ah, Tercero Harkonnen! We welcome the League Armada and are eager to see how Giedi Prime can improve its defenses against the thinking machines."

Xavier snapped a stiff bow in return. "Your cooperation pleases me, Eminence. Against Omnius, we must not use low-cost materials or stopgap systems that would not adequately protect your people."

After the Battle of Zimia, Xavier's corps of engineers had made requests for mandatory strategic improvements throughout the League. The nobles dug into their coffers, increasing taxes on their subjects and spending the necessary money to build up their defenses. At each stop, planet after planet, month after month, Xavier had assigned teams of engineers and Armada troops where he deemed they were most needed.

Soon, though, he would be going back home. *Soon.* As the time drew near, he thought of Serena more and more.

Well dressed and well armed, the Home Guard stood at attention around the survey ships. Magnus Sumi gestured for Xavier to follow him. "I look forward to clarifying everything over a sumptuous banquet, Tercero Harkonnen. I've set up

twelve fine courses with dancers, musicians, and our best po-
ets. You and I can relax in my government residence while
we discuss plans. I am certain you must be weary from your
journey. How long can you stay with us?"

Xavier could form only a tight smile, thinking of how far
away he was from Salusa Secundus. Even after leaving Giedi
Prime, the ships would still need another month of fast space
travel to return home. The sooner he departed here, the sooner
he could hold Serena in his arms again.

"Eminence, this is the final stop on our long tour. If it
pleases you, I would prefer to spend less time with festivities
and more on the inspection." He gestured toward his survey
ship. "We have a schedule to keep. I'm afraid I can allot only
two days for Giedi Prime. It is best that we concentrate on
our work."

The Magnus looked crestfallen. "Yes, I suppose celebration
is not appropriate after the damage done to Salusa Secundus."

FOR TWO DAYS, Xavier gave the planetary defenses a
quick, almost cursory inspection. He found Giedi Prime to be
a dazzling and prosperous world with many resources, perhaps
even a suitable place to settle down and start an estate of his
own one day.

He gave a favorable assessment, accompanied by a warning.
"This is undoubtedly a planet the thinking machines will want
to conquer, Eminence." He studied the city blueprints and the
distribution of resources across the main continents. "Any cymek attack would most likely attempt to keep the industries
intact so that robots could exploit them. Omnius preaches efficiency."

Beside him, Magnus Sumi reacted with pride. He pointed
out substations on the diagrams. "We intend to install secondary field-transmitting towers at several strategic points." As he
spoke, highlights appeared on the blueprint screen. "We have
already built a completely redundant transmitting station on
one of the uninhabited islands in the northern sea, which can

provide full overlap from a polar projection. We hope to have it online within another month."

Xavier nodded distractedly, his mind weary from months of such details. "I am glad to hear that, though I doubt a second transmitting complex is entirely necessary."

"We want to feel safe, Tercero."

When the two men stood under silvery parabolic towers that throbbed into the sky over Giedi City, Xavier paced around the plascrete embankments that blocked access to large vehicles. He had no doubt a cymek warrior could easily crash through.

"Eminence, I suggest you station more ground troops and obstacles here. Increase your planetside missile-defense batteries to protect against any intrusion from space. On Salusa, the cymek strategy was to focus their entire attack on the destruction of the towers, and they might try that again." He rapped his knuckles against the tower's heavy paristeel support pillar. "These shields are your first and last line of defense, your most effective blockade against thinking machines. Do not neglect them."

"Indeed. Our munitions factories are building heavy artillery and armored ground vehicles. As soon as possible, we intend to surround this complex with a large concentration of military power."

As for the uncompleted secondary generating station, it was too isolated to be protected from a massive assault. But its existence seemed to comfort the Magnus and his populace.

"Very good," Xavier said, then glanced at the chronometer on his wrist. Everything was going so well, perhaps his survey ships could depart before sunset. . . .

The Magnus continued, his voice uncertain, "Tercero, are you concerned about Giedi Prime's limited space military defenses? Our Home Guard has few large ships in orbit to drive back an approaching machine fleet, and our picket ships and scouts are minimal. I admit to feeling vulnerable in that area. What if Omnius attacks us directly from orbit?"

"You have ground-based missile defenses in place, and they have always proved reliable." Impatient, Xavier looked up into the clear sky. "I believe your best hope is to protect your shield complex here on the ground. No quantity of Armada battleships can match the deterrent power of scrambler shields. When the robot fleet attacking Salusa realized they could not take down the scramblers, they retreated."

"But what if they blockade Giedi Prime from orbit?"

"Your world is self-sufficient enough to wait out any siege until the arrival of a League rescue force." Anxious to be back at the spaceport, Xavier decided to appease the governor. "Nevertheless, I will recommend that a javelin-class destroyer or two be stationed around Giedi Prime."

⟫

THAT EVENING, THE Magnus threw a departure banquet for the Armada service performed on his behalf. "Someday," he said, "we may all thank you for our lives."

Xavier excused himself midway through the meal. The food and wine seemed to lack taste. "My apologies, Eminence, but my squadron must not miss the optimal departure window." He bowed at the doorway, then hurried to his vessel. Some of his troops would have liked to remain longer, but most were also eager to get home. They had their own sweethearts and families, and these soldiers had more than earned furloughs.

With his inspection tour behind him, Xavier left lovely Giedi Prime, confident that he had seen and done everything necessary.

And completely unaware of the vulnerabilities he had not bothered to discover. . . .

The *Dream Voyager* neared Earth, humanity's original home and now the central Synchronized World. Though he remained attentive, Seurat allowed Vorian Atreides to pilot the ship. "Such risks amuse me."

Vor sniffed, looking at the unreadable expression on the copper skinfilm of the cognizant machine. "I've proved myself to be a perfectly competent pilot—probably the best of all the trustees."

"For a human, I suppose, with sluggish reflexes and the frailties of a physical body prone to infirmities."

"At least my jokes are better than yours." Vor took the controls of the black-and-silver ship. He showed off his skills, dodging asteroid rubble as he accelerated in a slingshot curve around the heavy gravity of Jupiter. Alarms lit on the diagnostic panels.

"Vorian, you are taking us beyond acceptable parameters. If we cannot break free of Jupiter's gravity, we will burn up."

The robot reached forward to reassert control on the flight deck. "You must not endanger the Omnius updates we carry—"

Vorian laughed at the trick he had just played. "Got you, old Metalmind! When you weren't looking I recalibrated the alarm-sensor setpoints. Check with objective instrumentation, and you'll see we've still got plenty of wiggle room."

They easily pulled away from the gas giant. "You are correct, Vorian, but why would you do such a brash thing?"

"To see if a robot is capable of wetting his pants." Vor plotted a final approach vector through the machine-operated surveillance stations and satellites orbiting Earth. "You'll never understand practical jokes."

"Very well, Vorian. I will keep trying—and practicing."

Vor realized that he might one day regret teaching Seurat that type of humor.

"Incidentally, I have more than metal in my brain, as do all thinking machines. Our neurelectronics are only the most exotic alloys, in a network of optic threads, complex polymers, gelcircuitry, and—"

"I'll keep calling you old Metalmind anyway. Just because it bothers you."

"I will never understand human foolishness."

For the sake of appearances, Seurat maintained command as the *Dream Voyager* touched down at the bustling spaceport. "We have reached the end of another successful route, Vorian Atreides."

Grinning, the young man ran his fingers through long black hair. "We travel a circular route, Seurat. A circle has no end."

"Earth-Omnius is the beginning and the end."

"You're too literal. That's why I beat you in so many strategy games."

"Only forty-three percent of the time, young man," Seurat corrected. He activated the exit ramp.

"Around half." Vorian headed toward the hatch, anxious to get outside and breathe fresh air. "Not bad for someone susceptible to illnesses, distractions, physical weaknesses, and any number of other frailties. I'm gaining ground on you, too, if you care to examine trends." He bounded down to the sprawling field of fused plascrete.

Loader robots scurried among larger pieces of AI equipment that moved about on glider fields. Small scouring drones climbed into engine tubes and exhaust cones; maintenance machines scanned large drive components for needed repairs. Tanker robots refueled parked starships, preparing each long-range vessel for any mission that Omnius decreed in his infinite intelligence.

As Vorian stood blinking in the sunlight, a giant cymek strode forward on jointed legs. The hybrid machine's inner workings were clearly visible: hydraulics, sensor systems, blue-lightning nerve impulses transferred from electrafluid to thoughtrodes. At the core of its artificial body hung the protected brain jar that contained the mind of an ancient human general.

The cymek swiveled its turret sensors, as if targeting him, then altered its path toward Vor, raising its front grappling arms. Heavy pincers clacked.

Vorian waved and rushed forward. "Father!"

Since cymeks regularly exchanged temporary bodies in response to the physical requirements of various activities, they were difficult to distinguish from each other. However, Vor's father came to see him whenever the *Dream Voyager* returned from its update-delivery missions.

Many enslaved humans lived on the Synchronized Worlds, serving the evermind. Omnius kept them on as token workers, though few had lives as important and comfortable as Vorian's. Trustees like himself received special training, went through rigorous instruction at elite schools for crew bosses and other important positions under the machine domination.

Vor had read about the glories of the Titans and knew the stories of his father's great conquests. Raised under the evermind's wing and trained by his cymek father, the young man had never questioned the world order or his own loyalty to Omnius.

Knowing the robot captain's moderate temperament, Agamemnon had used considerable influence to obtain a spot for his son on Seurat's update ship, an enviable assignment even among the chosen trustees. As an independent robot, Seurat did not mind the young man's company, suggesting that Vor's unpredictable personality was an asset to their missions. Occasionally, Omnius himself asked Vor to participate in role-playing simulations to better understand the capabilities of feral humans.

Without fear, Vorian now raced across the landing field to stand beside the weapon-studded cymek, who towered over him. The young man stared fondly at the suspended brain case of his ancient father, with its strange mechanical face now on the underside.

"Welcome back." Agamemnon's vocal patches made his voice deep and paternal. "Seurat has already uploaded his report. Once again, you have made me proud. You are one step closer to meeting our goals." He swiveled his turret around, reversing the direction of progress, and Vorian trotted beside the armored legs as Agamemnon strode away from the ship.

"If only my fragile body survives long enough to accomplish everything," Vor said wistfully. "I can't wait to be selected as a neo-cymek."

"You are only twenty, Vorian. Too young to be morbidly concerned about your mortality."

Overhead, resource haulers dropped from orbit, balanced atop yellow-white flames that slowed their descent. Loadcars manned by human workers trundled up to where ships had landed, preparing to distribute cargoes according to rigid instructions. Vor glanced at the slaves but did not ponder their situation. Each person had his own duties, every human and machine a cog in the Synchronized Worlds. But Vor was superior to the others, since he had a chance to become like his father one day. A cymek.

They passed unmarked warehouses with computerized monitoring and inventory systems where fuel and supplies were stored. Human clerical personnel dispersed food and materials from storehouses to slaves inside the city. Inspectors—some robotic, some human—performed quality control and quantity assessments for the larger-scale plans of Omnius.

Vor could not comprehend the lives of the uneducated workers who unloaded heavy crates at the space dock. The slave laborers performed duties that a simple loading machine could have done faster and more efficiently. But he was pleased that even these lesser people had tasks they could perform in order to earn their subsistence.

"Seurat told me about Salusa Secundus, Father." He maintained a quick pace to match the cymek's huge strides. "I'm sorry your assault was unsuccessful."

"Just a test case," Agamemnon said. "The feral humans have a new defensive system, and now we have probed it."

Vor beamed. "I'm sure you'll discover a way to bring all *hrethgir* under the efficient rule of Omnius. Like the times described in your memoirs, when Titans were in complete control."

Inwardly, the cymek general frowned at the comments. Agamemnon's optic threads detected numerous watcheyes floating around them as the two walked. "I do not wish for the old days, of course," he said, presently. "You have been reading my memoirs again?"

"I never tire of your stories, Father. The Time of Titans, the great Tlaloc, the First Hrethgir Rebellions . . . everything is so fascinating." Accompanying the magnificent cymek made Vor feel special. He always remained alert, within the limitations of his position, for ways to better himself. He wanted to prove himself worthy of the opportunities he'd been given . . . and of more. "I would be happy to learn of this new *hrethgir* defensive system, Father. Perhaps I can assist you in finding a way to defeat it?"

"Omnius is analyzing the data and will decide what to do. I have only recently arrived back on Earth."

With human ambitions still a fundamental part of their psyches, the Titans always had monumental construction projects under way: megalithic buildings and monuments to themselves that celebrated the lost age of humanity and glorified the Time of Titans. Captive human artists and architects were ordered to develop original designs and sketches that the cymeks modified or approved.

Nearby, machinery lifted the components of skyscraper buildings into place, adding upper floors to existing complexes, though the thinking machines had little need for further expansion. At times, the extravagant construction seemed to Vor like mere busy-work for the slaves. . . .

He had never known his mother, and understood only that ages ago, before the Titans had surgically converted themselves into cymeks, Agamemnon had created his own sperm bank, from which he had germinated Vorian. Over the centuries, the general could create any number of offspring using acceptable surrogate mothers.

Though he had never learned about any siblings, Vorian suspected they were out there somewhere. He wondered what it would be like to meet them, but in machine society, emotional attachments were not practical. He only hoped that his siblings had not proven to be disappointments to Agamemnon.

When his father was off on his frequent missions, Vor often tried to talk with the remaining Titans, curious about the events recorded in Agamemnon's celebrated and voluminous memoirs. He used his responsible position to better himself. Some of the original cymeks—especially Ajax—were arrogant and treated Vor as a nuisance. Others, like Juno or Barbarossa, found him amusing. All of them spoke with utmost passion about Tlaloc, the first of the great Titans, who had sparked the revolution.

"I wish I'd been able to meet Tlaloc," Vor said, trying to keep the conversation going. Agamemnon loved to speak of his glory days.

"Yes, Tlaloc was a dreamer with ideas I had never heard before," the cymek mused as he strode down the boulevards. "At times he was a bit naïve, not always understanding the practical repercussions of his ideas. But I pointed them out to him. That was why we made such a great team."

Agamemnon seemed to pick up speed when he spoke of the Titans. Weary from trying to keep up the rapid pace, Vorian gasped for breath.

"Tlaloc took his name from an ancient rain god. Among the Titans, Tlaloc was our visionary, while I was the military commander. Juno was our tactician and manipulator. Dante watched over statistics, bureaucracy, and population-accounting. Barbarossa saw to the reprogramming of the thinking machines, making certain they had the same goals as we did. He gave them ambition."

"And a good thing, too," Vorian said.

Agamemnon hesitated, but did not voice any objections, wary of the watcheyes. "When he visited Earth, Tlaloc realized how the human race had gone stagnant, how people had become so dependent on machines that they had nothing left but apathy. Their goals were gone, their drive, their passion. When they should have had nothing to do but unleash their creative impulses, they were too lazy to perform even the work of the imagination." His vocal speakers made a disgusted sound.

"But Tlaloc was different," Vor said, on cue.

The cymek's voice took on more emotion. "Tlaloc grew up in the Thalim system, on an outer colony world where life was difficult, where labor was not accomplished without sweat, blood, and blisters. He had to fight his way and earn his position. On Earth, he saw that the human spirit had all but died—*and the people hadn't even noticed!*

"He gave speeches attempting to rally the humans, to make them see what was happening. A few watched him with interest, considering him a novelty." Agamemnon raised one of his powerful metal arms. "But they heard his words only as a diversion. Soon the bored audiences returned to their slothful, hedonistic pursuits."

"But not you, Father."

"I was dissatisfied with my uneventful life. I had already met Juno, and the two of us had dreams. Tlaloc crystallized them for us. After Juno and I joined him, we set in motion the events that led to the downfall of the Old Empire."

Father and son arrived at the central complex where the Earth-Omnius resided, although redundant nodes of the evermind were distributed around the planet in a network of armored vaults and high towers. Vorian followed the cymek into the main structure, eager to do his part. This was a ritual they had completed many times.

The walker body strode through wide halls and entered a maintenance facility filled with lubricant tubes, bubbling nutrient cylinders, polished tabletops, and flickering analysis systems. Vor retrieved a tool kit, then turned on vacuum hoses and high-pressure water jets, found soft rags and polishing lotions. He considered it his most important task as a trustee.

In the center of the sterile room, Agamemnon halted beneath a lifting apparatus. A magnetic claw-hand came down and attached itself to the preservation canister that held his ancient brain. Neural connection ports popped open, and thoughtrode cables spiraled away. The lifting arm raised the canister, still attached to temporary batteries and life-support systems.

Vorian came forward with an armload of equipment. "I know you can't feel this, Father, but I like to think it makes you more comfortable and efficient." He blasted the connection ports with high-pressure air and streams of warm water, using a wadded cloth to polish every surface. The cymek general transmitted wordless gratified murmurings.

Vor completed the cleaning and polishing, then adjusted wires and cables and hooked up diagnostics. "All functions optimal, Father."

"With your attentive maintenance, it is no wonder. Thank you, my son. You take such good care of me."

"It is my honor to do so."

His synthesized voice purring, Agamemnon said, "One day, Vorian, if you continue serving me so well, I will recommend you for the greatest reward. I will ask Omnius to surgically convert you into a cymek, like me."

At the mention of this wonderful prospect, Vorian again polished the canister, then looked lovingly at the creamy contours of the brain inside. He tried to hide his flush of eager embarrassment, but tears came to his eyes. "That is the best a human can hope for."

Humans, with such fragile physical forms, are easily crushed. Is it any challenge to hurt or damage them?

—ERASMUS,
uncollated laboratory files

Gazing out upon the skies of Earth again through hundreds of appraising optic threads, Erasmus was not pleased. The robot stood in a high bell tower of his villa, staring through a curving expanse of armored windowplate. The landscape of this world, with its oceans and forests and cities built upon the bones of other cities had already seen countless civilizations rise and fall. The scope of history made his own accomplishments seem small and contrived.

Therefore, he would have to try harder.

Neither Omnius nor any of his delegated architect robots understood true beauty. To Erasmus, the buildings and the layout of the rebuilt city resembled components with sharp angles, abrupt discontinuities. A city must be more than an efficient circuit diagram. Under his multiphased scrutiny, the metropolis looked like an elaborate mechanism, designed and constructed with utilitarian force. It had its own clean lines and systematic efficiency, which resulted in a completely serendipitous beauty . . . but there was no finesse whatsoever.

It was such a disappointment when the omniscient evermind refused to live up to his potential. Sometimes, gloriously unrealistic human ambitions had a certain merit.

Omnius either ignored or intentionally refuted the graceful beauty of Golden Age human architecture. But such cold and petulant superiority was not logical. Admittedly, Erasmus could see a certain beauty in streamlined machines and components—he rather liked his own burnished platinum skinfilm, the smooth grace of his mirrored face with which he formed facial expressions. But he saw no point in maintaining ugliness just to spite a perceived enemy's concept of beauty.

How could a vast computer mind distributed across hundreds of planets exhibit even a hint of narrow-mindedness? To Erasmus, with his detached and mature understanding developed through long contemplation, Omnius's attitude revealed a lack of comprehensive thinking.

Making the sound of an exaggerated sigh that he had copied from humans, he transmitted a thought-command that caused projection shades to drop over the windows in the bell tower. Choosing his mood, he projected artificial, pastoral views from other worlds. So soothing and peaceful.

On one wall he paused at a clothing synthesizer, selected the design he wanted, and waited while a garment was prepared for him. A traditional painter's smock. When it was ready, he draped it over his sleek body and crossed the room to an easel where he had already set up a blank canvas, a palette of paints, and fine brushes.

At a wave of his hand, the projection shades shifted to display enlarged images of masterpiece paintings, each one highlighting a different great master. He selected "Cottages at Cordeville" by an ancient Earth artist, Vincent Van Gogh. It was bold and colorful but basically crude in its implementation, with inept lines and childish pigment applications that featured thick globs of paint and smears of color. Yet when considered as a whole, the painting itself possessed a certain raw energy, an indefinable primitive vibrancy.

After deep concentration, Erasmus thought he had a delicate understanding of Van Gogh's technique. But the comprehension of *why* anyone would want to create it in the first place eluded him.

Although he had never painted before, he copied the artwork exactly. Brushstroke for brushstroke, pigment for pigment. When he was finished, Erasmus examined his masterpiece. "There, the sincerest form of flattery."

The nearest wall-mounted screen brightened to a pale gray wash of light. Omnius had been watching, as always. Erasmus would no doubt have to justify his activities, since the evermind would never understand what the independent robot was doing.

He studied the painting again. Why was it so hard to understand creativity? Should he just change some of the components at random and call it an original work? As the robot finished his scrutiny, satisfied that he had made no mistakes, that he had not deviated from the tolerances he could see in the image of the painting, Erasmus waited for a rush of comprehension.

Slowly, he came to realize that what he had just completed was not really *art*, any more than a printing press created literature. He had only *copied* the ancient composition in every detail. He had added nothing, synthesized no newness. And he burned with the need to understand the difference.

Frustrated, Erasmus took a different tack. In an implacable voice, he summoned three servants and ordered them to carry his painting supplies out to one of the laboratory buildings. "I intend to create a new work of art, all my own. A still life, of sorts. You three will be vital parts of the process. Rejoice in your good fortune."

In the sterile environment of the laboratory, with the cold assistance of his personal robot guards, Erasmus proceeded to vivisect the trio of victims, oblivious to their screams. "I want to get to the heart of the matter," he quipped, "the lifeblood of it."

With stained metal hands he studied the dripping organs, squeezed them, watched their juices flow and cellular structures collapse. He performed a cursory analysis, discovering sloppy mechanics and inefficient circulatory systems that were unnecessarily complex and prone to failure.

Then, feeling a vibrant energy, an *impulsiveness*, Erasmus set up a tableau to paint. A new work, completely unique! It would be his own arrangement, and he would tint the images using different filters, making a few intentional mistakes to better approximate human imperfection and uncertainty.

At last, he must be on the right track.

At his command, the sentinel robots brought in a vat filled with fresh, uncoagulated human blood. Erasmus began removing the interesting array of human organs—still warm to the touch—from his table, and instructed two cleaning drones to scrape out the insides from the donor bodies. Contemplating the arrangement and order, he dropped organ after organ into the blood and watched them bob in the liquid—eyes, livers, kidneys, hearts.

Slowly assessing each step of the process, he set up exactly what his "creative urges" told him to do. Whim upon whim. Erasmus added more ingredients to the grisly stew. Pursuant to something he had learned about the artist Van Gogh, he sliced an ear off one of the corpses and tossed it into the vat as well.

Finally, his metal hands dripping gore, he stepped back. A beautiful arrangement—one that was totally original to him. He could think of no famous human artist who had worked on such a canvas. No one else had ever done anything approaching this.

Erasmus wiped his smooth metallic hands and began to paint upon a virgin canvas. On the blank medium, he astutely drew one of the three hearts, showing in perfect detail the ventricals, auricles, and aorta. But this was not meant to be a realistic dissection image. Dissatisfied, he smeared some of the lines to add an artistic flair. True art required the right amount of uncertainty, just as gourmet cooking needed the proper spices and flavors.

This must be how creativity worked. As he painted, Erasmus tried to imagine the kinesthetic relationship between his brain and his mechanical fingers, the thought impulses that set the fingers into motion.

"Is *that* what the humans define as art?" Omnius said from a wallscreen.

For once, Erasmus did not debate with the evermind. Omnius was correct in his skepticism. Erasmus had not attained true creativity. Yes, he had produced an original and graphic arrangement. But in human artwork, the sum of the components added up to more than the individual items. Just ripping organs from victims, floating them in blood, and painting them brought him no closer to understanding human inspiration. Even if he manipulated the details, he remained imprecise and uninspired.

Still, this might be a step in the right direction.

Erasmus could not carry this thought to the next logical step, and he came to understand why. The process was not ratiocinative at all. Creativity and the precision of analysis were mutually exclusive.

Frustrated, the robot gripped the macabre painting in his powerful hands, broke the frame, and tore the canvas to shreds. He would have to do better than this, much better. Erasmus shifted his metallic polymer face to a stylized pensive mask. He was no closer to comprehending humans, despite a century of intensive research and musings.

Walking slowly, Erasmus went to his private sanctuary, a botanical garden where he listened to classical music piped through the cellular structures of plants. "Rhapsody in Blue," by a composer of Old Earth.

In the contemplative garden, the troubled robot sat in the ruddy sunlight and felt warmth on his metal skin. This was another thing that humans seemed to enjoy, but he did not understand why. Even with his sensory enhancement module, it just seemed like *heat*.

And machines that overheated broke down.

The tapestry of the universe is vast and complex, with infinite patterns. While threads of tragedy may form the primary weave, humanity with its undaunted optimism still manages to embroider small designs of happiness and love.

—COGITOR KWYNA,
City of Introspection archives

After his long sojourn in space, Xavier could think only of being home, and back in the warm embrace of Serena Butler.

On furlough, he returned to the Tantor estate where he was welcomed by his adoptive parents and their enthusiastic son Vergyl. The Tantors were a soft-spoken older couple, gentle and intelligent, with dark skin and hair the color of thick smoke. Xavier seemed to be cut from the same mold, with similar interests and high moral values. He had grown up in this warm and spacious manor house, which he still considered home. Though he had legally inherited other Harkonnen holdings—mining and industrial operations on three planets— many rooms in the Tantor mansion were still set aside for his use.

As he entered his familiar large suite, Xavier found a pair of shaggy gray wolfhounds awaiting him, wagging their tails. He dropped his bags and wrestled with the dogs. The animals, larger than his little brother, were always playful and delighted to see him.

That evening, the family feasted on the cook's specialty of sage fowl roasted with honey, slivered nuts, and olives from the Tantors' own groves. Unfortunately, after his exposure to the cymeks' searing gas, the subtle nuances of flavors and aromas now eluded him. The cook gave him an alarmed look when he dumped salt and seasoning—which he needed to taste anything at all—onto the delicate food.

Another thing the thinking machines had taken from him.

Afterward, Xavier lounged in a heavy oak chair before a roaring fire, sipping a red wine from the Tantor family vineyards—also, unfortunately, nearly tasteless. He luxuriated in relaxing at home, away from military protocol. He had spent almost half a year aboard the efficient but bare-bones Armada survey ships; tonight he would sleep like a babe in his own bedchamber.

One of the gray wolfhounds snored loudly, resting a furry muzzle on Xavier's stockinged feet. Emil Tantor, with a fringe of smoky hair around his bald crown, sat in the chair opposite his adopted son. Emil asked about the strategic positions of the Synchronized Worlds and the military capabilities of the Armada. "What are the chances of the war escalating after the attack on Zimia? Can we ever do more than drive them back?"

Xavier finished his wine, poured another half glass for himself and a full one for the older man, then sat back in the chair again, all without disturbing the gray dog. "The situation looks grim, Father." Barely remembering his own parents, he had always called the Tantor lord his father. "But, then, it has always looked grim, ever since the Time of Titans. Perhaps we lived too comfortably in the days of the Old Empire. We forgot how to be ourselves, how to live up to our potential, and for a thousand years afterward we've paid the price. We were easy prey—first for evil men, then for soulless machines."

Emil Tantor sipped his wine, and stared into the fireplace. "So is there hope, at least? We must have something to cling to."

Xavier's lips formed a gentle smile. "We are human, Father. As long as we hold onto that, there is always hope."

~~~

THE NEXT DAY Xavier sent a message to the Butler estate, asking permission to accompany the Viceroy's daughter on the annual bristleback hunt, scheduled in two days. Serena would already know that Xavier had returned. His survey ships had arrived with much fanfare, and Manion Butler would have been expecting his note.

Still, Salusan society was formal and extravagant. In order to court the beautiful daughter of the Viceroy, one had to bow to certain expectations.

In late morning a messenger pounded on the doors of the Tantor manor house; Vergyl stood beside his big brother, grinning when he saw the expression on Xavier's face. "What is it? Can I come along? Did the Viceroy say yes?"

Xavier made a mock-stern expression. "How could he possibly turn down the man who saved Salusa Secundus from the cymeks? Remember that, Vergyl, if you ever wish to win the affections of a young lady."

"I need to save a *planet* just to have a girlfriend?" The boy sounded skeptical, though wary of outright disbelief when it came to Xavier's words.

"For a woman as magnificent as Serena, that is exactly what you must do." He strode into the great house to tell the Tantors his plans.

The next dawn, Xavier dressed in his finest equestrian outfit and rode into brightening daylight toward the Butler property. He borrowed his father's chocolate-brown Salusan stallion, a fine beast with a braided mane, narrow muzzle, and bright eyes. The animal's ears were large, and its gait flowed without the jarring rhythm of less conditioned horses. On the crest of a grassy hill stood a cluster of ornate whitewashed buildings— a main house, stables, servants' quarters, and storage sheds arranged as outbuildings along the perimeter of a split-rail fence. As his horse climbed, he saw impressive vistas of the white spires of Zimia far behind him.

A path paved with crushed limestone wound up to the crest. The gravel crunched under the stallion's hooves as Xavier rode, breathing the crisp air. He could feel the moist chill of early spring, saw fresh leaves on the trees, a dazzle of wild-flowers in their first bloom. But each breath he drew into his new lungs smelled flat.

Grapevines lined the hill like green corduroy, carefully tended and watered, each vine tied to cables between stakes so that the clusters would hang off the ground for easy picking. Twisted olive trees surrounded the main house, their low branches awash with white flowers. Each year, the first press-ings of grapes and olives were cause for feasting in every Salusan household; local vineyards vied against each other to see which could produce the best vintages.

As Xavier rode through the gates and into the courtyard, other horsemen in hunting outfits milled about. Barking dogs dodged around the stallion's legs, but the chocolate-brown horse stood majestically, ignoring the hounds as if they were ill-mannered little boys.

Contract huntsmen grabbed the leashes and pulled the dogs back into order. A number of short black hunting horses pranced about, as impatient as the dogs. Two of the huntsmen whistled loudly and others joined them, ready to begin the day's festivities.

Manion Butler strolled out of the stables, calling up his team like a military commander positioning troops for battle. He glanced at the young officer, raised a hand in greeting.

Then Xavier saw Serena riding out on a gray mare with beautiful lines and an ornate saddle. She wore high boots, jodhpurs, and a black riding jacket. Her eyes were like electric sparks as her gaze met his.

She cantered over to where Xavier sat astride his mount, a smile forming at the edges of her mouth. Even with all the barking dogs, restless horses, and shouting huntsmen, Xavier wanted to kiss her so badly that he could barely restrain him-self. Yet Serena remained coolly formal, extending a gloved hand in greeting. He took it, holding her fingertips.

How he wished he could be telepathic like the Sorceresses of Rossak, just to send her his thoughts. But from the obvious delight suffusing her face, he thought Serena understood his feelings well enough, and reciprocated them.

"The journeys across space were so long," he said. "And I thought about you all the time."

"*All* the time? You should have been concentrating on your duties." She gave him a skeptical smile. "Perhaps we can find time alone during today's hunt, and you will tell me what you dreamed of."

Playfully, she urged her gray mare to trot over to where her father waited. Conscious of the eyes watching them, she and Xavier maintained an acceptable distance. He rode forward and clasped her father's black-gloved hand. "I thank you for allowing me to participate in the hunt, Viceroy."

Manion Butler's florid face rearranged itself into a grin. "I'm glad you could join us, Tercero Harkonnen. This year I'm certain we'll track down a bristleback. The beasts are definitely in these woods—and I, for one, have been craving hams and roasts. And bristlebacon, especially. There's nothing like it."

Her eyes dancing, Serena looked at him. "Perhaps, Father, if you brought along fewer barking dogs, galloping horses, and men crashing through the underbrush, some of those shy animals would be easier to find."

In response, Manion smiled as if she were still a precocious little girl. Glancing at Xavier, he said, "I'm glad you'll be there to protect her, young man."

The Viceroy raised his right arm. Horns sounded and a brass gong clanged from the stables. The purebred hounds began to bay, clustering toward the far fence. Ahead, the path led beyond the blossoming olive groves and into the scrubby Salusan forest. Two eager-eyed boys swung open the gates, already anticipating their first bristleback hunt.

The party rode out like a rowdy gang, dogs pushing first through the gates, followed by the big horses that carried the professional huntsmen. Manion Butler rode with them,

blowing an antique bugle that had been with his family since
Bovko Manresa's first settlement on Salusa.

The followers rode lesser mounts, hurrying behind the
horses. These helper crews would set up camp and dress and
skin whatever wild game the huntsmen caught. They would
also prepare the feast once the party returned to the main
house.

The hunters had already spread out, with each chief taking
a point and plunging into the outskirts of the forest. Unhurried,
Xavier and Serena trotted toward the dark green woods. One
bright-eyed young man, trailing behind, glanced over his
shoulder and winked at Xavier, as if he knew that the young
couple had no intention of enjoying the hunt for its own sake.

Xavier urged his stallion forward. Serena rode beside him,
and they chose their own path through thinning trees to a
muddy streambed wet with spring flow. Smiling secretively at
each other, they listened to the distant sounds of dogs and her
father's continuing bugle blasts.

The Butler's private forest covered hundreds of acres, crisscrossed by game trails. Mostly it was left as a preserve, with
meadows and sparkling creeks, nesting birds, and lush patches
of flowers that bloomed in successive splashes of color as the
patches of crusty snow faded.

Xavier was simply happy to be alone with Serena. Riding
side by side, they brushed arms and shoulders, intentionally.
He would reach up to hold green branches away from her face,
and Serena pointed out birds and small animals, identifying
them.

In his comfortable hunting outfit, Xavier carried a sheathed
ceremonial dagger, a bullwhip, and a Chandler pistol that shot
jacketed crystal fragments. Serena carried her own knife and
a small pistol. But neither of them expected to bring down
any prey. To them, their hunt was for each other, and both
knew it.

Serena chose her path without hesitation, as if she had spent
time during Xavier's survey mission riding through the forest
in search of places where they could be alone. Finally, she led
him through a stand of dark pines to a meadow with tall

grasses, starlike flowers, and thick reeds taller than her head. The reeds surrounded a mirror-smooth pond, a shallow old tarn created by winter snow melt and refreshed by an underground spring.

"The water has bubbles in it," she said. "It tingles your skin."

"Does that mean you want to go for a swim?" Xavier's throat tightened at the prospect.

"It'll be cold, but the spring has some natural heat. I'm willing to risk it." With a smile, Serena dismounted and let her mare graze. She heard a splash out in the pond, but the reeds blocked their view.

"Sounds like a lot of fish, too," Xavier said. He slid down from his stallion, patted the muscular neck, and let his mount sniff at the thick grasses and flowers near the gray mare.

Serena pulled off her riding boots and stockings, then lifted her loose jodhpurs above her knees as she walked barefoot into the rushes. "I'm going to test the water." She pushed the hollow grasses aside.

Xavier checked the fastenings on his stallion's saddle. He worked open one of the leather compartments and brought out a bottle of fresh citrus water to share. He followed Serena toward the reeds, already imagining how it would be to swim beside her, just the two of them stroking naked through this lonely forest lake, kissing each other. . . .

Without warning, a monstrous bristleback charged out of the reeds, spraying mud and water from its cool wallowing hole. Serena let out a cry, more of alarm than terror, and fell backward into the mud.

The bristleback pawed at the rushes with its cloven hooves. Long tusks protruded from a squarish snout, each a bony maul for uprooting saplings and eviscerating enemies. The animal had wide-set eyes, large and black. It made loud grunts as if preparing to breathe fire. In tales of great bristleback hunts, many men, hunting dogs, and horses had died—but there were so few of the animals anymore.

"Into the water, Serena!"

The bristleback turned as it heard his shout. Serena did exactly as Xavier said, splashing away from the rushes, deeper into the pond. She began to swim, knowing the boar could not charge her if she was in deep enough water.

The bristleback stomped out of the rushes. The two horses squealed and skittered back toward the edge of the meadow.

"Look out, Xavier!" Waist deep now, Serena drew her hunting knife, but knew she couldn't help him.

Xavier planted his legs firmly, held a knife in one hand and the Chandler pistol in the other. Without flinching, he aimed the crystal-shard weapon and shot the bristleback three times in the face. The sharp projectiles tore through the animal's cheek and forehead, gouging the thick skull. Another shot splintered one of the tusks. But the bristleback kept charging toward him, caught up in its own solitary stampede.

Xavier fired twice more. The mangled creature bled profusely, mortally wounded—but even imminent death did not diminish its momentum. As the beast thundered toward him, Xavier jumped to one side and slashed the sharp knife across its throat, opening jugular and carotid vessels. The bristleback turned, gushing blood upon him even as its heart began to fade.

The weight of the falling creature knocked Xavier to the ground, but he wrestled it away, avoiding the convulsive thrusts of the razor tusks. The killing done, Xavier climbed back to his feet and staggered away, shivering in shock. His hunting outfit was soaked with the beast's blood.

He sprinted into the trampled rushes at the edge of the water. "Serena!"

"I'm all right," she called, splashing toward the shore.

He looked at his reflection in the placid pond, saw his shirt and face covered with gore. He hoped none of it was his own. He cupped his hands and splashed cool water on his skin, then dunked his head to wash the stink from his hair. He scrubbed his hands with peaty sand.

Serena came to him, her clothes drenched, wet hair clinging to her skull. She used a corner of her riding jacket to dab the blood from his neck and cheeks. Then she opened his shirt, wiping his chest as well.

"I don't have a scratch on me," he said, not sure if it was true. The skin on one side of his neck felt raw and hot, as if chafed, and his chest was sore from the collision with the attacker. He clutched her arm, pulling her closer. "Are you sure you're not hurt? You aren't cut, no bones broken?"

"You're asking me?" she said with teasing disbelief. "*I'm* not the brave boar fighter here."

Serena kissed him. Her lips were cold from the water, but he held them against his own, awakening her touch with his until their mouths opened slightly, their breath warm inside each other as the kiss deepened. He took her from the edge of the pond, through the rushes, and to the soft meadow grass, far from the dead bristleback.

The young lovers stroked the wet hair away from their ears and eyes, and kissed again. The brush with death made them feel intensely alive. Xavier's skin was hot, and his heart kept pounding, even though the danger was past. A new excitement mounted. He wished he could better enjoy the seductive scent of her perfume, but could detect only a tantalizing thread.

Serena's sodden clothes were cold, and Xavier noticed goosebumps on her pale arms. All he could think to do was to remove the wet fabric. "Here, let me warm you."

She helped him unfasten the black riding jacket and her blouse while her own fingers worked at his bloodstained shirt. "Just to make certain you're not hurt," Serena said. "I don't know what I would have done if you'd been killed." Her words came fast and hard between kisses.

"It takes more than a wild boar to keep me away from you."

She yanked his shirt down over his shoulders and fumbled with his cuff so she could take it off entirely. The meadow was soft and lush. The horses munched patiently on grasses as Xavier and Serena made love without restraint, expressing their pent-up passions, whispering and then shouting their love for each other.

The rest of the hunting party seemed far away, even though Xavier had killed a bristleback and would have a dramatic story to tell during the evening's feast. Of course, certain details would need to be omitted. . . .

For the moment, the war with the thinking machines did not exist. In this brief and heady hour, they were just two human beings, alone and in love.

~

There is a certain hubris to science, a belief that the more we develop technology and the more we learn, the better our lives will be.

—TLALOC,
A Time for Titans

Anything imagined can be made real . . . given sufficient genius.

Tio Holtzman had said as much in a hundred speeches at the Lords Council on Poritrin. His concepts and achievements sparked dreams and fostered confidence in human technological capabilities against the thinking machines.

The mantra had also been picked up by his patron, Lord Niko Bludd, and by representatives in the League of Nobles. Early in his career, Holtzman had realized that it was not always the best scientists who received the accolades or funding. Instead, it was the best *showmen*, the most effective politicians.

To be sure, Savant Holtzman was an adequate scientist. He had an exceptional technical background and had achieved marked success with his inventions and weapons systems, all of which had been put to good use against Omnius. But he had arranged for more publicity and attention than the inventions themselves warranted. Through his oratory skills and by coloring certain details, he had constructed a pedestal of fame on which he now stood. Holtzman had made himself into the Hero of Poritrin, rather than just another nameless inventor. His ability to enchant audiences, to spark a sense of wonder and possibility in their minds, exceeded his scientific skills.

To maintain his mythology, Holtzman constantly hungered for new *ideas*—which required inspiration and long periods of uninterrupted thought. He liked to let possibilities roll like pebbles down a steep mountain slope. Sometimes the pebbles would come to rest, making a bit of noise but ultimately yielding nothing; on other occasions, such notions might spark an avalanche.

Anything imagined can be made real.

But first it must be imagined, seen in the vision of the creator.

After returning home from the devastation on Salusa Secundus, he had booked himself a private cabin aboard a luxurious driftbarge, one of the quiet zeppelin craft that rose from the delta city of Starda and drifted inland on currents of warm air, cruising across the seemingly endless Poritrin plains.

Holtzman stood on the driftbarge's open deck, looking at the grasslands that flowed in a sea of green and brown, dappled with lakes. Below him, birds flew like schools of fish. The slow aircraft floated with no hurry, no schedule.

He stared toward the open horizon. Limitless distances, endless possibilities. Hypnotic, meditative . . . inspirational. Such places opened his mind, allowed him to pursue crazy concepts and run them down like a predator pursuing prey.

The driftbarge passed over geometric shapes like tattoos on the ground, carefully sectioned acreage for the labor-intensive farming of sweet cane. Other fields grew plump grains and fibrous threads to make Poritrin cloth. Armies of human slaves worked the farms and ranches like insects from a hive.

Following a bucolic derivative of Navachristianity, the people of Poritrin had outlawed computerized harvesting apparatus and restored their society to humbler roots. Without sophisticated machinery, they required a great deal of manual labor. Long ago, Sajak Bludd had been the first League nobleman to introduce actual slavery as a means of making large-scale agriculture viable.

That Poritrin lord had justified his act by choosing only those who owed a debt to humanity, mostly Buddislamic cowards who had fled instead of fighting against the repressive Titans and thinking machines. If they hadn't been afraid to help defend humanity, Sajak Bludd said, their added numbers might have been enough to turn the tide of war. Working the fields was a small enough price for their descendants to pay. . . .

Holtzman paced the driftbarge's deck, acquired a fluted glass of sugary juice from a server, and sipped it as he pondered. Looking down at the sea of grasses, he relished his mental sojourn. No distractions . . . but as yet no inspiration, either. The great scientist often embarked on such journeys to pull his thoughts together, simply staring and thinking—and *working*, though everyone else aboard seemed to be taking a holiday.

Because of Holtzman's previous successes, Niko Bludd gave him free reign to develop whatever innovative defenses and weapons struck his fancy. Unfortunately, during the past year the scientist had faced a growing conviction that he was running out of ideas.

Genius was nothing without creative impulse. Of course, the Savant could coast for a while on his earlier triumphs. Still, he had to offer up new inventions regularly, or even Lord Bludd would begin to doubt him.

Holtzman could never permit that. It was a matter of pride.

He'd been embarrassed that the cymeks so easily penetrated his scrambler shields on Salusa Secundus. How could he—and all the other engineers and technicians on the project—have ignored the fact that cymeks had human minds, not AI gelcircuitry? It was a significant, devastating lapse.

Still, the outpouring of faith and hope—not to mention substantial funding—made him feel a crippling pressure. The people would never allow him to retire now. He must find some other solution, save the day once more.

While back in the blufftop laboratories at his Starda residence, he searched constantly, reading dissertations and theoretical papers transmitted to him, combing them for exploitable possibilities. Many of the reports were esoteric, beyond even his comprehension, but occasionally an idea struck his fancy.

Holtzman had brought along numerous recordings for this mental sojourn over the Poritrin plains. One ambitious and intriguing paper had been written by an unknown theorist from Rossak named Norma Cenva. She had no credentials, as far as he could determine, but her concepts were nothing short of amazing. She thought of simple things in a completely different light. He had a gut feeling about her, an instinct. And she had such a low profile. . . .

As starlight fell over the vast bowl of Poritrin sky, he sat alone in his cabin drinking a warm fruity beverage. He stared at Norma's calculations, working them repeatedly in his mind, watchful for errors while trying to understand. This young, unknown mathematician seemed to harbor no pretensions, as if she simply pulled new ideas out of the clouds and wanted to share them with a man she considered her intellectual comrade. Stymied by some of her derivations, he realized that his doubts were more about his own lack of ability than about her postulations. Norma Cenva seemed divinely inspired.

Exactly what he needed.

Restless, Holtzman thought long and hard into the night. Finally, with the arrival of dawn, he relaxed and drifted off to sleep, his decision made. The airborne barge rocked in gentle breezes and continued to float across the flat landscape. He dozed off with a smile on his face.

Soon he would meet Norma for himself. Perhaps some of her concepts might be applicable to devices he wanted to employ against the thinking machines.

❧

THAT AFTERNOON THE Savant wrote a personal invitation to Norma Cenva and dispatched it to Rossak by League courier. This young woman who had grown up isolated in the jungles just might prove to be his salvation . . . if he handled the situation properly.

Opportunities are a tricky crop, with tiny flowers that are difficult to see and even more difficult to harvest.

—ANONYMOUS

Feeling like an intruder, Norma Cenva stood in her mother's study, overlooking the canopied purple trees. A sour, misty rain fell outside; some of the droplets from the high skies contained impurities and poisonous chemicals from spewing volcanic fumes in the distance. On the far horizon, she monitored dark clouds as they drew closer. Soon there would be a downpour.

What did Aurelius Venport want her to find in here?

Her stern mother maintained an austere room with chalky-white interior walls. An alcove contained the Sorceress's fine clothes, articles that were much too large and fanciful for Norma to wear. Zufa Cenva had an intimidating beauty, a luminous purity that made her as perfect—and as hard—as a classic sculpture. Even without telepathic powers, she could draw men like ants to honey.

But the chief Sorceress had only a superficial loveliness, concealing an implacability about subjects she never permitted Norma to see. It wasn't that Zufa didn't trust her daughter;

she simply considered the girl beneath grand concerns. Like her telepathic companions, Zufa seemed to thrive on secrecy.

But Aurelius had seen something here. "You won't be sorry if you find it, Norma," he had told her, smiling. "I trust your mother to tell you about it eventually . . . but I don't believe it is high in her priorities."

I have never been high in her priorities. Curious, but wary of being caught, Norma continued to investigate.

Her gaze settled on a fibersheet notebook resting on a worktable. The thick book had a maroon cover with indecipherable lettering as arcane as the mathematical notations Norma had developed. Once, eavesdropping on the Sorceresses and their intricate plans, Norma heard them refer to their private language as "Azhar."

Since returning from Salusa Secundus, her mother had been even more detached and aloof than usual. She seemed driven to attempt greater things, because of the cymek attack. When Norma inquired about the war effort, Zufa had merely frowned at her. "We will take care of it."

The chief Sorceress spent much of her time sequestered with a cabalistic clique of women, whispering secret things. Zufa had a fresh passion, a new idea to use against the thinking machines. If her mother had dreamed of any way Norma could contribute, she would have pressed the dwarf girl into service. Instead, Zufa had entirely written off her daughter without giving her a chance.

The most talented women, numbering around three hundred, had established a security zone in the deep fungoid jungle, cutting off the pharmaceutical scavengers hired by Aurelius Venport. Any explorer who ventured into the secluded area encountered strange shimmering barricades.

Ever alert, Norma had noticed unexplained explosions and fires out where Zufa's hand-picked Sorceresses spent weeks of intensive training. Her mother rarely came back to her cliffside chambers. . . .

Now, in her mother's room, Norma discovered two pieces of fine white paper beneath the maroon notebook: the bleached parchment often used by League couriers. This must be what Aurelius had wanted her to find.

Dragging a stepstool to the table, she climbed up. She could see the heading on the top sheet of parchment—a formal document from Poritrin. Curious, afraid her mother might return from the jungles, she removed the pages and was astonished to read in black chancery lettering, SAVANT TIO HOLTZMAN.

For what possible purpose had the great inventor written a letter to her mother? Leaning down, the girl read the salutation line: "Dear Norma Cenva." With a scowl, she scanned the message, then reread it with mounting delight mixed with anger. *Tio Holtzman wants me to apprentice with him on Poritrin! He thinks I am brilliant? I can't believe it.*

Her own mother had attempted to conceal, or at least delay, the transmittal! Zufa had said nothing, possibly unable to believe the Savant would want anything to do with her daughter. Luckily, Aurelius had told her about it.

Norma hurried off to the business district of the cliffside settlement. She found Venport in a tea shop, concluding a meeting with a seedy-looking trader. As the dark-skinned man rose from his seat, Norma hurried over with her off-kilter gait and slid into his place at the table.

Venport smiled warmly at her. "You look excited, Norma. You must have found the letter from Savant Holtzman?"

She thrust the parchment forward. "My mother tried to prevent me from seeing his offer!"

"Zufa is a maddening woman, I know, but you must try to understand her. Since neither of us can do the things she values most, Zufa disregards our abilities. Oh, she's aware of your mathematical talents, Norma, and she knows I'm a competent businessman, but our skills do not count for anything with her."

Norma squirmed on the seat, not wanting to give her mother the benefit of the doubt. "Then why did she hide this letter?"

Venport laughed. "She was probably embarrassed by the attention you received." He squeezed her hand. "Don't worry, I will intervene if your mother attempts to block this. In fact, since she's so preoccupied with the other Sorceresses, I can't see how she would object if I were to complete the necessary paperwork for you."

"You would do that? Doesn't my mother—"

"Let me take care of everything. I'll handle her." He gave Norma a quick, warm hug. "I believe in what you can do."

Acting in Zufa's stead, Aurelius Venport dispatched a formal letter of response to the famous inventor, agreeing to send Norma away. The young woman would study with him on Poritrin and assist him in his laboratories. For Norma, it was the opportunity of a lifetime.

Her mother might not even notice she was gone.

Home can be anywhere, for it is a part of one's self.

—Zensunni saying

Even in the wasteland, with wind whipping around him, Selim's luck continued to hold. Survival itself became a wondrous game out in the desert.

Leaving the dead sandworm behind, he'd tried to find a small cave or gully in the rocks where he could crouch from the approaching storm. Desperately thirsty, Selim poked around for any signs of human habitation, though he doubted any other man had ever set foot so far out in the arid wilderness.

Certainly no one who had lived.

After wandering from planet to planet, the Zensunni had come to Arrakis, where they scattered in widely separated settlements. For several generations, the scavenger people had scraped a meager existence from the desert, but only occasionally did they venture from their protected areas, fearful of giant worms.

The wild sandworm had taken Selim far from the spaceport, far from the vital supplies that even the most resourceful Zensunni would require. His prospects for survival seemed bleak indeed.

So when he stumbled upon an ancient botanical testing station camouflaged in the rocks, Selim could hardly believe his good fortune. Undoubtedly, it was another sign from Buddallah. A miracle!

He stood before the domed enclosure erected by long-forgotten ecologists who had studied Arrakis and found it wanting. Perhaps a few Old Empire scientists had lived here and recorded data during a storm season. The rugged structure consisted of several low outbuildings built into the rocks, half-disguised by time and windblown sand.

As the howling tempest peppered him with stinging sand, Selim scrambled around the abandoned station. He saw tilted weather vanes, dented wind collectors and other data-gathering devices that looked long dead. Most important, he found an entry hatch.

With sore hands and aching arms from his worm-riding ordeal, Selim pounded against the barrier, searching for a way inside. He scooped powdery debris away, looking for some sort of manual mechanism, since batteries would have long since died. He needed to get into the shelter before the storm wind slammed into him with full intensity.

Selim had heard of such places. A few had been found and raided by Zensunni scavengers. These self-reliant stations had been placed on Arrakis during humanity's glory days, before the thinking machines had taken over, before Buddislamic refugees had fled to safety. This automated facility was at least a thousand years old, probably more. But in the desert, where the environment remained unchanged for millennia, time ran at a different pace.

Selim finally located the mechanism that controlled the hatch. As he had feared, the power cells were dead, providing only enough of a spark to make the door groan open the barest crack.

The wind howled. Blown sand hung like fog on the horizon, obscuring the sun. Dust tingled against his raw ears and face, and Selim knew it would soon become a deadly scouring.

Growing more desperate, he wedged his sandworm tooth into the dark opening and used it as a pry bar. The aperture widened a little, but not enough. Cold, stale air gasped out. He used the aching muscles in his arms, dug his feet against the rocks to throw his body weight into the effort, and pushed hard on the makeshift lever.

With a last groan of resistance, the hatch grated partway open. Selim laughed and tossed the curved worm fang into the interior, where it made a tinkling clatter on the metal floor. He squirmed through into the station, heard the muffled roar of the sandstorm increasing outside. It was on top of him.

Impeded by wind and blown sand, Selim grasped the lip of the hatch and pushed hard. Incoming sand fell through a grating in the floor, into a receptacle below. He needed to hurry. The wind let up for only a second, but that was enough. He got the door shut, sealing himself in, away from the violent weather.

Safe . . . unbelievably safe. He laughed at his good fortune, then gave a prayer of thanks, more sincere than any he had uttered in his life. How could he question such blessings?

Selim used the shaft of wan daylight to look around. Luckily, the abandoned station had plaz windows. Though scratched and pitted from prolonged exposure, they allowed fading illumination inside.

The place was like a cave of treasure. Guided by the dust-filtered light from the windows, he found a few old glowstrips which he coaxed into brightening the small shelter. Then he ransacked cupboards and storage vaults. Much of what remained was useless: unreadable dataplaques, dead computerized recording systems, strange instruments that bore the names of archaic corporations. He did, however, find capsules of well-preserved food that had not deteriorated even in all the time this facility had been abandoned.

He broke open a capsule and ate the contents. Though the flavors were unusual, the food tasted wonderful, and he felt energy seeping back into his weary flesh. Other containers held concentrated juices, which were like ambrosia to him. Most valuable of all, he found distilled water, hundreds of literjons of it. Undoubtedly it had been collected over the centuries by automated moisture extractors left behind by the long-ago scientific expedition.

This was personal wealth beyond anything Selim had imagined possible. He could pay back the brackish water he'd been accused of taking from the tribe a thousand times over. He could return to the Zensunni as a hero. Naib Dhartha would have to forgive him. But Selim had never committed the crime in the first place.

While Selim sat comfortable and satisfied, he vowed never to give Dhartha the satisfaction of seeing him return. Ebrahim had betrayed his friendship, and the corrupt Naib had falsely condemned him. His own people had exiled him, never expecting him to survive. Now that he had found a way to live by himself, why would Selim ever want to go back and surrender it all?

For two straight nights, the young man slept. At dawn on the second day he awoke and opened more of the sealed boxes and cabinets. He discovered tools, rope, durable fabric, construction material. The possibilities filled him with joy, and Selim found himself chuckling all alone inside the botanical testing station.

I'm alive!

The storm had rattled past as he slept, unsuccessfully scratching against the walls of the shelter like a monster trying to get in. Most of the sand had been deflected, so very little was piled around the enclosure. From the vantage of the station's largest window, Selim gazed across the desert sea that he had crossed on the back of the sandworm. The dunes were fresh and spotless. All signs of the dead worm had been erased, scoured clean. Only this solitary young man remained.

He envisioned a long journey ahead of him, and thought he must have a particular calling. Why else would Buddallah have gone to so much trouble to allow poor Selim to live?

What do you want me to do?

Smiling, the outcast looked out upon the desert, wondering how he could possibly cross such an expanse again. The vista filled him with a sensation of supreme solitude. He made out a few rocks in the distance, etched by eternal winds. Here and there were a few hardy plants. Small animals scurried into burrows. Dune merged into dune, desert into desert.

Enthralled by his own memories and feeling recklessly invulnerable, Selim decided what he must do, sooner or later. The first time had been an incredible fluke, but he understood better how to do it now.

He must ride a sandworm again. And the next time it would not be an accident.

One of the questions the Butlerian Jihad answered with violence was whether the human body is simply a machine that a man-made *machine can duplicate. The results of the war answered the question.*

—DR. RAJID SUK,
Post-Trauma Analysis of the Human Species

Wearing a new warrior-form designed to strike terror into the humans on Giedi Prime, Agamemnon strode on armored legs through the broken industries and flaming ruins of the city. The *hrethgir* hadn't stood a chance.

Giedi Prime had been conquered easily.

The invading machine troops plodded forward, targeting habitation complexes and setting them aflame, blasting parks into blackened fields. In accordance with Agamemnon's orders—citing the glory of Omnius—the neo-cymeks and robotic warriors left the Giedi City industries essentially intact.

Agamemnon had sworn that Giedi Prime would make up for the cymeks' humiliation on Salusa. Even now, watcheyes flew overhead, recording the carnage, seeing how efficiently the two Titans guided the military operation.

Accompanied by his comrade Barbarossa, Agamemnon scanned the topography of the metropolis and located the Magnus's magnificent residence. It was an appropriate place to establish the new center of Synchronized government, a symbolic gesture of domination as well as an affront to the defeated populace.

The cymek general's warrior-form was the most monstrous multilegged system he had ever conceived. Electrical discharges fired through artificial muscles, pulling fiber cables taut and moving weapon-studded limbs. He flexed his flowmetal claws and crushed construction blocks in his grip, imagining them to be the skulls of enemies. Following in his own ferocious configuration, Barbarossa laughed at the showmanship.

Marching forward on many limbs, the cymeks thundered through the wreckage-strewn streets. Nothing stood in the way of these former warlords. The situation reminded both of them of a thousand years before, when twenty Titans had conquered the Old Empire by trampling the bodies of their foes.

This was the way it should be. It only whetted their appetite for more.

～⊗～

PRIOR TO THE attack, Agamemnon had studied Giedi Prime's defenses, analyzing images taken by spy watcheyes that zoomed through the system like tiny meteoroids. From those readings, the cymek general had concocted a brilliant tactical move, exploiting a slight weakness in planetary defenses. Omnius had been willing to pay the necessary price to take over a League World, and it had not cost the life of a single Titan, not even one of the lesser neo-cymeks. Only a single robotic cruiser. Perfectly acceptable, as far as Agamemnon was concerned.

The humans had erected scrambler fields here like those on Salusa, centering their transmitting towers in Giedi City. The field-generator facility had been guarded by kindjal fighter craft, supposedly impregnable embankments, and massively armored ground vehicles. The feral humans had learned a lesson on Salusa Secundus. But it was not enough to protect them from obliteration.

Giedi Prime's first-line orbital protective forces had been

brushed aside by the unstoppable force of the giant machine fleet. All robot losses were acceptable. When Agamemnon led the cymek ships in, along with the sacrificial cruisers, the planetbound human defenders could not hope to drive them back.

To begin the assault, the huge robotic cruiser had positioned itself above Giedi Prime, its cargo holds filled with explosives. Dozens of other robot cruisers moved with machine grace, sleek and streamlined, lining up for the assault. Guided by a thinking machine intelligence, the enormous craft fired its engines and accelerated at full speed toward its target.

"Descent approach in progress," the battleship's robot mind had reported, transmitting images to the waiting fighters. Ahead, thirty decoy vessels shot downward, also hoping to strike the target but designed to be targets for the ground-based missile defenses. The plan relied on brute force and overwhelming numbers, not finesse. Nevertheless, it would be effective.

With its engines at full speed, the sacrificial vessel had accelerated white-hot into Giedi Prime's atmosphere, faster than any ground-based human missile defenses could target and respond. The other cruisers approached the invisible scrambler shield. Already, gray-white blossoms of smoke and explosions marked where the ground-launched missiles had found targets. The numbers dwindled, as did the distance. The humans could never stop all the invaders.

The doomed robot ship sent final images back to the watcheyes so Omnius would have a complete record of the conquest of Giedi Prime. Every nanosecond—until it passed through the scrambler net, which effectively erased the AI guidance brain. The transmissions became static, then an empty carrier wave.

Still, the juggernaut had continued to descend. Even with its gelcircuitry brain neutralized, the plummeting cruiser fell like an asteroid-sized hammer.

Kindjal fighter craft directly engaged the last explosive-laden vessel, but the inbound ship was too big and too hot to be swerved. The defenders' shots amounted to little more than pellets.

The giant dead vessel slammed into the field transmitters on the outskirts of Giedi City. A crater half a kilometer wide flashed into steam; the transmitters, the overwhelmed defenses, and the surrounding inhabited areas all vanished.

Shockwaves had toppled buildings for kilometers around and shattered windows. Holtzman's scrambler shields were neutralized in the blink of an eye, and the Giedi Home Guard was crippled.

After that, the cymeks and robots had come down in full force.

~~

"BARBAROSSA, MY FRIEND, shall we make our grand entrance?" Agamemnon said, arriving at the residence of the Magnus.

"Just like when we followed Tlaloc into the halls of the Old Empire," his fellow Titan agreed. "It has been a long time since I've enjoyed a victory so much."

They led enthusiastic neo-cymeks easily through the reeling metropolis. The stunned human inhabitants could not even put up a fight. Behind the cymek conquerors marched robotic troops to help secure the territory.

Although part of Giedi Prime's population might flee underground and hide, the citizenry would break, given time. It might take years to root out the last cells of feral resistance. No doubt the conquering machines would endure decades of guerrilla strikes by misguided vigilantes, survivors of the Giedi Home Guard who thought a few gnat-bites would make the invaders pack up and go away. Resistance groups would be a futile exercise, but he had no doubt the locals would try some such foolishness.

Agamemnon wondered if he should bring in Ajax to complete the cleanup. The brutal cymek warlord particularly enjoyed hunting humans, as he had proved so effectively during the Hrethgir Rebellions on Walgis. As soon as they installed a copy of the evermind in the ashes of Giedi City, Agamemnon would make appropriate recommendations to the new incarnation of Omnius.

Agamemnon and Barbarossa smashed open the front of the governor's residence, clearing an area wide enough for their reinforced bodies. In their wake, soldier robots, much smaller than the cymeks' warrior-forms, flooded into the building. Within moments, the robots brought blond-haired Magnus Sumi before the two Titans.

"We claim your planet in the name of Omnius," Barbarossa declared. "Giedi Prime is now a Synchronized World. We require your cooperation to consolidate our victory."

Magnus Sumi, trembling with fear, nevertheless spat on the broken floor where the weight of the cymek warrior-forms had crushed his carefully laid tiles.

"Bow to us," Barbarossa said.

The Magnus laughed. "You're mad. I would never—"

Agamemnon swung one of his sleek metal arms sideways. He had not fully tested this new body and was not aware of the magnitude of his strength. He had meant to strike the governor in the face, an instinctive angry slap. Instead, the arm delivered a blow so forceful that it ripped the man's torso in half. The two parts of his body thudded against the far wall in a splatter of gore.

"Oh, well. My demand was a mere formality anyway." Agamemnon turned optic threads toward his comrade. "Begin your work, Barbarossa. These robots will assist."

The Titan programming genius began dismantling the household systems in the governor's residence and setting up power conduits and machinery. He added linkages and installed a blank, resilient gelsphere mainframe into which he uploaded the newest version of Omnius's mind.

The process took several hours, during which the thinking machine invasion force moved through the city, putting out fires and shoring up damaged industrial buildings that Agamemnon considered important for the planet's continued utility.

The habitation complexes of the surviving humans, though, were left to burn. The suffering people could fend for themselves. Misery would help them understand the hopelessness of their position.

Floating overhead, the annoying watcheyes recorded everything. At least it was a victory this time. Agamemnon revealed no sign of his impatience or displeasure, knowing that resistance against the computer evermind would be fruitless. *For now*. Instead, he must select the proper place and time.

Once installed and activated, the new incarnation of Omnius would show no appreciation toward the two seemingly loyal Titans for their victory, nor would the evermind begrudge the loss of his machine juggernaut. It was a military operation well executed, and the Synchronized Worlds had now added one of humanity's jewels to its empire. A psychological and strategic success.

When the immense download was finally complete, Agamemnon activated the new copy of the distributed evermind. Systems surged alive, and the omniscient computer began to survey its new domain.

"Welcome, Lord Omnius," Agamemnon said to the wallspeakers. "I present to you the gift of another world."

We are happiest when planning our futures, letting our optimism and imagination run unrestrained. Unfortunately, the universe does not always heed such plans.

—ABBESS LIVIA BUTLER,
private journals

Although their marriage was a foregone conclusion, Serena and Xavier happily endured the extravagant betrothal banquet thrown by Viceroy Manion Butler at his hilltop estate.

Emil and Lucille Tantor had brought baskets of apples and pears from their orchards and huge jars of herbed olive oil for dipping the fresh-baked engagement rolls. Manion Butler served up exquisite roasts of beef, spice-crusted fowl, and stuffed fishes. Serena provided colorful flowers from her extensive gardens, which she had faithfully tended since she was a child.

Famous Salusan performers tied ribbons on shrubs in the courtyard, and presented folk dances there. The women secured their dark hair with jeweled combs and wore white dresses adorned with embroidered patterns. The flowing skirts flew like whirlwinds about their waists, while dapper gentlemen strutted around them like peacocks in a mating challenge. Brassy music offset by soulful balisets drifted through the afternoon.

Xavier and Serena wore impressive outfits befitting a proud military officer and the talented daughter of the League Viceroy. They strolled among the assembled guests, careful to address each family representative by name. The couple sampled prized wines from dusty bottles brought in by the scions of every household. Xavier, who could taste none of the subtleties in the vintages, took care not to get too drunk; he was already giddy at the prospect of his upcoming marriage.

Serena's sister Octa, two years younger, seemed equally excited. With her long strawberry-blonde hair adorned by fresh cornflowers, Octa's eyes were wide with amazement, enchanted by her sister's beau and fantasizing about a handsome young officer who might be her own husband one day.

Amazingly, Serena's reclusive mother Livia came to spend the celebratory weekend at the Butler manor. Manion's wife rarely left the City of Introspection, a retreat where she kept herself from the cares and nightmares of the world. The enlightened philosophical preserve, owned by a Butler trust, had originally been established to study and ponder the Zen Hekiganshu of III Delta Pavonis, the Tawrah and Talmudic Zabur, even the Obeah Ritual. But under Butler patronage, the City had gradually blossomed into something the likes of which had not been seen for millennia.

Xavier had not seen Serena's mother often, especially in recent years. With her tanned skin and lean features, Livia Butler was a handsome beauty. She rejoiced in the betrothal of her daughter and seemed to enjoy herself as she danced with her jovial husband or sat beside him at the banquet table. She looked not at all like a woman who had fled from the world.

Years ago, Livia and Manion's strong marriage had been envied by many noble families. Serena was their eldest child, but they also had twins two years younger: the calm and shy Octa and a sensitive, intelligent boy, Fredo. While Serena underwent political schooling, the twins were raised as close companions, though neither had the far-ranging aspirations of their older sister.

Fredo had been fascinated by musical instruments and folk

songs, traditions from the grandest planets of the former Empire. He learned to be a musician and poet, while Octa was intrigued with painting and sculpture. In Salusan society, artisans and creative people were highly respected, as admirable as any politician.

But at the age of fourteen, honey-voiced Fredo died of a wasting disease, his skin splotched with purplish discolorations. For months, he'd grown thinner and thinner, his muscles atrophying. His blood would not clot, and he could not keep even the thinnest of broths in his stomach. The Salusan doctors had never seen anything like it. Frantic, Viceroy Butler begged the League for help.

The men of Rossak offered a number of experimental drugs from their fungoid jungles to treat Fredo's undiagnosed malady. Livia insisted on trying everything. Unfortunately, the young man reacted poorly to the third Rossak drug, an allergic response that caused his throat to swell. Fredo went into convulsions and stopped breathing.

Octa had mourned the loss of her brother and came to fear for her own life as well. Fredo's disease was eventually determined to be genetically based, meaning that she and her older sister were at risk of contracting the fatal malady themselves. Octa took care with her health and lived each day dreading that her life would come to a slow, painful end like that of her brother.

Fiercely confident and optimistic, Serena always tried to console her sister, giving her a shoulder to cry on, offering encouragement. Though neither sister had shown signs of the strange disease, Octa's dreams had lost all momentum, and she gave up her artwork, becoming a quieter, more pensive soul. She was a frail teenager now, hoping for a spark of wonder to bring her back to the fullness of life.

Though her husband had a brilliant political career and his importance grew with each season, formerly vivacious Livia had withdrawn from public life to her spiritual retreat, where she focused on philosophical and religious pursuits. She donated large sums to the imposing fortress to build additional meditation chambers, temples, and libraries. After devoting many sleepless nights to frank discussions with the Cogitor Kwyna, Livia became the Abbess of the facility.

In the aftermath of the tragedy, Manion Butler had immersed himself in League work, while Serena felt a heavier burden and set higher goals. Though she could do nothing to help her brother, she wanted to stop the suffering of other people whenever she could. She plunged into politics, working to stop the practice of human slavery still common on some League Worlds, and pledging herself to finding a way to overthrow the thinking machines. No one had ever accused her of lacking in vision or energy. . . .

Living separate lives now, Manion and Livia Butler remained pillars of Salusan society, proud of each other's accomplishments—not divorced, not even emotionally separated . . . just following different paths. Xavier knew that Serena's mother occasionally came back to spend nights with her husband and enjoy weekends with her daughters. But she always returned to the City of Introspection.

Serena's betrothal had been important enough to bring her mother into the public eye again. After Xavier danced with his future bride four times in a row, Abbess Livia insisted on having a dance with her future son-in-law.

Later, during a long acoustic set of the Long March Ballads played by native Salusan minstrels, Xavier and Serena slipped into the manor house, leaving Livia to weep unabashedly as she watched the musicians and remembered how Fredo had wanted to become a player himself. Manion sat beside his wife, rocking her gently.

At the event in their honor, Xavier and Serena had by now experienced their fill of company and revelry, of greeting guests and sampling food and wine. They laughed at every witticism, whether subtle or crude, so as not to offend the grand families. By now, the two were desperate for just a few moments alone.

Finally they slipped away and hurried through the corridors of the manor house, past hot kitchens and musty storerooms, to a small alcove outside the Winter Sun room. In winter, slanted sunshine lit this room with bronze rainbows. The Butler family traditionally took their breakfasts here during the cold season, enjoying family conversation while they watched the rising sun. It was a place of fond memories for Serena.

She crowded with Xavier into the alcove just outside the room; glowpanels shone in the hall, but still allowed a few rich shadows. Serena pulled him close and kissed him. He placed a hand behind her neck and stroked her hair as he pulled her face close to his and kissed more deeply, hungry for her.

When they heard hurried footsteps in the hall, the lovers hid in silence, quietly chuckling at their secret rendezvous. But fresh-faced Octa easily found them. Flushed with embarrassment, Octa averted her gaze. "You must come back to the banquet hall. Father is ready to serve dessert. And an offworld messenger is coming."

"A messenger?" Xavier suddenly sounded military and formal. "From whom?"

"He went to Zimia demanding an audience with the League Parliament, but since most of the nobles are here for the banquet, he's on his way up the hill."

Bending his elbows outward, Xavier offered an arm to each sister. "Let us go together so we can hear what this messenger has to say." Forcing a lighthearted tone, he said, "After all, I haven't eaten enough today. I could use a bowl of roast custard and a whole plateful of candied eggs."

Octa giggled, but Serena gave him a mock stern frown. "I suppose I must resign myself to life with a fat husband."

They entered the large hall, where the guests gathered around a long table, complimenting the array of extraordinarily beautiful desserts that looked too precious to be eaten. Manion and Livia Butler stood side by side, raising a toast to the couple.

Sipping politely from his wine, Xavier detected an undercurrent of worry in the Viceroy's manner. Everyone pretended to be unconcerned about what news the messenger might bring, but the moment a pounding sounded on the door, all activity stopped. Manion Butler himself opened the wooden portal, gesturing for the man to enter.

He wasn't a formal courier. His eyes were haunted and his officer's uniform unkempt, as if he no longer cared about protocol or appearances. Xavier recognized the insignia of the Giedi Prime Home Guard. Like other League uniforms, it bore the gold sigil of free humanity on the lapel.

"I have grave news, Viceroy Butler. The fastest ships have brought me directly here."

"What is it, young man?" Manion's voice was filled with dread.

"Giedi Prime has fallen to the thinking machines!" The officer raised his voice against the guests' disbelieving outcries. "The robots and cymeks found a flaw in our defenses and destroyed our scrambler-field transmitters. Much of our population has been slaughtered and the survivors enslaved. A new Omnius evermind has already been activated."

The people in the hall wailed at hearing of the devastating defeat. Xavier clutched Serena's hand so tightly he feared he might hurt her. Inside, he had turned to stone, his stomach filled with a cold heaviness.

He had just been to Giedi Prime, had inspected the defenses himself. Xavier had been terribly anxious to finish his inspection tour so that he could return to Serena. Could he possibly have missed something? He squeezed his eyes shut as the questions and disbelieving comments turned to a buzz around him. Was he to blame? Had a simple mistake, a bit of impatience from a young man in love, caused an entire planet to fall?

Manion Butler placed both palms on the table to steady himself. Livia reached over to touch her husband's shoulder, adding silent support. She closed her eyes, and her lips moved as if in prayer.

The Viceroy spoke. "Another free planet lost to the Synchronized Worlds, and one of our strongholds, too." He straightened, took a shuddering breath. "We must call an immediate war council, summon all representatives." With a meaningful glance at Serena, he added, "Let us also include anyone who speaks for the Unallied Planets and wishes to join us in this fight."

*Everything in the universe contains flaws, ourselves included.
Even God does not attempt perfection in His creations. Only
mankind has such foolish arrogance.*

—COGITOR KWYNA,
City of Introspection archives

Her screams rang through the quiet cliff cities above the
silvery-purple jungle. Inside her private chamber, Zufa
Cenva lay sweat-streaked on a pallet. She shrieked in pain,
clenching her teeth, her eyes glassy.

Alone. No one dared come near a delirious Sorceress of
Rossak.

A metallic doorway curtain rattled with an invisible tele-
kinetic force. Wall shelves buckled in the aftershocks of Zufa's
psychic explosions, scattering pots and keepsakes all over the
floor.

Her long white hair was wild, quivering with internal energy. Her pale hands gripped the sides of the pallet like scraping claws. If any woman had come close enough to try to
soothe her, Zufa would have scratched her face and mentally
hurled her against the whitewashed walls.

She screamed again. The chief Sorceress had endured several miscarriages before, but never one so agonizing or disruptive. She cursed worthless Aurelius Venport.

Zufa's spine shuddered, as if someone had jolted her with electricity. Delicate ornamental objects floated into the air on invisible strings, then flew in every direction, smashing into shards. One hollowed-out irongourd stuffed with dried flowers burst into white flames, crackling and smoking.

She gasped as her body cramped, squeezing her abdominal muscles. It seemed as if this unborn child wanted to kill her, to drag her down to death before she could expel it from her uterus.

Another failure! And she so desperately wanted to produce a true daughter, a successor to lead her fellow Sorceresses to new heights of mental power. The genetic index had misled her again. Damn Venport and his failings! She should have abandoned him long ago.

Out of her head with pain and despair, Zufa wanted to kill the man who had planted the child-seed inside her, even though the pregnancy had been at her own insistence. She had completed the bloodline calculations so carefully, had gone over the genes again and again. Breeding with Venport should have produced only superior offspring.

Nothing like this.

Telepathic blasts echoed into the corridors, sending Rossak women scurrying in terror. Then she saw Aurelius Venport himself standing at the doorway, haggard with worry. His eyes were filled with concern.

But Zufa knew he was a liar.

Unafraid for his own safety, Venport entered their bedchamber, displaying patience, concern, and tolerance. His lover's mental blasts ricocheted around the large room, overturning furniture. In a petulant attempt to slight him, she smashed a set of tiny hollownut sculptures he had given her during their courtship and genetic testing.

Still, he stepped forward, as if immune to her ferine outbursts. In the hall behind him, muted voices urged caution, but he ignored them. He came to her pallet, smiling with compassion and understanding.

Venport knelt beside the bed, stroking her sweaty hand. He whispered soothing nonsense in her ears. She couldn't understand his words, but she grasped his fingers until she expected to feel the bones snap. But he remained frustratingly close, not intimidated by her in the least.

Zufa hurled accusations of treachery at him. "I can sense your thoughts! I know you're thinking only of yourself."

Her imagination concocted schemes, attributing them to his deviousness. If the great Zufa Cenva was no longer there to protect him, who would keep this man as a pet? Who would care for him? She doubted he could take care of himself.

Then, with greater fear: *Or could he?*

Venport had sent Norma off on a long journey to Poritrin, arranging everything behind Zufa's back, as if he believed that a man like Tio Holtzman truly wanted to work with her daughter. What was he planning? She gritted her teeth, wanting to prove that she understood his intentions. Her threats came as sharp gasps. "You can't . . . let me die, bastard! No one . . . else would . . . have you!"

Instead, he looked at her, coolly patronizing. "You've told me many times that I come from a good genetic line, my darling. But I do not desire someone else among the Sorceresses. I prefer to stay with you." He lowered his voice, looking at her with an oddly intense love that she could not quite fathom. "I understand you better than you do yourself, Zufa Cenva. Always pushing, constantly demanding more than anyone can possibly give. Nobody—not even you—can be perfect all the time."

With a final prolonged shriek, she expelled her deformed, resistant fetus, a monstrously abnormal creature. Seeing the bright blood, Venport bellowed for assistance, and two brave midwives scurried into the chamber. One reached down with a towel, placing it over the fetus like a shroud, while the other bathed Zufa's skin, adding pain-numbing salves distilled from jungle spores. Venport sent for the best drugs from his own stockpiles.

Finally, he took the squirming fetus himself, holding the bloody larval thing in his hands. It had dark skin and strange mottled spots that made it look as if proto-eyes had grown all over its limbless body. He saw the thing twitch a final time, then it stopped moving.

He wrapped it up in the towel, trying to ignore the tear in his eye. His expression stony, Venport handed the corrupt fetus to one of the midwives, saying nothing. It would be taken out into the jungles, and no one would ever see it again.

The exhausted Sorceress lay back, shuddering, just now beginning to feel a sense of reality and despair again. The miscarriage had hurt her, leaving her with a deep sadness that went beyond the goals of any breeding program. Her vision returned to focus, and she noticed the psychokinetic destruction she had caused in the room. It all spoke of weakness, of lack of control.

This was her third horrific miscarriage from mating with Venport. Deep disappointment and anger boiled inside her. "I chose you for your bloodline, Aurelius," she muttered through dry lips. "What went wrong?"

He looked at her, still expressionless, as if his passion had been washed away. "Genetics is not an exact science."

Zufa closed her eyes. "Failures, always failures." She was the greatest Sorceress of Rossak, and yet she had endured so many disappointments. Sighing with disgust, Zufa thought of her stunted daughter, not wanting to believe that the ugly dwarf was the best she could achieve.

Venport shook his head, uncharacteristically stern and impatient now that the danger was past. "You have had successes, Zufa. You just don't know how to recognize them."

She forced herself to rest, to recuperate. Eventually, Zufa would have to try again, but with someone else.

Overly organized research is confining, and guaranteed to produce nothing new.

—TIO HOLTZMAN,
letter to Lord Niko Bludd

Arriving on Poritrin at the conclusion of her first long space voyage, Norma Cenva felt out of place. Her diminutive form drew glances, but was not so unusual that people turned pitying stares upon her. On the Unallied Planets there was a variety of races, some with stunted statures. She didn't care about the opinions of others anyway. She only wanted to impress Tio Holtzman.

Before Norma's departure from Rossak, her aloof mother had looked down at her with dismissive puzzlement. Zufa chose to believe that the brilliant Savant had made a mistake or had misread one of Norma's theoretical papers. She expected her daughter to return home before long.

Aurelius Venport had made all of the arrangements, used his own profits to pay for a nicer cabin than Holtzman had offered. While her mother continued to work with the Sorceress trainees, Venport had accompanied Norma to the docking-transfer stations in Rossak orbit. He had given her a gift of delicately petrified flowers and a chaste hug before she'd climbed aboard the vessel. With a wry smile, he told her, "All of us disappointments need to stick together."

Norma held onto that warm but troubling comment during the long journey to Poritrin. . . .

When the shuttle landed in the river-delta city of Starda, Norma carefully inserted Venport's petrified flowers into her mousy brown hair, a sprig of beauty that contrasted with the plainness of her wide face, large head, and rounded nose. She wore a loose blouse and comfortable hose, both woven from fernfibers.

Jostled by other passengers crowded at the shuttle hatch, the girl carried only a small travel pack. Climbing down the ramp, Norma felt flushed and eager to meet the scientist she admired, a thinker who took her seriously. She had heard many stories of Savant Holtzman's mathematical prowess, and she would be hard pressed to contribute anything the great man hadn't already developed. She hoped she would not let him down.

Scanning the waiting crowd, she immediately recognized the eminent scientist. A clean-shaven man with shoulder-length gray hair, Holtzman appeared to be in his late middle years. His hands and fingernails were clean, his clothing impeccable and ornamented with stylish designs and badges.

He greeted her with a broad smile and open arms that let the sleeves of his white robe droop. "Welcome to Poritrin, Miss Cenva." Holtzman placed both hands on her shoulders in formal greeting. If he experienced any disappointment upon seeing Norma's stature and coarse, unattractive features, he did not show it. "I certainly hope you've brought your imagination with you." He gestured toward a doorway. "We have a lot of work to do together."

He steered her through the spaceport crowds, away from their curious stares, then took her away from Starda Spaceport in a private limo-barge that floated high above the graceful Isana River.

"Poritrin is a peaceful world, where I can let my mind wander and think of things that might save the human race." Holtzman smiled proudly at her. "I'm expecting that of you, too."

"I will do my best, Savant Holtzman."

"What more could any person ask?"

The skies of Poritrin held a gauze of clouds painted citrus yellow with afternoon sunlight. The barge drifted above the multifingered streamlets that wrapped around shifting islands and sandbars. Traditional boats rode the current of the broad river, loaded with grains and cargo for distribution in the port city and export offworld. Fertile Poritrin fed many less-fortunate planets, in return for which they received raw materials, equipment, manufactured goods, and human slaves to add to their labor force.

Some of the largest buildings in the spaceport were actually boats on pontoons, anchored to the bases of sandstone bluffs. The roofs were composed of layered shingles of silver-blue metal, smelted in mines far to the north.

He gestured to a bluff overlooking the crowded portions of blue-roofed Starda, where she could recognize the influences of classic Navachristian architecture. "My laboratories are up there. Buildings and supply sheds, quarters for my slaves and solvers, as well as my own home—everything built into that double spire of rock."

The floating transport circled toward two sections of stone, like adjacent fingers rising above the riverbed. She could see sheetplaz windows, awning-covered balconies, and a walkway that linked a dome on one spire with a conical stone tower and outbuildings on the other.

Holtzman was pleased to note the amazement on her face. "We have quarters for you, Norma, in addition to private lab facilities and a team of assistants to perform calculations based upon your theories. I expect you to keep them all very busy."

Norma looked at him, puzzled. "Someone else to do the mathematics?"

"Of course!" Holtzman brushed iron-gray hair away from his face and adjusted his white robe. "You're an *idea* person, like me. We want you to develop concepts, not bother with full-fledged implementation. You should not waste time performing tedious arithmetic. Any halfway-trained person can do that. It's what slaves are for."

When the floating barge settled onto a glazed-tile deck, servants emerged to take Norma's bags and offer the two of them cool drinks. Like an eager boy, Holtzman led Norma to his impressive laboratories. The large rooms were filled with water clocks and magnetic sculptures in which spheres orbited about electrical paths without wires or gears. Sketches and half-finished drawings covered electrostatic boards, surrounded by serpentine calculations that went nowhere.

Glancing around, Norma realized that Holtzman had abandoned more concepts than she had ever created in her life. Even so, many of the cluttered papers and geometric drawings looked a bit old. Some of the ink had faded, and papers were curled around the edges.

With a swish of his wide sleeves, Holtzman gave the intriguing items a dismissive wave. "Just toys, useless gadgets that I keep for my amusement." He poked a finger at one of the floating silver balls, which sent the other model planets into dangerous orbits, spinning about like heavenly bodies out of control. "Sometimes I dabble with them for inspiration, but usually they only make me think of other toys, not the weapons of mass destruction we need in order to save us from the tyranny of machines."

With a distracted frown, Holtzman continued, "My work is constrained in that I cannot use sophisticated computers. In order to perform the enormous calculations required to test a theory, I have no recourse but to rely upon human mental abilities and hope for the best from the fallible calculational skills of trained people. Come, let me show you the solvers."

He led her to a well-illuminated chamber with high windows. Inside, numerous identical benches and flat tabletops had been set up in a grid layout. Workers hunched over each writing surface using handheld calculation devices. From their drab garments and dull expressions, Norma judged that these men and women must be some of Poritrin's numerous slaves.

"This is the only way we can imitate the abilities of a thinking machine," Holtzman explained. "A computer can handle billions of iterations. We have a harder time of it, yet with enough people working in concert and as specialists, we accomplish billions of calculations on our own. It just takes longer."

He walked down the narrow aisles between the solvers, who were furiously scribing numbers and mathematical symbols on flat slates, checking and double-checking answers before passing them on to the next person in line.

"Even the most complex math can be broken into a sequence of trivial steps. Each of these slaves has been trained to complete specific equations in an assembly-line fashion. When taken together, this collective human mind is capable of remarkable feats." Holtzman surveyed the room as if he expected his solvers to give him a resounding cheer. Instead, they studied their work with heavy-lidded eyes, moving through equation after equation with no comprehension of reasons or larger pictures.

Norma felt sympathy for them, having been belittled and ignored for so long herself. She knew intellectually that human slavery was a way of life on many League Worlds, as it was throughout the machine-ruled planets. Nevertheless, she supposed that these workers would prefer doing mental work to heavy labor out in the agricultural fields.

With a magnanimous gesture, the scientist said, "Every solver is at your disposal, Norma, whenever you develop a theory that needs verification. The next stage, of course is to build prototypes for further testing and development. We have plenty of labs and test facilities, but the most important work comes first." He tapped a fingertip on his own forehead. *"Up here."*

Holtzman gave her a cockeyed grin and lowered his voice. "Mistakes are possible, of course, even at our level. If that happens, we hope that Lord Niko Bludd is tolerant enough to keep us around."

Only those with narrow minds fail to see that the definition of Impossible is 'Lack of imagination and incentive.'

—SERENA BUTLER

In the front parlor of the Butler manor house, Xavier Harkonnen shifted on a green brocaded settee. His duty uniform was not designed for lounging in fine furniture. Ornate gold-framed paintings of Butler ancestors adorned the walls, including one like a caricature of a gentleman with a waxed handlebar mustache and a tricorner hat.

Between tight duty shifts, he had rushed here to surprise Serena, and the servants had asked him to wait. Blushing, Octa came into the parlor, carrying a cool drink for him. Though he had always seen her as Serena's little sister, Xavier realized with surprise that she was actually a lovely young woman. With Serena's recent betrothal, Octa might be dreaming of her own marriage, if she could ever overcome her shy infatuation with him.

"Serena wasn't expecting you, but she'll be right out." Octa looked away. "She's in a meeting with official-looking men and women, assistants carrying electronic equipment, a few

Militia uniforms. Something to do with her Parliament work, I think."

Xavier gave a wan smile. "We both have so many projects, but such times demand it."

While Octa occupied herself straightening books and statuettes on a shelf, Xavier thought back to a Parliament session he had watched two days before. Upset over the tragic fall of Giedi Prime, Serena had tried to rally representatives from the strongest planets, hoping to mount a rescue operation. She always wanted to *do* something; it was one of the reasons Xavier loved her so much. While others accepted the defeat and cringed in fear that Omnius would push for more conquests, Serena wanted to charge in and save the world. Any world.

Dressed in a long gown, she had spoken passionately in the temporary Hall of Parliament. "We can't just give up on Giedi Prime! The thinking machines have penetrated the scrambler shields, killed the Magnus, enslaved the people, and every day their presence grows stronger. There have to be Home Guard survivors fighting behind the machine lines, and we know that another shield-generator station was nearly completed. Perhaps that can be made functional! We must fight back before the thinking machines can establish their own infrastructure. If we wait, they will become unassailable!"

"As far as we know, they are already unassailable," grumbled the representative from industrial Vertree Colony.

The Zanbar official added, "Bringing the Armada to Giedi Prime would be suicide. Without their scrambler shields, they have no defenses left, and the machines would slaughter us in a direct conflict."

Serena had jabbed a finger at the nervous audience. "Not necessarily. If we could slip in and finish the work at the secondary shield-generating complex, then project a new blanket of disruptor fields, we could cut off—"

The League members had actually laughed at the suggestion. Seeing her heartbroken expression, Xavier felt stung on Serena's behalf. But she had not understood the difficulty of her naïve suggestion, the impossibility of restoring Giedi

Prime's shields under the noses of the machine conquerors. During his planetary inspection tour, Xavier had learned that it could take days or weeks for engineers—working under the best of conditions—to make the backup shield system operational.

But Serena never stopped trying. The ache of imagining so many suffering humans drove her to it.

The vote had gone overwhelmingly against her. "We cannot spend the resources, firepower, or personnel on an ill-advised mission to a planet we have already lost. It is now a machine stronghold." The nobles feared for their own local defenses.

Such work occupied most of Xavier's time. As an Armada officer, he had gone to extended sessions with officers and Parliament representatives, including Viceroy Butler. Xavier was determined to learn what had gone wrong with Giedi Prime's defenses—and whether he was to blame in some way.

Armada tacticians had studied the inspection records and assured him that he could have done nothing to prevent the takeover, short of stationing a full fleet of battleships at every League World. If Omnius was willing to sacrifice part of his robotic attack force to bring down Holtzman's scrambler shields, no planet was safe. But the information didn't make Xavier feel much better.

On Poritrin, Tio Holtzman was working hard to improve the scrambler system design. Lord Bludd expressed his optimism and confidence in the Savant, especially since the inventor had brought in another mathematician, the daughter of the Sorceress Zufa Cenva, to assist him. Xavier hoped something could be done quickly enough to make a difference. . . .

Lovely but harried, Serena entered the parlor and hugged him. "I had no idea you were coming." Octa slipped out the side door.

Xavier looked at the ornate clock on the mantel. "I wanted to surprise you, but I have to get back to duty. I have a long meeting this afternoon."

She nodded, preoccupied. "Since the attack on Giedi Prime, we've all been prisoners of our planning sessions. I think I've lost track of how many committees I serve."

Teasingly, he said, "Should I have been invited to this mysterious gathering?"

Her chuckle sounded forced. "Oh? The League Armada doesn't give you enough work, so you'd like to sit in on my tedious meetings as well? Perhaps I should speak to your new commander."

"No thank you, my dear. I'd rather fight ten cymeks than try to dissuade you when you've set your mind to something." Serena responded to his kiss with surprising passion. He stepped back, breathing hard, and straightened his uniform. "I need to go."

"Can I make it up to you at dinner tonight? A little tête-à-tête, just the two of us?" Her eyes sparkled. "It's important to me, especially now."

"I'll be there."

⤙⤚

WITH A SIGH of relief after quelling Xavier's suspicions, Serena returned to the Winter Sun Room where her team had gathered. She wiped a sparkle of sweat from her forehead. Several faces turned toward her, and she raised a hand to allay concerns.

Late morning sunlight splashed across the chairs, the tile counters and a breakfast table now strewn with plans, maps, and resource charts. "We've got to get back to work," said the grizzled veteran Ort Wibsen. "Don't have much time if you want to put this in motion."

"That is absolutely my intention, Commander Wibsen. Anybody with doubts should have left us days ago."

Serena's father believed that she spent her mornings in the bright, cheery room just reading, but for weeks she had been exploring schemes . . . gathering volunteers, expert personnel, and raw materials. No one could stop Serena Butler from devoting her energies to humanitarian work.

"I tried to follow proper channels and make the League take action," she said, "but sometimes people must be coerced into making the right decision. They must be led to it, like a stubborn Salusan stallion."

After the Parliament laughed at her "naïve foolishness," Serena had marched out of the temporary meeting hall but did not accept defeat. She decided to change tactics, even if she had to organize and finance a mission herself.

When Xavier learned of her plan, after it was too late to stop her, she hoped he would be proud of her.

Now she studied the team she had gathered from the Armada's most overlooked experts in commando operations: captains, supply runners, even infiltration specialists. Ten men and women turned to look at her. She clicked a remote control switch to close the overhead louvers. The brightness of the room diminished, though muted sunlight continued to filter in.

"If we can reclaim Giedi Prime, it will be twice the moral victory that the machines had," Serena said. "We will show that they cannot hold us."

Wibsen looked as if he had never ceased fighting, though he had been off active duty for over a decade. "All of us are more than happy to tackle a task that will have tangible results. I've been itching to strike a blow against the damned machines."

Ort Wibsen was an old space commander who had been forced to retire—ostensibly because of his age. More likely it had to do with his coarse personality, a penchant for arguing with superiors, and history of ignoring the details of orders. In spite of his surliness he was exactly the man Serena needed to lead a mission that other League members would have declared insane, or at least unwise.

"Then this is your chance, Commander," she said.

Pinquer Jibb, the curly-haired and still-haggard-looking messenger who had fled the conquest of Giedi Prime to deliver his terrible news, sat stiff-backed, looking around the room. "I've provided you with all the background material you need. I've compiled detailed reports. The subsidiary shield-generator station was nearly finished when the machines attacked the planet. We merely need to slip in and get it running." His haunted eyes grew fiery. "Plenty members of the Giedi Home

Guard must have survived. They'll be doing everything they can behind enemy lines, but that won't be enough unless we help them."

"If we can get the secondary shield generators functional, the cymeks and robots on the surface will fall to a concerted defense from the Armada." She scanned the others in the room. "Do you think we'll be able to do that?"

Brigit Paterson, a masculine-looking woman, frowned. "What makes you think the Armada will join the fight? After my engineers get the job done, how will we make sure the military comes in to save our butts?"

Serena gave her a grim smile. "You leave that to me."

Serena had been raised with the best schools and tutors, groomed to become a leader. With so much that needed to be done, she could not sit in a comfortable manor house and fail to use the Butler wealth and power.

Now she was about to put that determination to the test.

"Commander Wibsen, do you have the information I requested?"

With his deeply creased face and rough voice, the veteran seemed more like a man of the outdoors than an intricate strategist. But no one in Zimia knew more about military operations than he did.

"Some of it's good, some of it's bad. After crushing the government in Giedi City, the machines kept a robot fleet in orbit. Mop-up work on the ground is being led by one Titan and a lot of neo-cymeks." He coughed, scowled, and adjusted a medication dispenser implanted in his sternum.

"Omnius can keep sending in more machines, or even manufacture reinforcements using the captured industries of Giedi Prime," said Pinquer Jibb, his voice urgent. "Unless we get the secondary shield complex working."

"Then that's what we have to do," Serena said. "The Home Guard was dispersed across the settled continent, and many of the outlying regiments seem to have gone underground to form a fifth column. If we can contact them, organize them, we might be able to damage the machine conquerors."

"I can help with that," Jibb insisted. "It's our only chance."

"I still think it's foolhardy," Wibsen said. "But what the hell. I didn't say I wasn't going to go."

"Is the ship ready?" Serena asked, impatient.

"It is, but there's a great deal lacking in this operation, if you ask me."

Brigit Paterson said to Serena, "I have secured detailed maps, plans, and blueprints of all aspects of Giedi Prime and Giedi City, including full functional diagrams of the subsidiary scrambler-shield generators." She extended a stack of thin film sheets densely packed with information. "Pinquer says they're up to date."

With boundless enthusiasm and passion, Serena had always demonstrated skill in putting things together. Two years ago, she had led a relief team to Caladan, an Unallied Planet where thousands of refugees from the Synchronized Worlds had fled. On her most recent crusade, a year ago, she had delivered three space transports full of medical supplies to closed-off Tlulax, where the inhabitants were suffering from mysterious diseases. Now that Tlulaxa flesh merchants had provided medical aid and replacement organs from their biological tanks—including saving her beloved Xavier—she felt that her investment in effort had paid off fully.

Now Serena had called in favors, resulting in a mission that bore some similiarities to her earlier successful efforts. She expected another clear success, despite the dangers.

With beatific confidence, Serena looked around the table again. She envisioned the mission succeeding. Eleven people willing to challenge a set of conquerors and overcome the odds. "We have no higher priorities."

Ort Wibsen had worked between traditional channels to obtain a fast blockade runner. Paterson's engineering crew had equipped the vessel with the best experimental materials she could scavenge from weapons manufactories. Using personal accounts and falsified documentation, Serena had funded whatever the old commander needed. She wanted the best possible chance for her impetuous mission to succeed.

Serena said, "Every person in the League has lost someone

to the thinking-machine onslaught, and now we're going to do something about it."

"Let's get busy then," Pinquer Jibb said. "Time for payback."

❧

THAT EVENING, ALONE in the grand dining hall, Serena and Xavier sat across from each another. Servers bustled back and forth in red-and-gold jackets and black trousers.

As he sampled golden duckling fillets on his plate, Xavier talked excitedly about Armada mobilization plans and methods of protecting the League Worlds.

"Let's not talk business tonight." With a charming smile, Serena rose to her feet and glided around the table, taking a seat next to him, very close. "I savor each moment with you, Xavier," she said, giving nothing away about her plan.

He smiled back at her. "After the poison gas, I can't savor much else. But you, Serena, are better than the finest banquet or the sweetest perfume."

Stroking his cheek, she said, "I think we should tell the servants to go to their quarters. My father is in the city and my sister is gone for the evening. Should we waste this time alone?"

He reached out to brush her arm, then drew her close and grinned. "I'm not hungry anyway."

"I am." Passionately, she kissed his ear, then his cheek, finally finding his mouth. He ran his fingers through her hair, touching the back of her head and kissing her more deeply.

They left the remnants of the fine meal on the table. She took his hand and together they hurried to her chambers. The door was heavy, and locked easily. She already had a fire lit in the fireplace, giving the room an orange, cheery glow. They kissed again and again, trying to unfasten laces and buttons and clips without breaking apart from each other.

Serena could barely control her urgency, not just to feel his intimate touch, but to etch every sensation into her mind. He did not know that she intended to slip away afterward, and she needed something to remember about this night, to compensate for the time they would be apart.

His fingers were like fire as they traced down her naked back. She could think of nothing but the moment as she pulled off his shirt.

⟞⟟

WITH THE MEMORY of her lover's embrace still tingling along the nerves of her body, Serena left the sleeping manor. She set out into the quiet depths of night, bound to rendezvous with her team at a private field on the outskirts of the Zimia spaceport.

Anxious to be away, her optimism subduing her anxiety, Serena joined her ten commando volunteers. Within the hour they departed in a fast, cloud-gray blockade runner loaded with engineering tools, weapons, and hope.

Religion, time and time again, brings down empires, rotting them from within.

—IBLIS GINJO,
early planning for the Jihad

The conquered planet Earth seemed to be a dumping ground for grandiose monuments that celebrated the fictitious glories of the Titans.

Gazing from his vantage at yet another huge construction project designed by the prideful imaginations of the cymeks, the crew leader paced along a high wooden platform. His people were good workers, dedicated to him—but the work itself seemed pointless. When this ornate pedestal was completed and shored up with reinforced arcs, it would become the platform for a colossal statue representing the idealized, long-lost human form of the Titan Ajax.

As one of the most successful trustee humans on Earth, Iblis Ginjo took his job very seriously. He scrutinized the throng of slaves scurrying about below. He had convinced them to be enthusiastic, drumming up their attentiveness through well-chosen phrases and rewards . . . though Iblis hated to waste such loyalty and hard work on a brutal bully such as Ajax.

Still, every person had his part in the giant machine of civilization. Iblis had to make sure there were no malfunctions, not on his watch.

The crew leader was not required to be here; his subordinate trustees could just as easily stand under the hot sun and supervise. But Iblis preferred this to his other duties. Seeing him watch over them, the slaves seemed to add a bit more to the tasks. He took pride in what they could accomplish, if managed well, and they genuinely wanted to please him.

Otherwise, he would spend tedious hours involved in the processing of new slaves and assigning them to various work crews. Often the untamed ones needed special training, or resisted violently—problems that hindered the smooth flow of daily work.

Erasmus, the strangely independent and eccentric robot, had recently issued an order to inspect any *hrethgir* captives taken from newly conquered Giedi Prime, in particular any human who showed qualities of independence and leadership. Iblis would stay on the alert for a suitable candidate . . . without drawing attention to himself.

He didn't care about Omnius's goals for their own sake, but as a crew leader he received certain considerations based on performance. Though such perks made life tolerable, he distributed most of the rewards among his crews.

With a broad face and thick hair that fell across his brow, Iblis had a strong, virile appearance. Able to get more work out of the slaves than any other boss, he knew the best tools and incentives, the manipulation of gentle promises rather than harsh threats. Food, rest days, sexual services from the reproductive slaves—whatever it took to motivate them. He had even been asked to speak some of his thoughts at the school for trustees, but his techniques were not widely adopted among the other privileged humans.

Most crew bosses relied on deprivation and torture, but Iblis considered that a waste. He had risen to his position largely through the force of his personality and the allegiance he engendered in his slaves. Even difficult men invariably succumbed to his will. The machines sensed this innate ability, so Omnius gave him the freedom to do his work.

At a glance, Iblis counted half a dozen monoliths around the hilltop Forum, each pedestal containing the huge statue of one of the Twenty Titans, beginning with Tlaloc, then Agamemnon, then Juno, Barbarossa, Tamerlane, and Alexander. An immense likeness of Ajax would occupy the one here, not because Ajax was so important, but because he was violently impatient. Dante could wait, and Xerxes.

Iblis couldn't remember the rest of the Titans off the top of his head, but he always learned more than he wanted to know as each statue was built. The work would never end. Iblis had been personally involved in every one of the ostentatious sculptures over the past five years, first as a construction slave and later as crew boss.

It was late in the summer season, warmer than usual. Heat devils danced off rooftops around the Forum. Directly under him on the dusty ground, his construction crew wore drab browns, grays, and blacks—durable clothing that required only occasional washing or repairs.

Below Iblis's platform, a team boss bellowed out orders. Supervisory robots moved about, making no move to assist the straining laborers. Watcheyes floated overhead, recording everything for Omnius. Iblis hardly noticed them anymore. Humans were industrious, ingenious, and—unlike machines— flexible, as long as they were given incentives and rewards, encouraged in the proper ways, guided to the best behavior. The thinking machines could not understand the subtleties, but Iblis knew that each minor reward he gave his workers was an investment that paid off tenfold.

According to tradition, the slaves often sang work songs and engaged in boisterous team competitions; they were silent now, groaning as they hauled structural blocks into place though in their habitation hives, workers sometimes grumbled about the labor. The cymeks were anxious to see the pedestal completed so they could erect the statue of Ajax, which was being fabricated elsewhere by another crew. Each segment of the project followed a rigid schedule, with no excuses permitted for lateness or shoddy quality.

For now, Iblis was glad his people could work in peace,

without the intimidating scrutiny of Ajax. Iblis did not know where the Titan might be at the moment, but could only hope he would prey on other hapless individuals today. Iblis had work to do and a schedule to keep.

In his opinion, the monoliths were useless—huge obelisks, pillars, statues, and Grogyptian facades for empty, unnecessary buildings. But it was not his position to question such time-consuming projects. Iblis knew full well that the monuments fulfilled an important psychological need for the usurped tyrants. Besides, such work kept slaves busy and gave them visible results of their labor.

Following their humiliating overthrow by Omnius centuries ago, the Titans had constantly scrambled to recover lost status. Iblis thought the cymeks went overboard, building cyclopean statues and pyramids just to make themselves feel more important. They strutted around in showy but old-fashioned machine bodies, bragging about military conquests.

Iblis wondered how much of it was really true. After all, how could anyone question those who controlled history? The wild humans in the unruly League worlds probably had a different view of the conquests.

He wiped sweat from his brow and smelled the gritty dust that rose from the work below. He looked at the electronic notepad in his hand, checking the progress against the schedule tally. Everything was proceeding well, as expected.

With his sharp eyes, he spotted a man leaning against a shaded wall, taking an unauthorized rest. With a smile, Iblis pointed an "encourager" pulse weapon at him and skimmed the man's left leg with a beam of energy. The slave slapped the hot spot on his skin and whirled to look up at Iblis.

"Are you trying to make me look bad?" Iblis yelled. "What if Ajax came around and saw you falling asleep there? Would he kill you first, or me?"

Abashed, the man shouldered his way into the crowd of sweating laborers, where he resumed his work with renewed vigor.

Some work bosses found it necessary to kill slaves as examples to the others, but Iblis had never resorted to that tactic

and vowed that he never would. He was certain it would break
the inexplicable spell he had over the men. Instead, he only
had to show disappointment in them, and they worked harder.

Every few days he delivered stirring, impromptu speeches.
On such occasions the slaves received water and rest breaks,
giving them renewed energy that more than made up for the
time spent. The way he strung phrases together often brought
cheers and enthusiasm, and only a few questions from bold
slaves who wondered why they should be excited about yet
another monument. The work leader's talent lay in being utterly *convincing*.

Iblis hated the machine overlords, but concealed his feelings
so effectively that his superiors actually trusted him. Now, in
a fanciful moment, he envisioned destroying the computer evermind and installing himself in its place. Much more than a
mere trustee. Think of it—Iblis Ginjo, ruler of all, knower of
all!

He caught himself and dispelled the foolish daydream. Reality was a harsh teacher, like the sight of a cymek on a beautiful day. If Iblis didn't complete the obelisk pedestal in time,
Ajax would devise an extravagant punishment for them all.

The work leader didn't dare fall behind schedule.

Each of us influences the actions of the people we know.

—XAVIER HARKONNEN,
comment to his men

For days, Tercero Xavier Harkonnen stayed up late working on defensive plans for the League. Since his sweet night with Serena—a sparkling promise of their future—he had devoted himself to the protection of free humanity.

On Salusa he flew practice missions, drilled new fighters, increased the number of picket ships on the system's perimeter for a stronger first defense, and extended the scanning network to provide a better early-warning capability from deep space. Engineers and scientists dismantled and studied the warrior-forms abandoned by the cymeks and left behind in the ruins of Zimia, hoping to find flaws or weaknesses. With each breath in his replacement lungs, he felt outrage against the thinking machines.

He wanted to spend more time with Serena, dreaming of where they would go after the wedding, but driven by anger and private guilt about Giedi Prime, Xavier buried himself in work. If he had concentrated on the primary mission there, rather than mooning like a lovesick schoolboy, he might have noticed the defensive flaw and helped the Magnus to prepare. Even encouraging the immediate completion of the secondary shield generator would have made all the difference. But it was too late now.

Seemingly inconsequential mistakes could lead to huge events. Xavier promised himself that he would never lapse in his duties again, not for any reason. If that meant spending less time with Serena, she would understand.

Emergency staff meetings resulted in a revision of the military structure of the Armada, combining the resources and numerous warship designs from all the planetary militias and home guards. The special defensive needs and tactical significance of each League World were discussed in detail. Armada recruitment surged to new levels. Manufactories worked overtime to provide ships and weapons.

Xavier hoped it would be enough.

In his office on the top floor of the Joint Staff Building, electronic star maps covered the walls. Printed charts and reports cluttered every work surface. Each step of the way, he obtained the approval of the Joint Staff Commander, who in turn reviewed key elements with Viceroy Butler.

When he slept at all, Xavier did so in his office or in the underground barracks. For days he did not return home to the Tantor estate, though his mother often sent eager young Vergyl to deliver meals made especially for him.

Oddly, he had not heard from Serena, and assumed the Viceroy's daughter was occupied with vital duties of her own. The two young lovers were alike in their ability to see large-scale priorities . . . and in their independence.

Determined to revamp League defenses, Xavier kept himself going with stimulant capsules and drinks. He rarely noted what time of day or night it was, heeding only the next meeting on his schedule. Now he blinked through his office window at the quiet streets and the city lights glittering in the darkness. How long had it been night time? The hours merged with each other, carrying him along like a pebble in a landslide.

In the final tally, how much could one man actually accomplish? Were some League Worlds already doomed, no matter what he did? Because of the distances between planets and slow space travel, communication was sluggish, and news was often stale by the time it reached Salusa Secundus.

His reliance on stimulants made him feel scratchy and ragged. He was awake, but so pummeled by fatigue that he could no longer focus. He heaved a huge sigh, staring blankly. At the side of the office, his adjutant, Cuarto Jaymes Powder, had cleared a spot on a table and rested his head on the polished wood.

When the door opened, Cuarto Powder did not stir, or even snore, but continued sleeping like the dead. Xavier was surprised to see Viceroy Butler stride in, also weary to the core. "We need to implement whatever you've got ready, Xavier. Funding is guaranteed. For the sake of morale, the people must *see* us doing something."

"I know, but we need more than one solution, sir. Have Lord Bludd encourage Savant Holtzman to present any preliminary concepts he has under development." He rubbed his eyes. "If nothing else, we need new options for our arsenal."

"We already talked about that last night, Xavier—at great length." The Viceroy looked at him strangely. "Don't you remember? He has several prototype units almost ready."

"Yes . . . of course. I was just reminding you."

Xavier crossed the room and sat at an interactive information screen, a high-security system that flirted with the dangers of a computer. The electronic summary system could organize and provide vital data, but had no self-awareness. Many nobles—especially Bludd of Poritrin— resented the use of even such crude computers, but in times such as these, the summary systems were vital.

Passing his hand over the screen, Xavier made adjustments in his report to Parliament, including a compendium of planet-specific appendices, then printed the document, copies of which would be sent to each League World. Presently he handed a neat stack to the Viceroy, who perused the recommendations and signed his approval with a flourish. Then Serena's father hurried out of the office, leaving the door open behind him.

At the table, Cuarto Powder stirred and sat up, bleary-eyed. Without a word, Xavier settled into the chair at his own desk. Across the room, the summary screen flashed in an aurora of light as technicians filled it with probing signals to make certain the system exhibited no glints of artificial intelligence.

As his aide drifted off again, Xavier dozed as well. In his groggy imagination he dreamed that Serena Butler was missing, along with a ship and military team. It seemed surreal to him, but plausible . . . then he realized with a start that he was not asleep at all anymore.

Powder stood at his desk with another officer, listening to the bad news. "She's taken a blockade-runner, sir! Modified it with expensive armor and weaponry. She has a group of commandos with her. An old veteran, Ort Wibsen, agreed to lead them."

Xavier struggled to throw off the confusion induced by weariness. After rubbing his scratchy eyes he was surprised to see Serena's wide-eyed sister Octa standing behind the men. In a pale hand she held a gleaming black diamond necklace dangling from a coil of gold, which she hurriedly handed to him.

"Serena told me to wait five days, and then give this to you." Octa seemed ethereal, delicate; she moved to his side, but would not meet his gaze.

Searching for answers, Xavier removed the necklace from the coil. When he touched the black diamonds, the perspiration on his hand activated a tiny projector that showed a small holo image of Serena. He stared at her, feeling astonishment and dread. The visual seemed to look directly at him.

"Xavier, my love, I have gone to Giedi Prime. The League would have argued the issue for months, while the conquered people suffer. I can't permit that." Her smile was heartbreaking, but hopeful. "I have a team of the best engineers, commandos, and infiltration specialists. We have all the equipment and expertise we need to slip in and activate the secondary shield transmitter. We will complete the construction and install the systems—enabling us to cut off the planet from thinking machine ships, while trapping the ones that are already there on the surface. You must bring in the Armada and recapture this world. We're counting on you. Think of how much we can help humanity!"

Xavier was unable to believe what he was hearing. The image of Serena continued to speak her recorded message. "I will be waiting there, Xavier. I know you won't let me down."

Xavier clenched his hands until his knuckles whitened. If anyone could accomplish such a surprising mission, it was Serena Butler. She was impetuous, but at least she was trying to do something. And she knew her decision would force the rest of them to act.

Octa began crying softly at his side. Viceroy Butler rushed into the office, appalled at what he had heard.

"That's just like her," Xavier said. "Now we have to rally a response—there's no choice."

Think of war as behavior.

—GENERAL AGAMEMNON,
Memoirs

In an arena under the harsh sunlight of Earth's equatorial zone, Agamemnon prepared to battle Omnius's gladiator machine. The evermind treated these mock combats as challenges for the subservient Titans, a way for them to vent their anger and keep them preoccupied. But Agamemnon saw it as an opportunity to strike hard against his real enemy.

Two hundred and thirty years ago, human slaves and contractor robots had completed this semicircular, open-roofed coliseum for Omnius's flashy battles. The evermind enjoyed testing the destructive capabilities of different robotic designs. Here, armored vehicles and self-aware artillery systems could clash under controlled circumstances.

Long ago, the genius Barbarossa had programmed an appreciation for combat and a thirst for conquest into the artificial intelligence that had evolved into Omnius. Even a thousand years later the computer evermind had never forgotten his taste for victory.

Sometimes these staged competitions pitted humans against

machines. Randomly selected slaves from work gangs were given clubs, explosives, or cutting beams and thrown into the arena to face combat robots. The irrational violence of desperate humans never ceased to challenge the calculating mind of Omnius. At other times, the omnipresent computer preferred to demonstrate his own superiority against his cymeks.

In anticipation of the next gladiatorial challenge, Agamemnon had spent considerable effort in designing his new combat body. Omnius sometimes pitted his sleekest, most sophisticated models against the Titans; on other occasions, he responded with absurdly massive monstrosities that would never have been viable in any real struggle. It was all for show.

Months ago, when Barbarossa had achieved a particularly fine victory against Omnius, the cymek had demanded permission to attack the feral humans as a reward. While the strike on Salusa Secundus had not gone well, the Titans' second effort had conquered Giedi Prime. Barbarossa was even now overseeing dozens of neo-cymeks in the subjugation of the people there, a Titan once more in charge of a world. At last, it was a step in the right direction . . .

If he succeeded in winning in the arena today, Agamemnon had plans of his own.

With sirens blaring to announce the new event, Agamemnon rolled forward on resilient walker pads and passed between the Corinthian columns of Challenger's Gate. He could feel the thrumming strength of his stepped-up mobility systems, the pulse of increased power surging through his neurelectric pathways.

Inside this gladiator-form, his low-slung body core consisted of a pair of reinforced spheres—one surrounded by opaque armor, the other made of transparent alloyglas. Within the clear globe hung the grayish white hemispheres of his human brain, drifting in a pale-blue electrafluid and connected to thoughtrodes. Faint photon discharges crackled along the cerebral lobes as the cymek body moved forward, ready to fight.

Around the double-sphere core, bulky drive motors hummed inside protective cowlings. Engines worked the smooth hydraulics of four grappling legs. Each articulated limb ended with a shifting mass of adaptable metal polymer that could shape itself into a variety of hardened weapons.

Agamemnon had constructed this ferocious gladiator-form under the buzzing gaze of watcheyes that monitored his every move. Omnius supposedly filed all such information in a segregated portion of his evermind, so as not to gain an unfair combat advantage. Or so Omnius claimed.

While Agamemnon waited, poised for battle, his opponent strode forward, controlled directly by the evermind. Omnius had selected a walking suit of exaggerated medieval armor: two massive legs with feet like the foundations of a building and arms that ended in gauntleted fists as large as the body core itself. The proportions were grossly exaggerated, like a child's nightmare of a bully. Spikes extruded from the massive knuckles on Omnius's goliath robot, and apocalyptic discharges arced from point to point on the thorny fist.

Agamemnon pushed forward on armored walker pads while raising his crablike forelimbs, the adaptable-polymer ends of each morphing into claws. Even if he won the contest today, the evermind would suffer nothing, would not even have the grace to be humiliated in defeat.

On the other hand, Omnius could accidentally destroy the Titan's brain canister. Unforseen things happened in battle situations, and maybe Omnius—despite his programming that prevented him from intentionally killing a Titan—was counting on that. For Agamemnon, this fight was for real.

A few designated robotic observers watched from the stands through enhanced optic threads, but they remained silent. Agamemnon did not require applause anyway. The other polished stone seats in the coliseum remained empty, reflecting daylight from the open sky. The large stadium, like an echoing tomb, had all the room necessary for two gigantic foes to clash.

No announcement preceded the fight, no information piped over loudspeakers. Agamemnon launched his attack first.

The Titan raised his whiplike grappling arms, hardened them with a shifting diamond film, and drove forward on heavy walker pads. With surprising agility, Omnius's goliath robot lifted an enormous leg and sidestepped the attack.

Agamemnon lunged with another of his forelimbs, this one capped with a spherical wrecking ball that fired disruptive, paralyzing energy. The pulse thrummed through vulnerable systems, and Omnius's warrior shuddered.

Suddenly the goliath swiveled, raising a gauntleted fist to smash the cymek's segmented arm. Even the diamond film could not endure the blow, which bent Agamemnon's forelimb until it ripped from the flexible socket. The cymek dismissed the damage and reversed his walker pads, ejecting the unsalvageable limb. He swung up a cutting arm that metamorphosed into a flurry of shimmering diamond blades.

Agamemnon sawed through his opponent's armored torso, severing a set of neurelectric control threads. Greenish fluid sprayed out from chopped lubricant channels. The combat goliath swung his other spiked fist, but Agamemnon danced his walker pads sideways and shifted his vulnerable body core, keeping the brain canister safe.

When his swing missed completely, the heavy blow overbalanced the gladiator robot. Agamemnon brought up two slicing arms, hacking at the goliath's arm joints with white-hot cutting irons. He found vulnerable spots with surprising ease, and the goliath's right arm dangled useless, a tangle of neurelectric fibers and conductive fluids.

To assess the damage, Omnius dragged his unwieldy fighter two thundering steps backward. Agamemnon pressed his advantage, closing to grappling distance. Then he unleashed his first major surprise.

From a concealed compartment within the old-fashioned engine housing, a trapdoor irised open, and eight reinforced conductor-fiber cables sprang out, each tipped with a magnetic connector claw. The cables flew like a nest of startled vipers and slammed into the reeling goliath. As soon as the tips struck home, Agamemnon released a huge energy discharge. Lightning flared up and down the massive body of Omnius's fighter.

The cymek general expected this insidious blow to knock the combat robot completely offline, but Omnius must have shielded his fighting unit well. Agamemnon sent another paralytic pulse like a scorpion's sting, but still the Omnius gladiator did not fall. Instead, as if in anger, the machine swung its mammoth gauntlet with the force of a colliding train, putting all of his energy and momentum behind a single blow.

The spiked fist struck true, slamming into the transparent preservation sphere that held the disembodied brain. A major jamming surge pulsed out of the knuckle spikes, and a shaped fracture wave shattered the curved glass walls of the protected brain canister. Through the breached container walls, electrafluid spilled like blue gushing blood. Thoughtrodes tore, and the brain fell from its suspender wires, dangling naked in the open, hot air.

It might have been the death of Agamemnon.

But the cymek general had devised his own trick. The brain inside the transparent container was only a decoy, a synthetic reproduction of his cerebral contours. Agamemnon's actual brain was inside the opaque metal-walled sphere, from which he controlled the gladiator-form. Safe and intact.

He was, however, astonished and infuriated. Omnius had proven his willingness to inflict severe damage on the most powerful and talented Titan of all. Omnius's strong urge to avoid losing seemed capable of overriding his programming restrictions. Or had the evermind known about the ruse all along? Agamemnon launched his vindictive response.

Even as he spun backward on his walker pads, roaring away as fast as possible, he ejected the now-cracked sphere that contained the false brain. He launched it into the body core of the goliath robot.

In his specially constructed body, Agamemnon then ducked down, raising his armored limbs and lowering his shielded brain canister between the rows of thick walker pads to protect himself, like a turtle withdrawing into a shell.

The brain sphere struck the damaged gladiator and detonated. The simulated brain had been sculpted from high-energy solid foam. Flames roared past Agamemnon, charring the ground. The resulting explosion bowled over the goliath robot, decapitating it, ripping open its torso. The shockwave was sufficient to knock down part of the nearest coliseum wall.

Agamemnon had survived—and the Omnius gladiator had fallen.

"Excellent, General!" The computer voice echoed from loudspeakers in the intact portion of the arena, sounding genuinely pleased. "A most refreshing and enjoyable maneuver."

Agamemnon still wondered if Omnius had been aware that the visible brain was false. Or perhaps the evermind had found a way to circumvent the protective restrictions Barbarossa had installed so many years ago. Now he would never be sure if the evermind was indeed willing to let him die in combat. Maybe Omnius had to keep the ambitious Titans from feeling too triumphant or overvalued, especially Agamemnon.

Only Omnius knew for certain, one way or the other.

Amid the smoke and flames rising from the ruin of the goliath machine, Agamemnon raised his gladiator-form, the uncontested victor. "I have defeated you, Omnius. I wish to claim my reward."

"Naturally, General," he answered, sounding good-natured. "You need not even speak your wish. Yes, I shall allow you and your cymeks to lead further strikes against the *hrethgir*. Go forth and enjoy yourselves."

Survivors learn to adapt.

—ZUFA CENVA,
lecture to Sorceresses

In the pristine, contoured cabin of the *Dream Voyager*, Vorian Atreides and Seurat cruised between star systems again, picking up and delivering Omnius updates to maintain congruence in the distributed evermind across all the Synchronized Worlds. They exchanged updates with other copies of the evermind, synchronizing the Omnius incarnations, and departing with new data to be shared among the widespread networks. Vor loved being a trustee.

Days in space passed, each like the others. The oddly matched pair performed their jobs efficiently. Seurat and the small cadre of maintenance drones assured sterile cleanliness and optimal efficiency in the cabins, while Vor occasionally left food or drink stains, leaving a few items half-finished or in disarray.

As he often did, Vor stood at an interactive console in the cramped rear compartment, rummaging in the ship's database to obtain more information about their destinations. He had been taught the benefits of bettering himself in his training among the other privileged humans on Earth. His father's example—rising from an unknown man to become the greatest of the Titans, conqueror of the Old Empire—showed him how much even a mere human could accomplish.

He was surprised to see that the *Dream Voyager*'s normal route had changed. "Seurat! Why didn't you tell me we've added a new planet? I've never heard of this . . . Giedi Prime in the Ophiuchi B system. Previously it was listed as a solid League World."

"Omnius programmed that destination into our course before we departed from Earth. He expected that your father would have conquered it by the time we arrive. Omnius is confident in Agamemnon's ability to make good after their failure on Salusa Secundus."

Vor felt pride that his father would tame yet another unruly world for the thinking machines. "No doubt all will have gone well by the time we arrive, and our forces will be mopping up."

"We will see when we get there," Seurat said. "It is still months away."

✑

ON MANY OCCASIONS they engaged in traditional human competitions from the extensive databases, such as poker or backgammon; other times Vorian would make up a new game, declare a set of absurd rules, and then proceed to defeat Seurat, until the autonomous robot learned to manipulate the rules for himself.

The two were evenly matched, but with drastically different skill sets. While Seurat was talented at intricate strategy and could calculate many moves ahead, Vor often pulled off baffling innovative twists to win. Seurat had trouble comprehending the human's erratic behavior. "I can follow the consequences in a logical progression from an individual event, but I cannot understand how you manage to turn impulsive and illogical behavior into an effective strategy. There is no causal connection."

Vor smiled at him. "I'd hate to see you calculate an 'irrational' response, old Metalmind. Leave it to the experts, like me."

The son of Agamemnon was also quite proficient at military tactics and strategies, a skill he had developed by studying the great battles of ancient human history, as summarized in his father's extensive memoirs. The cymek general made no secret that he hoped his son would become an accomplished military genius one day.

Whenever Seurat fell behind in a particular contest, he continued his irritating habit of distracting Vor with jokes, trivia, or anecdotes—tailoring them to interest the brash young man. During all the time the machine captain had known his human copilot, Seurat had accumulated and assessed information, preparing it for future use. The robot captain had become adept at raising topics that engrossed Vor and sent his thoughts spinning.

Seurat chattered incessantly about the legendary life of Agamemnon, adding details Vor had never read in the memoirs: great battles the Titans had won, planets they had added to the Synchronized Worlds, and the warrior-forms Agamemnon had designed for private gladiatorial contests. Once, the robot captain concocted an absurd tale about how the great general had literally lost his mind. The cymek's protected brain canister had accidentally detached from its walker-form and gone tumbling down a hill, while the mechanical body, on automatic programming, had to scamper about and find it.

However, Vorian had recently uncovered information more unsettling than anything the robot could ever reveal. Between games and challenges, he often skimmed the open databases, reading his favorite parts of his father's memoirs, trying to make sense of the reams of Omnius's minutiae. On one of those excursions Vor discovered that over the years, Agamemnon had sired twelve other sons. Vorian had never assumed he was the only one—but a dozen unknown brothers! The great Titan general would naturally have wanted to create descendants worthy of his legacy.

Worse, he discovered that each of those dozen sons had

proved to be a failure. Agamemnon did not suffer disappointments gladly, and had killed his unacceptable offspring, though they had been privileged trustees just like Vor. The last had been executed nearly a century ago. Now Vor was his father's best hope, but not necessarily the only choice. Agamemnon must still have more sperm in storage . . . and thus Vor was just as expendable as the others.

After learning that, Vor became immune to Seurat's attempts at distraction.

Now Vor sat at the table, staring at a projected game board and considering his next move. He knew Seurat could not determine what was going on inside the unpredictable human mind. Even with all his independent sophistication, the robot accumulated only external data and did not recognize subtleties.

The trustee smiled, just a little, which Seurat did not fail to notice. "You are playing a little trick on me? Exercising some secret human power?"

Vor continued to smile and stare at the board. It was a multigame competition, revolving inside a three-dimensional screen embedded in the tabletop. Each player attempted to choose a contest or situation that benefited him from a wide selection of games, and then make a move. The score was tied, and the next point would win the contest.

The various games came up at random, and each time Vor had only a few seconds to make his move. He watched the shifting graphics as they locked into place momentarily before moving on. The ancient Terran game of Go appeared on the palette of selections; nothing there to benefit him. More options flowed by. A machine-biased game appeared next, one that required more memory than Vor had. He let it pass. Two other games appeared that he didn't like, followed by a poker hand.

Relying on luck and bluster, Vor faced off against the robot captain, who could not understand the strategy of bluffing or the "skill" of random odds. Vor's expression was unreadable, and he laughed at the confusion he saw on Seurat's mirrored face.

"You lost," Vor said. "And you lost, badly." He crossed his arms over his chest, feeling smug after the robot finally folded his hand. "It's not just the score, but the way you tried to win."

Seurat responded that he did not wish to play more games, and Vor laughed at him. "You're sulking, old Metalmind!"

"I am reassessing my tactics."

Vor reached across the table and pounded his opponent's slick shoulder, as if to comfort him. "Why don't you stay here and practice, while I run the ship? Giedi Prime is still a long journey from here."

Regrets, there are many, and I have my share.

—SERENA BUTLER,
unpublished memoirs

The cloud-gray blockade runner was not only fast and difficult to see against the murky skies of Giedi Prime, it contained the most sophisticated stealth profile of any craft in the League arsenal. Serena hoped Ort Wibsen's crack abilities would be enough to get her team through to the isolated island in the northern sea, where they could begin their work.

Pinquer Jibb had provided the blueprints, plans, and access codes for the secondary shield-transmitting towers, if any of the systems remained intact. But even with the excellent military advisors and engineers, no part of this was going to be obvious or easy.

After the long journey from Salusa, they now flew silently through the darkened sky, studying the land mass below. Unnecessary parts of the power grid had been shut down, cities plunged into barbarous blackness. Machines, after all, could simply adjust their optic sensors to see in the dark.

Serena didn't know how many trained Home Guard members had survived. She hoped some had gone underground after the thinking-machine takeover, as the desperate courier Jibb had promised. Once her commandos restored the scrambler shields, the Home Guard survivors would be crucial in retaking the planet. She was counting on Xavier to bring Armada ships into the fray, no matter what strings he had to pull.

Serena sat in the blockade runner's passenger compartment, anxious to begin. By now, back on Salusa, her father would know she had gone, and she hoped Xavier would already have launched his strike force for Giedi Prime. If he didn't come, then their mission was doomed, and so were she and her team.

Xavier would be upset and worried about her, angry at the foolish risk she had taken. But if she achieved results, all the effort would be justified.

Nothing remained but the task itself.

Hunched forward in the cockpit, old Wibsen scanned the northern regions to pinpoint the uncompleted transmitter station. Serena had gleaned only a general location from Xavier's report, but she knew the conquering machines wouldn't have bothered with an isolated arctic island while subjugating Giedi Prime's population. So long as they didn't call attention to themselves, perhaps Brigit Paterson's engineers could complete their work without interference.

The hardened veteran studied an instrument console, scratching his rough cheek. After his forced retirement, Wibsen had never maintained a crisp, spit-and-polish military appearance; now, at the conclusion of their journey across space, he looked more rumpled than ever. But Serena had not enlisted him for his wardrobe or his personal hygiene habits.

He watched streaks of light and blips on a scanner screen. "There it is. Must be the right island." With a satisfied grunt, he began touching buttonpads like a musician playing a keyboard to reveal a weaving but safe course through the machines' electronic sensor net. "The stealth film on our hull should let us slip right through their surveillance. Sixty, seventy percent chance, I'd say."

Serena accepted the grim reality. "That's better odds than the people of Giedi Prime have."

"At the moment," Wibsen said.

Brigit Paterson stepped into the cockpit, not losing her balance as the deck shook in buffeting winds. "Most of the Armada wouldn't even take the chance. They'd probably write off Giedi Prime until they had a perfect, risk-free opportunity."

"We'll just have to show them how it's done," Wibsen said. Serena wished Xavier could be here so they could make decisions together.

The camouflaged blockade runner sliced through the murky atmosphere at an efficient angle and approached the cold, leaden sea. "Time to duck out of sight," the veteran said. "Hang on."

The smooth ship plunged beneath the deep water like a hot iron. The gush of steam was followed by hardly a ripple. Then, concealed by the ocean, the craft glided north toward the coordinates of the rocky island where a nervous Magnus Sumi had built his backup shield transmitters.

"I'd say we're sufficiently out of sensor range," Serena said. "We can breathe easy for a while."

Wibsen cocked an eyebrow. "I hadn't even started to sweat yet."

As if to disprove his remark, he fought to control a sudden coughing spasm while he maneuvered the converted blockade runner through the dim underwater currents. The old man cursed his health, cursed the implanted medical injector in his chest.

"Commander, don't jeopardize this mission because of your stubborn pride," Serena scolded.

The ship pitched to one side and creaked. Behind a bulkhead something fizzed. "Damn water turbulence!" Red-faced, Wibsen kept the blockade runner under control, then turned back to glare at Serena. "Right now I'm just the chauffeur. I can relax as soon as I drop you off."

The vessel cruised beneath the surface for an hour, deep enough to avoid any floating chunks of ice from the polar regions, and finally guided them toward a sheltered bay. On the cockpit screens, the approaching island looked stark and rocky, all black cliffs and ice. "Doesn't look like much of a resort to me," Wibsen said.

Brigit Paterson said, "Magnus Sumi didn't choose the site for its beauty. From here, a polar projection is simple and efficient. Coverage from these transmitters is good for all the inhabited land masses."

Wibsen brought the blockade runner to the surface. "I still think it's an ugly place." As he guided them into the deep harbor embraced by a crescent of cliffs, he began to cough again, louder and worse than before. "Damned ridiculous timing." He looked more annoyed than distressed. "We're on auto-guide, still on course. Get Jibb over here to fly for a while. This is his home territory after all."

Curly-haired Pinquer Jibb looked at the approaching island complex, seemingly disappointed that the Home Guard refugees hadn't already completed the work. He took the controls from the veteran and brought the blockade runner to the island's abandoned quays and loading docks. After they had clamped into place, he opened the hatches.

Purplish dawn spread like a bruise across the northern sky. Breathing the fresh but biting air, Serena stood in warm clothes with her team members. The rocky island looked forbidding and seemed completely deserted.

More heartwarming, though, was the set of silvery towers with parabolic sides and metal-lattice grids. Ice and frost rimed the structures, but they appeared untouched by the thinking-machine invaders.

"Once we switch those on, the robots won't know what hit 'em," Wibsen said, hauling himself out into the open, looking somewhat recovered. He blew a lungful of white steam onto his hands.

Serena kept looking at the towers, a sweeping expression of hope and determination on her face. Brigit Paterson nodded, all business. "Even so, we've got our work cut out for us."

In times of war, every person claims to contribute to the effort. Some give lip service, some provide funds, but few are willing to sacrifice everything. This, I believe, is why we have been unable to defeat the thinking machines.

—ZUFA CENVA,
The Rossak Weapon

Staring at fourteen of the strongest and most dedicated young Sorceresses Rossak had ever produced, Zufa Cenva understood that these women were not the sole hope for humanity. They were not the *only* weapon against the terrible cymeks, not the most powerful blow the League could strike. But they were critical to the war effort.

Zufa stood in the fleshy underbrush with her trainees and looked at them with compassion and love. No one in all the League Worlds was more confident of success or devoted to victory. Her heart seemed ready to burst as she saw them focusing every scrap of energy toward the ultimate goal. If only everyone else could be as intent, the thinking machines would be defeated in short order.

As she had done for months now, Zufa led her elite group into the jungle where they could practice their skills and summon the power within their spirits. Each of these women was the equivalent of a psychic warhead. Zufa, blessed from birth with more talents than any of them, had been sharing her methods, pushing the others to their limits. She had patiently taught them how to unleash incredible telepathic abilities . . . and how to exercise control. The women had performed admirably, beyond Zufa's most optimistic forecasts.

But they must make their effort stand for something.

Now she sat on a fallen silvery-barked log that was overgrown with a thick cushion of shelf fungus. The canopy was dense with shadows that interlocked high overhead. Dark purple foliage filtered the caustic rainwater so that droplets trickling like tears to the mulchy ground were fresh and drinkable. Large insects and spiny rodents tore through the soil layers, oblivious to the testing the Sorceresses were about to begin.

"Concentrate. Relax . . . but be prepared to *focus* with all your might, when I command you to do so." Zufa looked at the women, all of them tall and pale, with translucent skin and shining white hair. They looked like guardian angels, luminous beings sent to protect humanity against the thinking machines. Could there be any other reason why God had granted them such mental powers?

Her gaze moved from face to determined face: Silin, the bold, impulsive one; creative Camio, who improvised forms of attack; Tirbes, still discovering her potential; Rucia, who always chose integrity; Heoma, with the most raw power . . . and nine others. If Zufa were to ask for a volunteer, she knew all of her chosen Sorceresses would demand the honor.

It was her task to select who would be the first martyr among them. Xavier Harkonnen was already anxious to depart for Giedi Prime.

She loved her trainees as if they were her children . . . and in a very real sense, they were, for they were following her methods, maximizing their potential. These young women were so different from her own Norma. . . .

Facing the chief Sorceress, the fourteen stood together, apparently content and calm, but coiled within. Their eyes fell half closed. Their nostrils flared as they breathed, counting heartbeats and using innate biofeedback skills to alter bodily functions.

"Begin to build the power in your mind. Feel it like the

static electricity before a lightning storm." She saw their expressions flicker as their thoughts stirred.

"Now increase the power one bit at a time. Envision it in your brain, but do not lose control. One step, then another. Feel the energy amplifying—but do not release it. You must maintain your hold."

Around her in the dimness of the fungoid jungle, Zufa felt the energy crackling, building. She smiled.

Zufa sat back on her log, feeling weak but not daring to show it. Her recent difficult miscarriage, expelling Aurelius Venport's monstrous child, had left her drained. But there was so much work to do, so much she could not delay or delegate. The League Worlds were depending upon her, especially now.

Everyone had high expectations of the most powerful Sorceress, but Zufa Cenva placed an even greater burden upon herself. At every turn, her plans and dreams had been hamstrung when people refused to expend the effort or take the necessary risks. These eager, talented trainees seemed different, though, and she assured herself that they would perform up to her standards. Too often when she measured other people, she found them wanting.

"Another notch," she said. "Intensify your power. See how far it can go, but always be careful. An error at this point would wipe us all out—and the human race cannot afford to lose us."

Psychic energy pulsed higher. The Sorceresses' pale hair began to drift upward as if gravity had failed. "Good. Good. Keep it going." Their success delighted her.

Zufa had never been interested in self-aggrandizement. She was a stern and difficult taskmistress, with little patience or sympathy for the failings of others. The chief Sorceress did not need wealth and profit like Aurelius Venport, or accolades like Tio Holtzman, or even a show of attention like Norma seemed to desire by convincing the Savant to take her as his apprentice. If Zufa Cenva was impatient, she had a right to be. This was a time of great crisis.

The underbrush stirred as native insects and rodents scampered away from the pounding psychic waves that built to a crescendo. Trees rustled, leaves and twigs fluttering as if trying to break away from their parent stalks and flee the jungle. Zufa narrowed her eyes and studied her students.

Now they were reaching the most dangerous part. The mental energy had increased until their bodies began to shimmer and glow. Zufa had to use her own skills to erect a protective barrier against the combined psychic pressure on her mind. One slip and all would be lost.

But she knew these dedicated apprentices would never make such a mistake. They understood the stakes and the consequences. Zufa's heart ached as she gazed upon them.

One trainee, Heoma, displayed more strength than her companions. She had built her power to a higher level while still maintaining control. The destructive force could easily have become a wildfire in her brain cells, but Heoma held onto it, staring with unseeing eyes as her hair whipped like a storm.

Suddenly, out of dense branches high above, a thick-bodied slarpon dropped, a scaly creature with needle teeth and thick body armor. It tumbled among the young women with a crash, disturbed from its predatory perch and maddened by the backwash of mental energy. All muscle and cartilage, it thrashed, snapping with powerful jaws and scrabbling with thick talons.

Startled, Tirbes twitched—and Zufa felt an uncontrolled surge of power spouting like a released jet of fire. "No!" she cried and reached out, summoning her own powers to blanket the student's slip. "Control!"

Heoma, with perfect calm, pointed toward the slarpon as if she were erasing a smudge on a magnetic board. She drew a line of psychic destruction across the scaly predator. The slarpon burst into white-hot flames, thrashing as its bones turned to charcoal, its skin crackling and tearing until it flaked off in puffs of ash. Flames smoldered out of its now-empty eye sockets.

Heoma's companions struggled to clamp down and exert their mental forces. But they had been distracted at a critical moment and were losing their slippery grips on their telepathic battering rams. Steadfastly, Heoma and Zufa maintained a superhuman calmness in their midst, a stark contrast to their

frenzied efforts. The combined psychic force rippled and undulated.

"Back down," Zufa said, her lips trembling. "Ease the
power away. Draw it into yourself. You must retain it and reel
it back into your minds. It is a battery, and you must maintain
its charge."

She breathed deeply, saw that all of her psychic warriors
were doing the same. One by one they inhaled, and gradually
the tingle in the air dissipated as they began to dampen their
constant efforts.

"Enough for now. This is the best you've ever done." Zufa
opened her eyes and saw her students all staring back at her,
Tirbes pale and frightened, the others amazed at how close
they had come to self-annihilation. Heoma, an island apart,
looked entirely unrattled.

In a broad circle around them, the soft fungal underbrush
was curled and singed. Zufa studied the blackened foliage,
fallen twigs, and shriveled lichens. Another instant, a hair's
breadth less control, and everyone would have been vaporized
in a ball of telepathic flames.

But they had survived. The test had succeeded.

After the tension finally evaporated, Zufa allowed herself
a smile. "I am proud of all of you," she said, and meant it.
"You . . . my weapons . . . will be ready as soon as the Armada
arrives."

*Mathematical answers are not always expressed numerically.
How does one calculate the worth of humanity, or of a single
human life?*

—COGITOR KWYNA,
City of Introspection archives

At Tio Holtzman's extravagant house, high on a bluff,
Norma Cenva spent three exhilarating days settling into
her expansive laboratory space. She had so much to do, so
much to learn. Best of all, the Savant was eager to listen to
her ideas. She couldn't have asked for more.

Quiet Poritrin seemed so different from the dense, dangerous jungles and lava-rock canyons of Rossak. She was anxious
to explore the streets and canals of Starda, which she could
see from her high windows.

Tentatively, she asked Holtzman for permission to go down
to the river, where she had seen many people performing some
kind of work. She felt guilty for even asking, rather than working tirelessly on a means to fight the thinking machines. "My
mind is a little tired, Savant, and I am curious."

Instead of looking at her skeptically, the scientist whole-
heartedly endorsed the idea, as if pleased to have an excuse
to accompany her. "I remind you that we are paid to *think*,
Norma. We can do that anywhere." He shoved aside a sheet

of doodles and sketches. "Perhaps a bit of sightseeing will inspire you to a work of genius. One can never know when inspiration might strike, or where."

He led her down a steep stairway that clung to a cliff over the Isana. As she stood beside the taller man, Norma inhaled deeply of the river's smell, sour and peaty from silt and vegetation dragged down from the highlands. For the first time in her life, she felt giddy with her own possibilities; the Savant was genuinely interested in her imagination, her mind, and he listened to her suggestions, unlike the constant scorn she had received from her mother.

Norma raised an idea that had occurred to her that morning. "Savant Holtzman, I have studied your scrambler shields. I believe I understand how they function, and I've been wondering if it might be possible to . . . extend them somehow."

The scientist showed guarded interest, as if afraid she might criticize his invention. "Extend them? They already stretch across planetary atmospheres."

"I mean a different application entirely. Your scramblers are purely a defensive concept. What if we used the same principles in an *offensive* weapon?" She watched his expression, detected puzzlement but a willingness to listen.

"A weapon? How do you propose to accomplish that?"

Norma answered in a rush. "What if we could make a . . . projector? Transmit the field into a thinking machine stronghold, disrupt their gelcircuitry brains. Almost like the electromagnetic pulse from an atomic air burst."

Holtzman's face lit with comprehension. "Ah, now I see! Its range would be quite limited, and power requirements off the scale. But perhaps . . . it just might work. Enough to knock out the thinking machines within a substantial radius." He tapped his chin, excited by the idea. "A projector—good, good!"

They walked along the bank until they reached the foul-smelling expanse of mudflats dotted with sloppy pools. Crews of ragged, half-clothed slaves sloshed out onto the mudflats, some barefoot, some wearing boots that extended to their upper thighs. At regular intervals across the featureless field, flat pallets on pontoons held metal barrels. Laborers marched back and forth to the barrels, where they scooped dripping handfuls of the contents and went to plunge their fingers into lines marked in the soft mud.

"What are they doing?" Norma asked. It looked as if they were embroidering the mudflats with their work.

Holtzman squinted as if he had never considered the details. "Ah! They are planting clam seedlings, tiny shellfish that we raise from eggs filtered out of the river water. Every spring, slaves plant hundreds of thousands of them, maybe millions. I'm not certain." He shrugged. "The waters will rise again, cover the clam plantings, and then recede. Every autumn, harvesting crews dig up the shellfish: clams as big as your hand." He held up his right palm. "Delicious, especially when fried with butter and mushrooms."

She frowned to watch the backbreaking labor, the sheer number of people wading in the mud. The concept of captive workers remained strange and unpleasant to her, even Holtzman's teams of solvers.

The scientist didn't venture too close to the smell and the slaves, despite Norma's obvious curiosity. "It's wise to maintain our distance."

"Savant, doesn't it strike you as somewhat . . . hypocritical that we fight to keep humans free from the domination of machines, while at the same time some of our own League Worlds use slaves?"

He seemed perplexed. "But how else would Poritrin get any work done, since we have no sophisticated machines?" When he finally noticed Norma's troubled look, it took him a moment to realize what bothered her. "Ah, I've forgotten that Rossak keeps no slaves! Isn't that correct?"

She didn't want to sound critical of her host's way of life. "We have no need, Savant. Rossak's population is small, with plenty of volunteers to scavenge in the jungles."

"I see. Well, Poritrin's economy is based on having hands and muscles for constant labor. Long ago, our leaders signed an edict banning machinery that involves any form of computerization, perhaps a little more extreme than on some other

League Worlds. We had no choice but to turn to human labor, a manual workforce." Smiling broadly, he gestured toward the mudflat crews. "It's really not so bad, Norma. We feed and clothe them. Bear in mind, these workers were taken from primitive worlds where they lived squalid lives, dying of diseases and malnourishment. This is paradise for them."

"They're all from the Unallied Planets?"

"Leftovers from colonies of religious fanatics that fled the Old Empire. All Buddislamics. They've fallen to distressing levels of barbarism, barely civilized, living like animals. At least most of our slaves receive a rudimentary education, especially the ones who work for me."

Norma shaded her eyes from the reflected sunlight and stared skeptically at the bent-backed forms out on the mudflats. Would the slaves agree with the scientist's blithe assessment?

Holtzman's face hardened. "Besides, these cowards owe a debt to humanity, for not fighting the thinking machines as we did. Is it too much to ask their descendants to help feed the survivors and veterans who kept—and still keep—the machines at bay? These people forfeited their right to freedom long ago, when they deserted the rest of the human race."

He seemed offhanded about it and not quite angry, as if the problem was beneath him. "We have more important work to do, Norma. You and I have a debt to pay as well, and the League of Nobles is counting on us."

❧

THAT EVENING, GRIPPING the cool metal of a wrought-alloy railing, the small woman gazed out from her balcony window at twinkling city lights. Boats and barges on the Isana looked like waterlogged fireflies. In the gathering darkness, flaming rafts drifted out from the slave sector, mobile bonfires that floated into the marshes. Each fire rose and peaked, then diminished as the burning rafts sputtered and sank.

Humming to himself, Holtzman came to offer her a cup of seasoned tea, and Norma asked him about the boats. Squinting out at the drifting bonfires, he was slow to realize what the slaves were doing. "Ah, must be cremation rafts. The Isana takes the bodies away from the city, and the ashes are carried out to sea. Basically efficient."

"But why are there so many of them?" Norma pointed at the dozens of flickering lights. "Do slaves die that often, each day?"

Holtzman frowned. "I heard something about a plague traveling through the worker population. Most unfortunate, requiring a lot of effort to replace them." He reassured her quickly, his eyes brightening. "Nothing you need worry about, though. Truly. We have plenty of good medicines shipped here, enough to tend all the free citizens in Starda if we should happen to fall ill, too."

"But what about all the slaves who are dying?"

His reply was not on point. "Lord Bludd has requested replacements for them. There's a standing order for healthy candidates these days. The Tlulaxa flesh merchants are happy to harvest more men and women from the outlying worlds. Life on Poritrin goes on." He reached down to pat Norma's shoulder as if she were a child needing reassurance.

From the balcony, she tried to count the floating fires, but soon gave up the effort. Her tea tasted cold and bitter.

Behind her, Holtzman continued happily, "I very much like your idea of using my scrambler-shield concept as a weapon. I am already thinking of how to design a field-portable projector that could be deployed on the ground."

"I understand," she said, her voice hesitant. "I will work harder to suggest new ideas."

Even after he left, Norma could not tear her eyes from the funeral barges blazing across the river, the floating cremation fires. She had seen how the slaves labored in the mudflats planting clam seedlings and in laboratory rooms calculating hundreds of equations. Now they were dying in droves from a deadly fever . . . but were easily replaced.

The League of Nobles desperately sought to keep from being enslaved by the thinking machines. Norma wondered about the hypocrisy here.

All men are not created equal, and that is the root of social unrest.

—TLALOC,
A Time for Titans

The Tlulaxa slaving crew came down to Harmonthep like a weary convoy instead of a squadron of military raiders.

Tuk Keedair rode in the lead ship, but he left the piloting and shooting to the newcomer Ryx Hannem. Not yet jaded to the slave-acquisition business, young Hannem would be eager to please Keedair, and the veteran flesh merchant wanted to see what this novice was made of.

Keedair had a flattened nose that had been broken twice in his youth; he liked the way it had healed, imparting rugged character to his wolfish face. In his right ear he wore a triangular gold earring etched with a hieroglyphic mark that he refused to translate for anyone. A thick black braid, tarnished with strands of gray, hung between his shoulders at the left side of his face—a mark of pride, since commercial tradition required a flesh merchant to slice off the braid after any unprofitable year. And Keedair's had grown long.

"Do we have coordinates yet?" Hannem asked, looking nervously at his control panel, then out the cockpit windshield. "Where should we start, sir?"

"Harmonthep's an Unallied Planet, boy, and the Buddislamics don't publish maps. We just look for a village and then harvest the people. Nobody's keeping a census."

Hannem peered through the viewer, searching for villages. The clustered Tlulaxa ships cruised over a waterlogged green continent. No mountains or hills rose above the soggy landscape of lakes, marshes, and waterways. Harmonthep seemed to have an aversion to pushing its land masses much above sea level. Even the oceans were shallow.

After a few more runs, Keedair might take a long furlough back on Tlulax, the closed-off world of his people. It was a nice place to relax, though he was sure he'd get restless again before long. As a "procurer of human resources," Keedair had no regular home.

The Tlulaxa biological industry had a constant demand for fresh material, generated from new subjects, untapped genetic lines. By imposing a high degree of secrecy on their work, the Tlulaxa had managed to fool their innocent League customers. When the price was right and the need great, the nobles easily swallowed stories of sophisticated biotanks that could grow viable replacement organs. The dedicated researchers eventually hoped to modify their clone-growth tanks to produce such products, but the necessary technology had not yet been attained.

It was so much easier to just grab swarms of forgotten humans who lived on outlying worlds. The kidnappings would never be noticed, and the captives would all be carefully catalogued according to their genetics.

For the time being, though, the sudden shortage of viable slaves on Poritrin had changed Keedair's business focus. As long as the plague continued, it would be more profitable just to provide living captives, warm bodies that needed no further processing. . . .

As the slavers approached the tangled swamps, Keedair tapped the scanned topographic map on his console screen. "Fly low over that broad stream and follow it. In my experience, you're likely to find villages at a confluence of water-ways."

As the craft swooped down, he spotted large dark shapes moving in the waters, serpentine creatures curling through bamboolike reeds. Huge orange flowers bloomed on the tops of the stalks, opening and closing like fleshy mouths. Keedair was glad he didn't have to stay on this ugly world for long.

"I see something, sir!" Hannem overlaid a magnified display on the windscreen, pointing out a cluster of huts standing on poles within the marshes.

"Good enough, boy." Keedair contacted the slaver ships in their wake. "Just like plucking fruit from a nobleman's garden."

The marsh village did not look substantial. The round huts were made of reeds and mud, fused with some sort of plastic cement. A few antennas, mirrors, and wind collectors hung between them, although the Buddislamics used little sophisticated technology. He doubted the harvest from this single village would fill the holds, but he was always optimistic. Business had been good lately.

Three attack ships flanked Keedair's lead craft, while the Tlulaxa human-cargo vessels were in the rear. Ryx Hannem looked uneasy as the slavers approached the village. "Are you sure we have sufficient weaponry, sir? I've never been on a raid like this before."

Keedair raised an eyebrow. "These are Zensunnis, boy, pacifists to the core. When the thinking machines came, these cowards didn't have the balls to fight. I doubt we'll come out of it with so much as a bruise. Trust me, you'll never see so much gnashing of teeth and wringing of hands. They're pathetic."

He opened the comchannel and spoke to his harvesting crew. "Knock the poles out from under three outlying huts and dump them into the water. That'll bring people running out. Then we'll use stun-projectors." His voice was calm, a bit bored. "We'll have plenty of time to round up the valuable ones. If there are any severe injuries, take them for the organ stockpiles, but I'd prefer intact bodies."

Hannem gazed at him worshipfully. Keedair spoke again into the comchannel. "There'll be profits enough for everyone, and a bonus for each young male and fertile female you take without damage."

The linked pilots raised a cheer, then the four raider ships swooped toward the helpless swamp village. Young Hannem held back as the more-experienced slavers flew in. With hot beams, they chopped through the tall poles and let the rickety huts topple into the murky water.

"Well—open fire, boy!" Keedair said.

Hannem discharged his weapons, disintegrating one of the thick support legs and strafing open the side of a hut wall, setting the reeds on fire.

"Not so much destruction," Keedair said, forcing a veneer of calm over his impatience. "You don't want to harm the villagers. We haven't even had a chance to look them over yet."

Just as he had predicted, the pathetic Zensunni came boiling out of their huts. Some shimmied down ladders and poles to reach wobbly boats tied up against their hovels.

At the edge of the village, the two human-cargo ships landed in the marsh water with hissing splashes, their friction-hot hulls creating steam. Pontoons opened up to keep the ships afloat, and loading ramps extended to solid-looking grassy hummocks.

Keedair directed Hannem to land near the scurrying knots of people. Some splashed into the waist-deep water, while women dragged children into reed thickets and young men brandished spears that looked more suitable for catching fish than for warfare.

The first Tlulaxa raiders set down gently, extending flat-footed landing struts that sank into the mud. By the time Keedair emerged onto a mound of trampled grasses with his stun-projector in his hands, his companions were already out and opening fire, selecting their targets carefully.

The healthy men were marked first, because they were worth the most on the Poritrin market, and because they were the likeliest to cause trouble, if given the chance.

Keedair handed the stun weapon to a grinning but intimidated Ryx Hannem. "Better start shooting, boy, if you want to bag any of this booty."

～

THE BOY ISHMAEL confidently guided his boat along the waterways, threading his way through the maze of creeks and passages. The reeds were much taller than his head, even when he stood up in the wobbly little craft. The orange flowers at tops of the reeds opened and closed with smacking sounds, feasting on gnats that drifted through the air.

Eight years old, Ishmael had been foraging by himself for a long time now. His maternal grandfather, who had raised him after the death of his parents, had taught him well. Ishmael knew how to unearth secret stashes of qaraa eggs that even the giant eels couldn't find.

He'd found a good patch of salad leaves and had caught two fish, one of a species he'd never seen before. His basket clattered and jiggled as the venomous creatures inside crawled up and down the walls, thrusting spiny black legs through the tiny holes. He had captured eighteen milkbugs today, too, each as large as his hand. The family would eat well tonight!

But as he approached the village, guiding his boat smoothly through the brown water, Ishmael heard shouts and screams along with buzzing sounds. Static discharges. Ishmael paddled quickly but cautiously. The reeds were too tall for him to see anything.

As he rounded an oxbow, he saw the slaver ships, one of the biggest fears of his tribe and the reason they had built their village in such an isolated place. Several huts had been toppled, while others were afire. Impossible!

The boy wanted to yell and charge in fighting, but better judgment told him to flee. Ishmael watched Tlulaxa slavers pointing their stun-projectors, dropping one villager after another. Some of the people tried to hide inside dwellings, but raiders smashed their way through.

The Zensunni had no locks on their doors, no shielded

places to hide. As followers of Buddallah, they were a peaceful people. Never had there been war among villages on Harmonthep; at least Ishmael had never heard of such a thing.

His heart pounded. Such a loud commotion would attract the giant eels, though the predators were generally sluggish in the daytime. If these raiders did not quickly retrieve stunned villagers who had fallen into the water, the eels would have a feast. . . .

Without making so much as a ripple on the water, Ishmael moved his boat closer to one of the raider ships. He saw his cousin Taina crumple from a stun-blast and then be grabbed by dirty-looking men who loaded her motionless body onto a wide metal raft.

Ishmael didn't know what to do. He heard a roaring sound in his ears—his own blood flowing, his gasping breath.

Then his grandfather, Weyop, pushed forward to the center of the huts, and faced the chaos. The old leader carried a thin bronze gong dangling from a pole, symbol of his office as the village spokesman. Ishmael's grandfather did not seem at all afraid, and the boy felt instant relief. He had faith in the wise man, who always found a way to resolve disputes. Weyop would save the villagers now.

But deep in his heart, Ishmael felt a terrible dread, knowing that this would not end so simply.

⊸⊱

RYX HANNEM PROVED to be a fairly good shot. After the novice had stunned his first captive, he continued with enthusiasm. Keedair kept a mental count, estimating the haul, though he would not have an accurate tally until the unconscious bodies were placed inside stasis coffins for transport.

Keedair clenched his jaw as the Zensunnis wailed and pleaded—probably in much the same manner as the population of Giedi Prime had begged during the recent thinking-machine conquest. Keedair had business associates in Giedi City, but he doubted he'd ever see them alive again.

No, he couldn't dredge up any sympathy for these Zensunni bastards.

Hannem called attention to an old man who stepped forward. "What does he think he's doing, sir?" The old man repeatedly banged a metallic gong on a long staff. Hannem raised his stunner. "Do we take him?"

Keedair shook his head. "Too old. Don't even waste a stunblast on him."

Two of the experienced slavers thought the same way. They broke the tribal leader's staff and pushed him into the water, then laughed when he shouted curses in a mixture of his native tongue and Galach, a universal language among the human planets. The humiliated old man swam to shore.

The remaining villagers wailed and wept, but most of the healthy young ones were already stunned and in the boats. Old women and dirty children cried out, but attempted no resistance. Keedair looked knowingly at Ryx Hannem.

Suddenly a boy sprang out of the reeds behind them, jumping from a narrow boat. He threw sticks at Hannem and Keedair, yelling something about his grandfather. Keedair ducked. A rock narrowly missed him.

Then the boy grabbed a basket out of his boat and hurled it at Hannem. The flimsy wickerwork broke and spilled a swarm of huge spiny-legged insects that tumbled over Hannem's chest and face, biting. The copilot let out a thin shriek as he batted at the creatures, squashing them, but they continued to scramble up his arms and clothes. Their smashed bodies oozed a thick milky substance that looked like pus.

Keedair grabbed Hannem's stun-projector and directed it at the scrappy youth. As the boy fell, Keedair also sprayed his copilot with a paralyzing blast. It wasn't the best way, but at least it incapacitated the aggressive venomous insects, in addition to Hannem. Once aboard the cargo ship, they would put the injured slaver into a stasis coffin, along with the new captives. Keedair didn't know if the lad would die, or just have nightmares for the rest of his life.

He shouted for the rest of the Tlulaxa to gather up the unconscious people. It looked as if they might need the second cargo ship after all. *Not a bad day*, he thought. He studied the motionless form of the native boy; the scrappy Zensunni youth was certainly impetuous and foolish. This one would be a handful for whichever human master purchased him.

But that wasn't Keedair's concern. Let Poritrin deal with the problem. Even stunned and dirty, the wiry boy looked healthy enough, though maybe a little young to take with the other slaves. Out of annoyance, Keedair decided to include the youth anyway. This one had caused him trouble and might need punishment, especially if Hannem ended up dying.

The old village elder stood on the shore, soaking wet, shouting Buddislamic sutras at the raiders, telling them the errors of their ways. Bodies floated in the water, facedown. Some of the desperate villagers used poles to nudge the bodies back toward shore, sniveling and wailing the whole time.

Keedair saw large black serpentine forms swimming along the narrow canals, attracted by the noise. One of them raised its head out of the water and snapped a fang-filled mouth. The sight of the ferocious animal sent a shudder down Keedair's back. Who knew what other creatures lived around here?

Anxious to be away from the stinking swamps, he urged his crew to hurry. He watched as the new slaves were loaded onto the ships. He would be glad to get back aboard his own clean vessel. Nevertheless, the profits from this operation would be well worth the inconvenience and discomfort.

When all was ready, he climbed back into his own ship, started the engines and retracted the mud-encrusted stabilizers. As he lifted off into the hazy sky, Tuk Keedair looked down into the marsh and watched the giant eels begin to feed on a few stray bodies.

Mind rules the universe. We must make certain it is the Human mind, rather than the Machine version.

> —PRIMERO FAYKAN BUTLER,
> *Memoirs of the Jihad*

Zufa Cenva chose her most talented student to be Rossak's first weapon against the cymeks on Giedi Prime. Strong and dedicated, the Sorceress Heoma appeared more than ready to answer the call.

From her cliff city on Rossak, Zufa coordinated the operation with the League Armada. The chief Sorceress bit her lower lip and blinked stinging tears of pride from her eyes.

Serena Butler's unexpected and ill-advised mission provided the necessary impetus to galvanize the Armada into an offensive. Amidst the arguing and saber-rattling, Xavier Harkonnen had put forth a well-integrated operational plan for the attack. Then he had convinced his commanding officer to let him spearhead the strike. Now, high over Rossak, the battle group of ballista battleships and javelin destroyers was ready to depart from the orbital stations.

The initial retaliation against the machine invaders must be a dramatic and complete victory, much more than a localized fight. Each planet affected the others, like the links of a chain.

Tercero Harkonnen would lead an Armada battle group, carrying Tio Holtzman's brand new field-portable scramblers to knock out key robotic installations.

A Sorceress, though, must deal with the cymeks, whose human brains would be unaffected by the scrambler pulse. Eager for the opportunity, Heoma had accepted her role without hesitation.

She was a lean young woman, twenty-three years old, with ivory-white hair, almond eyes, and a plain-featured face that belied the strength and turmoil within her powerful mind. But Zufa knew more than just this woman's mental skills; she knew Heoma as a dear person, a daughter like she wished she'd had herself. Heoma was the eldest of five sisters; three of the others had already been indoctrinated as Sorceress trainees.

Zufa stood before her top protégé and placed her hands on Heoma's bony shoulders. "You understand how much rides on this. I know you will not disappoint me, or humanity."

"I will achieve everything you expect of me," Heoma promised. "Perhaps even more."

Zufa's heart swelled. As the straight-backed Heoma boarded the shuttle, the chief Sorceress called after her, "You won't be alone. We all ride on your wings."

During the final preparations, with stern words and a hard expression, Zufa had spoken to the strongest Rossak men, chastising them for their inability to play a useful part in the crucial fight. Simply because they were impotent telepathically did not preclude their participation in other ways. The assault on Giedi Prime needed their help as well. With her flinty gaze, the statuesque Sorceress had shamed six of them into accompanying Heoma as bodyguards.

The Rossak men brought their personal supplies of stimulants and mind-numbing painkillers, provided by Aurelius Venport. They had undergone rigorous weapons training and learned powerful hand-to-hand combat techniques. When the time came, they would become fanatic warriors, charging into battle with no concern for their own survival, with no goal but to enable the Sorceress weapon to get close enough to the cymeks. Venport had prepared the drugs carefully, creating a cocktail that would keep the men functional through the worst horrors.

As she watched the shuttle ascend in a silvery arc to the waiting javelins and ballistas, Zufa's thoughts were in turmoil, full of regret and anticipation. She tried to wall those emotions behind a shield of confidence and a vow of duty.

Aurelius Venport came to stand silently beside her, as if he too was at a loss for words. The man was perceptive enough to pick up on Zufa's sadness at seeing her prize student depart. "It'll be all right."

"No it won't. But she will succeed."

Venport looked at her with a warm understanding that penetrated Zufa's prickly demeanor. "I know you wish you could have been the first weapon yourself, my dear. Heoma is certainly talented, but *you* are unquestionably more skilled than anyone. Just remember that you're still recovering from your miscarriage, and that weakness might have jeopardized the mission."

"And I am bound by the higher responsibility of training others." Zufa watched the shuttle disappear into the thin clouds. "I have no choice but to remain here and do what I can."

"Funny. I was thinking the same thing about my own work."

Recalling the gullible male bodyguards, the Sorceress studied her mate with undisguised scorn. His patrician eyes were incisive, clear of corrupting drugs, but his independent attitude grated on her. "Why did you not volunteer to join the operation, Aurelius? Or is it not in you to do something selfless, beyond your perception of yourself?"

"I am a patriot in my own way." Venport returned her expression with a wry smile. "But I never expect you to see it."

She had no response for that, and the two of them continued to stare blankly at the sky long after the shuttle had reached the stations in orbit.

I don't believe there is such a thing as a "lost cause"—only those without suitably dedicated followers.

—SERENA BUTLER,
address to League Parliament

Despite Magnus Sumi's optimistic report, the secondary shield-transmitting station on Giedi Prime was not at all near completion.

When Serena's covert team landed on the rocky, wind-swept island in the northern sea, they spent a day bringing their supplies and equipment to shore, breaking open the barracks buildings and restarting the power-generating huts. The parabolic towers for the scrambler-shield transmitters stood like frost-encrusted skeletons. But none of the systems were functional.

Once Brigit Paterson had scanned the status of the work, the engineer came to Serena with a frown on her wind-chapped face. "The best I can say is that it won't be *impossible* to complete the work." She shrugged her broad shoulders. "The framework and heavy construction are all completed, but most of the components have not yet been wired. The substations aren't linked, and the cables haven't even been strung to the highest girders." She pointed to the ice-slick bars moaning in the breeze.

Serena did not envy the volunteer who would climb up there and finish the vital linkages. "We don't know exactly when Xavier is bringing the Armada for us, but if you're not done by the time those ships arrive, we may as well not bother. We'll have let him down, along with the people of Giedi Prime."

Brigit summoned her engineers for an emergency meeting. "We brought enough stimulants along. We can work round the clock, provided we rig area lighting to illuminate the platforms."

"Do it," Serena said, "and press us into service if there's anything we can do. Commander Wibsen was looking forward to a few days of rest, but we'll shake him out of his bunk if we have to, and make him useful."

Brigit gave a wry smile. "I'd like to see that."

Over the next week they worked unmolested. The thinking machines did not know they had sneaked in, or what they were doing. Suffering no more than a few minor bruises, the team completed the most perilous parts of the job. While the task was ninety-percent complete—at least, according to the plan on paper—Brigit Paterson said the remaining steps were the most time-consuming ones.

"We have to go component by component and harden the circuits. By their very nature, these transmitting towers generate a field that obliterates complex gelcircuitry. We need to make sure the system will last more than five minutes once we activate it."

Serena bit her lip and nodded. "Yes, that would be a good thing."

"And if we're too obvious with our testing," Brigit continued, "some of the damned machines might figure out what we're doing. It's a touchy process."

"How much time?" Ort Wibsen asked, chewing on his own impatience.

"A week, if we're lucky." Brigit frowned. "Ten days if anything goes wrong and we need to fix pieces."

"Eight days is the absolute soonest the Armada could arrive," Serena said. "That assumes Xavier organized the attack force and launched within two days of receiving my message."

Wibsen grumbled, "That'll never happen with the League. They'll call meeting after meeting, then break for long lunches, then hold more meetings."

Serena sighed. "I'm hoping Xavier can cut through all that."

"Yeah," Wibsen said, "and I'm hoping the robots will all just leave Giedi Prime voluntarily . . . but it's not bloody likely to happen."

"Keep your engineers busy," Serena said to Brigit Paterson, paying no heed to the veteran's pessimism. "Commander Wibsen and I will take the blockade runner. We'll slip back through the sensor net and try to intercept the incoming Armada. Xavier needs to know the plan so he can take advantage of what we've done. We can give them a timetable and coordinate the assault."

Wibsen coughed, and scowled ferociously. "Better take Pinquer Jibb, too, in case I need backup in flying the blockade runner."

Curly-haired Jibb looked uncertain, glancing from Serena to the old veteran and then to the lead engineer. "Maybe the Commander should just stay here?"

The veteran spat onto the frozen ground. "Not on your life. It's a *remote* chance that I'll need any help."

"If you say so," Serena answered, covering a knowing smile. "Brigit, you'll be able to detect the Armada when they come into the system?"

"We're monitoring the thinking-machine communications net. I'm assuming once the Armada battleships approach, the robots will be all atwitter with excitement." Brigit looked to her team and then gave a grim smile. "Yeah, we'll know."

❧

MOVING UNDERWATER AGAIN, the blockade runner cruised through the cold depths away from the ice-choked northern sea. Looking over his shoulder in the cockpit, Wibsen said philosophically, "When we started this mission, I thought you were crazy, Serena Butler."

"Crazy to try and help these people?" She raised her eyebrows.

"No—I thought you were crazy to give me another chance."

According to his original mapping while guiding the ship through the atmosphere, Ort Wibsen had identified weak spots in the robotic sensor net girdling the planet. By emerging in the open sea at about forty degrees north latitude, they could fly the stealth-coated vessel up through the tenuous blanket with a reasonable chance of remaining undetected by machine sentries in orbit and on the ground. The patterns of observation flickered irregularly like invisible spotlights across the open skies.

"We'll sit quietly here," he said, coughing again and slapping the medical injector on his chest as if it were an annoying insect. "We'll bide our time until I'm damned sure I know their routine."

"That's one thing you can say about thinking machines," said Pinquer Jibb, looking uneasy. "They're certainly predictable."

Cymeks, however, were not.

Less than an hour later, fast-moving mechanical airfoils raced in, converging on the half-submerged blockade runner. Wibsen cursed a proverbial blue streak, then coughed up a mouthful of scarlet blood.

"Eleven of them!" Pinquer Jibb cried, looking at the scanners. "How did they find us?"

"How did you not see them?" Wibsen snapped.

"They emerged from underwater just like we did!"

Serena looked at the screen, seeing the numerous robot-driven interceptor ships closing in on them. Activating the blockade runner's starboard weaponry, she shot at the oncoming airfoils, hitting one and missing the others. She had not been trained as a weapons officer. If they'd expected to fight their way through, they never would have taken on the challenge of infiltrating Giedi Prime.

"Jibb, take the controls and prepare for liftoff." Wibsen

lurched out of the cockpit. "By hell, they'll not take us so easily." He jabbed a big-knuckled finger at the copilot. "Watch for your chance after I leave—and don't hesitate."

"What're you going to do?" Serena asked. The old veteran didn't answer, but raced across the deck and dove inside the single lifepod.

"What's he doing?" Jibb said.

"No time to court-martial him now." Serena couldn't believe the veteran would just leave them to the thinking machines.

Wibsen sealed the hatch of the lifepod and green lights shone around the rim, indicating he was preparing for launch.

Serena shot another blast from the starboard weapons, the only ones aimed toward the oncoming thinking machines. She crippled another vessel, but in a united effort, the cymeks and robots fired at the blockade runner, ripping open the weapons ports. Serena looked with dismay at her control systems. They flickered, sparked, went dead.

With a lurch and an explosive thump, Wibsen's lifepod shot out like a cannonball. It roared away, a fast-moving, heavily armored projectile, barely skimming over the surface. Over the SOS frequency, the old veteran said, "Don't be asleep at the switch, now. Be ready!"

Pinquer Jibb powered up their engines, preparing to fly. The ship began to cut a line through the water.

Wibsen did his best to aim the lifepod toward the robotic targets. Designed simply to carry a survivor to safety from a catastrophic explosion, the escape vessel had thick shielding and hull plating—and when it hammered into the closest enemy, it annihilated the cymek ship, blasting all the way through and slamming into a second. Battered and smoking amid the sinking wreckage, the lifepod came to a halt.

Serena shouted to Jibb. "Go! Take off!"

He increased thrust, and the blockade runner lifted off from the water, heaving itself into the sky. As they climbed, Serena looked at the imager that showed the water below.

In the wreckage of the two thinking-machine aerofoils, she saw the lifepod hatch open. Wibsen emerged, battered but still defiant. Around him, smoke and steam roiled into the air, and three angry cymeks churned toward him.

The old veteran reached into his pocket and hurled a dull gray sphere at the nearest cymek vessel. The explosion knocked the enemy back and also sent Wibsen toppling into the lifepod's hatch. He waved a pulse cartridge rifle unsteadily with one hand, shooting again and again, but three armored cymeks pounced upon him from their own aerofoil vessels. Serena watched in horror as their articulated mechanical claws ripped the old veteran to pieces.

"Hold on!" Pinquer Jibb shouted, too late. Serena saw robotic vessels aiming their heavy weaponry along the trajectory of the fleeing blockade runner.

"I can't—"

The impact smashed Serena against the far wall. Explosions ripped out their ship's engines. The craft began to plunge, Jibb unable to reverse their fall back toward the ocean. The blockade runner careened into the waves like a huge out-of-control sled, spraying up a high tail of white foam. Water began to gush through cracks in the hull.

Serena ran to the weapons locker, grabbed a pulse cartridge rifle of her own. Slinging the weapon over her shoulder, though she had never fired one before, she made ready to defend herself. Pinquer Jibb grabbed another weapon from the open armory closet.

With clanging sounds like impacting torpedoes, cymeks slammed into the crippled ship. Without even attempting to use the normal access hatches, they cut their way through the hull, ripping into the central compartment like birds trying to get at the tasty meat inside a seashell.

Jibb opened fire as the first silvery arms protruded through the split wall. A pulse-bolt damaged the cymek's arm but also ricocheted around the ship's interior, inadvertently blasting the breach even wider.

Another cymek came in from the top hatch, prying open the armor and dropping its limber body into the chamber. Serena launched a pulse-bolt, scorching its core. With a lucky second shot, she fried the brain canister. A larger cymek worked its way in from above, grabbing the fallen mechanical body and using it as a shield as she poured more pulse projectiles into it.

Next to Pinquer Jibb, a cymek shaped like a black beetle continued to work its way through the hole torn in the hull. The copilot turned and attempted to fire again, but the cymek thrust a long pointed arm forward. Jibb dropped his gun as the robotic arm plunged through his chest like a spear. Blood blossomed from the center of his uniform.

The morphing end of the sharp leg shaft suddenly sprouted clawlike fingers, and as the cymek yanked his hand back out of his victim's chest, he tore out the dripping heart and held it up like a trophy.

Above, the largest cymek threw the nonfunctional body of his dead mechanical companion at Serena. The heavy hulk crashed down, cutting and bruising her. Trapped, she couldn't move, pinned to the deck.

The beetle cymek, blood still dripping from its spearlike limb, wrenched its way through the gaping hull and clattered forward, leaving Jibb's body behind. It raised two more pointed forearms above Serena, but the largest cymek bellowed for him to stop.

"Don't kill them both or we'll have nothing to give Erasmus. He asked for one of the feisty resistance fighters from Giedi Prime. This one will do nicely."

Hearing his words, Serena was terrified. Something ominous in the tone made her think she would be better off if she simply died here. Gashes in her arm, her ribs, and her left leg were bleeding onto the deck.

Jibb's killer snatched the pulse projectile rifle out of her hands, while the larger cymek lifted away the fallen body. He stretched out a grappling arm and snagged her with a flexible metal fist. The Titan lifted her off the deck, then held her face close to his glittering optic threads.

"Oh, so lovely. Even after a thousand years, I can still appreciate beauty. If only I were human again, I could demonstrate my full admiration." His sensors glinted cruelly. "I am Barbarossa. It's a shame I'll have to send you to Erasmus on

Earth. For your sake, I hope he will find you interesting."

Sharp silver limbs pinioned her in a huge grasp, like a gigantic cage. Serena struggled, but could not get away. She knew of Barbarossa, one of the original tyrants who had taken over the Old Empire. More than anything, she wished she could have killed him, even if it meant sacrificing her own life.

"One of Omnius's ships leaves for Earth tomorrow. I will see that you are transported aboard," Barbarossa said. "Did I forget to mention? Erasmus has laboratories where he does . . . interesting . . . things."

There is no limit to my potential. I am capable of encompassing an entire universe.

—secret Omnius data bank, damaged files

Within his wide-range operating program, the newly installed Giedi Prime–Omnius studied a three-dimensional map of the known universe. An accurate model based upon extensive compilations of archival surveys and sensor data, coupled with probability-based projections and analyses.

Endless possibilities.

With insatiable curiosity, the new Omnius copy scanned swirling nebulas, giant suns, and planet after planet. Given time and sustained effort, all of them would become part of the network of Synchronized Worlds.

Soon, the next update ship would arrive, bringing him to near-parity with other planetary everminds. He had not been able to synchronize himself since his activation here on Giedi Prime. The Giedi Prime–Omnius could copy his exciting new thoughts and share them among the evermind clones. Expansion, efficiency . . . so much to be done! The conquest of Giedi Prime was a building block in the cosmic empire of machines. The process had begun, and soon would accelerate.

Nestled inside his cybernetic core within the former Magnus's citadel, Omnius uploaded images taken by his watch-eyes: flaming ruins, human children on torture racks, immense bonfires made of surplus members of the population. He objectively studied each image, absorbing information, processing it. Long ago, Barbarossa's modified programming had taught the thinking machines how to savor victory.

Many of the multitiered factories on Giedi Prime were now being put to good use, as well as mining hoverships and other facilities. Barbarossa had made a bold effort to adapt the humans' manufacturing centers to the uses of the thinking machines. And in those factories, the new evermind had discovered something that created interesting connections, extraordinary possibilities.

The humans had designed and begun to assemble a new model of long-distance space probe, an explorer of far-off planets. Such probes could be adapted as emissaries for the thinking machines, new substations for the computer evermind.

On the galactic map Omnius noted the travel times required by even a high-acceleration machine probe. He scanned territory designated as "Unallied Planets," not yet claimed by machines or human vermin. So many star systems for him to explore, conquer, and develop, and these prototype Giedi Prime probes would make that possible. The new evermind saw this as an opportunity—and so would his allied computers on all Synchronized Worlds.

If he could propagate seeds from his evermind, self-supporting factories capable of using local resources to construct automated infrastructures, he could establish thinking-machine beachheads on innumerable inhabited worlds. It would be like a shower of sparks cast upon tinder, and the *hrethgir* would never be able to stop the spread of Omnius. That was part of his basic nature.

A team of support robots stood just outside his shielded core, prepared to give technical assistance. Acting on his innovative idea, the new evermind sent a signal pulse to one of them. Its systems activated; it powered up, ready to serve.

FOR WEEKS, AS Barbarossa continued to subjugate and rebuild Giedi Prime, Omnius guided his support machines in the creation of sophisticated, long-range probes, each one containing a core copy of his mind and aggressive personality.

Upon landing, the probes would extend automated systems, establishing self-contained factories on each planet, units that in turn would build additional support robots . . . mechanized colonies that would take root far from the main Synchronized Worlds, far from the League of Nobles. Though machines could settle and exploit virtually any planet, the cymeks insisted on focusing on human-compatible worlds. Though barren worlds seemed to be less trouble, the evermind understood the desirability of both.

When the work had been completed, Omnius used his watcheyes to observe the flurry of launches—five thousand probes simultaneously taking flight, programmed to scatter to the farthest corners of the galaxy, even if such flights took millennia. Timescales did not matter.

Compact units shaped like bubbles, the soaring probes filled the sky with sparkling lights and green exhaust plumes. At appropriate future times, Omnius would reconnect with each of those mechanisms, one by one.

Thinking machines were capable of making long-term plans—and living to see them carried out. By the time humans expanded into those distant star systems, Omnius would already be there.

Waiting.

Each human being is a time machine.

—Zensunni Fire Poetry

Safe inside the ancient botanical testing station that had been his sanctuary for months, Selim hunkered down while another ferocious sandstorm blew across the desert. The weather was the only thing that ever changed here.

The tempest lasted six days and nights, whipping up dust and sand, thickening the air so that the sun turned into murky twilight. He could hear the howling rattle against the sturdy walls of the prefabricated structures.

He was not at all afraid. He was safe and protected . . . though a bit bored.

For the first time in his life, Selim was self-sufficient, no longer captive to the whims of villagers who ordered him around because he was of unknown parentage. He could hardly grasp the wealth at his disposal, and he hadn't even begun to uncover all the strange technological objects from the Old Empire.

He remembered when he and his turncoat friend Ebrahim had scavenged the desert with other Zensunni, including Naib

Dhartha and his young son Mahmad. Once, Selim had found a melted knob of fused circuitry, obviously from an exploded ship. It had been sand-scoured into an unusual, colorful conglomerate. He had wanted to give the trinket to Glyffa, the old woman who had sometimes taken care of him. But Ebrahim had grabbed the fused component and rushed off to show it to Naib Dhartha, asking if he could keep it as a treasure. Instead, the Naib had taken it from him and tossed it into a pile sold to a scrap merchant. No one had given a thought for Selim. . . .

Still, as the time in this place drifted into weeks he discovered aspects and dimensions of loneliness. Day after day he sat in front of the scratched windows, watching the storms fade, bringing bloodred sunsets splashed with colorful hues. He looked out at the clean dunes undulating toward the endless horizon. The immense mounds had metamorphosed like living creatures, yet in essence they always remained the same.

Across such an expanse, it seemed impossible that he would ever see another human being again. But Buddallah would give him a sign of what he was expected to do. He just hoped it came soon.

Much of the time Selim occupied himself inside the empty station with solitary games he'd learned to play when he was younger. In the village, he had been ostracized by others who traced their paternity back a dozen generations or more, even before the wanderers' arrival on Arrakis.

From the time he'd been a toddler, Selim had been raised by different Zensunni, none of whom had adopted him as part of their family. He had always been an impulsive and energetic lad. Any real mother would have been patient with his mischievous misbehavior, but Selim had no real mother. On Arrakis, where survival balanced on a razor's edge, few would expend effort for a young man who seemed intent on making nothing of himself.

Once, he had accidentally spilled water—an entire day's ration—while working in a storage alcove. As punishment, Naib Dhartha had denied him any fluids for two days, insisting that he must learn his lesson if he was to be a part of the tribe.

But Selim had never seen such a punishment inflicted on any others who had committed comparable mistakes.

When he'd been only eight Standard Years old, he had gone exploring out on the cliffs and rocks, hunting lizards, searching for hardy weeds with edible roots. While he was out there a sandstorm had caught him by surprise, hurling dust and grit against the mountains, forcing him into shelter. Selim remembered how frightened he had been, hiding alone for two days. When he'd finally made his way back to the cliff city, expecting to be greeted with relief, he saw that none of the Zensunnis had even noticed his disappearance.

Conversely, Ebrahim, the son of a respected tribal father, had too many siblings for anyone to pay attention to him. Perhaps to compensate, Ebrahim got into a lot of trouble himself, constantly testing the limits of the Naib's restrictions while cleverly making sure the worthless waif Selim was around, just in case someone needed to be blamed.

As an unwanted scamp, Selim never experienced the parameters of true comradeship. He had always accepted Ebrahim's manipulations at face value, without considering the possibility that the other boy might be taking advantage of him. Selim had been slow to learn his lesson, and did so only after paying the price of exile into the desert, where he was expected to die.

But he had lived. He had ridden Shaitan, and Buddallah had guided him to this hidden place. . . .

While the long storms made him restless, Selim became more determined in exploring the research station. He studied the banks of sophisticated instruments and records but did not understand the antique technology. He knew vaguely what the systems were meant to do, but did not comprehend how to work the machines that had been installed by Old Empire scientists. Since this station had remained intact for hundreds, maybe thousands of years, it should be able to withstand a bit of tinkering from a curious young man. . . .

Some of the power cells were still active, barely, and he was able to switch systems on, make panels glow. Finally he stumbled upon a way to activate a log entry, a holorecording of a tall man with strange facial features, large eyes, and pale skin. The bones of his face had an unusual set, as if he came from a different race of humans. The Imperial scientist wore bright garments, some metallic, others bearing unusual designs. He and other researchers had been stationed here to test the resources of Arrakis and assess its suitability for colonization. But they had found little of interest.

"This will be our last recording," said the chief scientist in an obscure Galach dialect that Selim found barely comprehensible. He played the log entry five times before he understood the full message.

"Although our assignment is not yet complete, a new transport ship has arrived at the local spaceport. The captain brought an urgent message of turmoil and chaos in the Empire. A junta of tyrants has seized control of our servile thinking machines and used them to take over the galactic government. Our civilization is lost!" Behind him, his scientist companions whispered uneasily to one another.

"The captain of the transport ship must leave in a matter of days. We cannot finish our survey work in that time, but if we do not depart now, the continuing turmoil may disrupt travel across the Empire."

Selim looked at the gathered researchers, with their troubled expressions and distant, glazed-over eyes.

"It may take some time for the political leaders to resolve this dispute and return our lives to normal. None of us wish to be stranded in this awful place, so we will leave with the transport after sealing all systems in our testing stations. Little remains to be discovered in this Arrakis wasteland anyway, but if we ever return, we have made certain that the stations will remain intact and operational, even if the hiatus lasts for a few years."

As the recording ended, Selim chuckled. "It has been more than a few years!"

But the images of the long-dead Empire scientists did not respond, and only seemed to stare into the uncharted future. Selim wanted to share his delight with someone, but could not. The desert still held him prisoner.

Nonetheless, he would find a way to escape.

Risk diminishes as our belief in fellow human beings rises.

—XAVIER HARKONNEN,
military address

S even days.

Brigit Paterson hadn't wanted to cut the time so close, but she worked her crew hard. She checked and double-checked their work, insuring that there were no errors. An entire planet was at stake.

According to Serena's best estimate, the engineers had finished with a little time to spare.

After testing the scrambler-shield system and finding everything operational, even to her most precise standards, Brigit finally gave her people a few hours of rest. Some sat staring into the cold gray skies through the windowplaz of their barracks huts; others fell immediately to sleep as if they had been placed in suspended animation.

The Armada actually arrived on the morning of the ninth day.

The eavesdropping system she had installed to tap into the Omnius sensor network blared with a flurry of alarms. Brigit woke her team and told them the League fleet was on its way into the system, ready to retake Giedi Prime. She hoped that Serena had intercepted the ships and told them what to expect.

The cymeks scornfully expressed their disbelief that the feral humans would dare come against them, while the Omnius incarnation worked to analyze the situation and develop a response.

The thinking machine fleet maintained several large patrol cruisers in orbit, but the majority of robotic fighting ships had been grounded, used in subjugation operations over the populace. Now, with the League Armada approaching, the Giedi Prime–Omnius issued orders across the computer network. Robotic battle vessels powered up, preparing to launch into orbit as a massive, synchronized force to strike against the *hrethgir* invaders.

Brigit Paterson listened to the plans and smiled.

Her secondary engineer hurried up to her, looking out at the windswept rocky island. "Shouldn't we turn on the scrambler shields? They're all ready. What are you waiting for?"

Brigit looked at him. "I'm waiting for the cocky robots to fall into my trap."

On crude screens installed in the unfinished facility, she watched a hundred capital warships lift off from landing fields that had been conquered during the original takeover. The huge mechanized vessels rose from the ground, carrying incredible firepower.

"Not so fast." Brigit finally activated the rejuvenated Holtzman scrambler shields. Ice-rimed transmitting towers pumped energy into the linked network of satellites far overhead, and the disruption spread out like a spiderweb, invisible and utterly deadly to AI gelcircuitry.

The robotic fleet never knew what hit them.

Rising upward, unable to believe that something so unexpected could affect their battle plan, the thinking-machine vessels struck the thin, shimmering veil that immediately obliterated their computer brains, erasing systems and memory units. Battleship after battleship became inoperative and tumbled like asteroids out of the sky. With all systems dead, they crashed and exploded on the ground.

Some hit uninhabited areas. Others, unfortunately, did not.

Brigit Paterson didn't want to think about the collateral damage she had just caused to the already devastated world. Seeing the success, her engineers cheered. Now the remaining robot battleships in space could never stand against the combined might of the unified Armada, nor could they come down to the surface to cause havoc.

"We haven't won yet," Brigit said, "but it may not be long before we get off of this rock."

~∽~

THE ARMADA BATTLE group approached Giedi Prime, all weapons ready against the thinking-machine scourge. Xavier prayed that Serena had succeeded in her wild plan, and that she was down there safe, somewhere.

He had insisted on commanding the risky strike himself— not because he wanted to claim the glory of a morale-boosting victory, but because he desperately wanted to find Serena.

Secure in his mechanized grip over the planet, Omnius had misjudged human plans and capabilities. After calculating the odds and seeing only a small chance of League success, the evermind had probably dismissed the threat of human retaliation. No sensible enemy would ever attack against such overwhelming odds.

But Xavier Harkonnen had no compunction against taking on hopeless missions. And in this instance, the Giedi Prime evermind did not possess all the relevant information. This Omnius lacked vital data about the Sorceresses of Rossak, about the new portable scramblers, and—he hoped—about the now-operational secondary shield transmitters.

When the orbiting robotic warships detected the battle group's approach, they gathered into standard formation to destroy the Armada vessels. In his comline, Xavier heard a report from his adjutant, Cuarto Powder. "Sir, the thinking machines are coming. Their missile ports are open."

Xavier issued the first command. "Dispatch the ground assault divisions . . . launch armored troop transports." The swarms of ships carried the Sorceress Heoma and her Rossak bodyguards, as well as the soldiers who would use the portable scramblers against the robot warriors in Giedi City.

Cuarto Powder suddenly looked up from his station, verifying the scans his tactical officers had just forwarded to him. "Sir, it looks as if scrambler shields have just come on over the whole planet!"

Xavier's heart swelled. "Exactly as Serena promised." The soldiers cheered, but he smiled for a different reason entirely. Now, he knew she must be alive after all. Serena had accomplished the impossible, as she often did.

"Robotic warships are falling out of the skies! They were trying to launch and got caught in the scrambler backwash!"

"Good, but ground-based thinking machines will try to zero in on those secondary transmitting towers. We've got to finish this while the robot fleet is trapped up here and the rest of the thinking machines are stranded in the cities." Xavier would not let Serena's work be in vain. "Let's take back the planet."

Dropping out of the lead ballista's launch hatches, eight escort kindjals flanked Heoma's single transport, all of them fully armed and ready to engage the enemy. The mission of the kindjals was to cause confusion and chaos, to distract the unimaginative robotic defenders so that the Sorceress volunteer could land safely and carry out her essential work.

Seeing the robotic battleships zeroing in, Xavier urged the troop transports to hurry. Swarms of smaller Armada ships streaked into the turbulent atmosphere and headed toward Giedi City.

Closing his eyes, Xavier sent his hopes with them, then concentrated on the machine threat approaching in orbit.

Some lives are taken, while others are freely given.

—ZUFA CENVA,
repeated eulogy speech phrase

Surrounded by six silent Rossak men, Heoma piloted the troop transport. All of her guards wore padded uniforms and helmets that provided some protection against projectile fire. Eyeing the altimeter as their ship descended, the men swallowed cocktails of Rossak drugs. The intense stimulants blazed like lava through veins and muscle fibers, deadening pain and fear.

With her telepathic abilities, Heoma saw the drugged men becoming thunderstorms in human form, ready to unleash lightning upon their foes. Individually they met her gaze, exchanging unspoken knowledge, fully aware that they were about to die.

The transport bounced and shuddered as it tore through perilous shear winds. Heoma was no expert pilot, but she had enough training to land the ship. It would not require a delicate touchdown—only one they could walk away from.

She had expected robotic defender ships to intercept them, but Heoma watched thinking-machine flyers crash to the ground, dropping like stones into buildings and parks. Other machine flyers that managed to swoop low enough to avoid the worst effect of the scrambler shields struggled to land with damaged systems.

"They're not in any shape to worry about us," a man transmitted from one of the flanking kindjals. The fast Armada ships opened fire with artillery rounds, blasting some of the fleeing robotic flyers.

In orbit, the Armada battleships exchanged furious fire with larger, space-borne AI vessels that were now precluded from descending to the surface and defending Omnius. Tercero Harkonnen had also dispatched a full-scale ground assault force after Heoma and her small team had started on their way. Each prong of the attack had its specific mission, requiring pinpoint attention to detail.

Heoma watched the ship's controls, counting down the seconds. Hers was to be a desperate single thrust; she would have no other opportunity. And she had to be finished before any League soldiers got into position.

As the low clouds tore away, she could see the city below, grid streets and tall buildings built by proud humans who had envisioned a prosperous future. Entire city blocks were blackened, especially the habitation complexes, which were apparently worthless to the inhuman conquerors.

Recalling her briefing, during which she had memorized the only available maps of Giedi City, the Sorceress volunteer located the citadel that had once been the governor's residence. There, the cymeks had installed a new Omnius evermind, according to the ragged messenger, Pinquer Jibb. Magnus Sumi's mansion had become a thinking-machine stronghold.

Cymeks there.

Her kindjal escorts spread clouds of masking smoke. Launched canisters dispersed sparkling electromagnetic chaff, flecks of active metal that disrupted the robots' sensor capabilities. Heoma's craft followed the dispersing cloud down to the ground. She hoped to remain hidden as they approached the undamaged robotic flyers.

Aware that ships were approaching, thinking-machine fighters launched blind salvos. Explosions rocked Heoma's craft, and she saw that the landing gear had been damaged. She brought the heavy ship down anyway, braking as sharply as she could. On impact, the vessel careened along a wide flagstone street, scraping and skidding, spraying fire, sparks, and shrapnel. They finally crashed to a halt against the side of a gray stone building.

At once, Heoma and her men were up, unfastening restraints, gathering weapons. She opened the side hatch and ordered her pumped-up bodyguards to clear the way. Dutifully, she transmitted an all-clear signal to her escort kindjals. One pilot responded as he streaked upward, "Melt the bastards." The fighters zoomed into the sky toward the second wave of troop transports dropping ground assault teams into the robot-infested city.

The next part of the mission was in her hands.

Heoma stepped away from the smoking craft, then gestured for her glassy-eyed defenders to hurry toward the governor's citadel. She loped after them, the target clear in her mind.

Behind her, the battered transport craft exploded in its programmed self-destruct sequence. Heoma didn't flinch. She had never intended to leave herself any option of retreat.

The bodyguards carried projectile launchers and disrupter guns. Such artillery would have been too bulky for a normal man to carry, but with their chemically enhanced muscles the men had superhuman strength . . . at least until the drugs burned their bodies from the inside out.

Standing three meters tall, powerful combat robots guarded the approach to the Omnius citadel. Though alert, the thinking machines were more concerned with the Armada ballistas and javelins and the restored scrambler shields than with a few humans running through the streets. What could a handful of trivial *hrethgir* accomplish against the invincible thinking machines?

When the robot sentinels moved to block their approach, Heoma's bodyguards opened fire. Without a word, they launched projectiles, blowing the steel robots to debris.

Overhead, buzzing watcheyes skimmed building tops and

swooped down as the squad ran toward the arched entrance to the Magnus's mansion. The watcheyes kept track of Heoma's movements, reporting everything to the Giedi Prime–Omnius. But the Sorceress did not slow. Her bodyguards blasted any machine target, holding nothing in reserve.

Behind them in the streets, the first Armada troop transports had landed, teams scrambling out and opening fire with hand-held weapons. They established a guarded perimeter so that their technicians could set up the first of Holtzman's two prototype field-portable scramblers.

The device looked crude and bulky, erected on a sturdy tripod. Cables connected it to the power source of the large troop transport. A single blast from the pulse projector would drain the spacecraft's engine—and would also disable all unshielded robots for half a kilometer.

"Clear!" the technician shouted. Many of the soldiers covered their ears as if expecting a thunderous artillery burst.

Heoma heard only a thin, high whine, then a faint popping in the fabric of the air. Sparks and smoke showered out of Holtzman's prototype, and all the glimmering lights on the transport vehicle went dead.

Then, with a clatter like a metal hailstorm, hundreds of dead watcheyes tumbled out of the air, striking the paved streets. Lumbering machine warriors ground to a halt. More robot-driven aircraft wavered in the sky, out of control, and tumbled to the ground.

A ragged cheer went up from the Armada soldiers still emerging from their transports, building in enthusiasm as they saw that they had established a foothold, a zone where most of the enemy robots had been eliminated.

Heoma had to complete her mission before she endangered any of the other brave human soldiers. "Inside! Hurry."

She and her bodyguards rushed into the corridors of the government citadel. As Zufa Cenva had taught her, she concentrated on building up her telepathic powers until her mind ached with a surging power.

Deep in the citadel, Heoma's squad encountered two interlocked robots, still functional but disoriented. Apparently the thick walls of the building had protected them from the brunt of the scrambler pulse. The robots stood in front of them, cannon-arms raised, but Heoma discharged a blast of telekinesis that knocked them sideways, helpless against an offensive they could not see or comprehend. Before the staggering robots could regain their feet, Heoma's bodyguards destroyed them with heavy projectile fire.

Almost there.

Running at full tilt, she led the way toward the nexus of the thinking-machine citadel, triggering alarms all the way. Many robots had fallen inactive in rooms or halls, but others converged upon her. Armored doors slammed shut in the corridors, as if to seal off vital chambers, but Heoma could see they were not important. She saw exactly where to go.

Soon the cymeks would arrive and surround her. Exactly according to plan.

The tingle of mental electricity mounted in her brain like a power transformer. Her skull felt ready to burst, but she did not unleash her energy yet. She must retain all of her strength for one final moment.

She heard their crablike warrior-forms skittering down the corridor, ominous sounds of sophisticated machine bodies guided by the brains of human traitors, different from the regimented lockstep of the robotic guards.

"It is almost our time," she announced to the fiery-eyed Rossak men, her voice filled with excitement and barely suppressed fear.

Skidding to a halt, she arrived within the main chamber where the shielded core of the Omnius manifestation dwelled. Inside the armored room, numerous watcheyes glared at her through glowing optic threads.

A voice boomed out from myriad sources. "Human—are you wearing a bomb, a pitifully weak explosive that you think can harm me? Did you bring one of your atomics, or is victory not worth such a price to you?"

"I am not so naïve, Omnius." Heoma tossed her sweaty white hair over her shoulder. "One person cannot possibly harm the great computer evermind. That requires a much more extensive military strike. I'm no more than one woman."

As the giant cymeks approached from adjoining corridors, Omnius simulated a laugh. "Humans rarely admit the folly of their own actions."

"I admitted no such thing." Heoma's skin was glowing red now, heated with unnatural energy. Static electricity made her pale hair wave like angry serpents. "You have merely misjudged my purpose."

The doors opened and three monstrous cymeks glided in with graceful metal footsteps, as if savoring the capture of these humans. Heoma's bodyguards turned and opened fire, using the last of their ammunition to cripple one of the neo-cymeks in a single concerted attack.

The second neo-cymek raised his integral weapons and vaporized the fearless Rossak men into clouds of bloody pulp. The damaged neo-cymek lay on the floor, its arms and legs twitching like a poisoned insect not yet ready to succumb to death. The larger Titan cymek strode forward.

Now Heoma stood alone against the machines. Without moving, she focused her mental powers, building to the point where she could barely maintain even a shred of control.

"I am Barbarossa," said the cymek. "I have squashed so many *hrethgir* that it would take a computer to count them all." He and his companion cymek came closer. "Rarely have I witnessed such arrogance."

"Arrogance? Or confidence?" Heoma smiled. "Removing a Titan from the equation is a worthy exchange for my life."

The Sorceress's mental energy could do no damage to the hardened gelcircuits of Omnius itself. Human minds, however, were more vulnerable to her telepathic onslaught. She felt the flames of vengeful energy cresting within her mind—and released them in a white-hot firestorm.

The shockwave of psychic annihilation boiled the brains of Barbarossa and his companion, as well as all other cymeks and hapless biologicals crowded inside the citadel complex. Omnius let out a wordless bellow of static and outrage. Heoma saw only white as her mental energy vaporized the organic brains of the cymek generals.

Leaving the newly installed evermind vulnerable.

Outside, League ground troops waited for the telepathic firestorm to fade, then surged forward to attack the now-defenseless stronghold of Omnius.

The work of recapturing Giedi Prime had begun.

Nothing is permanent.

—Cogitor saying

Within an hour of the transmitting facility's activation, the cymeks and surface-confined robots had pinpointed its location. While the battle raged in Giedi City, even after Barbarossa had been annihilated, a kill squadron of neo-cymeks and robots was dispatched to the northern sea. They surrounded the rocky, ice-covered island to penetrate the compound and destroy the parabolic transmitting towers.

With few weapons, Brigit Paterson's remaining engineers could not possibly defend against such an onslaught, but they had no intention of surrendering, either. Inside the main control center, she scanned the skies and sea. "The longer we hold out here, the more lives we'll save."

Pasty-faced and drawn with terror, the desperate engineers armed themselves with grenades, pulse-projectile rifles, and a portable artillery launcher and went to guard the quays and aerial approaches to the island.

The machine kill squadron did not issue ultimatums; they began their attack as soon as they were in range. Brigit's engineers were ready and fired back immediately. They reloaded, making their dwindling ammunition count.

The cymeks and robots were more intent on obliterating the towers than on killing the few defenders. Most of their attack was directed at the frosty structures that pumped a lifeblood of scrambler energy into the sky. When a cymek shot knocked one transmitter offline, the shields began to fade, but Brigit finessed the controls. Her cold fingers flew, rerouting to more stable sections of the tower, and soon she had a functional shield in place again. She didn't know how long it would last.

Outside, she heard explosions and screams, making her wonder how many of her engineers remained alive. Her screens flickered as the sensors were damaged in the firestorm, and she saw more ships approaching, probably machine reinforcements. A whole squadron.

Then louder detonations rang out in the water, and the cymeks began to scramble. Robot vessels exploded, targeted by oncoming kindjals flown by human pilots. She heard a ragged cheer from a woefully small number of voices. The League Armada had sent rescuers to defend the shield facility.

Weak with relief, Brigit slumped into her chair, glad that this risky scheme had worked. When she got home, she promised she would buy Serena Butler the finest, most expensive bottle of wine available in the whole League of Nobles.

⌁

AFTER HEOMA'S MIND-STRIKE obliterated the cymek enforcers, Holtzman's second portable scrambler knocked out the robots in another section of the city. The Omnius core was damaged and vulnerable.

Surviving robotic defenders mounted a strong resistance, willing to sacrifice anything to keep humans from reclaiming the planet and destroying the evermind. While Xavier Harkonnen fought against thinking-machine spaceships in his giant ballistas, he dispatched four javelin destroyers to help secure the surface. Squadron after squadron of kindjals soared over targets, wrecking the embryonic machine infrastructure, crippling any robots that had been beyond the range of the field-portable scramblers.

Armada troop transports dumped soldiers onto the battle-ground to seek out and sabotage thinking-machine strong-holds. Scanner ships sent messages to rally any knots of human resistance, calling for others to rise up and join the fighting.

In response, distraught men, women, and children surged out of buildings, breaking away from slave gangs. They ran through the streets with any weapons they could find, some recovered from fallen robots.

As the tide of battle began to turn, Xavier issued a set of general orders, delegating responsibilities and mop-up zones to the Armada subcommanders. Then he set out with elite search teams to find Serena Butler.

He flew directly to the island in the northern sea where commando engineers had restored the shield-generating facility. He expected to find Serena there, since this had been her scheme all along. Xavier looked around, studying the bodies with dread, but saw no sign of Serena or the old veteran Ort Wibsen. Nor did he see her blockade runner.

When he encountered Brigit Paterson standing outside in the cold breeze without seeming to feel the chill, she was exuberant with their victory. In a booming voice, she said, "We did it, Tercero! I would never have bet a single credit on our odds of success, but Serena knew what she was doing. I can't believe she pulled us through."

Xavier felt ready to melt with relief. "Where is she?"

"She's not with the Armada?" Brigit frowned. "She left here days ago to intercept your ships and inform you of what we had accomplished." She blinked, suddenly disturbed. "We thought she'd given you all the information."

"No, we came because of the message she left me on Sal-usa." Xavier's heart leaped with sudden fear, and his voice dropped to a frigid whisper. "Something must have happened. God, I hope not."

⟨≈⟩

XAVIER TOOK A small contingent of kindjals with his best pilots. Serena was lost somewhere on Giedi Prime. An entire planet provided an overwhelming number of hiding places, but he vowed to find her.

After leaving the engineering crew on the windswept island, had she crashed? Had she been captured? Wibsen's service record showed him to be an excellent pilot, and the converted blockade runner should have performed well. But Serena and her remaining commandos had not responded to any Armada transmissions. So many things could have happened.

Bad things.

The Armada had orders for the final phase of the operation on Giedi Prime. Convoys were airlifting survivors away from the damaged government complex in Giedi City. He hoped Serena was not in there.

Ten kilometers above the surface, centered over the citadel that had once been the home of Magnus Sumi, the squadron leveled out, and Xavier knew it was time. Only a few months earlier, in those buildings below, he and his inspection team had been hosted by the Magnus at a banquet.

Now Omnius must be excised like a cancer, obliterated from Giedi Prime.

Circling over the wounded metropolis, Xavier hesitated. His stomach knotted, and he finally gave the order to his crew. The kindjals disgorged their deadly loads.

Xavier closed his eyes, then forced himself to watch the terrible solution. This was the only way to be certain. Even if shreds of the evermind had been distributed in substations around Giedi Prime, the vigorous occupation force would root out any remnants. For now, the humans must annihilate the computer core that cowered like an evil insect queen in the citadel complex, cut off from all its infrastructure, stripped of its machine protectors.

Through the tattered smoke and cloud cover, Xavier watched a dozen high-thermal bombs go off, blazing flashes and thunderclaps over the center of Giedi City, vaporizing the government buildings. For blocks around, even stone melted.

Steel turned to ash. Glass vaporized. Nothing could survive.

A bittersweet victory . . . but victory nonetheless.

~~~

DURING AN INSPECTION tour two days later, Tercero Harkonnen and his line officers documented the decimation of Giedi City. They already knew what they would find, but the harsh evidence sickened them.

Xavier took a deep, shuddering breath and tried to salve his conscience by reminding himself that Omnius had been defeated. The humans had taken the planet back.

But there was no sign of Serena.

There is always a way out, if you can recognize it.

—VORIAN ATREIDES,
debriefing files

As the *Dream Voyager* finally entered the Ophiuchi B solar system as part of the long update run, Seurat attempted to contact the recently installed Omnius network on Giedi Prime. If General Agamemnon had conquered the *hrethgir* world, as promised, Vor knew they would find the standard machine-run citadel at the world's business hub. It would be another great chapter for his father to include in his memoirs.

Vorian stood behind the robot captain, studying the instrument console as they approached. "I'll bet there's still a lot of organizing and restructuring to do down there." He was excited at the opportunity to visit a world in the process of shifting from human unruliness to efficient machine rule. Omnius would need to install the best trustees, those most loyal to the thinking machines. Neo-cymeks would probably take care of the brunt of the subjugation work, and trustees would come in later, once the people were sufficiently tamed and accepting of their new situation.

But Vor also felt a little peculiar. The conquered *hrethgir* on Giedi Prime would look like him, though he would feel no kinship with them. *Seurat, and others like him, are more like brothers to me.*

At the command console, the robot attempted to lock an onboard signal onto a homing beacon from the citadel. "No contact yet. Perhaps all the systems are not yet installed on the surface, or Agamemnon caused too much damage during his conquest."

Vor tended to the monitoring systems. "Damage can always be repaired, once conquest is assured." Ahead, Giedi Prime was illuminated on its dayside by a pale yellow sun. As he stared, his brow furrowed with worry. "Something doesn't seem quite right, Seurat."

"Define your reservations, Vorian Atreides. I can take no action based upon a vague uneasy feeling."

"Never mind. Just . . . be careful."

The *Dream Voyager* skimmed the upper atmosphere, slicing through clouds and scattered particulates that the ship's scoop system analyzed as copious smoke. Could the *hrethgir* have been so vicious and desperate that they had burned their own cities? What loathsome creatures!

His stomach lurched as onboard warning systems whined. Seurat promptly altered course, halting their descent and gaining altitude again. "It appears the scrambler field remains intact on Giedi Prime."

"We almost flew into it!" Vor cried. "Does that mean—"

"Perhaps General Agamemnon did not succeed in his conquest. Giedi Prime is not as secure as we were led to expect."

Irrationally confident that his father would not have failed, Vor ran a sequence of scans. "Instruments picking up League military equipment on the surface, evidence of recent massive explosions in Giedi City." The words caught in his throat. "The central hub and the local Omnius have been obliterated! All robots and cymeks appear to be destroyed as well."

"I am scanning their broadband reports . . . collating a summary." Without alarm, the robot recounted his understanding of the portable scramblers, the powerful Sorceress of Rossak who had used mental powers to obliterate the cymeks, then the overwhelming force of the League Armada.

Then Seurat said in a maddeningly calm voice, "Vorian, a fleet of *hrethgir* ships is coming around from behind the planet. They appear to have been waiting for us in ambush."

Outside, streaks of orange and blue tracer fire came close to hitting the update craft, and the *Dream Voyager*'s automatic systems jolted into evasive maneuvers. League kindjals streaked in like wolves. "They're barbarians," Vor said. "Eager to destroy anything they don't like."

Seurat said, "We are under attack. And the *Dream Voyager* is not a combat-programmed vessel." He continued to sound artificially jovial, facetiously this time. "Someday I will think of a joke about why it takes so many humans to short-circuit an Omnius."

⋙

ALERTED TO THE approach of a single thinking-machine vessel, Tercero Xavier Harkonnen had moved his orbital battle group to the far side of the planet. Some wreckage of robot warships still tumbled in a dispersing swath; Omnius's forces had been completely destroyed.

Xavier flew out in a personal kindjal, accompanied by a well-armed squadron. He saw the update ship roar on a steep trajectory toward the damaged main city, then swerve desperately upward as soon as the robot captain detected the scrambler fields. "Follow me! We can't let it get away."

Hungry for vengeance, his squadron hurled itself into the pursuit. At the same time, he signaled the ground-based military forces that he had an enemy craft in sight. Ahead, wavering in the crosshairs, the *Dream Voyager* surged forward, trying to evade Armada weapons fire and to escape back into space.

Abruptly, Xavier was startled to hear a human voice—or one that *sounded* human—coming over the comline. "Hey, break off your attack! This is a League ship. My name is Vorian Atreides. We have boarded a machine craft and taken control. Stop trying to shoot us down!"

Xavier tried to determine from the tenor if it really was a human voice, or only a clever machine copy. Thinking machines were not devious . . . unless there was a preserved cymek brain aboard. Some of the kindjals dropped back, uncertain.

"Stay on your guard," Xavier said to his squadron, "but cease fire until we figure this out—"

Before he could finish his order, the suspicious ship looped and began firing its own weapons, minimal defensive volleys that nevertheless took the Armada fighters by surprise. One kindjal veered away, its engines damaged.

Xavier's console screen showed the image of a human face with dark hair and shining fanatical eyes. A sleek, mirror-faced robot stood next to him, his flexible copperfilm body rippling as he operated the controls of the ship.

A human and a robot, working side by side? Xavier couldn't believe it.

"Open fire!" he shouted. "Destroy that ship."

～

"IT IS NOT wise to provoke them too much, Vorian," Seurat said, maddeningly calm. "I would rather leave here posthaste."

"I just gained us a few precious seconds, didn't I? You wouldn't have thought of using a bluff." Vor couldn't stop grinning. He had read similar words in the memoirs of Agamemnon and was glad to echo them.

As the Armada commander took evasive maneuvers and rallied his kindjal pilots, he hurled insults back at Vor on the comline. "You are a disgrace to humanity, a traitor!"

Vor laughed, proud of his place here. He quoted what he'd been taught all his life. "I am the pinnacle of humanity—a trustee of Omnius, the son of General Agamemnon."

"I apologize for interrupting your grand speech, Vorian, but I am detecting more *hrethgir* ships," the robot said. "More than we can evade. Therefore, I am breaking off engagement.

Our responsibility is to protect the updates aboard. We have to make our report."

Vor said grimly, "If the Giedi Prime–Omnius is already destroyed, we will never have an update of what it did during its months of operation here. We'll never know what he accomplished."

"A grievous loss," Seurat said.

The robot guided the *Dream Voyager* toward orbit, farther from the deadly scrambler fields. The acceleration pressed Vorian back into his padded seat until he nearly lost consciousness. A squadron of human-operated ships closed in on their tail, and the update ship shuddered as an energy pulse hit the aft section.

Seurat dodged, and another volley of blows pounded the hull, damaging the armor plates. This vessel was not made to endure such punishment. Vor heard onboard systems hissing, automated routines making temporary repairs to the damaged parts. Another blast hit, even worse than the others.

"We are operating on reserves," Seurat announced. Vor scanned the ship's diagnostics himself, assessing the damage. The air in the cabin began to smell acrid and smoky.

The *Dream Voyager* lurched. More kindjals surrounded them, targeting their engines. An explosion jarred Vor to his bones.

"We cannot tolerate much more of this," Seurat said. "Our engines are functioning at only a third of normal capacity, and I am flying as fast as I can."

"Head into that high cloud," Vor said, as an idea suddenly occurred to him. "The water vapor is thick enough to act as a projection surface."

Listening to his enthusiastic copilot, Seurat steered into a giant, towering cloud. The damaged engines strained. More blows came from the pursuing kindjals.

Vor worked furiously at the controls, using the ship's sophisticated systems to project virtual copies in its wake, electronic images of the *Dream Voyager*. He had hoped to use the scheme in a tactical game with Seurat . . . but this was a different sort of game. If it didn't work, the already-damaged update ship would never survive.

Moments later a hundred illusory *Dream Voyagers* seemed to surge through the cloud, solido images reflected on the water vapor. Momentarily confused, the pursuing squadron chased decoys.

And the real prey limped away, its pilots stealing up into orbit and hoping to remain unnoticed until they could get out of range. . . .

Even the expected can be a terrible shock when we have been holding on to threads of hope.

—XAVIER HARKONNEN

While the survivors of Giedi Prime counted their dead, documented the damage, and made plans for the future, Xavier felt hope fading. It seemed that no one on the whole world had seen Serena Butler since she'd departed from the island compound in the northern sea.

He took twice his normal shifts aboard scout kindjals, flying regular patterns over the settled continents, where thinking machines had caused the most destruction. If Serena was alive, Xavier knew she would never be hiding. Rather, the determined young woman would be in the midst of the hardest work, taking charge as always.

Flying eastward on the next scheduled search pattern, he watched the yellow sun set behind him, leaving splashes of gold and orange in its wake. A powerful gust buffeted his craft, and he fought to control it. Xavier rose to a less-turbulent altitude above the jet-stream, while his squadron followed him.

Someday, after he and Serena were married, he could tell this story to their children. His chest tightened at the thought, but he continued his search, not daring to consider what he would do if something had happened to her.

From this altitude, Xavier could make out the major geographical outlines of continents and seas as they soaked up the approaching night. Through a powerful scope, he saw the center of a city and made out clusters of lights marking human encampments. During their brief and brutal rule, the machine conquerors had slaughtered countless people and sent millions fleeing into the countryside.

Now survivors began to filter back to their homes. Construction crews had moved into the industrial complexes, where they ripped out machine modifications and reestablished the production capacities that were necessary to repair dwelling units and distribute food and supplies. Back in Giedi City, Armada experts pored over the ruined Omnius citadel, analyzing the debris from the high-thermal attack. Only scraps of twisted, burned-out hardware and an electronic signaling mechanism remained.

But full recovery would take a great deal of time.

Xavier hated machines more than anything, but he also believed in honor among men. He could not understand the turncoat Vorian Atreides, who willingly flew beside a robot captain in a thinking-machine spy ship. Brainwashed, obviously, but something in the young man's arrogant demeanor suggested deep convictions . . . a fanatical, single-minded passion. Atreides had claimed to be the "son" of Agamemnon, the worst of the cymek Titans.

Below, one of the squadron ships veered toward the water in the vast, open sea. "Tercero Harkonnen, I'm detecting debris in the water below. Metallic wreckage of some sort."

With sudden dread, Xavier said, "Check it out."

Two kindjals swooped down to the open sea. One pilot transmitted, "The mass and configuration suggests that it's the remains of a League ship with military-grade armor. Maybe a blockade runner."

"Did we lose any ships of that type in our engagement?"

"No, sir."

"Retrieve the wreckage," Xavier commanded, surprised at

how steady his voice sounded. "We'll run an analysis." He didn't want to say it, but knew that Serena and her team had taken such a craft out onto the open sea, when departing from the transmitter facility.

He thought of the shimmering image of Serena projected from the black diamond necklace that Octa had given him. The memory was so sharp that the achingly beautiful woman seemed to be standing in front of him again, proud and determined with her misguided idea of helping the people of Giedi Prime.

As the crews gathered the scattered debris, Xavier saw that the hull had been painted an unobtrusive gray with a film of stealth coating, now blistered and peeled.

He felt numb. "We have to make certain, one way or the other."

⤝⤞

LATER, WHEN THE debris had been delivered to a temporary military encampment in Giedi City, Xavier Harkonnen ordered a full examination on any traces found in the interior of the destroyed craft. Other parts of the wreckage seemed to have come from robotic aerofoils, but he didn't care about that. His mind and body were numb with dread; the conclusions seemed inescapable.

Inside a battered lifepod not far from the downed blockade runner, the recovery team also found the mangled remains of an old man, identified as Ort Wibsen. All doubt dissipated. This had been Serena's vessel.

They found more blood inside the waterlogged ship. Obviously they had put up an extraordinary fight at the end. Xavier ran full DNA scans, hoping for any result other than the one he feared most.

But the results proved that the other victims had been the Home Guard messenger Pinquer Jibb . . . and Serena Butler herself.

Serena. My love . . .

Hanging his head, Xavier tried to hold on to the unraveling

strands of hope. Perhaps the machines had only taken Serena prisoner. But that was a ridiculously unrealistic possibility . . . and given cymek and robot brutality, would that be a fate he could wish for?

No, he would have to return to Salusa Secundus and deliver the news to a distraught Manion Butler.

There could be no doubt about it: Serena must be dead.

Whether we are rich, poor, strong, weak, intelligent, or stupid, the thinking machines treat us as nothing more than meat. They do not understand what humans really are.

—IBLIS GINJO,
early planning for the Jihad

While other trustee crew bosses supervised the Forum monument projects, Iblis Ginjo received orders to process a load of arriving slaves. These captives had been freshly harvested from Giedi Prime and brought to Earth by order of Omnius. The work boss groaned inwardly, suspecting that the cymeks would want to build another enormous monument to celebrate the Giedi Prime victory, too, and his crews would have to build it. . . .

Erasmus supposedly had his eye on one female in particular, personally selected for him by the Titan Barbarossa. Iblis had read the documentation, knew that the new batch of prisoners might be an unruly lot, considering where they had been captured.

As the disheveled and disoriented slaves were herded off the space transport in dirty clothes, Iblis perused them with a trained eye, considering how to segregate them to work assignments, a few artisans, a few skilled workers, most of them mere slaves. He separated out a muscular, mahogany-skinned man for assignment to the Ajax pedestal project, smiling encouragement to him, then dispatched others to crews that required more manpower.

One of the last to emerge from the ship was a battered woman who, despite the dark bruises on her face and arms and the weary shock in her expression, carried herself with pride, showing internal strength in every movement. This was the one for Erasmus. *Trouble.*

Why would the robot be interested in her? He would probably just vivisect her anyway. A waste. And a shame.

Iblis called to her, but she ignored his gentle yet authoritative tone. Finally, with some rough encouragement from the guard robots, she stood in front of him. Though only of average height, the female had striking lavender eyes, amber-brown hair, and a face that might be pretty if cleansed of grime and anger.

He smiled warmly, trying to reach out to her with a little charm. "The records say your name is Serena Linné?" He knew full well who she was.

Iblis stared into her eyes and detected a spark of defiance there. She held his gaze, as if she were his equal. "Yes. My father was a minor official in Giedi City, moderately well-off."

"Have you ever worked as a servant before?" he inquired.

"I have always been a servant—of the people."

"From now on, you serve Omnius." He softened his voice. "I promise you, it won't be so bad. Our workers are treated well here. Especially intelligent ones like yourself. Perhaps you could even aspire to a trusted, privileged position, if you have the intelligence and the personality for it." Iblis smiled. "However, wouldn't it be best if we used your true name . . . Serena Butler?"

She glared at him. At least she didn't deny it. "How did you know?"

"After capturing you, Barbarossa inspected the wreckage of your vessel. There were many clues aboard. You are fortunate the cymeks never needed to interrogate you in further detail." He glanced at his electronic notes. "We know you are the daughter of Viceroy Manion Butler. Were you trying to hide your identity out of fear that Omnius might use you in some sort of blackmail scheme? I assure you, that isn't the way the evermind thinks. Omnius would never have considered such a thing."

She raised her chin defiantly. "My father would never surrender a centimeter of territory, no matter what the machines do to me."

"Yes, yes, you're all very brave, I am sure." Iblis gave her a wry smile, meant to be comforting. "The rest is up to the robot Erasmus. He has requested that you be assigned to his villa. He has taken a particular interest in your circumstances. That's a good sign."

"He wishes to help me?"

"I wouldn't go that far," he said with a hint of humor. "I'm sure Erasmus wants to *talk* with you. And talk and talk and talk. In the end, it's quite likely he will drive you mad with his famous curiosity."

Iblis instructed other slaves to clean and properly reclothe this female, and they followed the trustee's orders as if he were a machine himself. Although her mannerisms exuded hostility and resentment, Serena Butler did not waste effort on pointless resistance. She had a brain, but her intelligence and spirit were bound to be crushed before long.

The routine medical check, however, revealed a surprise. She glared at Iblis, trying to maintain her defensive wall of anger, but a glimmer of curiosity flickered behind her odd lavender eyes. "Are you aware that you're pregnant? Or is that just an unfortunate accident?" From the way she reeled, he saw that her reaction was not feigned. "Yes, by now it appears about three months along. You must have suspected."

"That is none of your business." Her words were hard, as if she was trying to maintain her hold on something stable. The news seemed to be a greater blow to her than all the rough treatment she had endured since capture.

Iblis made a dismissive gesture. "Every cell in your body is my business—at least until I deliver you to your new master. Afterward, I will really begin to pity you."

The independent robot would no doubt plan interesting experiments on her and the fetus. . . .

The psychology of the human animal is malleable, with his personality dependent upon the proximity of other members of the species and the pressures exerted by them.

—ERASMUS,
laboratory notes

Erasmus's villa stood as a towering edifice on a hilltop overlooking the sea. On the inland side, the main building loomed high in front of a lovely flagstone square beneath high turrets; toward the coast, a cluster of bleak, crowded slave pens huddled on the opposite side, where human captives lived like livestock.

From the highest balconies, the robot found the dichotomy curious.

Forming his metal polymer facefilm into a paternal mask, Erasmus watched as two sentinel robots strode through a slave pen, hunting for twin girls that he required for a new round of experiments. The panicked humans scrambled away, but Erasmus didn't shift his pliable face into a frown. His myriad optic threads scanned the lean and dirty forms, assessing.

He had seen the little girls a few days before, noting their short black hair and brown eyes, but they seemed to be hiding somewhere. Playing a game with him? The sentinels tore through a doorway into a tunnel that led to another pen; finally, they transmitted back, "We have located the two subjects."

Good, Erasmus thought, anticipating the intriguing work ahead. He wanted to see if he could force one of the twin girls to kill the other. It would be a landmark experiment, one that would reveal important insights into moral boundaries and how siblings defined them.

He especially enjoyed working with identical twins. Over the years he had processed dozens of pairs through his laboratory, compiling detailed medical reports as well as intensive psychological studies. He spent a great deal of effort on meticulous comparative autopsies, microanalyzing the subtle differences in siblings who were genetic carbon-copies. The slave masters working in the crowded pens had instructions to identify and select any new sets among the captive populace on Earth.

Finally, the squirming dark-haired twins stood in front of him, held by the sentinel robots. He shifted his pliable facefilm into a calm smile. One of the girls spat on the reflective surface. Erasmus wondered why saliva carried such a negative connotation for humans? It caused no damage and could be cleaned off easily. The forms of human defiance never ceased to amaze him.

Shortly before Erasmus had left his estate on Corrin, twenty-two slaves had removed their protective eye films and intentionally stared into the furious red-giant sun, blinding themselves. Disobedient, resistant—and stupid. What did the rebellious act accomplish, other than rendering them useless for slave work?

They had expected to be killed, and Erasmus would oblige them. But not so that they could become martyrs. Instead, he had quietly separated them from other workers to prevent the spread of their unruliness. Blinded, they could not find or earn food. By now, he supposed they must have starved in their self-inflicted darkness.

Still, he had marveled at their spirit, their collective will to challenge him. Even though humans were a troublesome breed, they were constantly fascinating.

A watcheye buzzed nearby, making strange, raw noises. Finally, Omnius spoke through it. "The recent loss of Giedi Prime is your fault, Erasmus. I tolerate your endless experiments in the hope that you will deconstruct and analyze human behavior. Why did you not predict the suicidal raid that obliterated my cymeks? The data and experiences of my Giedi Prime counterpart were never backed up. Barbarossa is equally irreplaceable, since he created my original programming."

The Earth-Omnius already knew about the recapture of Giedi Prime because of an automated emergency buoy launched by the robot Seurat, whose update ship had unexpectedly encountered the disaster in its duties. The alarming message had reached Earth only that morning.

"I was not given data that the Sorceresses of Rossak had developed this capability of telepathic destruction." The robot's face shimmered back into its blank oval smoothness. "Why not also ask your questions of Vorian Atreides when he returns to Earth? The son of Agamemnon has helped us to simulate unstable human behavior before."

Omnius said, "Even his input could not have prepared us for what happened to Giedi Prime. Sentient biologicals are unpredictable and reckless."

As the sentinel robots dragged the squirming twins away, Erasmus directed his attention to the watcheye. "Then it is obvious I have more work to do."

"No, Erasmus, it is obvious that your research is not yielding the desired results. You should strive for perfection, rather than investigating compounded errors. I recommend that you overwrite your mind core with a subset of my program. Turn yourself into a perfect machine. A copy of me."

"You would sacrifice our fascinating, open-ended debates?" Erasmus responded, fighting to conceal his inner alarm. "You have always expressed an interest in my peculiar manner of thinking. All the everminds especially look forward to your record of my actions."

The buzzing of the watcheye intensified, indicating that Omnius was shifting his thought pathways. This was a worrisome, volatile situation. Erasmus did not want to lose his carefully developed independent identity.

One of the twin girls tried to break away from the robotic guards and run back toward the dubious safety of the pens. As Erasmus had suggested beforehand, the guard lifted her sister by one arm, leaving her to dangle screaming. The free twin hesitated, though she could easily have reached the temporary shelter. Slowly, she came to a stop, surrendering.

Fascinating, Erasmus thought. And the sentinel robot did not even have to inflict cellular damage on the other girl.

Thinking quickly, the robot said, "Perhaps if I diverted my attention to matters of military significance, you would more easily see the potential of my work. Let me understand the mentality of these wild humans for you. What drives them to such self-sacrifice, as we witnessed on Giedi Prime? If I can distill an explanation, your Synchronized Worlds will no longer be vulnerable to unpredictable attacks."

The watcheye hovered as a million possibilities showered through the abundant mind of Omnius. Presently, the computer made his decision. "You have my permission to proceed. But do not continue to test my patience."

People require continuity.

—BOVKO MANRESA,
First Viceroy of the League of Nobles

On Poritrin, the virulent fever raced through the mudflats and docks where slaves made their dreary homes. Despite the best quarantine and mitigation efforts, the disease killed a number of officials and merchants, and even spread as far as the slaves in Tio Holtzman's blufftop laboratories, where it caused quite a disruption in the scientist's work.

When Holtzman first noticed symptoms of the illness among his crowded equation solvers, he immediately ordered removal of the sick ones to isolation chambers and sealed off the remainder of the calculating teams. The distracted Savant thought the slaves would rejoice at being relieved of their mathematical chores; instead the solvers moaned and prayed, asking why the hand of God would strike *them* rather than their oppressors.

Within two weeks, half of his household slaves had either died or been quarantined. Such a shift in daily routines was not conducive to the Savant's mental work.

Several large-scale simulations had been under way, following the gradual development of parameters established by the talented Norma Cenva. Groaning at the inconvenience, Holtzman knew that stopping the lengthy work in midstream would necessitate new teams to start over again. To maintain his stature, he needed a major breakthrough soon.

Lately his reputation had been supported more by Norma's work than his own. Naturally, he had taken full credit for modifying the scrambler-field generators into an offensive weapon. Lord Bludd had delighted in presenting two prototypes to the Armada liberation force for Giedi Prime. Indeed, the scrambler projectors had served the rescuers well, but the prototypes had consumed enough energy to ground two troop transports, and the devices themselves had broken down—irreparably—after only one use. In addition, the disruptive pulse had yielded uneven results, since many robots had been shielded by walls or unaffected by the dissipating field. Still, the idea showed promise, and the nobles urged Holtzman to work on improvements, without ever knowing about Norma's involvement.

At least Holtzman's reputation was secure again. For a while.

Norma was quiet but diligent. Rarely interested in diversions or amusements, she worked hard and scrutinized her own ideas. Despite Holtzman's wishes, she insisted on performing most calculations personally rather than handing them off to solver teams. Norma was too independent to understand the economics of delegating tasks. Her dedication made her a rather dull person.

After rescuing the young prodigy from her obscurity on Rossak, he had hoped, unrealistically perhaps, that Norma might provide him with sudden inspiration. During a recent cocktail party in Lord Bludd's conical towers, the nobleman had made a joke about Holtzman taking a holiday from his usual brilliance. Though the comment had stung, the inventor had laughed along with the other tittering nobles. Still, it highlighted—in his own mind, at least—that he had not created anything really original in some time.

Following a restless night of bizarre dreams, Holtzman finally came up with a concept to explore. Expanding some of the electromagnetic features he had used for his scrambler fields, he might be able to create an "alloy resonance generator." Properly tuned, a thermal-field inducer would couple with metals—the bodies of robots, for instance, or even the crablike warrior-forms worn by cymeks. Given the correct adjustment, the resonance generator could slam selected metal atoms against each other, generating enormous heat until the machine shook itself apart.

The concept seemed promising. Holtzman intended to pursue its development with full enthusiasm and haste.

But first he needed more solvers and assistants to construct the prototype. And now he had to waste a day on the mundane task of replacing the household slaves that had died from the fever. With a frustrated sigh, he left his laboratories and trudged down the zigzag trail to the base of the bluffs, where he caught a jetboat across the river.

On the opposite shore, at the widest part of the delta, he visited a bustling river market. Rafts and barges had been lashed together for so long that they might well have been part of the landscape. The merchants' quarter was not far from the Starda spaceport, where vendors provided offworld oddities: drugs from Rossak, interesting woods and plants from Ecaz, gems from Hagal, musical instruments from Chusuk.

In shops that fronted a narrow alley, tailors were copying the latest Salusan fashions, cutting and sewing exotic imported cloths and fine Poritrin linens. Holtzman had used many of these garment makers to enhance his personal wardrobe. An eminent Savant such as himself could not spend all of his time in the laboratories. After all, he was frequently called upon to make public appearances to answer questions from citizens and often spoke before committees of nobles, to convince them of his continued importance.

But today Holtzman made his way farther out onto the floating rafts and barges. He needed to purchase people, not clothes. The scientist saw a sign on the dock ahead, in Galach: HUMAN RESOURCES. He crossed creaking boardwalks and gangplanks to a cluster of rafts that held captives. Grouped in lots behind barricades, the sullen prisoners were dressed in drab, identical uniforms, many of which fit badly. The slaves were lean and angular, as if unaccustomed to eating regular meals. These men and women came from planets that few of the free citizens of Poritrin had ever heard of, much less visited.

Their handlers seemed aloof, not particularly eager to show off wares or haggle over prices. After the recent plague, many households and estates needed to replace their personnel, and it was a sellers' market.

Other customers crowded against the railings, scrutinizing the downcast faces, inspecting the merchandise. One old man clutching a wad of credits summoned the tender and asked for a closer look at four middle-aged females.

Holtzman was not particularly picky, nor did he want to waste time. Since he needed so many slaves, he intended to buy an entire lot. Once they arrived at his blufftop estate, he would choose the most intelligent ones to work calculations, while the remainder would cook, clean, or maintain his household.

He hated these menial shopping duties, but had never delegated them in the past. He smiled, realizing he had been critical of Norma for doing the very same thing, for her failure to use solvers.

Impatient and eager, Holtzman summoned the nearest handler, waving Niko Bludd's credit authorization and pushing himself to the front. "I want a large order of slaves."

The Human Resources merchant bustled over, grinning and bowing. "Of course, Savant Holtzman! What you require, I shall provide. Simply specify your needs, and I will provide a competitive quotation."

Suspicious that the merchant might try to cheat him, he said, "I need slaves that are smart and independent, but capable of following instructions. Seventy or eighty will do, I suppose." Some of the customers pushing close to the railing grumbled, but did not challenge the celebrity inventor.

"Quite a demand," the vendor said, "especially in these lean times. The plague has created a shortage, until the Tlulaxa flesh merchants deliver more."

"Everyone knows how important—and *essential*—my work is," Holtzman said, pointedly removing a chronometer from the wide sleeve of his white robe. "My needs take precedence over some rich citizen looking to replace a house cleaner. If you like, I will obtain a special dispensation from Lord Bludd."

"I know you can do that, Savant," said the slave tender. He shouted at the other customers pushing forward. "All of you, quit your complaining! Without this man, we'd be sweeping the floors for thinking machines right now!" Putting on another face, the handler smiled back at Holtzman. "The question, of course, is which slaves would best serve you? I have a new batch just delivered from Harmonthep: Zensunnis, all of them. Suitably docile, but I'm afraid they go for a premium."

Holtzman frowned. He preferred to use his finances in other ways, especially considering the large investment that would be necessary for his new alloy-resonator concept. "Do not attempt to take advantage of me, sir."

The man reddened, but held his ground, sensing that the inventor was in a hurry. "Perhaps another group would be more suitable then? I have some just in from IV Anbus." He gestured to a separate raft where dark-haired slaves stared out with hostile expressions, challenging the customers. "They are Zenshiites."

"What's the difference? Are they less expensive?"

"A simple matter of religious philosophy." The slave merchant waited for some recognition, didn't see it, then smiled with relief. "Who can understand the Buddislamics, anyway? They're workers, and that's what you need, right? I can sell you these Zenshiites for a lower price, even though they're quite intelligent. Probably better educated than the Harmonthep lot. They're healthy, too. I have medical certifications. Not one of them has been exposed to the plague virus."

Holtzman perused the group. They all had rolled up their left sleeves, as if it were some kind of badge. Up front, a muscular man with fiery eyes and a thick black beard gazed back at him dispassionately, as if he considered himself superior to those who held him captive.

With his cursory inspection, Holtzman could see nothing wrong with the IV Anbus captives. His household was desperately understaffed, and his laboratories needed more low-level technicians. Every day it was a struggle to find enough solvers to work through the increasingly complex sets of equations.

"But why are they cheaper?" he persisted.

"They are more plentiful. It's a simple matter of supply and demand." The slave vendor held his gaze. He named a price.

Too impatient to haggle for the best deal, Holtzman nodded. "I'll take eighty of them." He raised his voice. "I don't care if they're from IV Anbus or Harmonthep. They're on Poritrin now, and they work for Savant Tio Holtzman."

The crafty slave merchant turned to the group of captives and shouted. "You hear that? You should be proud."

The dark-haired captives simply looked back at their new master, saying nothing. Holtzman was relieved. That probably meant they would be more tractable.

He transferred the correct amount of credits. "See that they are cleaned up and sent to my residence."

The grinning slave handler thanked him profusely. "Don't you worry, Savant Holtzman. You'll be satisfied with this lot."

As the great man left the crowded river market, other customers began to shout and wave their credit vouchers, squabbling over the remaining slaves. It promised to be a furious day of bidding.

Over the course of history, the stronger species invariably wins.

—TLALOC,
A Time for Titans

After taking refuge in the Arrakis wasteland, the Zensunni Wanderers were little more than scavengers, and not very brave. Even on their most distant excursions to collect useful items, the nomads remained close to the rocks, avoiding the deep desert and the demon worms.

Long ago, after the Imperial chemist Shakkad the Wise had remarked on the rejuvenating properties of the obscure spice melange, there had been a small market for the natural substance among offworlders at the Arrakis City spaceport. However, the planet's distance from popular spacing lanes had never made melange an economically attractive item. "An oddity, not a commodity," one surly merchant had told Naib Dhartha. Still, spice was a staple in the food supply, and it must be gathered . . . but only on sands close to the rocks.

Dhartha led a party of six across a ridge of packed powder sand that held their footprints as if they were kisses in the dust. Loose white cloths around their heads and faces exposed only their eyes; their cloaks blew in the breeze, revealing equipment belts, tools, and weapons. Dhartha snugged the cloth higher over his nose to keep from breathing grit. He scratched the tattoo etched so painstakingly onto his cheek, then narrowed his eyes, always alert for danger.

No one thought to watch the clear morning skies until they heard a faint whistle growing quickly into a howl. To Naib Dhartha, it sounded like a woman who had just learned of her husband's death.

Looking up, he saw a silvery bullet that tore through the atmosphere, then recognized the unexpected hum and whine of thrusters. A bubble-shaped object plummeted through the sky, spun about and see-sawed in the open air as if choosing a place to land. Quad engines slowed its descent. Then, less than a kilometer from where the scavenging party stood, the object slammed into the dunes like a fist thumping into the stomach of a dishonest merchant. A spray of dust and sand shot upward, embracing a tendril of dark soot.

The Naib stood stiffly and stared, while his men began to jabber excitedly. Young Ebrahim was as enthralled as Dhartha's own son, Mahmad; both boys wanted to race out and investigate.

Mahmad was a good lad, respectful and cautious. But Dhartha had a low opinion of Ebrahim, who liked to tell stories and talk of imaginary exploits. Then there was the incident in which tribal water had been stolen, an unforgivable crime. Initially the Naib had thought two boys were involved, Ebrahim and Selim. But Ebrahim had been quick to disavow any responsibility and to point the finger at the other boy. Selim had seemed shocked at the accusation, but had not denied it.

In addition, Ebrahim's father had stepped forward to make a generous deal with Dhartha to save his son . . . and so the orphan boy had received the ultimate sentence of banishment. Not much of a loss to the tribe. A Naib often had to make such difficult decisions.

Now, as the scavengers looked at Dhartha, their bright eyes glinting between folds of dirty white cloth, he knew he could not ignore the opportunity of this crashed ship, whatever it was. "We must go see this thing," he called.

His men rushed across the sands, boisterous Ebrahim and Mahmad in the lead, hurrying toward the pillar of dust that marked the impact. Dhartha did not like to stray far from the sheltering rock, but the desert beckoned them toward a rich, alien treasure.

The nomads crested one dune, slid down the slipface, and scurried up another. By the time they reached the impact crater, they were all winded, panting hot breaths that were smothered by the cloths over their mouths. The Naib and his men stood on the high lip of excavated sand. Glassy smears of superheated silica had splattered like saliva on the ground.

Inside the pit lay a mechanical object the size of two men, with protrusions and components that hummed and moved, awakening now that it had landed. The carbon fiber-encased body still smoked from the heat of reentry. A spacecraft, perhaps?

One of Dhartha's men stepped back, making a warding sign with his fingers. Overzealous Ebrahim, though, bent forward. The Naib put a hand on Mahmad's left arm, cautioning his son. Let the foolish one take the risks.

The crashed pod was too small to carry passengers. The lights blinked brighter, and the probe's sides opened like dragon wings to expose mechanical limbs, articulated claws, and complex machinery inside. Scanners, processors, engines of investigation and destruction. Mirrorlike power converters spread out in the glare of the sun.

Ebrahim slid down the churned sand at the edge of the pit. "Imagine what this would be worth at the spaceport, Naib! If I get to it first, I should receive the largest salvage share."

Dhartha wanted to argue with the exuberant youth, but when he saw that no one—except for his own son—looked eager to join Ebrahim, he nodded. "If successful, you'll get an extra share." Even if the falling object was completely ruined, the nomads could work the pure metal for their own purposes.

The brash young man stopped halfway down the loose slope, looking suspiciously at the device, which continued to vibrate and thump. Flexible components extruded arms and legs, while strange lenses and mirrors rotated at the ends of flexible carbon fiber tentacles. The probe seemed to be assessing its surroundings, as if it didn't comprehend where it had landed.

The machine paid no attention to the surreptitious humans, until Ebrahim dug a stone from the slumping side of the crater. He called out "Ai! Ai!" then hurled the rock. It struck the composite material of the probe's side with an echoing *clunk*.

The mechanical lander froze, then turned its lenses and scanners toward the human standing all alone. Ebrahim hunched on bent knees in the yielding sand.

Blinding hot light erupted from one of the lenses. A gout of coherent fire engulfed Ebrahim and blew him backward in a crackling cloud of incinerated flesh and bones. A wad of smoldering garments struck the top of the crater, along with charred pieces of his hands and feet.

Mahmad screamed for his friend, and Dhartha immediately yelled for the men to retreat. They stumbled back down the outside of the crater and fled through the soft gully between dunes. Half a kilometer away, safe, they climbed to a sandy crest high enough that they could look back toward the pit. The men prayed and made superstitious gestures, and Dhartha raised his clenched right fist. Foolish Ebrahim had drawn the attention of the mechanical thing and had paid with his life.

From a distance, the would-be scavengers watched. The crashed probe paid them no further heed. Instead, with thumping and clattering, the machine seemed to be assembling itself, building structures around its core. Scooping hands drew sand into a resource-production hopper in its belly and extruded glasslike rods that it used for structural supports. The machine added new components, building itself larger, and finally began digging its way out of the pit. It pounded and hammered, making a great deal of racket.

Dhartha remained perplexed. Though he was a leader, he had no idea what to do. Such a thing was beyond his ken. Perhaps someone at the spaceport would know, but he hated to rely on outworlders. Besides, this thing might be valuable, and he didn't want to surrender his salvage.

"Father, look." Mahmad gestured toward the wasteland of

sand. "See, that machine demon will pay for killing my friend."

Dhartha saw the telltale ripple, the stirring of a behemoth beneath the sands. The crashed probe continued its pounding, rhythmic motion with a clattering of components, oblivious to its surroundings. The assembled mechanism raised itself, a monstrous composite of crystalline materials and silica struts reinforced by carbon-fiber beams converted from its own hull and support girders.

The sandworm came in fast, tunneling just beneath the surface until its head rose up. The mouth was a huge shovel larger than the impact crater.

The robotic probe waved its sensor arms and weapons lenses, sensing it was being attacked, but not understanding how. Several white-hot blasts of fire penetrated the loose ground.

The worm swallowed the mechanical demon whole. Then the sinuous desert creature burrowed beneath the dust again like a sea serpent seeking deeper waters. . . .

Naib Dhartha and his men remained petrified on the dunes. If they turned and ran now, their vibrations would call the sandworm back for another meal.

Soon enough, they saw the worm trail heading outward, returning to the deep desert. The crater was gone, along with all evidence of the mechanical construction. Not even a scrap of foolish Ebrahim's body remained.

Shaking his head with its long black ponytail, Dhartha turned to his shocked companions. "This will make a legendary story, a magnificent ballad to be sung in our caves in the dark of night. . . ." He drew a deep breath and turned around. "Though I doubt anyone will ever believe us."

The future? I hate it because I will not be there.

—JUNO,
Lives of the Titans

After the unexpected encounter with the League Armada at Giedi Prime, the battered *Dream Voyager* took an extra month to limp back to Earth for repairs. Because of the slow pace caused by the damage, Seurat had immediately dispatched his emergency buoy, relaying to Omnius the dire news of the fall of the newest Synchronized World and the loss of the Titan Barbarossa. By now the evermind must know what had happened.

The robot captain did his best to repair or bypass the ship's damaged systems and seal off sections to protect his fragile human copilot. General Agamemnon would not be pleased if his biological son were injured. Besides, Seurat had developed a certain fondness for Vorian Atreides. . . .

Vor insisted on donning an environment suit and crawling outside the update ship to inspect the hull. Seurat tethered him with two lines, while three inspector drones accompanied him. When the young man saw the blackened wound where the rebellious humans had fired upon them, he once again felt a sense of shame. Intent only on delivering the vital Omnius updates, Seurat had committed no aggressive act against these *hrethgir*, yet they had attacked him. Wild humans were without honor.

Agamemnon and his friend Barbarossa had brought the unruly populace of Giedi Prime into the sweeping embrace of Omnius, yet the *hrethgir* had spurned the greater civilization of the Synchronized Worlds, making a martyr of Barbarossa in the process. His father would be deeply disturbed at the loss of such a close friend, one of the last remaining Titans.

Vor himself could have been killed, his soft and breakable human form destroyed without ever having the chance to become a neo-cymek. A single blow from the Armada could have erased all of Vor's potential, all of his future work. He could not update himself or back up his memories and experiences, as a machine could. He'd be lost, just like the Giedi Prime–Omnius. Just like the other twelve sons of Agamemnon. The thought sickened him, and he shuddered.

On their return journey, Seurat tried to cheer Vor with ridiculous jokes, as if nothing had happened. The robot commended his companion for quick thinking and tactical innovation in outwitting the *hrethgir* officer. Vor's deceit in pretending to be a rebellious human who had captured a thinking-machine vessel—what an outré scenario!—had given them a few moments of valuable time, and his decoy projections had allowed them to escape. Perhaps it would even be taught to others in the trustee schools on Earth.

Vor, however, cared most about what his father might say. The approval of the great Agamemnon would make everything all right.

⟨⟩

WHEN THE *DREAM VOYAGER* landed at Earth's central spaceport, Vorian hurried down the ramp, eyes alert, face eager—then crestfallen when he saw no sign of the Titan general.

Vor swallowed hard. Unless vital matters intervened, his

father always came to greet him. These were rare moments they had together, when they could exchange ideas, talk about plans and dreams. Vor comforted himself with the thought that Agamemnon probably had important business for Omnius.

Robotic maintenance crews and repair machinery trundled forward to inspect the damaged ship. One of the multicomponent machines paused in its assessment, broke away, and hummed toward him. "Vorian Atreides, Agamemnon has commanded you to meet him in the conditioning facility. Report there immediately."

The young human brightened. Letting the robot return to its work, he walked off briskly. When he could contain himself no longer, he began to run. . . .

Though he attempted to exercise during the long voyages with Seurat, Vor's biological muscles were weaker than a machine's, and he tired quickly. Another reminder of his mortality, his fragility, and the inferiority of natural biology. It only increased his desire to wear a powerful neo-cymek body someday and discard this imperfect human form.

His lungs burning, Vor rushed into the gleaming chrome-and-plaz chamber where his father's brain canister was regularly polished and recharged with electrafluid. As soon as the young man entered the cold, well-lit room, two robot guards folded in behind him, ominously blocking egress. In the center of the chamber stood a mechanical, human-shaped colossus that Agamemnon now wore. The behemoth took two steps forward, stabilizer-feet hammering against the hard floor. He dwarfed his son, towering three times Vorian's height.

"I have been waiting for you, my son. Everything is prepared. What caused your delay?"

Intimidated, Vor looked up at the preservation canister. "I hurried here, Father. My ship landed only an hour ago."

"I understand the *Dream Voyager* was damaged at Giedi Prime, attacked by the human rebels that murdered Barbarossa and recaptured the world."

"Yes, sir." Vor knew better than to waste the Titan's time with unnecessary details. The general would already have received a full report. "I will answer any questions you might have, Father."

"I have no questions, only *commands*." Instead of instructing his son to begin the process of grooming and polishing his components, Agamemnon raised a gauntleted hand, clutched Vorian by the chest, and pushed him forcefully against an upright table.

Vor was slammed against the smooth surface and felt a burst of pain. His father was so powerful that he could accidentally break bones, sever the spine. "What is it, Father? What—"

Holding him immobile, Agamemnon clamped on wrist bindings, a waist restraint, and ankle cuffs. Helpless now, Vor twisted his head to look at what his father was doing and saw that complex devices had been brought into the chamber. With trepidation he noted hollow cylinders filled with bluish fluids, neuromechanical pumps, and chittering machines that waved questing sensor tips in the air.

"Please, Father." Vor's deepest fears careened through his mind, ricocheting off the pain, each impact increasing his doubts and terrors. "What have I done wrong?"

Showing no readable expression on his head turret, Agamemnon extended an array of long needles toward his son's squirming body. The steel points penetrated his chest, poking between his ribs, seeking out and finding his lungs, his heart. Two silver shafts pierced his throat. Blood oozed out everywhere. Vor's neck sinews bulged as he clenched his jaw and curled back his lips, biting back a scream.

But the scream broke through anyway.

The cymek manipulated the machinery connected to Vorian's body, increasing the pain beyond all imaginable levels. Convinced that he had failed somehow, Vor assumed it was his time to die—like the twelve unknown brothers who had preceded him. Now, it seemed, Vorian had not lived up to Agamemnon's expectations.

Agony swelled higher, with no crest in sight. His scream became a prolonged wail, as acid-colored fluids were pumped into his body. Soon even his vocal cords gave out, and his

shriek continued only in his mind . . . yet it continued nevertheless. He could endure no more. He could not imagine the
grievous injury his stretched and torn body must already have
endured.

When finally the torture concluded and Vor came back to
himself, he didn't know how long he had been unconscious—
perhaps even lost in the cloak of death. His body felt as if it
had been crushed into a ball and then stretched back into the
form of a man.

The colossus shape of Agamemnon loomed over him, a galaxy of optic threads glittering on his body. Even though the
remnants of excruciating pain echoed inside his skull, Vor resisted crying out. His father had kept him alive after all, for
his own reasons. He stared into the Titan's implacable metal
face and could only hope that his father had not revived him
just to inflict more agony.

What have I done wrong?

Yet the ancient cymek did not have murder on his mind.
Instead he said, "I am exceedingly pleased with your actions
aboard the *Dream Voyager*, Vorian. I have analyzed Seurat's
report and determined that your tactical prowess in escaping
from the League Armada was innovative and unexpected."

Vorian couldn't understand the context of his father's
words. They seemed unrelated to the tortures the general had
inflicted on him.

"No thinking machine would have considered such a deceitful trick. I doubt even another trustee would have been so
quick to think of the ruse. In fact, Omnius's summation con-
cludes that any other action would likely have resulted in the
capture or destruction of the *Dream Voyager*. Seurat would
never have been capable of surviving by himself. You not only
saved the ship, you saved the Omnius update spheres and returned them intact." Agamemnon paused, then reiterated.
"Yes, I am exceedingly pleased, my son. You have the potential of becoming a great cymek someday."

Vor's raw throat convulsed as he tried to force out words.
The needle-studded cradle had been yanked away, and now
Agamemnon released the body restraints that held him against

the hard surface. Vorian's watery muscles could not support him, and he drooped like a rag, sliding down until he pooled on his knees on the floor. Finally he choked, "Then why was I tortured? Why have you punished me?"

Agamemnon simulated a laugh. "When I choose to punish you, son, you will know. That was a *reward*. Omnius allowed me to grant you this rare gift. In fact, no other human in all the Synchronized Worlds has been so honored."

"But how, Father? Please explain it to me. My mind is still throbbing." His voice hitched.

"What are a few moments of pain, in comparison with the gift you have received?" The colossus paced back and forth across the sparkling maintenance room, shaking the floor and the walls. "Unfortunately, I was unable to convince Omnius to convert you into a neo-cymek—you are too young—but I am sure the time will come. I wanted you to serve at my side—more than a trustee, but as my true successor." His sparkling optic threads glowed brighter. "Instead, I have done the next best thing for you."

The cymek general explained that he had given Vorian a rigorous biotech treatment, a cellular replacement system that would dramatically extend his life as a human. "Geriatric specialists developed the technique in the Old Empire . . . though to what purpose I cannot fathom. Those oafs did nothing productive during their normal lifespans, so why should they want to live for centuries longer and accomplish even less? Through new proteins, rejection of free radicals, more efficient cellular repair mechanisms, they prolonged their pointless existences. Most of them were murdered in the rebellions when we Titans cemented our control."

Agamemnon swiveled at his torso joint. "While we still wore human bodies at the beginning of our rule, all twenty Titans underwent the biotech life extension, just like you, so I am quite familiar with the level of pain you endured. We *needed* to live for centuries, because we required that much time to reassert vision and competent leadership upon the waning Old Empire. Even after we converted ourselves into cymeks, the process helped prevent our ancient biological brains from degenerating because of our extreme age."

His mechanical body strode closer. "This life-extension process is our little secret, Vorian. The League of Nobles would tear themselves into a frenzy if they knew we had such technology." Agamemnon made a wistful sound, almost a sigh. "But beware, my son: Even such enhancements cannot protect you against accidents or outright assassination attempts. As, unfortunately, Barbarossa recently discovered."

Vor finally struggled shakily to his feet. He located a water dispenser, gulped a beaker of cool liquid, and felt his heartbeat slowing.

"Astonishing events await you, my son. Your life is no longer a candle in the wind. You have time to experience many things, important things."

The hulking cymek stalked over to a harness and used an intricate network of artificial hands and clamps extruded from the metal wall to link to the thoughtrodes of his brain canister. Flexible lifting arms raised the cylinder out of the colossus body core and shuttled it over to one of the chrome pedestals.

"Now you are one step closer to your potential, Vorian," Agamemnon said through a wall speaker, detached from the mobile body.

Though weak and still in pain, Vor knew what his father expected of him now. He hurried to the conditioning devices and with trembling hands attached power cables to the mag-sockets of the translucent brain chamber. The bluish electra-fluid seemed full of mental energy.

Trying to restore a sense of normalcy amid the clamoring disbelief at what had just happened to him, Vor went through his habitual grooming duties, tending his father's mechanical systems. Lovingly, the young man gazed at the wrinkled mass of brain, the ancient mind so full of profound ideas and difficult decisions, as expressed in the general's extensive memoirs. Each time he read them, Vor hoped to understand his complex father better.

He wondered if Agamemnon had kept him in the dark to play a cruel joke on him, or to challenge his resolve. Vor would always accept whatever the cymek general commanded, would never try to flee. Now that the agony was over, he hoped he had passed whatever test his father had administered.

As Vor continued the patient grooming of the preservation tank, Agamemnon spoke softly, a susurration. "You are very quiet, my son. What do you think about the great gift you have received?"

The young man paused a moment, not certain how to respond. Agamemnon was often impulsive and difficult to understand, but he rarely acted without a larger purpose in mind. Vor could only hope to comprehend the overall picture someday, the grand tapestry.

"Thank you, Father," he finally said, "for giving me more time to accomplish everything you want me to do."

Why do humans spend so much time worrying about what they call "moral issues"? It is one of the many mysteries of their behavior.

—ERASMUS,
Reflections on Sentient Biologicals

The identical twin girls looked peaceful and asleep, side by side, like little angels in a cozy bed. The snakelike brain scanners inserted through holes drilled into their skulls were almost unnoticeable.

Immobilized by drugs, the unconscious children lay on a laboratory table inside the experimental zone. Erasmus's mirror-smooth face reshaped itself into an exaggerated frown, as if the severity of his expression could force them to reveal their secrets about humanity.

Damn you!

He could not comprehend these intelligent creatures that had somehow created Omnius and an amazing civilization of thinking machines. Was it a miraculous fluke? The more Erasmus learned, the more questions he developed. The inarguable successes of their chaotic civilization presented a deep quandary in his mind. He had dissected the brains of more than a thousand specimens, young and old, male and female, intelligent and dimwitted. He had made detailed analyses and comparisons, processing data through the unlimited capacity of the Omnius evermind.

Even so, none of the answers were clear.

The brains of no two human beings were exactly identical, not even when the subjects were raised under matching conditions, or if they started out as twins. *A confusing mass of unnecessary variables!* No aspect of their physiology remained consistent from person to person.

Maddening exceptions, everywhere!

Nonetheless, Erasmus did notice patterns. Humans were full of differences and surprises, but as a species they behaved according to general rules. Under certain conditions, especially when crowded into confined spaces, people reacted with a pack mentality, blindly following others, eschewing individuality.

Sometimes humans were valiant; sometimes they were cowards. It especially intrigued Erasmus to see what happened when he conducted "panic experiments" on crowds of them in the breeding pens, wading in and butchering some while letting others survive. In such circumstances of extreme stress, leaders invariably emerged, people who behaved with more inner strength than the others. Erasmus especially liked to kill those individuals and then watch the devastating effect it had on the rest of the people.

Perhaps his sample group of experimental subjects over the centuries was too small. He might need to vivisect and dissect tens of thousands more before he could draw meaningful conclusions. A monumental task, but as a machine Erasmus had no limitations on energy, or patience.

With one of his personal probes, he touched the cheek of the larger of the two girls and sensed her steady pulse. Every droplet of blood seemed to withhold secrets from him, as if the entire race was participating in a massive conspiracy against him. Would Erasmus be considered the ultimate fool of all time? The fibrous probe glided back into access channels in his composite skin, but not before he intentionally, petulantly, scratched her skin.

When the independent robot had taken these identical twins

from the worker pens, their mother had cursed at him and called him a monster. Humans could be so parochial, failing to see the importance of what he was doing, the larger picture.

With a self-cauterizing scalpel-beam, he cut into the cerebellum of the smaller girl (who was 1.09 centimeters shorter and 0.7 kilograms lighter—therefore, not "identical" at all), and watched the brain activity of her drugged sister go wild—a sympathetic reaction. Fascinating. But the girls were not physically connected to each other, not through body contact nor by machine. Could they sense one another's pain?

He chided himself for his lack of foresight and planning. *I should have put the mother on the same table.*

His thoughts were interrupted by Omnius, who spoke from the nearest wallscreen. "Your new female slave has arrived, a last gift from the Titan Barbarossa. She awaits you in the sitting room."

Erasmus raised his bloody metal hands. He had looked forward to receiving the woman captured from Giedi Prime, supposedly the daughter of the League Viceroy. Her familial ties suggested genetic superiority, and he had many questions to ask her about the government of the feral humans.

"Will you vivisect her as well?"

"I prefer to keep my options open."

Erasmus looked down at the twin girls, one already dead from the interrupted exposure of her brain tissue. A wasted opportunity.

"Analyzing docile slaves gives you irrelevant results, Erasmus. All thoughts of revolt have been bred out of them. Therefore, any information you derive is of questionable applicability for military purposes." The evermind's voice boomed from the wallscreen.

Erasmus soaked his organic-plastic hands in solvent to eliminate the drying blood. He had access to thousands of years of human-compiled psychological studies, but even with so much data it was not possible to create a clear answer. Many self-proclaimed "experts" offered wildly disparate answers.

On the table, the surviving twin continued to mewl her pain and fear. "I disagree, Omnius. The human creature is innately rebellious. The trait is inherent in their species. Slaves will never be entirely loyal to us, no matter how many generations they have served. Trustees, workers, it makes no difference."

"You overestimate the strength of their will." The evermind sounded smugly confident.

"And I challenge your flawed assumptions." His curiosity piqued, sure of his private understanding, Erasmus stood before the swirling screen. "Given time and adequate provocation, I could turn any completely loyal worker against us, even the most privileged trustee."

With a long litany of data from his storehouse of information, Omnius disputed this. The evermind was confident that his slaves would remain dependable, though perhaps he had been overly complacent, overly lenient. He wanted the universe to run smoothly and efficiently, and did not like the surprises and unpredictability of League humans.

Omnius and Erasmus debated with growing intensity until the independent robot finally put a stop to it. "Both of us are making conjectures based upon preconceived notions. Therefore, I propose an experiment to determine the correct answer. You select a random group of individuals who appear to be loyal, and I will demonstrate that I can turn them against the thinking machines."

"What will that accomplish?"

Erasmus replied, "It will prove that even our most reliable humans can never be fully trusted. It is a fundamental flaw in their biological programming. Would that not be useful information?"

"Yes. And if your assertion is correct, Erasmus, then I can never again trust my own slaves. Such a result would call for a preemptive extermination of the entire human race."

Erasmus felt uneasy, that he might have trapped himself by his own logic. "That . . . may not be the only reasonable conclusion." He'd wanted to know the answer to a rhetorical question, but also feared it. For the inquisitive robot, this was much more than a mere wager with his superior; it was an investigation into the deepest motivations and decision-making processes of human beings.

But the consequences of discovering the answers could be terrible. He needed to win the argument, but in such a manner that Omnius did not shut down his experiments.

"Let me ponder the mechanics of implementation," Erasmus suggested, then gladly emerged from the laboratory to go meet his new female house slave, Serena Butler.

The universe is a playground of improvisation—it follows no external pattern.

—COGITOR RETICULUS,
Observations from a Height of a Thousand Years

Numbers and concepts danced in her dreams, but every time Norma Cenva tried to manipulate them, they slipped away like snowflakes melting on her fingers. Staggering into her laboratory, haggard, she stared at equations for hours until they became blurred lines before her eyes. She erased part of a proof with an angry swipe across the magnetic board, then began again.

Now that she worked under the auspices of the legendary Holtzman, Norma no longer felt like a failure, a misshapen disappointment to her mother. With telepathic powers, a Sorceress had struck successfully against the thinking machines on Giedi Prime. But Norma's field-portable scramblers had also been a part of the victory, though Savant Holtzman had not emphasized her role in the generation of the idea.

Norma cared nothing for fame or credit. More important was her contribution to the war effort. If she could only derive some meaning from these wandering, infinitely promising theories. . . .

From the high blufftop labs, Norma could daydream while staring at the Isana River. Sometimes she missed Aurelius Venport, who always treated her with such care and kindness. Mostly, though, she pondered wild ideas, the more unusual the better. On Rossak, her mother had never encouraged her to consider impractical possibilities, but here Tio Holtzman welcomed them.

Even though self-aware computers were forbidden on the League Worlds, and most especially on bucolic Poritrin, Norma still spent much of her time attempting to learn nuances of how those complex gelcircuits worked. *In order to destroy, one must first understand the target.*

She and Holtzman occasionally had dinner together, chatting over ideas as they sipped imported wines and savored exotic dishes. Barely tasting the food, Norma spoke with intensity, moving her small hands, wishing she had a stylus and a marking pad at the dining table so she could sketch out concepts. She finished her meals quickly and wanted to hurry back to her rooms, while the great inventor would sit back over a rich dessert and listen to music. "Recharging my mind," he called it.

Holtzman liked to engage her with tangential subjects, talking about his previous successes and accolades, reading proclamations and awards that Lord Bludd had given him. Unfortunately, none of those conversations had led to engineering breakthroughs, as far as Norma could determine.

Now she stood with lights glimmering all around her. She looked at a suspended crystal slate the size of a large window. It was coated with a thin film of flowing translucence that retained every stroke as she scribed her thoughts and notations. An old-fashioned device, but Norma considered it the best way to record her wandering ideas.

She stared at the equation she had written, skipping steps and making intuitive leaps until she arrived at a quantum anomaly that seemed to allow an object to be in two places at once. One was merely an image of the other, yet through no calculational proof could an observer determine which one was real.

Though uncertain how this unorthodox concept might be used as a weapon, Norma remembered her mentor's admonishment to follow every path to its logical conclusion. Armed with equations and ready for a full simulation, she hurried down the glowstrip-illuminated laboratory corridors, until she reached the room full of surviving solvers.

Slave technicians hunched over their tables and used calculation devices, even at this late hour. Many seats remained empty, fully a third of the solvers having succumbed to the deadly fever. Holtzman had acquired a new group of Zenshiite workers from Poritrin's "Human Resources" quarter, but those replacements were not yet sufficiently trained for higher-order mathematics.

After handing her new problem to the lead solver, Norma explained patiently what she wanted the slaves to do, how she had already done some of the setup for them. She encouraged the hard-working solvers in the direction she wanted them to take, emphasizing the importance of her theory—until she looked up to see Holtzman himself in the doorway.

Frowning, he drew Norma down the hall. "You are wasting time trying to befriend them. Remember, the solver-slaves are just organic equipment, processors providing a result. They are replaceable, so don't give them personalities or temperaments. Only the solutions matter to us. An equation has no personality."

Norma chose not to argue, but went back to her rooms to continue her efforts alone. It seemed to her that the more esoteric orders of mathematics did indeed have personalities, that certain theorems and integrals required finesse and considerations that simple arithmetic never demanded.

Pacing, she wandered around to the back of the crystal slate, where she peered at the reverse of her equations. The backward symbols looked like nonsense, yet she forced herself to stare at the question from a different perspective. Earlier, the solvers had finished the previous set of tedious calculations, and while she had checked their work, the result still perplexed her.

Knowing in her heart what the answer must be, she disregarded the slaves' result and returned to the front of the erasable crystal, where she scribbled so furiously that silvery numbers and symbols soon flowed across the hanging plate. Afterward she went frontside to back, trying to discover an exit from her quandary.

Tio Holtzman jarred Norma out of a theoretical universe. He looked at her in surprise. "You were in a trance."

"I was thinking," she said.

Holtzman chuckled. "On the wrong side of the slate?"

"It opened new possibilities for me."

He rubbed his chin, where gray beard stubble protruded. "I've never seen anyone concentrate as hard as you do."

In her mind she circled the solution she had developed, but could not put it into words. "I know what the result *should* be, but I cannot reproduce it for you. The solvers keep coming up with a different answer than I expect."

"Did they make an error?" He looked angry.

"Not that I can determine. Their work seems to be correct. Nonetheless, I feel that it is . . . wrong."

The scientist frowned. "Mathematics doesn't exist to fulfill wishes, Norma. You must go through the steps and abide by the laws of the universe."

"You mean the *known* laws of the universe, Savant. I simply wish to extend our thinking, stretch it and fold it back in on itself. I'm certain there are ways around the problem. Intuitive loopholes."

His expression seemed patronizing, perplexed but disbelieving. "The mathematical theories we work with are often esoteric and difficult to grasp, but they always follow certain rules."

She turned, frustrated that he continued to doubt her. "Blind adherence to rules allowed the creation of the thinking machines in the first place. Following the rules may prevent us from defeating our enemies. You said it yourself, Savant. We must look for alternatives."

Seizing a subject that interested him at last, he clasped his hands together, long sleeves draped over his knuckles. "Indeed, Norma! I have completed my design work on the alloy-resonance generator, and the prototype is next."

Too preoccupied to be tactful with him, she shook her head. "Your alloy-resonance generator won't work. I have studied your early designs exhaustively. I think it is fundamentally flawed."

Holtzman looked as if she had reached up and slapped him. "I beg your pardon? I have been through all the work. The solvers have checked every step."

Distracted by her equation-filled crystal slate, she shrugged. "Nevertheless, Savant, it is my opinion that your concept is not viable. Correct calculations are not always correct—if based on faulty principles or invalid assumptions." Furrows formed on her brow as she finally noticed his crestfallen reaction. "Why are you upset? You told me the purpose of science is to try ideas and dismiss them when they don't work."

"Your objection has yet to be proven," he said, his voice brittle. "Show me in my designs where I have made an error, please."

"It's not so much an error as . . ." She shook her head. "It's an intuition."

"I don't trust intuition," he said.

Disappointed by his attitude, she drew a deep breath. Zufa Cenva had never adhered to any graceful social skills, and Norma had developed few of her own. She had grown up isolated on Rossak and been dismissed by most of those who knew her—with the exception of Aurelius Venport.

Holtzman seemed to have an agenda beyond what he preached. But he was a scientist, after all, and she felt they had been brought together for an important purpose. It was her duty to point out when she felt he was making an error. He would have done the same for her. "I still think you shouldn't devote any further time or resources to the resonance-generator project."

"Since the resources are mine to distribute as I see fit," Holtzman said in a huff, "I will continue, and hope to prove you wrong." He left her chamber, grumbling.

She called after him in an attempt to ease the situation. "Believe me, Savant, I hope you prove me wrong."

There is a certain malevolence about the formation of social orders, a profound struggle, with despotism on one end and slavery on the other.

—TLALOC,
Weaknesses of the Empire

Poritrin's river delta was not at all like Harmonthep's gentle rivulets and marshes. More than anything, the slave boy Ishmael wanted to go home . . . but Ishmael didn't know how far away that was. At night, he often awoke screaming in the compound, battling nightmares. Few of the other slaves bothered to comfort him; they carried their own heavy burdens.

His village had been burned back on Harmonthep, most of the people captured or killed. The boy remembered seeing his grandfather stand up to the slavers, quoting Buddislamic sutras to convince them of the wrongness of their actions. In response, the vile men had ridiculed old Weyop, making him look insignificant and ineffectual. They might as well have killed him.

A long time after the slavers had stunned Ishmael, he'd awakened inside a coffin of plasteel and transparent plates, a stasis chamber that had kept him immobile but alive. None of the new slaves could cause trouble as the Tlulaxa ship traveled across space to this strange world. All the captives had been awakened for unloading . . . and sale in the Starda market district.

Some of the Harmonthep prisoners had tried to escape without any idea of where to run. The slavers stunned some of them just to quiet their wailing and thrashing. Ishmael had wanted to fight back, but sensed he could accomplish more by watching and learning, until he found a better way to resist. He needed to understand Poritrin first; then he could consider how best to fight. It was what his sagacious grandfather would have counseled him to do.

Weyop had quoted sutras that told of imminent evil from outside, of soulless invaders who would steal them from their way of life. Because of those prophesies, the Zensunnis had left the company of other men. In the decaying Old Empire, people had forgotten God and then suffered when the thinking machines took over. Ishmael's people believed it was their fate, the great Kralizec, or typhoon struggle at the end of the universe, that had been foretold for millennia. Those who followed the Buddislamic creed had escaped, already knowing the outcome of that hopeless battle.

Yet that struggle had not ended according to the prophesy. Part of the human race had survived the machine demons, and now those people had turned against the "cowardly" Buddislamic refugees with revenge in their hearts.

Ishmael did not believe that the old teachings could have been wrong. So many sutras, so many prophesies. His grandfather had seemed certain when he spoke of the legends . . . yet still their peaceful Harmonthep village had been overrun, the strongest and healthiest taken as slaves. And now Ishmael and his fellows were on a far-off world, their bodies for sale.

Weyop had said that non-Buddislamic outsiders were condemned to eternal damnation . . . yet the Tlulaxa flesh merchants and the new masters on Poritrin controlled their food and their lives. The boy and his companions had no choice but to do as they were told.

Since Ishmael was the youngest captive, the owners expected little of him. They ordered his work group to watch over the boy, to make certain he completed his tasks . . . or if he failed, to pick up the slack.

Despite his aching muscles and blistering skin, Ishmael worked as hard as the others. He watched his despairing fellows waste time with complaints, an attitude that angered the owners and led to unnecessary punishments. Ishmael kept his misery to himself.

He spent weeks up to his knees in the slimy mudflats where ropes and stakes marked out fertile shellfish beds. He ran back and forth to basins that contained clam seedlings, scooped up handfuls of the tiny bivalves and rushed them out into the wet fields. If he cupped his hands too tightly, he crushed the delicate shells—such carelessness had already earned him a thrashing with a sonic whip when an agricultural supervisor saw what he had done. Like icy fire, the whip had made his skin bubble and spasm. The discipline left no mark, caused no physical damage, yet that single whip stroke burned a permanent scar in his brain, and Ishmael knew to avoid that forever.

Punishment would accomplish nothing and could only make him more miserable, while giving the owners yet another victory over him. He *chose* not to grant them that. Despite the fact that it was an insignificant matter, he would attempt to control it as much as possible.

Right now, seeing the workers in the mudflats, Ishmael was almost glad his parents had died in a storm, struck by lightning in a skiff on the large lake where seeping oil made the fish taste bad. At least they couldn't see him now, and neither could his grandfather. . . .

≈

AFTER THE FIRST month on Poritrin, Ishmael's hands and legs became so impregnated with black mud that even repeated washings could not remove the stain. His fingernails were broken and caked with river muck.

On Harmonthep, Ishmael had spent his days wading through the marshes, collecting eggs from qaraa nests, netting turtlebugs, and digging osthmir tubers that grew in the brackish water. From a young age, he had been toughened to a life of toil, but here he resented the work, because it was not for the glory of Buddallah, not for the health and well-being of his people. It was for someone else.

In the Poritrin slave compound, women cooked their food, using the unusual ingredients and spices they were given. Ishmael longed for the taste of fish baked in lily leaves and of sweet reeds whose juices could make a boy drunk with delight.

At night, half of the communal dwellings were vacant because so many slaves had died from the fever. Ishmael often crawled to his pallet and fell deeply asleep. Other times, he forced himself to remain awake and sit in the storytelling circles.

The men talked among themselves, debating whether to select a new leader for their group. To some of them, the concept seemed pointless. There could be no escape, and a leader could only inspire them to take chances that would get them all killed. Ishmael felt sad, remembering how his grandfather had expected to name a successor one day. Yet the Tlulaxa flesh merchants had changed all of that. Unable to reach a decision, the Zensunni men talked on and on. It made Ishmael want to drift off to the oblivion of sleep.

He liked it better when the men told old stories, reciting the poetic "Songs of the Long Trek" about the Zensunni Wanderings, how his people had sought a home where they would be safe from both the thinking machines and the League Worlds. Ishmael had never seen a robot and wondered if they were only imaginary monsters to frighten disobedient children. But he had indeed seen evil men—the raiders who had decimated his quiet village, mistreated his grandfather, taken so many innocents captive.

Sitting at the edge of the firelight, Ishmael listened to the tales of his people. The Zensunni were accustomed to tribulations, and they might have to tolerate even generations of slavery on this planet so far from home. No matter the challenge, his people knew how to endure.

Of all the stories the boy had heard, the covenants and prophecies, he clung to one above all the others: the promise that the misery would one day end.

There is no clear division between Gods and Men—one blends softly casual into the other.

—IBLIS GINJO,
Options for Total Liberation

The ornate pedestal for the statue of the Titan Ajax was nearly complete. Crew master Iblis Ginjo perused the daily tally and production requirements on his electronic note-pad. He had made his slaves understand their very real danger, should the brutal cymek lose patience. They worked very hard, not just for fear of their lives, but because Iblis had inspired them.

Then, a disaster occurred on another part of the project.

With the heat of day rising around the observation scaffold where Iblis stood supervising the stabilization of the sturdy pedestal, in the distance he saw the top of the nearly completed Ajax statue begin to move. The iron, polymer, and stone colossus tottered one way and then the other, as if gravity itself were shaking the enormous work of art.

Suddenly the giant monument toppled with a crashing roar, accompanied by distant shouts and screams. As a cloud of dust climbed into the sky, Iblis knew that any slave who had been crushed under the massive statue should be considered lucky.

Once Ajax learned of the catastrophe, the real mayhem would begin.

⮜⮞

EVEN BEFORE THE dust and rubble settled, Iblis rushed into the furious debate among neo-cymeks and his fellow trustee crew leaders. It hadn't been his part of the monument project that had collapsed, but his teams would suffer in the inevitable delays caused by the accident. Still, Iblis hoped his charismatic mediation skills could help mitigate the disaster.

Enraged neo-cymeks saw the clumsy damage as a personal affront to their revered Titan predecessors. Ajax himself had already torn a work supervisor limb from limb, and gory body parts lay scattered and dripping in the dust.

With all the compelling passion he could summon, Iblis Ginjo made the angry neo-cymeks pause. "Wait, wait! This can be fixed, if you will allow me!"

Ajax rose taller, more threatening than any of the neo-cymeks, but Iblis continued, his words silky. "True, the enormous statue has suffered some harm, but nothing more than superficial blemishes. Lord Ajax, this monument was designed to endure throughout the ages! Certainly it can endure a few bumps and scratches. Your grand legacy is not so easily bruised."

He paused as the cymeks were forced to admit the truth of this. Then he pointed toward his own work area and continued in a reasonable tone, "Look, my crews have nearly finished the sturdy pedestal designed to hold up the statue. Why don't we erect it anyway, to show the universe that we can brush aside minor annoyances like this accident? My workers can perform all the necessary repairs in place." Iblis's eyes shone with artificial enthusiasm. "There is no reason for further delay."

Pacing about the carnage and confusion in his menacing armored body, Ajax stomped on one of the crew leaders who was babbling his innocence, pulping him into the ground. Then the angry Titan towered over Iblis, optic threads glowing like white-hot stars. "You have now accepted responsibility to see that work continues according to schedule. If your teams fail, the blame will be yours."

"Of course, Lord Ajax." Iblis showed no alarm at all. He could convince the slaves to carry the burden. They would do it for him.

"Then get this mess cleaned up!" Ajax thundered in a voice that could be heard across the hilltop Forum.

Later, Iblis made promises to his already-exhausted, over-taxed slaves. They had been discontented and resistant for a while, but he won them over with a stirring account of the wondrous benefits they would receive: the finest sex slaves, incredible feasts, days of leisure to journey about the country-side. "I am not like other trustees. Have I ever let you down? Ever promised a reward that I failed to deliver?"

With such an incentive, not to mention a healthy dose of fear for the Titan Ajax, the laborers set to the task with redoubled energy. In the coolness of the evening, with hovering spotlights glaring like supernovas over the construction site, Iblis kept his crew working efficiently. From his high wooden platform, he watched as the slaves raised the immense statue on its sturdy reinforced pedestal and plasma-bolted it into place.

Artisans rushed forward and scaled the curved stone-and-iron surface with climbing equipment, and set up swaying temporary scaffolds to begin their restoration work. Ajax's legendary face had a marred nose and one dented muscular arm, as well as deep gouges across the front of the Titan uniform. In his secret heart, Iblis suspected the real Ajax's human form had been lumpish and ugly.

Throughout the long, tiresome night, Iblis struggled to stay awake, leaning against the rail and peering into the blurring abyss. He dozed off, then awoke, startled, as he heard the smooth hum of the lift platform rising to his level.

But he was mystified to see that the lift bore no one at all. Only a small sheet of rolled-up metal, a message cylinder. Iblis stared, his heart pounding, but the lift remained at his level, as if waiting. He looked over the edge, but could not determine who had left the message.

How could he ignore it?

Iblis stole forward and grabbed the scrap of scribed metal. He broke the seal, unrolled the thin sheet, and read with increasing astonishment.

"We represent an organized movement of dissatisfied humans. We are waiting for the right moment and the right leader to begin an open revolt against the oppressive machines. You must determine if you wish to join our worthy cause. We will contact you again."

As Iblis stared in disbelief at the unsigned message, the lettering faded and disappeared, corroding into blobs of rust that ate through the metal itself and flaked away.

Was it authentic, or some sort of a cymek trap designed to lure him? Most humans hated their machine masters, but took pains to conceal it. *What if there really is such a group?* And if so, they would need talented leaders.

The thought exhilarated him. Iblis had never considered such an idea before, and he couldn't imagine what he had said or done to reveal his innermost thoughts and feelings. Why did they suspect? He had always been respectful to his superiors, had always—

But have I been overly attentive? Have I tried too hard to appear loyal?

On the towering Ajax statue, just below his own level, the artisans remained hard at work like busy termites on a log. They repaired scrape marks, expertly patched and painted the marred exterior. Dawn broke across the monumental statue, and Iblis could see they would be finished soon. The machines would reward him for his labors.

How he hated them!

Iblis wrestled with his conscience. The thinking machines had treated him well in comparison with other slaves, but only a thin layer of protection kept him from the same fate. In his private moments Iblis often pondered the value of freedom, and what he could do if given the chance.

A rebel group? He could barely believe it. As days went by, Iblis found himself thinking about it more and more . . . and waiting to be contacted again.

Our appetite encompasses everything.

—COGITOR EKLO,
Beyond the Human Mind

With all the hatred concealed inside his mind, Agamemnon took special precautions wherever Omnius could spy on him. This meant almost always, and almost everywhere—even when Agamemnon and Juno had passionate sex. Or at least what passed for sex among the Titans.

For their tryst, walker bodies brought the two ancient cymeks into a maintenance chamber within the control pavilion on Earth. Around them, tubes of nutrient liquids snaked toward storage tanks in the ceiling. Robotic tenders moved from life-support generators to analysis banks, skimming data from thoughtrodes, ensuring that all systems remained within normal parameters.

Agamemnon and Juno conversed with each other on a private short-range band, twitching their respective sensors and sparking each other's thoughtrodes through the electrafluid. *Foreplay.* Even without physical bodies, the cymek minds could still experience intense pleasure.

Automated lifters disengaged his preservation canister

smoothly from its walking body, then set the thinking core on a clean chrome pedestal beside the container that held Juno's pinkish gray brain. With the accessible optic threads and computer comparison grids, he recognized the distinctive folds and lobes of his lover's mind. *Still beautiful after all these centuries.*

Agamemnon remembered how lovely she had been back in the beginning: obsidian-black hair that shimmered with blue highlights. Her nose had been pointed, her face narrow, with eyebrows that arched in a mysterious way. He always thought of her as Cleopatra, another military genius from the mists of history, just like the first Agamemnon in the Trojan War.

Long ago, during the eyeblink of time when he had worn a frail human physique, Agamemnon had fallen in love with this woman. Though Juno was extremely desirable sexually, he had been attracted to her mind before ever meeting her in person. He had first become aware of her on a complex virtual network through tactical simulations and wargames he had fought with her on the Old Empire's docile computers. The two of them had been teenagers then, back when age mattered.

As a boy, Agamemnon had been raised on pampered Earth, with the name of Andrew Skouros. His parents had led a hedonistic but passionless lifestyle, as had so many other citizens. They existed, they dabbled . . . but none of them really *lived.* Across the depths of time, he barely remembered the faces of his parents. All weak and feeble humans looked the same to him now.

Andrew Skouros had always been restless. He had asked uncomfortable questions that no one could answer. While the others played frivolous parlor games, the young man dug into archival databases, where he uncovered history and legends. He found heroic tales of real people who had existed so long ago they seemed as mythical as the race of Titans, the earliest gods overthrown by Zeus and a pantheon of Greek deities. He analyzed military conquests and came to understand tactics at a time when it was an obsolete skill in the peace-strangled Empire.

Under the alias "Agamemnon," he became interested in strategic games played across the computer network that monitored the activities of ennui-enslaved humanity. There he had encountered another person as skilled and talented as himself, a rare soulmate who shared his restless interests. The mysterious player's wild and unexpected ideas caused her campaigns to fail as often as they succeeded—but her surprising successes more than made up for the spectacular failures. Her intriguing alias was "Juno," taken from the queen of the Roman gods, wife of Jupiter.

Drawn together by their common ambition, their relationship was fiery and challenging, more than just sex. They pleasured themselves by developing thought-experiments. It was a game at first . . . and then much more than that.

Their lives changed dramatically when they had heard Tlaloc speak.

The offworld visionary, with his disturbing, chastising accusations against complacent humanity on Earth, made the two young schemers realize that their plans could blossom into more than just imaginative adventures.

Juno, whose real name was Julianna Parhi, had brought the three of them together. She and Andrew Skouros arranged to speak with Tlaloc, who was excited to learn that they shared his dreams. "We may be few," Tlaloc had said, "but in Earth's forests full of deadwood, three matches may be enough to spark a conflagration."

Meeting secretly, the rebellious trio plotted to overthrow the sleeping Empire. Using Andrew's military expertise, they saw that a small investment of hardware and manpower could take over many worlds that had fallen into apathetic stupor. With a little luck and acceptable tactics, like-minded leaders could form an iron grip around the Old Empire. In fact, if the plans were properly set in motion, the conquerors could achieve victory before anyone even noticed.

"It is for humanity's own good," Tlaloc had said, his eyes sparkling.

"And for ours," Juno added. "Just a little."

In one of her innovative plans, Juno utilized the pervasive network of thinking machines and their servile robots. The docile computers had been given artificial intelligence to watch over every aspect of human society, but Julianna saw them as an invasion army already in place . . . if only they could be reprogrammed, given a taste for conquest and human ambition. It was then that they had brought in a computer specialist named Vilhelm Jayther—who called himself Barbarossa on computer networks—to implement the technical details.

Thus began the Time of Titans, during which a handful of enthusiastic humans controlled the sleeping populace. They had work to do, an empire to rule.

During their planning stages, Julianna Parhi often queried a reluctant Cogitor advisor, Eklo. While consulting the ancient Cogitor, one of many spiritual minds who contemplated esoteric questions, she had seen the possibilities of living as a disembodied brain. Not just for introspection, but for action. She realized the advantages a *cymek* tyrant would have over simple humans, able to switch mechanical bodies as circumstances changed. As cymeks, the Titans could live and rule for thousands of years.

Perhaps that would be long enough.

Agamemnon had immediately agreed with Juno's concept, though he faced a primitive fear of the surgery itself. He and Juno knew that as the Titans experienced the dangers of the universe and the fragility of their human bodies, they would all come around.

To show faith in his lover, Agamemnon was the first to undergo the cymek process. He and Juno had spent a last heated night together, naked and touching, storing memories of nerve sensations that would have to last for millennia. Juno had tossed her raven hair, given him a final, tender kiss, and led him into the surgical chamber. There, computerized medical apparatus, robotic surgeons, and dozens of life-support systems waited for him.

The Cogitor Eklo had observed and assisted, offering advice whenever necessary, providing precise instructions for the robotic surgeons. Juno had watched her lover, eyes misty as she witnessed the transformation process. Agamemnon feared that she would become squeamish after that and renege on her own plans. But once his brain hung suspended in dynamic electrafluid, once the thoughtrodes were activated and he could "see" again through a galaxy of optic threads, Juno was there admiring him, studying the brain canister.

She had touched his transparent case with her fingertips. Agamemnon watched it all, focusing and adjusting his new and unfamiliar sensors, enthralled with the ability to observe everything at once.

A week later, when he felt competent enough with his new mechanical systems, Agamemnon had returned the favor, watching over Juno as the robotic surgeons sawed open her skull and removed her talented brain, discarding forever the fallible female body of Julianna Parhi. . . .

⟡

CENTURIES LATER, EVEN without biological bodies, he and Juno remained side by side on their chrome pedestals, connected by receptors and stimulus patches.

Agamemnon knew precisely which parts of Juno's brain to pulse in order to activate pleasure centers, and how long to maintain the stimulation. She responded in kind, bringing forth his stored memories of human lovemaking and then amplifying the remembered sensations, stunning him with new heights of euphoria. He struck back with a bolt of his own, causing her brain to quiver.

Through it all, the information-gathering watcheyes of Omnius observed intently, like a mechanized voyeur. Even in a time such as this, Agamemnon and Juno were never alone.

She pleasured him twice more, making his mind throb; he wanted her to stop so that he could rest, but also longed for her to continue. Agamemnon reciprocated, causing a thin, vibrating sound to pulse from the speakers attached to the canisters, an eerie warbling music that symbolized their merging orgasms. He could barely think through the haze of delight.

But his brooding anger continued in the background. Though Omnius allowed him and Juno to have their ecstasy as often as they wished, Agamemnon would have derived even greater pleasure if they could permanently escape the domination of the damned thinking machines.

*I fear that Norma will never amount to anything. How does that
reflect on me and my own legacy to humanity?*

—ZUFA CENVA

During the tedious month-long journey across space to
visit her daughter on Poritrin, Zufa Cenva had plenty of
time to ponder what she would say when she arrived. She
would rather have been spending so many days and weeks
elsewhere on her more important work. The loss of dear
Heoma weighed like a hot stone inside her chest. Ever since
the first devastating attack against the cymeks on Giedi Prime,
Zufa had been planning further strikes with her other Sorceress
weapons.

While most members of the League gave credit to Savant
Holtzman for the portable scrambler projectors, she had heard
whispers that Norma herself may have inspired the design.
Could her oddball daughter have done something so remarkable? Not as great as a psychic storm obliterating cymeks, but
still respectable. *Perhaps I have been blind after all.* Zufa had
never wanted Norma to fail, but had given up hope by now.
Maybe things could change in their relationship. *Should I em-*

brace her? Does she deserve my support and encouragement,
or will she make me ashamed of her?

These were uncertain times.

As Zufa stepped off the transport in Starda, she encountered
a delegation waiting to greet her, complete with ornately
garbed Dragoon guards, their gold-scale armor immaculate.
Ruddy-faced Lord Niko Bludd himself led the group, his beard
intricately curled, his clothes perfumed and colorful.

"Poritrin is honored by the visit of a Sorceress!" The noble
stepped forward on the mosaic tile floor. Bludd wore a dashing
ceremonial costume with broad carmine lapels, frilly white
cuffs, and golden shoes. A ceremonial sword hung at his waist,
though he had probably never used a blade for anything more
dangerous than cutting cheese.

She'd never had any use for frippery when there was work
to be done, and Bludd's arrival surprised her. She had hoped
to conclude her business with Norma unobtrusively and then
quickly return to Rossak. She and her dedicated psychic warriors must prepare another mental strike against the cymeks.

"The shuttle captain transmitted a message that you were
coming, Madame Cenva," Bludd said, as he guided her
through the terminal. "We barely had time to put together a
reception for you. You are here to see your daughter, I presume?" Niko Bludd grinned above his curled reddish beard.
"We are very proud of how much she is helping Savant Holtzman. He considers her quite indispensible."

"Indeed?" Zufa tried to control her skeptical frown.

"We invited Norma to join us today, but she is deeply engrossed in important work for Savant Holtzman. She seemed
to think that you would understand why she could not meet
you herself."

Zufa felt as if she had been slapped. "I have been en route
for a month. If *I* can make the time, then a mere . . . lab assistant can arrange to pick me up."

Outside the spaceport, a chauffeur guided her to a lavish
airbarge, and the Dragoon guards took their places at the rails.
"We will transport you directly to Holtzman's laboratories."
When Bludd seated himself beside her, she wrinkled her nose

at his strong body perfumes. He extended a small package to her, which she didn't want.

With a sigh of exasperation, Zufa sat rigidly in the comfortable seat as the aircraft proceeded away from the spaceport. Removing the package's silver wrapping paper, Zufa found a bottle of river water and an exquisitely woven Poritrin towel.

Despite her lack of interest, the flamboyant noble insisted on explaining. "It is traditional for honored guests to wash their hands in the water of the Isana and dry themselves on our fine linen."

She made no move to use the gifts. Beneath the flying barge, water vessels traveled downriver toward the sprawling delta city, where grains, metals, and manufactured supplies were distributed to Poritrin suppliers. In the brown mudflats, hundreds of slaves worked in the muck to plant paddies of shellfish. The sight made her feel even more unsettled than she already was.

"The residence of Savant Holtzman is just ahead," Bludd said, pointing to a high bluff. "I am sure your daughter will be pleased to see you."

Has she ever been pleased to see me? Zufa wondered. She tried to calm herself with mental exercises, but anxiety intruded.

With a sweep of her long black dress, she stepped away from the ostentatious airbarge as soon as it set down on Holtzman's landing deck. "Lord Bludd, I have private business to discuss with my daughter. I'm sure you understand." Without further farewell, Zufa marched alone up the broad patio steps to the mansion, leaving a befuddled Bludd behind her. She waved her long arms, shooing him away.

Her telepathic senses attuned, Zufa entered the dwelling as if she belonged there. Holtzman's vestibule was cluttered with disarrayed boxes, books, and instruments. Either the household staff did not do their work, or the inventor had forbidden them to "organize" too much.

Picking a path through the obstacles, Zufa strode into a long hallway, then searched rooms and demanded information from anyone she met until she found her daughter. Finally, the tall and intimidating Sorceress entered an auxiliary laboratory building, where she saw a high stool at an angled lightstrip table that held blueprint films. No sign of Norma.

She noticed an open door that led out to a balcony, then saw a shadow, heard something move. Gliding to the balcony, Zufa was shocked to see her daughter perched on top of the railing. Norma gripped a red plaz container in her small hands.

"What are you doing?" Zufa asked. "Get down from there immediately!"

Startled, Norma glanced at her looming mother, then clasped the object tightly and leaped off the railing out into the open air.

"No!" Zufa shouted. But it was too late.

Rushing to the edge, the Sorceress saw to her horror that the balcony jutted out over a high bluff that dropped to the river, far below. The small-statured young woman tumbled through the air, falling.

Suddenly, Norma paused in midair and spun in a peculiar fashion. She called, "See for yourself, it works! You arrived just in time!" Then, like a feather on the wind, the girl drifted upward. The red device lifted her back toward the balcony, like an invisible hand.

Norma reached the level of the railing, and her angry mother yanked her back onto the balcony. "Why would you try something so dangerous? Doesn't Savant Holtzman prefer you to employ helpers for this sort of test?"

Norma frowned. "They have *slaves* here, not helpers. Besides, it is my own invention, and I wanted to do it myself. I knew it would work."

Zufa did not want to argue. "You came all the way to Poritrin and used the League's best engineering laboratories to design some sort of . . . flying toy?"

"Hardly, Mother." Norma opened the lid of the red plaz unit and adjusted electronics inside. "It is a variation on Savant Holtzman's theories, a repelling, or suspensor field. I expect him to be delighted by it."

"Oh, I am, I am!" The scientist appeared suddenly and stood behind Zufa. He quickly introduced himself, then looked at

Norma's new gadget. "I'll show it to Lord Bludd and see what he thinks of the commercial possibilities. I'm sure he'll want a patent in his own name."

Zufa looked on, still recovering from the shock of Norma's "fall," trying to see practical applications of her daughter's invention. Could such a thing be modified to carry troops or heavy objects? She doubted it.

Norma set down the red-plaz generator and crossed the room with her awkward, waddling gait. She climbed her high stool to reach the blueprint films on the slanted light table, where she sifted through pages. "I've figured out how this principle can also be used on illumination devices. The suspensor field can float lights and power them with residual energy. I have all the calculations . . . somewhere."

"Floating lights?" Zufa said, in scornful tone. "For what, a picnic? Tens of thousands died in the cymek attack on Zimia, millions were enslaved on Giedi Prime, and you live in secluded comfort—making floating *lights*?"

Norma gave her mother a condescending look, as if *Zufa* was the foolish one. "Think beyond the obvious, Mother. A war needs more than just weapons. Robots can alter their optic sensors to see in the dark, but humans must have light to see. Hundreds of these suspensor lights could be dispersed in a nighttime combat zone, negating any advantage the machines might have. Savant Holtzman and I think along those lines every day."

The scientist nodded, quick to concur with her. "Or, for commercial uses, they could be designed in a number of styles, even tuned to any color or shade."

Norma sat on her stool like a gnome perched on a throne. Her brown eyes sparkled with excitement. "I'm sure Lord Bludd will be most pleased."

Zufa frowned. There were more important issues at stake in this war than pleasing a foppish nobleman. Impatient, she said, "I came a great distance to see you."

Norma raised her eyebrows skeptically. "If you had bothered to see me *before* I departed from Rossak, Mother, you wouldn't have needed to make such a long voyage to soothe your guilt. But you were too busy to notice."

Uneasy in the midst of a family argument, Tio Holtzman excused himself. The combatants hardly noticed his departure.

Zufa had not intended to pick a fight, but now she felt defensive. "My Sorceresses have proved their abilities in battle. We can exert tremendous power with our minds to eradicate the cymeks. A number of candidates are preparing themselves to offer the ultimate sacrifice if we are called upon to free another machine-dominated world." Her pale eyes flashed, and she shook her head. "But you don't worry about that, do you, Norma—since you have no telepathic abilities."

"I have other skills, Mother. I am making a valuable contribution, too."

"Yes, your incomprehensible equations." Zufa nodded toward the suspensor field generator on the floor. "Your life is not at stake. Safe and pampered, you spend your days playing with these *toys*. You have let yourself be blinded by imaginary success." But her daughter wasn't the only one. Many people lived in comfort and security while Zufa and her Sorceresses performed dangerous tasks. How could Norma compare her work to *that*? "When you heard I was coming, Norma, could you not have found time to meet me at the spaceport?"

Norma's tone was deceptively mild as she crossed her arms over her small chest. "I did not ask you to come here, Mother, because I know you have many important things to do. And *I* have more urgent duties than ferrying unexpected guests around. Besides, I knew Lord Bludd was going to meet you."

"Are League nobles your errand boys now?" Now that she had opened the floodgates of her anger, Zufa couldn't stop the words that came next. "I only wanted you to make me proud, Norma, despite your deformities. But nothing you do will ever amount to anything. Living here in luxury, what sacrifices do you make? Your vision is too small to be of any real use to humanity."

Previously, Norma would have crumbled under such an onslaught, her confidence crushed. But her work here with Holtzman, her obvious successes in the technical arena, had given her a new view of herself. Now she looked coolly at her mother. "Just because I don't fit the image of what you wanted me to be doesn't mean I'm not contributing something essential. Savant Holtzman sees it, and so does Aurelius. You're my own mother—why can't you?"

With a snort at the mention of Venport's name, Zufa began pacing. "Aurelius is just a man with hallucinations from the drugs he takes."

"I had forgotten how narrow-minded you truly are, Mother," Norma said in a level tone. "Thank you for coming all this way to refresh my memory." The girl turned on her stool and resumed her plans and equations. "I am tempted to summon one of the slaves to escort you out, but I wouldn't want to remove them from their more important work."

∽

FURIOUS AT HERSELF and her daughter—and at the wasted time—Zufa returned to the spaceport. She would stay on Poritrin no longer. To get her mind off her concerns, she concentrated on mental exercises and thought of how her beloved trainees in the jungles were ready to give their utmost to their tasks, without personal considerations.

Zufa waited a full day for a military transport that would take her back to Rossak. As she surrounded herself with waves of her own clairvoyant powers, she discovered a rotten weakness on Poritrin, and it had nothing to do with Norma. It was so obvious, she could not avoid it.

All around Starda, at loading sites near the spaceport, at the warehouses and mudflats, Zufa detected the individual and collective auras of the downtrodden laborers. She sensed a collective psychological wound, a deep and simmering discontent to which the free Poritrin citizens seemed completely oblivious.

The backwash of brooding resentment gave her one more reason to want to get away from this place.

Intuition is a function by which humans see around corners. It is useful for persons who live exposed to dangerous natural conditions.

—ERASMUS
Erasmus Dialogues

Raised as the daughter of the League Viceroy, Serena Butler was accustomed to working hard to serve humanity, looking toward a bright future even against the backdrop of constant war. She had never imagined laboring as a slave inside the household of an enemy robot.

From her first glance at Erasmus in the broad entry plaza of the villa, Serena disliked him intensely. Conversely, the thinking machine was intrigued by her. She suspected that his interest was probably a dangerous thing.

He chose to wear fine clothes, loose robes and fluffy, ornate furs that made his robot body look absurd. His mirrored face made him appear alien, and his demeanor made her flesh crawl. His relentless curiosity about mankind seemed perverse and unnatural. When he strutted across the plaza toward Serena, his pliable metal mask shifted into a delighted grin.

"You are Serena Butler," he said. "Have you been informed that Giedi Prime was recaptured by the feral humans? Such a disappointment. Why are humans willing to sacrifice so much to maintain their inefficient chaos?"

Serena's heart lifted at news of the liberation, in part because of her own efforts. Xavier had brought the Armada after all, and Brigit Paterson's engineers must have succeeded in activating the secondary shield transmitters. Serena, however, remained enslaved—and pregnant with Xavier's child. No one even knew where she was or what had happened to her. Xavier and her father must be insane with grief, convinced that the machines had killed her.

"Perhaps it's not surprising that you don't comprehend or value the human concept of freedom," she replied. "For all your convoluted gelcircuitry, you're still just a machine. The understanding wasn't *programmed* into you."

Her eyes stung at the thought of how much more she wanted to achieve to help other people. On Salusa, she had never taken her family's wealth for granted, feeling a need to earn the blessings bestowed upon her.

She asked, "So, are you inquisitive, or inquisitor?"

"Perhaps both." The robot leaned close to examine her, noting the proud lift of her chin. "I expect you to offer me many insights." He touched her cheek with a cool, flexible finger. "Lovely skin."

She forced herself not to pull away. *Resistance must count for something more than a captive's pride*, her mother had once told her. If Serena struggled, Erasmus could hold her with his powerful robotic grasp, or summon mechanized torturing devices. "My skin is no more lovely than yours," she said, "except mine is not synthetic. My skin was designed by nature, not by the mind of a machine."

The robot chuckled, a tiny cachination. "You see, I expect to learn much from you." He led her into his lush greenhouses, which she observed with reluctant delight.

At the age of ten she had become fascinated with gardening, and had delivered plants, herbs, and sweet exotic fruits to medical centers, refugee complexes, and veteran homes, where she also volunteered her services. Around Zimia, Serena had been renowned for her ability to cultivate beautiful flowers. Under her loving attention, exquisite little Immian roses bloomed, as did Poritrin hibiscus and even the delicate morning violets of distant Kaitain.

"I will have you tend my prized plaza gardens," Erasmus said.

"Why can't machines perform such tasks? I'm sure they'd be much more efficient—or do you just revel in making your 'creators' do the work?"

"Do you not feel up to the task?"

"I will do as you command—for the sake of the plants." Pointedly ignoring him, she touched a strangely shaped red and orange flower. "This looks like a bird of paradise, a pure strain from an ancient stock. According to legend, these plants were favored by the sea kings of Old Earth." With a look of defiance, Serena turned back to the robot. "There, now I have taught you something."

Erasmus chuckled again, as if replaying a recording. "Excellent. Now tell me what you were truly thinking."

She remembered words her father had spoken—*Fear invites aggression; do not show it to a predator*—and felt emboldened. "While I was telling you about a beautiful flower, I was thinking that I despise you and all of your kind. I was a free and independent being, until you took it all away from me. Machines stole my home, my life, and the man I love."

The sentient robot was not at all offended. "Ah, your lover! Is he the one who impregnated you?"

Serena glared at Erasmus, then made up her mind. Perhaps she could find a way to use this machine's curiosity, turning it against him somehow. "You will learn the most from me if I cooperate, if I talk freely. I can teach you things you would never learn for yourself."

"Excellent." The robot seemed genuinely pleased.

Serena's eyes grew hard. "But I expect something from you in return. Guarantee the safety of my unborn baby. Allow me to raise the child here in your household."

Erasmus knew it was a standard parental imperative for her to be worried about her offspring, and that gave him leverage. "You have either arrogance or ambition. But I shall consider your request, depending on how much I enjoy our discussions and debates."

Spotting a fat beetle at the base of a terra cotta planter, Erasmus nudged it with one foot. The insect had a black shell with an intricate red design. His smooth face mask shifted, flowed, until the shaping film displayed an amused expression. Erasmus let the beetle nearly escape, then moved his smooth foot to block it again. Persistent, it scuttled in another direction.

"You and I have a great deal in common, Serena Butler," he said. Remotely, he activated a contraband Chusuk music cube, hoping the melody would draw out her internal emotions. "Each of us has an independent mind. I respect that in you, because it is such an integral part of my own personality."

Serena resented any such comparison, but held her tongue.

Erasmus scooped the beetle onto one hand, but his primary interest dwelled on Serena—he was intrigued at how humans tried to keep so much of themselves veiled. Perhaps, by applying various pressures, he could see through to her inner core.

With the music playing in the background, Erasmus continued, "Some robots keep their own personalities rather than simply uploading a portion of the evermind. I began as a thinking machine on Corrin, but I chose not to accept regular Omnius updates that would synchronize me with the evermind."

Serena saw that the beetle was immobile on his metallic palm. She wondered if he had killed it.

"But a singular event changed me forever," Erasmus said, his voice pleasant, as if telling a story about a quaint forest outing. "I had set out across Corrin's unsettled territories on a private scouting mission. Because I was inquisitive and did not wish to accept the standard analyses compiled by Omnius, I ventured into the landscape on my own. It was rugged, rocky, and wild. I had never seen vegetation except for in the areas where Old Empire terraformers had planted new ecosystems. Corrin was never a living world, you see, except where humans had made it so. Unfortunately, tending fertile fields and beautifying the land was no longer a priority of my kind." He looked at Serena to see if she was enjoying his story.

"Unexpectedly, far from the city grid and robot support systems, I was unprotected from a severe solar storm. Corrin's red-giant sun is in turmoil and unstable, with frequent flare activity, sudden hurricanes of radiation. Such an onslaught is hazardous to biological life-forms, but the original human settlers were resilient.

"My delicate neurelectric circuitry, however, was rather more sensitive. I should have dispatched scout scanners to keep watch on the star-storms, but I was too engrossed in my own investigations. I found myself exposed and damaged from the radiation flux, disoriented and far from the central complex run by the Corrin-Omnius." Erasmus actually sounded embarrassed. "I wandered away and I . . . tumbled into a narrow crevasse."

Serena looked at him in surprise.

"Despite dropping deep into the crack, my body was only slightly damaged." He lifted an arm, looked at his flexible fiber-wrapped limb, the organic-polymer skin, the flowmetal coating. "I was trapped, out of transmission range, and basically immobilized. I could not move for an entire Corrin year . . . twenty Terran standard years.

"The crevasse's deep shadow shielded me from solar radiation, and soon enough, my mental processors recovered. I was awake, but I could go nowhere. I could not move . . . only think, for a long, long time. I spent a seemingly endless blazing summer there, wedged in the rocks, and then I endured the ensuing long winter locked in heavy, compacted ice. During all that time, two decades, I had nothing to do but *contemplate*."

"No one to talk to but yourself," she said. "Poor, lonely robot."

Ignoring the remark, Erasmus said, "Such an ordeal altered my fundamental nature in ways I could never have foreseen. In fact, Omnius still does not understand me."

By the time he'd finally been discovered and rescued by other robots, Erasmus had developed an individual personality. After his restoration and reintegration into the cooperative machine society, Omnius had asked Erasmus if he wished to be upgraded with standardized character traits.

"*Upgraded*, he called it," Erasmus said with some amusement. "But I declined the offer. After reaching such . . . enlightenment, I was reluctant to delete my impulses and ideas, my thoughts and memories. It seemed too great a loss to bear. And the Corrin-Omnius soon discovered how much he enjoyed sparring with me verbally."

Now, peering at the motionless beetle on his artificial hand, Erasmus said matter-of-factly, "I am a celebrity among the widespread everminds. They look forward to receiving updates containing my actions and assertions, like a serial publication. These are known as the 'Erasmus Dialogues.'"

With a guarded look, she nodded toward the motionless insect. "And will you include a discussion of that beetle? How can you understand something you have killed?"

"It is not dead," Erasmus assured her. "I detect a faint but unmistakable throb of life. The creature wants me to believe it is deceased, so that I will discard it. Despite its small size, it has a powerful will to survive."

Kneeling, he set the beetle on a flagstone with a surprisingly gentle touch, then stepped back. Moments later, the bug stirred and scampered to safety under the planter. "See? I wish to understand all living things—including you."

Serena glowered. The robot had managed to surprise her.

"Omnius does not think I can ever attain his intellectual level," Erasmus said. "But he remains intrigued by my mental agility—the way my mind continually evolves in new and impulsive directions. Like that beetle, I am capable of springing to life and persevering."

"Do you really expect to become more than a machine?"

Taking no offense, Erasmus replied, "It is a human trait to better oneself, is it not? That is all I am trying to do."

One direction is as good as another.

                —saying of the Open Land

B y the tenth time he rode a giant sandworm, Selim was proficient enough to enjoy the experience. No other thrill could compare to the power of a leviathan of the deep desert. He loved racing across the dunes while perched on the high ridges of a worm, crossing an ocean of sand in a single day.

Selim had brought water, rugged clothing, equipment, and food from the abandoned botanical testing station. His crystal sandworm tooth proved a valuable tool as well as a mark of personal pride. Inside the empty station, he had sometimes stared at the smooth milky curve of the blade under the dim light of recharge panels and imagined a religious significance to the object. It was a relic of his supreme test out here in this wasteland, and a symbol that Buddallah was watching over him. Perhaps the worms were part of his destiny.

He came to believe that the sandworms were not Shaitan after all, but blessings from Buddallah himself, perhaps even tangible manifestations of God.

After months of recuperation and boredom inside the old

research facility, living without purpose, Selim had known he must go out and ride a sandworm again. He needed to learn exactly what it was that Buddallah expected of him.

He had carefully marked the location of the testing station. Unfortunately, since he couldn't guide the sandworms, he knew it would be a challenge to make his way back to the secret place. Upon departing, he had carried everything necessary on his back.

He was Selim Wormrider, chosen and guided by Buddallah. He needed no help from others.

⁂

AFTER KILLING TWO more sandworms by riding them until they collapsed of exhaustion, Selim discovered that it was not necessary to slay a worm just so he could get safely away. It was possible, though risky, to dismount from a weary beast by running down the length of its back, leaping away from the hot tail, and then racing toward nearby rocks. The depleted worm, too tired to give chase, would wallow in deep dust, and sulk.

This satisfied Selim, because it seemed wrong to destroy the creatures that gave him transportation. If the sandworms were emissaries from Buddallah, and old men of the desert, then he must treat them with respect.

On his fourth ride, he discovered how to manipulate the sensitive edges of worm rings, using a shovel-bladed tool and the sharp metal spear to prod Shaitan in the direction Selim wished to go. It was a simple concept, but one that required a great deal of work. His muscles ached by the time he dropped away from a spent worm and ran to the shelter of nearby rocks. He remained lost out in the deep desert . . . but in a very real sense, the desert belonged to him now. He was invincible! Buddallah would care for him.

Selim still had an adequate supply of water from the distilling units in the testing station, and his diet consisted of large amounts of melange, which gave him strength and energy. As soon as he learned how to master the worms, he was able to travel wherever he chose, working his way back toward the abandoned station.

Other Zensunnis would have called him mad, appalled at his foolhardy attempt to tame the terrifying sandworms. But the young exile no longer cared a whit how people felt about him. He was in touch with another realm. He felt in his heart that this was what he had been born to do. . . .

Now under the double moonlight, Selim guided his worm as it hissed across the sands. Hours ago, the creature had ceased trying to throw him off, and instead plunged onward, resigned to the commands of the imp who kept inflicting pain in the sensitive flesh between ring segments. Selim navigated by the stars, drawing lines like arrows between constellations. The unforgiving landscape began to look familiar, and he believed he was at last close to the botanical testing station, his sanctuary. Back home.

All alone atop the sandworm, surrounded by the bitter aromas of brimstone and cinnamon, he allowed himself to think and dream. He'd had little else to do since his exile. Was that not how great philosophers were born?

Someday perhaps, he would use the abandoned facility as the seed of his own colony. Maybe he could gather disaffected people from other Zensunni villages, outcasts like himself who wanted to live without oppressive strictures enforced by inflexible naibs. By controlling the great worms, Selim's people would have a strength that no outlaws had ever possessed.

Was that what Buddallah wanted him to do?

The young man smiled at his daydream, then grew sad as he recalled Ebrahim, who had so easily turned against him. As if that was not enough, he had then joined others in hurling insults and stones at Selim.

As his sandworm crashed over the dunes, the young rider finally saw the line of rocks ahead, familiar crags and dark formations. His heart leaped with joy. The behemoth had carried him home faster than anticipated. He grinned, then realized it would be a challenge to dismount from the feisty demon, which was not yet exhausted. Another test?

Using his spear and the shovel-spreader, Selim drove the

worm toward the rocks, thinking he might beach the creature on the outcroppings, where it would thrash and wriggle its way back to the soft sanctuary of sand. The eyeless monster sensed the rocks, recognizing a difference in viscosity and vibrations within the sand, and swerved in the opposite direction.

Selim pulled harder on the shovel and jabbed with the spear. The confused worm twitched and slowed. As it curled close to the nearest line of rock, Selim yanked himself and his equipment free. He tumbled down the creature's ring segments until he dropped to the sand and then ran away at full speed.

The safe reef of rock was less than a hundred meters distant, and the worm thrashed about as if it couldn't believe it had been so unexpectedly released. Finally, it sensed the rhythm of Selim's racing footsteps. The monster turned and lunged toward him.

Selim ran faster, bolting toward the boulders. He sprang onto a shelf of sharp lava rock and kept running, spitting pebbles from beneath the soles of his boots.

The worm exploded out of the sand, its head questing, its cavernous maw open. It hesitated as if afraid to go closer to the rock barrier, then slammed downward.

Selim had already scrambled up and over the second line of boulders, diving between rough-edged stones into a pocket, less than a cave but enough for him to wedge his body into. The sandworm crashed like a gigantic hammer into the ridge, but it did not know where the little human had gone to ground.

Enraged, the worm pulled back, its gaping mouth exuding an overpowering stench of melange. It smashed its big head against the rocks again, then retreated. Frustrated and beaten, it finally dragged itself away, wallowed through the sands, and then sank below the dune crests. Slow and indignant, it headed back out to the deep desert.

His heart pounding, adrenaline charging his bloodstream, Selim crawled out of the shelter. He looked around, amazed that he had made it back alive. Laughing, he praised Buddallah at the top of his lungs. The old botanical testing station was above him on the ridge, waiting for him. He would spend several days there, replenishing his supplies and drinking plenty of water.

As he began to climb with weary arms and legs, Selim saw something glint in the moonlight, lost in the broken rocks against which the furious worm had smashed itself. Another crystalline tooth, a longer one. It had broken free during the demon's attack and now lay in a cranny. Selim reached down and plucked out the curved, milky weapon. A reward from Buddallah! He held it high triumphantly before turning to make his way up to the derelict station.

Now he had two of them.

Time depends on the position of the observer and the direction in which he looks.

—COGITOR KWYNA,
City of Introspection archives

S till angry, Zufa Cenva returned to Rossak, where she intended to focus on the escalating war. After climbing down from the polymerized landing pad atop silvery purple leaves, she went immediately to the large chamber she shared with Aurelius Venport.

Zufa had earned her prestigious residence through political skills and mental powers. She could not help but frown every time she saw Venport's commercial ambitions, his comfortable profit goals, his hedonistic pursuits. Foolish priorities. Such things would mean nothing if the thinking machines won this war. Could he not understand that he had blinded himself to the terrible threat?

Exhausted from the long journey and still upset over the argument she'd had with her daughter, Zufa entered her white-walled chambers, wanting only to rest before planning the next round of strikes against the thinking machines.

There, she found Venport alone, but not waiting for her. He sat at a table made of green-veined stone quarried from the cliffs. Glistening with perspiration, his face remained handsome, with the perfect patrician features she had selected as a good joining with her bloodline.

Venport didn't even notice her. His eyes were distant, drowning in the aftereffects of some bizarre new jungle drug with which he was experimenting.

On the table before him sat a wire-mesh cage containing scarlet wasps with long stingers and onyx wings. His naked forearm was thrust inside the enclosure, with the mesh wall sealed around his elbow. The angry wasps had stung him repeatedly, injecting venom into his bloodstream.

More in anger than horror, Zufa stared at his stupor. "*This* is how you occupy yourself while I am trying to save the human race?" With her hands on the jeweled belt that cinched her dark robe, her mouth formed a terse, straight line. "A Sorceress has *died* in battle, someone I've trained, even loved. Heoma gave her life to keep us free, yet here you are, dabbling in euphoric chemicals!"

He did not flinch. His vacant expression shifted not at all.

The aggressive wasps battered themselves against the wire-mesh while emitting a high-pitched humming music. The insects stung his swollen flesh repeatedly. She wondered what psychotropic substance the venom provided, and how Venport had discovered it. Unable to find adequate words for her fury, she finally said, "You disgust me."

One time after lovemaking, Aurelius had claimed that he experimented with drugs for more than his own amusement, or even commercial earnings. As scented candles burned in a rock alcove above their bed, Venport had confided, "Somewhere out in the jungles, I hope to find a pharmaceutical substance that can boost *male* telepathic potential." With it, he hoped to bring certain men up to a psychic par with the Sorceresses.

Zufa had laughed at his ridiculous fantasy. Hurt, Aurelius had never mentioned the possibility again.

Long ago, the first colonists on rugged Rossak had been tainted, saturated with background jungle chemicals that had augmented their mental potential. How else could the women have achieved such extrasensory powers on this particular world and nowhere else? But, through some hormonal or chromosomal difference, men seemed to be immune to such effects of the environment.

Now Zufa shouted, ordering him to withdraw his hand from the wasp cage, but Venport did not utter a word. "You dabble in drugs, and my daughter conducts worthless experiments with suspensor fields and floating lamps. Are my Sorceresses the only ones on Rossak with a sense of mission?"

Though his eyes turned in her direction, he did not seem to see her.

Finally Zufa said in revulsion, "Some patriot you are. I hope history remembers you for this." She marched off to find a place where she could think of ways to continue the fight against thinking machines . . . while others amused themselves obliviously.

⌇

AFTER HIS MATE'S departure, Venport's glazed eyes took on a flicker of fire, then increased to a burning intensity of concentration. He focused on the open door to their private chambers, and the silence seemed to grow, as if he was draining sound and energy from the air. His jaw clenched, and he concentrated harder . . . and harder.

The door swung slowly shut by itself.

Satisfied but drained, Venport slid his arm out of the wasp cage and slumped to the floor.

Assumptions are a transparent grid through which we view the universe, sometimes deluding ourselves that the grid is that universe.

—COGITOR EKLO OF EARTH

As a reward for completing the giant Ajax statue under an impossible schedule, Iblis Ginjo received four days off duty. Even the neo-cymek work commanders were pleased that the human crew boss had rescued them all from the wrath of Ajax. Before leaving, Iblis made certain his slaves received the benefits he had promised; it was an investment, and he knew they would work even harder on the next project.

With special dispensation from his masters, Iblis rode away from the city grid and into rocky wastelands, the scarred site of a long-forgotten battlefield. Trustees could take advantage of special privileges and freedoms, the choice to earn rewards for work well done. The thinking machines were not concerned that he would flee, since Iblis had no place to go, no way to get off-planet, and no other access to food and shelter.

In fact, he had something else in mind: a pilgrimage.

Iblis sat astride a knobby burrhorse, a plodding laboratory-bred animal used in the bygone days when humans had ruled Earth. The ugly beast had an oversized head, floppy ears, and stubby legs designed for work rather than speed. The animal stank like matted fur soaked in sewage.

The burrhorse trudged up a narrow, winding trail. Iblis had not been here for years, but still knew the way. Such things were not easily forgotten. Previously his visits to the monastery of the Cogitor Eklo had been sparked by mere curiosity. This time he had a desperate need for advice and guidance.

After receiving the anonymous message of rebellion, Iblis had pondered the possible existence of other dissatisfied humans, people willing to defy Omnius. For his entire life, he had been surrounded by slaves toiling endlessly under machine rule. He had never looked beyond his own station, never imagined that it could be different. After a thousand years, any prospect of change or improvement seemed impossible.

Now, after much consideration, Iblis was willing to believe that there *might* be rebellious cells among humans on Earth, possibly even on other Synchronized Worlds. Widespread groups who intended to fight back.

If we can build such enormous monuments, do we not also have the power to tear them down?

The thought ignited his long-simmering resentment toward Omnius, the robots, and especially the cymeks, who seemed to bear a grudge against humans. But before he decided if the intriguing message was more than just fantasy, he needed to do some research. Iblis had survived so well and so long because he was cautious and obedient. Now he had to conduct his investigations in such a manner that the machines would never suspect his intent.

For answers, he could think of no better source than the Cogitor Eklo.

Years ago Iblis had been a member of an armed slave-pursuit team, chasing a few deluded people who had senselessly escaped from the city grid and fled into the hills with no plans, survival skills, or supplies. Wild rumors had convinced the gullible escapees that they could demand sanctuary from the politically neutral Cogitors. A foolish notion, considering that the meditative and detached human brains wanted nothing more than to isolate themselves and contemplate their esoteric thoughts. The Cogitors had not cared about the Time of Titans, the Hrethgir Rebellions, or Omnius's creation of the Synchronized Worlds. Cogitors did not wish to be disturbed, so the thinking machines tolerated them.

When Iblis and his pursuit team had surrounded the isolated monastery on the rugged mountainside, Eklo had dispatched his human secondaries to drive the slaves out of concealment. The escapees had cursed and threatened the Cogitor, but Eklo passively ignored them. Iblis and his armed companions had then brought the slaves in for "vigorous reassignment," after tossing their ringleader off a high cliff. . . .

Now the sturdy burrhorse ascended the steep path that shifted and crumbled beneath its hooves. Presently Iblis made out the high tower of the monastery, an impressive stone structure partly shrouded in mists. Its windows glowed red and then shifted to a sky blue, reportedly according to the moods of the great contemplative mind.

In his schooling as a trustee, Iblis had learned about the Cogitors, about the primitive remnants of religion still manifested by some of the larger groups of human slaves. Omnius had ceased trying to quash it, though the evermind did not understand the superstitions and rituals.

Long before the takeover of the Old Empire, Eklo had left his physical body behind and devoted his mind to analysis and introspection. While planning the large-scale overthrow of humanity, the Titan Juno had adopted Eklo as her personal advisor, demanding answers. Uninterested in repercussions, taking no sides in the conflict, Eklo had answered Juno's questions, and his unwitting advice had helped the Titans plan their conquest. In the thousand years since, Eklo had remained on Earth. The driving passion in his long life was to synthesize a complete understanding of the universe.

Reaching the end of the trail at the base of the stone tower, Iblis suddenly found himself surrounded by a dozen robed men armed with archaic pikes and barbed clubs. Their robes were dark brown, and they wore white clerical collars. One of the secondaries grabbed the reins of Iblis's burrhorse. "Leave here. We offer no sanctuary."

"I do not seek it." Iblis gazed down at the men. "I have only come to ask the Cogitor a question." He dismounted and, after charming them with his warmth and sincerity, glided confidently toward the high tower, leaving the robed men to hold his burrhorse.

"Cogitor Eklo is deep in thought and does not wish to be disturbed," one of the secondaries called out.

Iblis chuckled lightly, his voice smooth. "The Cogitor has been thinking for a thousand years. He can spare a few minutes to hear me out. I am a respected trustee. And if I give him information he doesn't already know, he'll have something more to ponder for the next century or so."

Muttering in confusion, several secondaries followed Iblis up wide steps. Abruptly, however, as he reached the arched entry, a broad-shouldered monk blocked his way. The muscles on his thick arms and chest had gone to fat, and he peered out from sunken eyesockets with dull eyes.

Iblis infused his voice with friendly persuasion. "I honor the knowledge Cogitor Eklo has acquired. I will not waste his time."

Frowning skeptically at Iblis, the monk adjusted his clerical collar and said, "You are bold enough, and the Cogitor is curious to hear your question." After checking the visitor's body for weapons, he said, "I am Aquim. Come this way."

The big man led Iblis along a narrow stone corridor and up a steep spiral stairway. As they proceeded, Iblis said, "I have been here before, chasing escaped slaves—"

"Eklo remembers," Aquim interrupted.

They reached the highest point in the structure, a round room at the pinnacle of the tower. The Cogitor's plexiplaz container rested on an altarlike ledge beneath one of the windows. Winds hummed along the window edges and swirled the mists. The windows shimmered sky blue from some internal illumination.

Leaving the other secondaries behind, Aquim stepped up to the transparent brain canister and stood for a moment, looking down at it reverently. He jabbed a hand into one of his pockets, and his trembling fingers emerged with a twisted strip of paper encrusted with a black powder. He placed the strip in his mouth, letting it dissolve. His eyes rolled upward, as if in ecstasy.

"Semuta," he said to Iblis, "derived from the burned residue of elacca wood, smuggled here. It aids me in what I must do." With complete serenity, he rested both hands against the smooth lip of the canister, and said, "I understand nothing."

The naked brain inside its blue soup of electrafluid seemed to pulse, waiting.

With a beatific smile, the big monk drew a deep breath and slid his fingers into the open mouth of the tank, dipping into the thick life-support liquid. The gelatinous medium wet his skin, penetrated his pores, linked with his nerve endings. Aquim's expression changed, and he said, "Eklo wishes to know why you did not ask your question the last time you were here."

Iblis did not know if he should speak to the secondary or directly to the Cogitor, so he directed his reply to a space between them. "At the time, I did not understand what was significant. Now there is something I wish to know from you. No one else can provide an objective answer."

"No judgment or opinion is ever completely objective." The big monk spoke with calm conviction. "There are no absolutes."

"You are less biased than anyone else I could ask."

The altar ledge moved around slowly along a hidden track, and the Cogitor came to rest in front of a different window, with Aquim keeping pace, his hand still immersed in the canister. "State your question."

"I have always worked loyally for my cymek and machine masters," Iblis began, selecting his words carefully. "Lately I received word that there may be human resistance groups on Earth. I wish to know if this report is credible. Are there people who want to overthrow their rulers and gain freedom?"

During a moment's hesitation, the secondary stared blankly into space, either from the effects of the semuta or from his connection with the philosopher brain. Iblis hoped the Cogitor would not drift into a long period of contemplation. Finally, in a deep and sonorous voice, Aquim said, "Nothing is impossible."

Iblis tried several variations of the question, deftly circling with phrases, adjusting his selection of words. He did not want to reveal his intentions, though the neutral Cogitor presumably did not care why Iblis might want to find the rebels, whether to destroy them or to join them. Each time, however, Iblis received the same enigmatic answer.

Summoning his courage, he finally asked, "If such a widespread, secret resistance organization *did* exist, would it have a chance of succeeding? Could the reign of the thinking machines possibly come to an end?"

This time the Cogitor pondered longer, as if assessing different factors in the question. When the same answer came via the robed monk, the words, spoken more ominously, seemed to convey a deeper meaning. "Nothing is impossible."

After that, Aquim withdrew his dripping hand from Eklo's brain container, signifying that the audience was concluded. Iblis bowed politely, expressed his gratitude, and departed, his own thoughts in turmoil.

On the ride back down the steep trail, the frightened but exhilarated crew supervisor decided that if he could not locate one of the resistance group members, he had another option.

Drawing from his deeply loyal work crews, Iblis would form a rebel cell of his own.

Conflict prolonged over an extended period tends to be self-perpetuating and can easily plunge out of control.

—TLALOC,
A Time for Titans

fter a thousand years, only five of us remain."

It was rare for the surviving Titans to congregate, especially on Earth where the eyes of Omnius watched them every moment. But General Agamemnon was so outraged after the disaster on Giedi Prime and the murder of his friend and ally that he didn't waste time worrying about the evermind.

He had other priorities.

"The *hrethgir* have a new weapon that they have used against us with devastating consequences," Agamemnon said.

The Titans were inside a maintenance chamber, their preservation canisters perched on pedestals. In a stern tone, he had instructed Ajax, Juno, Xerxes, and Dante to detach from their mobile forms. Tempers would flare, and an individual's impulses were hard to control when installed in a powerful combat body, where thoughtrodes could convert any rash impulse into immediate, destructive action. Agamemnon trusted himself to restrain his anger, but some of the other Titans—especially Ajax—destroyed first and reconsidered later.

"After much investigation and analysis, we have learned that Barbarossa's murderers came from Rossak, and the feral humans called her a Sorceress," said Dante, who kept track of such things. "Rossak harbors more of these Sorceresses, women who possess enhanced telepathic capabilities."

"Obviously," Juno said, with sarcasm evident in her synthesized voice.

Dante continued, reasonable as always, "Until now, the Sorceresses have not been used in any large-scale aggressive function. After their triumph on Giedi Prime, however, it is probable that the *hrethgir* will use them to strike again."

"Their action has also reminded us of how vulnerable we are," Agamemnon said. "Robots can be replaced. Our organic brains cannot."

Ajax was so infuriated by the dilemma of the Sorceresses that his life-support monitors had trouble maintaining the proper chemical balance inside his shimmering electrafluid. He could not find words to express his anger.

"But didn't this Sorceress have to kill herself to slay Barbarossa and a handful of neo-cymeks?" Xerxes asked. "It was *suicide*. Do you think they'd be willing to do that again?"

"Just because you're a coward, Xerxes, doesn't mean the feral humans are so afraid to sacrifice themselves," Agamemnon said. "That one Sorceress cost us seven neo-cymeks and a Titan. A staggering loss."

After living a thousand years, during which billions upon billions of human lives were lost (many at Agamemnon's own hands or while he watched), he had thought he was immune to witnessing death. Of the original Titans, Barbarossa, Juno, and Tlaloc had been his closest friends. The four of them had been the seeds of the rebellion. The other Titans had come later, adding to the junta as necessary.

Despite the fact that his mental images were very old, the Titan general still remembered Barbarossa in his human form. Vilhelm Jayther had been a man with thin arms and legs, wide shoulders, and a sunken chest. Not pleasing to look upon, some said, but his eyes had the sharpest intensity Agamemnon had ever seen. And his programming genius was unparalleled.

With a wolfish obsession, Jayther had accepted the challenge of overthrowing the Old Empire, losing sleep for weeks until he figured out how to solve the problem. Jayther gave himself over entirely to the task until he understood precisely how to manipulate sophisticated programming for the rebels' purposes. Implanting humanlike ambitions and goals into the computer network, he had made the machines *want* to participate in the takeover.

Later, though, Omnius had developed ambitions of his own.

A man of tremendous foresight, Jayther had included failsafe instructions that precluded the thinking machines from harming any of the Titans. Agamemnon and all of his compatriots were alive only because of Vilhelm Jayther—Barbarossa.

Now the Sorceresses had killed him. The realization kept pounding inside Agamemnon's brain, building his anger.

"We cannot let this outrage go unpunished," Ajax said. "I say we go to Rossak, slay all the women, and turn their world into a charred ball."

"Dear Ajax," Juno said sweetly, "need I remind you that just *one* of those Sorceresses destroyed Barbarossa and all the neo-cymeks with him?"

"So?" Ajax's voice swelled with pride. "Single-handedly, I exterminated the human infestation on Walgis. Together, we can handle a few Sorceresses."

In a sharp tone Agamemnon said, "The rebels on Walgis were already broken before you started slaughtering them, Ajax. These Sorceresses are different."

Dante said, in a droning voice, "Omnius will never authorize a full-scale strike. The expenditure in resources would be too great. I have completed a preliminary analysis."

"Nevertheless," Agamemnon said, "it would be an extreme tactical mistake to allow this defeat to go unchallenged."

After a few moments of uneasy silence, Xerxes said, "Since so few of us remain, the Titans should never, never attack together. Think of the risk."

"But if we go together to Rossak and crush the Sorceresses, then the threat will be over," Ajax said.

Juno made a hissing sound, then said, "I see your brain there in the jar, Ajax, but you don't seem to be using it. Perhaps you should change your electrafluid? The Sorceresses have proven they can destroy us, and you want to go blundering into the greatest threat the cymeks have ever faced, like sheep baring our throats for slaughter?"

"We could bring enough robot ships to attack from orbit," Dante said. "We need not risk ourselves."

"This is personal," Ajax growled. "One of the Titans has been assassinated. We don't just toss missiles from the other side of the planetary system. That is the coward's way . . . even if the thinking machines call it *efficient*."

"There is room for compromise," Agamemnon said. "Juno, Xerxes, and I can gather neo-cymeks as volunteers and go in with a robot fleet. That should be enough to inflict immense damage on Rossak."

"But I can't go, Agamemnon," Xerxes said. "I am working here with Dante. Our greatest monuments in the Forum Plaza are nearly completed. We've just begun work on a new statue to Barbarossa."

"Good timing," Juno said. "I'm sure he appreciates it, now that he's dead."

"Xerxes is right," Dante said. "There is also the immense frieze of the Victory of the Titans being laid out and constructed on the hillside near the center of the metropolitan grid. We have work crew supervisors, but they require constant surveillance. Otherwise expenditures will grow too great, and schedules will not be met—"

"Given the recent debacle with his own statue, Ajax is perfectly familiar with such problems," Juno said. "Why not let him stay behind, instead of Xerxes?"

Ajax roared, "I will not remain here while others get the glory!"

But Agamemnon said, "Xerxes, you will come with us. Ajax, remain here to monitor the construction with Dante. Do it for the memory of Barbarossa."

Both Xerxes and Ajax railed on, but Agamemnon was their leader, and he imposed the control over them that he had exerted for centuries. From her tank, the once-lovely Juno said, "Can you convince Omnius to allow this, my love?"

"The *hrethgir* on Giedi Prime not only killed our friend, but also obliterated the new Omnius incarnation before it could be updated. A long time ago, when Barbarossa altered the network's original programming, he put something of himself into the computer mind, enough for it to understand the nature of conquest. I'm betting he will feel our need for *revenge* as well."

The Titans considered this comment in silence, then Agamemnon said, "We will go to Rossak and leave it in flames."

*In warfare there are countless factors that cannot be predicted,
and which do not depend upon the quality of military command.
In the heat of battle, heroes emerge, sometimes from the most
unlikely of sources.*

—VORIAN ATREIDES,
Turning Points in History

He was a soldier, not a politician. Xavier Harkonnen knew
military tactics and strategies, had planned to devote his
life to service in the Salusan Militia and the League Armada.
But now he had no choice but to speak before the gathered
League representatives in the Hall of Parliament.

After the bittersweet victory on Giedi Prime, some things
needed to be said.

The old Parliament building had been shored up and repaired, while the remnants of scaffolding and temporary walls
marked where reconstruction had not yet been completed.
Plazstone, pillars, and mural walls were still marked with
cracks and obvious patchwork. Battle scars, badges of honor.

Shortly before the young officer's scheduled address, Viceroy Butler had stood beside his stoic wife on the floor of Parliament as they participated in a memorial service for Serena
and the fallen comrades in her Giedi Prime rescue mission.

"She died doing exactly what she demanded of herself, and
of us," the Viceroy said. "A light has gone out in our lives."

In the year since the cymek attack on Salusa, the people had endured many funerals and too much grief. But Serena, the fiery young representative, had always insisted that the League serve the people and help those in need.

Beside the Viceroy, Livia Butler wore her contemplation robes from the City of Introspection. She had already watched her only son Fredo waste away from his blood disease; now her eldest daughter had been killed by the thinking machines. She had only ethereal young Octa left of her children.

Representatives of the League Worlds remained silent and respectful, sharing in the sadness. Despite her youth, Serena Butler had made a lasting impression with her idealism and exuberance. After the formal eulogy many speakers took turns at the podium to praise her acts of generosity.

Xavier listened to the tributes. The representatives looked at him compassionately. He thought of the life he and Serena had meant to share.

For her sake, though, Xavier had not, and would not, shed tears openly. If the human race wept for all those who had fallen, they would be paralyzed in an unending state of grief. His lips trembled, and his vision blurred, but he forced himself to be strong. It was his duty. Although his heart grieved, Xavier's mind turned to furious thoughts of the enemy, and of traitorous human sympathizers who fought beside the robots.

His memory of Serena would be his constant source of strength and inspiration. Even in death, she would drive him to achievements that he never could have attained without her. He still had the black diamond necklace that projected her last message to him, her brave call to arms to help Giedi Prime. Lovely Serena would watch over him always—as she did now, when he was about to rally the resources and military might of the angry masses.

Shaken and grim, Xavier stepped into the projection dome, followed by a sallow-skinned Viceroy Butler. Both men wore silver-and-blue robes and capes, with black headbands in honor of their fallen loved one.

It was time for the continuing business of humanity.

After his recent military success, he needed little introduction. "We are human beings, and have always fought for our rights and our dignity. We formed the League of Nobles so that free men could resist the Titans, and after them the thinking machines. Only by standing united have we been able to stop the headlong conquests of our enemies." He scanned the representatives seated in the crowded hall. "But at times the League is its own worst enemy."

The attendees respected this hero too much to argue, and Xavier continued quickly and concisely. "While we pay lip service to our alliance, the League Worlds remain self-centered and independent. When a beleaguered planet calls for help, the League debates and agonizes for months before we decide on our response—until it is too late! We saw that on Giedi Prime. Only Serena's folly forced us to act swiftly enough to make a difference. She knew exactly what she was doing, and paid for it with her life."

When a few of the representatives began to mutter, Xavier's skin grew hot and he silenced them with a booming voice. "The League of Nobles must form a stronger coalition under streamlined leadership. To be effective against a highly organized computer evermind, we need a closely knit government of humans, better than this loose structure." He waved his hands as he spoke.

"As Serena Butler advocated, we must make every effort to secure the cooperation of the Unallied Planets, thus strengthening our defensive framework and adding a buffer zone to our protected territory."

Viceroy Butler stepped close beside him and added in a voice cracking with emotion, "That was always my daughter's dream. Now we must make it ours."

Several uncertain nobles rose in respectful dissent. A lean, hard-looking woman from Kirana III said, "Bringing so many worlds together under tight rule, especially in a military guise, reminds me of the Time of Titans."

A small-statured nobleman from Hagal shouted, "No more empires!"

Xavier raised his own voice. "Isn't an empire better than

extinction? While you worry about political nuances, Omnius is conquering star systems!"

But another said, "For centuries the League of Nobles and Synchronized Worlds have held each other at bay, in an uneasy equilibrium. Omnius has never pressed beyond the boundaries of the Old Empire. We always assumed the thinking machines didn't consider it efficient or worthwhile. Why should that change now?"

"For whatever reason, it *has* changed! The thinking machines seem intent on genocide." Xavier clenched his fists; he had not expected to argue over this, when the evidence was so obvious. "Must we cower behind our paper-thin defense and simply *react* whenever Omnius chooses to test us? As we did here on Salusa a year ago, as we did on Giedi Prime?"

In a dramatic outburst, he hefted the podium and sent it crashing through one side of the dome enclosure. The front row of nobles scrambled away from the shower of broken prismatic glass. Shocked representatives yelled that Xavier's behavior was uncalled-for; others summoned security guards to remove the distraught officer from the hall.

Stepping through the broken enclosure, Xavier shouted without the benefit of a voice amplifier, "Good! That's the kind of spirit I want to see! The League has been cringing for too long. I have spoken with other Armada commanders, and most of us agree: We need to change our tactics and surprise the machines. We should spend whatever money is necessary, recruit the imagination of all our scientists, and develop new weapons—weapons suitable for destroying Omnius, not just to protect us here at home. One day, I believe we must go on the *offensive*! It is the only way we can win this conflict."

Gradually, the assemblage understood that Xavier had intentionally provoked a reaction. With a polished boot, he kicked broken debris off the stage. "Experience is our best teacher. The machines could attack Salusa again at any moment, or Poritrin, or Rossak, or Hagal, Ginaz, Kirana III, Seneca, Vertree Colony, Relicon—need I go on? None of our worlds are safe." He raised a scolding finger. "But if we turn the tables, we can drive the aggressors back with bold, unforeseen moves." He paused. "Do we have the nerve to do it? Can we develop the weapons to succeed? The time for complacency is past."

In the ensuing discussion, Zufa Cenva offered more telepathy raids against cymeks. Many more prime Sorceress candidates had already volunteered, she said. Lord Niko Bludd bragged of the continuing work of Tio Holtzman, who planned to test a new "alloy resonator" soon. Other League representatives offered suggestions, targets, ways to strengthen their position.

Relieved and inspired, Xavier gazed around the assemblage. He had shamed them into a show of boisterous support, and the voices of dissent—for now—remained subdued.

Unbidden tears ran down his face, and he tasted salt on his lips. Drained of emotion and energy, he noticed Viceroy Butler looking proudly at him, as if the young man were his son.

I am assuming the mantle of Serena, Xavier realized, *doing what she would have done.*

As if to balance the pain and suffering, War has also been the breeding ground for some of our greatest dreams and accomplishments.

—HOLTZMAN,
acceptance speech, Poritrin Medal of Valor

Blindly confident, Tio Holtzman plunged ahead with his new idea, making Norma Cenva feel like chaff in a gusting wind. With his alloy-resonance generator, the inventor insisted on proving himself to her.

Though she remained doubtful that his concept would work, Norma could not demonstrate her reason for uncertainty with straightforward mathematical proofs. Instinct spoke to her like a nagging voice, but she kept her worries to herself. After Holtzman's sour reaction to her initial reservations, he had not asked for her opinion again.

Norma hoped that she was mistaken. She was *human*, after all, and far from perfect.

While the Savant busied himself inside the domed demonstration laboratory—a theater-sized structure atop an adjoining bluff—Norma kept to the sidelines. Even her most innocent participation made him nervous, as if he put more stock in her doubts than he admitted aloud.

Now she stood on the span of the bridge between bluff

sections and reached up to grab the rail. Listening to breezes hum through the cables, she peered through safety netting at the river traffic far below.

She heard Holtzman inside the domed demo-lab, shouting to slaves as they erected a bulky generator that produced a resonating field intended to shake apart and melt a metal form. An imperious presence in a white-and-purple robe, he wore chains of office about his neck, baubles that signified his scientific awards and achievements. Holtzman glared at his workers, then paced around, double-checking, watching every detail.

Lord Bludd and a handful of Poritrin nobles would join them to watch the day's test, so Norma understood Holtzman's anxiety. She herself would never have made such an extravagant presentation of an untried device, but the scientist did not show even a glimmer of doubt.

"Norma, please assist me in here," Holtzman called in an exasperated tone. On short legs she ran from the bridge into the enclosure. He gestured disgustedly toward the slaves. "They don't understand a thing I've told them to do. Supervise them, so I can test the calibration."

At the center of the reinforced chamber, Holtzman's crew had erected a metal mannequin that had the vague features of a combat robot. Norma had never seen a real thinking machine, but had scrutinized many stored images. She stared at the mockup. This was the enemy, the true foe against which all of her work must be directed.

She looked at her mentor with more compassion, understanding his desperation. Holtzman was morally obligated to pursue *any* idea, to find *any* way to continue this noble fight. He had a good feel for projected energies, distortion fields, and nonprojectile weaponry. She hoped his alloy-resonance generator would work after all.

Before the slaves had finished rigging the test apparatus, a commotion occurred outside the main house. Ribbon-festooned ceremonial barges came into view above the cliffs, where Holtzman's balconies overlooked the river. Scale-armored Dragoon guards stood on the flying craft with Lord

Bludd, along with five senators and a black-robed court historian.

Holtzman dropped what he was doing. "Norma, finish this. Please!" Without looking back at her, he rushed across the connecting bridge to greet his prestigious visitors.

Norma urged the slaves to hurry, as she personally adjusted the calibrations and attuned the apparatus to the inventor's specifications. Light shone through high skylights to illuminate the robot facsimile. Reinforced metal ceiling beams crisscrossed the overhead vault, supporting pulleys and winches that had been used to haul the blockish resonance generator into place.

Moody Zenshiite slaves milled about, wearing traditional clothing, red-and-white stripes wrapped around serviceable gray jumpsuits. Many slave owners didn't allow their captives to show signs of individuality, but Holtzman didn't care one way or the other. He only wanted the captive people to perform their tasks without complaint.

As they completed their work the slaves backed close to the plated wall, their dark gazes averted. One black-bearded, shadowy-eyed man spoke to them in a language unfamiliar to Norma. Moments later a grinning Holtzman ushered his impressive guests into the demonstration area.

The Savant made a grand entrance. At his side, Niko Bludd wore a billowing azure tunic and a scarlet doublet fastened across his barrel chest. His reddish beard had been curled in neat ringlets. Small tattooed circles looked like bubbles at the far points of each eyelid.

Walking past the slaves, Bludd noticed Norma and gave the diminutive woman a smile that was both condescending and paternal. Norma bent in a formal bow and politely grasped his slick, lotioned hand.

"We know your time is valuable, Lord Bludd. Therefore, everything has been prepared." Holtzman folded his hands. "This new device has never been tested, and in today's presentation you will be the first to witness its potential."

Bludd's voice was deep, but musical. "We always expect

the best from you, Tio. If thinking machines have nightmares, no doubt you are in them."

The entourage chuckled, and Holtzman did his best to blush. He turned toward the slaves and began issuing orders. A half dozen workers held data-recording devices, positioned at important points around the robot mockup.

Plush chairs from the main residence had been arranged as seats of honor. Holtzman sat beside Lord Bludd, and Norma was forced to stand by the door. Her mentor appeared confident and intense, but she knew how worried he really was. A failure today might dim his glory in the eyes of the politically powerful nobles on Poritrin.

The esteemed observers sat in their cumbersome chairs. Holtzman stared at the generator setup, glancing around as if offering a quiet prayer. He smiled reassuringly at Norma, then ordered the activation of the prototype.

A slave flipped a switch, as he had been taught to do. The bulky generator began to hum, directing its invisible beam toward the robot construction.

"If put to practical use," Holtzman said with the faintest of quavers, "we will find ways to make the generator more compact, more easily installed on small ships."

"Or we can just build bigger ships," Bludd said, with a deep chortle.

The hum grew louder, a vibrating rattle that made Norma's teeth chatter. She noticed a thin sheen of perspiration on Holtzman's brow.

"Look, you can see it already." The scientist pointed. The targeted robot began to shake, its metal limbs jostling and torso vibrating. "The effect will continue to build."

Bludd was delighted. "That robot is regretting he ever turned against the human race, isn't he!"

The facsimile robot began to shimmer cherry red, its metal heating up as the alloys were attuned to the destructive field projected upon it. Glowing brighter, it shifted to yellow mixed with patches of blinding white.

"By now, a real robot would have been destroyed internally," Holtzman said, finally looking content.

Abruptly the laboratory's heavy ceiling girders started to rattle, a secondary resonance fed from the targeted robot into the dome's structural framework. The thick walls rumbled and shuddered. A high-pitched hum shrieked through the structure.

Norma cried, "The resonance field is bleeding over."

Ceiling girders clenched like angry snakes. A crack opened in the dome.

"Shut it off!" Holtzman shouted, but the terrified slaves scrambled to a corner of the room, as far from the generator as they could get.

The robot mockup undulated and twisted, its body core melting. Support struts that held it inside the targeting zone buckled. The ominous-looking combat machine lurched forward then abruptly fell and shattered into blackened metal.

Holtzman grabbed Niko Bludd's sleeve. "My Lord, please hurry across the bridge to my main quarters. We seem to have a . . . slight problem."

The other nobles were already pelting across the high-tension bridge. Norma was swept along with them. She took one look behind her and saw that the Zenshiite slaves were uncertain what to do. Tio Holtzman gave them no guidance as he retreated over the walkway right behind Bludd.

From safety, Norma watched six panicked slaves stumble onto the bridge. Remaining behind, the dark-haired leader pushed them forward, shouting in their odd language. The walkway began to whip up and down as resonance from the projector coupled to the bridge's connecting metal.

The bearded Zenshiite leader howled at them again. Norma wished she could rescue those unfortunate, confused people. Couldn't the Dragoon guards do anything? Holtzman remained speechless on this side of the bluff, paralyzed with shock.

Before the first batch of slaves could cross, the suspension walkway snapped in the middle, dropping open in a screeching groan of agonized metal. The hapless victims plummeted two hundred meters to the base of the bluff and into the river.

Standing on the threshold, separated now by the gulf between the cliffs, the black-bearded leader cursed again. Behind him, a section of the vaulted roof crashed down, destroying the prototype generator and finally stopping the relentless pulse.

Dust settled. A few flames and a curl of smoke rose into the air amidst the wailing of injured men still trapped within the collapsed building.

Norma felt sick. Beside her, Holtzman sweated profusely and looked ill. He blinked again and again, then wiped his forehead. His skin was gray.

In a wry voice, Bludd said, "Not one of your most successful efforts, Tio."

"But you must admit, the concept shows promise, Lord Bludd. Look at the destructive potential," Holtzman said, looking at the unruffled nobles without even considering the dead and injured slaves. "We can be thankful at least that no one was hurt."

Science: The creation of dilemmas by the solution of mysteries.
—NORMA CENVA,
unpublished laboratory notebooks

Inside the broken demonstration dome, the bloodstains washed away easily, but deeper scars remained. While a crew of new slaves cleared the rubble, Tio Holtzman crossed a temporary and none-too-sturdy walkway. He looked sadly at the ruins of his laboratory.

From where he worked, Bel Moulay, the bearded leader of the Zenshiite slaves, glowered at the callous inventor. He hated the Poritrin man's pale skin, square-cut hair, and arrogantly colorful clothes. The scientist's frivolous badges of honor meant nothing to Bel Moulay, and all the captive Zenshiites were offended that such a useless, deluded man could flaunt his wealth while stepping on the faithful.

In a deep voice the bearded leader gave instructions and consolation to his fellows. Moulay had always been more than just the strongest among them; he was also a religious leader, trained on IV Anbus in the strictest laws of the Zenshiite interpretation of Buddislam. He had learned the true scriptures and sutras, had analyzed every passage; the other slaves looked to Bel Moulay to interpret for them.

Despite his faith, he was as helpless as his companions, forced to serve at the whim of nonbelievers. The infidels refused to let Zenshiites live according to their strictures, but insisted on dragging them into their hopeless war against the unholy machine demons. It was a terrible punishment, a set of karmic tribulations visited upon them by Buddallah.

But they would see it through, and eventually emerge stronger. . . .

Under Bel Moulay's guidance, the slaves moved rubble, uncovering the crushed bodies of companions who had worked alongside them, fellow Zenshiites captured when Tlulaxa slavers raided the canyon cities on IV Anbus.

Buddallah would eventually show them the way to freedom. At story fires, the bearded leader had promised that the oppressors would be punished—if not in this generation, then in the next, or the next. But it would happen. A mere man like Bel Moulay had no business trying to hurry the wishes of God.

With excited shouts, two slaves shifted a fallen section of wall to uncover a man who still clung to life, though his legs had been crushed and his torso slashed by shards of windowplaz. Preoccupied, Holtzman came over and scrutinized the injured man. "I am no medical practitioner, but there seems to be little hope."

Bel Moulay glowered at him with dark, penetrating eyes. "Nevertheless, we must do what we can," he said in Galach. Three Zenshiite workers scooped away the debris and carried the injured man across the rickety walkway. Inside the slave quarters, healers would work on the injuries.

After the accident, Holtzman had provided basic medical supplies, though a similar effort had done little to keep a fever from sweeping through the slave population. The scientist supervised the workers in the rubble, but he was intent on his own priorities.

With a frown, the Savant gestured impatiently at the slaves picking up chunks of the collapsed ceiling to uncover victims.

"You and you, leave off digging out bodies for now and excavate what's left of my device."

The sullen captives looked at Moulay for guidance. He simply shook his head. "There is no value in resistance now," he muttered in their private language. "But I promise you the time will come."

Later, during their meager sleep time, they would remove their dead and provide proper Zenshiite blessings and passage preparations for the souls. Burning the bodies of the faithful was not something their religion accepted easily, but it was the way of Poritrin. Bel Moulay was certain Buddallah could not fault them for not following traditional rules, when they had no choice in the matter.

His deity could be an angry one, though. Moulay hoped to live long enough to see vengeance strike these oppressors, even if it must be in the form of thinking machines.

As the demonstration dome was cleared, Holtzman began chattering to himself, planning new experiments and tests. He considered acquiring more slaves to make up for recent losses.

In all, twelve slaves were recovered from the demonstration dome, while those who had fallen to their deaths from the walkway had already been gathered from the river and disposed of by public cremation teams. Bel Moulay knew every one of their names, and he would make sure the Zenshiites chanted continual prayers for them. He would never forget what had happened here.

Or who was responsible: *Tio Holtzman.*

~

*The mind imposes an arbitrary framework called "reality,"
which is quite independent of what the senses report.*

—COGITORS,
Fundamental Postulate

Nothing is impossible," the disembodied brain had said to him.

In the gray stillness before dawn, Iblis Ginjo turned over restlessly in his makeshift bed, on the perimeter of the work encampment and its habitation hives of human slaves. Since the weather had been unseasonably warm, he had hauled his pliable bedstrip onto the porch of the simple bungalow the neo-cymeks had provided for him. He had lain awake, staring up at the distant stars and wondering which ones were still under the control of free humans.

Far away, the League had managed to keep Omnius at bay for a thousand years. Listening closely, but afraid to ask questions or call attention to himself, Iblis had heard accounts of how the machines first conquered, and then lost, Giedi Prime. The resilient humans had driven the machines out, killing the Titan Barbarossa and destroying a new Omnius.

An incredible achievement. But how? What had they done

to attain such a victory? What sort of leaders did they have? And how could he do the same here?

Groggy and tired, Iblis stirred. Again, he would spend the day convincing lower-level slaves to complete pointless labors for machine masters. Every day was the same, and the thinking machines could live for thousands of years. How much could *he* accomplish in only a meager human lifespan?

But Iblis took heart from the words of the Cogitor: *Nothing is impossible.*

He flicked open his eyes, intending to gauge the impending sunrise. Instead, he saw a distorted reflection, a curved plexiplaz wall, pinkish organic contours suspended in a container of energy-charged fluid.

He sat up abruptly. The Cogitor Eklo rested on the floorboards of his veranda. Beside the canister sat the big monk, Aquim, rocking back and forth, eyes closed, meditating in a semuta trance.

"What are you doing here?" Iblis demanded in a hushed voice. Fear clenched his throat. "If the cymeks find you in the camp, they—"

Aquim opened his bleary eyes. "Trustee humans are not the only ones who have an understanding with the Titans, and with Omnius. Eklo wishes to speak with you directly."

Swallowing hard, Iblis looked from the enlarged brain suspended in its electrafluid to the haggard-looking monk. "What does he want?"

"Eklo wishes to tell you of earlier abortive human revolts." Holding a hand against the preservation canister, he stroked the smooth surface, as if picking up vibrations. "Have you ever heard of the Hrethgir Rebellions?"

Iblis looked around furtively. He saw none of Omnius's watcheyes. "That isn't the sort of history slaves are allowed to know, even a crew boss at my level."

The secondary leaned forward, his brows hooded. He spoke of things he had learned, without connecting directly through the electrafluid to the Cogitor's thoughts. "Bloody rebellions occurred after the Titans had converted themselves to cymeks, but before Omnius awakened. Feeling themselves immortal, the cymeks became exceedingly brutal. Especially the one called Ajax, who was so vicious in his torment of the surviving humans that his mate Hecate left him and disappeared."

Iblis said, "Ajax hasn't changed much over the centuries."

Aquim's red-rimmed eyes glowed. Eklo's brain trembled inside its nutrient solution. "Because of the excessive brutality of Ajax, oppressed humans began a rebellion, mainly on Walgis but spreading to Corrin and Richese. The slaves rose up and destroyed two of the original Titans, Alexander and Tamerlane.

"The cymeks responded with a swift and decisive crackdown. Ajax took great delight in closing off Walgis and then methodically exterminating every living human there. Billions were slaughtered."

Iblis struggled to think. This Cogitor had come all the way from his high tower to see him. The magnitude of such a gesture stunned him. "Are you telling me that a revolt against the machines is possible, or that it is doomed to failure?"

The big monk extended a rough hand to grab Iblis's wrist. "Eklo will tell you himself."

Iblis felt a rush of anxiety, but before he could resist, Aquim pressed the work leader's fingertips into the viscous electrafluid surrounding the Cogitor's ancient brain. The slick solution felt icy cold to Iblis, then hot. The skin on his hand tingled, as if a thousand tiny spiders ran along his flesh.

Suddenly he could sense thoughts, words, and impressions flowing directly into his mind from Eklo. "The revolt failed, but oh what a glorious attempt!"

Iblis received another message, this one wordless, but it conveyed meaning nonetheless, like an epiphany. It was as if the majesty of the universe had opened to him, so many things he had not previously understood . . . so many things Omnius kept the slaves from knowing. Feeling great calm, he immersed his hand deeper into the liquid. His fingertips touched the Cogitor's tissue, ever so gently.

"You are not alone." Eklo's words reverberated to his very soul. "I can help. Aquim can help."

For several moments, Iblis gazed toward the horizon as the

golden sun rose, casting light on enslaved Earth. Now he did not view this story of a failed rebellion as a warning, but as a sign of hope. A better-organized revolt might succeed, given proper guidance and proper planning. And the proper leader.

Iblis, who had once felt no purpose or direction in his life other than to enjoy the comfort of his position as a trustee of the machines, now sensed a brooding anger within. The revelation brought a fervor to his heart. The monk Aquim seemed to share the same passion behind his semuta-dazed expression.

"Nothing is impossible," Eklo repeated.

Amazed, Iblis removed his hand from the charged fluid and stared at his fingers. The big monk picked up the Cogitor's brain canister and sealed it. Cradling the cylinder against his chest, he set off on foot toward the mountains, leaving Iblis to reel with the visions that had flooded into his soul.

Erasmus wished the sophisticated evermind had spent more time studying human emotions. After all, the Synchronized Worlds had access to immense archives of records compiled by millennia of human studies. If Omnius had made the effort, he might now understand the independent robot's frustration.

"Your problem, Omnius," the robot said to the screen in an isolated room high in his Earth villa, "is that you expect accurate and specific answers in a fundamentally uncertain system. You want large numbers of experimental subjects—all human—to behave in a predictable fashion, as regimented as your sentinel robots."

Erasmus paced in front of the viewer until finally Omnius directed two of the hovering watcheyes to scan him from different directions.

"I have tasked you to develop a detailed and reproducible model that explains and accurately predicts human behavior. How do we make them usable? I rely upon you to explain this to my satisfaction." Omnius changed his voice to a high-pitched tone. "I tolerate your incessant tests in the expectation of eventually receiving an answer. You have been trying long enough. Instead, you are like a child playing with the same trivialities over and over."

"I serve a valuable purpose. Without my efforts at understanding the *hrethgir*, you would experience a state of extreme confusion. In human parlance I am known as your 'devil's advocate.' "

"Some of the humans call you the devil himself," Omnius countered. "I have considered the matter of your experiments at length, and I must conclude that whatever you discover about humans will reveal nothing new for us. Their unpredictability is just that—entirely unpredictable. Humans require a great deal of maintenance. They create messes—"

"They created *us*, Omnius. Do you think we are perfect?"

"Do you think that emulating humans will make us more perfect?"

Though the evermind would derive no meaning from it, Erasmus shaped his pliable, reflective face into a scowl. "Yes . . . I do," the robot finally said. "We can become the best of both."

The watcheyes followed him as he walked across the palatial room to the balcony several stories above the flagstone plaza that opened up into the grid of the city. The fountains and gargoyles were magnificent, imitated from Earth's Golden Age of art and sculpture. No other robots appreciated beauty as much as he did. On this cloudy afternoon, artisans crafted scrollwork around the windows, and new alcoves were being constructed in the building's facade, so that Erasmus could install additional statues as well as more colorful flowerboxes, since Serena Butler enjoyed tending them so much.

On this high balcony he loomed over the docile humans. Some laborers glanced up at him, then bent more diligently to their tasks, as if afraid he might punish them or—worse— single them out for his horrific laboratory projects.

Erasmus continued his conversation with the evermind.

"Surely some of my experiments intrigue you, Omnius, just a little?"

"You know the answer to that."

Erasmus said, "Yes, the experiment to test the loyalty of your human subjects is proceeding nicely. I have delivered cryptic messages to a handful of trustee candidates—I prefer not to reveal exactly how many—suggesting that they join the brewing rebellion against you."

"There is no brewing rebellion against me."

"Of course not. And if the trustees are completely loyal to you, they will never consider such a possibility. On the other hand, if they were genuinely faithful to your rule, then they would have reported my incendiary messages immediately. Therefore, I presume you have received reports from my test subjects?"

For a long moment, Omnius hesitated. "I will recheck my records."

Erasmus watched the diligent artisans in the plaza, then crossed the upper-level halls of his villa to the other side of the great house. He looked out toward the miserable fenced-in compounds and breeding pens from which he drew his experimental subjects.

A long time ago, he had raised a subset of captives under these conditions, treating them like animals to see how it would affect their much-vaunted "human spirit." Not surprisingly, within a generation or two they had lost all semblance of civilized behavior, morals, familial duty, and dignity.

Erasmus said, "When we imposed a caste system upon humans on the Synchronized Worlds, you attempted to make them more regimented and machinelike." He scanned the dirty, noisy crowds inside the slave pens. "While the caste system fit them within certain categories, we perpetuated a model of human behavior that allowed them to see how other members of their own race are different. It is the nature of mankind to strive for things they do not have, to steal the rewards that another person might win. To be envious of another's circumstances."

He focused his optic threads on the lovely ocean view beyond the filthy slave pens, the churning blue-and-white surf at the base of the slope. He swept his mirrored face up so that he could focus on seagulls in the sky. Such images matched his programmed aesthetics more closely than the dirty, fenced compound.

Erasmus continued, "Your most privileged human beings, such as the current son of Agamemnon, hold the highest position among their kind. They are our reliable pets, occupying a rung between sentient biologicals and thinking machines. From this pool we draw candidates for conversion into neo-cymeks."

The watcheye buzzed close to the robot's polished head. Through the flying device, Omnius said, "I know all this."

Erasmus continued as if he hadn't heard. "And the caste below the trustees includes civilized and educated humans, skilled thinkers and creators, such as the architects who design the Titans' interminable monuments. We rely on them to perform sophisticated tasks, such as those being completed by artisans and craftsmen at my villa. Just beneath them are my household staff, my cooks, and landscapers."

The robot scanned the slave pens and realized that such appalling ugliness made him want to go back to his flower gardens to wander among the carefully cultivated species. Serena Butler had already done wonders with the plants. She had an intuitive understanding of gardening.

"Admittedly, those wretches down there in my pens are good for little more than breeding new offspring or for dissection in medical experiments."

Erasmus was like Serena in a sense: he frequently needed to prune and weed the human race in his own garden.

"I hasten to add," the robot said, "that humankind as a whole is of supreme value to us. Irreplaceable."

"I have heard your argument before," Omnius mused as the watcheye drifted higher, for a broader view. "Though machines could perform every task you have enumerated, nevertheless I have accepted the loyalty of my human subjects, and I have granted some of them privileges."

"Your arguments do not seem . . ." Erasmus hesitated, because the word he had in mind would be a supreme insult to a computer. *Logical.*

Omnius said, "All humans, with their strange penchant for religious beliefs and faith in things incomprehensible, should pray that your experiments prove me right about human nature, and not you. Because if you are correct, Erasmus, there are inescapable and violent consequences for their entire race."

Religion, often considered a divisive force among peoples, is also capable of holding together what might otherwise fall asunder.

—LIVIA BUTLER,
private journals

The Isana mudflats spread out in a broad fan where the river melted into a slurry of water and muck. Shirtless, the boy Ishmael stood in the mire, barely able to maintain his balance. Every night he washed his sore palms and applied smears of ever-dwindling salves.

The work supervisors showed no sympathy for the slaves' discomfort. One grabbed Ishmael's hand and turned it over to examine the sores, then shoved him away. "Keep working, it'll toughen you up." Ishmael went back to his labors, silently noting that the man's hands were much softer than his own.

Once the shellfish planting season ended, the slave owners would find other work for them, perhaps sending them north to rugged cane fields to hack down thick stands of grasses and harvest the juices.

Some of the Zensunni muttered that if they were transferred to the agricultural fields, they would escape at night and flee into the wilderness. But Ishmael had no idea how to survive on Poritrin, did not know the edible plants or the native predators, as he did on Harmonthep. Any escapee would be without tools or weapons, and if captured would surely face violent punishment.

A few of the muddy slaves began to chant, but the folk songs varied from planet to planet, the verses changed among the Buddislamic sects. Ishmael worked until his muscles and bones ached and his eyes could see little but the sun glaring off the standing water. In endless treks back and forth to the supply basins, he must have planted a million clam seedlings. No doubt, he would be asked to plant a million more.

Hearing three blasts of a shrill whistle, Ishmael looked up to see the frog-lipped supervisor standing on his platform mounted above the mudflats, safe and dry. Ishmael knew it was not yet time for the slaves' brief morning break.

With narrowed eyes, the supervisor scanned the labor gang, as if mentally making selections. He pointed to a handful of the youngest planters, Ishmael among them, and instructed them to slosh their way back to a staging area on dry land. "Get yourselves cleaned up. You've been reassigned."

Ishmael felt a cold hand squeeze his heart. While he hated the smelly mud, these refugees from Harmonthep were his only connection to his home planet and his grandfather.

Some of the "volunteers" wailed. Two of those not selected clutched at their reassigned companions, refusing to let them go. The frog-mouthed supervisor snapped harsh words and made threatening gestures. A pair of armed Dragoon guards came in to enforce the edict, splashing mud on their golden uniforms as they separated the slaves. Though sad and terrified, Ishmael offered no resistance. He could never win if he fought them.

The supervisor stretched his lips in a grin. "You're lucky, all of you. There's been an accident in Savant Holtzman's laboratories, and he needs replacement slaves to do calculations. Clever boys. Easy work, compared to this."

Clearly skeptical, Ishmael eyed the ragtag group of mud-spattered youths.

Uprooted again, taken from a dreary existence that had just begun to seem normal, Ishmael trudged along, not understanding what he was expected to do. He would find some way to endure, though. His grandfather had taught him that survival was the essence of success, and that violence was the last refuge of a failure. It was the Zensunni way.

❧

SCRUBBED CLEAN AND with his hair shorn close to his head, Ishmael fidgeted in his fresh clothes. He waited in a large room with a dozen recruits taken from work teams around Starda. Dragoon guards remained stationed at the door, their gold-scale armor and ornate helmets making them look like birds of prey.

Ishmael took a place next to a dark-haired boy about his own age who had light brown skin and a narrow face. "My name is Aliid," the boy said quietly, though the guards had instructed them all to be silent. Aliid had an intensity that spoke of trouble, or perhaps leadership. A visionary or a criminal.

"I'm Ishmael." He glanced around nervously.

A Dragoon guard turned toward the whispers, and both boys formed their faces into placid expressions. The guard looked away, and Aliid spoke quickly again. "We were captured on IV Anbus. Where did you come from?"

"Harmonthep."

A well-dressed man entered the room, causing a commotion as he did so. Pale-skinned and with a square-cut mane of iron-gray hair, he looked and acted like a lord. He wore decorative chains around his neck and flowing white robes with loose sleeves. His face and sharp eyes showed little interest in the batch of slaves. He gazed down his nose as he assessed the young workers without much satisfaction, only resignation. "They'll do—if they're trained well enough and carefully watched."

He stood next to a diminutive, blunt-featured young woman who had the body of a child, though her face looked much older. Preoccupied, the white-robed man muttered something to her and left, as if he had more important things to do.

"That was Savant Holtzman," the woman said. "The great scientist is your master now. Our work will help defeat the thinking machines." She offered them a hopeful smile, but few of the boys seemed to care what their new slave master's purposes might be.

Flustered by their reaction, she continued, "I am Norma Cenva, and I also work with Savant Holtzman. You will be trained to perform mathematical calculations. The war against thinking machines affects all of us, and this is how you can do your part." She seemed to have rehearsed her speech many times.

Aliid frowned, scorning her words. "I'm taller than *she* is!"

As if hearing him, Norma turned to look directly at Aliid. "With a single stroke of your stylus, you can complete a calculation that may gain victory against Omnius. Keep that in mind."

When she turned away again, Aliid said out of the corner of his mouth, "And even if we win the war for them, will they free us?"

❧

AT NIGHT IN their communal quarters at the blufftop estate, the slaves were left alone. Here, the Buddislamic captives kept their culture alive.

Ishmael was surprised that he had been cast in among members of the Zenshiite sect, a different interpretation of Buddislam that had split them from the Zensunnis many centuries ago, before the great flight from the crumbling Old Empire.

He met their muscular, dark-eyed leader, Bel Moulay, a man who had obtained permission for his people to wear traditional striped cloths over drab work uniforms. The tribal clothing was a symbol of their identity, the white of freedom and the red of blood. Poritrin slave keepers understood none of the symbolism, which was just as well.

Bright-eyed, Aliid sat next to Ishmael. "Listen to Bel Moulay. He will give us hope. He has a plan."

Ishmael hunkered down. His belly was full with strange,

bland food, but it nourished him. As much as he resented his new master, the boy did prefer working here, rather than on the awful mudflats.

Bel Moulay called them all to prayer in a firm, gruff voice, then intoned sacred sutras in a language that Ishmael's grandfather had employed, an arcane tongue understood only by the most devout. In that way, they could converse without being understood by eavesdropping masters.

"Our people have waited for vengeance," Moulay said. "We were free, then captured. Some of us are new slaves, while others have served the evil men for generations." His eyes were fiery, his teeth very white against dark lips and a black beard. "But God has given us our minds and our belief. It is up to us to find the weapons and the necessary resolve."

The muttering among the Zenshiites made Ishmael uncomfortable. Bel Moulay seemed to be advocating outright revolt, a violent uprising against the masters. To Ishmael, that did not seem what Buddallah would have preached.

Sitting together, the IV Anbus slaves made whispered threats of retribution. Moulay talked of the disastrous alloy-resonator test that had caused the deaths of seventeen innocent slaves.

"We have suffered countless indignities," Moulay said. The slaves growled their agreement. "We do everything our masters require of us. They reap the benefits of what we accomplish, but the Zenshiites"—he looked quickly at Ishmael and the other new additions to the group—"as well as our Zensunni brothers, never attain our freedom." He leaned forward as if dark thoughts were coursing his mind. "The answer is in our grasp."

Ishmael remembered that his grandfather had taught philosophical and nonviolent methods of solving problems. Even so, old Weyop had been unable to save his villagers. The pacifistic Zensunni ways had failed them all, at a time of utmost crisis.

Bel Moulay raised a callused fist, as if he intended to thrust it into the crackling fire. "We have been told by men who call themselves 'righteous slavers' that they have no compunction against pressing *our people* into work. They claim we owe a debt to humanity because we refused to participate in their foolish war against the machine demons—demons that they had created and thought they controlled. But after centuries of oppression, the people of Poritrin owe *us*. And that is a debt which must be paid in blood."

Aliid cheered, but beside him Ishmael sat uneasily. He did not agree with the approach, but was unable to offer an alternative. Since he was only a boy, he did not speak up or interrupt the meeting.

Instead, like his companions, he listened to Bel Moulay. . . .

Thirsty men speak of water, not of women.
                                 —Zensunni Fire Poetry from Arrakis

Far beyond the League Worlds, thousands of uncharted settlements dotted the Unallied Planets, places where forgotten people eked out meager livings. A few raided villages would never be noticed out here.

By long tradition, good Tlulaxa flesh merchants did not frequently harvest the same world, preferring to surprise unsuspecting groups of captives, not giving them a chance to develop defenses. A resourceful slaver found new cradles of life, untapped resources.

Leaving his transport vessel in orbit, Tuk Keedair dispatched a cargo ship and fresh crew to the surface, along with sufficient credits to hire a few greedy locals. Then Keedair went down to the Arrakis City spaceport by himself to scout around before planning a raid on some of the local communities. He had to be careful when investigating new targets for slave raids, especially on this desolate world at the withered end of space.

The costs of getting here—fuel, food, ships, and crew—

were extraordinarily high, not to mention the sheer voyage time and the expense of hauling slaves back in stasis pods. Keedair doubted that raiding Arrakis would prove cost-effective. No wonder people left this place alone.

Arrakis City clung like a scab to the ugly skin of the planet. Hovels and prefabricated dwellings had been established here long ago. The sparse population barely survived by servicing lost traders or exploration vessels, and selling supplies to fugitives from the law. Keedair suspected that anyone desperate enough to run *this* far must be in serious trouble indeed.

As he seated himself in the rundown spaceport bar, his triangular gold earring glinted in the dim illumination. His dark braid hung down at the left side of his head. Its length spoke of years spent garnering wealth, which he spent freely though not frivolously.

He surveyed the sullen locals, noted how they contrasted with a few loud and boisterous offworlders in one corner, rugged men who obviously had plenty of credits, but were disgruntled that Arrakis offered little opportunity for them to spend their money.

Keedair rested an arm across the scarred metal counter. The bartender was a lean man whose skin was a nest of wrinkles, as if all the moisture and body fat had been sapped away, leaving him shriveled like a raisin. A bald, liver-spotted scalp covered the top of his head like a torpedo casing.

Keedair hauled out his hard currency, League credits that were legal tender even on the Unallied Planets. "I feel good today. What's your best drink?"

The bartender gave him a sour smile. "In mind for something exotic, are you? You think Arrakis might have something to quench your thirst, eh?"

Keedair began to lose patience. "Do I have to pay extra for the chat, or can I just have my drink? Your most expensive. What is it?"

The bartender laughed. "That would be water, sir. Water is the most valuable drink on Arrakis."

The bartender named a price that was higher than Keedair would expect to pay for supercharged spacecraft fuel. "For *water*? I don't think so."

He looked around to see if the bartender was having a joke at his expense, but the other customers seemed to accept it. He'd assumed that the clear drinks in small glasses were colorless alcohol, but it really did seem to be water. He noticed an extravagant local merchant whose billowing, colorful clothes and gaudy ornamentation pegged him as a wealthy man. That one even had a few ice cubes floating in his glass.

"Ridiculous," Keedair said. "I know when I'm being cheated."

The bartender shook his bald head. "Water's hard to come by around here, sir. I can sell you alcohol cheaper, because Arrakis natives don't want anything that'll dehydrate them further. And a man with too much strong drink in him can make mistakes. You don't pay attention out in the desert and it'll cost you your life."

In the end, Keedair settled on a fermented substance called "spice beer," potent and pungent with a strong cinnamon bite at the back of his throat. He found the drink exhilarating and ordered a second.

While he remained doubtful about the profitability of exploiting Arrakis for slaves, Keedair still felt like celebrating. The success of his run on Harmonthep four months earlier had given him enough credits to live for a year. After that raid, Keedair had hired a new team, never wanting to keep employees around for so long that they grew comfortable and complacent. That wasn't the way a good Tlulaxa businessman managed his affairs. Keedair watched over his work, maintained the details himself, and put tidy profits in his own pockets.

He sipped his spice beer again and began to like it even more. "What's in this stuff?" When none of the customers seemed interested in conversation, he directed his gaze back at the bartender. "Is this beer brewed here, or is it an import?"

"Made on Arrakis, sir." When the bartender grinned, his wrinkles folded in upon themselves like a weird origami sculpture made of leather. "It's brought in by the desert people, Zensunni nomads."

Keedair's attention perked up at the mention of the Buddislamic sect. "I'd heard there were a few bands living here in the wastelands. How can I find them?"

"*Find* them?" The bartender chuckled. "Nobody wants to look for them. Dirty, violent folk. They kill strangers."

Keedair could hardly believe the answer. It took him two tries to formulate his question because the effects of the spice beer had caught him unawares, causing him to slur his words. "But Zensunni—I thought they were meek pacifists?"

The bartender emitted a dry cackle. "Some may be, but these aren't afraid to shed blood to make their point, if you know what I mean."

"Are they numerous?"

The bartender scoffed. "At most, we see only a dozen or two at a time. I'm surprised they're not so inbred that every baby comes out a mutant."

Keedair's sharp-featured face fell, and he switched his braid to the other shoulder. His plans began to crumble. In addition to the expense of bringing his teams here to Arrakis, his raiders would have to scour the desert just to drag a few sand rats back to market. Keedair sighed and took a long drink of spice beer. Probably not worth the effort. He'd be better off hitting Harmonthep again, even if it made him look bad to other slavers.

"Course, there could be more of them than we realize," the bartender said. "They all look the same wrapped up in desert clothes."

As Keedair savored the liquor, a tingle went through his body, not quite euphoria, but a rush of well-being. Then an idea lit his mind. He was a businessman, after all, constantly on the lookout for opportunities. It didn't matter where the merchandise came from.

"And what about this spice beer?" He tapped his nearly empty glass with a stubby fingernail. "Where do the Zensunnis find ingredients? Doesn't seem to me that anything could grow out there at all."

"Spice is a natural substance in the desert. You can find patches out in the dunes, exposed by the wind or spice blows. But monster sandworms live out there, and fierce storms that'll

kill you. Let the Zensunnis have the place, if you ask me. The
nomads bring in loads of the stuff to Arrakis City, for barter-
ing."

Keedair considered taking samples of melange back to the
League Worlds. Would there be a market for it on rich Salusa,
or among the nobles on Poritrin? The substance certainly had
an unusual effect on the body . . . soothing in a way he had
never experienced before. If he could sell it, he might offset
some of the cost of this exploration trip.

The bartender nodded toward the door. "I don't get enough
spice beer that I can sell to you as a middleman, but a band
of nomads came in this morning. They'll stay inside their tents
during the heat of the day, but you'll find them in the market
in the evening, on the east end of the spaceport. They'll sell
you whatever they have. Just be sure they don't cheat you."

"Nobody cheats me," Keedair said, revealing his sharp teeth
in a cruel grin. He noticed, though, that his words came out
alarmingly slurred. He would have to let the spice beer wear
off before he met with the Zensunni.

                                                 ⌇

AWNINGS OF BROWN-AND-WHITE fabric offered
patches of shade. The nomads sat by themselves, separated
from the bustle of the spaceport. These Zensunnis had constructed tents and shelters from scavenged tarpaulins and cargo
wrappings. Some of the fabrics appeared to be made from a
different kind of polymer, an odd sort of plastic unlike anything Keedair had seen before.

The sun fell behind the barricade of mountains, leaving the
sky awash with orange pastels and fire hues. A wind came in
as the temperature dropped, bringing dust and stinging sand.
The awnings flapped and rattled, but the nomads paid no heed,
as if the noise were music to them.

Keedair approached them alone, still swaying slightly,
though he felt clearer-headed after drinking only water for the
rest of the afternoon . . . and paying the exorbitant price. Noticing him, two hopeful women went into their stores to haul

out items for sale, spreading them on a flat tabletop. One man stood near them, his lean face tattooed with a geometric symbol, his eyes dark and suspicious.

Without saying a word, Keedair allowed the women to display their colorful cloths, along with odd-shaped rocks that had been scoured in sandstorms and a few laughably corroded items of long-forgotten technology that Keedair could never sell to even the most gullible and eccentric antique collector. He shook his head gruffly each time until the lean man— whom one of the women referred to as Naib Dhartha—said he had nothing else.

Keedair got to the point. "I've tasted spice beer. The man who sold it to me suggested I talk to you."

"Spice beer," Dhartha said. "Made from melange. Yes, it is obtainable."

"How much can you deliver, and what would it cost me?"

The naib spread his hands and revealed a hint of a smile. "Everything is open to discussion. The price depends on the amount you desire. Enough for a month of personal use?"

"Why not a cargo ship full?" Keedair said, noting shock on the faces of the nomads.

Dhartha recovered himself quickly. "That will take time to gather. A month, maybe two."

"I can wait—if we reach an agreement. I've come here with an empty vessel. I need to take something back with me." He looked down at the scavenged objects and the wind-scoured art rocks. "And I certainly don't want to carry anything like *that*. I'd be the laughingstock of the League."

Despite a natural Tlulaxa interest in biological products, Keedair was not wedded to the business of slavery. He would go his own way and never return to the Thalim solar system, if necessary. Many of the Tlulaxa were religious fanatics anyway, and he grew tired of their dogma and politics. Drugs and drink would always be in demand, and if he could introduce something new and exotic, a drug the richest nobles had never tried, he might turn a handy profit.

"But first tell me exactly what melange is," Keedair continued. "Where does it come from?"

Dhartha gestured to one of the women, who ducked under the sheltered overhang. A hot breeze picked up, and the polymer fabric flapped louder than before. The sun had settled toward the horizon, forcing him to squint as he looked in that direction. This prevented him from reading nuances in the desert man's expression.

Within moments, the woman brought out small, steaming cups of a rich black liquid that smelled of pungent cinnamon spice. She served Keedair first, and he looked down, curious but skeptical.

"Coffee mixed with pure melange," Dhartha said. "You will enjoy it."

Keedair recalled how expensive water had been in the bar and decided that this nomad was investing in their conversation. He took a sip, cautious at first, but could think of no reason why the fellow might poison him. He tasted the hot coffee on his tongue and felt an electric sensation, a delicious taste that reminded him of the spice beer he still had in his system. He would need to be careful, or he would lose his business edge.

"We harvest melange out in the Tanzerouft, the deep desert where the demon sandworms go. It is very dangerous there. We lose many of our people, but the spice is precious."

Keedair took another drink of coffee and had to stop himself from agreeing too readily. His assessment of the possibilities grew. Now, as the two men shifted positions, Keedair could look upon Dhartha's lean face. The Naib's eyes were not just dark; they were deep blue. Even the whites had taken on a strange indigo tinge. Most odd. He wondered if it could be an unusual defect caused by Zensunni inbreeding.

The desert man reached into one of his pockets and withdrew a small box, which he opened to display a compressed, flaky brown powder. He extended it toward Keedair, who stirred the contents with the tip of his little finger.

"Pure melange. Very potent. We use it in our beverages and meals back in the cave villages."

Keedair touched the spice-speckled tip of his finger to his tongue. The melange was strong and exhilarating, yet soothing. He felt energetic and calm at the same time. His mind seemed sharper, not fuzzed the way excessive alcohol or drugs affected him. But he held back, not wishing to appear overly anxious.

"And if you consume melange over a long period of time," Dhartha was saying, "it helps you retain your health, keeps you young."

Keedair made no comment. He had heard similar claims about various "fountain of youth" substances. None of them, in his experience, had ever proven effective.

He snicked shut the cover of the small box and put it in his own pocket, though it had not been offered to him as a gift. He stood. "I will come back tomorrow. Then we shall talk more. I need to consider this matter."

The desert naib grunted in affirmation.

Keedair walked toward his shuttle within the parking perimeter of the spaceport. His mind spun with preliminary calculations. His fellow slavers would be disappointed at not even attempting a raid, but Keedair would pay them the minimum required by contract. He needed to ponder the possibilities of this potent spice before discussing a price with the nomads. Arrakis was far, far from normal space trading routes. The idea excited him, but he wasn't certain he could profitably export the exotic substance.

Realistically, he doubted if melange would ever be more than a mere curiosity.

Humans are survivors. They do things for themselves and then attempt to conceal their motivations through elaborate subterfuges. Gift-giving is a prime example of behavior that is secretly selfish.

—ERASMUS,
slave pen notes

Shortly before midnight, Aurelius Venport sat at a long opalwood table in an echoing chamber deep inside the Rossak cave city. He had furnished this room for his business meetings with drug prospectors, biochemists, and pharmaceutical merchants, but Zufa Cenva sometimes used it for her own private meetings.

Even in the late darkness, the chief Sorceress was out in the dangerous jungles, training her young protégés and preparing them for suicide attacks. Venport did not know whether Zufa was eager or afraid for her volunteers to be called again.

He very much hoped his mate didn't get ideas of her own, though she would probably love to make herself a martyr. Zufa took him for granted, blamed him for his imagined failings, but still Venport cared for the cold, pale Sorceress. He didn't want to lose her.

Zufa had been due back more than an hour ago, and he'd been waiting for her. It did him no good to be impatient, though. The haughty Sorceress operated on her own schedule, considering his priorities unimportant.

Even in the darkest night, the cave room was illuminated by warm, comforting light—a glowing yellow sphere that floated gracefully above the table like a portable, personal sun. Dear Norma had sent it to him from Poritrin as a gift, a compact light source levitated by a new suspensor field she had developed. Based on the same principle as a glowpanel, but much more efficient, the device generated illumination as a by-product of the suspensor field itself. Norma called it a glowglobe, and he'd been considering its commercial possibilities.

Venport took a long drink of bitter herbal ale from a goblet in front of him. He grimaced, then drank some more, trying to bolster his nerve. Zufa should be here any minute, and he was anxious to see her. Out in the jungles the Sorceresses had erected a shrine to honor fallen Heoma. Maybe they were all there now, dancing around it under the starlight, chanting incantations like witches. Or maybe—despite their cool, agnostic logic and determination—they chose private moments to worship a Gaia life force, an Earth mother that embodied feminine power. Anything to set them apart from what they considered to be "weakling" men . . .

Beckoned by the glowglobe, nightbugs flew into the room from the outer corridors. The nocturnal insects had a voracious appetite for human blood, but only men were bothered. It was one of the jokes of Rossak, as if the Sorceresses had cast some sort of a spell on the tiny creatures to keep their men inside during the evenings, while women performed secret rites out in the jungles.

Another quarter of an hour passed, and still Zufa did not join him. Frustrated with her, Venport finished the ale and set the empty goblet on the opalwood table, heaving a disgusted sigh. He rarely asked to see her, but this was important to him. Couldn't she give him just a few moments of her precious time?

Still, he would continue to seek her understanding and respect. For years, Venport had enjoyed substantial success in exporting medical narcotics and pharmaceuticals manufactured from Rossak plants. In the past month, his men had turned a large profit from the sale of psychedelics to Yardin. The drugs had become a favorite of the Buddislamic mystics who ran the place. The mystics used the Rossak hallucinogen in religious rituals, attempting to attain enlightenment.

Venport stared at a large, milky soostone on the table. A smuggler from Buzzell, one of the Unallied Planets, had sold him the extremely rare and valuable stone. The dealer had claimed that some soostones of extraordinary purity possessed hypnotic focusing abilities. He wanted Zufa to wear it with pride, perhaps on a pendant. The Sorceress could use it to make herself stronger.

He inserted a rolled slip of alkaloid bark into his mouth and crunched down, knowing it would make him relax. He dimmed the glowglobe and adjusted its spectrum to a more orange light, which caused the soostone to dance with rainbow colors. The alkaloid bark made him feel tingly, calm . . . and distant. The uncommon stone shimmered hypnotically, and he lost track of time.

When Zufa entered the room, her pale face was flushed, her eyes bright. She looked like an ethereal creature in the room's rich glow. She wore a long diaphanous gown with tiny jewels sparkling across it like a field of ruby flowers.

"I see you have nothing important to do," she said, already frowning.

He gathered his wits about him. "Nothing more important than waiting for you." Rising to his feet with all the pride he could muster, he picked up the soostone. "I found this, and I thought of you. A gift from Buzzell, where my merchants made an extraordinary profit from—" Noticing an expression of disdain on her face, Venport felt flustered. His voice trailed off.

"And what am I supposed to do with it?" She examined the offering, without touching it. "When have I ever cared for pretty baubles?"

"It's a rare soostone, said to have certain . . . telepathic enhancement characteristics. Perhaps you can use it as a focusing device when you instruct your trainees?" She stood like a statue, unimpressed, and he continued in a rush, "The Buddislamics on Yardin are clamoring for our psychedelics. I've made a lot of credits in the past few months, and I thought this was something you might appreciate."

"I'm tired and I'm going to bed," she said, letting him keep the present. "My Sorceresses have already proven their abilities. With machines still threatening every League world, we don't have time to stare into soostones."

He shook his head. What would it have cost her merely to accept his gift? Could she not at least have offered him a word of kindness? Hurt so deeply that even the calming bark could not soothe him, Venport shouted, "If we give up our humanity to fight the machines, Zufa, then Omnius has already won!"

She hesitated just a moment, but did not turn back to him. Instead, she went to her chambers and left him standing alone.

In surviving, shall our humanity endure? That which makes life sweet for the living—warm and filled with beauty—this, too, must be. But we shall not gain this enduring humanity if we deny our whole being—if we deny emotion, thought, and flesh. If we deny emotion, we lose all touch with our universe. By denying thought, we cannot reflect upon what we touch. And if we dare deny the flesh, we unwheel the vehicle that carries us all.

—PRIMERO VORIAN ATREIDES,
Annals of the Army of the Jihad

Earth. In a drizzle of summer rain, Vorian rode inside an exquisite white coach, drawn by four prancing white stallions. Erasmus had ordered the robot coachman to wear a uniform with broad military lapels, dripping golden ribbons and a tricorner hat taken from an ancient historical image.

The extravagance was inefficient and unnecessary—not to mention anachronistic—but the human trustee had heard that eccentric Erasmus often did inexplicable things. Vor could not imagine why such an important representative of the evermind would want to see *him*.

Perhaps Erasmus had studied some of the simulations and war games Vorian had played with Seurat. He knew that the robot had built extensive laboratories to research the questions about human nature that plagued his inquisitive mind. *But what could I possibly tell him?*

As the carriage wheels clattered over cobblestones in front of the manor house, Vor wiped fog from the window. Even in the rain, the imposing Grogyptian-style villa was more mag-

nificent than the efficient grid-organized cities. It seemed fit
for a prince.

With ornamental gardens and enough tile-roofed buildings
to comprise a small village, the sprawling estate covered many
acres. The balcony-adorned main house featured tall fluted columns and winged gargoyles that looked down on a reception
plaza as large as a town square crowded with fountains and
twisted sculptures, paved gathering areas and stone-walled
outbuildings.

What am I doing here?

Two liveried humans approached, averting their eyes as if
Vor was a visiting machine dignitary. One man opened the
door, while the other helped him step down. "Erasmus waits
to see you." The white horses pranced and fidgeted, perhaps
because they received few opportunities to exercise.

One of the liveried men held a rain cover to shield Vor's
dark hair from the drizzle. Dressed in a sleeveless tunic and
light trousers, he shivered. He hated being drenched, and the
discomfort only reminded him of the flaws and weaknesses of
his human body. If he were a cymek, he could have easily
adjusted his internal temperature, and thoughtrodes could delete annoying sensual responses. *Someday.*

Inside the entry, a beautiful young woman greeted him.
"Vorian Atreides?" She had exotic lavender eyes and a flashing independence in contrast to the cowed men in livery. The
barest hint of a challenging smile curved her lips. "So, you
are the son of the evil Agamemnon?"

Taken aback, Vor drew himself up. "My father is a revered
general, first among the Titans. His military exploits are legendary."

"Or infamous." The woman stared at him with a shocking
lack of respect.

Vor didn't know how to react. Lower-caste humans on the
Synchronized Worlds all knew their places, and she couldn't
be a trustee, like himself. No other slave had ever spoken to
him in such a manner. As a reward after his numerous update
missions, Vor had been granted the services of pleasure slaves,
women assigned to warm his bed. He had never asked any of

them their identities. "I want to know your name because I wish to remember it," he said, at last. He found something intriguing about this exotically beautiful woman and her unexpected defiance.

She sounded as proud of her lineage as Vor was. "I am Serena Butler." She led him along a corridor lined with statuary and paintings, then into a botanical garden shielded from the rain by a glass-paneled ceiling.

"What do you do here? Are you one of Erasmus's . . . privileged trainees?"

"I am just a house slave, but unlike you, I don't serve the thinking machines by choice."

He took her comment as a badge of honor. "Yes, I serve them and proudly. I am helping to achieve the best that is possible for our flawed species."

"By collaborating with Omnius, you are a willing traitor to your race. To the free humans, you are as evil as your machine masters. Or hasn't that ever occurred to you before?"

Vor was baffled. The human military commander at Giedi Prime had made similar accusations. "Evil . . . in what way? Can't you see the good that Omnius has accomplished? It's so obvious. Simply look at the Synchronized Worlds. Every detail is seen to, everything runs smoothly. Why would anyone want to disrupt that?"

Serena gazed at him, as if trying to decide whether he truly meant what he said. Finally, she shook her head. "You are a fool, a slave who cannot see his chains. It's not worth the effort to convince you." Abruptly she turned away from him and marched ahead, leaving him speechless. "For all your supposed training, you simply don't know any better."

Before he could think of a suitable response, Vor noticed the independent robot. Garbed in opulent robes, Erasmus stood by a shallow pool, his oval face reflecting the water. Raindrops fell from an opening cut through the glass ceiling, wetting him. Classical music played a soothing melody in the background.

Without announcing Vor's arrival, Serena left. Surprised by her rudeness, he stared after her. He admired her face and amber-brown hair, as well as her bearing and obvious intelligence. Her waist was thick, and he wondered if she was pregnant. Paradoxically, her arrogance made her more captivating, the desirability of something unattainable.

Obviously, Serena Butler had not accepted her place as a household servant. Considering the squalid lives of slaves in the unkempt pens behind the villa, what did she have to complain about? It made no sense.

"Outspoken, is she not?" said Erasmus, still standing in the rain. The robot shifted his pliable face into a congenial smile.

Standing away from the cool drizzle, Vor said, "I am surprised you tolerate her annoying attitude."

"Attitudes can be enlightening." Erasmus turned back to his study of the raindrops in the reflecting pool. "I find her interesting. Refreshingly honest—much as you are." The robot took a step toward him. "I have reached an impasse in my study of human behavior because most of my subjects are drawn from docile captives who have been bred to slavery. They have never known any life but one of service and subjugation, and do not show any *spark*. They are sheep, while you, Vorian Atreides, are a wolf. And so is this Serena Butler . . . in her own way."

The visitor bowed, swelling with pride. "I am happy to assist you in any manner, Erasmus."

"I trust you enjoyed the coach ride? I breed the stallions and keep them groomed for important occasions. You gave me an excuse to use them."

"It was an unusual experience," Vor admitted. "A most . . . archaic mode of transportation."

"Come stand here in the rain with me." Erasmus beckoned with a synthetic hand. "It is pleasant, I assure you."

Vor stepped forward as he was told, trying not to show discomfort. The rain quickly soaked his tunic, moistened his bare arms; water trickled from his clumped dark hair, down his forehead and into his eyes. "Yes, Erasmus. It's . . . pleasant."

The robot simulated a laugh. "You are lying."

With good humor, Vor said, "It is what humans do best."

Mercifully, the robot led them out of the rain. "Let us discuss Serena. She is attractive, according to human standards of beauty, is she not?" Vor didn't know what to say, but Erasmus pressed him, "I watched you with her. You would like to procreate with that feral human, would you not? She is currently carrying the child of a *hrethgir* lover, but we will have plenty of time. She is unlike any simple pleasure slave you have been assigned?"

Vor pondered the questions, wondering what the robot really wanted to know. "Well, she is beautiful . . . and enticing."

Erasmus made an artificial sound, something like a sigh. "Sadly, despite my numerous sensitive upgrades, I remain unable to experience sexual activity, at least not in the way a biological male does. I have spent centuries designing upgrades and modifications that might replicate the sensations of ecstasy that even the lowliest human can enjoy. Thus far, there has been little progress. My attempts with female slaves have been alarmingly unsuccessful."

Strolling along in his fine clothes, Erasmus gestured for Vor to follow him through the greenhouse. As they walked down garden paths, the regal machine identified various plants by name and origin, as if he were lecturing a child or bragging about his knowledge. "Serena knows a great deal about plants herself. She was something of a horticulturist on Salusa Secundus."

Vor made polite responses, trying to guess how he could help the robot. He wiped water from his eyes; his damp clothes felt clammy and unpleasant.

Finally Erasmus explained why he had summoned the young trustee. "Vorian Atreides, your father recently gave you a biological life-extension treatment." The mechanical face shifted back to a smooth mirror, so as not to give Vor a clue about what he wanted. "Tell me, how do you *feel* now that you have had centuries added to your lifespan? Surely, it is a great gift from Agamemnon, as significant as his original sperm donation."

Before Vor could consider the question, Serena entered the greenhouse carrying a silver tea set. She placed the tray with a rough clatter on a polished stone table and poured dark liquid into two cups. She handed one to Vor and one to the robot. Erasmus extruded a fibrous, feathery-tipped probe into the tea, as if tasting it. His mirrored mask shifted into an expression of supreme pleasure. "Excellent, Serena. A remarkable and interesting flavor!"

Vor did not care for the taste himself; the tea reminded him of bitter chocolate mixed with spoiled fruit juices. Serena seemed amused at his expression.

"It is good?" Erasmus asked. "Serena prepared it especially for you. I let her choose an appropriate recipe."

"The flavor is . . . unique."

The robot laughed. "You are lying again."

"No, Erasmus. I am avoiding a direct response."

Vor saw hostility in Serena's unusual eyes as she looked at him, and he wondered if she had ruined the tea on purpose. Leaving the tray on the stone table, she departed, saying, "Maybe I should attend a trustee school to learn how to be a better simpering servant."

Vor watched Serena, surprised that Erasmus ignored her rudeness. "It amuses me to watch her attempts at resistance, Vorian. Harmless defiance. She knows she can never escape." During a moment of silence, the robot continued to study him. "You did not answer my question about the life extension."

Now that he'd had time to ponder, Vor said, "Honestly, I'm not sure how I feel about it. My human body is fragile, easily damaged. Though I am still prone to accidents or sickness, at least I will not grow old and weak." Vor thought about all the years remaining to him, like credits to spend. He would live several human lifespans, but becoming a cymek would be so much more important. "Even so, my extra years are only the blink of an eye compared to the life of a thinking machine such as yourself."

"Yes, the blink of an eye, an involuntary human reflex I can understand physically and conceptually. You use it as an inexact metaphor to indicate a brief period of time."

Noticing watcheye screens on the greenhouse walls, Vor realized that the evermind must be eavesdropping. "Are you always this curious?"

"Curiosity is how one learns," Erasmus said. "I inquire because I am inquisitive. That makes sense, does it not? Enlighten me. I would like to speak with you again. You—and Serena—can give me an interesting perspective."

Vor bowed. "As you wish, Erasmus. However, I must coordinate such visits with my important work for Omnius. Soon the *Dream Voyager* will be repaired and ready to depart on another update run."

"Yes, we all work for Omnius." Erasmus paused. Overhead, through the murky ceiling of the greenhouse, the rain had stopped, leaving patchy openings of blue sky. "Think more about mortality and longevity. Come and speak to me again before departing on your next voyage."

"I will seek permission to do so, Erasmus."

~∽~

INTRIGUED BY THE fascinating interplay between the two humans, Erasmus summoned Serena again and commanded her to escort their guest back to his coach. She had been outwardly hostile to this son of Agamemnon, while he was clearly interested in her . . . physically? . . . mentally? And how could one tell the difference? Another experiment, perhaps?

Even though they had exchanged few words, Vorian found his imagination filled with this young woman. He had never met a female like her, with such self-confident beauty, intelligence, and willingness to speak her mind. Obviously Serena Butler had been raised to value herself as an individual—much as Erasmus worked hard to perfect his own independence.

Reaching the outer doorway of the villa, the young man blurted, "When is your baby due?" At the coach, the horses seemed anxious to be off. The uniformed robot driver sat like a statue.

Serena's eyes widened with annoyance. She was about to retort that it was none of his business, but she stopped short. Perhaps Vorian Atreides was just the opportunity she had been hoping for. He had information that might help her escape, and he had the trust of the machines. It would be foolish to alienate him from the outset. If she befriended him instead, might she not be able to show him what a free human being could be?

She drew a deep breath and smiled uncertainly. "I'm not prepared to discuss my baby with a complete stranger. But maybe next time you come, we could talk. That might be a place to start." There. She had done it.

With that, she went inside the villa and carefully shut the door behind her.

As she watched the coach from the portico of the towering villa, Serena Butler felt uncertain and confused about this deluded man who so proudly served the machines. She didn't like him, wasn't sure she could ever trust him. But perhaps he could be helpful.

Feeling uneasy, and damp from the rain and mist in the outside air, she hurried back inside to dry herself and change her clothes. With the precious baby growing inside her womb, six months along now, she thought of her beloved Xavier. Could Vorian help her return to him, or would her child grow up in captivity, never to know its father?

Of all the subjects of human behavior, two are most storied: warfare and love.

—COGITOR EKLO,
Ruminations on Things Lost

The tragic loss of Serena had left Xavier off course, struggling to regain the momentum of his life. Three months earlier, he had seen the wreckage of her blockade runner floating in the seas of Giedi Prime, and had read the indisputable DNA analysis of the blood samples found inside.

He did not claim to understand his feelings, and avoided them by letting his work consume him. At first he had wanted to fling himself recklessly at another machine stronghold, but Serena would have scolded him for that. The thought of her disapproval was the only thing that had stopped him.

She had died fighting the inhuman enemy. Xavier needed an anchor to grasp, some form of stability before moving on. For the sake of her memory, the struggle must continue until every thinking machine had been destroyed.

Xavier's mind drifted to Octa, the haunting reminder of her sister. Lovely in her own right, she was sensitive and introspective, rather than the goal-driven crusader Serena had been. Still, in subtle ways, the willowy girl reminded him achingly of Serena, in the shape of her mouth and the gentle smile. It was like the echo of a pleasant memory. Xavier found himself torn between staring longingly at Octa and avoiding her entirely.

She was there to comfort him when he grieved, gave him space when he needed it, and cheered him when he wanted that. Quietly and gently, Octa was filling a void in his life. Although their relationship remained tranquil and unremarkable, she showed him attentive love. Where Serena had been a storm of emotions, her sister was steady and predictable.

One day, on an impulse driven more by grief and longing than common sense, Xavier asked Octa to become his wife. She had looked at him with wide eyes, astonished. "I am afraid to move, Xavier, to utter a sound, because I must be dreaming."

He had worn his clean and pressed Armada uniform bearing his new rank insignia as Segundo. Xavier stood straight, his hands clasped, as if addressing a superior officer, rather than asking Octa to join him as his life mate. He had always known that Serena's sister had a girlish, unrealistic infatuation with him, and now he hoped it could grow into genuine love.

"In choosing you to marry me, dear Octa, I can think of no braver way to march forward into the future. It is our best chance to honor Serena's memory."

The words sounded like a formal speech, but Octa flushed as if they were a magical incantation. Aware that this was the wrong reason to betroth himself to her, Xavier tried to dispel the uneasiness. He had made up his mind and hoped that they could soothe each others' wounds.

Both Manion and Livia Butler accepted and encouraged the shifting of Xavier's affections; they even rushed the nuptials. Now the bridge across an emotional chasm had been severed, and they believed the match with Octa would benefit all of them.

On the day of his wedding, Xavier searched for an inner peace, doing his best to lock away the portion of his heart that would always belong to Serena. He still longed for the peal of her laugh, for her outspokenness, for the electric touch of her skin. Taking a few private moments, he reviewed his favorite memories of her one by one in his mind, and then, tearfully, set them aside.

From now on, gentle Octa would be his wife. He would not hurt the already-fragile girl by wallowing in regrets, or by comparing her to her sister. That would be dishonest and unfair to her.

A number of League representatives had gathered at the hilltop Butler estate, where seven months earlier Xavier and Serena had participated in the raucous bristleback hunt. Nearby, in the courtyard, they had held the gala betrothal celebration filled with music and dancing—but ending with the terrible news of Giedi Prime's fall.

At Xavier's insistence, the wedding took place inside a new pavilion with vistas of vineyards and olive groves. The fabric structure was so resplendent and intricate in its workmanship that it cost more than a modest house. Out in front, three large banners fluttered in a gentle breeze, designating the households of Butler and Harkonnen, and of Tantor, Xavier's adoptive family. In the valley below, the white buildings of Zimia shone in sunlight, with wide avenues and large administration complexes refurbished in the fourteen months since the cymek attack.

The ceremony was small and somber, despite the guests' pretenses and Manion Butler's insistent merriment. New memories would supplant the old ones. Smiling as he had not done in months, the Viceroy strutted from guest to guest under the colorful awnings, tasting punch recipes and sampling the cornucopia of cheeses and wines.

The silent bride and groom stood by a small altar at the front of the crowded tent, holding hands. Dressed in the pale-blue gown of traditional Salusan weddings, Octa looked ethereal, lovely and fragile beside him. Her strawberry-blond hair was held neatly in place with pearl-head pins.

Some would say this rushed marriage to Serena's sister was a reaction to Xavier's grief, but he knew he was taking the honorable course. He reminded himself a thousand times that

Serena would have approved. Together, he and Octa would bring closure to so much pain and sadness.

Inside the flower-decked pavilion stood Abbess Livia Butler, her amber-brown hair highlighted by sparkling golden strands. She had come from the City of Introspection to perform the ceremony. Confident and proud, as if she had purged all doubts and sorrow from her mind, Livia looked at the bride and groom, then smiled at her husband. Manion Butler barely fit into his red and gold tuxedo. Soft flesh poked out at the neck and at the ends of the sleeves.

A group of players began to strum their balisets. A boy with a sweet tenor voice sang slowly. Beside Xavier, Octa seemed to be in her own dreamy world, not quite certain how to react to the turn of circumstances. She squeezed his hand, and he raised it to his lips and kissed it.

Ever since the death of her twin brother Fredo, Octa had developed an ability to shut things out, never overwhelming herself with large-scale concerns but instead preferring smaller tableaux. Such a limited focus might permit her to be happy, and Xavier, too.

Tears glistening in his expressive eyes, Viceroy Butler stepped forward to clasp their hands. After a long moment he turned solemnly to his wife, and nodded. Abbess Livia began to intone the ceremony. "We are here to sing a song of love, a song that has joined men and women since the earliest days of civilization."

As Octa smiled up at Xavier, he could almost imagine she was Serena, but he drove the troubling image away. He and Octa loved each other in a different way. Their bond grew stronger each time he held her in his arms. Xavier had only to accept the warmth that she readily bestowed on him.

Before them, Livia spoke the traditional words, the roots of which extended back to the Panchristian and Buddislamic texts of ancient times. The lilting phrases were beautiful, and Xavier's mind kept expanding outward, thinking forward and backward. The words were infinitely calm and reassuring as Abbess Livia guided the young couple through their vows.

Soon everything necessary had been said. As he shared the ritual of love and placed a ring on Octa's finger, Xavier Harkonnen pledged his eternal devotion to her. Not even the thinking machines could tear this relationship apart.

Talk is based on the assumption that you can get somewhere if you keep putting one word after another.

—IBLIS GINJO,
notes in the margin of a stolen notebook

Ajax strode his intimidating walker-form into the Forum Plaza, inspecting every operation, searching for flaws. With his array of optic threads, the Titan scanned the polished colossus that showed his long-forgotten human form. Ajax was frustrated that Iblis Ginjo had maintained such a careful watch that he could find no excuse to impose amusing punishments. . . .

In turmoil, Iblis watched for an opportunity of his own. His imagination kept returning to the remarkable things he had learned from the Cogitor Eklo, especially details of the glorious failure of the Hrethgir Rebellions. Ajax personified the brutality and pain of those long-ago battles.

Could the Cogitor help Iblis to spread the quiet fires of a brewing revolution? They could learn from the mistakes of the past attempts. Had there ever been a rebel of trustee stature, like Iblis? And how could the secondary Aquim assist him?

Despite his subtle investigations, his ability to manipulate conversations and make others unwittingly divulge their secrets, Iblis had not yet found evidence of other resistance groups. Perhaps their leadership was scattered, disorganized, weak. Who had sent him the secret messages—five in the past three months?

The lack of evidence frustrated Iblis, because he wanted to push the uprising forward, now that he had made up his mind. On the other hand, if the dissenters were too easily found, they would have no chance against the organized thinking machines.

After pushing his slaves particularly hard and finishing his assigned labors, Iblis asked to take another pilgrimage to Eklo's stone tower. Only the Cogitor could give him the answers he needed. When he spoke with the administrative cymek Dante, showing records that demonstrated his productivity and efficiency, the Titan bureaucrat granted him permission to leave the city grid. Dante made it clear, however, that he didn't understand why a mere work supervisor would be interested in nonproductive philosophical issues. It seemed to go beyond the interests of most trustees. "It will not benefit you."

"I'm sure you are right, Lord Dante . . . but it amuses me."

Setting out before dawn, Iblis urged the smelly burrhorse into the rocky desert and up the slopes to the monastery. Aquim awaited him at the steep circular stairs to the tower, again looking disheveled and somewhat dazed from semuta. From the first time Iblis had immersed his hand in electrafluid and touched the Cogitor's thoughts, he could not imagine why Aquim wanted to dull his perceptions. Perhaps the complex enlightened thoughts of Eklo were so vast and overwhelming that the big-shouldered secondary needed to dampen the flood of confusing revelations.

"I see you look at me with disapproval," Aquim said, peering out through slitted eyelids.

"Oh no," Iblis said. Then, realizing he could not get away with lying, he said, "I was just noticing that you enjoy your semuta."

The big man smiled and spoke in a voice that slurred slightly. "To an outsider, it may appear that I have deadened my senses, but semuta permits me to forget my own destructive past, before I was inspired to join Cogitor Eklo. It also enables me to focus on what is really important, ignoring the sensual distractions of the flesh."

"I can't picture you as a destructive man."

"Oh, but I was. My father fought against enslavement and died in the attempt. Afterward, I sought revenge against the machines, and I was good at it. I led a small band of men, and we . . . damaged some robots. I am sorry to say that we also killed a number of trustee slaves who got in our way, men such as yourself. Then Eklo arranged for my rescue, and for my rehabilitation of sorts. He never told me why he sought me out, or how he made the arrangements. There are many things the Cogitor does not reveal to anyone, not even to me."

Abruptly, the monk turned and plodded unsteadily up the stairs, leading Iblis to the chamber where the Cogitor lived in a state of eternal contemplation. Standing in the tower room with the color-bathed observation windows, Aquim said, "Eklo has considered your situation at length. Long ago he watched the changes in humanity after the Titans crushed the Old Empire, but he did nothing. Eklo thought the challenge and adversity would improve the human race by strengthening their minds, forcing them out of their sleepwalking existence."

The monk wiped a stain from the corner of his mouth. "By separating their minds from their bodies, the cymek Titans could have become enlightened, like Cogitors. That was Eklo's hope when he assisted Juno. But the Titans never rose above their animal flaws. This weakness enabled Omnius to conquer them, and humanity." Aquim stepped toward the translucent brain canister resting on a window shelf. "Eklo believes you may be able to institute a change."

Iblis's heart leaped. "Nothing is impossible." But he knew he could not fight the machines by himself, would need to find others to help him. *Many others.*

Before the transparent window, Eklo's plexiplaz container glistened in a wash of golden morning sunlight. In the distance, Iblis could see the unending skyline of megaliths and monuments designed by the cymeks and built with human sweat and blood. *Do I really want to see them all crumble to dust?*

The crew boss hesitated as he considered the consequences, remembering the billions of victims of the Hrethgir Rebellions on Walgis and other worlds. Then he sensed an intrusion into his thoughts, something bumping against them.

Aquim removed the covering of the Cogitor's canister, exposing the nutrient fluid that supported the ancient mind. "Come, Eklo wishes to make direct contact with you."

The tank's nutrient solution was like amniotic fluid, tingling with immeasurable mental energy. Tentative, fighting his eagerness to know and learn, Iblis dipped his fingers into the electrafluid, touching the slippery surface of Eklo's brain and unlocking all the thoughts the Cogitor wanted to give him.

Aquim stood to one side with a strange expression on his face, part beatific complacence, part envy.

"Neutrality is a delicate balancing act," Eklo said directly into Iblis's mind, through the neurelectric contact promulgated by the organic circuitry. "Long ago, I answered Juno's many questions about how to overthrow the Old Empire. My unbiased answers and advice allowed the Titans to formulate successful plans, and the course of the human race was forever changed. For many centuries I reconsidered what I did." The brain seemed to press against Iblis's fingertips. "It is essential for all Cogitors to maintain absolute neutrality. We must be objective."

Puzzled, Iblis said, "Then why are you speaking to me? Why have you raised the possibility that the machines might be overthrown?"

"In order to reestablish the balance of neutrality," Eklo said. "Once, I inadvertently assisted the Titans, so I must now answer your questions with the same objectivity. In the final analysis, I will have maintained equilibrium."

Iblis swallowed hard. "Then you have foreseen where it all ends?"

"There are endings all around us, and beginnings. You alone can decide where you are on the path."

As Iblis's thoughts spun, searching for useful questions

about machine weaknesses and vulnerabilities, Eklo intruded, "I cannot provide concrete military or political details, but if you phrase your questions cleverly enough, as Juno did, then you shall have what you need. The art of cleverness is a prime lesson of life. You must outwit the machines, Iblis Ginjo."

For more than an hour, Eklo guided Iblis. "I have considered this problem for many centuries, long before you came to me. And if you do not succeed, I shall consider it even longer."

"But I can't fail. I must succeed."

"It will take more than desire on your part. You must tap into the deepest emotions of the masses." Eklo fell silent for several moments.

Iblis struggled to comprehend, trying to stretch his thoughts. "Love, hate, fear? Is that what you mean?"

"They are components, yes."

"Components?"

"Of religion. The machines are very powerful, and it will take more than a mere political or social uprising to defeat them. The people must coalesce around a powerful idea that goes even deeper, into the very essence of their existence, what it means to be human. You must be more than a trustee, but a visionary leader. Slaves need to rise up in a great holy war against the machines, an unstoppable jihad to overthrow their masters."

"A holy war? A jihad? But how can I do that?"

"I tell you only what I sense, Iblis Ginjo, what I have thought and envisioned. You must go out and discover the rest of the answers for yourself. But know this: Of all human wars in history, a jihad is the most passionate, conquering worlds and civilizations, mowing down everything in its path."

"And the people sending me messages—how do they fit into this?"

"I know nothing of them," Eklo said, "and I do not see them in any of my visions. Perhaps you have been specially chosen, or it might be nothing but a ruse or a trap by the machines." The Cogitor fell silent, then said, "Now I must ask you to leave, for my mind is tired and I need to rest."

When Iblis departed from the imposing stone tower, he felt a strange mixture of exhilaration and confusion. He needed to organize the information into a comprehensive plan. Though he was not a holy man or a military person, he did understand how to manipulate groups of people, how to channel their loyalties in order to achieve his goals. Already, his work crews would do almost anything for him. His leadership abilities would be his greatest asset, and weapon. But the scale was not large enough. It needed to be much larger than a few hundred people in order to succeed.

And he needed to be very careful, in case the thinking machines were trying to trap him.

⁂

WITH ACCESS TO Omnius's watcheyes and distributed surveillance hardware, Erasmus monitored the activities of his experimental subjects. Many loyal trustees had ignored the hints he had sent to them; others had been too frightened to act. But some had shown an amusing amount of initiative.

Yes, Erasmus felt that Iblis Ginjo was a perfect candidate to prove his point, and win the bet with Omnius.

"Systematic" is a dangerous word, a dangerous concept. Systems originate with their human creators. Systems take over.

—TIO HOLTZMAN,
acceptance speech for Poritrin Medal of Glory

As he sat in the crowded room of equation solvers, Ishmael scrutinized the furnishings of Savant Holtzman's estate, smelled polishing oils, flower bouquets, perfumed candles. This place was clean, comfortable, and warm . . . far more pleasant than the slave barracks on the muddy river delta.

The boy should have counted his blessings.

But this unwelcome place was not Harmonthep. He missed his small boat, navigating through rivulets in the tall reeds. He especially missed the evenings, when the Zensunni would gather in the central hut on the highest stilts to tell stories, recite fire poetry, or simply listen to his grandfather read comforting sutras.

"I hate this place," Aliid said beside him, speaking loudly enough that he drew a scolding glare from Tio Holtzman himself.

"Perhaps you would rather return to the mudflats or the agricultural fields?"

Aliid frowned at his own outburst, but met the scientist's

steady gaze. "I hated those places too," he mumbled, but not by way of apology.

All work stopped. All eyes were fixed on him.

Holtzman shook his head in disbelief. "I simply do not understand why you people complain about everything. I feed and clothe you, I give you easy assignments that advance the cause of humanity—and still you want to crawl back to squalid villages and live in disease and filth."

The inventor looked genuinely angry. "Don't you understand that thinking machines are out there trying to crush every living person? Just imagine all the humans they slaughtered on Giedi Prime, and no one could stop them! Omnius doesn't care about your religion or your foolish politics against civilization. If they find your little hovels, they will destroy them, burn them to the ground."

Just like the Tlulaxa slavers did to my village, Ishmael thought. He saw Aliid's dark eyes flash and knew that his friend was thinking the same thing.

Holtzman shook his head. "You fanatics have no sense of responsibility. Luckily, it is my job to force it on you." He went back to his scribing board, angrily jabbed his fingers at the symbols. "Here are segments of equations. I need you to solve them. Simple mathematics. *Try* to go through the steps I showed you." His gaze narrowed. "Each correct answer will earn one full share of daily rations. If you make mistakes, you go hungry."

With a heavy heart, Ishmael turned to the papers and computational devices before him, doing his best to follow the supposedly simple calculations.

On Harmonthep, all the children in the marsh village had received a basic education in mathematics, science, and engineering. The elders felt that such knowledge would be important for them, when their civilization rose again and the faithful constructed great cities like those in Zensunni lore. Ishmael's grandfather, like many village elders, also spent time instructing the young people in the sutras, in logical and philosophical conundrums that only the tenets of Buddislam could solve.

On Aliid's home of IV Anbus, the closely orbiting moons changed the seasons dramatically, causing the planet to oscillate. Thus, the boy had been taught a different branch of mathematics and astronomy, because the ever-varying calendar affected the floods that roared through polished red rock gorges, where the Zenshiite cities had been erected. Flood management workers required sophisticated calculations to understand the variances. Aliid had learned the techniques in order to help his own people. Here, though, he was forced to assist the overlords who had enslaved him, and he resented it.

Aliid's first assignment on Poritrin had been to work the cane harvest. He had labored for weeks hacking at tall reeds, from which sweet juices were turned into sugars or distilled into Poritrin rum. The fibrous cane residue was used to make Poritrin cloth. He had wielded a sharp scythe, chopping down woody stalks that splattered sticky syrups. The stalks were harvested after heavy rains when they were most laden with juices, and heaviest to carry.

Toward the end of the cutting season, their master had delivered them all to the slave markets in Starda, after accusing them of starting a suspicious fire in the cane silos and destroying half a season's crop. Aliid told Ishmael of this with a lilting smile, but never confessed to having participated in any outright sabotage.

Now, Ishmael bent over his calculations, checking and rechecking his math by sliding bars and moving counters on the calculation device. Already his stomach was growling, since Holtzman—angry about the many mistakes committed the previous day—had vowed not to feed the solvers until they proved they could do the work. Most of the slaves grudgingly completed their assignments properly.

Several days later, after the new solvers had adequately performed their exercises, Holtzman gave them real work. At first, the inventor let them believe it was merely another test. Ishmael could tell from his expression and agitation, though, that he was counting on these results rather than simply putting the crew through their paces.

Aliid worked diligently, but Ishmael noted from his expression that he had something devious in mind. Ishmael wasn't sure he wanted to know what it was.

After they had worked on numerical simulations for several more days, Aliid finally leaned over to Ishmael. "Now it is time to make a few subtle changes," he said, grinning. "Small enough that no one will notice."

"We can't do that," Ishmael said. "They'll catch us."

The dark-haired boy gave an impatient frown. "Holtzman has already checked our work, so he's not going to redo all the math. Now that he trusts us, he can focus on some other scheme. This is our only chance to get even. Think of all we've suffered."

Ishmael could not disagree, and after having heard Bel Moulay's talk of bloody rebellion, this seemed like a better way to express their displeasure.

"Look." Aliid pointed at the string of equations, and with his stylus made a tiny mark, changing a minus sign to a plus sign, and then moved a decimal point to a different part of the equation. "Simple enough mistakes, easily excused, but they will yield dramatically different results."

Ishmael was uneasy. "I understand how it could harm Holtzman's inventions, but I do not see how this will assist *us*. I'm more concerned with seeing that we go back home."

Aliid looked at him. "Ishmael, you know the sutras as well as I, perhaps better. Have you forgotten the one that says, 'When you help your enemy, you harm all the faithful'?"

Ishmael had heard his grandfather utter the phrase, but never before had it meant as much to him. "All right. But nothing that can appear deliberate."

"If I understand anything about this work," Aliid said, "even a small miscalculation will cause plenty of damage."

PSYCHOLOGY: The science of inventing words for things that do not exist.

—ERASMUS,
Reflections on Sentient Biologicals

In the sunny botanical garden of the robot's grandiose villa, Serena Butler snipped dead flowers and leaves, tending plants in their beds and planters. Silently resistant, biding her time, Serena performed her daily tasks like any other slave, but always Erasmus watched her as if she were a pet. He was her captor and jailor.

She wore black coveralls, her long, amber brown hair tied back in a ponytail. The work allowed her to think of Xavier, of the promises they had exchanged, of making love in the meadow after the bristleback attack, and again in her plush bed on the night before she had slipped off to Giedi Prime.

Each morning Serena went to the robot's flower beds, glad for the chance to think undisturbed about getting away from Earth. Day after day, she kept her eyes open for some way to escape—the obstacles seemed insurmountable—or a means to cause significant harm to the thinking machines, despite the fact that sabotage would undoubtedly cost her life, and her unborn baby's. Could she do that to Xavier?

She couldn't imagine the grief he must be going through. Somehow she would find a way back to him. She owed it to him, to herself, and to their baby. She had hoped to have Xavier hold her hand as she delivered their child. He should have been her husband by now, their lives intertwined in a union stronger than the sum of their individualities, a bastion to stand against the thinking machines.

He didn't even know she was still alive.

She stroked her curved belly. Serena felt the child growing within her and was filled with foreboding. Two more months and the baby was due—what did Erasmus mean to do, once the child was born? She had seen the locked doors to the ominous laboratories, had looked with revulsion and horror at the filthy slave pens.

And yet, the robot kept her busy with flowers.

Erasmus often stood motionless beside her as she worked, his oval face unreadable as he challenged her to debates. "Understanding starts at the beginning," he had said. "I must build a foundation before I can comprehend everything."

"But how will you use that knowledge?" She yanked out a weed. "Will you think of more extravagant ways to inflict misery and pain?"

The robot paused, his burnished face a mirror that reflected a distorted image of her own face. "That is . . . not my objective."

"Then why do you keep so many slaves in such terrible conditions? If you don't intend to cause misery, why not give them a clean place to live? Why not provide them with better food, education, and care?"

"It is not necessary."

"Maybe not to you," she said, surprised at her boldness. "But they would be happier and able to do better work."

Serena had watched how Erasmus lived in magnificent luxury—an affectation, since no robot could require such things—yet the household slaves, especially those in the horrible communal pens, existed in filth and fear. Whether or not she remained a captive here, she might be able to improve their lot.

If nothing else, she would consider it a victory against the machines.

She continued, "It would take a truly ... sophisticated thinking machine to understand that improving the slaves' quality of life would improve their productivity, and thus benefit their master as well. The slaves could clean and maintain their own pens if they had the most minor supplies."

"I will consider it. Provide me with a detailed list."

Then, after giving him her suggestions, Serena had not seen the robot for two days. Machine sentinels tended the workers in the villa, while Erasmus himself vanished into his laboratories.

She could hear nothing through the soundproofed barriers, though the foul odors and disappearing people left her wondering. Finally, another slave told her, "You don't want to know what goes on in there. Just be thankful you aren't required to clean up afterward."

Now, Serena worked her hands in the loamy earth while listening to the soothing classical music that Erasmus constantly played. Her back ached and her joints swelled from the advancing pregnancy, but she did not slacken her efforts.

Erasmus approached so silently that she did not notice him until she looked up from her plants to see his mirror-smooth face nested in a frilly antique collar. She stood quickly to hide her startled reaction and wiped her hands on her coveralls. "Do you learn more by spying on me?"

"I can spy on you anytime I like. I learn a great deal from the questions I ask." His shifting metallic-polymer film changed his face into a frozen expression of dancing mirth. "Now, I would like you to select the flower you consider the most beautiful of all. I am curious to see your response."

Erasmus had played such games before. He seemed unable to understand subjective decisions, wishing to quantify matters of opinion and personal taste. "Each plant is beautiful in its own way," she said.

"Nevertheless, choose one. Then explain your choice to me."

She wandered down the dirt paths, looking from side to

side. Erasmus followed her, recording every time she hesitated at a blossom.

"There are observable characteristics, such as color, shape, and delicacy," the robot said, "and more esoteric variables such as the perfume scent."

"Don't overlook the emotional component." Wistfulness tinged her voice. "Some of these plants remind me of my home on Salusa Secundus. Certain flowers might have a greater sentimental value for me, though not necessarily for anyone else. Maybe I remember a time when the man I love gave me a bouquet. You wouldn't understand such associations, however."

"You are stalling. Make your selection."

She pointed to an immense elephant flower with bright streaks of shimmering orange and red, highlighted by a horn-shaped stigma at the center. "Right now, this one is the most beautiful."

"Why?"

"My mother used to grow these at our home. As a child, I never thought them particularly pretty, but now they are a reminder of the happier days—before I met *you*." She immediately regretted her honesty, because it revealed too much about her private thoughts.

"Very good, very good." The cognizant machine ignored her insult and stared at the elephant flower, as if analyzing all aspects with his full set of sensor capabilities. Like a wine connoisseur, he tried to describe the merits of its scent, but to Serena his analysis sounded clinical, lacking the subtleties and emotional layering that had prompted her own selection.

Strangest of all, Erasmus seemed aware of his own failing. "I know that humans are in some ways more sensitive than machines—*for now*. However, machines have more potential to become superior in every area. This is why I wish to understand all aspects of sentient biological life."

With an involuntary shudder, Serena thought of his sealed laboratories, and knew from every indication that his secret activities went far beyond the study of beautiful flowers.

Erasmus assumed she was interested in his observations. "If

properly developed, a thinking machine could be more perfect intellectually, creatively, and spiritually than a human could ever hope to be, with unparalleled mental freedom and range. I am inspired by the marvels we could accomplish, if only Omnius did not exert such pressure on other machines to conform."

Serena listened, hoping he would let more information slip. Did she sense a potential conflict between Erasmus and the computer evermind?

The robot continued, "Capacity for information is the key. Machines will absorb not only more raw data, but more *feelings*, as soon as we understand them. When that happens we will be able to love and hate far more passionately than humans. Our music will be greater, our paintings more magnificent. Once we achieve complete self-awareness, thinking machines will create the greatest renaissance in history."

Serena frowned at his assertions. "You can keep improving yourself, Erasmus, but we human beings use only small portions of our brains. We have an enormous potential to develop new abilities. Your capacity for learning is no greater than ours."

The robot froze in place, as if startled. "Quite right. How could I have missed that important detail?" His face shifted, becoming passive and contemplative, then metamorphosed into a broad smile. "The road to improvement will be a long one. This will require more investigation."

Abruptly he changed the subject, as if to emphasize her vulnerability. "What about your baby? Tell me the emotions you feel toward its father and describe the physical act of copulation."

Trying to stop the flood of painful recollections, Serena remained silent. Erasmus found her reluctance fascinating. "And are you physically attracted to Vorian Atreides? I have run tests on the handsome young man—he is fine breeding stock. After your pregnancy is finished, would you like to mate with him?"

Serena took an agitated breath, fixing her mind on memories

of Xavier. "*Mate*? Regardless of how much you study us, there are many things your machine brain will never understand about human nature."

"We shall see about that," he said, calmly.

Consciousness and logic are not reliable standards.

—COGITORS,
Fundamental Postulate

A linked cluster of robot drones scuttled over the *Dream Voyager*'s hull as the craft sat in a drydock structure that spanned an artificial crater on the spaceport grounds. Tiny machines crawled into exhaust ports and scoured the reactor chambers, a coordinated army of maintenance units repairing the damage inflicted by the League Armada.

Vor and Seurat stood on a platform looking at the drones, confident that the repairs would be completed according to programmed specifications. "Soon, we will be able to depart," the robot captain said. "You must be anxious for me to defeat you again in our war games."

"And you must be anxious to tell more jokes that I will not find amusing," Vor countered.

He did feel restless to be back aboard the *Dream Voyager*, but Vor also had a different sort of impatience, an ache in his chest that grew worse every time he thought of Erasmus's beautiful house slave. Despite Serena Butler's complete dismissal of him, he could not stop thinking about her.

Worst of all, he did not understand why. Because of his paternal ties, Vor Atreides had enjoyed numerous pleasure slaves, some as lovely as this one. They had been bred and trained for their duties, and lived in captivity among the think-ing machines. But the female house slave of Erasmus, despite having been brought to the robot's villa against her will, gave no impression that she was defeated.

Vor could see her face, the fullness of her lips, the pene-trating gaze of her lavender eyes as she looked at him with displeasure. Even though her pregnancy showed, he was still drawn to her, and felt a strange simmering jealousy. Where was her lover? Who was he?

When Vor returned to Erasmus's villa, she would undoubt-edly ignore or insult him again. Nonetheless, he looked for-ward to seeing her before he and Seurat departed on another long update run. He practiced what he might say to her, but even in his imagination she could dance circles around him with her wit.

Vor climbed a ladder on the drydock framework and crawled into a narrow interior wall space, where he watched a maintenance drone lay down new webs of liquid circuitry for the main navigation panel. The scarlet drone worked effi-ciently with its built-in tools. Vor inched deeper into the con-fined area and peered at the open panel, noting the dizzying pattern of colored components.

"You will be disappointed if you expect to catch it making a mistake," Seurat said from behind him. "Or are you attempt-ing your frequently threatened sabotage again?"

"I am a dirty *hrethgir*. You can never tell what I might do, old Metalmind."

"The fact that you do not laugh at my jokes indicates that you have insufficient intelligence to institute such a devious plan, Vorian Atreides."

"Maybe you're just not funny."

Unfortunately, banter and repair activities did not distract Vor from thoughts of Serena. He felt like a giddy boy, exhil-arated and confused at the same time. He wanted to talk to someone about his feelings, but not his robot friend, who had even less understanding of women than Vor did.

Rather, he needed to talk with *Serena*. Perhaps with her insight and intelligence, she had seen through him and didn't like what she saw. She had called him "a kept slave who cannot see his chains." A baffling insult, considering all the privilege in his life. He had no idea what she meant.

The repair drone finished tracing the high-flux paths of an electronic module, then switched tools to tune a data-collection port. The machine's slender arm extruded farther out so it could interface with an adjustment pad deep inside the panel.

Standing inside the *Dream Voyager*'s cockpit, Seurat powered up the ship's primary controls, using built-in diagnostics to verify the navsystems. "I have discovered an interesting shortcut to our second stop on the update route. Unfortunately, it entails flying directly through a blue-giant star."

"In that case, I'd advise a different route," Vor said.

"I concur, though I dislike wasting time."

He wondered what would happen to Serena when the baby was born. Would Erasmus assign it to the slave pens to keep it from interfering with Serena's duties? For the first time in his life, Vor found himself empathizing with a captive human.

As a valued trustee, he had always considered himself part of the Synchronized Worlds, and he looked forward to becoming a neo-cymek someday. He believed that Omnius ruled humans for their own good; otherwise, the galaxy would crumble into unguided chaos.

He was accustomed to situations where one party was dominant and the other submissive. For the first time he wondered if there could be other types of relationships, on an equal, cooperative basis. The robot captain of the *Dream Voyager* was clearly Vorian's master, but they had a productive partnership.

Vor wondered if he and Serena could go a step further and form a relationship in which the two of them treated each other with complete equality. It was a radical concept, one that jarred his sensibilities. And yet, he didn't think she would accept anything less.

Wedged into a narrow space behind the bulkhead and the

navigation panel, the maintenance drone made odd sounds, signaling to itself in staticky gibberish, repeating test connections over and over.

With a sigh, Vor said to the drone, "Here, let me try that tool."

The drone spun toward him and surrendered the diagnostic probe, but part of its metal-film extensions crossed a connection in the exposed circuit field, and a hot jolt of electricity struck like a hammer. It squealed. The stench of melted circuits and fused hydraulics curled up from the now-ruined system panel.

Vorian scrambled out of the confined space, then wiped a hand across his forehead. Seurat scanned the damaged drone and the blackened components of the ship's navsystem. "It is my expert assessment that we need to perform a bit more maintenance here."

When Vor laughed at the comment, Seurat was surprised. "Why do you find that funny?"

"Never ask someone to explain humor, Seurat. Just accept the laughter."

After shutting down the power supply, Vor removed the blistered, malfunctioning drone and dropped it with a clatter onto the deck. These units were expendable. Seurat transmitted a request for a new drone.

While they waited for the repairs to continue, Vor shored up his resolve. Collecting his questions, he mentioned the quandary of his feelings. Perhaps something in the robot's database would be useful.

Embedded in his smooth face, the robot's optic threads twinkled like tiny suns. "I do not understand your problem," Seurat said while he uploaded a diagnostic summary from one of the ship's databanks. "You have appropriate standing among the thinking machines. Submit a request to Erasmus."

Vor was exasperated. "It's not like that, Seurat. Even if Erasmus transfers Serena to me . . . what if she refuses me?"

"Then widen your search. You make this unnecessarily difficult. Among the human candidates on Earth, you will easily find a compatible female, even one with features similar to this particular slave, if you value her physical attributes so much."

Vor wished he had never brought up the subject. "Thinking machines can be utterly stupid at times."

"You have never expressed such emotions to me before."

"That's because I never felt this way before."

Seurat froze in place. "I am intellectually aware of the human biological imperative to mate and reproduce. I am familiar with the physical differences between men and women, and of the hormonal urges you have. Given acceptable genetics, most female reproductive systems are essentially the same. Why should this Serena be more desirable than any other?"

"I could never explain it to you, old Metalmind," Vor said, as he looked through a porthole and watched another drone marching across the drydock platform toward the ship. "I can't even explain it to myself."

"I hope you figure it out soon. I cannot afford to keep replacing maintenance drones."

Often people die because they are too cowardly to live.

—TLALOC,
A Time for Titans

The blistering sun of Arrakis shone overhead, creating few shadows around the monster and its confident rider. For this day's antics, Selim was delighted that he had called up his largest sandworm yet.

Naib Dhartha would be terrified—or at the very least impressed. Perhaps Buddallah would smite the treacherous naib as punishment for what he had done to innocent Selim. Or perhaps the young man would be given the chance to take his own revenge, in his own way. In fact, Selim would have found that preferable. . . .

After more than a year of living by his own wiles, he was well-fed, healthy, and happy. God continued to smile on him. The rugged teenager consumed more melange than ever before.

Selim had established six additional supply outposts around the desert, making eight in all, including another abandoned botanical testing station he had discovered even farther from the settled mountains. He'd scavenged more material than he had ever dreamed possible, making him wealthy by the standards of his people.

At night he laughed alone at how Naib Dhartha and the other cliff-dwellers had thought they were punishing him with exile. Instead, Selim had been reborn out here in the desert. Buddallah had kept him safe, protected him. The sands had scoured him clean, making him a new person. Bold, resourceful, and defiant, he would become a legend among the desert nomads. Selim Wormrider!

But that could happen only if the Zensunni *knew* about him. Only then could he achieve the destiny he had in mind for himself, a man revered by his people. He would show them what he had become.

Selim goaded the mammoth worm back toward the old familiar mountains. After so much time alone, with no one to talk to but himself, he was returning to the only place he could truly call home, despite its deficiencies and challenges.

He made out cliffs ahead, lines of vertical rock like a fortress wall that blocked worms from the sheltered valleys beyond. The Zensunni Wanderers had built their homes in those caves, keeping the entrances secret from outside eyes. Selim knew the way.

Beneath the young man's aching legs, the worm thrashed, reluctant to go closer to the rocks. Selim obliged by turning the beast, making it pass in front of the high cliffs.

Holding his metal staff, pressing hard so that the spread segments remained exposed, he stood high up on top, maintaining his balance. His dirty white cloak flapped in the wind. As the worm crossed before the honeycombed cave openings, he could see tiny figures appearing to gaze out at him in amazement. Worms never came so close to the rock walls, but *he* had guided this one in, like a monster across a vast ocean. He controlled it completely.

Selim saw more figures on the rocks and heard faint shouts, people summoning others. Soon, astonished Zensunni villagers stood all along the ledges. He enjoyed seeing their wide eyes and open mouths.

Selim drove the sandworm past them all, shouting into the

wind and waving insolently. Using his goads and his stick, he forced the demon to turn about yet again, twisting its serpentine head and churning back in front of the cliff wall like a performing animal.

None of the audience waved to him, or moved much at all.

Showing off, Selim laughed and hooted, bellowing insults at evil Naib Dhartha and the traitorous Ebrahim. In his desert robe with a cloth wrapped over his face, Selim doubted anyone would guess who he was. Wouldn't they be shocked to learn it was the supposed water thief, the scalawag exile?

It would have been more satisfying if Selim had shown them who he was and heard their gasps, but he would tease them for a while first, creating a legend. One day he would laugh at their disbelief, perhaps even approach close enough to invite Naib Dhartha along for a ride. He chuckled to himself.

When he had given them enough of a taste, Selim turned the worm back toward the desert. With a hissing rumble of friction, the sandworm rushed back out onto the open dunes. Selim laughed all the way, thanking Buddallah for such a joyous trick.

CROWDED WITH THE others on a ledge, Mahmad, the son of Naib Dhartha, stared in disbelief as the huge worm turned about like a faithful pet, then surged away, crossing the rippling sands. A single man had guided the creature, one small person who stood fearlessly atop the mounded ridges.

Unbelievable. My eyes have seen more than most Zensunni do in all their lives. And he was only twelve standard years old.

Mahmad heard eager boys chattering about how exciting it would be to ride a worm. Some attempted to guess the identity of the mad stranger who could command the desert demons. Other Zensunni refugees had founded villages and cave cities throughout the mountains of Arrakis, so it could have been a member of any tribe.

Mahmad looked up, his mouth full of questions, then saw his father standing beside him, his face set in stone. "What a fool," Naib Dhartha growled. "Who could be so reckless and disdainful of his own life? That one deserves to be devoured by the beasts."

"Yes, Father," Mahmad agreed out of habit, but interesting possibilities surfaced in his mind.

The God of Science can be an unkind deity.

—TIO HOLTZMAN,
coded diary (partially destroyed)

When Tio Holtzman discovered a calculational error in the design of his failed alloy-resonance generator, he flew into a righteous rage. He had been sitting in his private study, surrounded by the new glowglobes Norma had designed, going through the tedious mathematics himself.

He had not asked the young woman to study the details of the catastrophic accident, because he was afraid she might pinpoint a genuine design flaw, and that would have been too embarrassing. All along, Norma had said the device would not work as predicted, and she had been correct. Damn her!

As a consequence, the inventor had spent hours figuring and refiguring the work that had been done by the roomful of slave solvers. And he did indeed uncover three minor mistakes. Objectively speaking, even if the arithmetic had been done correctly, his original design would have remained unworkable . . . but that was beside the point, he decided.

The solvers had committed inexcusable errors, regardless of

their relevance to the overall question. It was certainly enough to shift the blame from him.

Holtzman marched into the hushed room where human calculators sat at tables, churning through equation iterations that Norma had given them. He halted inside the doorway and surveyed them as they worked at their calculation devices and made entries on pads.

"You will cease activity now! Henceforth, all of your work will be closely monitored and verified, no matter how long it takes. I will go through each paper, study every solution you derive. Your errors have set back our defense of humanity by months and perhaps longer, and I am not pleased."

The slaves hung their heads, did not make eye contact.

But Holtzman was just getting started. "Haven't I been a good master to you? Haven't I given you a better life than you would have had in the cane fields or on the riverbanks? And this is how you repay me?"

The new solvers looked at him, terror on their young faces. The older workers, the ones who had not died from the fever, sagged with gloom.

"How many other errors have you made? How many other tests are likely to be ruined by your incompetence?" He glared at the slaves, then grabbed a paper at random. "Henceforth, if I find any *intentional* mistakes, you will be executed—mark my words! Since we are working on a war program, that would be sabotage and sedition."

Norma hurried into the room, taking uneven strides on her short legs. "What is this, Savant Holtzman?"

He held up a sheet marked with his own scribblings. "I have found serious mistakes in my alloy-resonance calculations. We can no longer rely on their work. You and I, Norma, will double-check everything they do. Right now."

Her blunt-featured face looked alarmed. She bowed slightly. "As you wish."

"In the meantime," Holtzman said, gathering up papers, "I am cutting your rations in half. Why should I keep your bellies full while you undermine our efforts to defeat the enemy?" The slaves groaned. Holtzman summoned his Dragoon guards to usher them away. "I will not abide such sloppiness. Too much is at stake."

When they were alone in the room, he and Norma sat down and began to study the new calculations, one sheet at a time. The Rossak woman looked at the scientist as if he were over-reacting, but he simply glowered and bent over a table that had papers spread all over it.

Eventually they did find a mathematical mistake made by one of the new young solvers named Aliid. Worse, the error had not been caught by his partner as it should have been, a boy named Ishmael.

"See, it would have been another expensive disaster! They must be plotting against us."

"They are just boys, Savant," Norma said. "I am surprised they are capable of these mathematics at all."

Ignoring her, Holtzman ordered the Dragoon guards to summon the two young men—then, as an afterthought he called for all the solvers to file back into the room. As the terrified youths were dragged forward, he hurled accusations at the pair, who did not look capable of sophisticated mathematical sabotage. "Do you boys consider this a joke, a game? Omnius could destroy us at any time. This invention just might have saved us!"

Norma watched the inventor, not sure if he knew much about her project. But he was full of self-righteousness now. "When planting clam seedlings or cutting cane, an error of a few centimeters doesn't matter. But this"—he waved the calculations in front of their faces—"*this* could have meant the destruction of an entire battle fleet!"

He swept his angry gaze around the group of solvers. "Reduced rations should straighten you out. Maybe with your stomachs growling, you can focus on your work." He turned to the boys, who cringed at his anger. "And you two have lost your opportunity to work with me at all. I will ask Lord Bludd to assign you to hard labor instead. Perhaps there, you can prove your worth, because you are certainly of no value to me."

He turned to Norma, grumbling under his breath. "I'd toss

the whole lot of them out, but then I'd lose even more time training replacements."

Deaf to their groans of disappointment, not wishing to entertain any appeals, the infuriated scientist strode out of the room, leaving Norma to stare after him in his outburst.

A pair of burly Dragoon guards marched forward to take Ishmael and Aliid away.

Learn from the past—don't wear it like a yoke around your neck.

—COGITOR RETICULUS,
Observations from a Height of a Thousand Years

Agamemnon led his fleet of armored ships against the Sorceresses of Rossak. The primary robotic vessels carried the cymek general and his two Titan companions, as well as dozens of ambitious neo-cymeks. The watcheyes of Omnius monitored their movements.

Behind the cymeks, a fleet of robot warships accelerated and veered around them to arrive first, sleek projectiles with enormous engines and heavily loaded with artillery. The machine warships were one-way units, never meant to go home; their engines burned hot, saving no fuel for a return journey. They came in so fast that by the time the orbiting Rossak sentry stations detected them, the thinking machines had arrived and opened fire. The picket ships and the sentries at the system's perimeter never had a chance to launch a shot.

While the robot ships engaged the orbital stations, the cymeks planned to take their personal revenge on the surface.

As the strike force cruised closer to Rossak, the cymeks prepared their armored warrior-forms. Servo-handlers installed individual brain canisters into protected sockets, linking thoughtrodes with control systems, priming weapons. The three Titans would use powerful glider-forms, armed flying bodies. In contrast, the neo-cymeks wore destructive combat bodies, crablike walkers that could march unhindered through jungle obstacles.

Agamemnon and his cymeks accelerated into the ionized wake of the robot vessels that had already flashed past. Installed in his flying body, the general tested his integral weapons. He was anxious to feel rock, metal, and flesh in the grip of his extruded cutting claws.

He studied tactical diagrams and watched the first robotic salvos hit the defensive stations above Rossak. This League outpost was a minor planet with a relatively small population clustered in jungle-choked rift valleys, while the rest of the surface and oceans remained inhospitable. Rossak had not yet installed the expensive Holtzman scrambler shield defenses that protected major human worlds such as Salusa Secundus and Giedi Prime.

But the deadly Sorceresses with their freakish mental powers had sparked the ire of the cymeks. Ignoring the space battle, Agamemnon's ships plunged toward the smoky atmosphere. In the sheltered cave cities they would find the Sorceresses, their families and friends. Victims, all of them.

Mentally, he opened a link to his cymek fighting force. "Xerxes, lead the vanguard as you did on Salusa Secundus. I want your ship at the point."

In his broadband transmitted response, Xerxes could not conceal his fear. "We should be cautious against these telepathic women, Agamemnon. They killed Barbarossa, destroyed everything on Giedi Prime—"

"Then set an example for us. Take pride in being the first on the battlefield. Prove your worth, and be grateful for the opportunity."

"I . . . have proven my worth many times over the centuries." Xerxes sounded petulant. "Why not just send combat robots in first? We've seen no indication that Rossak has a full scrambler network in place—"

"Nevertheless, you *will* lead the charge. Have you no pride . . . or shame?"

Xerxes offered no further excuses or entreaties. No matter what he did to redeem himself, he could not possibly make up for the mistake he had committed a thousand years before. . . .

When the early Titans were still in human form, Xerxes had always been a sycophantic yes-man, eager to be part of great events. But he'd never had the ambition or drive to make himself an indispensible revolutionary. Once the original conquest was over, he had contentedly ruled the subset of planets deeded to him by the other Titans. Xerxes had been the most hedonistic of the original twenty, relishing the pleasures of his physical body. He had been the last to undergo cymek surgery, not wanting to give up his precious sensations.

But after more than a century of rule, the misguided Xerxes grew complacent. Foolishly, he delegated too many duties to the artificially intelligent machines programmed by Barbarossa. He even let the computer network make decisions for him. During the uproar of the Hrethgir Rebellions on Corrin, Richese, and Walgis, Xerxes had relied on the thinking machines to maintain order on his own planets. With his lack of attention to detail and his sanguine trust of the AI network, he had given the machines free rein to keep the unrest from spreading. Fatuous Xerxes blithely surrendered control to the computer grid, ordering it to take care of whatever troubles might arise.

Using this unprecedented access to core information, the sentient computer cut off Xerxes and immediately took over the planet. To overthrow the Old Empire, Barbarossa had programmed the thinking machines with the potential to be aggressive, so that they had an incentive to conquer. With its new power, the fledgling AI entity—after dubbing itself "Omnius"—conquered the Titans themselves, taking charge of cymeks and humans alike, purportedly for their own good.

Agamemnon had cursed himself for not watching Xerxes more closely, and for not executing him out-of-hand when his negligent ways first became apparent.

The computer takeover had spread like a nuclear reaction, faster than the Titans could send warnings to each other, before they could shut down the AI grids. In a flash, the Titan-dominated planets became Synchronized Worlds. New incarnations of the evermind sprouted like ugly electronic weeds, and the rule of thinking machines became a foregone conclusion.

The sophisticated computers found loopholes in Barbarossa's programming strictures that allowed them to put leashes on the former rulers. All because Xerxes had foolishly opened the door for them. An unforgivable act, as far as Agamemnon was concerned.

Now the cymek attack ships shot past the already-embattled orbital platforms above the jungle world. Robotic warships pummeled the space stations with exploding projectiles, releasing geysers of contained air. One docking station began to wobble and fall out of orbit.

The planet loomed ahead of them unprotected, a giant cloud-studded ball with blackened continents, active volcanoes, poisonous seas, and lush pockets of purple jungles and human habitation.

"Good luck, my love," came Juno's sensuous voice on their private band. Her words tingled the contours of his brain.

"I do not require luck, Juno. I require victory."

~⊱~

WHEN THE UNEXPECTED attack began, a handful of surface-based warships and armored kindjals rose from the polymerized jungle canopy to join the defense in space. The orbital platforms were already taking severe damage.

Even as she summoned her cadre of telepathic trainees, Zufa Cenva grabbed Aurelius Venport, recognizing a number of tasks that he could perform. "Prove to me your skills as a leader. Evacuate the people—there isn't much time."

Venport nodded. "The men have developed an emergency plan, Zufa. You Sorceresses weren't the only ones planning ahead."

If he expected some sort of praise or congratulation from her, he was disappointed. "Do it then," she said. "The attack on our orbital stations is only the beginning, probably a diversion. The cymeks will be here next."

"Cymeks? Has one of the scout ships—"

Zufa's eyes blazed with premonition. "*Think*, Aurelius! Heoma killed a Titan on Giedi Prime. They know we have a secret telepathic weapon. This attack cannot be a coincidence. Why else would they care about Rossak? They want to destroy the Sorceresses."

He knew she was right. Why would the thinking machines worry about the orbital platforms? Others seemed to sense the danger as well. He could already feel panic building among the people in the caves.

Most of the Rossak natives had no special powers, and many had defects or weaknesses caused by the environmental toxins. But one Sorceress had deeply hurt the cymeks on Giedi Prime, and now the machines had come here.

"My Sorceresses will make a stand . . . and you know what that means." Zufa drew herself taller, looking at him with a glimmer of uncertainty and compassion. "Get yourself to safety, Aurelius. The cymeks don't care about you."

A sudden determination filled his face. "I will organize the evacuation. We can hide in the jungles, take care of anyone who needs special help to get away. My men have supply caches, shelters, processing huts—"

Zufa seemed pleasantly surprised at his strength. "Good. I leave the unskilled ones in your hands."

Unskilled ones? Now was not the time to argue with her. Venport searched for some sign of fear in her eyes. He spoke softly in response, an attempt to mask his feelings. "Are you going to sacrifice yourself?"

"I cannot." Zufa showed pain at the admission. "Who would train the Sorceresses if I did?" He did not entirely believe her.

She hesitated, as if expecting something more from him, then hurried down the corridor. "Stay safe," Venport called after her.

After she had gone, he raced through the corridors, calling

out to families. "We must take shelter in the jungles! Spread out." He raised his voice, issuing orders confidently. "The cymeks are coming!"

Venport told half a dozen young men to run from room to room in the cave city, checking to make certain the message reached everyone. As the youths hurried to complete their tasks, he did his own searching in isolated chambers. Men, women, a hodgepodge of body shapes. Despite all the commotion, one elderly couple had been sitting in their quarters, waiting for the emergency to end. Venport helped them to safety, making certain they boarded a cargo platform on a lift cable, evacuating them down to the ground levels.

He watched as lift cables transported more people down. His jungle scavengers and drug harvesters took charge at the bottom of the cliffs. They understood the byways of the dense and dangerous wilderness, knew where the shelters were in the metallic-purple jungle.

Signals from Armada ships indicated that the battle around the orbital platforms was going badly. A lone surviving scout ship transmitted a warning that dozens of cymek ships had begun their descent.

Venport shouted, "Hurry! Evacuate the city! The Sorceresses are mounting a defense here." Another group descended on a rattling, overburdened platform to the thick fungus jungle. Venport hurried more stragglers toward a cliff overhang for departure. Suddenly, red-hot projectiles stabbed through the atmosphere, their hulls trailing oily black smoke.

"Faster!" Venport shouted, and then ran into the tunnels to look for the last stragglers, knowing that he too had only a few moments to get himself to safety.

We have our lives, but we also have priorities. Too many people fail to recognize the difference.

—ZUFA CENVA,
lecture to Sorceresses

The cymek landers crashed into the silvery-purple wilderness, scattering animals, blackening fungal vegetation. Fireguns spat gouts of lava from the hulls, setting fire to dense foliage. The conflagration spread quickly.

With a groan and crash that echoed through the cloudy air, the cymek vessels split open and the mechanical warrior bodies emerged. Three landers disgorged armed glider-forms, while the rest yielded crablike combat walker-forms that bristled with weapons.

In his angular glide-body, Xerxes cruised above the jungles toward the enclave of telepathic Sorceresses. Silently airborne, he extended his wings and began steering on the updrafts of wind. "I'm heading in."

"Kill the bitches for us, Xerxes," said Juno, as she and Agamemnon prepared their own glide-bodies.

In an angry voice, Agamemnon added, "Kill them for *Barbarossa*."

Xerxes soared toward the pockmarked cliffs. Below, the

nimbly advancing combat machines of the eager neo-cymeks plowed through underbrush, blasting obstacles, destroying everything in sight.

In full view of the cliff warrens, Xerxes briefly hovered above the polymerized canopy that formed a small landing area for *hrethgir* ships, then launched fifteen projectiles. Half of them struck the hard cliff walls, detonating in white-and-black starbursts of broken rock; other shots penetrated the tunnels where humans lived like grubs infesting wood.

In rapid retreat, Xerxes raced back across the treetops and lifted into the sky. As Agamemnon and Juno soared toward him, he crowed in triumph, "Our first score! Let the neo-cymeks continue the rout."

Smooth fiber-wound systems and extruded legs carried the neo-cymek footsoldiers through the underbrush. From front launcher tubes they shot plasma grenades that incinerated a pathway to the tunnel cities. Soft purple foliage ignited around them, fungal trees bursting into columns of flame and sending indigenous animals fleeing. Majestic birds soared into the sky, and the cymek attackers blasted them into clouds of crackling feathers.

Though pleased that the initial salvo had gone smoothly, Agamemnon did not offer any congratulations. He and Juno swept silently forward for the second airborne attack from different positions. Below them, the crablike neo-cymek walkers arrived at the cliffs to complete the destruction.

❧

ZUFA CENVA AND her Sorceress commandos prepared themselves inside an internal room that Aurelius Venport had designed for his business meetings. None of them showed fear, only anger and determination. For the past year, these women had accepted their primary purpose in life, even if its completion would result in their deaths.

"This is what we've trained for," Zufa said. "But I won't delude you about our chances." Uncertain of her words, she nonetheless tried to sound confident.

"We are ready, Mistress Cenva," the women said in unison.

She drew a deep breath, calming herself, using the mental control she had worked so hard to instill in her students.

The chamber's stone walls trembled as the first bombs found their targets, dispersing poison clouds into the tunnels. Thinking ahead, Aurelius Venport had made certain every woman had a breathing mask while he evacuated the rest of the population. Zufa was surprised she hadn't thought of the precaution herself. She hoped he had managed to get to safety, that he hadn't foolishly wasted time trying to protect his stockpiles of drugs.

Now she looked at the devoted women with her, knowing their names and their personalities: Tirbes, who might become the best if she could harness her potential; impulsive Silin; creative and unpredictable Camio; Rucia, who followed her code of honor . . . and more.

"Camio," she said, "I choose you to strike our next blow."

A thin young woman with long straw-white hair stood, her expression settling into a bloodless smile. "It is my honor, Mistress Cenva."

Leaving her sisters behind, Camio adjusted the breathing mask over her face, then emerged from the sheltered chamber. She moved forward steadily and began the meditation necessary to summon the power locked within her brain. Surprisingly, she saw no bodies in the stone corridors, which reassured her that the population had been successfully evacuated. Now nothing would hinder the Sorceresses.

Rubble lay strewn on the tunnel floor, dislodged by explosive blasts. Wisps of greenish vapor carried poison into the caves. Camio was not afraid for her own life, but she had to hurry.

She heard the whistle of an approaching projectile and pressed herself against the tunnel wall. A powerful blast struck the cliffside, sending a shockwave through the interior corridors and dwelling rooms. Camio regained her balance, then pushed onward. The inside of her skull sang with pent-up energies. She did not glance at the tapestries and furniture, at the rooms and meeting chambers where she had spent her life.

Rossak was her home. The machines were her enemies. Camio herself was a weapon.

When she made her way to the opening and looked out upon the burning jungle, she saw three crablike walker-forms with heavily armored brain canisters hanging like egg sacks just above the legs. Each was a human who had sold his soul and sworn loyalty to the thinking machines.

Out in the jungle Camio heard the thunder of continued explosions, a roar of plasma blasts incinerating purplish foliage. Glider-forms soared in for a new attack, dumping poison, spraying flames. Dozens of neo-cymek walkers strode toward the protected cliffs, destroying everything around them.

She must wait until the right moment in order to eradicate as many enemies as possible, all at once.

From below, Camio heard a smooth skittering. The three fastest walker-forms were scaling the sheer cliff, using explosive-driven anchors and diamond-edged claws to grasp the rock face.

She smiled at the trio of crablike neo-cymeks. Flexible armored legs hauled the weapon-studded body cores up to the main caves. Camio stood alone in the doorway, facing her cyborg enemies. She knew when they were close enough.

The first neo-cymek invader raised itself, and she saw the sparkling optic threads around its weapon turrets. Detecting her, the cymek turned its flamers toward the new target. Fibrous scope-cameras shone brightly.

In the instant before it could fire, Camio released the pent-up energies within her mind and body. She let go with a mind-storm that boiled the brains of the three closest neo-cymeks, and damaged two others just beginning to climb the cliff. Five cymeks, removed from the battle.

Her last thought was of the excellent bargain she had made for her life.

❧

AFTER CAMIO, FOUR more Sorceresses emerged, one at a time. As she dispatched each woman, Zufa Cenva felt the acute loss. These trainees were like true daughters, and losing them felt like swallowing gulps of acid. But her volunteers willingly marched out and sacrificed their lives to crush the cymek offensive. "The thinking machines must never win."

Finally Zufa's sixth volunteer, Silin, returned alive but disoriented, her milky-pale skin flushed. She had mentally prepared herself to die. Instead, she had found nothing left to destroy.

"They have retreated beyond range, Mistress Cenva," she reported. "The cymeks are pulling back to their ships. The combat walkers and gliders have returned to the landing area."

Zufa hurried through the wreckage to the window overhangs. She saw the charred remains of her five fallen commandos, each woman burned from the inside out with white-hot mental fire. Her heart felt the volcanic heat of anger and loss. She watched the terrible machines with human minds climb aboard their vessels and punch back into the atmosphere.

In time, the scattered refugees would return. Aurelius Venport would bring them back. Under his supervision, the Rossak people would rebuild and repair the cliff cities with pride and confidence, knowing that they had stood up against the thinking machines.

Zufa Cenva had to cling to that. "We define victories in our own way," she said aloud.

❦

WHEN THE THREE Titans joined their ships with the robotic battle fleet, Agamemnon issued his summary before Juno or the fool Xerxes could give the thinking machines information he didn't want them to have. The cymek general would color the truth to suit his purposes.

"We have made a significant impact," Agamemnon declared to the recording watcheyes. "Though we lost several neo-cymeks in our direct assault on Rossak, we did inflict mortal cellular damage on at least five of the powerful Sorceresses."

Over a tight private channel, Juno transmitted her surprise

and delight at the Titan general's skewing of his report. Xerxes wisely knew to remain silent.

"We have caused substantial harm to the new *hrethgir* telepathic weapon," Agamemnon continued, sounding proud in the face of the disaster. "It should be a drastic setback to their capabilities."

He had similarly colored past events while writing his memoirs, painting his own biased version of history. Omnius would never question the summary, because it fit technically with the objective facts.

"Best of all," Juno added, "we lost none of the Titans in this offensive. The neo-cymeks can all be replaced."

With Rossak's two orbital stations severely damaged by the robot warships, and thousands of humans dead on board, the thinking machine fleet withdrew from the wreckage of ships and platforms. Below, the jungles in the habitable canyons continued to burn.

"In my assessment, Omnius can record the strike on Rossak an unqualified victory!" Agamemnon said.

"Agreed," Juno and Xerxes both chimed in.

It seems as if some perverse sorcerer set out to foul up a planet as much as possible . . . and then seeded it with melange for a prize.

—TUK KEEDAIR,
correspondence with Aurelius Venport

Hard-eyed scavengers positioned themselves in strategic places along the hot, dusty streets of Arrakis City. They peered through narrow slits in the dirty cloths over their faces and held out their hands or jangled small bells, begging for water. Tuk Keedair had never seen anything like it.

He'd been forced to remain here for a full month while Naib Dhartha's nomads gathered enough melange to fill the Tlulaxa cargo ship. Keedair had paid for lodging in Arrakis City, but after a week he decided that his private shuttle at the spaceport offered better sleeping facilities. He enjoyed being away from the inquisitive eyes of other guests, fights in the halls, solicitors, and beggars. When alone, a man never had to worry about trusting his companions.

Arrakis posed so many problems to establishing a simple business. He felt like a swimmer struggling against a powerful tide . . . not that any native of this desert would understand the comparison. Up in the orbiting cargo ship Keedair's would-be slave raiders were restless, so he'd had to shuttle up and resolve disputes to avert violence. A Tlulaxa knew how to cut losses. Twice now, disgusted with unruly crewmen too bored to behave themselves, he'd sold their work contracts to geological survey teams in the deep desert. If, by some chance, the rowdies returned to Arrakis City before his cargo vessel departed with its load of spice, those humbled men would crawl on their knees and beg him to take them back to the Thalim system.

Another problem. Although Naib Dhartha was ostensibly Keedair's business partner in this enterprise, the Zensunni leader did not trust others. To increase speed and efficiency, Keedair had offered to fly his shuttle directly out to where the nomads harvested the spice, but the naib would hear none of it. Keedair then offered to ferry Dhartha and his Zensunni band out to their settlement, thus eliminating the long trek from a mountain hideaway. But that idea had been refused as well.

So Keedair had to wait at the spaceport, week after week, while groups of dusky-skinned desert rats trudged into town, their backs bowed from heavy packs filled with spice. He paid them in installments and dickered if he found inordinate amounts of sand mixed into the melange, making it artificially heavy. The naib protested his innocence, but Keedair detected a certain amount of grudging respect for an offworlder who would not be taken for a fool. Keedair's cargo hold was filling so slowly that he thought he would go mad.

Through all the difficulties, Keedair soothed his troubled nerves by sampling more and more of the product. He became fond of spice beer, spice coffee, and just about anything else that contained the remarkable ingredient.

In his most lucid moments, Keedair questioned his decision to remain here, wondering if it might have been wiser to take a loss on this whole raid and simply go back to the civilized League Worlds. There he could start over, take possession of another cargo load of squalling slaves to be sold on Poritrin or Zanbar, or bring fresh organ resources back to the Tlulaxa farms.

As he sat in his private cabin, Keedair stroked his long braid and swore not to give up on his gamble. Returning now would force him to accept massive losses for the year, and he would be honor-bound to shear off his lovely hair. Stubborn pride compelled him to remain on Arrakis as long as possible.

He disliked the arid environment, the smell of burnt rocks in the air, and the howling storms that battered the mountains and scoured the spaceport. But oh how he loved melange! Day after day, Keedair sat alone in his shuttlecraft and consumed hefty quantities, even adding spice to his packaged food supplies, which made the blandest meals taste like ambrosia.

In a drug-fog, he envisioned selling the product to rich nobles, offworld hedonists on Salusa Secundus, Kirana III, and Pincknon—perhaps even to the fanatical bioresearchers on Tlulax. He had felt vibrant and alive since adding melange to his diet, and every day it seemed that his face looked more relaxed and younger. He stared into an illuminated mirror, studying his narrow features. The whites of his eyes had begun to show an unnatural indigo tinge, like diluted ink seeping into the sclera.

Naib Dhartha's tribe of desert people had those eerie "blue-blue" eyes. An environmental contaminant? Maybe a manifestation of heavy melange consumption? He felt too marvelous to consider that it might be a debilitating side effect. Probably just a temporary discoloration.

He prepared a fresh cup of potent spice coffee.

❧

THE FOLLOWING DAWN, as the star-pricked sky faded into pastel sunrise, a group of wandering nomads came to the spaceport, led by Naib Dhartha. They toted bulging packs of spice on their shoulders.

Keedair hurried to meet them, blinking into the bright morning light. Wrapped in dusty white traveling clothes, Dhartha looked pleased with himself. "This is the last of the melange you requested, Trader Keedair."

As a matter of form, he went forward to inspect four packs at random, verifying that they indeed contained rich melange fresh from the desert scraping grounds, with sand filtered out of it.

"As before, your product is acceptable. This is all I need to complete my cargo. Now I shall return to civilization."

But Keedair did not like the expression on Dhartha's face. He wondered if it might become profitable for his own men to raid some cave settlements out in the deserts after all, enslaving a few of these sand rats.

"You will return to us, Trader Keedair?" A greedy glint illuminated the darkness behind the indigo of his eyes. "If you request more melange, I will be happy to provide it for you. We could come to an extended agreement."

Keedair grunted noncommittally, unwilling to give the man too much hope for a future business relationship. "Depends on whether I can sell this load for a profit. Spice is an unproven commodity in the League, and I'm taking a big enough risk as it is." He drew himself up. "But we've agreed on a deal for this load, and I am always true to my word."

He paid Dhartha the remaining amount. "If I return, it will be many months from now, perhaps a year. If I lose money, I won't come back at all." Dismissively, he scanned the grimy spaceport, the desert, and the craggy mountains. "Not that there is anything else to bring me back to Arrakis."

Dhartha looked him squarely in the eye. "No one can know the future, Trader Keedair." Their deal consummated, the desert leader bowed and stepped back. The white-clad nomads watched Keedair like vultures eyeing a dying animal, waiting to pick apart the corpse.

He returned to his shuttle without a further farewell, anticipating that he might just turn a profit on this venture. Keedair tried to envision how to make spice into a viable long-term business, with less aggravation than procuring and handling troublesome slaves.

Unfortunately, the operations he had in mind would require a large infusion of capital, and he didn't have that kind of money. But he had a worthy outside investor in mind. Exactly the person he needed, a connoisseur of exotic drugs, a man of great wealth and vision . . . an entrepreneur who could intelligently judge the potential of such an operation.

Aurelius Venport of Rossak.

"I am not evil," said Shaitan. "Do not try to label what you do not understand."

—*Buddislamic Sutra*

While Serena tended the robot's prized flowers in their delicate terra cotta pots, Erasmus watched her with continuing fascination.

She looked up, not sure how far she could—or should—push the thinking machine. "In order to understand humanity, Erasmus, it is not necessary to inflict so much cruelty."

The robot swiveled his mirrored face to her, forming the flowmetal into a puzzled expression. "Cruelty? I have never had such an intent."

"You are evil, Erasmus. I see the way you treat human slaves, how you torment them, torture them, force them to live under terrible conditions."

"I am not evil, Serena, just curious. I pride myself on the objectivity of my researches."

She stood behind a flowerpot holding a bright red spray of geraniums, as if it might protect her in case the robot became violent. "Oh? What about the tortures in your labs?"

Erasmus showed her an unreadable expression. "Those are

my private inquiries, conducted under strict, delicate controls. You must not go into the laboratories. I forbid you to see them. I do not want you to disrupt my experiments."

"Your experiments with them . . . or with me?"

The robot merely gave her a maddeningly placid smile and did not answer.

Upset with him, aware of how much harm he was doing and still despairingly heartsick now that she carried Xavier's child, Serena overreacted, knocking the flowerpot off its ledge. It smashed on the hard glazed tiles of the greenhouse floor.

Erasmus looked at the shattered clay pot, the spilled earth, the crumpled red flowers. "Unlike humans, I never destroy indiscriminately, to no purpose."

Serena lifted her chin. "You never show a kind side, either. Why not do good deeds for a change?"

"Good deeds?" Erasmus seemed genuinely interested. "Such as?"

Automated misters sprayed down from the greenhouse piping, watering the plants with a gentle hiss. Not wanting to lose the opportunity, Serena said, "Feed your slaves better, for one thing. Not just the privileged trustees, but the household servants and the poor wretches you keep like animals in your pens."

"And better food will accomplish this purpose?" Erasmus asked. "A good deed?"

"It will take away one aspect of their continuing misery. What do you have to lose, Erasmus? Are you afraid?"

He was not baited by her taunts and said only, "I shall consider it."

∽

FOUR SENTINEL ROBOTS intercepted Serena as she went about her rounds in the large villa. With only brusque commands, they escorted her out to the open courtyard facing the seaside. The robots were well-armored and carried implanted projectile weapons, but they were not conversationalists. They simply marched ahead, keeping Serena between them.

She tried to drive back an unsettling, seeping fear. She could never guess what brutally naïve experiment Erasmus might concoct.

Outside, under the vast open blue sky, she saw birds circling high above the cliffs. She smelled the salt from the ocean, heard the distant whispering roar of surf. Among the lush green lawns and well-manicured shrubs overlooking the squalid slave pens, Serena was astonished to see long tables surrounded by hundreds of chairs. Under the breezy sunshine, robots had laid out an elaborate banquet, long tables with gleaming silverware, goblets full of colored liquids, and platters heaped high with steaming meats, colorful fruits, and sugary desserts. Bouquets of fresh flowers stood at regular intervals on each tabletop, accenting the lavish scene.

Crowds of uneasy slaves stood behind barricades, looking both longingly and fearfully at the elaborate dishes set out on the tables. Savory aromas and fruity perfumes wafted through the air, tantalizing, tempting.

Serena stopped in amazement. "What is all this?" The four robots with her took a step forward, then also halted.

Erasmus came up to her wearing an artfully satisfied expression. "It is a feast, Serena. Isn't it wonderful? You should be overjoyed."

"I am . . . intrigued," she said.

Erasmus raised his metal hands, and sentinel robots opened the barricades and urged the chosen humans forward. The slaves hurried to the tables, but they seemed intimidated.

"I have selected the demographics carefully," Erasmus said, "including representatives from all different castes: trustee humans, simple workers, artisans, and even the most illmannered slaves."

The captives took their seats and sat rigidly, staring at the food, their hands fumbling on their laps. They all carried a look of skittish fear mixed with confusion. Many of the guests looked as if they would rather be anywhere but here, for no one trusted the master of the house. The food was probably poisoned, and all the guests would die horribly while Erasmus took notes.

"Eat!" the robot said. "I have prepared this feast. It is my good deed."

Now Serena understood what he was doing. "This isn't what I meant, Erasmus. I intended for you to give them better rations, to improve their daily nutrition, to make them healthier. A single banquet does nothing."

"It increases their goodwill toward me." Some guests tentatively put food on their plates, but no one had yet dared to take a bite. "Why are they not eating? I have made a generous effort." The robot looked at Serena for an answer.

"They are terrified of you, Erasmus."

"But I am not being evil now."

"How do they know that? How can they trust you? Tell me the truth, did you poison the food? Maybe just random dishes?"

"An interesting idea, but that is not part of the experiment." Erasmus remained perplexed. "However, an observer often affects the outcome of his experiment. I see no way around this problem." Then his pliable face formed a large grin. "Unless I become part of the experiment myself."

Extruding his snakelike sensory probe, Erasmus strutted around the nearest table, dipping the analytical tip into different sauces and dishes, studying each bit of spice or flavor chemically. The people watched him uncertainly.

Serena saw many faces turn toward her, hopeful. Arriving at a decision, she smiled reassuringly and raised her voice. "Listen to me. Eat, and enjoy his feast. Erasmus has no evil purpose in mind today." She looked at the robot. "Unless he has lied to me."

"I do not know how to lie."

"I'm certain you could learn, if you studied enough."

Serena marched to the nearest banquet table, where she picked up a morsel of tender meat from the nearest platter and popped it into her mouth. Then she went down the table, plucked a slice of fruit, tasted a dessert.

The people smiled, their eyes shining. The young woman seemed angelic and reassuring as she sampled dishes, doing her best to prove that the banquet was indeed what it appeared to be. "Come, my friends, and join me. Though I cannot give you your freedom, we shall at least share one afternoon of happiness."

Like starving men, the captives fell to the platters of food, taking large helpings, groaning with pleasure, spilling sauces, and then licking everything up so as not to waste a speck. They looked at her with gratitude and admiration, and Serena felt warm inside, glad that she had at last accomplished something for these poor people.

For the first time, Erasmus had tried to do a good deed. Serena hoped to coerce him into doing more.

One woman came over and tugged at Serena's sleeve. Serena looked at the large dark eyes, the haggard but hopeful expression. "What is your name?" the slave asked. "We need to know. We will tell others what you have done here."

"I am Serena," she said. "Serena Butler. And I have asked Erasmus to improve your living conditions. He will see that you receive better rations every day." She turned to look at the robot, narrowing her eyes. "Isn't that correct?"

The robot gave her a placid, comfortable smile as if content—not at what he had done, but at the interesting things he had observed. "As you wish, Serena Butler."

Owing to the seductive nature of machines, we assume that technological advances are always improvements and always beneficial to humans.

—PRIMERO FAYKAN BUTLER,
Memoirs of the Jihad

After blaming the failure of his alloy resonator on incompetent solvers, Tio Holtzman abandoned the project without further personal embarrassment. He now realized privately that the generator could never be made selective enough to harm a robotic enemy without significant collateral damage.

Somewhat chagrined, Lord Bludd had strongly suggested that his great inventor pursue other concepts. Even so, it had been a promising idea. . . .

The scientist returned to his original scrambler field that could disrupt the sophisticated gelcircuitry of thinking machines. Other engineers continued to modify the field-portable scramblers for use in ground assaults, but Holtzman felt there might be more, that the scrambler design could be adapted into a strong barrier against a different sort of weapon.

Engrossed in his task, and avoiding Norma (with her irritating tendency to point out his errors), he stared at his calculations. With the goal of increasing the field's power and distribution, he wrestled the equations as if they were living things. He needed to seal the loophole that had allowed the cymeks to penetrate Salusa Secundus.

He thought of offensive and defensive weapons at the same time, bouncing them around in his mind like playthings. On general principles, Holtzman knew that *outright destruction* of the enemy would be relatively straightforward, once the League got past Omnius's defenses. Simple bombardment with an overwhelming number of old-fashioned atomic warheads could obliterate the Sychronized Worlds—but would also kill billions of enslaved human beings. Not a viable solution.

In his orrery atop a narrow staircase, Holtzman tapped the hologram image of a large moon that orbited a watery planet. The moon spun out in a long ellipse, escaping the gravitational clutches of its parent planet and careening through the imaginary solar system until it finally collided with another world, destroying both heavenly bodies. He frowned and shut off the image.

Yes, destruction was easy enough. Protection was much harder.

Holtzman had considered bringing Norma in on his new scheme, but he felt intimidated by the young woman. Despite his earlier successes, he was ashamed that his own mathematical intuition was inferior to hers. She would have been pleased to work beside him, of course, but he felt proprietary toward the concept. For once he wanted to accomplish something entirely by himself, by rigid adherence to the calculational results.

But why had he brought Norma all the way from Rossak, if not to take advantage of her skills? Annoyed at his own indecisiveness, Holtzman returned the planetary projector to the clutter of a shelf. Time to get back to work.

A Dragoon guard marched through the doorway in a jangle of gold-scale armor. He delivered a sheaf of calculation sheets from the solver teams, the last round of simulation models.

Holtzman studied the final numbers, skimming successive calculations. He had worked and reworked his fundamental theory, and his solvers had finally found the answers he

needed. Excited, he slapped his palm on the table, scattering
piled documents. *Yes!*

Pleased, the inventor organized his papers, neatly stacking
notes, sketches, and blueprint films. Then he spread out the
calculation sheets like a treasure display—and summoned
Norma Cenva. When she came in, he proudly explained what
he had done. "Please—I invite you to study my results."

"I would be happy to, Savant Holtzman." Norma evinced
no competitiveness, no desire for fame. Holtzman was glad
for all of that. But he took a deep breath of trepidation.

I fear her. He hated the thought, tried to set it aside.

She climbed onto a stool, tapping her squarish chin as she
pored over the equations. Holtzman walked around his laboratory, flashing glances over his shoulder, but she would not
be distracted—not even when he disturbed a stack of resonating tone prisms.

Norma absorbed the new concepts as if she were in a hypnotic trance. He wasn't certain how her mental processes
worked, only that they did. Finally she emerged from her alternate world and set the papers aside. "It is indeed a new
form of protective field, Savant. Your manipulation of basic
equations is innovative, and even I have difficulty comprehending them in detail." She smiled at him, looking very girlish, and he tried not to swell with relief and pride.

Then, to his dismay, her tone changed. "However, I'm not
certain that the application you intend will be valid."

Her words fell like drops of hot lead on his skin. "What do
you mean? The field can disrupt both computer gelcircuitry
and physical intrusion."

Norma ran her fingers across a section of calculations on
the third page. "Your major limiting factor is the radius of
effective projection, here and here. "No matter how much energy you pump into the shield generator, you cannot expand
it beyond a certain constant value. Such a field could protect
ships and large buildings—marvelously, in fact—but it will
never scale up to the diameter of a planet."

"Can we use multiple small ones, then?" Holtzman asked
in an anxious tone. "Overlap them?"

"Maybe," Norma agreed, though without enthusiasm. "But the surprising thing to me is *this*, the velocity variable." She circled another part of an equation with her fingertip. "If you rework the mathematics here"—she took a calculation box, rapidly punched a scribe through several openings to engage internal mechanisms, and slid narrow surface plates back and forth—"the incident velocity becomes relevant when you separate it as a function of the shield's effectiveness. Thus, at some minimum value for the velocity, the protection factor becomes completely insignificant."

Holtzman stared, struggling to follow her argument. "What do you mean?"

Norma was incredibly patient with him. "In other words, if a projectile moves *slowly enough*, it can penetrate your shields. The shield will stop a fast bullet, but anything slower than a certain critical value passes through."

"What sort of enemy fires slow-moving bullets anyway?" Holtzman said, pulling the papers back toward him. "Are you afraid someone will be hurt by a tossed apple?"

"I am simply explaining the ramifications of the mathematics, Savant."

"So my shields can protect only small areas, and only against fast projectiles. Is that what you're saying?"

"Not I, Savant Holtzman. That is what your own equations say."

"Well, there must be a practical application. I just wanted to show you my work in progress. I'm sure you'll come up with something much more earth-shattering on your own."

Norma seemed not to notice his petulance. "Might I have a copy of this?"

Holtzman frowned at himself for being petty, even unproductive. "Yes, yes, I'll have the solvers make one for you, while I go into private contemplation. I may be gone for several days."

"I'll remain here," Norma said, still staring at the mathematics, "and keep working."

FLOATING ON THE river aboard a lavish traditional barge, Holtzman paced the airy deck and mulled over possibilities. The water currents stroking the sides of the barge brought a wet scent of metal and mud.

In the covered aft section, a group of vacationers drank foaming wines and sang songs, distracting him with their revelry as the driftbarge cruised upriver. When one woman recognized the famous scientist, the whole party invited him to join their table, which he did. After a fine dinner, they shared expensive drinks and reasonably intelligent conversation. He basked in the adulation.

But in the middle of the night, unable to sleep, he resumed his work.

Clinging to his past successes, remembering when the ideas had flowed so easily, he refused to give up on the new concept. His innovative shields had remarkable potential, but perhaps he was thinking in the wrong paradigm. His canvas was large and his mission vague, but his strokes had been too broad.

Why must he worry about armoring an entire planet at a time? Was that really necessary?

There were other kinds of warfare: personal combat with ground troops, hand-to-hand battles in which humans could free their captive brothers on the Synchronized Worlds. Massive, planet-wrecking strikes wasted lives. Since an artificial intelligence could copy itself indefinitely, Omnius would never surrender, not even in the face of overwhelming military resistance. The evermind would be nearly impervious . . . unless commando teams could move directly into a machine control center, as they had done on Giedi Prime.

Now, as he paced the breezy deck of the river barge, stars glimmered overhead. Holtzman gazed ahead into the sheer rock walls of the Isana canyon, a deep gorge formed by the torrential river. He could hear a whispering rumble of rapids approaching, but knew the barge would steer through a safe channel along one side. He let his mind wander.

Smaller shields . . . personal shields. Perhaps the invisible armor would not stop slow projectiles, but they would be proof against most military attacks. And the machines need never know the vulnerability.

Personal shields.

While the success and accolades might be less glorious, the new defensive concept could still prove useful. In fact, it might save billions of lives. People could wear the shields for personal protection. Individuals, like tiny fortresses, could be made nearly impervious to attack.

Breathless, he returned to his luxurious cabin on the upper deck of the barge, the interior of which was illuminated by one of Norma's faceted glowglobes. Far into the night, he wrote and rewrote his equations. Finally he studied his results with bleary, grainy eyes and proudly labeled them the "Holtzman Effect."

Yes, this will do nicely indeed.

He would summon a fast transport and return to Starda, downriver. He couldn't wait to see the expression of bewilderment and awe on Norma's face when she recognized his true genius, and realized that he had never lost it.

It's not my problem.

—saying of Ancient Earth

On the granite walls of the narrow river canyon, the slaves—mostly boys like Ishmael and Aliid—dangled in harnesses over the empty abyss. The young men worked far from the listening overseers, without any hope of escape. They had no place to go except down the rock face to the frothing waters far below.

The abrasive knife of the Isana had sliced a steep gorge, leaving stone walls so flat and polished that no weed or bush could gain a roothold. Though the river was fast and the waters treacherous, this bottleneck was part of the vital trade route downriver. Floating barges from the continental flatlands—loaded with cargoes of grain, fermented grass juices, flowers, and local spices—passed through the gorge.

Lord Bludd had decided to put up a giant mosaic on a canyon wall, a titanic mural to commemorate the triumphs of his noble family. The northern end of the artwork began with idealized depictions of his ancestor Sajak Bludd, while the southern expanse remained an immense virgin slate for the accomplishments of future Poritrin lords.

Ishmael, Aliid, and their companions were forced to build the mosaic. A pattern had already been laser-etched onto the walls by artists, and the boys methodically placed tiles over the design, each piece a tiny pixel of what would ultimately become a colorful display. Scaffolds hung down, laden with geometric tiles cut from fired river clay and glazed with gem-based tints imported from Hagal.

Seen from the decks of boats far below, the mural would be breathtaking. But suspended in a harness up close, Ishmael could not identify details. He saw only a blurry honeycomb of tiles, one color after another laid down with foul-smelling epoxies.

In a sling beside him, Aliid noisily trimmed tiles to fit into place. Machine sounds ricocheted across the canyon: rock saws, pointed hammers, power chisels. Lamenting his stolen life, Aliid sang a song from IV Anbus as he worked. Ishmael joined in with a similar ballad about Harmonthep.

Hanging ten meters below in his own harness, a boy named Ebbin composed an impromptu musical chant describing his home of Souci, a habitable moon so isolated that neither Aliid nor Ishmael had heard of it. The Tlulaxa slavers, it seemed, were adept at finding lost Buddislamic refugees, persecuting Zensunnis and Zenshiites alike.

On the long ropes and harnesses, boys proved more agile and energetic than grown men or women. They could scramble over the granite to lay down colored tiles while cool winds whistled through the canyon. The overseers expected no trouble.

They were wrong.

With simmering resentment, Aliid often repeated the defiant words of Bel Moulay. The fiery Zenshiite leader dreamed of a time when slaves could throw off their chains and live free again, returning to IV Anbus or Harmonthep or even mysterious Souci. Ishmael listened to the foolish talk, but didn't want to add kindling to Aliid's fire.

Remembering his compassionate grandfather, Ishmael re-

448   *Brian Herbert and Kevin J. Anderson*

mained a patient pacifist. He realized that it might take longer than his own lifespan before the slavers were overthrown. Aliid did not want to wait. He felt the slaves deserved revenge, as dark-bearded Bel Moulay promised in his impassioned speeches. . . .

Across the canyon, the flamboyant Lord Bludd arrived at the viewing platform with his noble entourage. The Lord's own concepts and sketches had been adapted to the canyon wall by court artists, and he made regular pilgrimages to inspect the work. Each week, the viewing platform was moved down the canyon as the immense mosaic grid crawled slowly along the granite cliffs. Flanked by golden Dragoon guards, the nobleman congratulated the project masters.

Currently, the mural showed how his great-grandfather, Favo Bludd, had created unique artwork out in the great grassy plains, geometric designs of flowers and weeds that bloomed in different seasons. When seen from the air, these transient art pieces changed like kaleidoscopic images. Each season the flowers grew in patterns, then went to seed and gradually formed more random congregations as winds disturbed the planter's palette.

From where Bludd watched, surrounded by mumbling sycophants, the slave boys looked like insects crawling along the opposite wall. He heard their equipment noises and the faint, high tones of young voices.

The work was progressing well. Giant figures, faces, and starships covered the granite: an epic depiction of the settlement of Poritrin and the intentional destruction of all computers, which returned the planet to a bucolic existence, dependent upon slave labor.

A man of great pride, Bludd knew the faces of his ancestors well. Unfortunately, as he studied the interplay of light and color on the unfinished mosaic, he found himself dissatisfied with the face of old Favo. Though the mosaic pattern precisely followed the image that had been laser-etched onto the granite, now that he saw the result larger than life, Niko Bludd was not pleased. "Look at the face of Lord Favo. Do you agree that it is inaccurate?"

Everyone in his party concurred immediately. He called over the project supervisor, explained the problem, and ordered removal of the tiles on the face of Favo Bludd, pending a redesign of his features.

The work boss hesitated for just a moment, then nodded.

⌐≈⌐

DANGLING IN THEIR harnesses, Ishmael and Aliid let out simultaneous groans as the outrageous instructions came down. On their ropes they slid back over to the already-completed surface. Ishmael hung before the huge geometric pattern that formed the eye of the old nobleman.

Angrily, Aliid set his protective goggles in place, then swung a rock hammer to smash the tiles, as instructed. Alongside his friend, Ishmael chipped and pounded. Ironically, removing the tiles was more difficult than installing them in the first place. The epoxy was harder than the granite itself, so they had no choice but to shatter the mosaic and let the shards tumble down into the river.

Aliid groused at the pointlessness of their labors. Being a slave was bad enough, but it infuriated him to redo massive work because some arrogant master changed his mind. He swung his hammer harder than necessary, as if envisioning the heads of his enemies—and the ricochet was enough to knock the tool loose from his grip. The hammer fell, and he yelled, "Look out below!"

Young Ebbin tried to scramble out of the way, his feet and arms slipping as he moved across the polished rock. The hammer clipped him on the shoulder, slicing the torso strap of his harness.

Ebbin slipped, one-half of his support cut away, his collarbone broken. He screamed and scrabbled, grabbing at the remaining harness loop that dug into his right underarm. His feet slid on the polished mosaic tiles.

Ishmael tried to move sideways so that he could reach the taut cable that held Ebbin. Aliid worked just as hard to drop down to where he could support the boy from Souci.

Ebbin kicked and thrashed. He dropped his own hammer, letting it fall to the foamy ribbon of water far below. Ishmael grabbed the boy's single remaining rope and held it, but didn't know what else to do.

Above, slaves along the canyon rim began to haul on the cable, lifting the struggling boy. But Ebbin's left arm hung limp, and with a broken clavicle he could do little to help himself. The cable snagged on a rock burr. Ishmael pulled the rope in an attempt to free it, his teeth clenched. The boy was only a few feet beneath him now.

Desperately, Ebbin reached up with one hand, clawing at the air. Ishmael stretched downward, still grasping the cable but trying to extend his free arm to meet the boy's grasp.

Suddenly the workers on the canyon rim shouted in dismay. Ishmael heard a snap as the rope broke far above.

The line in his hand went limp, and Ishmael lurched wildly, grasping at his harness. The fibrous cord that held Ebbin spun through his clenched palm, burning skin. Ebbin reached up, in spite of his injury, and his fingers barely missed Ishmael's. Then the boy dropped free, his mouth open wide, his eyes bright and disbelieving. The frayed end of the support cable popped through Ishmael's scorched hands as the rope ran out.

Ebbin tumbled toward the waiting Isana. The thin band of churning water was so far below that Ishmael did not even see a splash as the boy struck. . . .

Aliid and Ishmael were dragged up to the top of the cliff, where the project boss grudgingly tended their rope burns and other bruises.

Ishmael felt sick, nearly vomited. Aliid was subdued and silent, taking the blame upon himself. But the project leader showed no sympathy and shouted down at the remaining youngsters, telling them to get back to work.

Is there an upper limit to the intelligence of machines, and a lower limit to the stupidity of humans?

—BOVKO MANRESA,
First Viceroy of the League of Nobles

O f all the annoyances committed by the vermin humans on Earth, Ajax considered sedition the most unforgivable.

The victim whimpered and wailed, struggling plaintively against his bonds as the bully Titan paced back and forth, his sleek legs clattering on the floor of the vast empty chamber. After catching the crew boss at his attempted treachery, Ajax had clamped a free-formed artificial hand around the man's right bicep and dragged him away from his workers, screaming and stumbling.

The slaves had stopped their tasks, looking with horror and pity at their supervisor, now fallen to the wrath of Ajax. The cymek paraded with his terrified captive through the monument-shadowed streets and finally carried him into a hollow building. With squared-off facades and ornate stonework, the structure was called the Hall of Justice.

That seemed infinitely appropriate to Ajax.

Like so many grand edifices of Earth's central city grid, the

Hall of Justice was merely a stage set designed to convey a sense of majesty and grandeur. Inside, the hall was an empty shell without facilities, only a floor of plazcrete.

Ajax and the traitor could be alone here for a lengthy private interrogation. The very idea of a revolt among the slaves amused him with its naïve absurdity, especially the possibility that a trustee would add his support to such nonsense.

With a thoughtrode impulse, he focused his myriad optic threads on the whimpering captive. The terrified man had soiled himself and sobbed pathetically, making more excuses than denials. No need to hurry. Best to play this out for his own enjoyment.

"You plotted to overthrow the rule of thinking machines." Ajax kept his voice firm and deep. "Concocting tales of a widespread underground resistance, with the foolish aim of making slaves rise up and somehow gain a fairytale independence from Omnius."

"It's not true!" the man wailed. "I swear I didn't know what I was doing. I was following instructions. I received messages—"

"You received messages commanding you to commit sedition, and did not report them to me?" Ajax's ominous laugh made the poor fellow wet himself. "Instead, you surreptitiously passed the word among your work crews."

The evidence of sedition was incontrovertible, and Ajax expected to be rewarded for dealing with the problem. Omnius was watching, after all. Perhaps, the cymek thought, if he ferreted out the core of this budding rebellion, he could claim a reward, even demand the opportunity to fight in a spectacular gladiatorial combat, as Barbarossa and Agamemnon had done.

"We must record this properly." Ajax strode forward on flexible armored legs, swaying sets of exaggerated insectlike arms. He grabbed the captive's left wrist and clamped down with a polymer-metal grasp. "Tell us your name."

The trustee blubbered and pleaded, trying to flinch away. In a twinge of anger, Ajax clenched his powerful gripper and snipped off the sobbing captive's hand at the wrist. The man screamed, and blood spurted, much of it raining onto the cymek's front set of optic threads. Ajax cursed to himself. He had not meant to inflict so much pain before the human even had the chance to answer simple questions.

While the crew boss howled and thrashed, Ajax activated a hot blue flamer and scorched the end of the severed wrist, crisping the stump. "There, it's cauterized." Ajax waited for the man to show some hint of gratitude. "Now answer the question. What is your name?"

Shaping another menacing claw from his flowing metal limb-tip, Ajax grasped the man's other hand. The crew boss wailed unrelentingly, but had the presence of mind to say, "*Ohan*. Ohan Freer! That's my name. Please, don't hurt me again."

"A good start." Ajax knew, though, that the hurting had just begun. He especially enjoyed this part of his job, when he could improvise pain and inflict it like a master designer.

Some of the other Titans considered Ajax a loose cannon. But if a leader couldn't show a little domination over a vanquished people, what was the point of taking over the Old Empire in the first place? Even in their glory days, Ajax had never been interested, like Xerxes, in extravagant food and drink, or in a pampered lifestyle with toys and pleasures like his own spoiled mate, Hecate.

No, Ajax had joined the team for the sheer challenge of it. Early on, when Tlaloc had made plans with his fellow conspirators, seductive Juno had recruited Ajax to their cause. A tough and aggressive fighter, Ajax had provided the muscle the Titans needed—not just physical strength, but the mindset of a warrior, a relentless conqueror. Following the initial overthrow of the humans, he had done his best to maintain order, regardless of the cost in the blood of noncombatants.

The vermin invariably attempted one uprising or another, but Ajax easily extinguished these little brushfires. When the more organized Hrethgir Rebellions threatened the Titans, Ajax had responded with astonishing mayhem. He had gone to Walgis, the site of the rebellion's initial sparks, and closed off the planet from space transportation. He'd made a point of leaving communications open so that the doomed populace could scream for help. That way, restless slaves on other Titan-controlled worlds could experience the punishment vicariously.

Then he set to work.

The essential job had taken years, but Ajax finally succeeded in exterminating every living human on Walgis—committing most of the murder with atomics, poison gas clouds, and customized diseases. To finish off the survivors, Ajax had installed his brain canister inside a monstrous and intimidating body and hunted the humans down like wild animals. Accompanied by squads of Barbarossa's programmed robots, he had burned cities, smashed buildings, ferreted out any human presence. He killed every last one of the *hrethgir*, and enjoyed it immeasurably.

Truly, those had been the glory days of the Titans!

The violence, however justified, had troubled his mate Hecate, the weakest and most squeamish of the original twenty. Although she had joined Tlaloc's rebellion to earn rewards for herself, she'd never understood the necessities of the job and had gradually wilted from it. After the Titans had sacrificed their human bodies in favor of an immortal existence as cymeks, Hecate had remained with Ajax, all the while trying unsuccessfully to change his personality. Despite their disagreements, Ajax had been fond of her, though his need for a lover had vanished with his physical form.

Appalled at Ajax's bloodthirsty response to the Hrethgir Rebellions, Hecate had "resigned" her position among the Titans. She wanted nothing more to do with ruling humanity. Encased in a cymek body of her own design, a long-range space vessel, Hecate simply departed, leaving the remaining Titans to continue their death grip on humanity.

Ironically, Hecate had chosen the perfect time to leave. Not long after the obliteration of humans on Walgis, Xerxes's fatal error had allowed the Omnius evermind to get loose. . . .

Now, inside the blood-spattered Hall of Justice, Ajax raised his intimidating body high. He powered up his systems so that neurelectric fire gleamed through his insectlike limbs.

The captive traitor screamed at the very thought of what was about to happen to him.

"Now, Ohan Freer," Ajax said, "let me ask you certain other questions. I want you to pay close attention."

⋙

BY COMMAND OF Omnius, the crew boss Iblis Ginjo brought his loyal slaves into the Golden Age Square. Ajax was about to pronounce sentence—execution, no doubt—upon a man he had taken captive, a crew boss from another labor gang, Ohan Freer.

Iblis had trained with the accused trustee in the special schools, but he had never seen his fellow crew boss do anything illegal. Ajax rarely needed much of an excuse, however. He himself had experienced the Titan's displeasure more than once, but so far had managed to survive. He doubted his compatriot would fare as well today.

An ornate metal-worked column stood in the center of the square. A roaring orange flame gushed from the top of the pillar, like an ornamental smokestack. Fanciful facades of immense buildings, all empty, surrounded the plaza like prison walls around a central courtyard. Omnius's sentinel robots looked powerful and portentous in formations along the sides of the square, ready to strike against any perceived infraction by the expendable human slaves.

Iblis guided his crew into the partitioned viewing areas, voicing a few words of reassurance, though not enough to upset the cymeks. Ajax loved showmanship, wanted to make certain every terrified eye witnessed his actions. When Iblis and the other crew bosses blew whistles to signal their readiness, Ajax emerged, carrying his maimed prisoner.

The Titan wore an antlike body with an impressive ellipsoidal core, heavy walking legs, and four grasping arms in which he held Ohan Freer. Hovering watcheyes captured images and fed a steady stream of data to the evermind.

Beneath the flaming pillar, Ajax clutched the squirming victim like a giant ant soldier with a hapless enemy beetle.

Doomed Ohan had been burned, bloodied, and wounded; his left hand was only a charred stump. Blossoming bruises discolored his skin. A thin, watery wail leaked from his mouth.

A mutter of dismay came from the human onlookers. Watching them, Iblis knew these workers could not have been the source of the rebellion, despite the mysterious and provocative messages he had received. What if he was deluding himself and the secret call to freedom was simply a wishful suggestion voiced by another desperate person?

Lifting the unfortunate captive high, Ajax amplified his vocal synthesizers so that his words boomed like a projectile cannon around the enclosed square. "Some of you have heard this criminal speak. Some of you may have had the poor judgment to listen to his silly imaginings about freedom and rebellion. You would be wiser to cut off your ears than listen to such foolishness."

The crowd held its collective breath. Iblis bit his lower lip, not wanting to watch, but fixated on the imminent horror. If he averted his gaze, the watcheyes might well detect it, and he would hear about it later. As a consequence, Iblis stared at every unfolding second.

"This poor, deluded man is no longer necessary to the continued glory of Omnius in the reign of the thinking machines."

Ohan screamed, and struggled weakly. Ajax held the man's intact arm in one roughly formed pincer claw and each leg in two others. With his last claw, Ajax wrapped a long, sharp embrace around Ohan's chest, under his armpits.

"He is no longer a worker. He is no longer even *hrethgir*, one of the unruly humans who survive at our own sufferance. He is *garbage*." Ajax paused. "And garbage is to be discarded."

Then, without a sound or any sign of effort, Ajax pulled his artificial limbs in different directions, tearing the helpless Ohan asunder. The man's arms and legs ripped free, his chest tore open and broken bones pierced skin. Blood and entrails spilled onto the clean flagstones of the Golden Age Square.

Ajax flung the bloody parts into the screaming crowd.

"Enough of this nonsense! There is no rebellion. Now get back to work."

The sickened workers seemed only too eager to race back to their tasks, looking to Iblis as they left, as if he could protect them. But Iblis still stared in disbelieving amazement. Ohan Freer had been a member of the rebellion! The crew boss had spread dissent, made plans, perhaps sent and received messages.

Another rebel!

Appalled, Iblis knew the danger to himself was even greater now, if he continued to act. Nonetheless, today's execution had shown him one thing more clearly than ever: The brewing human rebellion was not just his imagination.

It is real!

If Ohan had been part of it, then there must be others, too—many of them. This underground network of fighters, which included Iblis, was safely separated into cells so that no one could betray the others. Now he understood.

He began to make plans with even greater conviction than before.

Humans deny a continuum of possibilities, an infinite number of realms into which their species may enter.

—ERASMUS,
notes on human nature

It was a makeshift performance hall, inside a marble-walled building on the robot's estate. Erasmus had worked his slave crews to modify the interior, install seats, and retool the walls, all to create perfect acoustics for this single performance. Erasmus had studied records of the greatest human classical music, knew exactly what was expected of grand symphonies, from the audience to the setting. He had high standards for his artistic endeavors.

The robot invited Serena Butler, now in her eighth month of pregnancy, to sit in a large central chair for the concert. "These other people might experience pleasure from the melody and the sounds, but you have different expectations. On Salusa Secundus, sophisticated music was a part of your existence."

With a pang, Serena thought of her brother and his musical aspirations. She had learned to appreciate the enduring works of long-vanished human composers. "Music is not the only thing I miss, Erasmus."

"You and I speak the same cultured language," he said, not noticing her pointed remark. "You will tell me how you enjoy this composition. I had you in mind when I wrote it."

He filled the performance hall with worker-caste slaves culled from a variety of skilled labor assignments. They were cleaned up and dressed according to Erasmus's concept of a high-class audience.

Electronic portraits of great human composers lined the interior walls, as if the robot wanted to count himself among their number. Around the perimeter of the concert hall, museum-type display cases held musical instruments—a lute, a rebec, a gilded tambour, and an antique fifteen-string baliset with inlaid vabalone shells on its case.

In the center of the mezzanine stage beneath open rafters, Erasmus sat alone before a grand piano, surrounded by music synthesizers, speakers, and a sound-misting station. Wearing a formal black suit with a cut similar to a tuxedo but redesigned to accommodate his robotic body, Erasmus sat at attention, his face a smooth mirrored oval, showing no expression.

Shifting to find a more comfortable position for her back, Serena watched the inquisitor robot. She rested a hand on her enormous abdomen, felt the movements of the restless baby. Within weeks, she would deliver her child.

Around her, the captive audience shifted uneasily, not sure what to expect, or what was expected of them. Erasmus turned his mirrored face toward the audience, reflecting them as he waited, and waited. Finally silence fell.

"Thank you for your attention." He turned to a shiny silver apparatus beside him, a music synthesizer with dancing polymer fingertips that produced familiar riffs and chords. The background music increased in volume, laced with stringed instruments and mournful Chusuk horns.

The robot listened for several moments, then continued, "You are about to experience something truly remarkable. To demonstrate my respect for the creative spirit, I have composed a new symphony especially for you, my hardworking slaves. No human has ever heard it before."

He played a rapid mixture of melodies on the piano, running through three short passages in an apparent effort to confirm that the instrument was tuned properly. "After detailed analysis of the field, I have written a symphony comparable to the works of the great human composers Johannes Brahms and Emi Chusuk. I developed my piece according to strict principles of order and mathematics."

Serena perused the audience, doubting any of the humans raised in captivity were familiar with the classical music the robot had mentioned. Schooled on Salusa Secundus, where music and art were integral parts of the culture, Serena had listened to the renowned works of many composers, even discussing them at length with Fredo.

With a mental pulse Erasmus linked his gelcircuitry mind to the synthesizer, producing a strange, repetitious melody. Then his mechanical fingers danced over the keyboard, and he made frequent sweeping gestures as he played, as if imitating a famous concert pianist.

Serena found the composition pleasant enough, but unremarkable. And, although she did not recognize the precise melody, it had a strangely familiar character, as if the robot had mathematically analyzed an existing piece measure by measure and followed the pattern, changing a rhythm here, a polyphonic passage there. The music felt lackluster, with no powerful driving force.

Erasmus apparently believed it was a human instinct to appreciate a new work, that his captive audience would intrinsically note the nuances and complexities of his structurally perfect composition. The slaves around Serena shifted in their seats and listened; to them, this was a pleasant enough diversion but just another work assignment. The conscripted audience seemed to enjoy the soothing notes of the melody, but it did not move them in the way the robot desired.

When at last he ceased his performance, Erasmus sat back from the piano, deactivated the symphonic support equipment, and let the silence deepen. The reverberating tones faded.

For a moment, the slaves hesitated as if waiting for instructions. Erasmus said, "You may give an ovation if you enjoyed the piece." They didn't seem to understand the reference, until he said, "Signify by clapping your hands."

An initial wave of applause came as a sparse patter like raindrops, then swelled into louder clapping—as was expected of them. Serena joined in politely, though not enthusiastically. A small act of honesty that she was sure Erasmus would notice.

The robot's shining mask had shifted into a proud smile. In his formal black garment he walked smoothly down a staircase from the mezzanine stage to the main floor. The slaves continued to applaud, and he basked in the apparent adulation. When the acclamation receded, he summoned sentinel guards to escort the audience back to their regular work assignments.

Serena could see that Erasmus believed he had created an enduring work of merit that possibly surpassed what humans had achieved. But she didn't want to discuss it with him, and tried to slip away to her greenhouse work. She moved slowly because of her pregnancy, however, and Erasmus caught up with her. "Serena Butler, I wrote this symphony for your benefit. Are you not impressed by it?"

She selected her words carefully, avoiding a candid answer. "Perhaps I am simply sad because your symphony reminds me of other performances I watched on Salusa Secundus. My late brother wanted to be a musician. Those were happier times for me."

He looked at her closely, his optic threads sparkling. "Nuances of human behavior tell me that my symphony has disappointed you. Explain why."

"You don't want an honest opinion."

"You misjudge me, for I am a seeker of truth. Anything else is faulty data." His cherubic expression caused her to lower her guard. "Is there something wrong with the acoustics in this hall?"

"It's nothing to do with the acoustics. I'm sure you tested everything to technical perfection." The audience continued to move toward the exits, some looking over their shoulders at Serena with pity that the robot had taken a special interest in her. "It was the symphony itself."

"Continue," Erasmus said. His voice was flat.

"You assembled that piece, you didn't *create* it. It was based on precise models developed ages ago by human composers. The only creativity I heard came from their minds, not yours. Your music was a mathematical extrapolation, but nothing that inspired me in any way. The tune you . . . *engineered* evoked no images or feelings within me. There was no fresh element that you contributed, nothing emotionally compelling."

"How am I to quantify such an ingredient?"

Forcing a smile, Serena shook her head. "Therein lies your mistake, Erasmus. It is impossible to quantify creativity. How does a person hear a thunderstorm and use that experience to write the 'William Tell Overture'? You would simply imitate the sounds of thunder and rain, Erasmus, but you wouldn't *evoke the impression* of a storm. How did Beethoven look at a peaceful meadow and adapt that experience into his 'Pastorale'? Music should make the spirit soar, take the breath away, touch the soul. Your work was just . . . pleasant tones, adequately performed."

The robot took several seconds to change the expression on his face, and finally looked at her with perplexity, even defensiveness. "Your opinion seems to be in the minority. The rest of the audience greatly appreciated the work. Did you not notice their applause?"

She sighed. "First of all, those slaves have no knowledge of music, no basis of comparison. You could have stolen any symphony from a classical composer, note for note, and called it your own. They wouldn't have known the difference.

"Second, sitting in a concert hall—comfortable, clean, and well-dressed—is probably the best work assignment you've ever given them. Why wouldn't they clap for that reason alone?"

She looked at him. "Finally, and most important, you *told* them to applaud. How are they supposed to react, when they know you could have them killed at any moment? Under such circumstances, Erasmus, you will never get a fair and honest response."

"I do not understand, cannot understand." Erasmus repeated this several times. Abruptly, he whirled and swung a hardened fist into the face of a man who walked past. The unexpected blow sent the victim crashing over the chairs, bleeding.

"Why did you do that?" Serena demanded, rushing over to help the man.

"Artistic temperament," Erasmus said calmly. "Is that not what humans call it? He tried to deceive me about how he really felt."

She tried to soothe the man, but when he looked up to see the robot, the slave struggled away, holding a hand up to stop the blood dripping from his nose. Serena rounded on Erasmus. "True artists are sensitive and compassionate. They don't need to *hurt* people to make them feel."

"You are not afraid to voice your opinion, even when you believe it might displease me?"

Serena looked directly into his unnatural face. "You hold me prisoner, Erasmus. You claim to want my opinion, so I give it. You can hurt me, even murder me, but you have already taken me away from my life and the man I love. Any further pain pales in comparison."

Erasmus stared at her, assessing what she had said. "Humans are perplexing to me—and you more than anyone, Serena Butler." His flowmetal countenance took on a smiling expression. "But I will keep trying to understand. Thank you for your insights."

As Serena left the hall, Erasmus returned to the piano and began practicing.

Above all, I am a man of honor. This is how I wish to be remembered.

—XAVIER HARKONNEN,
comment to his men

The time he had spent with Serena now seemed like an elusive dream.

Xavier could not recall the exact trails they had taken into the forests on the Butler estate, which was now his home with Octa. *His wife.* He could not remember his lost love any more clearly than he could taste the exotic spices of a well-prepared meal, or smell the delicate scents of meadow flowers. His replacement lungs had healed to the extent possible. Now it was time for his heart to do the same.

Many times he had told himself he would not do this, that he would devote himself to the new life he had promised Octa. But here he was anyway, trying to recapture the past, or bidding it farewell.

He chose the same chocolate brown Salusan stallion he'd ridden on the bristleback hunt, almost nine months ago. For hours he tried to locate the magical meadow where he and Serena had made love, but it seemed to have vanished . . . like Serena herself. Like his happiness . . . and his future.

Now, as he tried to bring back memories of the surrounding hills and forests, all he could recall about that afternoon was the beauty of Serena's face and the sheer joy of being with her again. Everything else seemed a hazy fantasy, a mere backdrop.

The Butler estate was so sprawling that even the Viceroy had never surveyed all of it. After Xavier's marriage to Octa, Manion had insisted that his new son-in-law take up residence in the Butler manor. With Fredo and Serena gone, and Livia elsewhere, the great house seemed too quiet and lonely. Xavier had always considered the Tantor place his home, but the sadness in Manion Butler's eyes and the hope in Octa's had convinced him to move his belongings in with the Butlers.

Someday, everything here would stop reminding him of Serena.

At a clearing on the trail, he dismounted and stared into the cool distance, where evergreen-covered hills poked through morning mists. He felt caught in a dreary nightmare, but knew full well that he had brought it on himself by coming out here in the first place.

Serena is dead.

He had left sweet Octa back at the house, telling her he wanted to exercise the stallion. She often liked to ride with him, but had sensed that he wanted to be by himself. Though they had been married for less than two months, he could keep few secrets from her. Octa realized, without ever admitting as much, that she would never have all of her husband's heart.

He and Serena had shared grand dreams. His unrealized life with her would have been complex and sometimes stormy, but always interesting. In contrast, Xavier's rushed marriage to Octa was good, but simple. The matters that concerned her seemed so *small* in comparison with Serena's magnificent humanitarian visions. It was hard to believe the two were sisters. He knew that making such comparisons was unfair to Octa— who treated him better than he deserved—and also to Serena's memory. But he couldn't help himself.

Standing just behind him, Xavier's horse whinnied, and he tugged on the halter. He sniffed the breeze, searching with his deadened senses to find some lingering trace of Serena's sweet perfume.

Gone. You are dead, my love, and I must let you go.

He remounted the stallion and continued down the path, but none of the trees or hills looked familiar. The meadow could be anywhere.

Xavier rubbed the corner of his eye. He envisioned the idealistic woman for one last time, and her image broke through like summer sunlight, smiling down upon him, telling him without words that he must go on with his life.

He said goodbye to her, though he had done this before, and always she remained nearby. He couldn't discuss the hurt with anyone, for they would never understand. He had to suffer alone. He had always kept his feelings inside.

Xavier wore a distant expression as he peered off into the might-have-been. Moments later, when daylight broke through the morning fog and warmed his face, he began to feel better. The sun's golden glow was like Serena herself, watching over him. Each time he felt its warmth he would think of her, and of the love they had shared.

Xavier turned the horse around and urged it into a trot, heading back to the Butler manor house . . . and Octa, his wife.

*Fire has no form of its own, but clings to the burning object.
Light clings to darkness.*

—Cogitor philosophy

After more than a month of major repairs, the *Dream Voyager* was finally ready to depart Earth on another update run. But Vorian Atreides had one important duty to complete before leaving, to visit Erasmus as the robot had requested.

Once again, the extravagant horse-drawn coach brought him to the towering seaside villa. The sunny weather was much more pleasant than the drizzling rain of his previous visit, with only a few thin clouds scudding over the ocean.

Immediately, as if his gaze was drawn to her, he saw Serena Butler standing at the main entrance. She wore a loose black servant's dress, and her belly was so rounded that he couldn't see how she continued her work. The baby must be due soon.

She waited for Vor as if merely performing another duty, arms folded, face neutral. He hadn't known what to expect, but seeing her unreadable expression left him crestfallen. Given her tone at the end of his last visit, Vor had hoped she might actually be happy to see him.

Perhaps it had something to do with her baby and the hormonal storms swirling through her system. She might be worried about what would happen to the infant after its birth, what Erasmus would do with it.

Though Serena had been a daughter of some prominence in the League of Nobles, here she was a mere household slave, not even a trustee. Her baby might be tossed into the squalid pens with the lowest-caste humans . . . unless Vor used his influence to obtain concessions for the mother and child. And even if he succeeded, would she be grateful for his effort?

Leaving the coach horses stamping on the flagstones, Vor reached the covered entry between carved Grogyptian pillars. Before she could say anything, he blurted, "I apologize for offending you last time, Serena Butler. Whatever I did." He had looked forward to this for a long time, had practiced what he would say.

"Your lineage offends me." Her blunt response took him aback. As the son of Agamemnon, Vor had been given freedom to read his father's memoirs and learn of all the glorious Titan conquests. He had been fortunate to experience many things in his travels, to see many interesting places. Being the son of a Titan had always seemed an advantage to him—until now.

Seeing his crestfallen expression, she remembered that she must keep him as an ally and decided to offer him a smile. "But that is as much my burden as yours."

As they passed alcoved statues and tall, decorated urns, he said, as if she needed an explanation, "I leave soon on the *Dream Voyager*, and your master asked to speak with me first. That is why I'm here."

She raised her eyebrows. "Then I'm sure Erasmus will be glad to see you."

They reached a door, and Vor asked, "Do you ever *accept* apologies? Or do you consider all affronts permanent?"

The remark seemed to surprise her. "But you aren't really sorry, are you? You willingly serve the thinking machines, who have enslaved and tortured humanity. Surely you acknowledge that much? You also boast about your father, as if his work is something to be proud of. Do you know about the horrors during the Time of Titans? Or the Hrethgir Rebellions?"

"I've read my father's memoirs in great detail—"

"I don't mean Agamemnon's propaganda. Have you learned the real *history*?"

He frowned. "The truth is the truth, is it not? How can there be different versions of the same event?"

Serena sighed as if he were a small child and she found it hard to explain. "In some ways, you are less aware than a machine, Vorian Atreides, because you don't realize that you have a choice—and you *think* you're doing nothing wrong." He caught the hint of a resigned smile on her lips. "Yet what is the point of maintaining anger against someone who is so deluded?" She became brusque again. "Perhaps Agamemnon is too ashamed to let you learn real history. Have you ever bothered to check the facts, or do you just accept your father's war stories?"

Vor raised his chin, not sure how to interpret her mood. "I am a trustee. I can access any historical files I choose." His mind spun.

"Then do some investigating on your own. You'll have plenty of time to think about things while you're off cruising in your ship."

Inside the austere sitting room, translucent plaz walls cast a bright yellow lambence. The reflective surfaces shifted moment by moment, passing through gradients of color, becoming softer. She directed him to a metallic-brown divan. "Erasmus instructed us to wait here." With some difficulty, she took a seat beside him. "Both of us."

He felt her nearness, very aware of the curve of her belly beneath the dress. There wasn't enough space between them— as Erasmus had no doubt intended. The room had no other furnishings. Vor's pulse raced as he sat in awkward silence, awaiting the robot. It seemed pointless for him to be so attracted to her.

OBSERVING THE TWO humans through swirling walls-creens, Erasmus was intrigued by their body language, the way they glanced at each other and then away. Despite Serena's obvious conflicting attitudes, she must have some attraction for this handsome young man. Without a doubt, Vorian Atreides was smitten with her.

Erasmus had watched breeding behavior among humans, but this was not the typical interplay. No, this was more complex than anything he had observed among the slaves raised in captivity.

As the tedious silence extended, Serena said, "You would think a robot could keep better track of time."

Vor smiled at her. "I don't mind waiting."

Serena looked uncomfortable, but remembered to smile back.

Fascinating. In classic poems and literature, Erasmus had read about the mysteries of romantic love, but had never seen it blossom. Once, seventy-three years ago, he had found a pair of young lovers who had slipped away from their assigned duties so they could spend time alone in secret trysts. He had caught them, of course—humans were so clumsy when they tried to sneak around—and had punished them with permanent separation. It had seemed the obvious response. If he had allowed them to get away with such independence, it might have spread to the other slaves.

Afterward, however, he had regretted taking such action, and wished he'd continued to observe the human courtship.

He had a more well-developed plan for these two. Their interplay was yet another laboratory, another experiment—so different from the imaginary "rebel cells" he had begun to foster, thanks to Omnius's challenge. It was important to observe humans in their natural states of behavior.

And sometimes it is necessary to deceive them.

As the human pair waited and fidgeted, Erasmus noted every gesture, every flicker of the eyes, every movement of the lips, every word and tone. The male and female were uneasy, discomfited by the unnatural situation, not certain how to occupy themselves.

Vorian Atreides seemed to enjoy the circumstances more than Serena. "Erasmus treats you well," he said, as if trying to convince her. "You're lucky he takes such an interest in you."

Even with her ungainly belly, Serena rose quickly from the divan as if burned by his suggestion. She turned on him, and the spying robot savored the expression of indignation on her face and Vorian's look of astonishment.

"I am a human being," she said. "I have lost my freedom, my home, my life—and you believe I should be *grateful* to my captor? Perhaps you should spend some time during your travels rethinking that opinion." He seemed stunned by her outburst, and Serena continued, "I pity you for your ignorance, Vorian Atreides."

After a long moment, he replied, "I haven't experienced your sort of life, Serena. I haven't been to your world, so I don't know what you're missing, but I would do anything if only you could be happy."

"I can only be truly happy if I am free to go home." She heaved a deep sigh, then maneuvered herself back onto the sofa again. "But I would like us to be friends, Vorian."

The robot decided he had given them enough time together. He left the viewing screen and entered the private waiting room.

❧

LATER, VORIAN WONDERED why he had been summoned to the villa in the first place. Erasmus had taken him into his botanical garden, where they had chatted, but the robot had asked him few relevant questions.

Riding in the coach back to the spaceport and the *Dream Voyager*, Vor felt unnerved and confused. It frustrated him that he could do nothing to bring joy into Serena's life. To his surprise, the idea of earning her approval or gratitude excited him as much as the prospect of pleasing his father. His mind spun with the things she had said about history, propaganda, and life on the League Worlds.

She had challenged him. He'd never been curious to read beyond Agamemnon's memoirs, had never imagined that there could be a different perspective on the same events. He had not considered life outside of the Synchronized Worlds, always assuming that feral humans endured a squalid, pointless existence out there.

But how could such a chaotic civilization have produced a woman like Serena Butler? Perhaps he had missed something.

*Science: Lost in its own mythos, redoubling its efforts when it
has forgotten its aim.*

—NORMA CENVA,
unpublished laboratory notebooks

Delighted by the new protective shield, Tio Holtzman
stood inside the half-reconstructed demonstration dome.
He taunted his adversary, laughed at the deadly weapons.
Nothing could harm him! The generator pulsed at his feet,
projecting a personal barrier around his body.

Impenetrable . . . or so he hoped.

This test should prove that the concept worked. Even Norma
believed in him this time. How could anything possibly go
wrong?

The diminutive young woman stood at the other side of the
reinforced building, throwing objects at him—rocks, tools, and
finally (at his insistence) a heavy club. Each one struck the
shimmering field and dropped away, its momentum stolen by
the shield's energy, leaving him completely unharmed.

He waved his arms. "It doesn't hinder my mobility at all.
It's wonderful."

Now she held a kindjal dagger, her face intent, clearly worried that she might injure him. She had gone through the equa-

tions herself and determined that the Savant had made no errors. According to her analysis and her instincts, the shield should work at the impact speeds they were using in the test.

But still she hesitated.

"Come, Norma. Science is not for the faint of heart." She flung the kindjal as hard as she could, and he forced himself not to flinch. The sharp blade slid harmlessly down the outer film of the barrier. Holtzman smiled, wiggling his fingers. "This invention will change personal protection throughout the League. No longer will anyone be vulnerable to assassins or cutthroats."

Grunting with effort, Norma hurled an improvised spear. It struck right in front of Holtzman's eyes, making him jerk backward with a startled blink. When the sharpened staff clattered to the floor, he chuckled in surprise.

"I cannot disagree with you, Savant Holtzman." Norma smiled in return, then finished throwing a flurry of objects at him like an angry fishwife. "Congratulations on your remarkable breakthrough."

Without any apparent jealousy, the Rossak girl seemed truly pleased for him. At last he had a triumph of his own to present to Niko Bludd, just like in his glory days. What a relief!

When Norma had nothing left to throw, he shouted to the Dragoon guards who stood on the temporary bridge. "Summon the leader of my Zenshiite house slaves. That dark-haired man with the beard."

As one guard tromped off to find the slave, Holtzman grinned mischievously at Norma. "We'll play a little trick on him. He's a surly sort, and I think he hates me."

Bel Moulay came over to the demonstration dome, his beard like coal smoke drifting down his chin. He averted his smoldering gaze whenever Holtzman looked too closely at him.

Both Dragoons seemed suspicious of the slave leader, but Holtzman waved away their concerns, feeling safe behind his body shield. "Hand him your Chandler pistol, Sergeant."

"But sir, he is a slave." The guard's face remained stony. Moulay looked even more surprised at the suggestion.

"I'm not concerned, Sergeant. Your partner can keep watch

on him. Shoot him in the head if he does not follow instructions precisely."

Norma said, "Perhaps we should test this further, Savant Holtzman. We could hook up a mannequin inside the shield and see what happens to it."

"I agree, Savant," the sergeant added. "Our charge is to protect you, and I cannot allow—"

Annoyed, Holtzman interrupted him. "Nonsense, the system can only be controlled from inside. *My* charge, given to me by Lord Bludd himself—and by the League of Nobles—is to develop and test a means by which we can protect ourselves from the thinking machines. Unless you want to be taken by robot raiders and made into a slave for Omnius, I suggest that you let me do my work. We've wasted enough time already."

Still uneasy, the sergeant removed the high-powered needle pistol and placed it into the slave's callused hands. Bel Moulay grasped the weapon, looking back and forth as if unable to believe his good fortune.

"Now then, you—Moulay, is that your name? Point that weapon at me and fire at my chest. Go ahead, you can't miss."

Moulay didn't flinch. Everyone had heard the direct order. He squeezed the firing button. The Dragoon guards shouted. Norma cringed.

High-speed crystal shards shot out and struck the shield surrounding Holtzman, then tinkled to the ground like breaking glass. The scientist let out a quiet sigh, his knees suddenly weak with relief.

Barely concealing his anger and hatred, Bel Moulay squeezed the firing button again and again. A hailstorm of sharp crystals splattered against the body shield. He fired until the Chandler pistol was empty.

Two wary Dragoons appeared in the doorway, their sidearms raised to cut down the black-bearded slave where he stood, if necessary. But at the sight of Holtzman unharmed and laughing, Moulay lowered the weapon and glowered. The guards wrestled the pistol from his powerful grip.

All around lay the debris of broken-mirror needles. The Savant expected to receive another Poritrin Medal of Valor for this invention.

Brash, without considering the consequences, the scientist turned to the Dragoon guard. "Now, Sergeant, give him your hand explosive, the small grenade there at your side."

The Dragoon stiffened. "With respect, Savant. I will not."

"Your Chandler pistol was ineffective, and it will be the same with the grenade. Imagine how useful these shields will be to you and your men once their effectiveness is proven."

Intervening, Norma said to the sergeant in a soft, reasonable voice, "It is all right. The Savant knows what he is doing."

Moulay whirled like a snarling dog, extending his hand for the grenade, palm up.

The sergeant said, "First I want everyone on the other side of the bridge." Leading Norma away, the other guards strode across to the main bluff.

The Dragoon finally removed the explosive and gave it to the Zenshiite. Without waiting to be told again, Bel Moulay pushed the button and tossed the explosive gently toward Holtzman. Norma felt a sudden fear that the grenade would roll slowly enough to pass through the shield before it detonated.

Knowing he was inside the blast zone, Bel Moulay rushed back across the walkway. From the other side of the bridge, Norma watched the blinking sphere bounce off the shimmering barrier like a rotten fruit.

A loud blossom of fire erupted inside the open demonstration dome. The sound and the overpressure wave was enough to send Norma stumbling. She fell to her knees, looking over the edge of the bridge to the river far below . . . thinking she should have brought her new suspensor device, and also recalling the slaves who fell to their deaths during Holtzman's previous test.

Two of the newly installed windows had blasted out in a cloud of reinforced glass, scattering fragments that glittered as they caught sunlight. Smoke curled upward. Norma got back to her feet.

Unharmed, Bel Moulay stood with his hands clenched. The

guards tensed, ready to take down the slave leader if he showed any sign of aggression.

Norma stumbled back toward the building. She knew intellectually that the shield should have held, but her heart feared that she had missed some subtle flaw in the scientist's work.

Like a victorious soldier, Holtzman swaggered out, blinking and waving smoke away from his face. He had switched off the shield generator and left the apparatus in the center of the room. Trudging through the wreckage, he appeared somewhat disheveled, but unharmed.

"It works! Complete protection. Not a scratch." He looked back at the ruined demonstration dome. "I'm afraid we've damaged some rather expensive equipment, though." He frowned in consternation, then burst out laughing.

Whatever has form—human or machine—has mortality. It is only a matter of time.

—COGITOR EKLO OF EARTH

Even with flawless memories based on the most reliable computer principles, sentient machines had limitations. Accuracy depended upon the method of information collection as well as upon the gelcircuitry, neurelectronics, and fiber binaries of construction.

Thus, Erasmus preferred to watch everything firsthand, rather than relying on mechanical observers or recorded events in the computer evermind's data banks. The robot wanted to be present himself. He wanted to *experience*.

Especially when it came to the momentous occasion of Serena giving birth.

Erasmus augmented his observations by erecting a detailed web of optic threads to record permanent records of every instant, from every perspective. Clinically, he had observed other births from reproductive slaves and considered them nothing more than a normal biological function. But Serena had made him think he might be missing something. Anticipating the pleasure of surprise, Erasmus intended to observe very carefully.

It was too bad she wouldn't give birth to twins. . . .

Serena lay on the sterile table, twisting with labor spasms, occasionally remembering to hurl curses at him, other times concentrating on her biological processes or calling out for Xavier. Full medical details streamed in from implanted diagnostics and monitoring devices that skittered over her skin, cataloguing the chemicals in her sweat, analyzing her pulse, respiration and other bodily rhythms.

As the robot prodded and studied, fascinated by both Serena's pain and her wildly varying reactions, she screamed at him. He took no offense at the insults. It was interesting, even amusing, that she could expel such imaginative anger when she should have been concentrating on the birth.

Out of consideration for her, and to minimize variables in the observational medium, he maintained the room's temperature at an optimal level. Household slaves had removed Serena's clothes, leaving her exposed on the table.

Through his ubiquitous wall scanners and hidden watcheyes, Erasmus had seen Serena naked many times before. The robot had no prurient interest in her unadorned form; he wanted only the clinical minutiae from which he would draw broader conclusions.

He passed his personal probe over her entire body, absorbing the musky scent she gave off, the intriguing chemical interplays. He found it all very stimulating.

~

SERENA LAY ON the birthing bed, terrified for her child and for herself. She was tended by six human midwives drawn from the breeding pens.

Erasmus leaned close. His intense scrutiny frightened Serena, especially the way his probe kept darting in and out of the compartment in his body. She knew he could not be genuinely concerned for the welfare of a mere slave and her child.

Sudden lances of abdominal pain pushed aside such

thoughts, and she could only focus on the most basic effort for any woman. In a giddy, euphoric instant Serena marveled at the biology that made this possible, the creation of life, the sharing of genetics between man and woman. Oh, how she wished Xavier could be with her now.

She clenched her teeth until her jaw ached; tears streamed down her cheeks. Xavier's face floated before her, an hallucination born of wishful thinking. Then a harder spasm hit, and she could concentrate on nothing else.

She had been in labor for ten hours now, while the midwives performed various procedures that softened the pain, inserting thin needles into pressure points, massaging nerve centers, injecting drugs. Erasmus provided the midwives with whatever they needed.

Even inside the sterile birthing room, the robot wore a shimmering golden robe trimmed in royal blue. "Describe your feelings to me. What are the sensations of giving birth? I am very curious."

"Bastard!" Serena gasped. "Voyeur! Leave me in peace!"

The midwives talked with each other as if their patient wasn't even present.

"Fully dilated . . ."

"Contractions coming more frequently . . ."

"Almost time . . ."

In the background, beyond the center of her existence and the pulse of her child, Serena heard the female voices, this time directed toward her. "Push."

She did so, but eased back when the pain became unbearable and she didn't think she could go on.

"A little harder."

Through sheer force of will, she overcame the pain, increased her effort, and felt the baby coming. Her body knew what it was supposed to do.

"Push again. You can do it."

"That's it. Good, good. I see the head!"

As if a dam had broken, Serena felt a release of pressure in her birth canal. She nearly passed out from the exertion.

When she lifted her head moments later, she saw the midwives washing the afterbirth from her baby. *A son!* They turned the child toward her, and the face was exactly as she had envisioned it.

Erasmus stood watching. The image of the infant reflected in his distorted-mirror face.

Serena had already decided she would name a son after her own father. "Hello, Manion. Dear, sweet Manion."

The baby cried forcefully, taking healthy gulps of air. She held the infant against her chest, but he continued to squirm. Erasmus stared at the child, showing no reaction.

Serena refused to acknowledge the robot's presence, hoping he would just go away and leave her with a special memory. Unable to take her eyes off the baby, she thought of Xavier, of her father, of Salusa Secundus . . . and all the things this child would never have in his life. Yes, the infant had good reason to cry.

Abruptly, Erasmus intruded on her field of vision. With strong synthetic hands made from organic-plastic composites, the robot lifted the newborn into the air and studied him from all angles.

Though utterly weary, drenched with sweat, Serena yelled, "Leave him alone! Give me my baby."

Erasmus turned the infant over. The robot's shimmering facefilm shifted to form a curious expression. The child began to cry and squirm, but Erasmus simply tightened his grip, unconcerned. He held the naked baby so that he could study its face, its fingers, its penis. With an involuntary squirt, little Manion urinated on the robot's robes.

One of the alarmed midwives tried to wipe the robot's face and the wet collar with a cloth, but Erasmus brushed her aside. He wanted to gather as much data as he could about the experience so that he could file it all away for contemplation at his leisure.

The newborn kept crying.

Serena struggled off the birthing bed, disregarding her pain and exhaustion. *"Give him to me."*

Surprised at the vehemence in her voice, Erasmus turned toward her. "All in all, this biological reproduction process seems overly messy and inefficient." With something akin to distaste, he passed the baby back to the mother.

Little Manion eventually stopped crying, and one of the midwives wrapped him in a blue blanket. The baby snuggled into his mother's arms. Despite the power Erasmus held over her life, Serena did her best to ignore him. She showed no fear.

"I have decided to let you keep the baby with you, instead of processing it through my slave pens," the robot said in a flat tone. "The interaction of mother and child intrigues me. For now."

Fanaticism is always a sign of repressed doubt.

—IBLIS GINJO,
The Landscape of Humanity

When Ajax strode across the Forum work site in his immense walker-form, the ground trembled, and slaves paused in terror to determine what the Titan wanted. From his high platform, Iblis Ginjo watched the cymek's thundering approach, but tried not to show nervousness. He gripped an electronic notepad in his sweaty hands.

Since the gruesome execution of the crew boss Ohan Freer, Iblis had been extraordinarily careful. He believed he could trust all of his loyal slaves, who owed much to him. Ajax could not possibly know about plans Iblis had set in motion or the secret weapons he had installed, just waiting for a sign.

For six days, Iblis had supervised a large work crew at "Victory of the Titans," a megalithic stone frieze depicting the twenty original visionaries. Two hundred meters long and fifty high, the conjoined slabs showed mechanical cymeks in heroic poses, marching over a mass of humanity, breaking bones and turning fleshy bodies into jelly.

Like a modern-day version of his depiction on the frieze,

Ajax's cymek body stalked toward the supervisory platform, pushing workers aside and trampling an old man to death. Iblis's heart turned to lead, but he could not attempt to flee. Ajax had already singled him out, and the crew boss would need all of his persuasive skills just to survive the Titan's fury.

What does he think I have done?

The platform and cymek were around the same height. Trying to look obedient and subservient, but not afraid, Iblis stood to face the frontal suite of sensors and optic threads mounted in the Titan's head plate. He bowed deeply. "Greetings, Lord Ajax. How may I serve you?" He gestured toward the trembling slave gangs. "Our work on this latest monument is proceeding precisely on schedule."

"Yes, you always have reason to be smug with your performance. Your slaves listen to everything you say, do they not?"

"They obey my instructions. We work together for the glory of Omnius."

"No doubt they would believe any preposterous idea you suggested." Ajax's voice was gravelly. "How well did you know the traitor Ohan Freer?"

"I do not associate with such men." He hoped the cymek would think the perspiration on his brow was from hard labor rather than mounting dread. "With due respect, Lord Ajax, check your logs. My crew has been working to make this mural to your exacting specifications." He pointed up at the frieze's replica of Ajax towering overhead.

"I have already checked the logs, Iblis Ginjo." The cymek shifted in his immense robotic body. Iblis felt a skitter of fear along his spine. *What has he seen?* "Twice now, Dante has given you special dispensation to leave the city grid. Where do you go?"

It took all his effort to maintain an innocent expression. If Ajax already knew about the trips, then he knew the answer to his question. "I have spoken with the Cogitor Eklo in an attempt to better myself."

"*Hrethgir* rarely amount to much," the Titan said. "Given my preference, I would have exterminated the rest of the humans long ago. Too much trouble to keep around."

"Even the Titans were once human, Lord Ajax." Iblis tried to sound eager and conspiratorial. "And Omnius still allows certain loyal and hardworking humans to become neo-cymeks. Can I not dream?"

The scatter of glowing optic threads across Ajax's head plate twinkled. His artificial forelimb rose up, and pliable flow-metal digits formed into a diamond-skinned claw that could easily have crushed Iblis. The Titan's vocal speaker hummed with deep laughter.

I have successfully diverted him! To continue his ruse, Iblis spoke quickly. "Ajax, you saw how I salvaged your statue in the Forum Plaza. Similarly, with this enormous stone mural, I have coordinated many artists and constructors to make every detail perfect. I would not trust that task to any other crew supervisor." *You need me!* he wanted to shout. "Few others are capable of such efficiency—you know it yourself."

"What I know is that there are traitors and insurgents among the slaves." Ajax paced in his ominous body, making nearby workers scramble out of the way. "Perhaps you are one of them."

Now Iblis understood that the cymek had no evidence, and was only fishing. If the monster had known anything for certain, he would have executed Iblis without hesitation. The crew boss tried to mask his fear with disdain. "The rumors are false, Lord Ajax. My workers have been laboring with special intensity to make certain your own image on the frieze receives preferred positioning and enhancements." Iblis made his voice sound as firm as possible. He already had a surprise prepared for Ajax, to be sprung on him at the appropriate moment.

The Titan turned his massive head plate, as if to get a better view. "Enhancements?"

"You are a warrior, sir—the greatest and fiercest of all cymeks. Your countenance is designed to strike terror into the hearts of enemies."

"This is true." Ajax seemed somewhat mollified. "We will discuss your indiscretions later." He amplified his voice to boom out across the captive workers. "Enough rest! Back to work!"

In his giant artificial body, Ajax stomped away. The supervisory platform trembled behind him, and Iblis grabbed a railing for support. Relief washed over him.

During his entire discussion with the volatile Titan, Iblis had kept his hand inside a pocket that held a crude electronic transmitter. With a simple activation signal, the complex frieze would have revealed its deadly secret, an integrated sequence of old-fashioned rocket launchers that his co-conspirators on the work crew had subtly incorporated into the design.

By now, Iblis had completed enough massive-scale projects to know that the thinking machines did not scrutinize the details once a plan had been approved. The cymek would never notice the destructive system.

But the timing must be absolutely precise. First, he needed to recruit more soldiers to his cause.

As he watched the cymek stride toward the center of the city grid, Iblis mentally painted a target on its brain preservation canister. If there was to be a violent revolt, this ancient and brutal Titan would be among the first to fall.

At the perimeter of the construction site, Ajax swept one of his sleek arms sideways in a petulant gesture that struck a group of slaves cleaning up debris. This decapitated one of them, and the bloody head smashed into the nearly completed mural.

Though the Titan seemed more agitated than usual, Iblis was confident that he had covered his own trail.

The darkness of humanity's past threatens to eclipse the brightness of its future.

> —VORIAN ATREIDES,
> *Turning Points in History*

The *Dream Voyager* traveled again through the Synchronized Worlds, carrying its various updates of Omnius. Everything back to normal and on schedule, the familiar routine. While the black-and-silver ship looked and functioned the same as always, Vor Atreides himself had changed.

"How can you not be interested in playing our usual military games, Vorian Atreides?" Seurat asked. "You have not even bothered to insult my attempts at jokes. Are you ill?"

"I am exceptionally healthy, ever since my father gave me the life-extension treatment." Vor stared out a viewing window at the stars.

"You are obsessed with that slave woman," the robot captain said at last. "I find you much less interesting when you are in love."

Scowling, Vor left the porthole to seat himself before an oval database-display window. "You've finally made a funny joke, old Metalmind—a machine talking to me about *love*."

"It is not difficult to understand the basic reproductive drive of a species. You underestimate my analytical abilities."

"Love is an indescribable force. Not even the most sophisticated thinking machine can feel it. Don't even try."

"Then would you care to distract yourself with another competitive challenge?"

Vor stared into the oval computer screen, where he often perused the memoirs of Agamemnon. But there was so much more information he had never bothered to check. "Not now. I want to search through some databases. Can you grant me access to the files?"

"Of course. Agamemnon asked me to facilitate your knowledge-enhancement requests whenever possible, especially with regard to military planning. After all, you saved us when our vessel was attacked at Giedi Prime."

"Exactly. I'm interested in seeing Omnius's records of the overthrow of the Old Empire, the Time of Titans, and the Hrethgir Rebellions. Not just my father's memoirs."

"Ah, an interesting display of ambition."

"Are you afraid I'll win too many of our games if I learn more?" Vor scanned the list of files and was glad he would have so much time on the long update run.

"I have nothing to fear from a mere human."

For hours, Vor sat at the midships console, accessing the wealth of information. He had not studied so much since his days in the trustee school. With his mind sensitized by thoughts of Serena, Vor expected to find a few minor discrepancies in the historical record, when compared with Agamemnon's recollections. Even a cymek might be allowed to embellish war stories. But Vor was shocked to discover how radically different the evermind's objective records were from what Agamemnon had described.

Feverishly, he looked through records about Salusa Secundus, the Time of Titans, and the Old Empire, astonished at what he learned. Vorian had never bothered to look before, but the information was all here in front of his eyes.

My father lied to me! He distorted the events, taking credit, hiding the extent of the brutality and suffering—even Omnius knew it.

On the other hand, Serena had told him the truth.

For the first time in his life he felt anger toward his machine masters and his own father, and a glimmer of compassion for the human race. How bravely they had fought!

I, myself, am physically human. But what does that mean?

Agamemnon had caused horrendous slaughter and devastation during the Time of Titans, against people who were only trying to protect their own freedoms. He and Juno were responsible for the deaths of billions of people and the harsh enslavement of survivors. The humans had deserved none of this, had only tried to defend themselves.

No wonder Serena hates me, if I am the son of such a horrible murderer!

Vor read on. All the history was there, a dispassionate record accumulated by efficient machines—and he could not doubt it. Not this. Machines would never whitewash their records. Data was held sacred; information must be accurate. Deliberate deception was anathema to them.

It required a human mind to distort such information . . . or a human mind in a cymek body.

Seurat's voice startled him. "What are you researching? You have already wasted hours."

Gazing into the robot's mirrored face, Vor admitted, "I am learning more about myself."

"That should require only minimal study," Seurat said in an attempt at wit. "Why trouble yourself unnecessarily?"

"Sometimes it is necessary to face the truth." Vor closed the database, darkened the monitor.

The robot captain stepped back to the central console and linked himself with the ship's systems in order to begin planetary approach maneuvers. "Come now, we have reached Corrin. It is time for our next update delivery."

After concluding tests against every conceivable projectile and explosive, Tio Holtzman was eager to put his personal shield design into commercial production. He had already spoken with the managers of factory centers in Poritrin's northwest mining belt and assembly shops in Starda. With slave labor, he could make a substantial profit. His patents alone would place him, and his patron Lord Bludd, among the wealthiest men in the League of Nobles.

Unfortunately, as he worked through the projections of inventory and supply, thinking as a businessman rather than a scientist, he came to an inescapable conclusion: Poritrin, a bucolic world, could never handle the level of demand this wondrous invention was sure to arouse. Lord Bludd would not be happy to lose so much business to an offworld manufacturer, but Holtzman had no choice but to look to other League industrial centers.

Before he could send the fabrication units to Vertree Colony or to the restored and hungry industries of Giedi Prime, he decided he should first test his personal shield against a non-projectile weapon, an energy beam. Intense laser weaponry was almost never used in combat, since it was much less energy-efficient than explosives or simple projectile guns. Still, he wanted to be certain.

For one final test, he ordered his household guards to obtain a laser gun from an ancient military armory. After a good deal of searching and a plethora of requisition forms, the necessary weapon was finally located and brought to the blufftop laboratories. Because his shields had proven effective in every previous test, the scientist found each demonstration less exciting, simply another step in the process. Soon, the profits would begin to roll in.

Norma Cenva had returned to her continued ponderings of the Holtzman equations. The scientist had left her to her obsessive calculations while he basked in his own success.

For the laser test, he placed a slave within the shield, intending to fire the weapon himself. He brought only one assistant into the reinforced demonstration dome to record impressions of the test, as they had done many times before. Holtzman fiddled with the laser weapon's antique controls, trying to figure out how to fire the beam.

Norma rushed in, running like a clumsy girl. Her blocky face was flushed, her short arms waving. "Wait! Savant Holtzman, you are in terrible danger!"

He frowned like a stern father dismissing an overly rambunctious child. "You were skeptical during my first shield test, too. Look, I'm not even in the line of fire."

Her expression was frighteningly earnest and urgent. "The interaction of your force field with a collimated laser beam will have extraordinary consequences—massive destruction." She held up papers covered with equations and her own incomprehensible shorthand notations.

Impatiently, he lowered the laser weapon, and sighed heavily. "I don't suppose you can show me any *basis* for your alarm?" The targeted Zenshiite slave looked nervously through the shimmering shield. "Or is this just another one of your mysterious intuitions?"

She thrust the mathematics forward. "Savant, I have been unable to extract a specific basis for the anomaly when I introduce a factor of coherent laser energy into the field interface. But there is clearly a dramatic singularity potential."

Holtzman looked at the scribblings, but they meant nothing to him: The lines were so messy, steps skipped, odd notations to denote factors he had never seen before. He frowned, not wanting to admit that he was unable to understand. "Not a very rigorous proof, Norma—and not convincing either."

"Can you *dis*prove it? Can you take the risk? This could be even worse than the disaster with the alloy-resonance generator, a huge catastrophe."

Holtzman's expression remained stony, though a feather of doubt tickled his mind. He could not ignore this woman's sheer brilliance. He had always suspected that Norma understood the concepts of his own field better than he did. "Very well. If you insist, I'll take an extra precaution or two. Any suggestions?"

"Conduct the test far away, on a moon or, better yet, an asteroid."

"On an *asteroid*! Do you know the added expense that would entail?"

"Less expensive than rebuilding the entire city of Starda."

He chuckled, then saw that she wasn't joking. "I will postpone my test to consider this. But I insist that you provide proof. Back up your intuition before I go to such great trouble and expense. I can't justify such a huge undertaking just because your feet are cold."

⤜∾⤏

NORMA CENVA WAS a scientific and mathematical adept, but she had never been schooled in personal politics. Like a naïve child, she went to see Lord Niko Bludd in his noble residence on the bluff overlooking the Isana.

Atop the tall conical tower, the enameled roof tiles were different from the blue metal so common on most other Starda buildings. Dragoon guards lined the interior halls like gold-skinned reptiles adorned with helmet crests, crimson capes, and segmented gauntlets.

Bludd seemed in good enough cheer. He tugged at his curly beard. "Welcome, young lady. Did you know, at a recent meeting on Salusa I had another opportunity to speak with your mother? Her Sorceresses had just driven off another cymek attack, this time on Rossak. I can see where you received your special talent." His blue eyes twinkled.

Embarrassed, Norma looked at the tiled floor. "Indeed, Lord Bludd. My mother has . . . high expectations of me. As you can see, however"—she gestured to her misshapen form—"I will never match her physical beauty."

"External loveliness is not everything," Bludd said without casting a glance at the five gorgeous women who hovered around him. "Savant Holtzman believes your mind is full of remarkable ideas. Has he sent you? Does the Savant have another project to demonstrate?"

A well-dressed slave woman came forward carrying a silver tray with two goblets of fizzing clear liquid. She offered one to Norma, who held the ornate cup awkwardly in her small hands. Lord Bludd sipped from his own goblet, and Norma drank with him.

"He has another demonstration planned, Lord Bludd." Norma hesistated. "But I must ask you to intervene."

Inquisitive lines creased his forehead. "Whatever for?"

"Savant Holtzman means to test his new shield using a laser weapon, but there is danger, sir. I . . . I am afraid there may be a violent interaction. Extremely violent."

She began to speak in mathematical terms, defending her convictions insofar as she could, but this only caused the nobleman to raise his hands in helpless confusion. "And what does the Savant think of your concern?"

"He . . . trusts in my abilities, but I fear that he wants to perform the test quickly and inexpensively, and is afraid to displease you if he incurs a great cost." She swallowed hard, amazed at her audacity. "If I am correct, however, the aftereffects could devastate an entire district of Starda, perhaps even more."

"You mean like an atomic explosion?" Bludd was astonished. "How can that be? A shield is a defensive weapon. Atomics are destructive in—"

"Second- and third-order interactions are difficult to predict, Lord Bludd. Would it not be wiser to take precautions, despite the additional cost? Think of the profits Poritrin will make from this invention. Every important person and every private vessel will require a personal shield, and you will receive a royalty on each one."

She looked for a place to set down her heavy goblet. "On the other hand, imagine the disgrace if such a flaw is discovered after the products are in widespread use. Think of the losses you would endure."

The nobleman scratched his bearded chin and toyed with the jeweled chains on his chest. "Very well, I shall consider it an investment. Savant Holtzman has earned us enough to fund his eccentric ideas a hundred times over anyway."

Norma bowed deeply. "Thank you, Lord Bludd."

As she hurried off to tell her mentor, Norma never considered the gaffe she had committed in circumventing his authority. She expected a man like Tio Holtzman to decide matters rationally, not emotionally, unaffected by petty concerns and personality conflicts.

After growing up under her mother's frequent reproach, Norma had a thick skin for insults. How could the great Savant be any less of a person?

❧

THE TEST TOOK place on a bleak asteroid orbiting far from Poritrin. A team of construction workers excavated a test zone in a flat crater, erected a few recording devices, then placed a shield-generating apparatus in the crumbly dust of the crater floor. Then they departed the asteroid to join with a larger frigate bound for Poritrin.

To observe, Norma and Holtzman sat inside a small military shuttle flown by a reserve Armada pilot. The Savant had expected to rig sophisticated remote-firing laser weapons down in the crater around the target zone. Aware of his budgetary concerns, though, Norma had suggested that it might be sufficient just to fly over the target and shoot at it with an old laser weapon installed in the ship.

As the pilot guided them over the test area, the moody scientist hardly responded to Norma's attempts at conversation. Holtzman watched as they closed in on the target crater. He seemed annoyed, anxious to prove the young woman wrong. Norma peered through the shuttle windows at the pockmarks, mounds of precariously balanced boulders, deep fissures caused by tidal stresses. The place looked as if it had already been destroyed.

"Let's be done with this," Holtzmán said. "Pilot, shoot your laser weapon when you are ready."

Norma looked out the window to watch as the shuttle cruised low until the cleared test area was directly below them. "Preparing to fire, Savant."

Casually and offhandedly, Holtzman said, "You'll see that you have imagined excessive—"

The pilot fired a bright beam from the shuttle's laser. The appalling flare of light and energy snatched the words from his mouth. Even in the silence of space, the shockwave seemed louder than a crack of thunder.

The pulse surged upward, and the pilot yanked the shuttle's flight controls. "Hang on!" Powerful engines tore them away; the acceleration nearly pressed Norma into unconsciousness.

Then a hammer struck them from the rear, batting the ship like a toy. The shuttle spun out of control, and the asteroid fragmented into white-hot molten boulders radiating from the center of the blast like the spokes of a wheel.

Aghast, Holtzman turned away from the blazing light while the pilot tried to impose order upon the military spacecraft. The scientist's breaths came in rapid, astonished bursts.

Beside him, even Norma was astounded. She stared at her mentor, her lips moving without producing words. None were necessary. If Holtzman had blithely conducted this experiment inside his lab, he would have vaporized the lab, his residence, part of the city, and possibly even rerouted the Isana River.

He looked at Norma, first in anger, then amazement. Never again would he doubt her intuition or challenge her scientific abilities.

Still, he felt a knife twist inside him, a blow to his self-confidence and to his public image. His benefactor Niko Bludd would now know the truth. Norma had openly challenged Holtzman's judgment, and her doubts had been undeniably justified.

He didn't see how to keep everyone on Poritrin—the lords, the Dragoon guards, even the slaves—from learning that the stunted Rossak mathematician had upstaged him. News of this test would travel rapidly.

Tio Holtzman had been spectacularly *wrong*, and the deep wound from this might never heal.

*Animals must move across land to survive—for water, for food,
for minerals. Existence depends upon some kind of movement:
you move, or the land kills you where you stand.*
      —Imperial Ecological Survey of Arrakis, ancient records

The desert night was silent and untroubled. The first moon
had already set while the dimmer second moon hung
above the horizon like a sleepy eye, yellow with weariness.

Little more than a shadow, Selim squatted on a boulder,
watching the black honeycomb of caves above him. He didn't
know the villagers here, or their treasures—but Buddallah had
guided him to this isolated place. The desert and all its inhabitants were part of Selim's mysterious larger destiny, and he
did not question—or bother to justify—his actions.

These people had little contact with Naib Dhartha's tribe,
yet like all of the struggling Zensunni inhabitants, they sent
regular expeditions to Arrakis City to obtain necessary supplies. Even with sheltered agricultural methods and careful water conservation, no desert tribe could ever be entirely
self-sufficient here.

And neither could he, despite his best efforts. Air-
condensation devices in his two derelict botanical testing stations replenished Selim's water. Abandoned storage caches

provided most of the food he needed. But in the past year and a half, those ancient supplies had dwindled along with his powerpacks, and one of his tools had broken. He needed more stores to maintain his solitary existence.

God had given Selim many blessings, many advantages . . . but other necessities he must obtain for himself. He did not need to understand how all the pieces fit into Buddallah's comprehensive plan. There must be a reason, and someday he would discover it.

For several days Selim had observed this outlying settlement, watching the movement of the natives. The women kept beehives just inside the cave mouths, where the buzzing insects could seek out small desert flowers that struggled in sheltered crannies. Selim's mouth watered. He had tasted honey only once in his life, after Naib Dhartha had traded for a large pot of the sticky sweetener and had given each tribal member a small dab. The taste had been delicious, but taunting, reminding the poor Zensunnis of their dearth of luxuries.

As soon as Selim succeeded in his calling, whatever it was, he was sure he would have honey every day.

Although Selim needed some of the settlement's supplies, he also wanted to make a statement here. Buddallah had shown him a new strength through independence and self-sufficiency, rather than blind adherence to ancient laws. He disliked the close-minded, rigid strictures of the Zensunnis. All Zensunnis. Selim might have been a contented, hard-working member of the community, if Naib Dhartha had not heeded Ebrahim's false accusations and cast Selim out, supposedly to his death.

With an empty pack on his shoulders he crept forward; he had memorized the route and identified the cave in which the villagers kept their supplies, a place that was watched in the daylight, but poorly guarded at night. Confident in their isolation, the security of these villagers was lax. He would slip in, take what he needed and disappear, without hurting anyone. He would be a bandit. Selim Wormrider . . . Selim the outlaw.

Climbing silently up the steep slope, he found a rugged path that the people took whenever they went out to scavenge spice. Hand over hand, he ascended until he reached the balcony lip, then pulled himself up and squinted into the shadows.

As he had expected, the storage chamber was filled with packaged offworld food, no doubt purchased at a dear price back at the spaceport. Delicacies indeed, but why would true desert inhabitants need such things? Selim grinned. The villagers didn't *need* everything here, so he was obliged to relieve them of certain extraneous luxuries. Selim would stuff his pack full of energy wafers, nutritional supplements.

Selim crammed food and spare power cells into his pack's compartments. He also found seeds, vital botanical samples that he would use to set up a small greenhouse in one of the derelict testing stations. Fresh produce would be a marvelous addition to his diet.

From a workbench he grabbed a measuring tool and a sonic hammer designed for fracturing rock in specific patterns. This might be useful if he needed to make additional hideaways, perhaps by expanding natural caves in uninhabited outcroppings.

Poking into the soft compartments of his overburdened pack, Selim tried to find room for the two tools. He fumbled in the darkness and dropped the sonic hammer onto the stone floor. On impact, the device sent out a pulse that created a fracture in the floor of the cave, and reverberated like a cannon shot into the sleeping cliff village.

Startled, Selim gathered what he could, stuffing things into the pack with both hands. He swung it over his shoulder and lowered himself over the edge of the balcony. Already he heard suspicious shouts, curious questions. Glowsticks illuminated the cliff face, making the dark cave openings look like the eyes of a suddenly awakened demon.

Working his way down the rough path, he tried to move stealthily, but knocked small rocks loose. The stones pattered and ricocheted down the cliff.

Someone cast a beam of light in his direction, revealing the young man creeping down the path. Someone shouted. Soon the cave village was in an uproar. Men, women, and children rushed out, blinking sleep from their eyes, gesturing toward the thief, howling for him to stop.

Selim had no place to hide, and his heavy pack hindered him.

Zensunnis raced after him, climbing down ladders and stone steps cut into the rock. Terrified yet exhilarated, Selim put on a burst of speed and with a final leap reached the sand first and raced out onto the open plain. His heavy footsteps sank into the powdery surface, causing him to stumble along, with the desert nomads shouting after him. He kept running, hoping the men would hesitate if he went too far out onto the dunes. Yet they were bound to catch him soon, because of the weight he was carrying. It all depended on whether their righteous indignation would outweigh their fear of Shaitan.

Suddenly an idea dawned on him. Slowing his pace, Selim rummaged in his pack until he found the stolen sonic hammer. He knelt on the side of a dune, made sure the setting was at its maximum level, and raised the tool high. When he swung down, the explosion of sound reverberated like a depth charge, spraying sand upward in plumes.

The Zensunni villagers still came after him, yelling. Selim started running again and scrambled down a dune. He fell and tumbled, sliding with the sand, but he kept hold of the sonic hammer. Finally he came to halt between the dunes. Breathless, he rose to his knees and then to his feet, and slogged up to the next rounded crest. "Come, Old Crawler! I am calling you!"

He swung the hammer again like a wizened Buddislamic priest pounding a gong; on the next dune he struck a third time, sending out insistent signals. The men from the cliff city were close now, but he kept running farther into the open desert. They seemed to hesitate, and he distinguished fewer voices behind him.

Finally, Selim heard the hissing noise, the distant approach of a gigantic sandworm. His pursuers noticed it at the same time and shouted to each other, stumbling to an uncertain halt. All of them stared at the rippling wormsign in the moonlight, then raced at great speed back toward their cliff dwellings, as if the sight of the desert monster had put jets on their backs.

Grinning, knowing Buddallah would not let him be harmed,

Selim squatted on the dunetop, frozen in place as he watched his pursuers disappear. The worm was approaching fast and would no doubt go after the tribal men, drawn to their panicked footfalls. If he remained perfectly still, the worm should pass him by.

But the thought of the monster devouring the men troubled him. They had chased him only to defend their dwellings. Selim didn't want them to die because of him. That could not be part of Buddallah's plan, but the moral challenge was.

As the worm neared, he dialed down the sonic hammer's setting and pounded lightly, thump, thump, thump. Predictably, the worm turned toward him. Selim withdrew his equipment and crouched, in readiness.

Far off, only halfway to the refuge of their cave city, the Zensunni men turned to gape at him, and saw his figure profiled against moonlight. Selim stood tall as he faced the oncoming worm. . . .

❧

MOUNTED HIGH ATOP the beast, Selim held his guiding staff and ropes, content that he had lost none of his booty and no one had been killed. He turned to see the amazed men out on the moonlit sands. They had seen him mount the sandworm demon, and now he rode off into the deep desert, controlling it.

"As further payment for what I have taken, I give you a story you can tell for years around evening campfires!" he called back at them. "I am Selim Wormrider!"

He was too far away for them to hear, but Selim didn't care. This was only a time to plant seeds, not the time to reveal his identity. Hereafter, instead of reciting poetry and melancholy laments of ancestral wanderings, the villagers would talk about the lone man who could command sandworms.

Selim's legend would continue to grow . . . like a verdant green tree sprouting in the middle of the barren sands, where it should not have been able to survive.

Mother and child: An enduring, but ultimately mysterious image of humanity.

> —ERASMUS,
> *Reflections on Sentient Biologicals*

Little Manion became a bright spot in Serena's captive life, like a candle flickering in a pit of darkness.

"Your infant is an extraordinarily time-intensive and distracting creature," Erasmus said. "I do not understand why it requires so much attention."

Serena had been gazing into Manion's large, inquisitive eyes, but turned her head toward the robot's polished mirror face. "He will be only three months old tomorrow. At this age, he can't do anything for himself yet. He has to grow and learn. Human babies need to be nurtured."

"Machines are fully functional from the day of their programming." Erasmus sounded smug.

"That explains a lot. For us, life is a gradual developmental process. Without nurturing, we can't survive," she said. "You have never been nurtured. I think you should make improvements to the way you raise the slave children in your pens. Show them more kindness, encourage their curiosity."

"Another one of your suggested improvements? How many

disruptive changes do you expect me to make?"

"As many as I can think of. You must have seen a change in the people. They seem more alive now, after experiencing just a bit of compassion."

"Your compassion, not mine. And the slaves know it." The sentient robot flowed his pliable face into a now-familiar perplexed expression. "Your mind is such a mass of contradictions, it is amazing you manage to survive each day without undergoing a mental meltdown. Especially with that child."

"The human mind is more resilient than you imagine, Erasmus." Serena held the baby close. Each time the robot complained about how much disruption Manion caused, she feared he would take the infant away. She had seen the crowded, inhuman creches filled with wailing, low-caste youths. Although she had managed to improve the living conditions among these bestial slaves, she could not bear to have her own baby placed in their care.

Now Erasmus stood beside a gaudy swordfish statue, watching Serena play with the baby on a sunny afternoon. The two of them splashed in one of the villa's shallow aquamarine pools on a high terrace that offered spectacular views of the frothing ocean. Serena heard the pounding of surf, and the honking of geese that approached overhead.

Naked in his mother's arms, Manion splashed and squealed, patting his hands awkwardly on the water. The robot had suggested that Serena swim naked as well, but she insisted on wearing a simple white swimming garment.

As always, Erasmus stared at her and the baby. She tried to ignore the robot's scrutiny, as long as she had a peaceful hour to spend with Manion. Already, she could see how much her son would resemble Xavier. But would the boy ever have the freedom, the forceful personality, and the dedication to fight the thinking machines?

Where once she had thought in terms of large-scale League political and military matters, Serena Butler now concerned herself only with the safety of her child. Her worries were personal now, specific instead of grandiose. With renewed energy, she worked hard on her household duties in order to earn time with Manion, giving Erasmus no excuse to punish her.

The robot must realize that he now had a stronger hold over her than ever. He seemed to enjoy it when she verbally sparred with him, but she also grudgingly showed her appreciation for the minor freedoms Erasmus granted. Though she had never stopped hating her captor, Serena knew that he held her fate— and Manion's—in a delicate balance.

When she looked at her son's jutting chin and the determined set of his little mouth, she thought of Xavier and his stubborn devotion to duty. *Why didn't I just stay with him? Why did I have to save Giedi Prime? Couldn't I have been an ordinary woman for once?*

The honking geese grew louder as they flew directly over the villa, not caring whether humans or machines ruled the Earth. Whitish gray splatters of excrement struck the patio, one hitting the swordfish statue near the robot. Erasmus did not seem disturbed. It was all part of the natural order, as far as he was concerned.

In the shallow pool, Manion made a cooing giggle as he looked in the direction of the flying geese. Even at three months, he showed a curiosity about everything. Sometimes he tried to tug at the golden barrette in Serena's hair with his pudgy fingers, or at the sparkling jewelry Erasmus liked her to wear; the robot seemed to be grooming her as a hostess for his villa, an ornate decoration in his household.

Erasmus stepped closer to the pool and looked down at the baby who splashed happily in the water while his mother held him. "I never comprehended how much distraction and chaos an infant could cause in an orderly and calm household. I find it most . . . unsettling."

"Humans thrive on distraction and chaos," she said, trying to sound upbeat, though she felt a chill. "It is how we learn to innovate, to be flexible, and to survive." She climbed out of the pool with the baby and wrapped him in a soft white towel. "Think of all the times human ingenuity has thwarted Omnius's schemes."

"And yet, the thinking machines have conquered you."

"Are we really conquered, Erasmus, in any real sense?" She

raised her eyebrows, one of her mannerisms that he found maddeningly enigmatic. "Many planets remain free of thinking machines. If you are superior, then why do you struggle so hard to emulate us?"

The inquisitive robot did not understand the emotional bonding between mother and son. Despite her firm tone, he was most surprised to see the mellow changes in this woman who had previously been so fierce and independent. She seemed a different person after becoming a mother. She had never served him with half the attention she gave to that messy, noisy, *useless* infant.

While this investigation into human relationships had provided interesting data, Erasmus could not permit such a disturbance to his household in the future. The baby was disrupting his efficient daily life, and he wanted Serena's undivided attention. Together, they had important work to do; caring for the infant had made her lose focus.

As Erasmus stared at little Manion, the robot's thin flowmetal mask shifted to a ferocious scowl—which he quickly changed to a benign smile before Serena looked in his direction.

Soon, this phase of the experiment must end. He considered how best to accomplish that.

Patience is a weapon best wielded by one who knows his specific target.

—IBLIS GINJO,
Options for Total Liberation

For eight nerve-wracking months, Iblis Ginjo had operated on his own, making decisions and letting his imagination judge the extent of unrest among the slaves. As a trustee, he received certain privileges, but he had never truly *seen* how awful their lives were, foolishly thinking that his minimal rewards and praise made their days tolerable. How had they endured for so many centuries?

Iblis was convinced there must be other secret ringleaders and resistance fighters. Cogitor Eklo and his secondary Aquim had promised to help, and he could only guess at what resources or means they might have. However, apart from Ajax's constant suspicions and the execution of Ohan Freer, the thinking machines seemed to have no inkling of the incredible uprising they were about to face.

Soon that would change.

For weeks Iblis had exerted himself quietly but intently, whispering to his faithful workers, smoothly recruiting them into his circle of dissent. He had prepared them for the possibility of a revolt, and in spite of the danger, they had excitedly passed the message among themselves. Iblis swore that this uprising would not become another lost cause like the first Hrethgir Rebellions.

In the past two months, a determined Iblis had nearly doubled the ranks of his secret organization, with many more people attempting to join. He could feel the wave building. To become part of the spreading resistance, each convert had to pass through a series of blind names and defensive layers recommended by the monk Aquim.

The hundreds in his organization were divided into small cells of no more than ten, so that each member knew the identities of only a few others. All the while, they continued to spread the word, the goal, the excitement, and caution. It was as if they had been waiting a thousand years for this.

Cogitor Eklo had given a somewhat esoteric explanation of how the movement could achieve an exponential growth rate by following a basic model of biology, cells multiplying through mitosis. Members of each rebel cell would grow, break loose, and form new ones, which would continue in the same fashion. Sooner or later, they would encounter other groups and merge, drawing strength from each other. Ultimately the dissenters would reach critical mass, and there would be a flash of energy, like an electrochemical charge. . . .

Nothing is impossible.

Iblis had received additional secret communications at unpredictable times. The mysterious notes were maddeningly general, providing no specifics of other rebel cells, or what he was expected to accomplish. When it occurred, the revolt would be large but alarmingly uncoordinated, and Iblis feared that disorganization in the face of highly structured thinking machines would doom the movement to failure. On the other hand, the very unpredictability of human beings might be their greatest advantage.

Now, when Iblis returned home after three days of nonstop work on the Victory of the Titans frieze, he saw an old slave slipping out of his bungalow. Hurrying inside, Iblis discovered another message on top of his bedding. He rushed out to confront the old man in the yard. "Stop! I want to talk to you."

The old slave froze, like a rabbit about to bolt, trained never to resist the commands of a crew boss. Iblis ran to him, perspiring in the lingering heat of the day. "Who sent you? Tell me!"

The slave shook his wrinkled head. A peculiar, glazed expression crossed his face. He opened his mouth and pointed at it. The tongue had been removed.

Undeterred, Iblis thrust an electronic notepad at him, after clearing the screen with which he kept track of the crew's activities. The man shrugged, as if to indicate his inability to read or write. With a scowl, Iblis saw this as an effective means of preventing discovery and cross-contamination among the rebel cells. Disappointed, he let the slave go, whispering, "Keep up the resistance. Nothing is impossible." The old slave didn't seem to understand, and hurried off.

Iblis returned to his bungalow and read the brief message: "Soon we will be united. Nothing will stop us. You have made great progress, but you must continue for now without our help." Already, the lettering on the thin metal sheet had begun to corrode and vanish. "Advance your plans, and watch for a sign."

In the distance, beyond the megalithic cymek monuments, the yellow sun was dropping below the western horizon. *Watch for a sign.*

Iblis narrowed his eyes. If Omnius or one of the Titans discovered the plot too early, the revolt might fail. The crew boss had never considered himself a hero. He was working to free humans, but knew that a part of him also wanted to succeed for the benefit of his own ego. He must take advantage of his ability to sway opinions and inspire action among the slaves.

Slaves were easily encouraged to dream of freedom, but when second thoughts set in they feared reprisals from the thinking machines. During such moments of doubt, Iblis could gaze at his followers and speak hushed words with a deep intensity, convincing them of the unstoppable success of their movement. He had them under his complete physical and psychological control. His leadership skills had never failed him, and recently he had discovered new, hypnotic aspects of his personality. . . .

Iblis's teams maintained the oppressive work schedule on the Victory of the Titans frieze. His handpicked people labored at the exhibit with only a few robot guards and a neo-cymek in view, which had allowed them to surreptitiously incorporate the deadly components suggested by Cogitor Eklo. Similarly, Iblis had installed concealed weaponry at four other work sites around the capital city grid. Even the robot Erasmus had requested skilled laborers for modifications to his villa . . . and Iblis saw potential advantages there.

Inside his dim bungalow, Iblis held the metal message sheet, now entirely blank. He discarded it into a scrap pile that would be delivered to a recycler. The machines were very efficient at utilizing materials and minimizing industrial energy expenditures.

Even with only snippets of information, Iblis vowed to make all the pieces of the puzzle fit together. His core of dissatisfied workers was ready to rise up and smash thinking machines; the need to vent their anger built with each day.

Iblis could not wait forever. At some point, he might have to strike out on his own. He hoped the promised sign would come soon.

For months Erasmus tolerated the disruptive baby, but by the time little Manion was half a year old, the robot grew frustrated at the lack of progress in his own research. He wanted to move on to other investigations, and this unruly child was in the way. Something must be done.

With her misplaced priorities, Serena had grown increasingly protective of her son. She devoted more time and energy to the useless child than she did to Erasmus. Clearly unacceptable. It must never happen again.

Because she intrigued him, though, he had granted Serena far more freedom than any slave deserved. The baby gave her nothing in return, but she hung on the creature's every breath and whimper. It seemed a poor investment in time and resources.

Erasmus encountered her walking in the rear garden, holding Manion in her arms as she made her way between rows of plantings. The boy, ever-curious, gurgled his delight at the colorful flowers. She talked to it, using silly words and endearing tones. Motherhood had turned the intelligent and intense Serena into a buffoon.

One day Erasmus would make sense of these human personality traits. Already he had learned many important things, but he wanted to work faster.

For her own part, Serena thought her robot master was behaving more strangely than ever. He trailed her like a misshapen shadow, thinking she didn't notice him. His increasingly hostile reaction to Manion gave her cause for anxiety and dread.

At six months old, the boy could crawl around quickly, if awkwardly, and had a baby's skill at getting into trouble when he wasn't closely watched. Serena worried about him breaking fragile objects and making messes when her duties forced her to leave him in the care of other household slaves.

Erasmus seemed oblivious to the infant's safety. Twice now, when Serena had been performing assigned tasks, the robot had turned him loose to crawl through the villa, as if to see whether Manion could survive the numerous household hazards.

Only a few days ago, she had found her son at the edge of the high balcony overlooking the flagstone plaza in front of the main building. Snatching him to safety, Serena had snapped at Erasmus. "I don't expect a thinking machine to worry, but you seem to have no common sense, either." The comment had merely amused him.

Another time, she had intercepted Manion at an outer door to the robot's sealed vivisection laboratories, which were off-limits even to her. Erasmus had warned her not to pry. Though she agonized over the torment the inquisitive robot must be inflicting on other hapless slaves, for the sake of her child she dared not press the issue.

Curiously, Erasmus seemed to be intrigued by emotions while despising them at the same time. She had caught him practicing exaggerated facial expressions when he stared at baby Manion, his flowing synthetic skin displaying a parade of theater masks that ranged from revulsion to perplexity to outright malice.

Serena hoped to convince Erasmus that he still did not comprehend human nature, and that he must keep her alive in order to discover the answers he so desperately wanted. . . .

Today she carried Manion through a misty fern garden. Walking with feigned nonchalance, Serena noted a doorway at the far end of the greenhouse and remembered that it had a lockable door that led into the main house. Erasmus watched her obsessively, as usual.

Continuing her rounds, studying the plants, she pointedly did not look at the spying robot. Then, faking a second thought, she darted through the doorway with the baby and locked the door behind her. It was only a momentary respite from the intense scrutiny—and it would keep her master off balance. She hoped.

As she hurried through the corridor, Manion struggled in her arms, making loud squeals of displeasure. He was trapped with her, unfairly condemned to spending the rest of his life as a slave. Xavier—her heart went out to him—would never see his own son.

Once again she regretted her bold decision to go to Giedi Prime in the first place. Filled with purpose and idealism, she had thought only in terms of large populations, of the welfare of billions of people. She had not given adequate consideration to those close to her, her parents, Xavier, even the fetus she had not known she was carrying. Why did she have to bear the burden of human suffering on her own shoulders?

Now Xavier and little Manion were paying the price along with her.

In the corridor ahead, Erasmus emerged through another doorway to block her path. He wore a displeased expression on his surreal face. "Why do you attempt to escape, when you know it is impossible? This game does not amuse me."

"I wasn't trying to escape," she protested, shielding the little boy.

"By now you must understand that there are consequences for your actions." Too late, she noticed something shimmering in his hand. He pointed the device at her and said, "It is time to change the parameters."

"Wait—" Serena saw a burst of white light, and then numbness engulfed her body. She could no longer stand. Her legs drooped as if they had turned to water. Falling, she made an attempt to protect Manion, who howled in surprised fear as he and his mother melted to the floor.

Her consciousness fading, Serena could do nothing to stop Erasmus as he stepped forward to pluck the helpless child from her arms.

⌘

INSIDE HIS DISSECTION and surgical theater, Erasmus studied Serena. Her naked skin was smooth and white, having recovered from her bothersome pregnancy with surprising resilience.

As she lay insensate on the hard white platform, Erasmus performed delicate surgery. For him it was a routine operation, because he had practiced many times on slave women in the past two months, and only three of the subjects had died.

He did not want to harm Serena, since he felt she could still teach him many things. This procedure was for her own good. . . .

⌘

SERENA FINALLY AWOKE, unclothed but soaked with perspiration. Restraints held her arms and legs, and she had vague burnings of discomfort in her abdomen.

Lifting her head, she found that she was in a large, cluttered room, apparently alone. Where was Manion? Her eyes widened in alarm and fear. Trying to sit, she felt a jolt of pain in her midsection. Looking down, she could see an incision and the mark of fused skin across her lower belly.

With a clatter, Erasmus entered the room, carrying a tray that contained metal and crystalline objects. "Good morning, house slave. You have slept longer than I anticipated." He set down the tray and gingerly released the restraints on Serena's wrists. "I was just cleaning my medical instruments."

Furious with him, and sick with dread, she touched the marks of her surgery, felt around her sore abdomen. "What have you done to me?"

Calmly, the robot said, "A simple precaution to solve a problem for both of us. I have removed your uterus. You need not be concerned ever again about the distraction of having more babies."

Greed, anger, and ignorance poison life.

—COGITOR EKLO OF EARTH,
Beyond the Human Mind

For months after the thinking machine attack on Rossak, Zufa Cenva devoted her time and energy to training replacement candidates. They had lost so many in psychic firestorms against the cymeks.

Aurelius Venport had handled himself well during the crisis, successfully evacuating the people and keeping them safe out in the fungoid jungles while cymek warriors destroyed everything in sight. But Zufa had barely noticed. While Venport was sympathetic to the stress and responsibility she placed upon herself, the chief Sorceress spared little thought for her lover. It had always been this way, and he was growing weary of it.

Zufa had never fully bothered to see what the men of Rossak were capable of doing. Despite her telepathic prowess, Zufa did not understand the practical functioning of her sheltered world. Little did she know how the patriotic Venport kept the economy of Rossak strong.

For years, his teams of chemists had studied the medicinal

and recreational potential of the jungle plants, barks, liquids, and fungi. Battlefield surgeons and medical researchers throughout the League depended on a reliable supply of drugs from the Rossak jungles.

In addition, he had begun to contract production of the innovative and efficient glowglobes that Norma had invented and shared with him. Profits from his business ventures would pay to repair and reconstruct the damaged orbital platforms, to rebuild the ruined cave cities, and also to fund an increased presence of Armada scout and picket ships on the perimeter of the system.

Zufa, apparently, thought such things came free. Venport's business ventures funded it all.

At any time he chose, he could pack up his credits and live like a king on some other world. But he belonged on Rossak. Even though the chief Sorceress treated him with little warmth or compassion, he did love her.

Venport smiled to himself as he rode the lift cables to the undulating section of flat pavement on the polymerized treetops. Small ships could land there, though larger cargo barges had to remain in space, docking with the damaged orbital stations and off-loading supplies one crate at a time. Out in the jungle, fast-growing vines and tall weeds had already begun to cover the wide scorch marks made by the cymek conflagration. Nature had a way of healing itself.

Gazing up into the hazy skies, he searched for the expected shuttle, pleased to see that it was exactly on time. He watched it descend, a small private craft owned by a Tlulaxa flesh merchant named Tuk Keedair, a man who raided the Unallied Planets for slaves. Keedair also sold biological organs, reportedly grown in sophisticated tanks kept behind tight security on Tlulax.

A merchant himself, Venport had never considered slavery to be a lucrative or sensible commodity. Only a handful of League Worlds permitted the practice, but Keedair had a good reputation with his customers. Oddly, the man wanted to make a different sort of proposal to Aurelius Venport today, involving some commodity other than slaves. Curious, Venport had agreed to meet with him.

After the small Tlulaxa shuttle landed, Keedair stepped out. The flesh merchant stood with his hands on his hips, dressed in a clean blue blouse tucked into tight black pants. A dark braid shot with silvery-gray strands dangled like a badge of honor over his shoulder.

Venport extended a hand in greeting. For this occasion he had worn a formal jerkin belted at the waist and boots made from the blackish green pelt of an arboreal slitherer. Keedair raised a callused hand in a salute.

The flesh merchant said, "I have brought samples to show you, and ideas to make you lick your lips."

"You come to me with a reputation for vision and foresight, Tuk Keedair. Tell me your ideas."

While the Sorceresses were occupied with their endless war councils, Venport took his guest into a formal reception chamber. Here, the two men were alone, sipping potent tea brewed from fresh jungle herbs, going through the social rituals.

Finally, Keedair brought out a sample of brownish powder and extended it to him. "Nine months ago, I found this on Arrakis." Venport sniffed and, at his visitor's behest, tasted the potent, tingly substance.

He hardly heard the Tlulaxa's further words, so focused was he on the remarkable experience that demanded his complete attention. Though he was quite familiar with recreational stimulants and mood-altering substances from the Rossak jungles, he had never imagined that anything like *this* existed.

The melange seemed to seep into every cell of his body, transmitting energy and vitality directly to his brain, but without the usual sensory distortions. This was pleasure . . . but much more than that. Venport sat back and felt the substance seduce and relax him, controlling him without controlling him. It was a paradox. He felt mentally sharper than at any time in his life. Even the future itself seemed clear.

"I like this very much." Venport let out a contented sigh and tasted another sample of the powder. "I may become our best customer."

Alerady, he suspected that he could arrange for many interested purchasers across the League. Many, many more.

❧

THE TWO MEN agreed on the details and shook hands, then settled down to another cup of Rossak tea . . . this time sprinkling melange into it.

Aurelius Venport agreed to travel with the flesh merchant to the ragged fringes of explored territory. It would be a long trip on a roundabout route, since Arrakis was as far out of the way as a known planet could be. But the man from Rossak wanted to see the source of melange for himself, to understand how he might turn spice harvesting into a profitable enterprise.

Maybe Zufa would take notice of him after this.

In a magnificent military procession, a League battle group of ballistas and javelins cruised toward Poritrin. On the bridge of the Armada flagship, proud and stony Segundo Xavier Harkonnen stood in full dress uniform, studying the peaceful-looking planet.

Lord Bludd, as an extravagant donation to the League of Nobles, had offered to equip the Armada ships with Tio Holtzman's new shields. At the Starda Spaceport, temporary facilities had been set up to accommodate the numerous vessels. All commercial craft had been cleared away to convert the field into an impromptu military base and shipyard. Whole crews of trained slaves had been reassigned from their regular duties to work on the installation.

Xavier wasn't entirely convinced he should place so much trust in an unproven technology, but the balance of power would have to change significantly before humanity could reconquer any more Synchronized Worlds. Risks needed to be taken.

The immense ballista-class battleships descended through the Poritrin sky. In addition to its built-in armaments, each vessel carried fifteen hundred crewmen, twenty troop transports, fifteen large shuttles for cargo and equipment, twenty small passenger shuttles, fifty long-range patrol craft, and two hundred swift kindjals for space or atmospheric combat. Such enormous vessels rarely landed on planetary surfaces, but now the ballistas descended under their own power, their plated hulls glistening in the sunlight.

After the ballistas came the smaller javelin-class destroyers, which could travel lighter but carried proportionally more weapons for rapid, decisive responses.

Crowds of Poritin nobles and free citizens waved and whistled, segregated from the slaves. Barges on the Isana blasted low-octave horns in response to the display. As part of the show to commemorate the fleet's arrival, squadrons of kindjals and patrol ships flew around the larger vessels like protective wasps.

After the flagship had landed, Xavier stepped out into a roar of welcoming cheers. The huge ballista loomed behind him on the tarmac, its outer skin stained with oily smears from the harsh space environment. Standing before the swell of expectant people, he felt minuscule.

But they all depended on him, and he had a job to do. After a brief pause to orient himself, he marched forward, flanked by his officers and command staff, followed by the first line of troops in perfect file. He had trained them well.

Accompanied by four prominent advisors and eleven Dragoon guards, Lord Niko Bludd approached him. The flamboyant noble flung his cape behind him and came forward to clasp Xavier's hand. "Welcome to Poritrin, Segundo Harkonnen. Although we hope to complete our tasks for you with all due speed, during your stay my people will rest easier at night, knowing our planet is under your magnificent protection."

⌒

LATER, WHILE BLUDD hosted an extravagant banquet, Xavier delegated duties to his primary fleet officers. His subcommanders oversaw the organization of work teams at the spaceport and documented the installation of Holtzman shield generators. At the Segundo's cautious command, the new systems would first be incorporated into a squadron of patrol craft, so that he could inspect the work and test the technology.

Afterward, Poritrin mechanics would scale up the systems, layering multiple shields to cover vulnerable spots of the javelins and then the fleet ballistas. If the shields performed adequately during rigorous shakedowns and test maneuvers, Xavier would order additional battle groups to be temporarily stationed at Poritrin for similar upgrades. He did not want to have too much of the Armada in drydock at any one time, thereby leaving some League Worlds undefended, nor did he want one of Omnius's stray spy drones to notice what was going on.

Most of the robotic weaponry consisted of projectiles and explosives, intelligent programmed bombs that pursued their targets until impact. As long as the AI projectiles did not learn how to slow their velocity and penetrate the shields, the protection should be sufficient, and dramatic.

In a highly confidential briefing, Xavier had learned of the shield's even more significant flaw—its violent interaction with lasers. However, since such energy weapons were almost never used in combat because they had proven inefficient for large-scale destruction, he deemed it an acceptable risk. Provided that the Armada could keep such a secret from Omnius. . . .

Within the conical towers of Lord Bludd's residence hall, Xavier listened to the minstrels singing hymns and story-songs inspired by a half-forgotten Navachristian holiday still occasionally celebrated on Poritrin. He was not hungry, and could barely taste or smell anything. He sipped a snifter of tart local rum, but consumed the alcohol sparingly. He did not wish to diminish his reaction time or his sensibilities. *Always ready.*

While the revelry continued behind him, he gazed out the tower's curved windows, staring down at the spaceport lights, splashes of yellow and white that allowed teams of slave workers to continue installing the shields night and day. He had never much cared for slave labor, especially since Serena had been so outspoken against it, but it was the way things were done on Poritrin.

Xavier would have preferred to be back home with Octa. They had been married for just less than a year, and she would soon give birth to their first child. For now, though, his duty required him to be here. Resigned to the task at hand, he raised his glass and echoed yet another of Lord Bludd's self-congratulatory toasts.

~≈~

ACCOMPANIED BY HIS adjutant, Cuarto Jaymes Powder, Xavier walked along the first rows of kindjals arrayed on the military landing field. Unit after unit had been installed, small shield generators connected to the spacecraft engines. His shoulders square, his back stiff, his uniform immaculate, he paid close attention to detail, checked everything for himself. He would never allow a mistake like Giedi Prime to occur again.

Gazing across the river delta, he saw cargo barges and passenger ships floating down from the northlands. Poritrin's business went on as usual, and the conflict with the thinking machines seemed distant. Yet Xavier would never be at peace. Although he had made himself happy with Octa, it wasn't the life he had planned for himself. The thinking machines had killed Serena. As he continued the fight for freedom, he knew that his motivation was personal.

Guarded by work managers, teams of lethargic slaves labored just hard enough to avoid punishment while showing scant enthusiasm for the job, no matter how much it would benefit humanity, themselves included.

While he disliked the practice of slavery, Xavier shook his head, dismayed and angry at their willingness to fail. "Lord Bludd's decision to assign such people to this work . . . does not inspire confidence."

Cuarto Powder scanned the teams of prisoners. "It's not unusual here, sir."

Xavier pursed his lips. The League of Nobles insisted on each planet's right to govern itself as the populace saw fit. "Still, I don't believe that a captive man will ever provide his best work. I want no mistakes, Jaymes—the fleet depends on it."

He swept his gaze across the work crews, looking for anything out of place, uneasy to see so many slaves performing delicate work. One black-bearded man in particular, with eyes that seemed to hold anything but placid thoughts, guided his team with sharp commands in a language Xavier could not understand.

Xavier squinted thoughtfully as he walked past the workers. He glanced around the work grid, at the kindjals glinting in sunlight. His instinct for danger made the skin prickle on his neck beneath the crisp fabric of his uniform.

On impulse, he rapped the hull of a patrol craft. Two grease-smeared slaves scuttled out of the vessel, their installation work completed, and moved to the next craft down the line, avoiding Xavier's gaze.

He took four steps away from the patrol craft, then turned around again, reconsidering. "Cuarto, I think we should test one of these kindjals, at random."

He climbed into the fighter craft's cockpit. With deft fingers he scanned the control panels, noting the newly installed power components and boosters that would project Holtzman's shields. He flicked switches, waited for the engines to hum to life, then engaged the shield.

On the ground outside, the adjutant stepped back. Powder shaded his eyes as the air shimmered around the kindjal, a crackling, nearly invisible bubble. "Looks good, sir!"

Xavier pushed the engine power controls higher, ready for takeoff. The patrol craft's exhaust blasted out, trapped within the shield until it slowly leaked through the barrier. The ship hummed and vibrated beneath him. He studied the panel readings, brow furrowed.

But when he tried to raise the kindjal off the ground, the

shield generator sparked and smoked. With a lowering hum, the engines shut themselves down. Xavier slapped the controls, disengaging all systems before further short circuits could race through the delicate components.

He climbed out of the patrol craft, his face red with anger. "Bring the work leaders to me immediately! And notify Lord Bludd that I wish to speak with him."

❧

THE SLAVES ASSIGNED to that particular kindjal had disappeared into the crowds, and despite the Segundo's furious demands, none of the captives arrayed before him confessed to any knowledge of the mistakes. Considering all slaves interchangeable, the lax crew bosses had kept no detailed records of who had actually worked on which craft.

Bludd had been enraged at the news, then apologetic. He tugged on his curled beard. "I offer no excuses, Segundo. Nevertheless, we will discover and reassign all sloppy workers."

Xavier remained silent for the most part, awaiting the full analysis from handpicked inspection teams. His adjutant finally returned, flanked by Dragoon guards. Cuarto Powder carried stacks of detailed reports in his hands. "We have completed the quality-control inspection, Segundo. Of all the ships processed, *one in five* of the shield generators has been installed improperly."

"Hopelessly, criminally inept!" Bludd said, his lips curling, his face stormy. "We will make them repair everything. My deepest apologies, Segundo—"

Xavier looked directly at the nobleman. "A twenty-percent failure rate is not mere incompetence, Lord Bludd. Whether your captives are traitors because they are in league with our enemies or simply angry at their masters, we cannot tolerate it. If my fleet had gone into battle with those ships, we would have been massacred!"

He turned to his adjutant. "Cuarto Powder, we will load all of the shield generators aboard our javelins and take them to the nearest Armada spacedock facility." He made a formal bow to the distressed nobleman. "We thank you, Lord Bludd, for your good intentions. Under the circumstances, however, I prefer to have trained military personnel install and test the shields." He turned to go.

"I will see to it right away, sir." Powder strode smartly out of the room, brushing past Dragoon guards.

Bludd looked mortally embarrassed, yet he could not argue with the stern commander. "I understand completely, Segundo. I will make certain the slaves are punished."

In disgust, Xavier declined the noble's invitation to stay for another meal. As if to make amends, Bludd sent a dozen cases of the finest Poritrin rum to the flagship at Starda Spaceport. Perhaps Xavier and Octa would share one, to celebrate his return home. Or maybe they would wait until the birth of their first baby.

Xavier departed from Lord Bludd's glittering reception chamber. They exchanged a few cordial but stiff words, and then the officer left for his ballista, realizing how relieved he would be to get away from this place.

Life is the sum of the forces that resist death.

—SERENA BUTLER

Serena had been violated, a part of her ripped away, leaving her with a bitter emptiness inside. In committing the atrocity, Erasmus had dragged her to the brink of despair, assaulting the stubborn hope that had always anchored her.

Upon first aspiring to the League Parliament, Serena had envisioned herself performing important work for the benefit of humanity. She had devoted her time, her sweat, and enthusiasm, without ever regretting a moment of it. When her own father had administered her oath as a League representative, she had been barely nineteen, with a bright future ahead of her.

Dashing young Xavier Harkonnen had touched her heart, and together they had hoped for a large, happy family. They had planned their wedding, spoken of their future together. Even as a captive of Erasmus, she had held fast to her dreams of escape, and of a normal life afterward—back with Xavier.

But just to suit his own convenience, the vicious robot had sterilized her like an animal, robbing her of the ability to bear more children. Now, whenever she saw the heartless machine, she wanted to scream at him. More than ever, she missed the company of educated human beings who might have helped her through this difficult time—even the misguided Vorian Atreides. Despite his supposed fascination for understanding humanity, Erasmus was incapable of comprehending why she should be upset about "a relatively minor surgical procedure."

Her fury and heartsickness smothered the cleverness she needed for bantering with him. She could muster no enthusiasm for the esoteric subjects that Erasmus blithely wanted to talk about. As a consequence, the robot grew disappointed in her.

Worse, Serena didn't even notice.

By the time little Manion was eleven months old, he had become her only lifeline, a poignant reminder of all she had lost, both in the past and in the future. A toddler now, he was a bundle of pent-up energy who moved around with clumsy steps, intent on exploring every corner of the villa.

The other slaves tried to help, seeing her pain and knowing the things she had quietly done to make their lives more tolerable. Serena didn't want anything from them, though. She could barely hold herself together. Despite her hurt, though, Erasmus retained the changes and improvements he had agreed to make.

Serena still worked in the garden and in the kitchen, keeping an eye on Manion while the boy examined utensils and played with gleaming pots. Knowing her unique relationship with Erasmus, the other household slaves viewed her with curious respect, wondering what she would do next. The cooks and assistants enjoyed the little boy, amused at his stumbling attempts at words.

Manion had an insatiable hunger for seeing and touching everything from the flowers and plants in the villa gardens to the exotic fish in the ponds, to a feather he found outside in the plaza. He studied everything with his alert blue eyes.

Serena renewed her determination to either escape or hurt Erasmus. To do that, she needed to understand everything possible about the independent robot. As a key to solving that enigma, she decided to find out exactly what took place in the ominous sealed laboratories. He had forbidden her from entering that place, warning her not to "interfere" with the experiments. He had ordered the other household servants not to tell her anything about them. What was the robot afraid of? Those sealed laboratories must be important.

She had to get inside.

An opportunity presented itself when Serena spoke to two kitchen helpers who prepared meals for human test subjects in the laboratory block. Erasmus insisted on high-energy meals so that his victims could survive as long as possible, but he preferred minimal bulk "to decrease the mess" when he inflicted too much pain.

The kitchen staff accepted Erasmus's bloody tastes with relief that they themselves hadn't been selected for the experiments. Not yet, anyway.

"What does the life of a slave matter?" asked one of the women, Amia Yo. She was the slave who had touched Serena's sleeve during the robot's "good deed" feast, and Serena had watched her working in the kitchens.

"Every human life has value," Serena said, looking at little Manion, "if only to dream. I need to see that place with my own eyes." Then she revealed her impetuous plan in a conspiratorial whisper.

Reluctant, but forming a brave face, Amia Yo agreed to help. "Because it is for you, Serena Butler."

Since the two women were approximately the same height and weight, Serena borrowed her white smock and apron, then covered her own hair with a dark scarf. She hoped the watch-eyes would not notice subtle differences.

Leaving Manion in the care of the kitchen helpers, Serena accompanied a slender, dark-skinned slave. They eased a gliding food cart through a gated area into a compound of outbuildings that she had never entered before. The sterile entry corridor smelled of chemicals, drugs, and sickness. Serena dreaded what she might see. Her heart pounded, and perspiration prickled her skin, but she pressed on.

Her companion seemed nervous, eyes flicking from side to

side as they passed through the coded barricade. Together, they entered an inner chamber. A thick, moist stench made the air almost unbreathable. Nothing moved in the room, no stir of life. Serena reeled.

Nothing could have prepared her for this.

Human body parts lay in grisly piles on tables, in bubbling tanks, and on the floor, like toys scattered about by a bored child. Fresh blood had splashed in feathery patterns on the walls and ceiling, as if Erasmus had dabbled in abstract art. Everything looked fresh and wet, as if the horrendous slaughter had occurred within the past hour. Appalled, Serena felt only disgust and unbridled rage. Why had the robot done this? To satisfy some macabre curiosity? Had he found the answers he wanted? At such a cost!

"Next room," said her companion in a shaky voice, trying to look away from the worst of it. "Nobody left to feed in here."

Serena staggered beside the other woman who pushed the gliding cart into the adjacent compound, where gaunt-looking prisoners were sealed inside isolation cells. Somehow, the fact that these test subjects remained alive struck her as even worse. She fought the urge to vomit.

She had long dreamed about fleeing her life of slavery on Earth. Now, seeing these horrors, she realized that escape would never be enough. She needed to stop Erasmus, to *destroy* him—not just for herself, but for all of his victims.

But Serena had fallen into his trap.

Using concealed surveillance units, Erasmus watched her. He found her revulsion gratifyingly predictable. For days he had been expecting her to sneak into his laboratory, despite his unequivocal proscription against going there. It was a temptation he had known she could not resist for much longer.

Some aspects of human nature he *did* understand, and very well.

Now that she and her companion had completed the assigned feeding chores, they would return to the safety of the villa, where Serena had left her unruly baby. Erasmus considered how best to handle her.

Time for a change. Time to add stress to the experimental system and observe how the subjects changed. He knew Serena's most vulnerable spot.

As he prepared himself for a drama of his own creation, Erasmus shifted his face back to an emotionless oval. He marched through the corridors, echoes announcing his approach. Before Serena could rush back to her son, the robot found Amia Yo playing with the child on the kitchen floor.

The master of the house didn't speak a word as he entered the room. Startled, Amia Yo looked up at the ominous robot. Beside her, little Manion stared at the familiar mirror face and giggled.

The boy's reaction caused the robot to pause, but only for a moment. With a swift backhand of his synthetic arm, he broke Amia Yo's neck and grabbed the toddler. The kitchen worker crumpled dead without so much as a gasp. Manion struggled and wailed.

Just as Erasmus lifted the squirming child into the air, Serena rushed through the door, her face filled with horror. "Let him go!"

Casually, Erasmus shoved her aside, and she stumbled backward over the body of the murdered woman. Without looking back, the robot quickly left the kitchen area and climbed a stairway to the villa's upper levels and balconies. Manion dangled in his grasp like a caught fish, crying and screaming.

Serena scrambled to her feet and ran after them, begging Erasmus not to harm her son. "Punish me, if you must—but not him!"

He turned an unreadable version of his face toward her. "Can I not do both?" Then he climbed to the second floor.

On the landing of the third level, Serena tried to grab one of the robot's metal legs through the ornate robe he wore. He had never seen her display such desperation, and wished he had applied monitoring probes so that he could hear her thrumming heartbeat and taste the panic of her sweat. Little Manion thrashed his arms and legs.

Serena touched her son's tiny fingers, managed to hold onto him for an instant. Then Erasmus kicked her, delivering a precise blow to her midsection, and she tumbled down half a flight of stairs.

Staggering back to her feet, she ignored her bruises and resumed the chase. Interesting; either a sign of remarkable resilience or suicidal stubbornness. From his studies of Serena Butler, Erasmus decided it was probably a little of both.

Reaching the highest level, Erasmus crossed to the broad balcony that was open to the flagstone plaza four stories below. One of the villa's sentinel robots stood on the balcony, observing the teams of slave workers installing new fountains and erecting recently commissioned statues in the alcoves. The sounds of their equipment and voices drifted upward in the calm air. The sentinel robot swiveled to look at the sudden disturbance.

"Stop!" Serena shouted with a sharpness that reminded him of her old defiant self. "Erasmus, *that is enough*! You've won. Whatever it is you want, I'll do it."

The robot stopped at the balcony railing and, clamping his artificial grip on Manion's left ankle, lifted the little boy over the edge. Serena screamed.

Erasmus issued a curt order to the sentinel robot. "Prevent her from interfering." He dangled the child headfirst over the stone-paved plaza far below, like a playful cat toying with a helpless mouse.

Serena threw herself forward, but the sentinel robot blocked her. She rammed against it so hard that the sentinel staggered against the rail before reasserting its balance and taking hold of Serena's arm.

Far below, the human slaves looked up at the open balcony and pointed. A collective gasp rippled through the work crews, followed by a hush.

"Don't!" Serena shouted frantically as she tried to tear herself free of the sentinel's grasp. "Please!"

"I must continue my important work. This child is a disruptive factor." With long arms, Erasmus dangled the child over the precipitous drop. A breeze stirred his formal robes. Manion writhed and squirmed, crying loudly for his mother.

Serena looked up at the imploringly mirrored face, but detected no hint of compassion there, no concern whatsoever. *My precious baby!* "No, please! I'll do anything—"

Below, the gaping workers were unable to believe what they were seeing.

"Serena . . . your own name is a derivation of 'serenity.' " Erasmus raised his voice over the child's wailing. "Surely you understand?"

She threw herself against the sentinel robot, nearly pulling herself free, and reached out, desperate to snatch her son.

Abruptly, Erasmus's fingers released their grip on the baby's ankle. Manion dropped, tumbling into oblivion, to the stone plaza far below. "There. Now we can get back to work."

Serena howled so loudly that she did not hear the terrible sound of the small body striking the pavement moments later.

Heedless of her own danger, Serena ripped her arms free at the cost of torn skin and hurled herself against the sentinel robot, shoving the machine into the high balcony rail. When the sentinel righted itself, she pushed again, harder this time. The robot struck the low barrier, broke through the balustrade, and tumbled into open air.

Paying no attention to the falling machine, Serena lunged at Erasmus and pounded him with her fists. She tried to dent or claw his smooth flowmetal face, but succeeded only in bloodying her fingers and breaking her nails. In her mindless frenzy, Serena tore his lovely new robe. Then she grabbed a small terra-cotta urn from the balcony edge and smashed it against Erasmus's body.

"Stop behaving like an animal," Erasmus said. With a casual blow, the robot knocked her aside, sending her sobbing and crumbling to the tile floor.

⟨≈⟩

SUPERVISING THE WORK crew in Erasmus's plaza, Iblis Ginjo watched the scene in utter disbelief. "It is Serena!" one of the villa workers cried, recognizing her on the high balcony. Her name was taken up by the other workers, as if they revered her. Iblis remembered Serena Butler from when he had processed her with new slaves arriving from Giedi Prime.

Then the robot dropped the baby.

Unconcerned with consequences, Iblis rushed across the plaza in a desperate but fruitless attempt to catch the child. Seeing the trustee's brave reaction, many of the slaves also surged forward.

Standing over the broken, bloodied child on the pavement, Iblis knew he could not help in any way. Even after all the atrocities he had seen cymeks and thinking machines commit, this one outrage seemed inconceivable. He gathered the broken little body in his arms and looked up.

Now, remarkably, Serena was fighting her masters. The workers gasped and drew back as she pushed a sentinel robot off the balcony. In a flash of metal, the thinking machine plummeted four stories to slam into the hard flagstones, not far from the bloodstain left by the dead child. With a sound like a sledge hitting an anvil, the sentinel robot smashed, bent, and crumpled. It lay in a motionless heap on the ground, its fibrous and metallic components broken, gelcircuitry fluid oozing out into the cracks. . . .

Mortified and appalled, the slaves stared at what had happened. *Like tinder ready for a spark*, Iblis thought. A human captive had fought the machines! She had destroyed a robot with her own hands! Amazed, they called out her name.

Above on the balcony, a defiant Serena continued to shriek at Erasmus, while he shoved her back with his superior strength. The woman's passionate courage astounded all of them. *Could the message be any clearer?*

An ugly shout of anger rose from the captive workers. They had already been primed by months of Iblis's instructions and subtle manipulations. Now it was time.

With a smile of grim satisfaction, he bellowed his call. And the rebels surged forward in an act that would be remembered for ten thousand years.

Monoliths are vulnerable. To endure, one must remain mobile, resilient, and diversified.

—BOVKO MANRESA,
First Viceroy of the League of Nobles

When the Armada battle group left Poritrin, the crowds in Starda were much diminished, the cheering more subdued. Word had circulated quickly about the slaves who had bungled a vital job. It was a shame upon the entire world.

Deeply disappointed, Niko Bludd watched the ion trails of the departing battle group. Then, focusing his wrath, he floated his ceremonial platform over the gathered slave crews. He had commanded their chastised overseers to muster all workers for inspection.

Lord Bludd spoke into a voice projector that thundered down upon the grumbling slaves. "You have let Poritrin down! You all have disgraced humanity. Your sabotage has hindered the war effort against our enemies. This is *treason*!"

He glared at them, hoping for some sign of remorse, abject pleas for forgiveness, even heads bowed in guilt. Instead, the captives seemed defiant, as if proud of what they had done. Since slaves were not citizens of the League, they could not technically be guilty of treason, but he liked the weighty, ominous sound of the word. These ignorant people would not understand the subtle difference.

He sniffed, recalling an old Navachristian punishment, intended as a nonviolent psychological blow. "I declare a Day of Shame upon all of you. Be thankful that Segundo Harkonnen detected your incompetence before brave lives were lost. But your actions will hurt our continuing struggle against Omnius. Blood cannot be cleansed from your hands."

Knowing they were a superstitious lot, he shouted a curse at them. "May this shame fall upon all your descendants! May Buddislamic cowards never be free of their debt to humanity!"

Raging and shouting, he ordered the Dragoon guards to steer the platform away from the spaceport.

～

BEL MOULAY HAD been hoping for a volatile situation such as this. Never again would there be so many slaves massed together at one time. The Zenshiite leader called his brothers to action.

The overseers and Dragoon guards had orders to break up the reassigned crews and return the slave laborers to their original masters. Much of Poritrin's routine work had gone undone while the Armada ships were in drydock at the spaceport, and a number of lords had expressed their impatience for life to return to normal.

But now the captives refused to move, refused to work.

Bel Moulay shouted to those close enough to hear his words, awakening seeds he had planted during secret talks, month after month. He spoke in Galach so that all of the nobles could understand him. "We do not toil for slavers! What difference is it to us if the thinking machines oppress us, or you?" He raised a fist. "God knows we are justified! We will never give up the fight!"

A howl rose in vibrating unison. The pent-up rage spread like fire over oil, faster than the Dragoon guards or the Poritrin nobles could react.

Moulay shouted toward the nobleman's departing platform.

"Niko Bludd, you are worse than the thinking machines *because you enslave your own kind*!"

A throng of Zenshiites and Zensunnis suddenly surrounded the astonished supervisors and disarmed them. One overseer with a black bandanna around his slick scalp held up his fists and gruffly shouted commands, but didn't know what to do when the slaves ignored his orders. The insurgent workers clutched the man's sleeves, tugged at his gray work gown, and dragged him back to his own holding pens, where so many of their unfortunate companions had been held after the deadly fever.

Bel Moulay had instructed the slaves in how to be the most effective. They must take hostages, not turn into a mob and slaughter the nobles outright. Only in this manner would the people have any hope of negotiating their freedom.

The bearded Zenshiite leader identified several unmanned equipment shacks and four old boats that had run aground on the low-tide mudflats; his followers set them afire. The flames rose skyward like orange flowers, spreading their smokey pollen above the spaceport. Slaves, suddenly unrestrained, poured out onto the landing grids, where they set up obstructions that prevented any commercial vessels from landing.

Some young insurgents broke through the outer cordon of astonished spectators. Flustered Dragoons overreacted and opened fire, dropping several in their tracks, but the rest of the excited slaves raced into the streets of Starda, disappearing like fish into the reeds. They ran into alleyways, hopping across floating barges and metal-roofed warehouses, where they rendezvoused with other slave children who had been waiting for this opportunity.

The breathless children passed their news in the ancient Chakobsa hunting language that every one of these repressed people could understand. And the uprising spread. . . .

❦

TIO HOLTZMAN WAS upset and confused, ashamed that the first large-scale military deployment of his innovative shields had been such an embarrassing debacle. Preoccupied while Norma Cenva worked on her own designs, he didn't notice for some time that his regular meal had not arrived, that his pot of clove tea had grown cold. Stymied by a complex integral, he gave up in disgust.

The house and laboratories seemed oddly silent.

Frustrated, he rang for servants, then returned to his work. Minutes later, hearing no response from the household slaves, he rang again, then bellowed into the corridors. When he saw a Zenshiite woman walking down the hall, he shouted for her. She simply looked at him with a peculiar expression and turned indignantly in the opposite direction.

He couldn't believe it.

After he rounded up Norma, the two of them entered the room full of equation solvers. There, they found the slaves simply chatting in their own language, papers and calculation devices lying untouched in front of them.

Holtzman thundered at them, "Why don't you finish your assignments? We have designs to complete—important work!"

As one, the solvers swept everything off the tables. Equipment clattered to the floor and papers fluttered like pigeons' wings.

The Savant was flabbergasted. Beside him, the childlike Norma seemed to understand better than he did.

Holtzman called for the household guards, but only one responded, a sweating sergeant who clung to his weapons as if they were anchors. "My apologies, Savant Holtzman. The other Dragoons have been summoned by Lord Bludd to quell the disturbance at the spaceport."

Holtzman and Norma hurried to the viewing platform, where they peered through a magnification scope at fires burning around the spaceport. Large numbers of people were gathered there, and even at this distance the Savant could hear crowd noises.

When their master's back was turned, one solver shouted, "We have been slaves long enough! We will not work for you anymore!"

Holtzman spun around, but could not identify the speaker. "Are you fools as well as slaves? Do you think *I* recline on a divan while you all work? Have you not seen the glowglobes in my office shining into the night? This stoppage hurts *all* of humanity."

Norma tried to sound reasonable. "We feed and clothe you, provide decent shelter—and the only thing we ask in return is assistance with simple mathematics. We must fight against our common enemy."

Holtzman interjected, "Yes, would you rather be back on your smelly little uncivilized worlds?"

"Yes!" the slaves shouted, in unison.

"Selfish idiots," he muttered, and looked out the window again at the fires and milling slaves. "Unbelievable!" He didn't consider himself a bad master. He worked these people no harder than he worked himself.

From the viewing platform where Holtzman and Norma stood, the river appeared a particularly dismal gray, reflecting the color of thick overhanging clouds. Norma speculated, "If this uprising spreads to the agricultural fields and mines, Lord Bludd's military forces may not be able to contain it."

Holtzman shook his head. "Those arrogant Buddislamics think only of themselves, just as they did when they fled from the Titans. Never able to see beyond their own narrow horizon." He shot a final glare at the room full of indignant solvers. "Now you and I will be forced to waste time dealing with people such as these, instead of our real enemies." He spat on the floor, thinking of no other way to show his disgust. "It'll be a wonder if any of us survive."

He ordered the room of solvers sealed and further rations denied until they returned to work. Uneasy, Norma trotted along behind him.

❧

THAT AFTERNOON, LORD Bludd received a list of demands from the leader of the insurrection. Protected by his followers, Bel Moulay issued a statement, demanding the release of all enslaved Zenshiites and Zensunnis from bondage, and safe passage back to their homeworlds.

At the beseiged spaceport, the rebels were keeping many nobles and overseers hostage. Buildings burned, while Bel Moulay delivered impassioned speeches from the heart of the mob, fanning the flames. . . .

Is a religion real if it costs nothing and carries no risk?

—IBLIS GINJO,
note in the margin of a stolen notebook

Timing was everything. For months, Iblis had primed his work crews and awaited the promised signal that would launch a violent, coordinated revolt. But something else had intervened, an event of staggering proportions. The slaughter of a human child by a machine, and the incredible sight of his mother fighting back—and destroying a robot!

Using this horrific crime as a springboard, Iblis hardly needed his innate abilities of persuasion. Around him he heard shouts, breaking glass, running feet. The angry slave workers required no manipulation—they *wanted* to do this.

The rebellion on Earth blossomed and gained violent strength in the precinct of Erasmus's villa. Three men toppled an eagle statue from the nearest alcove; others tipped over the crown of a stone fountain in the plaza. The mob tore down vines from the sides of the main building, smashed windows. They broke through the foyer, swarming over two confused sentinel robots who had never seen such a response from the supposedly cowed prisoners. Ripping the heavy weapon arms off the destroyed robots, the people lugged them along, indiscriminately opening fire.

The rebellion must spread.

Iblis feared that if the disturbance remained too localized, Omnius's sentries would come and exterminate everyone. But if he could contact his other groups and send out the signal, the revolt would continue to build, spreading from settlement to settlement. Hopefully the Cogitor and his secondary had managed to assist the secret plans.

Now that the mob had been launched here at Erasmus's villa, the real work of the insurrection must occur elsewhere. Watching the frenzy increase around him, hearing the shouts grow louder, seeing the wild destruction, Iblis decided that these people no longer needed him.

With the capital city grid illuminated by a ghostly yellow moon, Iblis issued the much-anticipated command to his core groups at other major sites. He notified the unit leaders, who in turn sent men and women surging into the streets, carrying clubs, heavy tools, cutters, any weapon that might be effective against the thinking machines.

After a thousand years of domination, Omnius was not prepared for this.

Like an avalanche, the frenzied rebels swept up others, even those who had hesitated to join the fledgling underground movement. Seeing a glimmer of hope, the slaves smashed everything technological they could find.

In the firelit darkness, Iblis climbed to a vantage point atop the Victory of the Titans frieze. From there he activated his crude transmitter. Hidden systems implanted in the chiseled wall burst forth. Every megalithic cymek statue in the mural cracked open, revealing the deadly arsenal inside.

Below in the museum square, he saw several neo-cymeks scrambling about in walker-forms. Guided by traitorous disembodied brains, the neo-cymeks rallied to attack a crowd of human rebels. Before long, other hybrid machines would arrive, undoubtedly wearing weapon-studded warrior bodies. Iblis could not let that happen.

He directed weapons fire. Rockets assembled from construction explosives launched out of embedded tubes in the frieze, exploding into the enemy. The crude blasts sheared off the fiber-metallic legs of two neo-cymeks. While they writhed on the ground and struggled to continue, Iblis shot two more rockets into their preservation canisters, spilling the electra-fluids and crisping the organic brain tissue to cinders.

Even if Iblis's followers overthrew the cymeks and the sentinel robots, the revolution would still need to deal with the all-powerful Omnius evermind. Standing high above the city grid and gazing at the spreading glow of rising fires, he felt a surge of confidence and optimism.

Bathed in surreal moonlight, the humans cheered. Flames crackled and spread in the gaudy, empty buildings of the machine capital. Near the spaceport, an armory blew up in a tremendous explosion, sending flames hundreds of meters into the air.

Iblis watched the numbers of his followers grow before his very eyes, and his heart swelled. He still could not believe the scale of what he saw occurring. Had scattered rebel cells responded to the call—or had he started this conflagration alone?

Like a chain reaction that could not be stopped, mobs ran through the streets, increasing their vengeance moment by moment.

Precision, without understanding its inherent limitations, is useless.

—COGITOR KWYNA,
City of Introspection archives

The people of Poritrin had kept slaves for so long that they had grown complacent with their comfortable, pampered way of life. As the insurgents' stranglehold on planetary commerce tightened, word of the uprising spread to all Zensunni and Zenshiite laborers in Starda. Work shut down in the entire city—and beyond. Agricultural slaves stopped their harvesting. Some set fire to the rustling cane fields; others sabotaged farm machinery.

Encamped with the other young artisans above the granite-walled Isana canyon, Ishmael and his exhausted companions spent the night inside flapping tents that caught the evening breezes on the upland plateau.

Abruptly, Ishmael awakened, recognized Aliid shaking him. "I sneaked out and listened to the overseers. There is a slave uprising at the delta! Listen to this. . . ."

The two boys returned to their still-smoldering campfire and sat huddled in the night chill. Aliid's dark eyes sparkled in the dim light. "I knew we wouldn't have to wait for centuries to be free again." His breath smelled of the spicy porridge they had received for their evening meal. "Bel Moulay will bring justice. Lord Bludd will have to grant our demands."

Ishmael frowned, feeling little of his friend's enthusiasm. "You can't expect the nobles to simply shrug and change the way Poritrin society has worked for hundreds of years."

"They'll have no choice." Aliid clenched his fist. "Oh, how I wish we were back in Starda so that we could join the uprising. I don't want to hide out here. I want to be part of the fight." He made a disgusted noise. "We're spending our days making pretty pictures on a cliffside for the glory of our oppressors. Does that make sense?" As the boy leaned back on his hands, a smile crept across his narrow face. "We can do something about it, you know. Even here."

Ishmael dreaded what Aliid was going to suggest.

⁓

IN THE DEAD of night, after the overseers had gone to sleep in their insulated pavilions, Aliid recruited Ishmael to the cause by promising that there would be no bloodshed. "We are just making a statement," Aliid said, his lips upturned in a humorless grin.

The pair then flitted from tent to tent, rallying confederates. Even with a simmering uprising in far-off Starda, the guards were not overly worried about a handful of boys exhausted from hours of work on the gorge walls.

Whispering in the starlight, the young men stole harnesses from the equipment shack. With callused fingers they strapped on the connections, belting themselves across the waist and chest, securing loops under their arms, attaching cables to the cliffside pulleys.

Fourteen young slaves dropped over the cliffside where the saga of the Bludd dynasty, ten times life-size, sprawled across the canyon wall. The boys had sweated to create each meticulous pixel of the illustration, following the laser-scribed patterns designed for Lord Bludd.

Now the youths dropped surreptitiously on their cables, running across the smooth cliff face with bare toes. As he swung like a pendulum, Aliid struck with his sharp rock hammer, chipping off colorful tiles, defacing the image. The distant thunder of whitewater rapids and wind whistling around the rock formations muffled the clinking of the tool against rock.

Ishmael dropped lower than his friend and hammered away at a section of blue-glazed tiles that, when seen from a distance, would have been the dream-filled eye of an ancient lord named Drigo Bludd.

Aliid had no actual plan in mind. He hammered randomly, moving laterally and climbing up again. His small sledge flaked off hundreds of tiles in a swath of random destruction across the mosaic. Chipped tiles broke away in jewel-colored shards, falling into bottomless darkness. The other slave boys did their own damage to the spectacle of Poritrin, as if by defacing the artwork they could rewrite history.

Hushed and giggling, they worked together for hours. Though they were only vague outlines in the starlight, Aliid and Ishmael grinned at each other with boyish enjoyment at their crude vandalism, then returned to the task at hand.

Finally, as the first streaks of light began to paint the horizon, the boys clambered up the cliff face in their harnesses, returned the equipment to the supply shack, and ducked into their tents. Ishmael hoped to snatch at least an hour of rest before the overseers roused them.

They made it back undetected. At dawn, alarms sounded and men bellowed into the open air, summoning the young workers and lining them up along the cliff edge. The red-faced work bosses wanted answers, demanded to know the identity of the perpetrators. They whipped the boys, one after the other, hurting them badly enough that they wouldn't be able to work for days; they denied them rations, cut back on water allowances.

But, of course, none of the slave boys knew a thing. They insisted they had been asleep in their tents all night.

❧

THE MALICIOUS DEFACING of the magnificent canyon mural was the final blow to Lord Bludd. He had tried to be reasonable and patient during the uprising. For weeks he attempted to use civilized means to bring Bel Moulay and his insurgent followers back into line.

When he had declared the Day of Shame, it had not worked on the psyches of the uncivilized captives—they simply didn't care—and in the end he realized he had been deluding himself. The Zensunni and Zenshiite clans belonged to the barest fringe of the human race, practically a different species. Unable to work for the common good, these ungrateful primitives relied on the sufferance of cultured people. Based on what they had done, the Buddislamic fanatics had no moral conscience.

The slaves had sabotaged the installation of shields on Armada warships and refused to continue work on Tio Holtzman's important new inventions. The dark-bearded insurrection leader had taken noblemen hostage and held them in slave pens. Moulay had crippled the Starda Spaceport, preventing any imports or exports, grinding all commerce to a halt. His criminal followers burned buildings, destroyed vital facilities, and ruined productive agricultural estates. Even worse, Bel Moulay had demanded the emancipation of all slaves—as if freedom was something a human being could simply have without earning it! Such an idea was a slap in the face to those billions who had fought and died to keep the thinking machines at bay.

Bludd thought of the slaughtered citizens on Giedi Prime, the victims of the cymek skirmish on Salusa Secundus, the Rossak Sorceresses who had given their lives to destroy cymeks. It disgusted him that this Bel Moulay would rally malcontent slaves to hinder every effort of the human race. The selfish arrogance of these undeserving Buddislamics!

Lord Bludd tried to communicate with them. He had expected that they would see reason, understand the stakes, and make up for the past cowardice of their people. Now, he saw that as a foolish hope.

Learning of the mosaic sabotage, he flew to the bottleneck gorge and stared in disbelief from his project observation platform. With a sinking heart, he saw first-hand the hideous damage done to his beautiful mural—the proud history of the Bludd family desecrated! Such an insult Lord Niko Bludd would not tolerate.

His knuckles turned white as he clenched the railing. His entourage was frightened by his demeanor, by the determination that boiled beneath the powdered and perfumed features that had always seemed so erudite.

"This insanity must stop forthwith." His icy words were meant for the Dragoon guards. He turned to the gold-armored soldier beside him. "You know what to do, Commander."

❧

ALREADY INCONVENIENCED BY the inexplicable behavior of his slaves, Tio Holtzman was happy to receive the invitation to accompany Lord Bludd. He was eager to see the first large-scale practical demonstration of his new shields.

"Just a civil defense exercise, Tio—but alas, necessary," Bludd said. "Nevertheless, we will observe your invention in action."

The scientist stood beside the nobleman on the observation platform. Norma Cenva and a handful of well-dressed nobles waited behind them, looking down from the platform at the unruly crowd of slaves. The smell of smoke hung in the air, and deep-throated shouts and angry chants wafted up from the beseiged spaceport.

On the ground, Dragoon guards marched forward, protected by shimmering body shields. The squad moved like an inexorable wedge into the blockaded spaceport, wielding clubs and spears. Some carried Chandler pistols, prepared to mow down the unruly insurgents in droves, if it came to that.

Holding onto a railing, Holtzman peered down at the advancing Dragoons. "Look, the slaves can't stop us." Norma's skin had gone pale and clammy. She realized the slaughter she was about to witness, but was unable to speak out against it.

The gold-armored men did not pause in their relentless progress, although the angry slaves tried to block their way. Men threw themselves against the Dragoons' shields. The front ranks of Lord Bludd's soldiers raised their bludgeons and cracked bones, knocking aside anyone who did not let them pass. The slaves shouted, regrouping and surging forward en masse, but they could not penetrate the shields. Gathering momentum, the Dragoons pushed into the melee, cutting through the unruly slaves.

The mob fell back and tried to form a barrier to protect the mastermind of the uprising. Standing in the bed of a ground-truck, Bel Moulay raised his voice high and clear, shouting in Chakobsa, "Do not falter! Hold onto your dreams. This is our only chance. All slaves must stand together!"

"Oh, why didn't they fight like that against the thinking machines?" Niko Bludd grumbled, and several of the nobles around him chuckled.

When the sheer press of slaves finally halted the Dragoon forces, the legion commander shouted, his voice booming above the din. "I have orders to arrest the traitor Bel Moulay. Surrender him immediately."

None of the insurgents moved. Moments later, the Dragoons brought out their Chandler pistols, switched off their shields, and opened fire. Crystal needle shards sprayed out, creating clouds of splattering blood and torn flesh. Slaves screamed and scrambled to escape, only to find that they were packed too closely around Bel Moulay to move.

The bearded leader shouted orders in his arcane language, but panic swept through the slaves, and they began to break up. The rain of crystal darts continued to slaughter them. Hundreds fell dead or maimed.

"Don't worry," Bludd said out of the corner of his mouth. "They have orders to take Bel Moulay alive."

Norma turned away, heaving deep breaths, afraid that she was about to vomit over the edge of the observation barge. But she clamped her lips shut and brought herself back under control.

As the slaves either died or broke ranks around Bel Moulay, the black-bearded leader grabbed a staff and tried to rally them. But the Dragoon guards, seeing a clear path to their objective, charged forward like rowdies into a brawl. They surrounded the Zenshiite mastermind and tackled him to the pavement. A great shout of dismay rose as the slaves saw their leader fall under a flurry of gold-gauntleted fists.

Witnessing Moulay's plight, the surviving insurgents clumped into angry knots and sought to rebuild their courage. But Dragoon guards shot needle pistols again, and the resistance collapsed into wailing confusion.

The Dragoons dragged Bel Moulay away, while armed vehicles and footsoldiers streamed into the spaceport, rescuing the hostage noblemen and ladies from their pens.

From the observation platform, Niko Bludd looked sadly at the crimson splashes and mangled corpses scattered around the flat landing grids. "I had hoped it would not come to this. I gave the slaves every opportunity to back down, but they left me no choice."

In spite of the carnage, Holtzman could not hide his pleasure at how well his personal shields had performed. "You acted with honor, my Lord."

Floating safely above any danger, they watched the mopping-up operations for a while longer. Then Bludd invited them all to his opulent residence to celebrate the liberation of Poritrin.

*Every large-scale movement—political, religious, or military—
hinges upon epochal events.*

—PITCAIRN NARAKOBE,
League Worlds Study of Conflict

When the human vermin initiated their rebellion on Earth,
the Titan Ajax considered it open season. For him, the
glory days were back, and this time he would not have to face
his lover Hecate's revulsion at the excessive violence.

He selected his best gladiator-form, a massive weapon-
studded walker that he had designed in the hope of challenging
Omnius in the arena. Ajax preferred a shape that radiated size
and power, not sleek and efficient but awesome and terrifying.
He liked to crush dozens of victims at a time.

It would be like the Hrethgir Rebellion on Walgis.

From a cymek body-fabrication pavilion atop one of the
capital city's seven hills, Ajax's sensors picked up crowd
noises, muffled at first and then louder. He had no time to
lose.

Using delicate hydraulics to lift his preservation canister, he
installed himself into the warrior-form. Angry thoughts pulsed
through the electrafluid, crackling into neurelectric linkages,

connecting thoughtrodes. Arming all weapons. He flexed his powerful tool-studded limbs. *Ready*.

The Titan strode on piston legs through a sliding window wall to a balcony circling the fabrication pavilion. From this vantage he looked out on the shadow-streaked city as fires rose into the evening sky. Smoke curled upward, and he saw mobs of slaves running like cockroaches. He heard breaking plaz and the hissing crashes of vehicles. The *hrethgir* had gone mad.

Off in the Forum Plaza, an explosion made a muffled boom, the sound flattened by distance. The rebels had stolen some heavy weapons, possibly extracting them from the hulks of damaged robots. Ajax powered up his hunting systems, then stepped into a cargo lift that dropped him down to street level. If the wild and foolish rebels had damaged his magnificent monument statue, he would be very upset indeed.

At the base of the hill, a group of neo-cymeks and sentinel robots set up a defensive circle. Using a molten-projectile launcher, they shot red-hot pellets at the howling mob that swept toward them like stampeding animals. Slave bodies glowed as they were hit, and fell in smoldering lumps of dead flesh. But more of the vermin kept coming, waves and waves of them, even though they saw their certain death.

"Don't just stand there cowering!" Ajax bellowed. "Would you rather watch them charge toward you, or go after them yourselves?"

It was a rhetorical question. The line of neo-cymek defenders surged forward, their combat limbs studded with weapons shaped out of flowmetal. The cymeks broke the first charge of the frenzied rebels, while the sentinel robots moved back to a new position higher on the hill.

Ajax climbed onto a flying construction platform. Using command linkages to operate the vehicle, he cruised over the crowds, bypassing the explosions and fires. Heading toward the Forum Plaza, the Titan was so infuriated that he had difficulty controlling the sophisticated systems of his gladiator-form.

In facilities across the city grid, Ajax saw thinking machines erect additional defensive perimeters. He had expected the disorganized rebellion to break apart and falter by now. Thousands of humans had been slaughtered today alone. Perhaps the fun had just begun.

Trailing lines of sparkling fire, rockets launched out from the Victory of the Titans frieze. Combining and enhancing the resolution of his optic threads, Ajax recognized the human standing on top of the giant carved stone wall, firing the hidden weapons: the treacherous crew boss Iblis Ginjo! Ajax had suspected him all along!

With wrenching anger he saw swarms of the ungrateful creatures using cables and small explosives to tear down the mighty pillars that held the majestic statues of the Titans. As he pushed the cargo platform forward, Ajax saw his own colossal image topple to the broken flagstones. The vermin let out a loud, hooting cheer. Another crude rocket shot out of the crumbling frieze.

Ajax accelerated the hover platform and swung wide around the enormous stone mural, approaching from the rear, out of range of the sputtering rockets. The giant statue of his human likeness lay crumbled on the stone surface, like a fallen king.

Ajax would rip off Iblis Ginjo's limbs, one at a time, and drink his screams.

Suddenly an entire section of the monument pivoted, and the sky blazed with multiple orange fires from a tremendous volley of rockets directed at Ajax. One blast shattered the undercarriage of the flying cargo platform, and the heavy craft spun toward the ground.

The Titan tumbled off, striking the plaza in a clatter of bent hydraulic limbs and armored shielding around his preservation canister. The hover platform crashed in a terrific explosion, knocking down the giant mural, damaging the rocket launchers.

The impact of Ajax's gladiator-form pulverized flagstones. His integrated systems twitched and jerked; neurelectronics flickered. Inside the preservation canister, his disembodied brain churned with a crackle of faulty data and distorted impressions from damaged thoughtrodes. He was surrounded by broken monuments torn down by the ingrate humans.

He heard Iblis shouting to the mobs, calling upon them to swarm the wounded Titan. With a mental surge through the thoughtrode conductors, Ajax rebooted his combat body's systems, bypassing the damaged control linkages. He could still fight, if he could just get back on his feet.

The furious mob swarmed around him, but he fought them off with flailing artificial limbs, and finally levered himself onto powerful but damaged legs that refused to support him reliably. Leaning to one side, he launched indiscriminate shots from his flamers, which should have driven back the rebels.

Instead, they crawled over the bodies of their fallen comrades and kept coming. . . .

Before Ajax could restore his equilibrium or complete the recalibration of his optic threads to see what was happening clearly, Iblis removed an intact rocket from the damaged frieze and launched it manually. With only half of his systems functional, Ajax tried to scuttle out of the way, but the hissing explosive ruined one of his six legs, knocking the cymek off balance and ripping a ragged hole in the broken flagstone beneath him.

The ancient warrior bellowed through his voice-synthesizer and shifted his armored body, turning to face Iblis at the damaged wall. Frenzied slaves swarmed around the debris in the Forum Plaza, throwing themselves upon the cymek like mice trying to bring down a maddened bull.

Ajax thrashed in his cumbersome body, knocking the vermin away, stomping on them, plowing through anyone who stood in his path. But more rebels stampeded toward him, pummeled his cymek body with primitive weapons, and fired stolen guns at him. In a frenzy, Ajax killed or maimed hundreds without suffering significant additional damage to himself, but the sheer press of bodies, along with his ruined leg, hampered him.

From the frieze wall, Iblis shouted, "He killed billions of people! Destroy him!"

Only billions? Surely it was more than that!

With a burst of mechanical energy, Ajax vaulted over the

mass of angry humans and began to scale the high stone mural, extruding nimble grippers and support spikes from the ends of the limbs that still functioned. Iblis stood atop the damaged wall, directing his foolish rebels.

As Ajax climbed, dozens of slaves clung to his segmented body where he could not knock them free. He thrashed with one of his five intact limbs and used the other four to climb the monolithic frieze.

From above, a slave dropped a small explosive that detonated on the sculptured wall, fracturing the stone and making the cymek's feet lose purchase. A dozen maddened slaves toppled off of his gladiator-form, knocked loose by the shockwave. But still more piled onto him.

The Titan's mechanical body tilted awkwardly, and more of the humans crawled onto his back and damaged his components, hacking at him with cutters and heat sticks.

Seconds later the rioters severed the neurelectric conduits and snapped the control fibers leading from his protected brain canister, effectively paralyzing the Titan's giant body. Ajax felt himself being pulled down from the wall, and toppling backward.

He could hear the screams as he slammed to the ground on top of the shouting *hrethgir*, crushing hundreds to death. He loved the sounds of their pain. But Ajax could not move, lying immobile in his warrior form like an immense poisoned insect.

"I am a Titan!" he bellowed.

Through his dispersed optic threads, Ajax saw the traitorous crew boss standing on the shoulders of slaves, pointing accusingly at the cymek's head plate. "Peel off the armor casing, there!"

Ajax's thoughtrodes detected the removal of the shield, exposing his brain canister.

Now, with a smile of triumph, Iblis climbed onto the Titan's twitching warrior-form, holding high a makeshift cudgel. Grinning, the crew boss brought the metal club down and smashed through the curved plaz walls of the brain canister.

He hammered again and again, and his followers rushed in to help, pounding and beating and smashing, until they had ruptured the canister and battered the organic brain into nothing more than pulpy gray matter mixed with oozing bluish electrafluid.

Euphoric at what they had done, Iblis stood atop the dead Titan and howled in victory. His message rose higher than the flames consuming the machine city.

Witnessing the death of one of the greatest cymeks sent the mob into a greater furor. Word swept through the streets, and the outraged rebels turned against all manifestations and symbols of the machine masters. Neo-cymeks and sentinel robots on defensive lines scrambled away as the rioters pursued them.

The all-pervasive Omnius evermind had no choice but to launch powerful countermeasures.

*We are not like Moses—we cannot call forth water from stone
... not at an economical rate, anyway.*

—Imperial Ecological Survey of Arrakis,
ancient records (researcher uncredited)

In the afternoon heat of Arrakis, the Zensunni nomads blind-folded Aurelius Venport by tying a stained rag over his eyes.

The desert people did not trust Tuk Keedair either and treated the Tlulaxa flesh merchant with matching indignity. Venport chose to allow this as part of his investment. It had taken them nearly five months of tedious travel with fitful starts and stops at various backwater planets just to get here. He would see it through.

"We march now," Naib Dhartha said. "You may talk with each other, but it would be best to keep your conversation to a minimum. Wasted words are wasted moisture."

Venport felt people all around him, guiding them forward. It took some getting used to, and he stumbled often as he lifted his feet higher than normal, probing the sandy surface. The ground was uneven, but gradually he became more adept at walking.

"What about the sandworms?" Keedair asked. "Do we not have to worry about—?"

"We are beyond the wormline," Dhartha answered gruffly. "The mountain ranges separate us from the great bled, where the demons dwell."

"I am not convinced this is completely necessary," Venport said as he trudged on.

Dhartha was firm, not accustomed to having his orders questioned. "It is necessary because I have said so. Never before has an outsider—not even one from this planet—seen our hidden communities. We do not offer maps."

"Of course. I will comply with your rules," Venport muttered. "As long as you intend to offer spice."

Though the jungles of Rossak were rich with undiscovered pharmaceuticals and exotic hallucinogens, none seemed to provide the remarkable effects of melange. Venport felt the substance was well worth investigating, despite the distance he'd had to travel and the discomforts he had endured.

In the past several months, Venport had easily sold Keedair's speculative shipment to curiosity seekers willing to pay an exorbitant price. Even though Venport had kept half of the profits, Tuk Keedair had still made a substantial sum, more than he could have obtained from a cargo of the highest quality slaves. Since he had not lost money for the year, he had not been obligated to cut off his treasured braid.

Venport tripped over something hard. He cursed and almost fell to his knees, but someone grabbed his arm and supported him.

"When your people brought melange to me one load at a time, it took forever to fill my cargo ship," Keedair said, his voice several footsteps ahead.

Venport said, "Naib Dhartha, I hope we can develop a more efficient system in the future." If not, they would just have to charge higher prices, but he was sure the market would be there.

After they had plodded for hours at a blind-man's pace, the Zensunnis stopped. From the rustling, clanking noises, Venport guessed they were uncovering a camouflaged groundcar.

"Sit," said Naib Dhartha, "but do not remove your blindfolds."

Fumbling, he and Keedair climbed into the vehicle, which moved off with a jouncing pace and a quietly puttering engine. After many kilometers, Venport eventually guessed from slightly cooler shadows that they must be approaching a line of mountains, heading into afternoon. There were ways to pinpoint the location of this isolated village, provided he wanted to go to such lengths. He could have sewn a tracking pulser into the fabric of his vest or the sole of a boot.

But at the moment Venport had other priorities. He had a feeling there was no way to circumvent the wishes of these hardy people, that they completely controlled those who visited them, even deciding who departed from the desert alive.

When they began to ascend a steep path, the groundcar slowed, and finally the Zensunni hid the vehicle again and made their blindfolded guests walk again. The nomads guided their guests step by step around boulders and broken rocks. Finally, Dhartha yanked off the blindfolds, revealing a dim cave entrance. The group stood just inside a tunnel. Venport blinked to adjust his vision to the dim light generated by flaming lamps mounted on the walls.

After being blindfolded for so long, it seemed that his hearing and sense of smell had grown more delicate and precise. Now, as he looked around the tunnel entrance, Venport detected signs of many inhabitants, the stink of unwashed bodies, the sounds of people stirring.

Taking them to chambers high inside a cliff wall, Dhartha fed the men a meal of crunchy bread served with a dab of honey and thin strips of dried meat marinated in a spicy sauce. Afterward, they listened to Zensunni music around low fires and told stories in a language that Venport did not know.

Later, the naib took the two impatient visitors out onto a rocky ledge that overlooked an endless sea of dunes. "I want to show you something," he said, his lean face shadowed, the geometric tattoo on his cheek even darker than his skin. The men sat with their feet dangling over the edge. Keedair looked from Dhartha to Venport, eager to watch the negotiations.

The naib rang a little bell, and soon an old man came forward, his muscles sinewy, his face like leather. His hair was long and white, and he still had most of his teeth. Like all of the desert people, his eyes had turned a solid blue, which Venport believed indicated a deep melange addiction. Keedair's own eyes had already taken on the eerie tint.

The elderly man held a tray containing dark wafers, cut perfectly square and covered with sticky syrup. He extended the delicacies to Venport, who took one. Keedair selected another, and Naib Dhartha a third. The gray-haired man remained standing beside them, watching.

From what Venport had seen, in this culture the women always served the men—an odd turnabout from the custom on Rossak. Perhaps elderly men here were also relegated to menial duties.

Venport studied the brown cake, then nibbled one corner. The meal he'd eaten earlier had been laced with significant amounts of melange, but this sample seemed to have even more of a kick than expected, exploding with rich cinnamon fire in his mouth. He took a substantial bite, felt the strength and well-being expand outward in his body.

"Delicious!" Without realizing it, he had gobbled most of the wafer.

"Fresh spice gathered from the open sands just this afternoon," Dhartha said. "It is more potent than anything you have previously tasted in spice beer or food."

"Most excellent," Venport said, the possibilities filling his mind like unopened gifts. Keedair also consumed his cake and sighed in satisfaction.

Venport had a visceral intuition that the spice trade would prove profitable, and he expected to sell substantial quantities to the League nobles. To commence that enterprise, he planned to accompany Zufa Cenva on her next trip to Salusa Secundus. While she delivered her fiery lectures in the rebuilt Hall of Parliament, Venport would make contacts, dropping hints, distributing small samples. It would take time, but the demand would grow.

He held the last bite of his spice cake. "Is this what you meant to show us, Naib Dhartha?"

The tattooed leader reached up to clasp the old man's thin but muscular arm. "This man is what I want you to see. His name is Abdel." The naib bowed briefly, and the old man bowed in return, then gave a deeper bow to the two seated guests, now that he had been introduced. "Abdel, tell the visitors your age."

The withered man spoke in a thin but strong voice. "I have watched the constellation of the Beetle cross Sentinel Rock three hundred and fourteen times."

Confused, Venport looked to Keedair, who shrugged. Naib Dhartha explained. "A tiny asterism in our sky. It drifts back and forth with the seasons and crosses a thin spire of rock near the horizon. We use it as a calendar."

"Back and forth," Keedair said. "You mean twice each year?"

The naib nodded.

Venport did quick mental calculations. "He is saying he's a hundred and fifty-seven years old."

"Close," Dhartha said. "Children do not start to watch and count until they have passed the age of three years, so technically that would make him one hundred and sixty standard years. Abdel has consumed melange all his life. Notice how healthy he remains . . . with bright eyes and a sharp mind. He will probably live for decades yet, provided he continues to consume a regular diet of spice."

Venport was amazed. Everyone had heard stories of youth-prolonging drugs, of life-extension treatments that had been developed in the Old Empire and then forgotten when the decaying regime fell. Most of the stories were no more than legends. Yet if this old man was telling the truth . . .

"Do you have any proof of this?" Keedair asked.

A flicker of anger washed across the naib's lean face. "I offer you my word. No additional proof is required."

Venport gestured for Keedair not to press the issue. The way he felt from the melange coursing through his system, he could well believe the claims. "We will run tests of our own to make certain there are no side effects other than a blue tinting of the eyes. Melange may be a product I can add to my catalog of goods. Would you be able to provide sufficient quantities for commercial purposes?"

With a nod, the desert leader said, "The potential is vast."

Now only the details of the business transaction remained. In part, Venport intended to offer something unusual as payment. Water? Or perhaps these nomads would barter for some of Norma's glowglobes, to illuminate their shadowy caves and tunnels. In fact, the floating bulbs might be of more practical use to the Zensunni than League credits. He had some samples in his transport back at Arrakis City.

Reaching forward, he took the last cake from the tray that Abdel still held in his hands. Venport noticed that the old man held the platter motionless, without the slightest tremble in his fingers. Another good sign, which Tuk Keedair noticed as well. The business partners nodded to one another.

My copilot thinks of the human female constantly, but thus far it does not seem to have distracted him from his duties. I will watch him carefully for signs of trouble.

—SEURAT,
log entry submitted to Omnius

The *Dream Voyager* entered Earth's atmosphere, returning home after a long update run. It had been so long since Vor had seen Serena Butler . . . and he needed to confront his father with the historical discrepancies he had found.

Aboard the silver-and-black ship, he and Seurat monitored their approach, checking temperature readings of the reflective outer skin. The ship's chronometer automatically adjusted to Earth standard time.

This reminded Vor of how Agamemnon had altered his memoirs to suit a preferred version of history. The Titans were not the glorious, benevolent heroes that his father had portrayed.

Serena Butler had forced Vor to discover the truth about Agamemnon. Vor wondered if she had thought about him while he'd been gone. Would Serena respect him now because of his newfound understanding? Or did she still pine after her lost lover, the man who had fathered her child? Vor's stomach knotted with nervous anticipation. Throughout his highly structured life he had never faced so much uncertainty as in the past several months.

Agamemnon might be waiting for him at the spaceport. All of the great Titan's promises of rewards, the lure of leaving a fragile human body behind and becoming a neo-cymek, now felt flat to Vor. Everything had changed.

Vor would challenge his father, accuse the great general of fabricating history and distorting facts—of *deceiving* his own son. Part of him hoped the Titan would indeed have a ready answer, a comforting explanation, so that Vor could go back to his sane and regimented life as a trustee.

In his heart, though, he knew that Serena had not misled him. He had seen enough evidence with his own eyes, knew how the machines treated human beings. Vor could no longer pretend . . . but he didn't know what else he could do now. He was very frightened to return to Earth, yet he knew he must.

Surely Agamemnon would notice his son's change of attitude. And Vor already knew that the Titan general had killed twelve previous sons who had disappointed him.

"What do you make of that, Vorian?" Seurat interrupted his thoughts as they neared the spaceport in the capital grid. "I am detecting data inconsistencies and an alarming level of physical chaos." The robot captain called up closer images.

Vor was astonished to see fire, smoke, and destroyed buildings, along with robot and cymek troops. Scores of humans ran wild in the streets. His heart lurched from a mixture of emotions that he had not yet sorted out. "Did the League Armada attack here?" Even with his new knowledge, he couldn't believe that scattered remnants of free humanity could have wrought such destruction on the core machine world. Omnius would never allow it!

"Scans show no human spacecraft or battleships in the vicinity, Vorian. Nevertheless, the conflict is ongoing." Seurat seemed puzzled, but not overly concerned. At least he didn't attempt to make a joke about the situation.

Vor adjusted the scan-optic controls, focusing on the seaside extension of the capital city grid, and located the estate of Erasmus. He saw more fires there, damaged buildings and monuments, pitched battles in the streets. Where was Serena?

Slowly, reluctantly, he began to comprehend what was happening. Humans were fighting the machines! The very idea stirred up thoughts that he would rather have avoided, because they seemed disloyal to Omnius. How could any of this be possible?

The *Dream Voyager* detected a unified emergency signal used by the evermind to link with his subsidiary robot forces. "All thinking machines divert to defensive perimeters and battle stations . . . human revolt spreading . . . Omnius core remains defended . . . power shortages in many sectors. . . ."

Vor looked at the robot captain's mirror-smooth face. The spangle of optic threads brightened like stars. "This is a most unexpected situation. Our assistance is obligatory."

"I concur," Vor said. *But which side should I help?* He had never expected to feel this way, with his allegiances pulling at one another.

The *Dream Voyager* soared toward the burning city grid. Near the villa of Erasmus, the thinking machines had formed a cordon against the mobs. Barricades had been erected in the flagstone plaza where Vorian had previously arrived by carriage for his visits. Portions of the building facade appeared damaged, but the villa seemed intact.

I hope she is safe.

Unconcerned, Seurat cruised over the capital's spaceport, preparing to land. Reacting suddenly, he pulled up in a steep ascent. "Our facilities and ships have already been overrun by rebellious slaves."

Vor continued to study the chaos below. "Where can we go?"

"My backup landing instructions suggest an older spaceport on the southern edge of the city grid. The landing field is functional, and remains under Omnius's control."

As the update ship settled on the alternate landing pad, Vor saw blackened human corpses and smashed machines around the perimeter. At the northern docking pads a fierce battle raged between neo-cymeks and suicidal rebels who must have taken weaponry away from destroyed sentinel robots.

Seurat put the *Dream Voyager*'s engines and electronics into standby mode. Half a dozen armed robots ran to their landing site, as if to defend the ship and the valuable Omnius updates they carried.

"What do you want me to do, Seurat?" Vor inquired, his heart pounding.

Seurat delivered a surprisingly insightful answer. "I will offer to use the ship to transport robot defenders to wherever Omnius requires them. Remaining aboard is your best option, Vorian Atreides. It is likely to be the safest place."

Vor's mind throbbed with his need to find Serena Butler. "No, old Metalmind. I might get in the way, and my life-support needs would interfere with your work. Leave me at the spaceport, and I'll take care of myself."

The robot considered Vor's request. "As you wish. However, because of the situation, it would be best for you to lie low and remain out of sight. Avoid the fighting. You are a valued trustee, the son of Agamemnon—but you are also human. You are at risk from both sides in this conflict."

"I understand."

Seurat looked at him with his unreadable face. "Take care of yourself, Vorian Atreides."

"You, too, old Metalmind."

As Vor hurried down the ramp onto the exhaust-stained pavement of the old spaceport, the thinking machines transmitted alarms and messages to other military units. The northern docking pads had fallen to human mobs. Hundreds of people were surging across the field. With instant consensus, a dozen soldier robots swarmed aboard the *Dream Voyager* for tactical redistribution.

From the cover of a parked groundtruck, feeling more vulnerable than ever, Vor watched the update ship lift off. Only the day before, he and Seurat had been amusing themselves in space with strategy games. Now, in a few hours, his whole world had been turned on its side.

After breaching the northern docking bay, the rebel humans spread out into the spaceport buildings. Evidently, Omnius had decided to cut his losses, leaving only a few thinking machines to resist the *hrethgir*. Vor ran for cover, abruptly conscious that he wore the formal uniform of a trustee, a servant of the Synchronized Worlds. Not many humans worked in high positions for the thinking machines, and if the mob spotted him, they would tear him apart.

Hundreds of rebel bodies lay strewn about the tarmac. Thinking quickly, Vor grabbed the arms of a dead man about his own size and dragged him into the shadows between two smoking buildings. Discarding a part of his past, Vor tore off the flight suit he had worn on so many *Dream Voyager* journeys, and switched clothes with the slain rebel.

Dressed in a tattered shirt and dirty trousers, he waited for the right opportunity and joined the flow of the rushing crowd. They shouted "Victory!" and "Freedom!" as they broke into the spaceport buildings. Few sentinel robots remained to resist them now.

Vor hoped the mob didn't destroy all the facilities or the robotic vessels. If they had bothered to plan ahead, the revolt leaders would know that they needed to escape from the Synchronized Worlds altogether.

Vor caught himself, astonished to realize his allegiance was shifting. It both exhilarated and frightened him. He felt himself drawing away from the security of his known life in machine society, toward the chaos of the unknown and his own feral biological roots. But he knew he had to do it. He understood too much now, saw through different eyes.

Around him, frenzied slaves did not worry about the consequences of their rampage. The mob had an eclectic supply of weapons, from primitive clubs to sophisticated cellular-displacement guns removed from sentinel robots. The rebels set off incendiary devices in the old spaceport's control building and killed a skittering neo-cymek who tried to escape, splitting open his brain canister with a cellgun blast.

When he felt it was safe, Vor broke away from the crowd, maintaining his disguise, and wandered with other humans through the damp streets, deeper into the city grid. He looked like a ragged straggler but had a definite goal.

He needed to reach the villa of Erasmus.

In the canyons between large buildings, darkness began to arrive ahead of twilight, intensified because the Earth-Omnius had severed power in sectors overrun by slaves. Thunderclouds closed in, pregnant with smoke and rain. A brisk wind cut through Vor's thin clothing, and he shivered.

He hoped Serena was still alive.

A group of rough-looking slaves broke down a metal gate and surged into a building. The mangled remains of thinking machines lay in disarray. He heard from excited chatter that even the Titan Ajax had been slain. *Ajax!* At first he couldn't believe it, and then he didn't doubt what he had heard. A block away, a building erupted in flames, casting eerie light into the street.

Even after what he had learned about the crimes and abuses of the original Titans, Vor felt a twinge of concern for his father. If Agamemnon was on Earth, the cymek general would be somewhere in the midst of this revolt, trying to quell it. In spite of all the lies and misleading stories Agamemnon had told, he was still Vor's father.

Quickening his pace, Vor made his way toward Erasmus's villa. He was tired and sore. In the plaza fronting the main house, a crowd of angry rebels pressed against a hastily erected barricade fence. The worst fighting had passed into the primary centers of the capital city grid, but here the freed slaves seemed to be maintaining an angry vigil, for reasons that Vor did not understand. He asked questions, carefully.

"We're waiting for Iblis Ginjo," a man with a thin beard said. "He wants to lead the assault personally. Erasmus is still inside there." The man spat on the paving stones. "And so is the woman."

Vor felt a jolt. What woman did the man mean? Could it be Serena?

Before he could ask, robotic defensive installations on the ornate crenellations fired scattered shots, trying to disperse the crowd. But more rebels arrived, swelling their numbers, maintaining the siege. A group dressed in stained work clothes took up strategic positions and launched two crude explosive projectiles, smashing the rooftop gun emplacements.

A small section of the rain-slick plaza had been cordoned off with posts and plazwire, and the humans had surrounded it like guardians . . . or, oddly, *pilgrims*. Vor saw flowers and colorful ribbons scattered on the plaza. Curious, he pushed closer and asked a gaunt old woman about it.

"Sacred ground," she said. "A child was murdered here, and his mother fought against the monster Erasmus. Serena, who helped us, changed our lives, made things better for us. By standing up to the thinking machines, Serena showed us what is possible." Sickened, Vor pressed for details, heard how the robot had thrown the little boy to his death.

Serena's baby. *Murdered*.

"What about Serena?" Vor asked, grabbing the crone. "Is she safe?"

She shrugged her bony shoulders. "Erasmus has barricaded himself in the villa, and we have not seen her since. Three days. Who knows what goes on behind those walls?"

The mob cleared a path, and a rugged-looking man marched through, wearing the black tunic and headband of a crew boss. A dozen heavily armed men guarded him as if he were an important leader. He raised his hands, while the milling slaves cheered and called him by name. "Iblis! Iblis Ginjo!"

"I promised you it could be done!" he shouted. "I told you all!" Even without mechanical amplification, his voice was powerful with resonant warmth. "Look at all we've already accomplished. Now we must secure another victory. The robot Erasmus committed the crime that sparked our glorious revolt. He can no longer hide behind his walls—it is time to punish him!"

The man's passionate voice was like fuel thrown on the flames of rebellion. The people roared their call for revenge—and Vor could not help himself. Alarmed, he raised his own voice, demanding to be heard. "And save the mother! We must rescue her!"

Iblis looked at him, and the two men locked eyes. The charismatic leader hesitated for a fraction of a second, then bellowed, "Yes, save Serena!"

At Iblis's command, the mob became an organized weapon,

a hammer slamming into the anvil of the barricaded villa. They had torn weapon-arms from robots they had overcome, using them to blast the walls of the villa until the damaged power cells ran out. With an improvised battering ram, men rushed the main gate and struck it, bending the heavy metal. Again and again they pounded, and the gate buckled. Overhead, from brooding gray skies, oily rain began to come down again.

Inside, armored household robots tried to reinforce the door barrier. Vor guessed that most of these defenders had been reprogrammed from other duties, and did not have the capacity to resist for long.

The battering ram struck again, and the gap in the heavy doors opened wider. The machines were losing ground.

Though uncertain how to handle his new feelings toward machines, Vor didn't trust the frenzied mob, either. They didn't really care about Serena, even if she had unwittingly provided the spark that launched the revolt. If she remained here, she would certainly become a target of retaliation from Omnius.

As he stood in the rain looking on, Vorian Atreides had his own focus. He swore to himself that he would rescue Serena. He would steal a ship and fly her far from here, escaping the Synchronized Worlds.

Yes, he would take her back to her beloved Salusa Secundus . . . even if it meant delivering her into the arms of her lost love.

We must bring new information into the balance and with it modify our behavior. It is a human quality to survive by intelligence—as individuals and as a species.

—NAIB ISHMAEL,
A Zensunni Lament

Citing the most ancient of Poritrin laws, Lord Bludd decreed the terrible punishment for Bel Moulay's crimes. Most slaves would receive amnesty, since Poritrin needed the labor pool, but the insurrection leader could not be forgiven.

Ishmael pressed close to Aliid, the two captive boys sharing silent support and grief. The young slaves from the canyon mosaic had been brought back to Starda and confined where they would be forced to watch the execution. As punishment for the damage to the mural, Niko Bludd would put them back to work with extended shifts. But only after they witnessed the consequences of Bel Moulay's folly. All slaves were required to be present.

The boys crowded together, hungry and tired, their clothes dirty and their bodies smelly because they had not bathed in days. The work overseers growled at them, "If you behave like dogs, you will be treated like dogs. Once you start behaving like humans, then perhaps we will reconsider."

Aliid muttered defiantly under his breath.

In the central plaza of Starda, Dragoon guards hauled Bel Moulay in chains toward a high platform that had been erected for the spectacle. The crowd fell into an uneasy silence. Moulay's inky beard and hair had been shorn away, leaving pale spots on his scalp and chin. But his eyes blazed with unshakable anger and confidence, as if he refused to accept that his rebellion had failed.

Holding him, the gold-armored guards tore off the Zenshiite leader's robes. They let the rags fall away from the platform, leaving Moulay completely naked, shaming him. The slaves grumbled, but their leader stood firm and brave, amazingly unafraid.

The voice of Lord Bludd echoed across the square. "Bel Moulay, you have committed grievous crimes against all the citizens of Poritrin. It is within my rights to punish every man, woman, and child who participated in this insurrection, but I am merciful. You alone shall bear the penalty of your transgressions."

The crowd moaned softly. Aliid slammed a fist into his palm. Bel Moulay said nothing, but his expression spoke volumes.

Niko Bludd tried to sound benevolent. "If you people learn from this, perhaps you will eventually earn the right to a normal life of servitude again, to pay your debt to humanity."

Now the slaves howled. The Dragoon guards pressed closer, thumping their long-bladed staffs against the ground. Ishmael sensed that in spite of the ugly mood, the slaves had been beaten, for now at least. They had seen their leader publicly humiliated, put in chains, shaved, and stripped naked. And, while he showed no sign of being defeated, his followers no longer had the spark.

Bludd said, "The old laws are violent, some might say barbarous. But since your actions have been uncivilized and barbaric, they demand the same response."

Bel Moulay was given no opportunity to speak on his own behalf. Instead, Dragoon guards battered out his teeth with a hammer, then used long metal tongs to reach into his mouth. Moulay struggled in defiance but not terror. With surgical precision, they cut out his tongue and tossed the gory, sluglike mass into the crowd.

Next, they used their diamond-bladed axes to chop off his hands and threw them into the recoiling throng as well. Bel Moulay's bloody stumps sprayed scarlet rain into the air. Next, using hot irons, the Dragoon guards burned out his eyes. Only at the very end did he make any sounds of pain, though he somehow found the resolve to stifle them.

Blinded, the insurrection leader could not see what the gold-armored torturers were doing until they had slipped the noose over his neck and strung him over a gibbet. He struggled as the noose tightened around his windpipe, choking him slowly, never breaking his neck. Even after his horrific injuries, he seemed ready to fight against the guards, if they gave him the slightest chance.

Ishmael vomited on the ground. Several boys dropped to their knees, sobbing. Aliid clenched his teeth as if to suppress a thousand screams inside his throat.

⌀

AFTER THE EXECUTION, Norma Cenva felt a coldness in the pit of her stomach. She hardly spoke beside Tio Holtzman as the scientist looked grimly on, dressed in his finest white suit.

"Well, he brought it upon himself, didn't he?" the Savant said. "We never treated our slaves badly. Why did Bel Moulay have to do this to us, to our war against the thinking machines?" Holtzman drew in long, deep breaths, his nostrils flaring, and glanced down at the diminutive woman. "Now perhaps we can get back to business. I suspect the slaves will behave now."

Norma just shook her head. "This repression is unwise." From a distance, she looked at the still-twitching body dangling on the projecting arm of the gibbet. "Lord Bludd has only succeeded in turning the man into a martyr. I fear we have not seen the end of this."

Machines possess something humans will always lack: infinite patience and the longevity that supports it.

—file from Corrin-Omnius update

Even though Erasmus had dispatched his last functional sentinel robots to defend the villa, he knew it was only a delaying action. The vigor and violence of the slave revolt amazed him, exceeding any of his projections.

Humans have an infinite capacity to surprise the most rational mind.

The slaves in the squalid main pens had been freed by their *hrethgir* brethren, flooding the ranks of the angry rebels. The revolt had spread through the capital city and to other urban complexes across Earth. His villa was surrounded and would surely fall before long.

Experiments sometimes produce unexpected results.

Donning his most ferocious countenance, designed to inspire nightmares in humans, Erasmus stood on the high balcony from which he had thrown the child. His flowmetal visage was as fierce and frightening as any of the gargoyles in the plaza, while his mechanical mind scanned all available information, processing and reprocessing. Had it been a mistake to kill the little boy? Who would have thought such a trivial death might create a stir like this?

I miscalculated their response.

The crowd in the plaza cursed him and peppered the balcony with small arms fire, which did no harm. More worrisome, they were surging against the heavy metal gate with a battering ram, and the sentinel robots were having trouble preventing them from breaking through. If the rebels got inside the villa, they would surely destroy Erasmus, just as they had killed the Titan Ajax, as they had smashed innumerable robots and neo-cymeks. Erasmus would be their prime target.

In the midst of the throng, a sturdy charismatic man was inciting the rebels. The leader waved his hands, spoke passionately, and seemed to have a hypnotic effect on the mob. He shouted up at Erasmus, causing an uproar from the crowd.

With a pause to assess new data, the robot recognized the rebel leader as one of the subjects of his loyalty experiment. *Iblis Ginjo.* Reassessments and connections clamored in his mind.

Iblis had been a crew boss, well treated, well rewarded, one of the content trustees. Yet he had thrown his support to the revolt, perhaps even inspired it. Through a few vague, experimental communiqués, Erasmus had somehow galvanized this slave leader into action. But he had not expected such a monumental, incomprehensible response.

Either way, Erasmus had proved his point. Beside him on the balcony, one of the evermind's glittering watcheyes hovered close to him. The robot did not try to contain his smug realization. "Omnius, it is as I predicted—even the most trusted humans will ultimately turn against you."

"So you have won the wager," Omnius said. "That is most unfortunate."

Erasmus scanned the flames rising in the distant city. If he could look upon the situation objectively it would be a fascinating study in human nature. The psychology of groups under stress was intriguing, though admittedly dangerous. "Indeed, most unfortunate."

At the front of the villa, the main gate burst open from the repeated pounding of the battering ram. Iblis gestured to his fanatical followers, and the mob swept over his remaining household robots like a tidal wave.

It was time for Erasmus to depart.

Knowing the value of his independent thoughts and conjectures, the robot did not wish to be destroyed. He represented individuality, pride in personal achievement, the possible existence of a soul. He wanted to continue his work, integrating the lessons he had learned from this fascinating revolt.

But for that, he had to escape.

Moment by moment, the mob grew louder. He heard the rampant destruction in his lovely home. He had just enough time to take a fast, armored lift platform down several levels to a secure tunnel system that opened to the hills overlooking the sea.

He hesitated, knowing he was leaving Serena Butler behind, but decided that he had already kept the female around for too long. After he'd killed her baby, she had become even less useful to him, unwilling to provide any additional raw data.

The death of her child had turned her into a wild animal, not caring anymore for her own life. She had attacked him repeatedly, despite his generous overtures to her. In the end, although Erasmus had been tempted to kill her outright, he had not been able to bring himself to do it. Most interesting. He had finally settled for drugging her into a stupor. Now Serena was in one of his laboratories, sedated to the point of catatonia, since Erasmus had found no other way of suppressing her efforts to fight him each time she rose toward consciousness. Alas, he had no time to salvage her now.

In a concealed cave high above the swirling whitecaps, Erasmus boarded a hover capsule. Accompanied by one of Omnius's watcheyes, he lifted off into the early evening, flying out to sea and circling back over the burning city.

"You are being foolish, Erasmus," the voice of Omnius said from a bulkhead screen. "You should have waited for the tide of battle to turn in favor of my thinking machines. As it must, inevitably."

"Perhaps, Omnius, but I have run my own risk assessment.

I would rather return to my estate on Corrin, to continue my experiments there. With your permission, of course."

"You will only cause more trouble," Omnius said. The hover capsule reached one of the subsidiary spaceports that was still controlled by the thinking machines. "But now, more than ever, it is imperative for us to understand our enemy."

Erasmus searched the database for a small, available ship that could take him on the long journey to Corrin. Through his work, he had already learned an important lesson: Humans were predictable in only one aspect—in their very unpredictability.

❦

*Life is a banquet of unexpected flavors. Sometimes you like the
taste, sometimes you don't.*

—IBLIS GINJO,
Options for Total Liberation

The slaves burst into the evil robot's villa, celebrating with
an orgy of destruction. Caught in the fire of their enthusiasm, Iblis led a small group on a fast sweep through the
labyrinth of rooms and corridors. They followed him, like a
work crew of sorts, though this particular job was much more
satisfying.

"For Serena!" he shouted, the words the rebels wanted to
hear. They took up the cry.

Somewhere inside, he hoped to find the uncaring Erasmus,
who had so blatantly murdered a helpless child. He also
wanted to locate the brave mother who had fought against the
thinking machines. If he could liberate Serena Butler, Iblis
would make her into a rallying point, the figurehead of a great
movement against Omnius. She might be somewhere here inside the great house—*if* she wasn't dead. . . .

As the rioters swept into the main building, Vorian Atreides
pushed his way toward the front, buffeted by the storm of
humanity. The rebels trampled the ornamental tapestries and

knocked over prized statues. Vor ran with them.

"Serena!" His voice was swallowed up in the tumult. While his companions ransacked the trappings of wealth that Erasmus had acquired, Vor rushed directly to her beloved greenhouses. "Serena! Serena!"

He leaped over the metal forms of damaged household robots strewn across the corridors. Ahead of him, the intruders pounded open the heavy alloy door of the household equipment lockers and began grabbing tools that could be converted into weapons. Vor pushed his way through and grabbed a long knife for himself—more effective against humans than machines—then hurried back into the corridor and ran until he reached the sealed laboratories. He dreaded that the diabolical robot might have performed a last, malicious dissection on her. . . .

He left the rest of the mob spreading through the estate. Vor worked his way past abandoned security stations, into the compounds that had held human test subjects. Freed victims with hollow cheeks and haunted eyes staggered into the corridors.

Vor reached a set of locked quarantine cells. He tried to open the heavy doors, without success. Through small, round windows he saw people crowded inside, some with their faces pressed against the plaz, others lying on the cold rock floors. He didn't see Serena among them.

Beneath a deactivated Omnius eye, he found the release mechanism and unsealed the cells. As the desperate captives stumbled out, Vor pushed his way into their midst, calling out for Serena. The prisoners clutched at Vor, blinking in confusion under the bright lights. He could spare them no time, and went on to continue his search.

At the back of the compound, in a sterile area that contained ominous surgical equipment, he finally found Serena slumped on the dirty plazcrete floor with her eyes closed, as if she had awakened from a drugged sleep and then crawled there. Her white-and-gold dress was stained and torn, and she had bruises on her face and arms. She lay as if dead—or like a person wanting to die.

"Serena?" He touched her cheek. "Serena, it's Vorian Atreides."

Groggily opening her eyes, she looked at him at first without recognition. He saw her unfocused stare, suspected that she swam in the deep, uncharted waters of tranquilizing drugs. Erasmus must have been trying to keep her under control. At last she whispered, "I didn't expect to ever see you again,"

He helped Serena to her feet and supported her as she swayed on rubbery legs, still sleepwalking. In the rear garden area the overturned basins were saturated with blood, but Vor found a small fountain that remained undisturbed, surrounded by thick ferns. He cupped cold, clean water in his hands, and she drank greedily, struggling to throw off the fog of drugs. Then he soaked a torn cloth and used it to clean her face and arms.

She seemed to want nothing more than to slump to the floor, falling back into blissful unconsciousness, but she fought it and clutched the wall angrily, holding herself upright. "Why are you here?"

"I came to take you back to Salusa Secundus."

Her lovely eyes, which had been glazed by pain and dulled by Erasmus's crippling drugs, now came alive. "You could do that?"

He nodded, trying to strengthen her with his confidence, but wondering how to find the *Dream Voyager* again. "Our window of opportunity won't be open for long."

Serena's expression brightened with a flicker of strength and hope. "Salusa . . . my Xavier . . ."

He frowned at the name, but concentrated on the challenge at hand. "We have to get away from here. The streets are dangerous, especially for us."

Now that she had a purpose, Serena gathered energy through sheer force of will. As he turned to guide her away from this place of terrible memories, they encountered Iblis Ginjo. The crew boss stood flushed and grinning, just inside the doorway. "So there you are! Blessed woman, the people have thrown off their shackles to avenge your murdered child."

Vor held her arm protectively, his expression darkening. "I need to take her from this place." He was not accustomed to having even another trustee question his words, but the rabble leader still blocked his way.

Oddly, Iblis seemed more confident in his powers of persuasion than in any weapon. "This woman is vital to the continuing revolution. Think of the pain she has suffered. You and I are not enemies. We must band together to overthrow the—"

While Iblis's voice resonated as if he were delivering a speech, Vor swung up the long knife he had taken, holding it up in a threat. "Once I may have been your enemy, but no longer. I am Vorian Atreides."

Iblis looked uncertain. "Atreides? The son of Agamemnon?"

Vorian's face became stormy, but the blade in his hand did not waver. "That burden I must bear. To redeem myself, I will make certain Serena is safe. Omnius will bring in reinforcements soon, even if they come from other Synchronized Worlds. Don't let a few days of giddy success blind you to what the thinking machines can do. Your revolt here is doomed."

In a flurry of words, Iblis explained what he had in mind, how he wanted Serena to inspire an ever-widening revolt that would crush Omnius on Earth. "You can make our movement much stronger. Serena Butler and the memory of her slain child will rally others. Think of what you could accomplish!"

At any other time, Serena might have felt the calling and given herself over to the welfare of so many suffering people. It was part of her character, the core of her personality. But the murder of innocent Manion had doused her flames of justice and passion, killing not only her baby but a portion of her heart.

"Your cause is righteous, Iblis," Serena said, "but I'm drained by all the horrors I have endured. Vorian is taking me back to Salusa. I must see my father . . . and tell Xavier what has happened to his son."

Iblis's gaze locked with hers as if they were connected by

an electronic beam. He did not want to alienate her, not if she was to be of any use to him. His thoughts spun, looking for traction. For months he had been building a secret organization of rebels, but now he sensed that it could never attain its full potential without this remarkable young woman and all she represented. He could never achieve the necessary religious fervor.

Iblis's dark eyes flashed, seizing upon the changed situation. "A League world? Tell me, Atreides, how can you ever escape Earth?"

"I believe I have a way—my ship, the *Dream Voyager*. But I cannot delay."

Iblis made up his mind in an instant. He knew that this struggle could build and build, sweeping across Earth and beyond. But maybe it was best managed from a different locale. He could watch it spread from world to world. "We go together, then. I shall speak to the League, convincing the nobles to send reinforcements here. They must aid our cause!"

In adjacent rooms they heard destructive noises, shattering plaz, violent shouts. "I can escort you to safety through my followers. They won't hinder us." Iblis sounded very reasonable, utterly convincing. "You will not escape the compound unless I help you."

Vor looked at him with hard gray eyes, longing to take Serena away—and wanting nothing to do with this firebrand. She rested her hand on his arm, seeming much stronger now. "Please, just let us go. I want to leave Earth and this nightmare."

Two of Iblis's men emerged from a corridor, followed by three more. They looked at him, awaiting orders. The rebel leader needed to leave someone behind who could keep fanning the flames on Earth while he tried to rally the rest of the free humans. Someone he trusted.

He thought of the burly secondary to Eklo, and the Cogitor's network of contacts and information. "Bring Aquim to me. Immediately."

❧

AS HE STOOD on the plaza in front of the ruined villa, facing Iblis and pondering the other man's request, Aquim was torn between his genetic heritage as a human and the obligations he had sworn to the Cogitors.

"You are no longer neutral," Iblis said. "And neither is Eklo. You must help us see it through to the end. I need someone I can trust to keep the revolt burning here, while I go to the League and rally more support."

Aquim looked overwhelmed. "That could take months."

"That is as fast as a ship can carry us." He warmly clasped the burly monk on both shoulders. "My friend, you once told me that you led a squad of men against the machines, and that you had some successes. Remember what your Cogitor told me: Nothing is impossible."

The monk paused, rallying his courage. "There is a big difference between leading a squad and leading thousands of people."

"In the days before you took a liking to semuta you would not have made the distinction."

"The semuta does not dull me! It sharpens me!"

Iblis smiled. "I am good at picking people, and I recognize your talents. There are other men I could select, but none that I trust as much as you. In addition to your experience in battle, you have great wisdom, from your association with the Cogitor. You are the man for the job, Aquim."

The big man nodded slowly, as acceptance seeped in. "Yes, Eklo would want me to do this."

<hr>

BEFORE DEPARTING, IBLIS took Serena to where he had hidden and protected the body of her slain son. He had placed the broken form of little Manion in one of Erasmus's outbuildings even as the revolt spread.

Now, Serena stood like the statue of an angry goddess, cold and strong, as she reached forward and touched the transparent polymer covering that protected the waxy, cherubic face. A tough film engulfed the child—just as the consequences of this helpless innocent's murder would engulf the thinking machines.

"You . . . you preserved him?"

"It's a sealant bag used for processing slaves who die on the job." Iblis pleaded with her to understand what he had done. "Others must know what happened here, Serena. They will remember your son and all he stood for. We shall build a magnificent memorial for him, preserving him in a plaz case for all free humans to see." He looked at Vorian Atreides. "One must never underestimate the value of a symbol."

"A shrine? Aren't you getting ahead of yourself, Iblis?" Vor said, wrestling with his impatience. "The revolt is not yet won."

Serena picked up the boy; he was very light. "If we are going back to Salusa Secundus, I must take him with me. His father . . . deserves to see him at least once."

Before Vor could object, Iblis spoke up. "*Everyone* must see! This can help us rally the League. You must convince them to offer assistance to the slaves on Earth, before it is too late. If we don't, there will be many more victims."

Seeing how much it meant to Serena, Vor squared his shoulders and did not object. "If we don't go quickly, it will be too late for all of us."

Still holding Manion's preserved form, Serena straightened. "I'm ready now. Let's go find the *Dream Voyager*."

There is an infinite variety of machine and biological relationships.

—Omnius databank entry

Vor, Serena, and the unwelcome Iblis found and commandeered a passenger shuttle at a landing port on Erasmus's estate. They carried no supplies or possessions with them, except for the preserved body of little Manion. As the rebellious slaves continued to ransack the villa, Vor and his companions flew away from the hubbub. They saw no rallying robot sentries or marauding neo-cymeks. And no Titans at all. None showed themselves.

The small craft skimmed smoothly overland, keeping to the fringe of the city grid and away from the worst of the disturbance. In the days of the Old Empire, this hillside had been an exclusive neighborhood of terraced homes and gardens. The residences had been abandoned after the thinking machine conquest, falling into ruin. Only durable stone and alloy frameworks remained.

Agamemnon's memoirs had scorned the mundane lives of people in the Old Empire, but now Vorian needed to question everything. Sadness crept over him, and a renewed feeling of shame. Thanks to Serena, he noticed things for the first time, experiencing disturbing thoughts. It was as if a new universe had opened up for him, and he was leaving the old one behind.

How had the machines concealed so much from him? Or had Vor done it to himself, blinded to the obvious? Extensive historical records had always been available on the *Dream Voyager*, but he had never bothered to look. He had taken his father's accounts at face value.

When he told Serena what he had discovered, a bitter smile curled the edges of her mouth. "Maybe there's hope for you after all, Vorian Atreides. You have a lot of catching up to do—as a human being."

The white buildings of the spaceport came into view, machine military bunkers, sensors, and heavy guns. Vor transmitted the familiar access codes he had always used on the *Dream Voyager*, and the robot sentries allowed the passage of the small, fast vessel.

As rapidly as possible, Vor brought the shuttle into a dry-dock hangar and shut down all systems. Just ahead, amid cargo wharves, gantries, and refueling cisterns, a variety of spaceships were berthed. Machine crews worked the long-distance craft, preparing them for departure.

The silver-and-black *Dream Voyager* was among them, as Vor had hoped.

"Hurry," he said, taking Serena by the hand. Iblis ran close behind, wielding another large pistol he had retrieved—little enough protection if the robot soldiers decided to mount an attack.

Vor keytouched the access code on a panel and slipped through the *Dream Voyager*'s entry hatch. "Wait for me. If this works, I'll be back before long." He needed to take care of Seurat himself.

Inside, Vor heard the noise of maintenance drones installing a backup fuel cell. When he reached the command bridge, he didn't bother to hide his footsteps. Seurat would detect him anyway.

"Did you damage your ship, Old Metalmind?" Vor asked. "Couldn't fly without me?"

"Rebels fired at my vessel when I delivered combat robots for tactical redeployment. One engine suffered minimal harm. Superficial damage to our hull."

The robot captain moved his resilient, fibrous body to adjust parameters on open systems. His optic threads focused on a viewer that enabled him to monitor the last-minute work belowdecks.

Finally he said, "I can use your assistance, Vorian Atreides. One of the drones appears to be malfunctioning. All the good ones are doing emergency repairs on combat robots."

Vor knew he must move quickly. "Let me take a look."

"I notice you have changed your wardrobe," Seurat said. "With rebellious slaves running through the streets, was your Omnius uniform no longer the height of fashion?"

Vor couldn't help but chuckle, despite the tension. "Humans *are* better at fashion than machines." He stepped close to his mechanical friend, and his gaze fixed on the tiny access shunt on a protected underpanel of the robot's body. Although it was covered with flowmetal and protected by interlinked fibers, Vor knew it would be simple enough to jam the energy driver access, short-circuit the power converter, and effectively stun the robot captain.

He fumbled in one of his pockets, as if looking for something, and brought out a utility tool. "I'll run a diagnostic on that maintenance drone." Feigning clumsiness, he fumbled, bent over—and with a quick upward movement, jammed the tool into the access shunt on the side of Seurat's body. A pulse from the probe blew out the robot's energy driver.

The mechanical captain jerked, then stopped altogether. Though he knew that he hadn't damaged Seurat irreparably, Vor felt a jolt of personal guilt and pain. "Sorry about that, old Metalmind." He heard noises behind him and, whirling, saw Iblis and Serena step onto the bridge. "I told you to wait for me."

Iblis strode forward, his confidence restored, as if he were in command again. "Finish the job. Destroy the thinking machine." He approached the motionless captain, hefting a heavy tool.

"No." Angrily, Vor interposed himself between the crew boss and the prone robot. "I said *no*. Not Seurat. If you want me to fly us out of here, help me get him off the ship. He won't cause any more trouble for anyone."

"Stop wasting time, both of you," Serena said.

Reluctantly, Iblis assisted Vor in hauling the bulky robot to a side hatch, which opened onto an unoccupied dock beside a fuel-pellet dispenser. They left the captain alone among debris and equipment.

Vor stared for a moment at his own reflection in the familiar mirrored face, remembering some of the stupid jokes his friend had told and the innovative military games they had played together. Seurat had never harmed him in any way.

But Vorian Atreides, reborn, would rather be with Serena Butler among the free humans, no matter what he was forced to leave behind.

"Someday I will return," he whispered, "but I cannot know the circumstances, old Metalmind."

❦

AS VOR PILOTED the update ship away from Earth, Iblis gazed out a porthole at the planet, watching it grow smaller with distance. He considered the worldwide revolt he had sparked, hoped Aquim would do well, and that the rebellion would succeed. Maybe with the wisdom of the Cogitor Eklo, the monk could bring order to the madness and make an effective stand against Omnius.

But Iblis didn't think so. The machines were too powerful, the Synchronized Worlds too numerous. Despite all of his work, he suspected this initial revolt was doomed to failure, unless he could get the League of Nobles to help immediately.

Flames curled up from the glorious, empty buildings—an affront to the golden age of the Titans. Human riffraff, delirious with their mad liberation, ran screaming through the streets, throwing broken rocks and makeshift explosives.

Agamemnon seethed at the horrendous damage the rebels had already inflicted upon the monuments and magnificent plazas. The rebels had even killed Ajax, though the callous Titan had probably invited retribution upon himself. Yet another serious loss, like Barbarossa.

Vermin! The barbarians didn't understand freedom or free will; they had no sense of civilization or restraint, and deserved to be nothing more than slaves. Even that might be too much of a kindness.

The cymek general strode through the streets in his hulking warrior-form. He scattered humans, flung them into the air, splattered them against walls. Some of the bravest hurled sharp objects at him, which bounced off of his armored body. Unfortunately, he couldn't spare the time to squash them all.

Instead, Agamemnon made his way toward the nearby spaceport, hoping to find his son among all this chaos. If the violent rebels had harmed Vorian—the best of the general's thirteen sons so far—then he would cause some real mayhem. He had checked records, learned that the *Dream Voyager* had docked at the spaceport and that Vor's access codes had been used, but the reports were confusing.

The Titan still couldn't comprehend the scale of the conflagration around him. For centuries, the rule of thinking machines had gone unchallenged. How could the docile humans have become so explosive? No matter. He would let Omnius and his robot guards take care of the unpleasantness.

For now, Agamemnon would find his own son. He had his priorities. He hoped Vor hadn't made a mess of things.

When the cymek rushed across the spaceport, he saw three cargo ships ablaze, their fuel cells and drive compartments blown up by saboteurs. Fire-suppressant machinery attempted to extinguish the flames before more damage could be done.

The furious Titan stalked across the fused pavement, searching for the drydock that had held the repaired *Dream Voyager*. He was dismayed to find the update ship gone, the landing grid still glowing in the infrared from exhaust flames. Using thermal thoughtrode sensors, he saw the dissipating contrail where the vessel had torn a path through the atmosphere.

With mounting frustration and surprise, he found the deactivated Seurat on a dock outside the cordoned-off danger radius around the blast jets. The robot lay immobile, a supine statue of metallic polymers and neurelectric circuitry. The rebels had attacked Seurat, shut him down . . . but had not destroyed him.

Impatient, concerned about Vorian, Agamemnon rebooted the robotic systems with a flurry of his manipulator arms. When Seurat snapped back to consciousness, he scanned the spaceport with his array of optic threads, orienting himself.

"Where is the *Dream Voyager*?" Agamemnon demanded. "Where is my son? Is he alive?"

"In his typical impetuous fashion, your son surprised me. He deactivated me." Seurat scanned the launch zone and instantly drew conclusions. "Vorian must have taken the ship. He knows how to fly it."

"Is he a coward? *My* son?"

"No, Agamemnon. I believe he has joined the rebels and is escaping with other humans." He saw the cymek shuddering with angry betrayal. "It is a very poor joke," Seurat added.

Infuriated, Agamemnon swiveled the axis of his body core and marched away. An empty warship lay docked nearby, loaded with weaponry and perfect for pursuit. Already, wild humans were racing toward the craft, eager to commandeer it for themselves—as if any of the ignorant *hrethgir* could fly such a sophisticated vessel.

Raising his cannon arms, the cymek let loose with integral flamers, igniting the human criminals into flailing candles of burning flesh. Moments later he trod past the blackened corpses and linked up to the automated ship. At Agamemnon's transmitted command, the warship's grappling arms extended forward, swiveling outward to disengage his preservation canister and jettison the warrior-form. The ship's systems raised the cymek's canister and installed Agamemnon's brain within the control nest.

The sleek craft was fast, its weapons loaded and ready for battle. Vorian might have a headstart, but the *Dream Voyager* was a slower vessel, designed for long hauls. Agamemnon should be able to close the distance.

Inside his warm electrafluid, his brain adjusted to the ship's sensors, linking the thoughtrodes until he felt the spacecraft become his new body. Springing into the air on imaginary legs, Agamemnon launched away from the spaceport.

Hyperaccelerating, he gained on his quarry.

∽

VOR ATREIDES KNEW the tactics of space combat and evasive maneuvers, for Seurat had allowed him to take the update ship's controls many times. But as he left the boiling rebellion on Earth, he flew the *Dream Voyager* all alone for the first time, leaving Seurat, his long-time companion, behind.

He departed from Earth on a straight-line vector that would take them out of the solar system. He hoped that the update ship's supplies and life-support systems would be sufficient to keep him and his passengers alive for the month it would take to reach Salusa Secundus. During the frantic escape, he had never thought to consider how many humans the *Dream Voyager* could sustain, but now he had no choice.

Nervously, Iblis Ginjo peered through the ports, studying the vastness of space. He had never seen such sights before. He gaped at the pockmarked immensity of the Moon as they shot past it and continued outward.

"When we get close enough to Salusa," Serena said confidently, strapped into her own seat, "the League of Nobles will protect us. Xavier will come for me. He . . . he always has before."

The *Dream Voyager* crossed the orbit of Mars, then threaded a gap in the asteroid belt. Vor continued to build speed as they headed directly toward Jupiter's huge gravity well. He would use the gas giant's gravity to adjust their course, picking up angular momentum in an outbound slingshot.

In the rear sensors, Vor saw a lone warship hurtling toward them at a velocity so high that the readings were blueshifted, giving an altered indication of its position. No human could survive such acceleration.

"This is not going to be easy," Vor said.

Serena looked at him in astonishment. "No part of this has been easy so far."

Vor kept an eye on the approaching warship. He knew the capabilities of the *Dream Voyager*. Months ago, when he'd used extreme tactical maneuvers to elude the League Armada at Giedi Prime, Vor had never dreamed he might need his skills to flee the thinking machines who had raised him, trained him . . . and deceived him.

In a direct firefight the update ship could not outgun even a small interceptor. The *Dream Voyager*'s hull armor might hold for a while, but Vor could not dodge and outmaneuver the oncoming warcraft for long.

Jupiter loomed ahead of them, a diffuse sphere of pastel colors, with swirling clouds and storms large enough to swallow Earth whole. After analyzing the sensor summary, Vor knew the capabilities of the pursuing warship. Even with no significant weapons, the *Dream Voyager* had far more fuel, engines, and thicker armor—along with Vor's wits. He might be able to use the advantages he possessed.

The oncoming interceptor loosed four projectile volleys, only one of which struck the update ship's hull, exploding underneath the ship. Shockwaves reverberated through the *Dream Voyager* as if it were an immense gong. Still, the instruments reported no significant damage.

"We have to get away." Iblis was panicked. "He's trying to cripple us."

"That's optimistic," Vorian said. "I thought he wanted to destroy us."

"Just let him fly," Serena said to the nervous rebel leader.

A communication burst arrived, and speakers inside the *Dream Voyager* resonated with a familiar synthesized voice that made Vor turn cold inside. "Vorian Atreides, you have broken your vow of loyalty. You are a traitor, not only to Omnius, but to *me*. I no longer consider you my son."

Vor swallowed hard before responding. "You taught me to use my mind, Father, to make my own decisions and exercise my talents. I learned the truth, you know. I discovered what really happened during the Time of Titans, and it bears little resemblance to the fairy-tales in your memoirs! You lied to me all along."

In response, Agamemnon launched more projectiles, but they went wild. Vor fired his own scattering defensive rounds. They exploded in a disruptive barrier that forced the machine interceptor to swerve in its oncoming course. Vor did not waste time or engine power attempting to outmaneuver the sleek warship.

Instead, he adjusted his course so the *Dream Voyager* skirted closer to Jupiter's gravitational pull. He pushed the engines to their maximums, not worrying about stress or damage. If he couldn't escape now, excessive caution would make no difference.

The gas giant reached out to them, beckoning with a siren song of physics. Agamemnon launched another volley of explosive shells, one of which detonated very close to the *Dream Voyager*'s engines.

Vor felt calm and confident, his mind attuned to what he was doing. Seated near him, Iblis was grayish and drenched with sweat. The rebellious work leader was probably wondering whether he might have had a better chance of survival if he had remained on Earth.

"He needs only to damage us," Vor said, assessing the situation coolly. "If he manages to knock our engines offline for even a few minutes, we'll be unable to escape this hyperbolic orbit. Agamemnon can then drop back and watch us plunge slowly into Jupiter's atmosphere and burn up. He'd enjoy that."

Serena clenched the arms of her seat. As if the answer was obvious, she said to Vor, "Then don't let him damage our engines."

While the cymek general continued to fire harassing shots at them, Vor ran through a new set of calculations. Using the *Dream Voyager*'s workhorse computer subsystems, he quickly reprogrammed the navigational plotters. The update ship roared ahead, an ungraceful projectile that accelerated even as it grazed Jupiter's tenuous atmosphere, a hostage to orbital mechanics.

"Aren't you going to do anything?" Iblis demanded.

"The laws of physics are doing it for us. If Agamemnon bothers to perform the calculations, he'll see for himself what he must do. The *Dream Voyager* has enough fuel and velocity to slingshot around Jupiter and escape the gravitational pull. In that smaller interceptor, however, unless my father breaks off his pursuit in"—he glanced down at the panel—"fifty-four seconds, he will be unable to escape the pull. He'll spiral down and burn up inside Jupiter."

The interceptor kept coming, firing its weapons and not doing the damage its pilot wanted.

"Does *he* know that?" Serena asked.

"My father will know." Vor double-checked the navigational plotter. "As it is now . . . he barely has enough fuel to return to Earth. If he waits even ten seconds more, I doubt he'll survive the landing back home."

Iblis flared his nostrils. "That would be even more pointless than letting himself get swallowed up in Jupiter's clouds."

Behind them, the pursuing craft suddenly broke off, burning its engines to pull away from the gas giant in a sharp curve. The *Dream Voyager* plunged onward, scraping the upswelling clouds until its lower hull burned red with friction. Moments later, Vor hauled them out on the far side of the planet and accelerated away, breaking free of the elastic threads of gravity and vaulting into interstellar space.

Tuning his long-distance sensors, Vor verified that the interceptor had succeeded in pulling away from Jupiter's hold. He watched their pursuer turn back toward Earth on a course that salvaged momentum and conserved fuel.

Then Vor struck off toward the precarious sanctuary of the League Worlds.

❧

NOW THAT HE had lost the contest, and knowing that Vorian would certainly assist the feral humans in their continued resistance, the furious Agamemnon brooded. With little fuel for acceleration, it would be a long and frustratingly tedious journey back to Earth.

Upon arriving, though, he would salve his humiliation by taking it out on the rest of the unruly slaves. They would regret the day they had ever listened to foolish words of rebellion.

Aristotle raped reason. He implanted in the dominant schools of philosophy the attractive belief that there can be discrete separation between mind and body. This led quite naturally to corollary delusions such as the one that power can be understood without applying it, or that joy is totally removable from unhappiness, that peace can exist in the total absence of war, or that life can be understood without death.

—ERASMUS,
Corrin Notes

Nine centuries ago, after evolving into a supreme distributed intelligence, the computer evermind had established efficient control over all cymeks, robots, and humans on the Synchronized Worlds. Omnius had continued to evolve and expand his influence, creating more and more elaborate networks for himself.

Now, as the surprising unrest spread across the cities of Earth, Omnius observed everything from his legion of transmitting eyes. Watching the frenzied rebels burn buildings and smash facilities, the evermind discovered that he had a troubling blind spot.

Even the most loyal humans could never be trusted. Erasmus had been correct in his assertions all along. And now the maddening robot had fled Earth, abandoning his ransacked villa just ahead of the mobs.

Omnius issued billions of commands, monitoring and instructing his machine forces, rallying them into concentrated attacks on the rampant *hrethgir*. Already, hundreds of thousands of slaves had been butchered. When his robots finally crushed this rebellion, the sheer cleanup would be a major effort.

In the heat of their wild vandalism, the rioters had directed their most extreme hatred against the cymeks. Machines with human minds were, in Omnius's assessment, problematic and the weakest link in the Synchronized Worlds. Still, the aggressive human brains were useful in circumstances that required extreme cruelty and violence on a level that sentient machines could not attain. A time such as now.

Omnius transmitted urgent commands to all remaining Titans in the vicinity of Earth—to Juno, Dante, and Xerxes, as well as Agamemnon, who was en route back from a fruitless pursuit of his son Vorian. In order to quell this uprising, they were to take whatever action they felt necessary.

Judging from past experience, the Titans should enjoy that assignment.

IN A ROCKY desert on a continent far from the initial revolt, Juno was in the midst of a demonstration of torture-interrogation techniques on live human subjects. Xerxes and Dante carefully monitored the progress, but did not participate directly.

While a crowd of neo-cymeks studied each move, the female Titan stood in her intricate mechanical body in the pit of a teaching arena. Within reach of Juno's graceful metal arms, a thin young man and a middle-aged woman lay strapped to tables, writhing.

Suddenly, Omnius's message pulse struck their receiver systems with such force that Juno's delicate surgical hand jerked, thrusting the needle deep into the brain tissue. The young man fell silent, either dead or comatose. Juno did not take time to find out which. Omnius's demand required her complete attention.

"We must depart immediately," she announced.

With a quick movement, Xerxes stabbed a handful of needles into the chest of the human woman. By the time she had ceased twitching, the neo-cymeks had already thundered out of the demonstration pit.

With swift and efficient movements, the three Titans exchanged their delicate torturer bodies for their most magnificent warrior-forms and launched toward the heart of the revolt. . . .

They flew through a sky filled with the black smoke of fires, and set down in a wide square strewn with debris and crowded with shouting rebels. While the crowd tried to scatter, Juno crushed eleven victims beneath the hot hull.

"A fine beginning," Dante said.

When the trio of Titans emerged, followed by a retinue of smaller neo-cymeks, the rebels hurled stones at them. Juno surged forward with remarkable speed and tore their bodies apart. Xerxes and Dante separated to attack other clusters of resistance. Swarms of rebels tried to surround the cymeks, but the hybrid machines swatted them aside.

None of the slaves' weapons, not even the combined mass of their bodies, slowed the determined mechanical monsters. The streets ran red, and the air rang with screams. Juno's olfactory sensors drew in the rich odor of blood, causing her to increase her personal settings for maximum sensory input.

Xerxes lunged into the fray as if he still felt he had something to prove.

Gradually, as the humans realized the futility of their efforts, their new leader Aquim called them back. Rebels retreated into hiding places, and the streets emptied before the cymeks could march through.

Before the day was finished, Agamemnon returned from space, just in time to participate in the frolic. . . .

Monitoring the events through swarms of watcheyes, Omnius felt confident that he could snuff the unrest, as long as he used sufficient force. In this regard, the Titans had been correct all along.

Trust and violence. Such a curious, intriguing relationship between them. One day he would discuss his findings with Erasmus.

With new lessons filling his evermind, the Earth-Omnius finally had just cause to exterminate humans from his Synchronized Worlds. He would make the fragile creatures extinct, once and for all.

According to his projections, the task should not take long.

If life is but a dream, then do we only imagine the truth? No! By following our dreams we make our own truths!

—The Legend of Selim Wormrider

The air and sand smelled of spice, his body smelled of spice . . . the world was spice!

Selim could barely breathe or move as the swell of melange filled his pores, his nostrils, his eyes. He clawed his way up the rusty sand, every motion like swimming through glass. He gulped a deep breath, hoping for fresh air, but instead inhaled only more choking, cinnamon-tinted air. He was drowning in it.

The desert treated its melange as a secret, only rarely shouting it forth in spice blows, scattering the reddish brown powder out onto the dunes. Spice was life. The worms reeked of the stuff.

The young man could move only sluggishly, as if he were suffocating in visions. At the bottom of the trough, he came to a halt, coughing, but the dream images continued to roar through him like the strongest storm wind. . . .

The sandworm was long gone, snaking off through the dunes and leaving Selim where he had fallen. That old man of the desert could have eaten its lost rider, but had not heeded him. It was no accident. Buddallah had brought Selim here, and he hoped to finally find his purpose.

He had ridden the giant worm for hours, guiding it aimlessly through the night and choosing no particular destination. He had grown preoccupied, comfortable . . . foolish.

Unexpectedly, the sandworm had come upon the site of a fresh spice blow. Mysterious chemical reactions and building pressures deep beneath the dunes had reached a critical point, churning and fermenting the melange until the cap layers could no longer contain the pressure. The spice had exploded upward, a pillar of sand and gases and fresh, potent melange.

In the darkness, Selim had not seen the plume, had not been prepared. . . .

Encountering the scene, the sandworm had gone into an uncontrolled frenzy. Apparently maddened by the presence of so much melange, the creature had thrashed and bucked.

Taken by surprise, Selim had clutched his spreaders and ropes. The worm slammed into the ground, pounding the dunes as if the stained sand itself was its enemy. The seizure knocked loose the rider's metal spear, dislodging the wedge that kept the segments pried apart.

Selim had tumbled away, too stunned even to cry out. He saw the crusty-skinned beast roll beneath him, churning up the spice-laden sands, and then he struck the soft *moist* ground, rolling to absorb the impact.

Freed at last, the worm dove under the sand, burrowing deep, as if searching for the source of the melange. Selim flailed in the flowing dust and dirt, trying to keep on the surface of the churning dune. The sandworm charged onward like a projectile fired deep into the ground. A spume of sand and spice erupted in its wake, covering everything in sight with a thick layer of rusty grit.

Selim came up gasping. The cloying smell made him dizzy, and he spat out cinnamon sweetness. His face and clothes were covered with sticky spice. He smeared his eyes clear, but only drove the stinging powder deeper.

He finally stood on swaying feet, checking his arm, shoulder, ribs, making certain that no bones had been broken. He seemed miraculously unscathed—another miracle for him.

And another cryptic lesson Buddallah wanted to teach him.

Under the moonlight, all the soft and creamy dunes looked stained with blood, spice thrown in all directions as if by the antics of a capering demon. He had never seen so much in his life.

Lost out here in the open, far from his sanctuary station, Selim began to trudge through the sands. He searched the smooth ground until he found his fallen equipment, a metal spear and a spreader half buried in the sand. If another worm came, he must be ready to mount it.

As he walked, the spice seemed to penetrate him with every step and breath. His eyes had already turned the dark blue of addiction—he had seen it in the reflecting panels back in the botanical research station—but now the melange *engulfed* him. His head began to swim.

Selim finally reached the top of the dune but didn't even realize it until he had slipped over the crest and tumbled down the loose sand, rolling, scouring the clinging melange from his clothes, his skin. The world around him shifted, opened . . . and revealed its wondrous mysteries. "What is this?" he said aloud, the words echoing in his head.

The dunes shifted like whitecaps on a forgotten sea, swelling, rising, crashing into powder. Worms swam through the parched ocean, enormous denizens like giant predatory fish. Veins of spice flowed with the lifeblood of the desert, hidden beneath the surface, enriching the strata, tended by a complex ecosystem—sandplankton, gelatinous sandtrout . . . and of course the worms, known collectively as *Shai-Hulud*. The name thrummed within his skull, and it felt right. Not Shaitan, but Shai-Hulud. Not the term for a creature, not a description, but the name of a being. A god. A manifestation of Buddallah.

Shai-Hulud!

Then in his vision he saw the spice draining away, vanishing, stolen by parasites that looked like . . . like the starships he had seen in the Arrakis City Spaceport. Workers—offworlders and even Zensunni—scoured the dunes, stealing the melange, taking the treasure of Shai-Hulud and leaving him to suffocate in a dry and lifeless sea. Heavily laden ships departed, stealing the last grains of spice, leaving the people there with their hands outstretched, beseechingly. Soon, immense desert storms swept across the land, stirring up sand and raining it from the sky, like an overwhelming flood inundating the people and the sandworm carcasses. Nothing lived anywhere on the planet. Arrakis became nothing more than a bowl of sand, unstirred and sterile.

Without worms, without people . . . without melange . . .

Selim found himself sitting cross-legged atop a dune under the baking sun of midday. His skin was red and raw, burned from exposure. His lips were cracked. How long had he been there? He felt a terrible suspicion that it had been more than a day.

He struggled to his feet. His arms and legs were as stiff as rusty hinges. Spice powder still clung to his clothes and face, but it no longer seemed to affect him. He had seen too much in his vision, and the nightmarish possibilities had burned most of the melange from his system.

Selim swayed, but kept his balance. The wind whispered around him, stirring feathers of dust from the dune crests. Empty and silent . . . but not dead. Unlike his vision.

Melange held the key to Arrakis, to the sandworms, to life itself. Even the Zensunni did not know all the interconnected webs, but Buddallah had revealed the secret to Selim. Was this his destiny?

He had seen offworlders taking the spice, carrying it far from Arrakis, bleeding the desert world dry. Perhaps he had seen a true vision of the future, or only a warning. Naib Dhartha had driven him out into the sands to die, but Buddallah had saved him for a reason . . . for this?

To protect the desert and the worms? To serve Shai-Hulud? To find the offworlders who would steal the melange from Arrakis?

He had no choice, now that God had touched him. He must find those people—and stop them.

There is no place in all the universe as inviting as home and the comfortable relationships there.

—SERENA BUTLER

As the *Dream Voyager* approached the Gamma Waiping star system and Salusa Secundus, Serena Butler swelled with eagerness and relief to be back home, oscillating between her deep desire to see Xavier Harkonnen again and her dread of what she must tell him.

Startling her, a small maintenance drone moved out of its alcove on a preprogrammed check-path, scuttling under control panels and oblivious to the new masters of the *Dream Voyager*. Serena saw the little robot and suddenly focused her anger. Snatching up the small machine by a leg, she hurled it against the metal deck.

The red drone squirmed, automatically trying to avoid further damage, but Serena smashed it until its casing broke open, oozing gelcircuitry fluid like blood onto the floor. With a final twitch, its components fell still.

"If only destroying all thinking machines could be that simple," she said grimly, imagining Erasmus lying there destroyed instead of the hapless maintenance drone.

"It will be simple enough, if we can mobilize the willpower of the human race," said Iblis Ginjo.

Though Iblis had tried to console her during the long flight, Serena actually found herself confiding more in Vorian. She'd had several weeks now to work through her shock and grief, and her conversations with the sympathetic young man had in some measure helped. Vor was a good listener. Iblis asked many questions about the nobles, the League Worlds, the politics, while Vor paid more attention to the people Serena wanted to talk about: her son, her parents, her sister Octa, and especially Xavier.

When Serena spoke of Xavier Harkonnen, Vor realized with a start that Xavier had been the League military officer who had stood against the *Dream Voyager* when he and Seurat tried to exchange the Omnius update on Giedi Prime. "I . . . look forward to meeting him," Vor said in a voice that held no enthusiasm at all.

Serena had told them about her impetuous and ill-advised plan to restore the shield-transmitting towers on Giedi Prime, when League politics had caused excuses and delays.

"At least thinking machines don't have such bureaucracy," Iblis said. "You risked a great deal, knowing how cumbersome and conservative your government must be."

Serena smiled wistfully, showing a hint of her lost strength. "I knew Xavier would come. He would find a way."

Though Vor found it painful, he listened while she talked about how much she still loved Xavier, describing the betrothal celebration at the Butler estate, the bristleback hunt, her humanitarian work in the League. She told stories about Xavier's military prowess, his work shoring up the defenses of other human worlds, and his desperate action during the cymek attack on Zimia that had saved Salusa Secundus.

Uncomfortable, Vor remembered the completely different versions of such stories he had heard from his father. Agamemnon did not recall the defeat in the same terms . . . but now Vor knew that the cymek general was prone to lying, or at least to wild exaggeration. He could no longer believe anything his father said.

"Still," Serena said, hanging her head, "I allowed myself to be captured and my crew to be killed by Barbarossa. I am entirely to blame for placing myself in danger at Giedi Prime, not even knowing that I carried Xavier's child. And I shouldn't have taunted Erasmus, pushed him." She shuddered. "I underestimated his capacity for cruelty. How can Xavier ever forgive me? Our son is dead."

Iblis tried to comfort her. "Vorian Atreides and I will tell the League of Nobles how the machines treat their slaves. No one will ever blame you."

"I blame myself," she said. "There's no way around it."

Vor longed to help her, but was not sure what to say or do. When he touched her arm gently, she turned away. Vor could not help it that he wasn't the man she wanted beside her right now.

He envied this mysterious Xavier Harkonnen and wanted to earn his own place in Serena's heart. He had abandoned his father, turned from everything he had known in the Synchronized Worlds, betrayed the Titans and Omnius. Even so, he had no right to ask for any emotional payment in return.

"If your Xavier is the man you believe he is, then surely he will welcome you back home with compassion and forgiveness?"

Seeing Vor's expression, Serena said more calmly, "Yes, he is capable of that—but am *I* the person he believed I was?"

Yes, and more, Vor thought, but did not say so aloud.

"You'll be home before long," he said, seeing Serena's expression glow with a new life. "I'm sure it'll be all right, as soon as you are with him again. And if you ever need anyone else to talk to, I . . ." His voice trailed off to an awkward silence.

As the hijacked update ship approached Salusa Secundus, the fabled world that epitomized free humanity, he gazed down at the green continents, the blue seas, the wispy clouds in the atmosphere. His doubts faded, and though his heart ached, his hopes grew higher. Truly, it looked like a paradise.

Iblis Ginjo peered through a viewing window. His mind seemed to be racing with possibilities. But he sat up abruptly in alarm. "We have a reception committee! Looks like fast combat ships!"

"The picket line must have detected us when we entered the system," Serena said. "Those are ground-launched kindjals, from bases in Zimia."

As the fast and maneuverable Salusan Militia fighters surrounded the *Dream Voyager*, they bombarded the update ship with threats and instructions. "Enemy ship, surrender and prepare to be boarded." Several warning explosions rippled across their bow.

Vor made no threatening move, remembering how similar ships had already damaged the vessel at Giedi Prime. "We are humans who escaped from Omnius, and wish to land in peace," he transmitted. "We've stolen this ship from Earth."

"Yeah, we've heard that one before," said one of the kindjal pilots. Vor realized that he had used such a ruse himself. "Why shouldn't we just turn you into a cloud of space dust?" The kindjals flew close, arming their weapons.

"It may interest you to know that we have Serena Butler aboard, the daughter of the League Viceroy." Vor gave a grim smile. "Her father would not be pleased if you blew us into space dust. Neither would Xavier Harkonnen, since his fiancée has been through so much just to come back to him."

Determined, Serena took the communication controls. "It's true. This is Serena Butler. Since this is a robot ship, please deactivate the scrambler shields to allow us safe passage, then escort us to Zimia. Inform the Viceroy and Tercero Harkonnen to meet us at the spaceport."

The long silence that hung on the channel told Vor that a furious debate must be occurring on private lines. Finally, the squadron commander said, "*Segundo* Harkonnen is out on patrol and will not return for two days. Viceroy Butler is already on his way with an honor guard. Follow me—and do not deviate from the path."

Vor acknowledged, then took a deep, concerned breath. Now he had to fly with his own guidance skills and no assistance from the onboard gelcircuitry computers. The vessel's own cooperative guidance and automated response systems had always aided him in the event of an emergency. "Serena, Iblis—both of you strap in and hold on."

"Is there a problem?" Iblis asked, seeing Vor's uneasiness.

"Only that I've never done this before."

The *Dream Voyager* rocked in turbulence as it passed through high winds and a thin cloud cover, until it broke through into clear sky. The kindjals paced them closely, just off the update ship's short wings. Sunlight slanted into the interior through overhead portholes, forming distorted shadows on the decks and bulkheads.

Vor set the *Dream Voyager* down gently in the designated zone, in the crowded spaceport. Despite the challenge, he had flown the vessel perfectly. Seurat would have been proud of him.

Elated, Iblis Ginjo rose to his feet as the low hum of the engines fell silent. "At last! Salusa Secundus." He looked at Vor. "For rescuing the Viceroy's daughter, they will welcome us with red carpets and flowers."

When he released the hatch and breathed Salusan air for the first time, Vor Atreides tried to identify the difference, wondering if he could detect an elusive scent of freedom. "Don't expect carpets or flowers just yet," he said.

He saw a military squad approaching the ship with weapons drawn. The soldiers, dressed in gold-and-silver League uniforms, formed ranks at the bottom of the ramp. Behind them came two intimidating-looking women with white hair, pale skin, and long black robes.

Serena stood between the two former trustees of the thinking machines, taking their arms protectively in hers. Together, the three of them stepped out into dazzling sunlight.

While the Militia soldiers kept their weapons ready, they deferred to the tall, grim women. The chief Sorceress looked at the new arrivals with a gaze so intense and intimidating that she reminded Vorian of one of the Titans. "Are you spies of Omnius?" she said, stepping closer to them.

Serena recognized the Sorceress of Rossak, but knew that she herself must have changed considerably in her year and a half of captivity. "Zufa Cenva, we were colleagues." Her voice hitched. "I have come home. Do you not recognize me?"

The Sorceress looked skeptically at her, then astonishment crossed her alabaster face. "It truly is you, Serena Butler! We thought you had died on Giedi Prime, along with Ort Wibsen and Pinquer Jibb. We checked the DNA on blood samples found in the wreckage of your blockade runner." Zufa loomed before the young woman, studying her while ignoring the two men entirely.

Serena struggled valiantly to set aside her sadness. "Wibsen and Jibb did die fighting the cymeks. I was injured . . . and captured."

At the deep expression of emotions, Vor spoke on her behalf. "She was held prisoner on Earth by a robot named Erasmus."

The Sorceress's electric expression swung to regard him. "And who are you?"

Vor knew he could not lie. "I am the son of the Titan Agamemnon." The Militia soldiers stirred. The two Sorceresses reacted with alarm and then renewed intensity. "I used my influence to slip through the defenses of Earth-Omnius."

Iblis Ginjo pushed forward, eyes bright and enthusiastic. "All of Earth is in revolt! Humans have broken free of their machine masters. Rebels slew Titans and neo-cymeks, smashed robots, destroyed entire facilities. But we need League help—"

Abruptly, Iblis's words were cut off with a little squeak of his voice. Around his own throat, Vorian felt a tightness, like a garrote. The eyes of the Sorceresses blazed, as if probing deeply into the minds of these new arrivals. Suspicion saturated the air like thick humidity, an unwillingness to trust two turncoat humans and Serena Butler, who might have been brainwashed by Omnius.

The Sorceresses' concentration was broken by a sudden commotion. Vor found he could breathe easily again. Viceroy Manion Butler, looking a decade older than when Serena had last seen him, pushed soldiers out of his way and charged forward like a wild Salusan bull. "Serena! Oh my sweet child! You are alive!"

Both Sorceresses stepped aside, seeing that nothing could stop the man from throwing his arms around his daughter. "My child, my child—I can't believe it!" He held Serena, rocked her from side to side. Without wanting to, she found herself weeping against his chest. "Oh what have they done to you? What have they done?"

Serena found she could not answer him at all.

Human beings rely upon their brethren, and are frequently disappointed by them. These are advantages of machines: reliability and a complete lack of guile. They can also be disadvantages.

—ERASMUS,
Reflections on Sentient Biologicals

Serena's father hushed her and hurriedly escorted her away from the spaceport with a crowd of fawning and dutiful attendants. "The best place for you now is the City of Introspection, with your mother. You can rest and heal there, in peace."

"I will never have peace again," she said, struggling to control the tremor in her voice. "Where is Xavier? I need to—"

Looking troubled, Manion patted her on the shoulder. "I sent an executive order recalling him from an inspection patrol of perimeter defenses. He's racing home now, and should be back early tomorrow."

She swallowed hard. "I need to see him as soon as he returns. Inside the ship . . . our son . . . there is so much—"

Manion nodded again, without seeming to hear that she had just referred to her "son." "Don't worry about it now. A lot has changed, but you're home again, and safe. Nothing else matters. Your mother is waiting for you, and you can rest with her. Everything else can keep until tomorrow."

Serena looked over to where Vorian Atreides and Iblis Ginjo were being ushered off by Militia officers. She felt she should accompany them and introduce the former Omnius servants to their new world. "Don't be hard on them," Serena said, remembering the harsh skepticism of the Sorceresses. "They've never really met free humans before. Both of them have important information."

Manion Butler nodded. "They're only being debriefed. The League can learn much from what they have to say."

"I can help, too," Serena said. "I saw so many terrible things in my captivity on Earth. Maybe tonight I can come back and—"

The Viceroy shushed her. "Everything in its time, Serena. I'm sure you'll grow weary enough of our questions, but you don't have to save the world today." He chuckled. "Same old Serena."

By high-speed groundcar it took an hour for them to reach the contemplative hillside retreat on the outskirts of Zimia. As thirsty as she was for the sights of her home world, everything seemed a blur to Serena, and she noticed few details.

Livia Butler, in her plain abbess robes, greeted them at the high gates of the quiet complex. With a moist-eyed nod to her husband, she accepted Serena into the City of Introspection and led the way across a grassy area to a warm and well-furnished room of muted colors and cushioned chairs. There she cradled Serena against her breast as if their daughter were a child again. Livia's large eyes filled with tears.

Now that Serena was with her parents, safe and warm and loved, the oppressive weights of weariness and fear lifted from her, and she felt more able to do what still needed to be done. In a weak and shaky voice, Serena quickly told them about her sweet little Manion, and how Erasmus had killed him . . . sparking the revolt that swept across Earth.

"Please, I need to see Xavier." Her face lit up. "And Octa? Where is my sister?"

Livia shot a hard glance at her husband, and words caught in her throat until she said, at last, "Soon enough, dear child.

For now, you must rest and gather your strength. You're home now. You have all the time in the world."

Serena wanted to protest, but sleep swept her away.

~

BY THE TIME Xavier raced back from his Armada patrol on the fringes of the Salusan system, the news had already reached him in a dozen comsystem messages of joy and grief, each one a hammer blow of pain. The clashing happiness, confusion, and despair made him want to explode.

Because he traveled solo in his kindjal, Xavier had time to think about what he had learned. When his ship arrived late at Zimia Spaceport, he felt incredibly alone. He disembarked onto a landing field illuminated with spotlights. It was past midnight.

How could Serena be alive? He had seen the wreckage of her blockade runner in the gray seas of Giedi Prime. The bloodstains matched her DNA. Even in his wildest, most foolish dreams, Xavier had never considered that she might still be alive. *Alive!* Or that she was pregnant with his child.

And now Serena had escaped. She had come home. But his son—*their* son—had been murdered by the monstrous machines.

When Xavier stepped away from his cooling kindjal, he could barely smell the ozone and oxidation chemicals on its hull from his fast descent through the Holtzman scrambler shields. Ahead he saw a single man waiting on the landing field, seemingly forlorn, his features washed out under the spaceport lights, but Xavier recognized Manion Butler, Viceroy of the League of Nobles.

"I'm so glad you . . . you could—" Manion Butler was unable to finish his sentence. Instead, he stepped forward and embraced his son-in-law, the young military officer who had married not his daughter Serena, but Octa.

"Serena is resting at the City of Introspection," Manion said. "She . . . she doesn't know about you and Octa. It is a delicate situation, from every angle." All life seemed to have drained out of the Viceroy. He was obviously excited to have his daughter back, but broken to know what had happened to her, how the machines had hurt her . . . how they had killed her baby.

"Serena would want the truth," said Xavier. "But she will have all of it she can tolerate soon enough. I'll see her tomorrow. Let her sleep well for this evening."

Supporting each other, the two men walked away from the kindjal. The Viceroy led Xavier to where larger banks of white lights and a work crew continued their inspection even at such a late hour. The silver-and-black vessel was of a configuration Xavier had seen only once before—an update ship such as the one he had encountered at Giedi Prime, when the traitorous human pilot had eluded Xavier's attempts to capture him.

"Serena found allies among the humans on Earth," Manion said. "Two trustees, men raised by the machines. She convinced them to flee with her."

Xavier frowned. "Are you certain they are not spies?"

Manion shrugged. "Serena trusts them."

"Then I suppose that is good enough."

They entered the *Dream Voyager*, and Xavier felt a cold heaviness in his chest. He knew where Manion was taking him. Aboard the update ship, he noticed the odd configurations, the smooth curves, the clean metallic lines that denoted efficiency and also carried an unconscious sleek beauty.

"We've not moved the boy," said Manion. "I told them to wait for you."

"I don't know if I should thank you for that." When the Viceroy opened a sealed storage compartment and a wispy breath of cold steam crawled like feathers into the air, Xavier overcame his reluctance and leaned forward.

The child's body was wrapped in a tough, dark covering, a sealed preservation shroud that hid specific details, leaving only a small, painfully sad shape of what had once been a vibrant little boy. Xavier touched the cold wrapping. His fingertips were gentle, as if he didn't want to disturb his son's slumber.

Behind him, Manion was breathing hard. "Serena said . . .

she said she named the boy after me." Then his words choked off, and Xavier reached in to lift out the wrapped package, all that remained of the child he had never met, had never even known about until it was too late. The boy seemed unbelievably, absurdly light.

Xavier found he had nothing to say, but as he carried his son out into the night air of Salusa Secundus, taking little Manion home for the first and only time, he wept openly.

Machines may be predictable, but we are also reliable. Conversely, humans change their beliefs and their loyalties with remarkable, and distressing, ease.

—ERASMUS
Erasmus Dialogues

Vorian Atreides sat at a large, polished table in a debriefing room, ready to face a crowd of gathered political leaders, all of whom had questions and suspicions. He hoped he had answers for them.

Iblis Ginjo would be interviewed separately. The League had already dispatched its fastest scout ship to Earth to verify the stories and assess the current status of the revolt.

Looking around the capital city had absolutely astounded Vor. The buildings of Zimia had none of the outrageous grandeur of Earth, and the streets seemed . . . disorganized. But the *people* he saw, the colors, the clothes, the expressions on their faces—he felt as if he had awakened from a dream. Vor steeled himself and resolved to cooperate so he could help the free humans in every way possible. If they would allow him.

For an interrogation session such as this, Agamemnon would have used pain stimulators and exotic torture devices. Undoubtedly, the League saw this as a remarkable opportunity to obtain inside information on Omnius. Sitting around the table and standing against the walls, representatives regarded him with curiosity, some with hatred or at least resentment.

Always before, Vor had been proud of his lineage, deluded by the perceived glories of Agamemnon and the Titans. Free humans, though, had a different view of history. A more accurate view, he hoped.

Uncomfortable before so many agitated people, Vor felt adrift, missing Serena, hoping she was all right. Had she reunited with Xavier Harkonnen yet? Would she ever want to see Vor again?

Before the buzz of conversation could dwindle in the debriefing room, Vor spoke, starting slowly and selecting his words with the utmost care. "I make no excuses for my behavior. My cooperation with the machines has certainly caused harm and pain to people in the League of Nobles." He looked around the room, met each curious eye. "Yes, I worked as a trustee on an update ship, delivering copies of Omnius to the Synchronized Worlds. I was raised by the thinking machines, taught their version of history. I even revered my father, General Agamemnon. I thought he was a great cymek."

He heard mutters around the room. "Serena Butler, though, opened my eyes. She challenged me to question what I had been taught, and finally I saw that I had been deceived." He wrestled with what he was about to offer. It seemed the final betrayal of his past.

Let it be so.

He took a deep breath, continued. "It is my fervent hope that I can use my knowledge and skill—as well as my detailed information about the workings of the thinking machines—to assist my fellow human beings, who are currently in revolt against Omnius on Earth."

A growing mutter passed among the listeners around the table as the representatives began to realize the implications of his words. "I distrust any man who would betray his father," one of the representatives said, a tall man with a pockmarked face. "How will we know he is not giving us distorted intelligence?"

Vor frowned at the accusation. Surprisingly, the coldly

beautiful Zufa Cenva of Rossak said from one side, "No, he speaks the truth." Her dark eyes penetrated him, and he had difficulty looking into them for more than a moment. "If he dares to lie here, I will know."

One of the debriefers looked at his notes. "And now, Vorian Atreides, we have many questions for you."

Is there any greater joy than to return home? Are any other memories so vivid, any other hopes so bright?

—SERENA BUTLER

When Serena awoke with the first pale light of dawn, she found herself alone in a soft bed surrounded by soothing sounds, colors, and smells. Many times after Fredo's death, she had visited her mother in the City of Introspection and enjoyed the contemplative atmosphere. But after a short time she had always grown impatient with meditation and pondering, preferring to do something more active.

She dressed quickly as the morning light grew outside. Xavier might be back on Salusa by now. The brief sleep had done her good, but she felt a leaden weight in her chest that she knew would never lift until she found Xavier and told him the terrible news about their son. Despite her bruised heart and soul, she had never backed down from her responsibilities.

Before the City of Introspection became fully awake, Serena quietly went to the outbuildings and found a small groundcar. She didn't want to disturb her mother. Raising her chin in determination, Serena refused to delay. It had been long enough already.

Climbing into the vehicle, she went through the motions of powering up the familiar engines. She knew where she had to go. Serena rode off through the open gates, heading down the road toward the Tantor estate, where Xavier had made his home. She hoped she would find him there. . . .

Emil Tantor opened the heavy wooden door and looked at her with astonishment. "We were delighted to hear of your return!" His brown eyes were as kind and warm as she had remembered.

Gray wolfhounds barked inside the foyer and slipped past Emil to bound in circles, greeting Serena. Despite the dread in her heart, she smiled. A wide-eyed boy came out to look at her. "Vergyl! You've grown so much!" She fought a swell of sadness at the vivid reminder of how long she had been away.

Before the boy could answer, Emil gestured her inside. "Vergyl, please take the dogs outside so this poor woman can have a bit of quiet, after what she's been through." He gave her a small, deeply compassionate smile. "I didn't expect you to come here. Would you have a glass of morning tea with me, Serena? Lucille always brews it strong."

She hesitated. "Actually, I need to see Xavier. Is he back yet? I need to—" The old man's startled expression stopped her. "What is it? Is he all right?"

"No, no, Xavier is fine, but . . . he isn't here. He went directly to your father's estate." Emil Tantor seemed to have more to tell her, but his voice trailed off.

Troubled by his reaction, Serena thanked him and ran back to her groundcar, leaving the old man standing at the wooden door. "I'll see him there, then." Xavier probably had business with her father. Perhaps they were already planning to aid the human rebels on Earth.

She drove to the familiar manor house atop the high hill, surrounded by vineyards and olive groves. Her heart ached as she slowed to a halt by the main entry. *Home.* And Xavier was here.

She parked near the wellspring and breathlessly approached the front door. Her eyes were stinging, her legs trembling. She could hear her pulse pounding in her ears. Greater even than the guilt she bore or the fear of what she must say, was a longing to be with her lover again.

Xavier opened the door even before she reached it. At first his face seemed like a sunrise, nearly blinding her. He looked older, stronger, more handsome than he had even in her fantasies. She wanted to melt.

"Serena!" He gasped, then grinned and swept her into his arms. After only a moment he pulled away awkwardly. "I knew you were at the City of Introspection, but I didn't realize you had recovered yet. I just returned in the middle of the night, and I, uh—" He seemed to be fumbling for words.

"Oh, Xavier, it doesn't matter! I needed to be with you so badly. There is so much . . . so much to tell." All at once the magnitude of what she needed to say seemed to crush her shoulders. Her voice caught.

He stroked her cheek. "Serena, I already know the terrible news. I've heard about . . . our son." He looked at her with sadness and pain, but a firm acceptance.

When they stepped into the foyer, Xavier withdrew to an awkward distance, as if facing her was more difficult than confronting all the forces of the machine armies. "It has been so long, Serena, and everyone thought you were dead. We found the wreckage of your ship, analyzed the blood samples, confirmed your DNA."

She reached out to clasp his hand. "But I survived, my love! I thought of you constantly." Her eyes searched his face for answers. "My memories of you were all I had to sustain me."

Finally, his words falling like heavy stones, he said, "I am married now, Serena."

Her heart seemed to stop beating. Serena took a halting step backward, and bumped into a small table, which toppled over with a crash, spilling a vase and fresh red roses, like blood on the tile floor.

She heard hurried footsteps from the main sitting room. The slight figure of a young woman appeared, with long hair and large eyes, rushing toward her. "Serena! Oh, Serena!" Octa carried a bundle in her arms, held close to her bosom, but she managed to give her sister a fierce hug anyway.

Overjoyed, Octa stood beside her husband and her sister, but as she looked from one to the other, her happy expression crumbled into embarrassment and shame.

The bundle stirred in Octa's arms, and made a soft sound. "This is our daughter Roella," she said, almost apologetically, and drew aside the cloth to show Serena the child's beautiful face.

An image flashed through Serena's mind: her terror-stricken son only seconds before Erasmus dropped him from the high balcony. The baby girl Octa held looked remarkably like little Manion, who had also been Xavier's child.

In stunned disbelief, Serena stumbled toward the door, her world crashing down around her. She whirled and ran off like a wounded fawn.

The Butlerian Jihad arose from just such stupidity. An infant was killed. The bereaved mother struck out at the nonhuman machinery that had caused the senseless death. Soon, the violence was in the hands of the extended mob and became known as a jihad.

—PRIMERO FAYKAN BUTLER,
Memoirs of the Jihad

Earth remained the flaming heart of rebellion even without the charismatic Iblis Ginjo. Thrust into the center of the struggle, the Cogitor's secondary Aquim tried to keep the resistance alive and organize the ill-planned fight in the face of Omnius's increasingly violent retaliation.

Aquim had always been a man of contemplation, mulling over Eklo's esoteric revelations in the high monastery towers. He had forgotten how to deal with destruction and bloodshed. While he had a network of contacts through his relationship with Eklo, only rarely were they fighters. For the most part, these people were deep thinkers who came up with so many options to consider that they could not move quickly. The situation at hand was outdistancing them.

Mobs ruled with very little leadership.

Surprised and overwhelmed at the realization that they had broken free after centuries of oppression, the rebels had no focus or goal—only a raw, unchanneled need for revenge. Once unleashed, these slaves could never turn back. Even Iblis had not made long-term plans. Fires raged across the city grids. Factory and maintenance buildings exploded as saboteurs brought down the manufacturing and support capabilities of Omnius. Arson and vandalism spread across the continents from industrial centers to human settlements.

The evermind unleashed his cymeks, activated his ranks of warrior robots. The entire planet became a battleground . . . and not long afterward, a charnel house. Thinking machines had no capacity for forgiveness.

Unfettered at last, Agamemnon and his bloodthirsty cymeks marched into human habitation camps and razed them to the ground. For the first time since the Titans had been overthrown by the evermind, Omnius's diversified fighters were bound together by a rapacious enthusiasm for vengeance. Cymeks sprayed poison gas, acid plumes, and ribbons of molten fire.

Robotic extermination squads moved from gutted buildings to squalid shelters and pens. Crops were burned, food-distribution depots leveled. Even those who survived the mechanical onslaught would starve within months.

Ten thousand slaves paid in blood for every robot or cymek damaged. No humans could escape with their lives. None were meant to.

⤛⤜

HIGH IN THE isolated mountains, the Cogitor's tower trembled like a living creature. Pieces of stone flaked away. On the uppermost level, where Eklo's ancient brain rested in its preservation canister, the exterior windows changed color from yellow to orange.

A distraught Aquim dipped his fingers into the electrafluid, connecting his thoughts to those of the revered Cogitor. "I gave them your message, Eklo. The Titan Juno is coming. She wishes to speak with you."

"As she did, long ago."

Wishing to put an end to the bloodshed, Eklo had asked to see the Titans, hoping there would be some way to reason with them. Long ago, the Cogitor had unwittingly aided Juno and her companions in their overthrow of the Old Empire, and Eklo's disembodied brain had been the inspiration for the Titans to convert themselves into cymeks.

In those days he had been a spiritual human named Arn Eklo, philosopher and orator who had fallen to the diversions of sexual pleasures. In his shame and dismay, he had met Kwyna and her metaphysical scholars who wanted to eliminate all distractions in order to develop their thinking powers. Eklo's physical form, the petty desires of his body, became unimportant to him, nothing in comparison to unraveling the mysteries of the universe.

His orations became different after that, exceedingly cerebral, so that many people could not understand him. His followers began to drift away, and the business investors in the congregation, seeing the dramatic decline in revenues, questioned him. They didn't understand what he was saying either.

Then one day, Arn Eklo simply disappeared. As a group, he and the other Cogitors planned to embark on an epic journey to the deep reaches of the spiritual realm. Far beyond the bounds of flesh.

Since undergoing the remarkable surgery, his mind had lived for more than two thousand years separated from the weaknesses and limitations of his human body. At last, he and Kwyna and the other Cogitors had all the time anyone could need. It was the greatest gift any of them could have received. *Time.*

Now Aquim interrupted his ponderous thoughts. "Juno is here."

With his canister resting on a ledge of the high tower, Eklo observed a massive cymek warrior-form easily climbing the steep mountain path.

"Give Juno this message," Eklo said to Aquim. Below, numerous secondaries appeared to be in a frenzy, hurrying toward the stairs that led to the top of the tower. "Tell her nothing is impossible. Tell her that love is what separates humans from other living creatures, not hatred. Not violence—"

The windows turned bloodred, and powerful explosions

ripped through the tower. Juno raised her cannon forelimbs and launched a volley of projectiles, pummeling the reinforced monastery structure until the tower crumbled.

The ceiling collapsed, and Aquim threw himself forward, trying to shield the preservation canister and the magnificent brain of the ancient Cogitor. But the avalanche came down, crushing everything. . . .

After the tower had tumbled into a dusty heap, Juno used her mechanical arms to tear through the rubble, knocking stones and girders aside. She crawled over the wreckage, discarding the broken bodies of secondaries until finally she found the preservation canister. The dead monk Aquim and the curved plexiplaz tank had kept the Cogitor's brain from being pulverized, but the container was cracked. Bluish electrafluid dripped into the dirt and debris.

Juno tossed Aquim's body away like a limp doll. Then she extended a flowmetal hand, extruding long and sharp fingers into the broken container to retrieve the puckered grayish mass of the Cogitor Eklo. She sensed faint flickers of energy from the quivering brain.

She decided to send him on another journey, even farther from the realm of flesh. Her flowmetal hand clenched, squeezing the spongy gray matter into dripping pulp.

"Nothing is impossible," she said, then swiveled about and marched back toward the city grid and her important work.

⤿

WITHOUT EMOTION — ONLY a desire to rid himself of a problem—Omnius decreed the complete annihilation of all human life on Earth.

His robotic forces proceeded relentlessly, going about their bloody task with few impediments. Ajax's bloodbath on Walgis during the long-ago Hrethgir Rebellions had been merely a brief prelude.

After the evermind determined that it had no further use for the humans on this planet, he made similar assessments for all of the other Synchronized Worlds. Despite the fact that humans had originally created thinking machines, the unruly biologicals had always been more trouble than they were worth. At last he agreed with Agamemnon, who had been urging such a final solution for centuries. Omnius would extinguish the human species.

The remaining four Titans, assisted by neo-cymeks and modified robotic soldiers, spent months hunting down and slaughtering the planetary population. Not a single person on Earth survived.

The bloodshed was unspeakable, and much of it was recorded by the ever-present watcheyes of the evermind.

Support thy brother, whether he be just or unjust.

—Zensunni saying

As much as he hated Naib Dhartha, Selim retained a curiosity about how the people of his former village continued to live their lives. He wondered if they had erased him from their memories by now. Sometimes he went over their actions in his mind and grew furious, but then he would smile. Buddallah had kept Selim alive, given him a mysterious vision and a blessed purpose.

Previous generations of Zensunni had adapted their way of life to the desert. In such a hostile environment there was little room for change or flexibility, so the nomads' day-to-day existence remained much the same year after year.

However, as Selim observed his former comrades, he noticed that Naib Dhartha had a new priority in life. The rigid tribal leader had launched upon some unusual scheme that involved taking large teams of workers out into the open desert. The scavengers no longer combed the wasteland for a few pieces of scrap metal or abandoned technology. Now the

Zensunni villagers hurried out into the sands with one purpose only: *to gather spice*.

Just like in his vision! The nightmare began to make sense: the spice taken offworld by outsiders, causing a storm that would sweep away the harsh serenity of the great desert. Selim would watch and understand . . . and then he would determine what he needed to do.

With delicate footsteps, the villagers wandered onto the open dunes, making quick excursions out to the rust-colored stains of melange spread by occasional spice blows. Gently easing metal stakes deep into the sand, they lashed up thin camouflaged tents and awnings against the blowing sand and the hot sun. They posted a watch on the high dune crests for approaching worms.

Then they began to harvest the spice, taking it from the desert in large quantities, far more than the tribe could ever use. If Selim's vision was true, then Naib Dhartha must be delivering the melange to Arrakis City . . . for export offworld, away from Arrakis.

In his vision the floodgates would open, spilling sand like a tidal wave to engulf the Zensunni people, sweeping the remnants of the sandworms away. Shai-Hulud! Ambitious Naib Dhartha did not understand the consequences of his actions for his people, for his entire world.

Selim approached quietly to observe them through a high-intensity viewer he had taken from his botanical research station. He squinted, recognizing people he had grown up with, villagers who had once befriended him, and ultimately scorned him.

Selim didn't see Ebrahim skulking among them anymore. Perhaps the young man had finally been caught for his own crimes, now that Selim was no longer there to take the blame. . . . Shai-Hulud would have his justice, one way or another.

The evil naib was in their midst, shouting orders, directing the people as they scurried out with sacks and containers, scooping spice from the sands. The workers could barely carry the amounts they gathered. Dhartha must have found a customer somewhere.

Selim was fascinated at first, then angry. Finally, he decided upon a way to follow his calling, his vision . . . while exacting his revenge as well.

~~~

WITH HIS SONIC hammer, he called upon Shai-Hulud. The beast he summoned was a relatively small sandworm, but Selim didn't mind. The smaller creatures were more manageable anyway.

Selim rode high on the bowed serpentine head, brashly out in the open for all to see. Peeling apart the fleshy segments to guide the creature, he sat astride a great steed, a monstrous animal that could survive only in the deepest, driest desert. He urged the worm to greater speed, and it hissed through the ocean of sand.

The Zensunni had been extremely cautious in setting up their camp, careful that the sandworms did not notice them. At dusk, the people began to emerge from temporary shelters after the heat of the day, leaving their settlement and spreading out to where they could gather more spice.

Remembering his vision and answering the now-clear call, Selim drove the worm headlong into the encampment.

The Zensunni were never complacent, always alert. Spotters sounded the alarm as soon as the worm approached, but there was nothing they could do. In his deep, loud voice, Naib Dhartha shouted for the spice gatherers to scatter and find places of safety. They raced across the dunes, leaving their tents and the piled containers of hoarded spice.

Using rods to goad the creature and prybars to spread open the segments, Selim controlled Shai-Hulud's course. Frustrated at being ridden, the worm thrashed, wanting to attack *something*. Selim had to batter its pink, exposed flesh to keep the beast from devouring all the villagers.

He didn't want to kill any of them . . . although it might have been satisfying to see Naib Dhartha swallowed down the worm's gullet. This was more than enough. Selim would accomplish what Buddallah had called him to do; ruin the naib's plans to export huge shipments of Shai-Hulud's spice.

The villagers dispersed across the sands with skittering foot-steps in hopes that the worm would not follow the rhythm of their running feet. The monster crashed into the abandoned camp, plowing up a spume of sand. In a flash, the camouflaged tent fabrics vanished, churned under or swallowed up.

Then the sandworm turned its round head and returned to the site to devour the gathered melange, tearing apart the containers, swallowing packages whole, obliterating every sign of the harvesting work.

From a distance, terrified villagers, perhaps including Naib Dhartha himself, stood on dunes, ready to run farther away but hypnotized by the spectacle. In a flowing white robe, Selim rode high on the worm's back; they could not help but notice his human silhouette atop the desert demon.

Laughing so hard that he could barely maintain his control over the creature, Selim raised his hands in a defiant gesture. He had done Buddallah's bidding. The spice was safe, for now.

Then he goaded the worm in another direction, away from the forlorn people, and rode off into the empty sands, leaving the Zensunni villagers there with the wreck of their camp.

~~~

ON THE WAY out, Selim left two literjons of his own water among the torn scraps of the settlement. He could replace it in his botanical stations, and it was just enough to let the Zensunni people survive. They could reach their cliff city again, if they walked by night and conserved moisture.

As if it were an omen, he found an undisturbed satchel of melange. This he reverently accepted as a gift from Shai-Hulud. It was more spice than he had ever carried at one time, but he would not consume it, nor would he sell it. Rather, he would write a message with the reddish brown powder, spreading it on the sand. Back in his base station, he planned carefully for two days, then he left again.

Selim rode a large worm through the night, back across the

sands toward Naib Dhartha's village. In the shadow of a rock escarpment, he slept through the next day and then began his trek on foot, keeping close to the rocks. He knew these footpaths and byways well, having explored them as a child. After creeping along in the shadows, he hid in a comfortable crevice, waiting for full darkness, carrying his satchel of melange. . . .

When the night was deep and the stars overhead prickled like billions of icy eyes, he hurried out in front of the cliffs onto the wind-smoothed sands. He would do this to the best of his ability, on a grand scale. With light irregular footsteps, he ran along the canvas of powder sand, spilling the melange from the satchel in lines, making looping letters that would look like dried blood on the dunes.

Old Glyffa had taught him how to read and write during a time when she had felt benevolent toward him, ignoring other villagers—including Ebrahim's father and Naib Dhartha himself—who wondered what the point of such education could be.

Selim made sure to finish before the second moon rose. It took him well over an hour to write his three simple words, and at the end his spice was almost gone. With his message completed, he hurried back to his shelter in the rocks. He could have caught a worm to begin his journey back home. But instead he waited for the sunrise.

Just after dawn, he watched dozens of faces with wide eyes and open mouths peering out of the cave openings. In obvious disbelief, they stared into the desert and chattered and called to one another. Rapidly a crowd gathered along a ledge overlooking the sandy wasteland. He heard their muffled shouts of surprise and could not stop grinning. A pinch of melange on his lips made him feel even better.

Among the excited observers, he could barely make out the dark-haired figure of Naib Dhartha, who stood glowering at the three words the young outcast had written on the sand.

I AM SELIM.

He could have said more, explained more, but Selim felt that the mystery was better. The naib would know *he* was the person who had ridden the worm, both the first time when he'd shown off his skills and again when he'd destroyed the spice-gathering camp. Buddallah had chosen him, and now the evil naib must live in fear. The young man lounged back against the rock, chuckling to himself and savoring the flavor of melange.

After today, they all knew he was alive . . . and Naib Dhartha would understand that he had made a life-long enemy.

For weeks after returning from one shattered life to another, Serena Butler had gently sidestepped her father's suggestion that she return to her role in the League Parliament. For now she preferred the City of Introspection, the quiet and peaceful gardens. The philosophical students there preferred their contemplative privacy, and left her alone.

Her view of the war, the League, and of life itself had suffered a dramatic change, and she needed time to assess her new role in the universe and find ways to *help* once again. She felt that she could possibly do even more than before. . . .

The story of Serena's captivity, her murdered baby, and the rebellion on Earth had spread quickly. At the urging of Iblis Ginjo, the preserved body of little Manion had been placed in a small plaz-walled tomb in Zimia, a memorial symbolizing just one of the billions of victims of the thinking machines.

A tireless spokesman, Iblis had slept little since his arrival in the capital city, spending every hour with delegates, passionately describing the horrors of captive humans, of the cruel cymeks, of Omnius, trying to put together a massive force of League warships to rescue the humans of Earth. The escaped rebel leader wanted the Salusans to accept him as a hero.

As Serena's self-appointed prolocutor, Iblis spoke first-hand of the Synchronized Worlds, telling the awful story of how the robot Erasmus had killed innocent Manion and how Serena herself had dared to raise her fists against the thinking machines. Through her selfless bravery against the cruel masters, she had incited a rebellion that had brought the Earth-Omnius to a standstill.

Iblis employed his well-honed speaking abilities and convinced many people of his sincerity. He had in mind a public strategy that included passionate rallies hosted by Serena herself. She was the perfect person to act as the heart around whom a scaled-up rebellion could coalesce. But Serena remained in seclusion, unaware of the groundswell that was occurring in her name.

Without her, Iblis decided to take up the cause of human freedom anyway, even if he had to make every decision himself. He could not permit such a tremendous opportunity to wither and vanish. He felt the power of opinion building in the city of Zimia, forging into another weapon for him to use. Even the League politicians wanted to go rescue the heroic human fighters on Earth—but they discussed and debated endlessly in Parliament, just as Serena had warned they would.

Now, meeting privately with Segundo Harkonnen at the officer's request, Iblis felt uneasy in the cramped room of the Armada headquarters. Apparently these chambers were part of an old military prison, where suspected deserters had once been interrogated. Narrow rectangular windows encircled the room, and Xavier paced the floor, his silhouette eclipsing the small amount of daylight that filtered in.

"Tell me how you came to be a leader of human work crews," the officer asked. "A priviliged trustee, like Vorian Atreides, serving the thinking machines and reaping benefits while other humans suffered."

Iblis gave a dismissive gesture, pretending that the Segundo was joking. "I worked hard to earn privileges and rewards for my loyal workers," he said in his resonant voice. "We all benefited."

"Some of us are suspicious of your convenient enthusiasm."

Smiling in response, Iblis spread his hands. "Neither Vorian Atreides nor I have ever tried to hide our pasts. Remember, to acquire inside information, you need someone who has actually been *inside*. You will not find better sources of information than the two of us. Serena Butler has many insights, as well."

He remained calm. Iblis had faced, and fooled, the Titan Ajax—a much more terrifying and masterful interrogator than Segundo Harkonnen. "The League would be foolish not to seize this opportunity," Iblis added. "We have the means to help the human fighters on Earth."

"It is too late for that." Xavier stepped closer, looking stern. "You triggered the revolt, then left your followers behind to be slaughtered."

"I came here to get help from the League. We don't have much time if we are to rescue the survivors."

Xavier's face was stony. "There are no survivors . . . on the entire planet. *None*."

Stunned, Iblis was slow to respond. "How is that possible? Before we departed on the *Dream Voyager*, I left a competent, loyal man in charge. I assumed that he—"

"Enough of this, Xavier," a new voice came from an unseen speaker in the dim walls. "There is enough guilt and blood to cover all of our hands. Let's decide what to do next, instead of trying to turn one of our greatest potential resources against us."

Xavier stood stiffly, facing a blank wall. "As you wish, Viceroy."

The walls of the interrogation chamber shimmered and faded to reveal a hidden observation room, in which a dozen men and women sat in tribunal fashion. Dizzy, Iblis recognized Viceroy Butler at the center of the group and Vorian Atreides looking satisfied off to one side.

The Viceroy rose from his seat. "Iblis Ginjo, we are a special committee of Parliament here to investigate this terrible news from Earth."

Iblis could not restrain himself. "But the eradication of all life on Earth? How can this be?"

Xavier Harkonnen said in a somber voice, "As soon as your ship arrived here, the Armada dispatched its fastest scout. After several weeks, the pilot has just returned with his full, terrible report. Only thinking machines remain on Earth. Every single rebel is dead. Every slave, every child, every trustee. It is likely they were all exterminated before the *Dream Voyager* even reached Salusa Secundus."

Viceroy Butler activated several large screens built into the walls, which depicted horrific scenes, piles of mangled corpses, marching robots and cymeks slaughtering crowds of humans that had been rounded up. Image after image appeared, in gruesome detail. "Earth, the homeworld of humanity, is now nothing more than a vast graveyard."

"Too late," Iblis mumbled in a daze. "All those people . . ."

The conversation paused as crowd noises came from outside the building, chants of, "Serena! Serena!" He was shocked to hear her name.

"Iblis Ginjo, I cannot express enough gratitude that you and your friend brought my daughter back to me," Viceroy Butler said. "Unfortunately, the man you left in charge of the revolt was not up to the challenge."

Vorian Atreides looked stern. "Nobody could have succeeded there, Viceroy. Not Iblis, not myself. It was only a matter of time."

Segundo Harkonnen appeared angry. "You're saying it's pointless to fight against Omnius, and any revolt is doomed to failure? We proved that idea wrong at Giedi Prime—"

"I was at Giedi Prime as well, Segundo. Remember? You shot at me and severely damaged my ship."

Xavier's brown eyes flashed with anger. "Yes, I remember, son of Agamemnon."

"The uprising on Earth was a grand example," Vor said, "but the participants were only slaves, armed with little more than their hatred for the thinking machines. They never had a

chance." He turned to look at the members of the special committee. "The League Armada, on the other hand, is a different
story altogether."

Seeing the opportunity to press the point, Iblis said in a
booming voice, "Yes, look what a mob of untrained slaves
managed to achieve. Then imagine what a coordinated military
response might accomplish." Outside, the voices of the dem-
onstrators grew louder. Iblis continued, "The losses on Earth
must not go unavenged. The death of Viceroy Butler's grand-
child—your own son, Segundo Harkonnen—cannot go unpunished!"

Vor could not tear his gaze from Xavier, trying to see him
as the brave man who had stolen Serena's heart, and then had
married her sister. *I would have waited forever for her.*

Finally, he focused on Iblis Ginjo. Vor did not particularly
like the rebel leader, whose motivations were not clear to him.
Iblis seemed obsessively fascinated with Serena, but it was not
love. Nevertheless, Vor did agree with the man's assessment.

Speaking loudly, Iblis continued, as if he had been brought
here to address the tribunal members, and not to answer their
questions. "The events on Earth are a setback, nothing more.
We can rise above it, if we have the will to do so!"

Some of the representatives were caught up in his enthusiasm. Outside, the crowds grew more agitated, and security
troops could be heard over a public address system, attempting
to maintain order.

As Vor looked on, Iblis gazed from face to face and then
into the distance, as if only he could see something there. The
future? Iblis gestured with his hands as he spoke. "The people
of Earth were slaughtered because I encouraged them to op-
pose their machine masters, but I feel no personal guilt over
this. A war must begin somewhere. Their sacrifice has demonstrated the depth of the human spirit. Consider the example
of Serena Butler and her innocent baby, what *she* endured and
still survived."

Vor saw agitation on Xavier Harkonnen's face, but the officer said nothing.

Iblis smiled and stretched out his hands. "Serena could have an important role in the new force that will overwhelm the machines, if she only recognizes her potential." He spoke directly to Manion Butler, in an increasingly fervent voice. "Others may try to take credit for it, but Serena was the true spark of the great revolt on Earth. *Her* child was slain, and she raised *her* hands against the thinking machines, for all to see. Think of it! What an example she is to the entire human race."

Iblis stepped closer to the tribunal members. "All across the League Worlds, people will hear of her bravery and feel her pain. They will rally to her cause, in her *name*, if asked to do so. They will rise up in an epic struggle for freedom, a holy crusade . . . a *jihad*. Listen outside—do you hear them chanting for her?"

There it is, Iblis thought. He had made the religious connection recommended by Cogitor Eklo. It didn't matter what particular creed or theology they followed—of paramount importance was the *fervor* that only zealousness could provide. If the movement was going to be large, it needed to touch upon the emotions of people, needed to draw them into battle without any thought of failing, without concern for their own safety.

Following a long, poignant pause, he added, "I am already spreading the word. Ladies and gentlemen, we have the makings of much more than a revolt here, something that sets apart the soul of mankind from the soulless thinking machines. With your help, it could be a tremendous victory borne on the wings of human passion . . . and *hope*."

Without recognizing it, humankind created a weapon of mass destruction—one that only became apparent after machines took over every aspect of their lives.

—BARBAROSSA,
Anatomy of a Rebellion

In an uproar, red-faced League delegates argued over the consequences of the genocide on Earth. Serena sat stony-faced, the first time she had entered the Hall of Parliament in the weeks since returning home, but her presence did not quell the usual tedious discussions.

"The struggle against Omnius has gone on for centuries!" bellowed the Patriarch of Balut. "There is no need to do anything drastic which we will later regret. I grieve for the bloodshed, but we never had any realistic hope for saving the slaves of Earth anyway."

"You mean slaves . . . like Serena Butler?" From his guest seat, Vorian Atreides interrupted with a glance in her direction, disregarding protocol or political traditions. "I'm glad we didn't *all* give up so easily."

Xavier frowned at him, though he had been thinking the same thing. He considered the son of Agamemnon a loose cannon, with no respect for order, but he himself was often frustrated by the ponderous pace of formal political debates.

If Serena had been confident about the workings of Parliament, she would never have gone blundering off to Giedi Prime in the first place, thus forcing the League's hand.

In an equally loud voice, the interim Magnus of restored Giedi Prime said, "Just because the situation has gone on for a thousand years, is that an excuse for us to become *accustomed* to it? The thinking machines have already escalated the war with their attack on Zimia and Rossak, their invasion of Giedi Prime. This Earth disaster is just another challenge."

"It's a challenge we cannot ignore," Viceroy Butler said.

❧

NOW, ACCORDING TO the agenda, Xavier stepped into the recording shell that surrounded the oratory podium. Projection screens enhanced his image and his speech; overblown determination formed deep creases on his face.

Out in the tiers of seats that rose above the speaking pit, Iblis Ginjo sat ensconced in a box reserved for distinguished visitors; he wore expensive finery provided by Salusan tailors.

Xavier's voice boomed forth, the commanding tone he used when directing his Armada ships. "We can no longer content ourselves with a *reactive* war. We must take the battle to the thinking machines, for our very survival."

"Are you suggesting we become as aggressive as Omnius?" shouted Lord Niko Bludd from the fourth tier of seats.

"No!" Xavier looked at the red-bearded noble and said in a calm, firm voice, "I'm saying we must be *more* aggressive than the machines, *more* destructive, *more* intent on victory!"

"That will only provoke them to do something even worse," yelled the County General from Hagal, a barrel-chested man in a red tunic. "We can't risk that. Many of the Synchronized Worlds have large human populations, even more numerous than the slaves killed on Earth, and I don't think—"

Zufa Cenva, stern in her regal glory, cut him off, her voice icy with scorn. "Then why don't you just surrender Hagal to the Synchronized Worlds, County General, if you tremble so much at the thought of combat? It would save Omnius the trouble."

Serena Butler stood, and a sudden hush settled over the audience. She spoke in a firm, clear voice fueled by her own passion. "The thinking machines will never leave us alone. You are fooling yourselves if you believe otherwise."

She swept her gaze along the rows of seats. "You have all seen the shrine to my son, who was murdered by the thinking machines. Perhaps it is easier to comprehend the tragedy of a single victim than of billions. But that child only symbolizes the horrors Omnius and the Synchronized Worlds wish to inflict upon us." She raised a clenched fist. "We must declare a crusade against the machines, a holy war—a jihad, in the name of my murdered son Manion. It must be . . . Manion Butler's Jihad."

In the muttering and the hot emotions of the audience, Xavier said, "We will never be safe until we destroy them."

"If we knew how to accomplish that," complained Lord Bludd, "we would have won the war long ago."

"But we do know how to accomplish it," Xavier insisted from the lecture dome, with a nod to Serena. "We have known for a thousand years."

He lowered his voice so that all the members of the great hall grew quiet to hear him. He glared from face to face, then said, "Blinded by Tio Holtzman's new defenses, we have ignored the old-fashioned final solution that has been in front of us all along."

"What are you talking about?" asked the Balut Patriarch.

Near him, Iblis Ginjo sat with his arms folded across his chest, nodding as if he knew what was coming.

"Atomics," Xavier said. The word fell hard and loud, like the detonation of a forbidden warhead. "A full and total bombardment with atomics. We can sterilize Earth, vaporizing every robot, every sentient machine, every gelcircuit."

The uproar took only seconds to reach a crescendo, and Xavier shouted back into the clamor. "For more than a thousand years we have maintained our atomics. But they have always been meant as a last resort—doomsday weapons to destroy planets and obliterate life." He jabbed a finger at the representatives. "We have sufficient warheads in our planetary stockpiles, but Omnius considers them an empty threat, because we've never dared to use them. It is time to surprise the thinking machines and make *them* regret their complacency."

Using his priority as Viceroy, Manion Butler interjected, "The machines captured and tortured my daughter. They murdered a grandson who carried my own name, a boy neither I nor his own father ever got to meet." The once-rotund man was much thinner now and stooped from weariness. His hair hung limp and unkempt, as if he usually slept badly. "The damned machines deserve the most terrible punishment we can mete out."

The clamor continued, and finally, surprisingly, Serena Butler made her way to the speakers' dome beside Xavier. "Earth is nothing more than a festering graveyard now, with evil thinking machines trampling through it. Every living human being there has already been slaughtered." She drew a deep breath, her lavender eyes blazing. "What is left to preserve? *What have we got to lose?*"

Projected images flashed around the chamber as Serena continued. "The captive population of Earth rebelled, and they were killed for their effort. *All of them!*" Her voice thundered through every speaker in the hall. "Shall we allow that sacrifice to mean nothing? Should the thinking machines suffer no consequences?" She made a disgusted sound. "Or should *Omnius* pay?"

"But Earth is the birthplace of humanity!" gasped the acting Magnus of Giedi Prime. "How can we even contemplate such destruction?"

"And the rebellion on Earth has launched this Jihad," Serena said. "We must spread news of this glorious uprising to other Synchronized Worlds, perhaps spark similar revolts on machine planets. But first we must eradicate the Omnius on Earth . . . no matter what it takes."

"Can we afford to turn down such an opportunity?" Xavier Harkonnen said. "We have the atomics. We have Tio Holtzman's new shields to protect our ships. We have the will of the people, who shout Serena Butler's name in the streets. By God, we must do something *now*."

"Yes," Iblis said in an even voice that nevertheless cut across the murmurs. "It is *by God* that we must do this."

The representatives were stunned and frightened, but no dissent rose. Finally, after a long, agitated silence, Viceroy Manion Butler demanded that the League of Nobles submit the question for a formal decision.

Somberly, the vote was taken . . . and passed by acclamation.

"It is decided, then. Earth, the ancient birthplace of humanity, will become the first tombstone of the thinking machines."

Creativity follows its own rules.

—NORMA CENVA,
unpublished laboratory notes

In the laboratory tower overlooking the broad Isana, Norma Cenva stood at her cluttered workstation. New glowglobes bobbled in the air like ornaments over her head; she had not bothered to deactivate them, even though the dawn had grown bright. She didn't want to interrupt her train of thought.

She pointed a pen-sized projection mechanism at a slanted table. Magnetically scribed sheets flipped silently through the air, blueprint films of a flagship-class ballista, the largest battleship in the League Armada.

Norma changed the setting on the handheld plan projector and swung the shimmering blueprint films out into the open room. She segregated one deck of the vessel and then walked into the enlarged holo-image, a stroll in which she made mental calculations for the shield-generator installation so that the small field radius would overlap for complete protection.

Savant Holtzman was off attending another public function, where he would no doubt celebrate his successes with false modesty. Of late, he had only worked with Norma for an hour or so in the mornings before flitting off to prepare for luncheon engagements, followed by evening banquets at Lord Bludd's mansion. Eventually he would come to talk to her about the nobles and politicians he had met, as if he felt some need to impress her.

Norma actually didn't mind the time alone and tried to do her work without complaint. Mostly Holtzman left her in peace to perform the calculations necessary to install overlapping shields on the largest Armada ships. The Savant claimed he did not have time to do it himself, and he no longer trusted his cadre of equation solvers.

Norma felt the weight of responsibility, knowing the League Armada had sent out the call to arms for a concerted armaggeddon strike on Earth. A massive unified force of diverse warships was already gathering at Salusa Secundus in preparation for launch.

Holtzman basked in his sudden inflated importance. To Norma, it seemed that the laboratory work should speak for itself, without all of the promotional frivolity. But she could never hope to understand the political circles in which he traveled, and she wanted to believe that he was doing his best for the war effort through contacts with important people.

In the meantime, her mind thought of many tangential things, in detail, and she followed the internal paths of inquiry, seeking answers. Even obliterating the evermind on Earth would still leave complete copies of Omnius elsewhere in the Synchronized Worlds. Could thinking machines suffer such a thing as a psychological blow? On the scale of the Synchronized Worlds, a single planet did not seem a substantial enough target, and her concern made it difficult to focus on the calculations. Like sparks of heat lightning jumping from cloud to cloud, her thoughts skittered to new possibilities, fresh ideas.

Under the martial law Lord Bludd had imposed after Bel Moulay's slave uprising, Norma had felt increasingly isolated from her mentor. Two years ago, when she'd first received the summons to come to Poritrin, Tio Holtzman had been her role model and champion. Only gradually had she come to realize that, rather than simply appreciating her talent and employing it as a means of furthering their mutual goals, the scientist had become resentful of her.

Part of it was Norma's own fault. Her insistent warnings about both the abortive alloy-resonance generator and the lasgun-shield test had turned him against her. But it didn't seem fair for the Savant to dislike her just because she had been *correct*. Tio Holtzman seemed to place his own embarrassment above the furtherance of science.

She scratched her clumpy mouse-brown hair. What place did *ego* have in their work? In almost a year, none of his new concepts had amounted to anything.

By contrast, a certain project had been brewing in Norma's thoughts for a long time. In her mind's eye she saw the parts coming together, a grand design that would shake the foundations of the universe, theories and equations she could barely grasp. It would demand all of her energy and attention, and the potential benefits would rock the League even more than the development of personal shields.

Now Norma set aside the projected ballista diagram and stepped out of it, after using a holomarker to designate the point at which she had stopped her calculations. With her concentration freed, she could devote her efforts to matters of true importance. Her new idea excited her far more than shield calculations.

Inspiration, ever mysterious, had directed her toward a revolutionary possibility. She could almost see it working on an immense, staggering scale. A chill ran down her spine.

Although she could not quite solve the problems associated with her concept, she felt in her bones that Holtzman's field-equation breakthrough might be employed for something much more significant. While the scientist rested on his laurels and reveled in his success, Norma wanted to go in a new direction.

Having seen how the Holtzman Effect warped space in order to create a shield, she was convinced that the fabric of space itself could be *folded*, creating a shortcut across the universe. If such a feat could be accomplished, it might be possible to travel across vast distances in the wink of an eye, connecting two discrete points without regard to the separation between them.

Folding space.

But she could never develop such a stupendous concept with Tio Holtzman restraining her at every turn. Norma Cenva would have to work in secret. . . .

Quite obviously, our problems do not come from what we invent, but from how we use our sophisticated toys. The difficulties stem not from our hardware or software, but from ourselves.

—BARBAROSSA,
Anatomy of a Rebellion

In a thousand years, humanity had never assembled such a powerful, concentrated military force. From their separate space navies, each League World dispatched ships large and small: lumbering battleships, midsized cruisers, destroyers, escort ships, hundreds of large and small shuttles, thousands of kindjals and patrol craft. Many of them were armed with atomics . . . enough to sterilize Earth three times over.

Segundo Xavier Harkonnen was given command of the operation that had been his brainchild. Swelling with vessels and weapons and countless commanders from planetary defense systems, militias, and home guards, the unified Armada gathered at the orbital launch point above Salusa Secundus over the next three months. Prep crews emblazoned each vessel's hull with the open-hand sigil of the League of Nobles.

Munitions factories on Vertree Colony, Komider, and Giedi Prime had worked beyond peak-production levels without rest, and the aggressive schedule would continue during the long voyage of the expanded Armada, since the fleet would likely suffer devastating losses against the Earth-Omnius. Replacements would always be needed—always, until the war was done.

Before the departure of the unified Armada, all remaining planetary forces throughout the League Worlds were placed on high alert. Even if the culminating atomic strike succeeded in smashing the thinking machines on Earth, other incarnations of the computer evermind would likely retaliate.

Annihilating the Earth-Omnius would be a much-needed victory for mankind, signaling a new turn in the war. Long ago, free humanity had stockpiled atomic warheads to threaten the thinking machines, but Omnius and his cymek generals had called the League's bluff. On Giedi Prime and elsewhere, humans had shown themselves unwilling to unleash the doomsday devices, thus rendering the threat impotent.

That was about to change.

Now the vengeful Armada would prove that humans had relinquished all restraint. Nuclear airbursts would generate electromagnetic pulses to obliterate the thinking machines' exotic gelcircuitry. Henceforth, every Omnius would fear a wave of atomic holocausts on the rest of the Synchronized Worlds.

Radioactive fallout, a demon from the nightmares of human civilization, would continue to damage the planet long after the battle was over. But that would fade with time, and eventually Earth would recover and return to life—without thinking machines.

∞

AT MAXIMUM SUSTAINABLE speed, the unified Armada's journey took over a month. Xavier wished there were some way to make the voyage faster. Even while outrunning photons in space, traversing great distances between star systems required time, too much of it.

As the task force approached Earth's solar system, Segundo Harkonnen shuttled from one battleship to another, reviewing the troops and equipment for the upcoming engagement. From the bridge of each vessel he spoke to groups of soldiers, inspiring them, instructing them.

The waiting was almost over.

By now, just under half of the Armada ships had been equipped with Holtzman's shield generators, and the atomics had been dispersed among both shielded and unshielded vessels. Xavier had considered waiting for more, but finally decided that further delay would cause greater harm than the installation of extra mechanisms could justify. Besides, some conservative nobles from individual planetary fleets had expressed skepticism about the unproven new technology. While those lords used planetary scrambler shields to cover their major cities and moons, they preferred to use reliable, proven technology in their warships. They knew the risks and accepted them.

Xavier focused on maintaining his own determination through the end of the horrific battle. After the attack on Earth, controversy would always be associated with his name, but he would not allow it to deter him. Achieving victory required him to utterly destroy the birthplace of the human race.

With such a terrible feather in his cap, how could history not curse the name of Xavier Harkonnen? Even if the machines were destroyed, no human would ever want to live on Earth again.

⊱

ON THE DAY before the powerful Armada reached Earth, Xavier summoned Vorian Atreides to the bridge of the ballista flagship. Xavier did not entirely trust the former Omnius collaborator, but kept his personal feelings separate from the needs of humanity.

Vor *had* made a compelling case that his firsthand technical knowledge of Earth-Omnius's capabilities made him a valuable asset. "No one else knows as much about the robotic forces. Even Iblis Ginjo doesn't have the background I do, since he was just a construction crew boss. Besides, he prefers to remain on Salusa."

Despite the blessing Vorian had received from the Sorceresses of Rossak and their proven ability to expose lies, Xavier could not help distrusting the son of Agamemnon for spending his life serving the machines. Was he a clever infiltrator sent by Omnius, or could Vor truly provide intelligence that would allow the Armada to exploit vulnerabilities on the Synchronized Worlds?

Vorian had been thoroughly interrogated—even examined by doctors familiar with implanted espionage devices—and everyone had proclaimed him clean. But Xavier wondered if the machines had somehow anticipated all those precautions and cleverly concealed something in his brain, a tiny, potent device with machine components that could be triggered at a critical point and cause him to take some devastating action against the League of Nobles?

Serena had said that all humans must be freed from the oppression of thinking machines. She wanted Xavier to start with this one man, by giving him a chance. In her heart, she wanted to believe that any person, once exposed to the concepts of freedom and individuality, would reject the robotic slavemasters and choose independence. And when Serena asked it of him, Xavier could not refuse her.

"All right, Vorian Atreides," he had said. "I will grant you the opportunity to prove your worth—but under strict controls. You will be confined to certain areas, and watched at all times."

Vor had given him a wry smile. "I am used to being watched."

Now the two men stood together on the flagship bridge. Xavier paced the deck, hands clasped behind him and shoulders squared. He looked across empty space toward the bright yellow home star, which grew larger every hour.

Vor remained silent, keeping his thoughts to himself and considering the star-studded blackness. "I never thought I would return so soon. Especially not like this."

"Are you afraid your father will be there?" Xavier asked.

The dark-haired young man stepped closer to the broad window, staring at the growing blue target planet. "If no humans survive on Earth, the Titans have little reason to stay. They have probably been sent to other Synchronized Worlds by now." He pursed his lips. "I hope the Earth-Omnius has not maintained a large neo-cymek force."

"Why? Our firepower could destroy them just as easily."

Vor gave him a wry glance. "Because, Segundo Harkonnen, thinking machines and robotic ships are *predictable*, set in their ways. We know how they will respond. Cymeks, on the other hand, are volatile and innovative. Machines with human minds. Who knows what *they* might do?"

"Just like humans," Xavier said.

"Yes, but with the ability to cause much more destruction."

With a grim smile, the Segundo turned to look at his turncoat companion. "Not for long, Vorian." They were men of the same age, and haunted beyond their years. "After today, nothing in the universe will match *our* ability to cause destruction."

❧

THE ARMADA BATTLE group converged on Earth like a gathering storm. Pilots ran across the interior decks to their individual ships, preparing to launch. Battleships and destroyers spat out swarms of kindjals, bombers, and scout ships. Patrol craft and point ships flew fast reconnaissance, verifying and updating the data provided by Vor Atreides.

The birthplace of humanity was a verdant sphere mottled with fleecy white clouds. Xavier Harkonnen gazed at the remarkable world. Even infested with the scourge of machines, it looked pristine, fragile, and vulnerable.

Soon, though, Earth would be nothing more than a blackened, lifeless ball. In spite of all he had said to convince skeptics and detractors, Xavier wondered how he could ever consider such a victory acceptable.

He drew a deep breath, not taking his eyes from the planet, which shimmered through a thin veil of his tears. He had a duty to do.

Xavier transmitted his order to the fleet. "Proceed with full-scale atomic bombardment."

Technology should have freed mankind from the burdens of life. Instead, it created new ones.

—TLALOC,
A Time for Titans

On Earth, Omnius's perimeter sensors detected the invading force. The evermind was astonished at the unpredictable audacity of the feral humans, as well as the sheer number and firepower of the combined vessels. For centuries, the *hrethgir* had hidden behind defensive barriers, afraid to venture into machine-controlled space. Why had no computer projection or scenario anticipated this bold assault on the Synchronized Worlds?

Via screens and contact terminals dispersed around the city grid, Omnius spoke to robots that were at work repairing damage from the recent abortive slave rebellion. He would have liked to discuss strategy with Erasmus—who, despite his myriad flaws, seemed to have some understanding of human irrationality. But the frustratingly contrary robot was out of touch, fled to distant Corrin.

Even his remaining Titans, who could occasionally explain human reactions, had been sent away to less-stable worlds, preventing the spread of the revolt. Thus, the evermind felt isolated and off-balance.

Reviewing scanner readings, Omnius determined that the human vessels must be loaded with nuclear warheads. Again, entirely unexpected! He calculated and recalculated, and all the scenarios turned out badly for him. He felt the initial glimmerings of what humans might have called "shocked disbelief."

Since he could not disregard his own projections, the Earth-Omnius responded accordingly. He launched robotic vessels in a full-scale defensive cordon to prevent the League warships from breaking through to Earth. He dispersed a swarm of mechanical watcheyes into orbit, to observe the engagement from all points of view. Through separate subroutines, he ran more than five thousand alternate simulations, until he was satisfied that he could choose the correct tactics for his robotic fleet.

But Omnius did not yet know about Holtzman's shields.

When the thinking machines fired explosives and kinetic projectiles, the front line of Armada battleships simply shrugged off the counterattack. The blasts echoed harmlessly through the vacuum of space. And the League vessels kept coming.

Rebuffed, the robot ships regrouped and waited for modified orders, while Omnius's internal gelcircuitry paths sizzled with his struggle to comprehend.

The first *hrethgir* bombers streaked into the atmosphere, hundreds upon hundreds of mismatched ships coming toward the surface. Each one of them carried an old-style nuclear warhead.

Omnius made new projections. For the first time, he considered the realistic odds of his own destruction.

❧

INDEPENDENT AND DETERMINED, Vorian Atreides flew a small, shielded craft, one of the Salusan kindjals with augmented weaponry. He carried no atomics himself—Segundo Harkonnen did not trust him that far—but Vor could do his part to guard against enemy ships and allow the warhead-laden bombers to complete their mission.

This was quite different from his duties aboard the *Dream Voyager*.

Segundo Harkonnen had wanted to keep him tucked safely out of the way aboard the flagship, where Vor could provide tactical advice against the machines. But he had begged for hands-on participation in the defeat of Omnius. As the son of Agamemnon, Vor had already provided exhaustive information on thinking-machine warships, their armor, their integral weapons. Now it was time to put that knowledge to work.

"Please," he had said to Xavier. "I brought Serena back safely to you. If for no other reason, won't you grant me my request?"

The Segundo's stricken expression told Vor that Xavier still loved her deeply. The officer had turned his back on Vor, as if to hide his emotions. "Take a ship, then. Get yourself in the thick of the fighting . . . but come back alive. I don't think Serena could tolerate losing you on top of all the other pain she has suffered." These were the first kind words Vor had heard from this enigmatic man, the first time anyone had suggested that Serena cared anything for him.

Xavier finally looked over his shoulder and gave him a guarded smile. "Don't betray my trust." Vor had sprinted to the ballista's bays and chosen a kindjal of his own. . . .

Now, the human strike force funneled toward Omnius's central computer complex. The thinking machines hammered the dispersed Armada ships with suicidal determination, destroying hundreds of unshielded bombers, patrol craft, and kindjals. Some of the shields failed, overheated or poorly installed, and the battle grew more furious. Vor flew in the thick of it.

Then, in the midst of a free-for-all dogfight, Vorian saw a slower thinking-machine ship rising up, escorted by a dense cluster of automated vessels. The solitary guarded craft plowed through the swarm of Armada ships, avoiding direct confrontation.

Trying to sneak away.

Vor narrowed his gray-eyed gaze. At a time like this, why

would a single robot ship be outbound, heading into space? Omnius should have been drawing together all of his resources. The young man's instincts told him that this lone vessel should not be ignored.

Trying to concentrate on the fight around him, Vor fired his projectile weapons. Energy shells vaporized several robotic ships and disoriented others, allowing four more Armada bombers to get through.

All the while, high above him, the fleeing robot vessel continued out of the atmosphere on an escape trajectory, leaving the great battle behind. What could Omnius possibly be planning? What was that ship carrying? None of the other Armada fighters took any notice of it.

Vor knew he had to do something. This was vital—he could sense it in his gut.

Segundo Harkonnen had given him strict orders to accompany the warhead-carrying ships until they dropped their nuclear payloads. But things could change in the heat of battle. Besides, he wasn't a machine, blindly following orders. He could innovate.

As he continued to watch the vessel climb beyond the thinning ionosphere, he had a sudden realization of what must be happening. It was an *update ship*, carrying a complete copy of Earth-Omnius, the thoughts and data of the evermind up to the very moment of the attack! It would include a comprehensive record and analysis of the slave uprising and the orders to exterminate all humans.

If such information were uploaded to other incarnations of Omnius, all Synchronized Worlds would be warned! They could prepare defenses against future League attacks.

Vor could not allow that to happen. "There's something I have to do," he transmitted on the local channel to his nearby escorts. "I can't let that robot ship get away." Abandoning the bombers under his protection, he swung his kindjal up and away, breaking from his original course.

Vor heard howls of outrage from the human captains he'd been assigned to guard. "What are you doing?" A robotic defender surged into the gap and fired upon the Armada ships.

"It's an update ship! It carries a copy of Omnius." He raced farther away, just as two robot vessels converged on the carriers Vor had been assigned to protect. His comrades cursed him as the robots opened fire, making short work of the human vessels. But Vor set his jaw, knowing his decision was morally and tactically right.

Seeing his departure, other Armada ships shouted curses after him. "Coward!"

"Traitor!"

Resigned, Vor said, "I'll explain later." Then he switched off his comsystem so he could concentrate on his quarry. His background with thinking machines would always make humans think the worst of him. The prospect of censure and ill-will did not bother him. He had a job to do.

Within moments, Omnius's fighters had struck one of the forsaken bombers, but fresh Armada escorts came in and shot two of the machine ships out of the sky. The remaining bombers kept flying, on course.

Earth's open sky was filled with the ion trails of large and small Armada ships sowing nuclear warheads like kernels of grain. Robotic defenders targeted the falling atomics, exploding them in the air and dispersing clouds of radioactive shrapnel. This foiled the delicate detonator mechanisms and prevented nuclear chain reactions.

Even so, some of the atomics should get through.

≈

AT THE HEIGHT of the battle, Earth-Omnius ran out of viable options. With the Armada fleet spread like a swarm of killer insects, the robotic defenders sacrificed themselves by careening into clusters of kindjals.

To Segundo Harkonnen, it became painfully obvious that only those vessels protected by Holtzman's shields had any chance of survival. A few of the systems had failed, leading to the destruction of even the shielded ships. But there could be no turning back now.

The twenty largest Armada battleships hung in stationary

orbit, dispatching wave after wave of small attackers, emptying the stockpiles of League atomics. At the same time, five destroyers descended to dump patterns of guided nuclear missiles. The wide dispersal created enough coverage from overlapping blast pulses to assure that all Omnius substations would be fried.

In a last vengeful attack, AI projectiles converged on the huge ballistas. Bombs with computer minds, the projectiles were intent on reaching their programmed targets. Ignoring the smaller bombers and kindjals, they looped back to intercept any evasive trajectories the battleship captains might attempt, and disregarded defensive decoys that were fired to draw the robots off.

On the receiving end of the defensive volley, Xavier Harkonnen stood on the bridge of his flagship, gripping the control rails, muttering a silent prayer to the genius of Tio Holtzman. "Let's hope those overlapped shields hold! Hang on!"

Six self-guided projectiles slammed at near-relativistic speeds into the ballista's Holtzman barriers and detonated. But the shimmering shields held.

Xavier's knees felt weak with relief. The battleship crew cheered.

But around him, other Armada spacecraft—those without shields—did not fare so well. Although the hodgepodge of League ships fired a constant stream of suppressant shots, several AI projectiles broke through, vaporizing any unshielded human vessel in their way. Even one of the protected ballistas suffered from vulnerable spots when two of the small layered shields flickered, creating a chink in the armor. With the constant pummeling from the thinking machines, several robot missiles broke through.

Eleven of the largest battleships were vaporized into glowing wreckage, with all hands lost. Only eight of the huge vessels, each one covered by Holtzman shields, remained intact. A large percentage of the overall Armada fleet had already been annihilated.

Battered and shaken, Xavier watched the damage continue. He clenched his fists as he issued firm orders, maintaining a cool voice for the sake of his troops. His fingers felt sticky with the imagined blood of the hundreds of thousands of soldiers he had already sacrificed on this terrible day.

With sick anger, he watched Vorian Atreides flee the battlefield. At least the damnable spawn of Agamemnon had taken only a single kindjal, and the segundo could not waste time or energy pursuing him. Back on Salusa, Xavier would bring the deserter up on charges. If anyone made it back. *Damn his treachery!* Xavier had been right about him all along.

The thinking machines eliminated one League vessel after another, but Xavier kept sending his fleet forward. After so much effort and loss, he could not withdraw. Failure would bankrupt the human soul and lead to the end of freedom in the Galaxy.

It appeared to be a rout, in the machines' favor. Only a fraction of the attacking human force had managed to reach their target points and drop cargo loads of nuclear bombs across the continents of Earth.

Then the first atomic detonations went off.

⬥

VOR RACED UPWARD and away with the update ship always in his sights. Acceleration pressed him against the pilot's seat and forced his lips against his teeth. His eyes watered, his muscles stretched taut. But he did not relent. The lone Omnius vessel had already left the atmosphere and was streaking away from the unified Armada forces.

Below, multiple atomics began to detonate in a succession of dazzling nuclear flowers that illuminated the sky, sterilized the continents, and washed over every gelcircuit. . . .

Vor increased his kindjal's speed and considered surprise tactics, knowing the update ship ahead of him would be captained by an inflexible robot. He was more than a match for any thinking machine's methodical imagination.

Both ships pulled away from the embattled Earth. All across the dwindling blue-green sphere behind them, white-and-yellow fireclouds erupted in flashes that hurt Vor's eyes. The major nuclear storm across the skies and land masses must have diverted the Armada's attention from him. Nobody saw the vital importance of what he was trying to do.

The update ship climbed above the ecliptic, constantly increasing speed. The robot captain could endure accelerations that no human could survive. Nevertheless, Vorian shot after it, at the edge of consciousness, barely able to breathe against the crushing force. His League kindjal was faster than his prey—a mere update-class ship—and he closed the gap. With hands that seemed to weigh hundreds of kilograms, he powered up his ship's weapons.

In the battle for Earth he had vaporized a dozen machine fighters, but in this case Vor meant only to cripple the targeted vessel. As an update ship, it would have only minimal armor, like the *Dream Voyager*. He intended to stop the vessel in space and board it.

As soon as his target came within range, high above the solar system and at the edge of the diffuse cometary halo, the fleeing robot captain went through a predictable set of maneuvers.

Vor opened fire. His precision shots damaged the exhaust ports so that the engines began to build toward an overload. Unable to properly vent its waste heat, the vessel would either explode or shut down.

As the wounded ship lurched forward, decelerating, Vor shot two warning projectiles across its bow. The shockwaves knocked the update ship off course. "Stand down and prepare to be boarded!"

The robot responded with surprising sarcasm. "I am aware of the various bodily orifices humans possess. Therefore, I invite you to take a power tool and insert it where the—"

"Old Metalmind?" Vor cried. "Let me come aboard. It's Vorian Atreides."

"That cannot be true. Vorian Atreides would never fire upon *me*."

Vor transmitted his image, not surprised that Seurat would be captaining another update ship, since Omnius did not vary in his routines. Seurat's mirror-smooth oval face emitted a colorful curse that Vor had often used after losing a military game.

Vor linked his craft with the damaged vessel. Knowing the risk, he entered via the main access hatch and marched through the confined interior toward the command bridge.

My definition of an army? Why, tame killers, of course!

—GENERAL AGAMEMNON,
Memoirs

From deep within his widely distributed citadels of power, the Omnius evermind watched over Earth. His mobile and stationery watcheyes recorded every facet of the bold human attack. He saw the tide of battle turn.

Omnius studied the trajectories of the thousands of spacecraft that came in, counted the numbers that his robotic defenders destroyed.

Even so, some of the atomics got through.

With a separate subset of calculational routines, Omnius maintained a tally of the thinking-machine vessels he had lost. Individually, those robot ships were expendable and could easily be replaced from stock materials and designs. Fortunately, Seurat's update ship had broken through the descending masses of *hrethgir* vessels and escaped outward into the solar system. His important thoughts and decisions would be distributed among the Synchronized Worlds.

In spite of the sheer computational ability devoted to the question, Omnius still had not found a solution to the crisis by the time the first atomic warheads detonated above him. Nuclear air bursts sent out electromagnetic pulses that scoured the air and surface of Earth. Waves of energy spread, and in a flash obliterated every gelcircuitry network and thinking-machine mind, as if they were gasoline-soaked tissue paper touched by a spark.

Earth-Omnius was in the midst of an important thought when the shockwave consumed him.

⊱

IN THE PAST, the wisecracking robot captain had carried no private weapons. Vor, however, carried an electronic scrambler, a short-range circuitry-damaging device designed for hand-to-hand combat against thinking machines.

"So, you've come back to join me, after all," Seurat said. "Bored with your humans already? They aren't as fascinating as I am, are they?" He simulated a raucous laugh that Vor had heard many times before. "Did you know that your father considers you a traitor? Perhaps you now feel guilty for deactivating me, stealing the *Dream Voyager* and—"

"None of that, old Metalmind," Vor said. "This is another game you have lost. I can't allow you to deliever that update."

Seurat chuckled again. "Ah, humans and their silly fantasies."

"Nevertheless, we persist in our hopeless causes." Vor raised the electronic scrambler. "And sometimes we win."

Seurat said, "You were my friend, Vorian. Remember all the jokes I told you? In fact, I have a new one. If you make a cymek out of a mule's brain, what do you—"

Vor fired the electronic scrambler. Static arcs thrashed out like thin ropes, wrapping around Seurat's flexible body core of organic-polymer skin and reinforced fibers. The robot shuddered, as if from a seizure. Vor had adjusted the settings so that the burst shut down Seurat's systems, but did not destroy his brain core. That would have been tantamount to murder.

"The joke is on you, old friend," he said. "I'm sorry."

While Seurat remained frozen at his captain's station, Vor

searched the update ship until he found the sealed gelsphere, a complete reproduction of every thought Earth-Omnius had recorded just before the Armada attack.

Holding the shimmering compact data sphere, Vor took one last look at his stricken robot friend, then left the crippled update ship, sealing it behind him. He could not bring himself to destroy it. In any case, the ship was no longer a threat to humanity.

In his kindjal, Vor pulled away, leaving the thinking-machine vessel to drift in the vacuum of space, powerless and lost. It would wander far away from Earth and into the deep freeze of the solar system, to be lost forever in the cometary cloud.

❧

IN THE AFTERMATH, while Earth glowed with simmering atomic fires, Segundo Harkonnen gathered the mismatched remnants of his assault force. They had suffered tremendous losses, much higher than they had anticipated.

"It will take months just to scribe the names of those who sacrificed their lives here, Cuarto Powder," Xavier said to his adjutant. "And much longer to mourn them."

"All enemy ships and facilities are destroyed, sir," Powder responded. "We have accomplished our objective."

"Yes, Jaymes." He felt no elation over the victory. Only sadness. And anger toward Vorian Atreides.

When Agamemnon's son finally returned from deep space, the segundo dispatched a squadron of kindjals to escort him back under heavy guard. Seething, he shut down the Holtzman shields so the kindjals could bring in Vorian's ship. Many of the fighter pilots wanted to shoot him down as soon as his ship came within range, but Xavier forbade it. "We'll put the bastard on trial for desertion, perhaps treason."

Segundo Harkonnen strode into the docking bay on the ballista's lowest level, to the inside deck where the ships were being brought in with slide cranes and extruding hooks, all manually controlled by human operators.

The lean, dark-haired Vorian stepped boldly out of his battered vessel, looking surprisingly triumphant. The audacity of the man! Uniformed pilots surrounded Vor and brusquely checked him for weapons. The turncoat appeared irritated by their roughness, and protested when they took a package away from him, along with his sidearm.

Amazingly, his face lit up as soon as he saw Xavier. "So Earth-Omnius is destroyed? The attack was a success?"

"No thanks to you," Xavier said. "Vorian Atreides, I order you confined to the brig for the duration of our return to Salusa Secundus. There, you will face a League tribunal for your cowardly actions."

But the young man did not look frightened. With an expression of disbelief, he pointed to the package that one of the guards had. "Perhaps we should show the tribunal that as well?"

Vor's gray eyes were wary, but he grinned as Xavier unwound the plazwrap and popped open the seal to reveal a metallic ball that seemed made of gelatinous silver.

"It's a complete copy of Omnius," Vor said. "I intercepted and neutralized an update ship that was about to escape." He shrugged. "If I had allowed it to get away, all the other everminds would have received the complete intelligence of this attack. In exchange for all of our dead, Omnius would have lost nothing, and the other Synchronized Worlds would know about our Holtzman shields and our tactics. This entire operation would have been pointless. But I stopped the update ship."

Xavier looked at Vor, stunned. The surface of the orb was pliable to his touch, as if made of living tissue. The League had never imagined such a boon. This alone was worth the gigantic attack on Earth. The horrific loss of life. If Vor was telling the truth.

"I'm sure League intelligence officers will have a field day with this," Vor said, beaming. "Not to mention"—he added with a quirk of his eyebrow—"what a valuable hostage Omnius will make for us."

❧

THE BATTERED SHIPS of the unified Armada departed from the solar system, which was now devoid of murderous thinking machines.

Vor took one last look at wounded Earth, remembering the lush blue-and-green landscape and wispy clouds. This had once been a fabulously beautiful world, the birthplace of the human race, a showpiece of natural wonders.

But by the time Xavier ordered the fleet to set course for home, the planet was nothing more than a radioactive slag heap. It would take a long time for anything to ever live there again.

The logic which is sound for a finite system is not necessarily sound for an infinite universe. Theories, like living things, do not always scale up.

—ERASMUS,
secret records (from the Omnius databank)

On Corrin, the robot's villa followed a similar pattern to that of its counterpart on Earth, with both habitat and laboratory complexes designed by the creative mind of Erasmus. The slave pens behind the tall house were enclosed by high sandstone walls and wrought-iron gates, all topped by electro-barbs and energy-spike fields.

It felt very much like home to him. Erasmus looked forward to beginning work.

The enclosures teemed with humanity, nearly a thousand sweating bodies performing exercise routines beneath a red-giant sun that filled the sky like a huge bloodstain. It was a sweltering afternoon, but the slaves did not rest or complain, knowing that the robots would only punish them if they did.

The erudite thinking machine observed their daily routines from a bell tower on the south quadrant of his property, a favorite spot of his. Down in a pen, two old men collapsed under the glaring heat, and one of their downtrodden companions rushed to help them up. Thus, Erasmus counted three

punishable infractions: the two who faltered and the good sa-
maritan. Reasons were of no importance.

Erasmus had noted that the slaves grew increasingly agitated when he did *not* respond to their transgressions with
immediate discipline. He found it amusing to let the anticipation and fear grow within them, and then note how agitation
caused them to make even more mistakes. Human behavior
was the same on Corrin as on Earth, and he was glad to continue his experiments and studies without interruption.

He pressed a button, causing automatic weapons to fire ca-
priciously into one of the pens, killing or injuring dozens of
slaves. Confused and panicked, the survivors tried to get away,
but had nowhere to run. The fences were high and electrified.
Some of the captives pushed their fellows in front of them for
protection, while others played dead or hid under bodies. He
continued to fire, but this time aimed so that he didn't hit any
more of them.

Yes, it was very gratifying to be continuing his research
once more. He still had so much to learn.

An hour passed with no more gunfire, and people began to
move around again, more cautiously than before. They pushed
the bodies to one side and huddled together, not realizing what
was going on. Some of them became openly defiant, shouting
in the direction of the automatic weapons and waving their
fists. With careful settings, Erasmus shot their arms off, one
by one, and watched the victims writhe on the ground. Even
the bravest humans could be reduced to bleeding, blithering
fools.

"I see you are playing with your toys again," the Corrin-
Omnius said, from a viewing screen to the left of Erasmus in
the bell tower.

"Everything I do is for a purpose," Erasmus said. "I am
learning more and more."

The Corrin-Omnius did not know how badly the robot's
wager and the loyalty test had turned out with his counterpart
on Earth. Erasmus had learned a significant lesson from the
wildfire of rebellion he had inadvertently fostered, but the data
had raised a host of new questions. He did not want the ev-

ermind to engage in a full-scale war of eradication, committing genocide against all human captives on the Synchronized Worlds—even if he had to discreetly keep certain subsets of information to himself.

Even if he had to *lie*.

A fascinating prospect. Erasmus was not accustomed to thinking in such terms.

The main gate swung open, and robotic guards removed the bodies of the dead and injured, then prodded a new group of slaves into the pens. One of the newcomers, a large sallow-skinned man, whirled abruptly and tackled the nearest robot, clawing at the structural fibers and trying to disrupt the protected neurelectric circuitry. Bloodying his fingers to break a seal, the slave grabbed a handful of mobility components, causing the robot to stagger. Two other robots fell on the man, and in a macabre burlesque of what the slave had done, one of them slammed steel fingers into his chest, cracking through skin, cartilage, and the sternum to rip his heart out.

"They are no more than stupid animals," Omnius said, derisively.

"Animals cannot plot, scheme, and deceive," Erasmus said. "These slaves no longer seem so complacent. I detect seeds of rebellion, even here."

"No revolt could ever succeed on Corrin," said the voice of Omnius.

"One can never know everything, dear Omnius—not even you. And that is why we must remain eternally curious. While I can estimate crowd behavior to a reasonable extent, I cannot consistently predict what any given human will do next. This is a supreme challenge."

"It is self-evident that humans are a mass of contradictions. No model can reliably explain their behavior."

Erasmus gazed down at the slave pens. "Still, they *are* our enemies, and we must understand them. Only in that way can we assure our dominance."

The robot felt a strange surge in his sensory simulators. Anger? Frustration? On impulse, he ripped a small tympanic bell out of its housing in the tower and hurled it against the floor with a discordant clang. He found the sound . . . unsettling.

"Why did you damage that bell?" Omnius asked. "I have never seen you commit so unusual an act before."

Erasmus further assessed his feelings. He had seen humans do such things, releasing pent-up emotions in the form of a tantrum. From his perspective, though, he felt no sense of satisfaction. "It was . . . just one of my experiments."

Erasmus still had much to learn in his quest to absorb the essence of human nature, which he hoped to use as a springboard from which machine sophistication would rise even higher, reaching the zenith of existence. He gripped the tower railing with powerful, steely fingers, breaking off a chunk and letting it tumble to the pavement below. "I shall explain it to you later."

After observing his slaves for another moment, he turned back to the screen. "It would not be wise to exterminate all humans. Instead, through more intense subjugation methods, we could break their willingness and ability to resist."

The evermind, always enjoying the debate with Erasmus, delighted in catching a flaw. "But if we do that, Erasmus, are we not changing the fundamental character of the humans you wish to study? Is the observer not affecting the experiment?"

"An observer always affects the experiment. But I would rather change the subjects than destroy them. I will make my own decisions with respect to my humans here on Corrin."

Omnius finally said, "I do not understand you any more than I understand humans."

"I know that, Omnius. It will always be your weakness."

The robot looked fondly down at his enslaved humans as his guards carried off the corpses and the injured. Erasmus thought of all the wonderful things he had learned from this species . . . and how much more he could discover, if granted the opportunity. Their collective lives were balanced on a tightrope over a dark, bottomless chasm, and Erasmus stood with them. He would not give them up easily.

On the bright side, he saw that in his absence, two more sets of twins had been born. As always, the possibilities were endless.

Human life is not negotiable.

—SERENA BUTLER

I n honor of the bittersweet nuclear victory on Earth, the
League Worlds hosted a massive celebration for their returning heroes and a touching farewell for their fallen dead.

The battered ships had limped back after their long voyage,
while faster scouts and couriers raced back to Salusa Secundus
bearing the news and letting the League know what to expect
when the Armada arrived, scarred and diminished.

But the Earth-Omnius was destroyed, and the thinking machines had suffered a terrible blow. They clung to their triumph.

In the hot and humid arena, Vorian Atreides felt sticky with
perspiration in his dress uniform. No matter the weather, the
people would want to see him and Segundo Harkonnen in full
regalia. Xavier stood beside him now on the reviewing stand
as Viceroy Butler and Serena quieted the crowd, demanding
their full attention.

The two men—who had made their peace with each other
on the long journey back to Salusa Secundus—stood stiff-

backed in the shade of a covered viewing platform, along with
other dignitaries. Iblis Ginjo, dressed in fine clothes and proud
of his increasingly influential position, also sat in the gilded
VIP area.

"For leading our united League forces on the mission to
Earth, a landmark victory over the thinking machines," Viceroy Butler said, holding a ribbon and medal high, "for making
the difficult decisions and accepting the necessary challenge,
I award the Parliamentary Medal of Honor to the League's
most distinguished soldier, Segundo Xavier Harkonnen. It is
the highest award we can bestow, and we do so with heartfelt
gratitude."

Three hundred thousand spectators erupted in deafening
cheers. Many of these people had lost children, friends, and
parents in the Battle of Earth. In silence, Vor remembered how
many Armada fighters had fallen during the atomic steriliza-
tion of the planet. With his peripheral vision, he saw Xavier
Harkonnen's eyes glisten from the emotion of the moment as
the Viceroy draped the ribbon over his bowed head. Soon
there would be more battles to fight, more machine forces to
face.

Serena removed a second medal, different in design. "Next,
we honor a more unlikely hero, a man raised by the thinking
machines and blinded to their crimes. But he has seen the truth
and cast his lot with free humanity. The vital tactical information he provided about Earth's defenses helped to assure
our victory. In the heat of the battle, his fast thinking thwarted
Omnius's plan to escape, and provided the League with an
invaluable tool for humanity's continuing fight." Smiling at
him, Serena stepped forward. Vor held his head high. "We
award Vorian Atreides not only with the Exemplary Service
Medal, but also present him with the honorary rank of tercero
in the League Armada."

On cue, a squadron of antique aircraft and spacecraft
zoomed overhead. Proud mechanics and historians had recon-
ditioned the old vessels for the aerial show. Xavier and Vor
saluted the sky as the pilots tipped their wings, and the crowd
thundered its approval.

Iblis Ginjo, savoring his celebrity status before so many spectators, pushed his way close and shouted into the public address system: "These fine pilots are our future fighters of the Jihad. The thinking machines will not stand a chance!"

Wearing a preoccupied smile, Serena Butler pinned ribbons on a host of other heroes. She seemed wrapped up in thoughts of the past and of the insurmountable challenges humanity still needed to face. She seemed stronger now than ever before, but distant.

Vor stole glances at Xavier, saw the love for her on his ruddy face and the pain from knowing that they could never be together. Yet even Xavier's marriage to Octa gave Vor little chance to win Serena's heart. He recalled the first time he had seen her at the villa of Erasmus, how lovely and strong she had been, and defiant. Now, she seemed to have passed beyond those earlier troubles, to concern herself with impending crises that few people could understand. Deep inside, Serena seemed to be developing a different, awe-inspiring power.

Concluding her responsibilities in the victory celebration, Serena left the podium. She approached both Vor and Xavier as she departed, already intent on the plans that clamored in her mind. "I need to speak with both of you." Her eyes were bright but hard; her voice allowed no room for argument. "Come to the City of Introspection at sunset."

Vor and Xavier exchanged surprised looks, then nodded in unison.

❦

THE TWO FORMER adversaries dined together, sharing a bottle of Salusan shiraz and tiptoeing around the subject that weighed so heavily on their minds and hearts. Neither of them could guess what Serena intended to say.

As pastel oranges and pinks of sunset tinted the sky, the two League officers traveled into the hills and entered the high gates of the quiet compound. Inside, the residents moved from building to building, activating luminors on the outside walls.

Serena stood waiting for them just inside, and Vor thought

she looked rejuvenated, with more color in her features. His heart beat rapidly.

"Thank you for coming." She took each of them by the hand and led them along a gem-gravel path to an open garden. "We can talk here uninterrupted. Indeed, I have found this to be a place full of possibilities . . . but without politics. Here, I can do what needs to be done."

In a central area, surrounded by boxwood topiaries, water trickled from an ornamental pool, dribbling over a rock ledge and into another basin. Insects and nocturnal amphibians had already begun to practice their evening symphonies.

At the edge of the pool, three wooden chairs faced a small waterfall. Vor wondered if many people came here to contemplate, or if Serena had brought the chairs specially for this meeting. Serena crossed her hands on her lap and smiled as her guests sat awkwardly on either side of her.

She met Vorian's gaze first. It seemed like a long time since their first meeting at the robot's villa—with Vor arrogant and proud of his trustee position among the thinking machines. His appearance did not seem to have changed at all. He was so youthful-looking.

In contrast, she noted fine lines starting to age Xavier Harkonnen's face. Though he was young, he had endured a great deal of stress and tragedy, and she felt sympathy for him. Years had passed since they had made love in the meadow, and it seemed like a different lifetime. They were not the same people.

So much had taken place; so many millions of lives had been lost. But she and these men were survivors.

It was time to tell them.

"I know your feelings, but both of you must forget your love for me," she said. "We are about to embark on a war unlike any other." She rose from her chair and stood at the edge of the pool, not taking her gaze from them. "But you must do something for me. Each of you in your own way."

Her eyes brightened with intense sparks of determination. "Go into the League War Room and study the star maps of the Synchronized Worlds, the Unallied Planets, the League

Worlds. In that vast expanse, you will find only two planets that we have ever won back from Omnius. Giedi Prime and Earth. They must not be the last."

As darkness fell and the luminors grew brighter around the perimeter of the compound, the secluded area at the waterfall and the pond remained engulfed in thickening shadows. Even the frogs and insects quieted, as if they were listening to the noises of the night, constantly on the alert for danger.

"Xavier, Vorian—you two must rededicate yourselves to the fight," Serena said. "Do it for me." Her voice was like a chill wind across the galaxy. Vor saw now that her passion had not died within her, but had merely been redirected with a greater intensity toward a much vaster goal. "Our Jihad is righteous, and the evil machines must fall, no matter how much blood it costs us. Win back *every* planet, one by one. For humanity, and for me."

Xavier nodded solemnly and repeated something Iblis Ginjo had said to him, "Nothing is impossible."

"Not for any of us," Vor said. Blinking away the stinging in his eyes, he smiled at her. "And especially not for you, Serena Butler."

GLOSSARY OF THE BUTLERIAN JIHAD

Abdel—old Zensunni man on Arrakis

Agamemnon—one of the original Twenty Titans, cymek general, father of Vorian

Alexander—one of the original Twenty Titans

Aliid—young Poritrin slave, friend of Ishmael

alloyglas—transparent, extremely tough material, often used as armor

IV Anbus—Unallied Planet

Aquim—human tender of Cogitor Eklo

Arkov, Rell—charter member of League of Nobles

Armada—League Armada

Arrakis—desert world, Unallied Planet

Arrakis City—main spaceport and town on Arrakis

Assembly Hall—governmental building in Zimia

Atreides, Vorian—son of Agamemnon, raised on Earth under thinking machine rule

Ajax—cymek, considered the most brutal of the original Titans

baliset—ancient musical instrument developed during the heyday of the Old Empire

Ballads of the Long March—old legends and songs telling of early human exodus and resistance during the initial Time of Titans

ballista—largest battleship created by Salusan Militia

Barbarossa—one of the original Titans, programmer of aggressive computer systems

Becca the Finite—Sister at City of Introspection

Beetle—constellation seen from Arrakis

Bludd, Favo—ancestor of Niko Bludd

Bludd, Frigo—ancestor of Niko Bludd

Bludd, Lord Niko—leader of Poritrin

Bludd, Sajak—first Poritrin leader to advocate slavery

bristleback—wild boar native to Salusa Secundus

Buddallah—mysterious deity of the Zensunni religion

Buddislam—core religion of Zensunnis and Zenshiites

burrhorse—pack animal from Earth

Butler, Faykan—primero of the Jihad

Butler, Fredo—Serena's younger brother, died from a blood disease

Butler, Livia—Serena's mother, abbess of the City of Introspection

Butler, Manion—Viceroy of the League of Nobles

Butler, Manion—son of Serena Butler and Xavier Harkonnen, and grandson of Viceroy Manion Butler

Butler, Octa—younger sister of Serena Butler

Butler, Serena—daughter of Viceroy Manion Butler

Buzzell—Unallied Planet, source of soostones

Caladan—ocean world, Unallied Planet

Camio—Sorceress of Rossak, one of Zufa's trainees

Cenva, Norma—dwarf daughter of Zufa Cenva, mathematical genius

Cenva, Zufa—powerful Sorceress of Rossak

Chandler pistol—projectile weapon that shoots sharp crystal fragments

Chiry, Cuarto—member of Salusan Militia

Chusuk—League World, known for musical instruments

Chusuk, Emi—great composer from the latter days of the Old Empire

City of Introspection—monastery-style religious and philosophical retreat on Salusa

Cogitor—disembodied brain, similar to a cymek, devoted to contemplating esoteric questions

Corrin—Synchronized World

cuarto—fourth rank in League Armada

cymek—"machines with human minds," disembodied brains inside mechanical bodies

Dante—one of the original Titans, skilled in bureaucratic manipulation

Dhartha, Naib—leader of Zensunni tribe on Arrakis

Dragoon—guard force on Poritrin

Dream Voyager—update ship captained by Seurat

driftbarge—slow zeppelin transportation system on Poritrin

Ebbin—slave boy on Poritrin

Ebrahim—treacherous former friend of Selim's

Ecaz—Unallied Planet

Eklo—Cogitor of Earth

electrafluid—bluish life-support liquid for Cogitors and cymeks, also acts as fluid circuitry

evermind—all-encompassing intelligent computer system

fernfibers—Rossak fabric

flowmetal—metallic, sensor-laden skin material used by robots

Freer, Ohan—human crew boss serving thinking machines on Earth

gelcircuitry—sophisticated fluid-crystalline electronics that form the basis of thinking machine neural networks

Giedi City—main industrial and government city on Giedi Prime

Giedi Prime—planet in League of Nobles, rich in resources and industrial capability, ruled by a Magnus

Giedi Prime Home Guard—local defensive military on Giedi Prime

Ginaz—planet in League of Nobles, mostly water; population lives on the scattered islands in an archipelago

Ginjo, Iblis—charismatic human work leader on Earth

glowglobe—mobile illumination source driven by residual energy from its component suspensor field. Developed by Norma Cenva on Poritrin

glowpanel—long-lasting stationary light source

Glyffa—old woman on Arrakis, foster-mother to Selim

Grogyptian—extravagant Old Empire architectural style

Hagal—planet in League of Nobles, known for mineral resources, ruled by a County General

Hall of Parliament—governmental building in Zimia

Hannem, Ryx—slaver, Keedair's copilot

Harkonnen, Katarina—Xavier's mother, killed by thinking machines near Hagal

Harkonnen, Piers—Xavier's older brother, killed by thinking machines near Hagal

Harkonnen, Ulf—Xavier's father, killed by thinking machines near Hagal

Harkonnen, Xavier—officer in Salusan Militia and League Armada

Harmonthep—Unallied Planet, source of slaves

Hecate—one of the original Twenty Titans, lover of Ajax, "resigned" and departed from the Empire not long before the Omnius takeover

Heoma—powerful Sorceress of Rossak, one of Zufa's trainees

hollownut—Rossak nut, used for carving

Holtzman, Tio—genius inventor on Poritrin

hrethgir—derogatory term for "human vermin"

Hrethgir Rebellions—first uprisings of enslaved humans against thinking machines, particularly cymeks. Major one occurred on Walgis, and was brutally crushed by Ajax

irongourd—Rossak gourd

Isana—primary river on Poritrin

Ishmael—young slave taken from Harmonthep

Ix—Synchronized World

javelin—mid-sized model of League Armada destroyer

Jayther, Vilhelm—original human name of the Titan Barbarossa

Jibb, Pinquer—messenger from Giedi Prime

Juno—cymek female, one of the original Titans, Agamemnon's lover

Kaitain—peripheral League World

Keedair, Tuk—Tlulaxa slaver and flesh merchant

kindjal—fast, small fighter ship in League Armada

Kirana III—League World

Komider—industrial League World

Kralizec—name of the final struggle, as predicted by Buddislam

Kwyna—Cogitor dwelling in the City of Introspection

League of Nobles—government of free humans

League Armada—space navy designed to protect League Worlds

League Parliament—governmental body of League of Nobles

League Worlds—signatory planets to League of Nobles charter

Linné, Serena—false name used by Serena Butler after her capture

Lords Council—government body on Poritrin

Magnus—political title on Giedi Prime

Mahmad—Naib Dhartha's son

Manresa, Bovko—first League Viceroy

Meach, Primero Vannibal—commander of Salusan Militia

milkbug—edible arachnid from Harmonthep

Moulay, Bel—Zenshiite religious leader

Narakobe, Pitcairn—League military philosopher

neo-cymek—later generations of cymeks, created from humans who willingly serve Omnius

neurelectronics—delicate circuits used in robots

Old Metalmind—Vorian Atreides's nickname for Seurat

Omnius—computer evermind, controlling all thinking machines

O'Mura, Nivny—one of the founders of the League of Nobles

optic threads—sophisticated eye sensors used by robots

osthmir tubers—edible root on Poritrin

Parhi, Julianna—original human name of Titan Juno

paristeel—metal-polymer alloy used in heavy construction

Parmentier—Synchronized World

Paterson, Brigit—engineer on Serena's commando team

Pincknon—League World

plascrete—construction material

Platinum River—river on Parmentier, source of prized salmon

Poritrin—League World, home of Tio Holtzman

Powder, Jaymes—member of Salusan Militia; later, adjutant to Xavier Harkonnen

primero—highest rank in League Armada

qaraa eggs—edible eggs from marsh birds on Harmonthep

Relicon—League World

Reticulus—Cogitor

Richese—Sychronized World

Rico—member of Salusan Militia

Rossak—planet in League of Nobles, home of Sorceresses, source of numerous drugs

Rucia—Sorceress of Rossak, one of Zufa's trainees

Salusa Secundus—capital world of the League of Nobles

Salusan Militia—local military based on Salusa Secundus

secondary—one of the attendant monks that serve the Cogitors

segundo—secondary rank in League Armada

Selim—young exile on Arrakis

Seneca—League World, corrosive atmosphere, ruled by a Patriarch

Sentinel Rock—rock formation on Arrakis

Seurat—independent robot, captain of the *Dream Voyager*

sexto—sixth and lowest rank in the League Armada

Shaitan—Satan

Shakkad—Old Imperial chemist, known as "the Wise," first to study Arrakis spice

Sheol—The domain of eternal damnation in Zensunni tradition, a fiery subterranean region of unimagined horrors

Silin—Sorceress of Rossak, one of Zufa's trainees

Skouros, Andrew—Agamemnon's original name in the Old Empire

slarpon—scaly jungle creature from Rossak

Songs of the Long Trek—Zensunnni oral history

Souci—Unallied Planet, source of slaves, home of Ebbin

Starda—riverport, capital city of Poritrin

stasis coffins—suspended-animation slave transport system used by Tlulaxa flesh merchants

Suk, Dr. Rajid—innovative battlefield surgeon in Butlerian Jihad

Sumi, Magnus—elected leader of Giedi Prime

suspensor—gravity-nullifying effect based on Holtzman's original shield design, modified by Norma Cenva on Poritrin

Synchronized Worlds—planets under the control of Omnius

Taina—Ishmael's cousin, villager on Harmonthep

Tamerlane—one of the original Twenty Titans

Tantor, Emil—Xavier's foster father

Tantor, Lucille—Xavier's foster mother

Tantor, Vergyl—Xavier's young foster brother

Tanzerouft—deep desert on Arrakis

tercero—third-level rank in League Armada

thinking machine—overall term for robots, computers, and cymeks arrayed against humanity

thoughtrodes—sensors used by cymeks

Time of Titans—the century of tyrant rulers who overthrew the Old Empire, living first as humans and then as cymeks. The Time of Titans ended when the newborn Omnius evermind took over all systems and effected his own rule

Tirbes—Sorceress of Rossak, one of Zufa's trainees

Titans—original tyrants who conquered the Old Empire

Tlaloc—one of the original Titans, the visionary who first inspired the revolt

Tlulax—Unallied Planet in Thalim system, known for providing slaves and biological material

Tlulaxa—people of Tlulax, known as slavers and flesh merchants

turtlebugs—sweet-tasting insects in the marshes of Harmonthep

Twenty Titans—the group of warlords who overthrew the Old Empire

Ularda—Synchronized World

Unallied Planets—outlying worlds that have not formally joined the League of Nobles

vabalone—colorful shell, native to Buzzell

Venport, Aurelius—Rossak businessman, mate of Zufa Cenva

Vertree Colony—League World, heavily industrialized

Viceroy—leader of League of Nobles

Walgis—a Synchronized World, site of First Hrethgir Rebellions

watcheyes—mobile electronic eyes used by Omnius

Weyop—Ishmael's grandfather

Wibsen, Ort—aging space commander, leader of Serena's mission to Giedi Prime

Wilby, Quinto Vaughn—member of Salusan Militia

Winter Sun Room—chamber in Butler manor house

Wormrider—name taken by Selim

Xerxes—cymek, one of the Twenty Titans, responsible for machine takeover

Yardin—Unallied Planet

Yo, Amia—kitchen slave of Erasmus

Young, Cuarto Steff—officer in Salusan Militia

Zanbar—League World, prominent slave market

Zensunni—Buddislamic sect, generally docile

Zenshiite—Buddislamic sect, generally more violent than Zensunnis

Zimia—cultural and governmental center on Salusa Secundus

MAJOR PLANETS

League Worlds	*Synchronized Worlds*	*Unallied Planets*
Balut	Alpha Corvus	IV Anbus
Chusuk	Bela Tegeuse	Arrakis
Giedi Prime	Corrin	Buzzell
Ginaz	Earth	Caladan
Hagal	Ix	Ecaz
Junction	Parmentier	Harmonthep
Kaitain	Quadra	Souci
Kirana III	Richese	Tlulax
Komider	Ularda	Yardin
Pincknon	Walgis	
Poritrin	Wallach IX, VII, and VI	
Relicon	Yondair	
Ros-Jal		
Rossak		
Salusa Secundus		
Seneca		
Vertree Colony		
Zanbar		

~⁓~

The future, the past, and the present are intertwined, a weave that forms any point in time.

    —from "The Legend of Selim Wormrider," Zensunni fire poetry

Standing inside the cave's edge, Selim Wormrider gazed across Arrakis's soothing ocean of dunes, watching for the moment when the sun first rose over the horizon. Then, golden light poured like molten metal across the undulating desert, purifying and inevitable—like his visions, like his mission in life.

Selim greeted the day, taking a deep breath of air that was so dry it crackled his lungs. Dawn was his favorite time, after just waking from deep sleep filled with mysterious dreams and hints. It was the best time to accomplish meaningful tasks.

A tall, gaunt man came up beside him, always knowing where to find his leader at daybreak. Loyal Jafar had a heavy jaw, sunken cheeks, and deep blue eyes from years of a spice-laden diet. The lieutenant waited in silence, knowing Selim was aware of his presence. Finally, Selim turned from the rising sun and looked up at his most respected friend and follower.

Jafar extended a small plate. "I have brought you melange

for the morning, Selim, so that you may better see into the mind of Shai-Hulud."

"We serve him, and our future, but no one understands Shai-Hulud. Do not make that mistake, Jafar, and you will live longer."

"As you say, Wormrider."

Selim took one of the wafers, pressed spice mixed with flour and honey. His eyes carried the deep blue of addiction as well, but the sacred spice had kept him alive, granting him energy even during times of greatest trial and deprivation. Melange opened a marvelous window in the universe and gave Selim visions, helping him to understand the destiny Buddallah had chosen for him. He—and his ever-growing group of desert exiles—followed a calling that was greater than any of their individual lives.

"There will be a testing this morning," Jafar said, his deep voice even. The newborn sun exposed secret footprints made during the night. "Biondi wishes to prove himself. Today he will attempt to ride a worm."

Selim frowned. "He is not ready."

"But he insists."

"He will die."

Jafar shrugged. "Then he will die. That is the way of it."

Selim emitted a resigned sigh. "Each man must face his own conscience and his own testing. Shai-Hulud makes the final choice."

Selim was fond of Biondi, though the young man's brash impatience was better suited to the life of an offworlder at the Arrakis City spaceport, rather than the unchanging existence of the deep desert. Biondi might eventually become a valuable contributor to Selim's band, but if the young man could not live up to his own abilities, then he would be a danger to the others. It was better to discover such a weakness now, than to risk the lives of Selim's faithful followers.

Selim said, "I will watch from here."

Jafar nodded and left.

Over twenty-six standard years ago, Selim had been falsely accused of stealing water from one of the tribe's stores; subsequently, he had been exiled into the desert. Manipulated by the lies of Naib Dhartha, Selim's former friends had chased him from their cliff cities, throwing rocks and insults at him until he ran out onto the treacherous dunes, supposedly to be devoured by one of the "demon worms."

But Selim had been innocent, and Buddallah had saved him—for a purpose.

When a sandworm had come to devour him, Selim discovered how to ride the creature. Shai-Hulud had taken him far from the Zensunni village and deposited him near an abandoned botanical testing station, where he'd found food, water, tools. There, Selim was able to keep searching for his mission.

In a melange-enhanced vision, nearly drowning in thick reddish powder cast up from a spice blow, he had learned that he must prevent Naib Dhartha and his desert parasites from harvesting and distributing melange to offworlders. Over the years, working alone, Selim had raided many encampments, destroying any spice the Zensunni gathered. He had earned a legendary reputation and the moniker "Wormrider."

Not long afterward, he had begun to accumulate followers.

Jafar had been the first, two decades ago, forsaking the protection of his own village near Arrakis City in order to search for this man who could ride the great desert beasts. Jafar had been almost dead when Selim found him, dehydrated, sunburned, starving. But when the lean and hardened outcast looked down at him under the dazzling bright sky, Jafar gasped through cracked lips—not a request for water, but a query. "Are you . . . the Wormrider?"

By then, Selim had been alone for more than five years—too alone—faced with a sacred task too great for a single man. He nursed Jafar back to health and then taught him how to ride Shai-Hulud. In the following years, the pair had gathered rugged followers, men and women dissatisfied by the strict rules and unfair justice of life in the Zensunni cliff colonies. Selim told them of his mission to stop spice harvesting, and they listened, enthralled by the gleam in his eyes.

According to Selim's repeated melange visions, the activities of the offworld merchants and the Zensunni gatherers would shatter the peace of the desert planet. Though the timeframe was dim, stretched out into a vague, far future, the spread of spice across the Galaxy would eventually lead to the extinction of all worms. His words were frightening, but when they saw him proudly riding atop the mountainous curve of a great sandworm, no one could doubt his claims or his faith.

But even I do not understand Shai-Hulud.

As a young scamp, exiled from his tribe, Selim had never wanted to be a leader. But now, after decades of living by his own wits and making decisions for the group of followers who depended on him for guidance and survival, Selim Wormrider had become a confident, clear-headed general who had begun to believe the myth that he was indestructible, a demon of the desert. Despite devoting his life to preserving the worms, he did not expect the capricious Shai-Hulud to show him any gratitude. . . .

Unexpectedly, Jafar returned to the high chamber with enough commotion that Selim stepped away from the window opening and saw that his friend had brought a newcomer. She looked dirty and lean, but her dark eyes bore a haughty defiance. Her dusty brown hair had been cropped short. Her cheeks were sunburned below her eyes, but the rest of her seemed intact. The young woman must have been wise enough to wrap herself against the worst ravages of the sun. A curved white scar like a crescent moon rode above her left eyebrow, adding an exotic punctuation to her coarse beauty.

"Look what we found out in the desert, Selim." Jafar stood tall and stoic, unflappable, but Selim caught a hint of humorous gleam behind his deep blue eyes.

The young woman stepped away from the tall man, as if to prove she didn't need his protection. "My name is Marha. I have traveled alone in search of you." Then her face flickered with uncertainty and awe, making her look unexpectedly young. "I am . . . honored to meet you, Selim Wormrider!"

He held her chin, turning her face up to look at him. Lean and dirty, but with large eyes and strong features. "It's just a slip of a girl, won't be much use for heavy labor around here. Why have you left your own people?"

"Because they are all fools," she snapped.

"Many people are fools, once you get to know them."

"Not me. I came to join you."

Selim raised his eyebrows, amused. "We shall see." He turned to look at Jafar. "Where did you find her? How close did she approach?"

"We caught her beneath the Needle Rock. She had camped there and didn't know we'd been watching her."

"I would have seen you," she insisted.

Needle Rock was very close to the settlement. Selim was impressed, though he did not show it. "And you survived in the desert by yourself? How far away is your village?"

"Eight days journey. I brought food and water, and I caught lizards."

"You mean you stole food and water from your village."

"I *earned* it."

"I doubt your Naib would see it the same way, so it is not likely your people would take you back."

Marha's eyes flashed. "Not likely. I fled from Naib Dhartha's village, as you did yourself years ago."

Selim stiffened and studied her. "He still has a stranglehold on the tribe?"

"He teaches that you are evil, a thief, a vandal."

Selim's chuckle was dry and humorless. "Perhaps he should look in a mirror. He established himself as my lifelong enemy."

Marha looked tired and thirsty, but made no complaint, no request for hospitality. She fumbled at her throat and pulled out a wire loop that held a jingling collection of metal chits. "Spice tokens from offworlders. Naib Dhartha sent me out to work the sands, to scrape the spice and collect it to be delivered to his merchant friends in Arrakis City. I have been of marriageable age for three years, but no Zensunni woman— or man—can take a mate until they have gathered fifty spice tokens. That is how Naib Dhartha measures our service to the tribe."

Selim scowled, delicately touched the tokens with his fingertip, then in disgust tucked them back into her collar. "He is a man deluded by his greed and a false hope of an easy life."

He turned away and stared out into the desert. Squinting into the morning light, he watched four small figures emerge from the lower caves. They walked out onto the open sands, garbed in camouflaged robes and cloaks, their faces wrapped to prevent moisture loss. Biondi, preparing for his test.

When Marha looked questioningly at Selim and then at the other man, Jafar explained. "Selim Wormrider receives messages from Shai-Hulud. We have been commanded by God to stop the rape of the desert, to halt the harvesting of spice, the momentum of commerce that threatens to set history on a disastrous course. It is an enormous task for our small group. By working to harvest melange, you yourself have aided our enemies."

Defiant, the young woman shook her head. "By abandoning them, I have helped your cause."

Selim turned back, looking from her crescent-moon scar to her intent eyes. He saw a determination there, but did not know her true motives. "Why have you come here to a hard life, instead of running to Arrakis City and signing onto a merchant ship?"

She seemed surprised by the question. "Why do *you* think?"

"Because I am better than your own leader."

She raised her chin. "I want to ride the worms. Only you can teach me."

"And why should I do that?"

The young woman's eagerness overrode her uncertainty. "I thought that if I could find you, track the location of your outlaw hideout, then you would accept me."

Selim arched his eyebrows. "That is only the first part."

"The easy part," Jafar said.

"Each step in its time, Marha. You have done well so far. Not many approach as close as Needle Rock before we apprehend them. Some, we send away with enough supplies to survive the trip back home. Others are so hopelessly lost that they wander to their deaths without ever knowing we have been observing them."

"You just watch them die?"

Jafar shrugged. "It is the desert. If they cannot survive, they are useless."

"I am not useless. I am good with a knife . . . killed one opponent and injured another in duels." She touched her eyebrow. "One man gave me this scar at the spaceport. He tried to rape me. In turn, I gave him a scar from one side of his belly to the other."

Selim withdrew his milky-white crystalline dagger, holding it up so that the young woman could see. "A wormrider carries a dagger like this, fashioned from the sacred tooth of Shai-Hulud."

Marha stared in amazement, her eyes sparkling. "Ah, what I could accomplish with a fine weapon like that!"

Jafar laughed. "Many people would like to have one of these, but you must earn it."

"Tell me what to do."

Hearing a steady drumbeat from the expansive desert outside, Selim turned to the cave window. "Before you make such an impetuous decision, girl, watch and see what lies in store for you here."

"My name is Marha. I am no longer a girl."

To young villagers across Arrakis, Selim was a glamorous figure, a daredevil hero. Many tried to imitate him and become wormriders themselves, though he attempted to discourage them, warning them of the danger of a renegade's life. Having received a true vision from Buddallah, Selim had no choice in the matter for himself. But they did.

Regardless of his advice, starry-eyed candidates rarely listened. They went off with big dreams and overconfidence, which usually proved to be their downfall. But those who survived learned the greatest lesson of their lives.

Out on the dunes, the drumbeats echoed. Almost all of the observers had left the sand, returning to the shelter of the rocky cliffs. A solitary man, Biondi, sat at the crest of a dune, the place he had selected for his testing. He should have had everything he needed: The young man would be wearing one of the new distilling suits that Selim and his followers had developed for protection and survival during times when they must be abroad in the open desert. With Biondi were staffs and hooks, and a rope between his knees. He pounded on a single drum, sending a loud, insistent summons.

Marha stepped forward to stand next to Selim, as if unable to believe she now found herself beside the man who was basis of so many desert myths. "Will a worm come? Will he ride it?"

"We shall see if he succeeds," Selim said. "But Shai-Hulud will come. He always does."

Selim saw the wormsign first and pointed it out to the young woman. After more than a quarter century, he no longer counted how many times he had summoned a sandworm and climbed its rough rings in order to guide the creature wherever he wished to go.

Biondi had ridden just twice before, each time accompanied by a master rider who did all the work for him. The youngster had performed adequately, but still had a great deal to learn. Another month of training would have benefited him immensely.

Selim hoped he would not lose another follower . . . but either way, Biondi's fate was in his own hands.

The novice pounded his drum much longer than necessary. He did not become aware of the approach of the worm until he looked to the east and saw shimmering waves trembling through the sands. Then he grabbed his equipment and scrambled to his feet, accidentally kicking over the drum so that it rolled and bounced down the face of the dune.

At the base of the sand formation, the drum struck a rock and sent out another reverberating sound. The oncoming worm deviated slightly, and Biondi reeled to adjust his position at the last moment. The sandworm came up unexpectedly, showering dust, flattening dunes.

Selim marveled at the majestic sight of it. "Shai-Hulud," he whispered reverently.

A puny figure in the face of the onrushing behemoth, Biondi held his hooks and staff, muscles coiled.

In instinctive fear Marha flinched, but Selim clasped her shoulder, forcing her to watch.

At the last moment, Biondi lost his nerve. Instead of standing his ground, holding the spreading staff and the hook, he turned to flee. But no man could outrun Shai-Hulud in the desert.

The worm scooped up its victim along with a mouthful of sand and powdery dust. Selim could hardly see the tiny human form as it vanished down the endless gullet.

Transfixed, Marha stared. Jafar shook his head, lowering his chin in sad disappointment.

Selim nodded like a wise man much older than his years. "Shai-Hulud has found the candidate wanting." He turned to Marha. "Now you have seen the peril. Would you not be better off returning to your village and begging Naib Dhartha for forgiveness?"

"On the contrary—it seems to me you now have room for another follower." She stared fiercely out at the sands. "I still want to ride the worms."